Chronicles of
THE LAST LEGEND
Awakened
Unto the End
Forever

את

An Epic Trilogy
by
Joshua B. Wichterich

Chronicles of The Last Legend is a trilogy in its entirety, consisting
of book one Awakened, book two Unto The End, and book three Forever.
The characters and events portrayed in this book are fictitious. Any similarity to real persons,
living or dead, is coincidental and not intended by the author.

Scripture Bible versions - KJV
Poem quotes – The Lady of Shalott
By Alfred, Lord Tennyson

ISBN / SKU: 9780578715353

I thank God for loving me.
He has blessed me in so many ways while leading me through this
literary journey.
For many years I've worked on this trilogy,
tweaking things here and adding things there,
ultimately putting together this masterpiece:
Chronicles of The Last Legend.
Jesus has inspired me on so many levels and transformed my broken
pieces into inspiring art.
God has turned my darkness into light.
Yeshua is my heart.

To my brothers & sisters in Christ
*Always keep the light within your heart and let them know Him through
you…then show them the way.*

The Last Legend
Chronicles

†

<u>AWAKENED</u>
7

†

<u>UNTO THE END</u>
330

†

<u>FOREVER</u>
541

← To Far off lands
The Golden Lands
The Kingdom of Minslethrate
Harbor Village
The Coast
Crown
The Great Fields of Minslethrate
cottage
Weeping Road
rosemary bush
Forest Provence
Ducre' Provence
Forest of Old
Minslethrating River
Lake Iris
To Prat &
The Kingdom of Hanon
Haifen Springs
The Great Wall
The Forbidden Lands
The Black Forest
Provence of the Old Ways
Temple of Dolsia
Here once dwelled the Garden of Nede
Temple of Fiara
Haifen Falls
Entrance to Temple of Haifen
King's Tree
Skull Hill
Fiara Mountains
The Black Field of Old Blood
Dark Tower of Sacrifice
Lands of Wild Mountains

History is the past that unravels the present, opening the doors to an unstoppable future... But there is some history that has been long forgotten—like the gifts of nature. This history has been taken for granted and passed down as a legend—an age-old tale, like the seasons of earth. And then, just like the small details of earth and the many phases it entails, legend is soon forgotten. For the world has witnessed so many great wonders—and has forgotten them... Pity to those who do not know it, for they are lost—pity to those who have forgotten it, for they are weak—and pity to those who do not heed it—for they are cursed...

...The Legend is this... So long ago, before the beginning of time—before the lives and dreams of man, when the being of earth was but a thought, and before the great veil of night was sprinkled with light—before life itself began to dwell, there was a kingdom of light that never vanished. This divine domain was called Nevaeh, and sparkled in the deepest region of the great veil, on the outskirts of the still darkness. A great king of light ruled over this kingdom with his tangible love and kindness. In all of his splendor and bravura, he was passionately worshiped by his people. And among this grandeur kingdom were his warriors, beings of light called legna. These legna were his knights, his Legion of Light who followed him till no end, who fought for him and the freedom and love he bestowed upon them.

But among these warriors of light was a knight whose heart did not shine as bright as the rest, an Archlegna called Lucif. He was captivating and gifted, commander-in-chief of the Legion of Light and at the Great King's right hand. But just like the dim and blistering tip of a flame, the Archlegna's heart was also dim and blistering—and above anyone else, craved power, to be worshiped like that of the Great King.

The deceiving Archlegna presented to the Great King all of his fabrications, of what he could do for him, what great things he would grant him—like that of the earth and all of its magnificence—under one condition—if he would bow down and worship him, praise him for everything he did...

The king knew of what was in Lucif's heart, for he foresaw it—he knew everything that was and was to come—including that of the creation of man and earth and all that was imparted upon it. Lucif did not understand that everything he did was through the Great King's spirit, that the Great King could do any mysterious and impossible thing on his own will. the Great King saw the wickedness in Lucif's heart and the jealousy in his eyes, and he had compassion and sympathy in his heart for Lucif—for the Great

King is always good. He pitied Lucif and casted him and his followers out, exiling them unto the darkness and away from Nevaeh, the Great Kingdom of Light.

…Many years had passed like a faint breeze, and within those years the king had done many great and mysterious things—like that of the creation of Earth and man and everything that it consists of. So many miracles were done by the king of light—so many that one merely cannot count them…

Lucif and his followers fell upon the earth like an angry bolt of lightning, ravaging the mighty king's creations. Lucif's revenge was great and he loathed the Great King, doing everything in his power to stop the king's good works. He came upon the earth to steal, kill and destroy— everything that was good… With malice in his heart and nastiness on his tongue, Lucif conjured up an immense plan to conquer the Great King, a scheme that was even more intricate than one's lifetime. He spread his fabrications to his followers, his nomeds, who ate up every word from his black tongue. All it acquired was timing, the perfect sacrifice and the perfect place—the Kingdom of Minslethrate.

Minslethrate was an ancient kingdom and was called the Golden Lands, for it was the land where the Great King first bestowed his people upon, establishing the first settlement of light. Even though Minslethrate was small, it was very beautiful and prosperous, blessed, having an abundance of vegetation and livestock and was amongst the purest of rivers. Out of spite, these were the lands Lucif chose to infiltrate and plant his seeds of iniquity—to ravage like a great disease… And so, those seeds gave birth to darkness. After years of torment and pandemonium, the dark lord waited in the darkness for a thousand years in the deep chasms of Minslethrate until that time came…to reign in darkness and in flesh…

The time is now… Catching the scent of the perfect innocent and lost blood, Lucif ascended from the dark chasms and the shadows of the forest…finally snatching up what he yearned for…

†

PROLOGUE
So It Begins

All she could do was run—as fast as she could. Screaming would do her no good; no one was around. How did she get there? Where was she? Who or what was she running from?! All of these questions ripped through her throbbing head as she ran away from—something…

It was cold, too cold—and dark. Her hands and bare feet were like ice as she ran through the great stone halls of the castle. At least she thought it was a castle… The wet, cold air was heavy and smelled of thick mildew in the dark spaces around her. The halls were long and the stone walls reached high up until they disappeared into the darkness of the black abyss above her. There were torches scattered about the hall which barely lit the horrifying and damp place. The torches seemed to laugh at her as they cascaded dancing shadows across the stone walls. Spider webs and deep cracks stretched along the walls, creating a mural of twisted shapes and images.

The breathless girl had to stop, just for a moment, to breathe, to rest her aching feet and legs, but not for too long—because it was coming, closer. She could feel a presence growing in the dark air, a presence that she had never felt before. It didn't feel good—it felt horrifying and evil, like all feelings of hope, love, and happiness were sucked from the world, away from her. She could feel it everywhere, all around her now, like she had been shrouded in a thickly woven mantle, made from prickly ivy and course hair. Her chest burned as she sucked in the stale, cold air of the atmosphere that masked her whole body.

Scaling alongside the moist, spider-webbed stone wall, she began to run again, but couldn't. Her burning legs wouldn't allow her to run anymore. She made her way to the nearest torch. The fiery light burned bright above her head as it crackled and popped. The warmth emitting from the fire felt somewhat comforting against her frozen skin as it sent rays of goose-bumps through her flesh. She leaned against the stone wall, not caring about the fuzzy mildew that seemed to be covering the moist stones. She looked at her hands and bare feet which protruded out from beneath the long black gown she was wearing. Her hands and feet were bruised and scraped raw. Dirt and dried blood were scattered upon her once clean and smooth skin. But she couldn't sense the pain, for the feeling of fear and numbness of the cold was too strong upon her frail body.

Her chest, half covered, heaved to and fro as she breathed heavily. The front of the black bodice she was wearing was loosely fastened, revealing her pale skin. Instead of the usual white material of an under garment, her milky skin was revealed. A red pendant that hung upon her chest showed elegantly against the ghostly complexion of her skin. The blood-red pendant she wore sparkled under the fire light, revealing its splendor. These weren't her garments. She would never wear such ragged and inappropriate garbs, especially her being of royal blood from a very respected and powerful family.

It seemed that she had just arrived to the kingdom, marrying young and beautiful, learning their ways and customs, their language and religion. She was confused and frightened, wondering what had happened and how she had gotten in the predicament she was in. It was morning when she had snuck off to explore the strange and beautiful lands of Minslethrate. Content and curious, she wandered off into the fields and forests, yearning to find something new—and that she did. A dark presence caught the scent of her innocent blood. Having a weak flame burning in her heart, she fell asleep in a strange and dark forest, and awakened in fear and in darkness in a cold and wet chamber, alone and scared, and seemingly…hunted.

Her long black hair cascaded down her back and chest, making her beauty appear haunting and dark. Her mysterious almond-shaped eyes were dark, lined with thick lashes, and her elegant bone structure of her face was brushed red from the cold air.

"I see you…" said a low and whispering voice.

The voice seemed to come from everywhere! It echoed down the dark and morbid hallway, making her numb skin crawl.

Her heart pounded even more as she began to cry hysterically. The whites of her eyes were stained red as heavy tears flowed, and her hands shook as if electricity ran through them.

"What do you want?!" she screamed out in the Minslethratian language. Her accent was thick and shook with fear, making her words barely recognizable.

She began to walk backwards, away from where she thought the treacherous whispers came from.

"Carnage…" The haunting voice emitted from a black figure which stood still and menacingly down the hallway.

The whisper pierced her heart with fear.

She could see that the figure was covered in a long, black hooded cloak. The torch above it barely allowed her to see who or what it was. The terrified girl's breath showed in the cold air as she attempted to run again. The dark and narrow hall only went one way. All of the massive wooden doors on either side of the hallway were locked, or stuck! As she attempted each door, she glanced back. Horror shot through her body as the figure came closer! She could see it as it passed beneath each torch. It didn't seem to be running or even walking, but motionless, gliding across the stone ground.

She ran until the hallway ended abruptly, past two long flowing, tattered curtains. She was outside. She panicked as she realized that she was on a balcony, a dead end! The moon was deviant, dim and red, peeking in and out of the black clouds. The wind moved through her long black hair and gown as she ran into the cement railing of the balcony, nearly falling over into the darkness below. She leaned over the ice-cold cement balustrade, screaming out. Parts of the old balustrade crumbled and crashed down into the blackness of the night. The balcony was high, overlooking an abyss of dark trees and a black river that ran alongside the jagged rocks of the cliff's base, on which the small castle rested on.

Her intuition was correct; she was in some sort of castle, a tall and treacherous tower which seemed to be high atop the bottom cliffs of a mountain side. The sphere of the ice-cold moon revealed its face brilliantly now as the clouds passed by it. It seemed to gawk at her, laughing with its blood-red orb. Where was she? She didn't recognize anything. She couldn't see anything but moonlit trees and miles of field as far as the eye could see.

"We have been waiting," a low and frightening voice said from behind her.

The terror-stricken girl turned quickly to discover that the black figure was standing right in front of her, her face nearly touching it. The smell of death emitted from the thing, burning her nostrils and eyes, and her heart.

The girl's screams echoed across the dark and cold night sky, carried by the wind to the black trees and fields beyond. The only witnesses of what had happened that night were that of a flock of bats that flickered through the strange ominous sky…

Almost thirty years went by like the passing of an ill wind. Like in the days of the ancestors when the lands were much younger, innocent blood was spilled upon the earth by the malevolent hearts of man, who ate from the insidious seeds that Lucif had planted. Sorrow and sin continued to ravage the earth and the lands of Minslethrate as the ancient wanderer, Lucif, whose wicked heart was still enveloped by blackness and envy, lived like man upon the Golden Lands.

He had possessed the body of a young queen named Karnidge, and ruled the Golden Lands of Minslethrate after the death of King James, with a lust for innocent blood and absolute supremacy. Drunken by evilness and power, Queen Karnidge demanded to be venerated like that of a god, having anyone brutally burned at the stake if she was denied her idolization. Then, after five years of foul ruling and pandemonium, subsequent to the thirty-year reign of the late King James, the body of Queen Karnidge was cursed and became deathly ill. She could reign no more; her wicked flesh finally died…

The kingdom was taken up by her young son and heir to the throne, Prince Julpen, who tried to light the flame of Minslethrate once again. As time passed, Julpen became an acceptable king, and he married the beautiful Princess O'nessa. They were the new successors of Minslethrate. During the beginning of the forty years of King Julpen's reign, Queen O'nessa spread her love and kindness upon the people.

After some time, they had a daughter whom they called Marrisa. After the first two years of Princess Marrisa's life, Queen O'nessa mysteriously became ill and died. She left the kingdom and the royal family in a state of sadness and darkness. As Marrisa grew to the tender age of six, she began to show traits of her mother, becoming lovelier at every waking moment. The people of Minslethrate began to see a pattern of love and kindness in her, giving them a glimpse of hope once again.

But over the forty-year reign of King Julpen, the wicked spirit that had been dwelling in the darkness, lingered on still like a foul scent. The darkened spirit traveled from one lost and barren heart to another, waiting for the era when darkness would have the chance to reign over all creation; when the lake of fire and deep pits of hell would be full and earth would be lost and all on it would bow down and worship the Lord of Darkness.

Book One
Awakened

†

CHAPTER 1
The Burning

The strange sky looked haunting as the people of Minslethrate began to congregate in the town square. The sky had many shades of dark-gray with billowy clouds that loomed over the small kingdom. Some of the clouds were such a dark-blue and heavy looking, that they seemed as if rain would come pouring out of them at any minute. The air was cold and bitter winds blew, sending cold shivers down the backs of the onlookers.

The town's people crowded around a small wooden platform. A large stake ran straight through the center of the platform which stood a couple of feet above the ground. Stacks of dried sticks and straw circled around the bottom of the stake, drenched in oil.

"It's a good day for a burning," an overweight peasant woman said to her stick-like husband as she placed her large basket of apples down onto the ground.

"I wonder who it is?" her husband responded. "There's been no burning since that mad woman of a queen ruled many years ago. I remember that young beauty be killing everyone when we were youngins. Remember?" he said, taking a puff from his wooden pipe.

"Oh yes, I do, I do. I was just a wee girl on my mother's arm," she said as she shook her head slowly. "I wonder who the unlucky soul is?"

"It be the head-maid of the royal family and household," a small old woman said, standing next to the larger woman.

"What a shame that is," the overweight woman said, shaking her round face slowly. "The royal family just has to make a horrid scene and burn some poor soul."

"Entertainment!" the stick man shrieked as he picked at one of his six crooked teeth, flicking whatever came out, onto the ground.

His overweight wife nudged his arm as she chuckled. Small drops of saliva shot out of her large mouth and landed on the old woman's face. The shrew didn't seem to notice as she stared off into the crowd, stuck in thought.

"She be killing other handmaidens of the royal family. Yes... It's happening again. Evil things be brewing, like in the old days. When I was much fairer, before the many rough years got the best of me, these same things be happening," the old woman said, interrupting the large woman's chuckles.

The odd couple became quiet, wide eyed, as if shocked but fascinated by what the old woman was saying.

"A servant found her performing some kind of ritual deep down in that old dungeon of the castle, lit candles everywhere. A poor young maid was found lying on her back, a bloody gash from ear to ear. Poor hussy—it be evil craft I tell you!"

The startled woman hugged up against her little husband. Her plump pink hand cuffed over her mouth; eyes still wide open like that of a fish.

"They found other dead maids hidden in strange places in that dark old dungeon. The stink probably be telling on that witch. They be finding some old skeletons and dead animals too, under piles of dirt and stone. That old castle be full of secrets and horrid acts!" The old woman shivered, from either the cold or from her own tale, and then pulled her ragged shawl tightly around her bony frame.

"That same thing be happening about forty or so years ago. After the death of his grace, King James—the mighty God rested his soul—the evil poured out of that queen then! Queen Karnidge was her name and she tore this kingdom apart. She be burning everyone at the stake for five years, I believe it was. I remember, as a young maiden, how horrid the kingdom be smelling because of the burning flesh of the people. My poor mother was burned. Gossip had it that she started hiring many young peasant girls as help in the castle. They say she sacrificed those poor young darlings to the dark father himself, bathing in their blood. She did this for five years! When she died the whole kingdom celebrated." Amused at what she just said, the old woman let out a loud cackle as she shook her shriveled little head.

The couple just glanced at each other.

"Can you believe that trollop thought she would stay beautiful and live forever if she be doing such a thing?!" She let out another cackle, creating more wrinkles on her face then she already had.

They noticed that the sky began to get a little darker. The blue-gray sky looked as if it were about to pour an ocean down. The winds picked up, making the atmosphere even colder. The town's people began to light more torches. Nearby pub and shop owners lit their lamp posts, making sure that the people could see that they were still open.

"I have heard some old legends and stories of what happened long ago; they used to frighten me as a child. But what a shame, the poor dears," the large woman said, shaking her swollen head.

Her cheeks looked like two bright-red apples as the chilly wind hit against them.

"How do you be knowing such things, old woman?" the stick man asked as he took another puff from his pipe.

"I be a very old woman, around for a long time. I be knowing all the gossip around this kingdom."

The town's people grabbed their attention. With all the commotion, it seemed as if festival season had just arrived.

"Oh, but what about that poor dear?" the woman asked, pointing her plump finger at a small red-headed girl across the way.

The young girl shyly stood, snuggling up against a young servant woman's dress. Her long red hair fell in waves over her little white gown. She looked about six years old or so. She seemed scared and timid even though she was among her five personal handmaidens, as well as courtiers and other important people associated with the royal family. The handmaidens comforted her and would lean over to talk to her every now and then to console her.

"Oh, Princess Marrisa, the little jewel," the old woman said with a crooked smile. Her rotten teeth looked like little raisins between two flaps of dried bread.

"The poor deary is probably scared to death," the large woman said with a frown. She tried to get the young girl's attention by waving to her without being noticed by any of her several handmaidens. "She is too young to understand such things. She shouldn't have to be out here in this mess! Oh, without her mother and all, she should be so terrified," the large woman fussed, watching every move of the small child.

"It be a sad thing," the old woman said, shaking her head. "I do remember when the poor Queen O'nessa died from illness. That day be a sad day. That beauty was a loving one too. She always be there for us people in this kingdom. She spread her love and faith till no end. But she do be in a better place now, with the Holy Father of Light." She looked up to the sky while smiling her odd smile again, then back at the crowded scene of the marketplace. "Ever since she died, strange things be going on around here. And the king," the old woman said with that glazed look in her eyes again, "oh, has he changed. You can feel the sadness coming from him when he comes into town. The king must be going mad from everything that be happening in that castle. That little red beauty child be the only light of hope in that castle."

✝✝✝

The crowd was loud and filled with strange excitement. Everyone seemed to be talking at once and about the same subject, but different versions. Along with the ruckus of the people, there was the sound of music. A small bard and musicians were dressed in odd costumes with masks, playing music and acting out a strange scene of what they thought was about to happen that evening. Many people circled around the scene, watching, laughing, and dancing all around the strange performance.

The racket of nearby pubs could be heard as well, with the sound of laughter and drunken gibberish. Although the odd weather and nippiness of the air continued to hurry in, the people of Minslethrate didn't seem to want to rush away to their warm homes. It had been many years since a burning, and this one seemed to strangely excite the people.

The king and his band of soldiers finally arrived on horses. The throngs of town's people slowly split as they made their way into the town square. The soldiers stopped their horses at the small platform, pushing the people away from it. The king stayed where he was at, a couple of yards away from the soldiers, still sitting on the large black horse.

The jewels on his velvet red tunic sparkled as the many torches of the marketplace gleamed off them. A long golden chain with a brilliant deep-red pendant dangled on his chest. He was middle-aged and had a stern face. He looked fierce and intimidating, but still had a glimpse of sadness in his black eyes. He always looked that way. His eyes had dark circles under them, indicating stress and lack of sleep. His beard and long wavy hair were dark-brown with a touch of gray. The crown on his head gleamed elegantly as he sat straight up on his large horse.

Marrisa was excited to see her father. Because, even though they lived in the same abode, they rarely saw each other. Marrisa only saw her father at dinner, Sunday church, and sometimes in the halls of the castle. She tried to wiggle away from the band of handmaidens, but they held her back, worried that she would come up missing in the ruckus of the town square. But Marrisa knew she couldn't go see her father anyway. She could tell something bad was going to happen. She could tell by the look on her father's face, the sadness among her servants and the number of people in the town square.

Instead of fighting her handmaidens to get to her father, she decided to stay tightly gripped to Lilith. Lilith was the new head-maid of Marrisa's servants. She was younger than her other maids but acted older. Even though Lilith was strange she was usually sweet and gentle. But lately, she wasn't as warm and kind as Marrisa remembered her to be.

Marrisa's other handmaidens kept asking her questions while touching her hair and face. They kept trying to talk to her. She didn't like any of it; she didn't understand what was going on. All she knew was that Moira had done something awful…

Her father had told her that Moira was a bad woman, and then told her that Lilith was her new guardian—replacing her beloved Moira. But she didn't understand how Moira could do anything remotely wrong. How could she be a *bad* woman? Moira was like a mother to her, the only source of comfort she had ever known. After the death of Queen O'nessa, Moira watched over Marrisa. Moira was always there by Marrisa's side, feeding her, bathing her, and telling her bed-time tales while she brushed her long red hair. How could she do anything bad? Marrisa had this question whirling around in her young brain as she looked around at everyone.

The crowd seemed to quiet down now that her father arrived. Marrisa looked around at everyone; some people were shouting, some laughing and dancing, some even still shopped around at the random carts and small shops.

"Do you want to leave, Princess?" Katrinka the handmaiden asked, while bending over to look straight into Marrisa's clear blue eyes.

"No, she does not!" Lilith snapped as she rudely put her hand in front of Katrinka's face. "I mean, she needs to learn," she said, in a now softer tone. "She is a princess after all, Katrinka, a young queen; she will see this again..."

"Lilith, this is no environment for a young maiden, princess or not," Katrinka said, trying to be bold. Her face was down, not even looking into Lilith's dark-brown eyes.

The silence between them was intense for a couple of seconds, feeling like an hour. Marrisa peered up, looking at the two women. Lilith's face was straight with no sign of emotion, just blank, which made her look frightening to Marrisa for the first time. Katrinka slowly moved back to the other side of the group of handmaidens, hoping not to be chastised later for talking back to her new superior. Lilith's stare seemed as if it could burn a hole straight through Katrinka's face.

"Do you want to leave, my lady?" Lilith now asked with a smile, breaking the silence.

Marrisa's bottom lip began to quiver as fat tears swelled up in her big blue eyes. It used to be Moira's kind face she would look up to. It would be Moira who used to console her. Marrisa's sweet face turned sour in a quick second.

"No! I want my Moira!" she screamed as she folded her arms.

Lilith just patted the top of her head, looking up to the platform of wood with a strange smile. "You will, soon enough," Lilith said, then looked back down at the teary-eyed child.

Marrisa glanced back up at her and noticed how different she looked. Her dark-brown eyes seemed darker than usual, almost black, and her smile was scary.

Just then the crowd roared as a small carriage was pulled in by a large bald man sitting atop a black horse.

"There she is now," Lilith said, with that same strange smile and dark eyes.

Even though Marrisa didn't want to, she held tightly onto Lilith's gown as the crowd got louder.

As the warden pulled the small carriage next to the wooden platform, two armed soldiers walked up next to it, ready to pull whomever out of it. The large bald man hopped off the horse and stood between the two soldiers. His massive shoulders and broad back blocked the view of the small carriage door. A ring of keys hung from a rope around his waist. He looked through the keys, found the right one, then unlocked the rusty lock-pad that hung from the door. He pulled the small, heavy door open, and then hopped back onto his horse as one of the soldiers pulled a middle-aged woman out.

It was Moira. She was crying and pitiful looking, with her hands tied behind her back. Her long dark hair was down and knotted and she wore a long black dress. Her head faced down, allowing her tangled hair to cover most of her countenance.

One of the soldiers shoved her towards the platform, not caring when she fell to the ground. Her face hit the rough cobblestone, marking a gash on her left cheek and bottom lip.

"Get up, witch!" the other soldier yelled as he yanked her up by her bounds.

He shoved her as well, but she didn't fall this time. Her face looked strange, as if she had no idea what was going on. She looked confused and shocked at the same time. She appeared innocent, as if she had been wrongly accused. Bright red blood trickled down her cheek and lip. Tears flowed down her dirty cheeks, leaving streaks of dirt behind.

"Moira!" Marrisa shrieked as she tried to run towards her. Lilith held onto her tightly.

The atmosphere screamed with pandemonium. The crowd roared and shouted obscene words at Moira as the soldiers shoved her against the splintered stake, tying her tightly to it. The crowd seemed to be angry at the woman, hating her, and she appeared as if she had no idea why. People began to throw things at her, like rocks and even their fresh apples and other produce that they had just purchased. Some of the people even threw their mugs of brew at her.

"Let me go!" she screamed, shaking her frazzled head.

Blood poured from her cheek and lip and she became sopping wet from the thrown brew.

"I've done nothing to no one I tell you! No one!" she cried out to the king who was still sitting on his horse.

King Julpen's face was blank, as if his mind was whirling with questions and thoughts—and doubts. His eyes looked sad and dark.

"My king, do not let this happen!" she screamed out. She then lowered her head and began to weep uncontrollably.

The king said nothing, didn't even look at her. He then raised his hand into the air as if signaling something, then rode off between the crowds, not even looking back. The two soldiers nodded their heads, then signaled to a soldier who was holding a torch, next to the platform. The soldier lit the oil-drenched sticks and hay beneath the hysterical Moira.

Marrisa's servants began to cry as they covered their mouths with their shaken hands, some not even looking but burying their faces into each other's shoulders as they consoled one another.

The aggressive flames rose up quickly, becoming bigger and angrier.

Moira became devoured in it.

"So, it begins," Lilith said in a low voice to herself as she held a crying and screaming Marrisa.

"She will cry out to Him through her black, burning and gnashing teeth. Her heart shall pump no more.   And she will go straight to the lake of fire and scream out in eternal darkness…"

21

Ten years had now passed upon the earth—ten peaceful and silent years. The burning of Moira was the first and last burning that had ever been ordered by King Julpen, leaving him in a state of heavy sadness.

But Princess Marrisa became to be the most beautiful and loving woman to ever walk upon Minslethrate. Just like her mother, the princess spread her love and kindness upon the kingdom—giving them a glimpse of hope.

Minslethrate finally began to become whole again… The people of Minslethrate began to live their lives in peace, going about their everyday business in a state of happiness… Every day was just a normal day.

And so, our story begins…

The time is now that the kingdom shall be stirred and the earth will be shaken.

Undisturbed and sleeping, the land of Minslethrate was about to be awakened by a forbidden and dark power that had long been forgotten—a quiet and hidden ancient evil which lurked in flesh upon the Golden Lands…

†

CHAPTER 2
Princess Marrisa

The sun was barely up, making the dark-blue sky look strangely beautiful. The clouds had flecks of dark-red and orange, illuminating off of the mountains on the silhouetted horizon. Cool air came in through the large doorway which opened out to a balcony, overlooking the Kingdom of Minslethrate. The beautiful but eerie sky of the early morning made the courtyard of the castle and village beyond look dark and gloomy. Long scarlet-colored curtains that hung in the large entryway fluttered in the early morning breeze, appearing like clots of dancing blood that were caught up into the air. Silhouettes of leaves from vines that grew around the balcony danced in the breeze, as well as two huge potted rose bushes that grew on either side of the balcony.

Marrisa stood before the massive threshold of the balcony, staring out into the world beyond—lost in thought. The cool breezes of the morning felt good against her body. Her long red wavy hair fell below her bosom and down her back, and her long white night gown fluttered in the breeze. She looked angelic, like a being of light.

That day was her sixteenth birthday, and the first day of the rest of her life as a woman. That day was supposed to be a happy day, a great day that would involve lavish gifts and full attention, ending in a great feast and a grand ball that would be held in her honor. But to Marrisa, that day was a day of great change, and change she did not want. It was her last day as a free person in Minslethrate, to do whatever she wanted with her friends, to love whomever she wanted, and to just be—free.

Before the great feast she would meet her future husband whom she had been betrothed to since birth, for the very first time. After the great feast there would be a royal ball, then they would be introduced to the courtiers and everyone else associated with the royal family as the new king and queen of a whole other kingdom that she didn't even care about. Then bright and early the very next morning they would be off to that kingdom to be married—and that is where she would live for the rest of her life.

Marrisa didn't know what kind of people lived in that kingdom; she didn't even know what kind of husband she would have. All Marrisa knew was that Prince Phillip was from a whole other country, a rather large kingdom by the name of Ishkar. She didn't even know if they spoke the same language! That day was the day she had been dreading, for a very long time. Marrisa knew that day would come, but instead of coping with it emotionally, she had been pushing it in the back of her mind, and now that it was there, she thought it was insufferable.

Marrisa wrapped her arms tightly around her bosom as shivers went down her back. The early morning breeze made the opened room chilly and filled with the scent of the outside air, which was actually pleasing to her even though she grew cold. She walked to the bathing room of her chamber which was not too much smaller than her actual room. An opened arch-doorway led to it.

Her bathing room consisted of a bathtub, a large washing basin that sat on top of a tall standing table, a large standing mirror and a small wooden vanity that had a smaller mirror on it; along with candles, a hairbrush and other things a young maiden might need. With the candles unlit, the room barely had any light. A small window above the commode on the far wall let in as much light as the early morning would allow.

She walked into the small room, wishing that hot water was ready for her in the tub. Lilith usually had the water ready for her every day when she woke up in the morning, with a lovely breakfast waiting for her when she was done bathing. She would miss that too even though she was not too fond of Lilith. She wanted to fetch Lilith to start her morning routines, but decided to leave her alone. The bright sun would be peeking out over the mountains soon anyways.

That morning was different; she woke up way earlier than normal because of the anxiety that lingered in her heart and soul. Marrisa stood in front of the mirror, studying herself from head to toe. She imagined herself as being a queen over a totally different county. She tilted her head slightly, still looking into the mirror, wondering if anyone in Ishkar had red hair. Her long red curls were lovely as they hung just below her chest. Her clear blue eyes pierced into her own reflection as she began to think more, but not of what she would be gaining as a queen, but of what she would be losing as a princess…and she hated what she would be losing. Marrisa detested the fact that she wouldn't see her father or the people of Minslethrate anymore after that day. She also couldn't stand how she would never see her sister-like friend, Natalia, ever again or even Tairren for that matter…

†††

Marrisa and Natalia were the same age and had known each other since they were small children. As young children they would always run and skip through the halls of the great castle or sneak out into the courtyard to play. Lady Natalia was a courtier and belonged to the Ducre' family. The noble family consisted of noblewoman, Lady Christianne, and nobleman, lord Fernund. Natalia and her family always attended every party, dinner, and social event that was hosted by the king. Marrisa and Natalia were always together; even so when they met Tairren for the first time.

Tairren was a couple of years older than both Marrisa and Natalia. He wasn't part of the aristocracy of Minslethrate, but only a common boy. Tairren and his mother, Moral, owned a small shop in the marketplace of Minslethrate. They sold all kinds of trinkets, fresh herbs and natural remedies, as well as things like fresh honey and preserves and even natural spring water all the way from Haifen Springs from across the land of Minslethrate. Their shop wasn't a big shop like some of the other entrepreneur's, but a small quaint little tent with a wooden frame and a large piece of fabric that hung over the top. They made just enough money to buy food, if they didn't get it from the land, and cheap fabric to make their clothes with.

Tairren and Moral lived in a small little cottage in the Forest Provence that was built by Tairren's father. As a child, Tairren did everything his father did. He learned everything from his father, everything dealing with nature, hunting, and The Holy Father of Light. He showed him what was edible that God put on the earth and what wasn't. Tairren was also taught how to fish and how to clean them afterwards. During each lesson Tairren's father would tell him many stories and legends, some true and others too outrageous to even be true. He also learned how to read and write from his father, the Book of Light being the first book he had ever read.

Tairren's father taught him so much, but everything changed when he was twelve years old. Tairren's father died from an accident in the woods when he was that age, leaving him as the man of the house.

Tairren wasn't as social as his mother or anyone else for that matter. He would always be found either in the marketplace, town square, or in the forests, continuing where his father left off, or just expanding his knowledge of the great outdoors even more.

On much of his time Tairren would be found resting under the trees or by the fountains playing his wooden flute in the town square.

And that was where Marrisa and Natalia met Tairren for the first time when they were carefree adolescents—in the town square. Tairren was sitting beneath a tree eating an apple and reading an old-looking book, while Marrisa and Natalia spotted him while shopping for new brooches. The two girls were accompanied by three handmaidens, two of them were Marrisa's: Lilith and Katrinka, and the other was Natalia's, who was called Sora...

✝✝✝

Marrisa smiled as tears began to form in her blue eyes. Her mind drifted away even more as she thought of Tairren. She still remembered everything so clearly. She remembered being amazed at how well Tairren knew how to read, considering that he was a young peasant boy.

✝✝✝

Her and Natalia had just purchased new brooches and were moving on to the next shop when she noticed a dark-haired boy reading beneath a flowering tree. She noticed the small, thick book he was reading, and how old it looked...

"What are you reading boy?" asked Marrisa.

She noticed how surprised he looked as he peered up at her, realizing who she was. His face was fresh and handsome, shy and humble. He stood up quickly and bowed down to her. She remembered that her and Natalia giggled, covering their mouths so not to embarrass him. She also remembered the looks of disapproval that the handmaidens had on their plane faces, because of her talking to a peasant boy.

Strangely, Lilith stood a little way away, covering her mouth and holding her stomach as if she were sick. Marrisa never understood why she never went near Tairren that afternoon or any time after that...

"What is your name boy?" Marrisa asked, still smiling.

She remembered how red his face was, making his blue eyes look even bluer.

"Tairren—your royal Highness," he said, looking very nervous.

Marrisa remembered what book he was reading, because she had to study copies of its pages, as well as other things, every day. She walked past her family's book, the original book, many times in the castle library, because it always sat in the same spot, on a little table below a massive stained-glass window: the legendary Book of Light.

"I see you love the tenacious words of our father of radiance," Marrisa said, sounding mature and well educated for a young princess.

He nodded, and she noticed him looking around at the other women who were staring at him, especially Lilith, who gave him an unpleasant but nervous look.

"Yes, your ladyship," he answered. "The book was passed down to me from my father, and my ancestors."

"Strange how you come about it. It's such a rare book to come by indeed. Your family is wise and able... I am Princess Marrisa, but you can just call me Marrisa if you are comfortable enough to; and this is The Lady Natalia Ducre'," she said, motioning towards her petite, dark-haired friend.

She remembered that he blushed again, lowering his face.

"Your Royal Highness, we must go!" Lilith snapped, still covering her mouth and nose, nauseated by the presence of Tairren.

"It was enchanting to have met you," Marrisa said with a smile as they began to walk again.

Tairren's cheeks appeared as a red rose.

Marrisa remembered that they left quickly, and as they left, she turned back at Tairren, waving goodbye.

After that day the three of them became secretly inseparable.

✝✝✝

Marrisa still looked into the mirror, coming out of her thoughts and daydreams. She was startled as she noticed a dark figure in the reflection of the mirror, standing behind her in the doorway. She inhaled a rush of air as she turned around quickly.

"Lilith, you frightened me!" Marrisa fussed as she held her chest.

She could feel her heart beating quickly beneath her hand.

"I am sorry your Highness," Lilith said as she came closer to Marrisa. "Daydreaming again I see," Lilith said, her black eyes just staring.

"No—I'm just frantic about today," Marrisa said, walking back into her room.

Lilith followed her, fetching a red robe made from the finest fabric in Minslethrate. She held the robe out, allowing Marrisa to slip her elegant arms into the sleeves.

"It is a big day for you—for all of us... I wish you a happy birthday, my lady."

"Oh Lilith, don't wish that upon me. How I wish today didn't even come," Marrisa said as she let herself fall backwards onto her bed. "I hate today—and have been dreading this day for some time."

"Today is a happy day," Lilith said as she lit the fire place on the far side of the room, getting it ready to heat some water for Marrisa's bath. "Today is a day of great change, a day that celebrates a new beginning, a new way of things…," Lilith said as she smiled her odd smile.

She seemed more excited about that day than Marrisa did. Lilith walked over to the side of the bed, still smiling. "A day of great change? A new way of things? What is she talking about?" Marrisa thought to herself as she just lay there, staring out of the balcony at the sun rise.

The sky was a brilliant orange now, with flecks of crisp blues scattered about it.

"Don't say such things, "Marrisa said, turning towards Lilith.

As long as Marrisa had known her, that was the very first time Lilith had ever seemed to be so excited about something. "I believe I have never seen you smile Lilith, and today you seem to be laughing on the inside. Why are you so happy, and why do you insist that it is a great day?" Marrisa thought, noticing how much Lilith had physically changed over the years. Her face was strange looking.

Marrisa thought that Lilith once looked pleasant, but now with the dark rings under her dark eyes, and the contrast of her ghostly white skin against those wide, coal-colored eyes, she didn't look so pretty anymore. Her once vibrant blonde hair was pulled back into a pile of braids and she wore her usual plain, dark-blue servant gown. All the handmaidens wore the same thing, except Lilith, who wore a thin leather belt around her waist, accompanied with a large ring of keys that hung from it. She held the keys to every door in the castle.

"I'll fetch some water to warm for your bath, my lady." She quickly walked out of the room, closing the large wooden door behind her.

Marrisa continued to just lay there, unimpressed and saddened, staring at the canopy of fabric that was draped over the top of her bed.

She thought of what would happen if she were to just run away. She probably wouldn't get too far, and would have nowhere to go. She could ask Tairren to guide her and Natalia to accompany her, but they couldn't possibly live in the forests for the rest of their lives—or maybe they could… Tairren knows everything about the forest, and what to do and what to eat.

Marrisa's thoughts of what would happen that day and running away whirled through her mind, giving her a headache. Besides, what would odd Lilith do then? Lilith was to come with her to the new kingdom to continue her status as head handmaiden. Lilith would probably hunt her down if she did run away; she was the type of person to do that. But even though Lilith submitted to Marrisa, there was still something about her that Marrisa didn't like. She was strange and cold, and carried an eerie presence about her. Her demeanor was uptight and—different. She never attended Sunday church with Marrisa, she never ate with Marrisa and she always refused to go near Tairren when they saw him in the marketplace. And there was something about her that sent chills down Marrisa's spine, sometimes. There seemed to be no life behind her dark-brown, almost black, eyes.

Marrisa turned on her side towards the fireplace. The large mouth of the fire place roared with a bright orange fire. The flames seemed to dance as they crackled and popped. The feelings of sadness and anxiety welled up inside of her, lingering like an illness as she stared into the dancing fire. She didn't like that Lilith used her fireplace to heat up her bath water. But she knew that it would be a huge hassle for Lilith to carry huge vats of hot water up and down from the kitchen to her room. Lilith insisted that this way was much easier, which it was, but Marrisa didn't like it. Lilith knew that Marrisa hated fire, but seemed not to care. She just kept away from fireplaces, and fire for that matter. She would rather freeze to death than sit in front of a fire place. There was something about fire that terrified her. It reminded her of death and sadness and for some strange reason—her childhood. Marrisa never really talked of her childhood, except for the experiences she had with Natalia. The only good memories of her childhood seemed to be just of her companions.

She didn't even have any memories of her mother, but only the knowledge of how great of a woman she was, and the stories she heard from her father and other courtiers around the palace. Moral, Tairren's mother even had lots of great things to say about her. By the many haunting paintings of her mother around the castle, Marrisa could see how beautiful she was; and that she resembled her mother greatly, which she was proud of. The only difference was that her mother had darker red hair and her eyes weren't as vibrant of a blue as Marrisa's. Marrisa would ask her father sometimes about her mother, when she would have the chance to actually sit down and talk with him. But he would never say too much about the deceased queen. She would even ask him about her grandmother and grandfather sometimes, but he always changed the subject abruptly, as if he was hiding something...

She kept a large family portrait painting in her room, hanging right above the fireplace. She was only a baby in the painting, but loved to look upon it anyways. Marrisa didn't like the painting being above the mantle of the fireplace though, but that was the only spot in her room that she could clearly see from her bed. Her father looked happier in it, as well as her mother, who had a lovely smile. They seemed to be in love by the looks of the painting and by what everyone had said. "Maybe my future husband won't be so horrid... And maybe we can fall in love like mother and father," Marrisa wondered as she put her hands beneath her head, still lying on her back. "Maybe he will be handsome, and fall in love with me, but not because he has to but because he truly wants to—and I him. Hopefully he is caring, and loves the Holy Father—like Tairren... Oh, Tairren, how I will miss you and everything that you do for me...," Marrisa's eyes became flooded with tears as she continued to think of—everything. "I think I will miss you most of all, Tairren..., and how I feel so free when I am with you. Nothing will ever be the same, nothing. I will have no one in Ishkar... Even though we are just friends, I will miss you so badly, more than you would ever know."

Marrisa continued to look at the painting above the roaring fire.

"I am half sick of shadows..." she said to herself.

Her eyes became red as tears trickled down the sides of her face. She longed for her mother, and her company through this dubious day, her birthday. She wished it was her mother whom she could talk to, and not just daunting Lilith. She wished it was her mother who would be the one to comfort her, but she knew she would never see her mother. She was tired of looking at her world through the family portrait that smiled at her. The only loved ones in her life were her friends, whom she would have to leave the very next morning. She would even miss her father, who seemed too busy to pay any attention to her during these times, or any time at all for that matter.

Marrisa rolled onto her stomach and buried her face into her pillow— feeling alone. Even though she was a princess and looked upon with great respect, she felt alone and never had anyone to really talk to in the great, cold castle. At times she even felt lost... She knew that crying would do nothing to help her, but that was the only thing she could do.

†

CHAPTER 3
Tairren

The early morning sun-light leaked in through the window brightly as Tairren opened his eyes. He was too tired to start his early morning chores before going to set up shop. He couldn't sleep during the night; he had too much on his mind. His restless mind seemed to only think of Marrisa. It bothered him that Marrisa was betrothed to another man, and had to move to another kingdom. Tairren couldn't stand that he wouldn't be able to see Marrisa anymore, or be able to talk to her, or even be able to have long walks through the woods with her anymore. Natalia would be there for him and he there for her, but it just wouldn't be the same. Marrisa was so much sweeter, and understanding, and just so much more—beautiful.

He stayed up all night thinking about her long red hair and crystal blue eyes, and the way she would smile at him. He would miss those things, and didn't even realize it until she was almost gone. She was sixteen now, and a woman, and a very beautiful and caring one at that. Even though Marrisa and Tairren were just friends, he still cared deeply for her; more than what a friend usually would care. He loved her. He knew this because of the way he felt when they were together, and the way his heart pounded so rapidly when she touched him. He loved the way she smiled and blushed when she did something silly. He loved that she didn't even know how beautiful she was, and that she didn't let her social stature get to her head. He loved her long red hair and the way it fluttered in the breeze when they went for walks. Most of all, he loved that she wasn't even embarrassed by him being poor. He just loved her, and she didn't even know it.

"Tairren, honey, are you up yet?! I made some tea and tartlets." Moral hollered from the kitchen.

Tairren slept in the upstairs compartment, which only had one way in and out, up a ladder and through a hatch door. He could hear his mother rummaging through cabinets, and the sounds of pots and dishware crashing together.

"Yes, mother," Tairren replied as he continued to just lay there on his homemade, stuffed goose feathered mattress, beneath his knitted quilts.

Even though he was eighteen and considered a man, he still chose to live at home and take care of his mother. He didn't feel comfortable with the thought of her living alone in the woods. He knew she would never move out, his father's spirit seemed to live in the walls and grounds of that little cottage. It wasn't just a house; it was a home that symbolized his father, and would stand forever.

"Come on down Tairren, before your tea gets cold!" she hollered.

He heard another crash of dishes, as if she dropped a pot or two. He knew that he wouldn't be able to sleep anymore so he got up to pull on his trousers and tunic. Tairren could see through his small window that it looked like it was going to be a beautiful day, but under the circumstances, he knew that the day wasn't going to be as beautiful as it should be.

The sun illuminated through the tree tops, marking shadows of leaves on the grass. The leaves of the trees danced in the breeze and dragonflies and butterflies fluttered to and fro about them. Little birds dove in and out of the tall grass that waved back and forth. Tairren loved mornings like that in the forest, wishing it could look that way every day. But even as the cheery sunlight touched his face, he still felt sad inside, as if his heart was slowly losing something. He knew his heart wouldn't be the same after the day was over with.

"Coming mother!" he hollered back as he fastened the front of his trousers.

He looked into a small mirror that hung on the wall of his little attic-like room. He ran his hands through his shaggy black hair to try to comb it a little. He was a handsome young man with black hair and blue eyes. His teeth were not too bad, and his bone structure in his face was nice to look at, at least that's what his mother told him—and that he resembled his father greatly.

As he looked into the mirror, he wondered why Marrisa didn't love him the way he loved her. But he knew it was of no use to love a princess as beautiful as she; society and rules would never allow it. The first-born daughter of the king was always betrothed to a prince from another country; and if the king had a son, he would be the first in line to take the kingdom, and a princess would be set up to come to him on her sixteenth birthday—like sweet Marrisa… That was the way they did things, and had been doing for generations. That was how different kings from different lands negotiated, making sure they had stability and a partner kingdom to trade goods with. Tairren didn't like it, and thought it unfair.

He smiled in the mirror to check out his teeth, he knew he had to clean them as soon as he went outside to freshen up at the washing bowl. Today was the day that he knew he had to look his best for Marrisa. He wanted her to remember him as a strapping young poor boy instead of just a poor boy. He fastened the top of his tunic, and then slipped on his heavy boots.

A large dagger and a heart shaped stone necklace that he made especially for Marrisa, hung on the wall of his little room. The dagger was his father's, and a beautiful one at that. The hilt was made of a smoothed out black stone that his father had found far off in the mountains before Tairren was born. The blade was sharp and Tairren made sure he kept it that way. He took the dagger from the wall and put the silver sheath on it which was also beautiful, and embedded with smaller black stones. There was a thick leather strap that was attached to the sheath, which he fastened around his waist. The dagger was one of his favorite things in the whole world, besides the blue stone necklace that he made himself. He put the necklace around his neck, tucking the blue heart shaped stone underneath his tunic.

When he was a child, exploring the far-off land of Minslethrate with his father, he found a blue stone that was wedged in the rough base of a cliff. He saved it all that time, just because it was the first special thing he had found with his father, and not to mention it was lovely to look at. One side was rough with tiny light blue crystals all over it and the other side was a darker blue that was not as rough. He spent a lot of time chiseling at it and forming it into the shape of a heart. He fastened a long thin strip of leather around it, making it into a necklace. He made it especially for that day, Marrisa's sixteenth birthday. Tairren had told Marrisa the story of how he came about the blue crystal once. She loved the story, and he knew that she would think the gift was even more special just because of it.

Opening the small hatch door of Tairren's room was like opening a door to an oven, but just not as hot. The smell of sweet tartlets and freshly steeped tea rushed into his room, hitting his nose like how the taste of sweet honey would on his taste buds.

"Good morning, it smells wonderful mother," Tairren exclaimed as he made his way down the ladder from his loft.

"Good morning, son. I made some fresh berry tartlets. And there is some tea ready for you at the table," Moral said, taking a batch of the berry tartlets out of the stone oven.

Tairren sat down at the small wooden table that was in the center of his small cozy home. Even though their house was small, it was a very lovely looking house. Bouquets of pansies and roses sat here and there, and small clay vases of dried herbs and flower petals filled the room with lovely smells. Bundles of dried herbs hung upside down from the ceiling, giving the small home an earthy and pleasant feeling. A small window on each wall allowed the bright sunlight to pour in; and candles sat here and there for light during the dark nights. One side of their house was the kitchen area, with a small stone fireplace oven that was built into the wall, and a washing basin for the dishes, and the other side of the house was Moral's small room which was closed off with an embellished quilt, hanging from the ceiling.

The quilt was a magnificent piece of art, which had a scene of a castle with a prosperous land surrounding it. Tairren and Moral were very talented and made many things, not only to sell in their shop, but for their home as well. Tairren created things which he used from nature and Moral created things by sewing and embroidering, as well as creating different remedies, elixirs and concoctions which always did good things for their minds and bodies. Moral also made their clothes, curtains, blankets and just about everything else that dealt with fabrics.

Tairren sipped at his tea, sniffing the light scent of coriander and lavender and other herbs as wisps of steam rolled out. He began to think of Marrisa—coriander and lavender tea was her favorite. She would sometimes come over to have tea with them, and to eat whatever his mother made that day, which was usually something sweet. He loved every moment he had with Marrisa, and didn't want it to ever end. But he knew that day was the last day that he would ever see her beautiful smile ever again.

"Here we are," Moral said as she placed a covered basket of tartlets on the table.

She sat on the bench across from her son. Tairren said nothing as he still sat in a daze, lost in deep thought. Moral moved the vase of flowers that was sitting in the center of the table over to the side, so that she could see her son better. She noticed how sad and off he looked and she knew why, but didn't want to bring it up; she was waiting for him to. Instead she uncovered the basket of tartlets. Steam rose from the basket, whirling up into the air, releasing the aroma of sweet berries and buttery pie crust. Moral served them both, placing two tartlets on each plate. The little topless pies looked delicious as the thick juices from the berries oozed over the sides of the crust. Tairren brought one of them to his mouth, then put it back onto his plate.

"Mother, can I ask you a something?" Tairren asked, looking into his mother's eyes. She was in the middle of fixing up her tea with some fresh cream and sugar, but stopped, looking up to him.

"Yes, son?"

"How…," he paused, looking down at his tartlets. He knew that the question he was about to ask might not be such a favorable one. "How does your heart heal—after losing someone whom you are in love with?"

Tairren watched his mother's eyes. He knew it took his mother a long time to get over his father's death. He always wondered how her heart felt because they never really talked about…

Moral was quiet for a second, or two, and then took a sip of her tea.

"Well, son—you continue to live your life every day, and think of the other things in your life that is worth waking up in the mornings for. And you talk to the good Lord, and ask him to mend your broken heart. And everything happens for a reason, you know. You just have to ask God what that reason is, and then you meet him half way to figure it out. And you thank him for it—you must always thank God… Loving God and trusting him with your whole heart is the only thing that matters…"

Tairren just nodded his head. He briefly thought about what his mother said, and the comment that what happened was supposed to happen. He didn't like that part too much. He knew that even though he loved Marrisa with all of his heart, he was not allowed to. He wasn't allowed to be with her for that matter. He knew that Marrisa probably didn't feel the same way for him as he did for her. How could a princess even grow to love a commoner? But, even if she were to love him the same way, it didn't really matter. The only thing that mattered was what was supposed to happen... And the important thing was that Marrisa was destined to be the queen of a whole other country, far, far away.

"Tairren, I know how you feel about The Princess Royal, but her Highness has to be married to that prince, and she has to live in that other kingdom. She has had no choice ever since she was born. Living a royal life seems charming and wonderful, but when it comes down to it, it's a life filled with rules and regulations. Living that life comes with specific obligations."

"I know that, I just don't think it should be this way… I don't want her to leave, but I know that she has to." Tairren took another bite of his tartlet, and then drank the rest of his tea. "And you are right, mother. I just need to live my life, which reminds me, I need to get going to open up shop,"

Tairren said, then stood up, cramming his other tartlet into his mouth, not caring when the hot juices from the berries burned him.

"But it's early still, sit down and have another tartlet, son," Moral said has she wiped her mouth with a handkerchief.

"No, I want to wash up then get started early. The weather is beautiful, which means people will want to start their shopping early."

Tairren kissed his mother on her cheek, and then walked to the door.

"Alright son, I will see you in a while then," she said as she brought her cup of tea to her lips.

That was what they usually did. Tairren would open up the shop in the morning, and Moral would come later to help with business. Then they would close in the early evening before it got dark. But Tairren thought that he might close a little earlier that day, just so that he could spend quality time with Marrisa before she had to get ready for her big social event that night.

Tairren walked out, shutting the door behind him. He really didn't need to leave early, and he really didn't care that customers wanted to shop early—he just wanted to leave. He didn't want to talk with his mother about Marrisa leaving anymore. He shouldn't have even brought it up, he thought. He knew one thing, that he didn't care if Marrisa was a princess or not, he was going to tell her how he had been feeling about her since the very first time he met her four years ago. He had to let her know how he felt about her. Even though his heart would be broken, it would make him feel better that she knew.

Tairren walked over to the side of the cottage to where the water well was. He pulled up a bucket of fresh, cold water and poured it into a large bowl. He sat the bowl on top of a small table that sat next to the back wall of the house. He washed his face with a bar of lavender soap his mother had made and washed his mouth and teeth with mint, rosemary, and caraway seed paste which was contained in a small covered glass jar. The paste was strong and refreshing, smelling of sweet spearmint and evergreen. After freshening up, he walked through the beautiful sunlit forest and thought some more. He decided to go the long way through the forest to the marketplace.

The leaves and grass of the forest fluttered in the soft breezes, allowing the sunlight to sparkle through the thick overhang. The feathery wind felt wonderful against his skin. He loved when the leaves would scatter on the earth when the breezes burst through the timber. He also loved the sounds of the trees and critters that were scattered throughout the serene atmosphere. The forest's animal companions always darted through the bushes and tall grasses, every once in a while, poking their furry faces out. The Forest Provence was one of the most beautiful parts of Minslethrate.

Tairren thought of Marrisa once again, and remembered how he saw her strolling through the forest by herself for the first time. That was the first time that he had ever seen a royal walk through the forest without a companion, servant, or guard following close behind. He always saw the random lovers, travelers, or even children of the kingdom, but never Princess Marrisa. He remembered how that day was an extra ordinarily beautiful day, and how after an exhilarating and swift year of knowing Marrisa, it was the first time that she had ever come into the Forest Provence looking for him… He would never forget it… He remembered it in detail as if it had just happened. His mind drifted away to that sweet moment…

✝✝✝

Tairren walked through the forest, coming from the great rosemary bush he had planted many years ago with his father when he was but a small child. He remembered how his father came home one morning after a long journey with his guild from a great trade fair. He brought home many things, and rosemary was one of them. He and his father had planted it in an opened area in the forest, along the steep side of a very small cliff and away from the shade, in full sunlight.

Tairren contained sprigs of the aromatic herb in a leather satchel that hung over his shoulder. Moral had asked him to get as many as he could, the tips of the rosemary that had the most blooms. Not only did she use the scented gray-green leaves in home remedies, but kept a vessel of them around the cottage to chase away any bad smell.

As Tairren made his way to his home, he could hear a beautiful voice. It was the voice of a young maiden, singing a piece of music that he had heard before many times. He had usually heard the catchy melody from the bard that would come and entertain in the town square and marketplace. He had also remembered hearing Marrisa and Natalia singing it together once before, harmonizing beautifully. The maiden's voice traveled softly through the forest, dancing with the breezes…

> Are you going to the spring-time fair?
> Rosemary, love, and sunshine.
> Remember me when you go there,
> For he once was a hero of mine.
> Tell him to make me a golden crown,
> Rosemary, love, and sunshine.
> Without no metal—and made with feather-down,
> Then he'll be a true love of mine…

Her voice was beautiful and soft and hypnotizing, sounding like a forest nymph from ancient stories. Tairren followed it, catching a glimpse of the songstress. At first glance he knew who the girl was; her red hair and lovely countenance gave it away.

His heart began to pound, excited and surprised to see her in the Forest Provence, his abode. He quickly began to finger-comb his black hair and smooth out his old tunic. He tried to rub the dirt from his hands and trousers, but knew it would be of no use without his mother's herbal cleansing soap.

He dashed up a small slope and hid behind a large oak tree, apparently catching Marrisa's attention. He grunted at himself. He was irritated, knowing that Marrisa must've caught a glimpse of him. She had to have, because she stopped singing for a moment, and then giggled.

Tairren could feel his face turning bright red with embarrassment as he leaned up against the tree. He held his breath, then peeked around the tree to see what she was doing. She started singing again as she made her way through some tall grass and flowers, picking a bouquet as she slowly came closer. He went to walk out from behind the massive oak, but hesitated. He knew he should have made himself present, but he didn't want her to stop singing…

He rarely heard her beautiful singing voice. She usually would only sing for royalty or nobility at concerts that would be held in the castle on a random occasion. Hearing her angelic voice amongst the enchanted forest was like magic. He fell in love with her all over again.

> Tell him to find me a castle of lace,
> Rosemary, love, and sunshine.
> By the saltwater—on a mountain's face,
> Then he'll be a true lover of mine.

Tell him to clean it with a fine feather,
Rosemary, love, and sunshine.
And sprinkle the halls with sprigs of heather,
Then he'll be a true hero of mine…

Tairren began to come out from behind the tree, worried that Marrisa would realize that he'd been watching her. She continued to sing, passing the tree a couple of yards away. Tairren went to take a step, still fixated on Marrisa. His foot got caught on a large knotted root of the oak, making him fall towards the ground, and down the small leafy slope. Defeating the purpose of not wanting to look like a strange idiot, he caught Marrisa's attention again, making her look over at him with curiosity. She rushed over to him, smiling. Embarrassed, Tairren got to his knees like a frazzled old woman who had just dropped a basket of fruit. He began to quickly pick up some of the sprigs of rosemary that spilled from his satchel, blowing the dirt from each one.

"What are you doing, Tairren?" Marrisa giggled, kneeling down to help him pick up the herbs.

She softly placed her bouquet down, trying not to scatter her flowers.

"I—I was just picking some herbs for my mother. Umm… What is a royal princess like yourself doing in the forest alone?" he asked, shyly catching a glimpse of her sparkling blue eyes.

"And what is a boy like *yourself* doing spying on a princess—*like myself?*" she teased, smiling at him. "I've come looking for your companionship…"

They simultaneously went to pick up the last sprig, her hand touching the spiny rosemary first, and his hand on hers. She could feel the roughness of his hand as he felt the elegance of hers. They were quiet, looking into each other's eyes. After what seemed like eternity, Tairren quickly pulled his hand away. They both stood up, dusting the gritty earth off themselves.

Tairren cleared his throat nervously. "Forgive me—I was just captivated by your—beautiful voice," he said, swallowing down his nervousness, glancing away from her tender blue eyes for a second. "You had my ears under some kind of spell."

After an intense moment, Tairren noticed her bouquet still lying on the ground. He picked it up, giving it to Marrisa.

She smiled at him again, excepting it from him as if he had picked it for her himself. She brought the rosemary up to her nose, smelling it and admiring the small dusty-blue colored blossoms. It carried the strong aroma of spicy sweet evergreen, lemons and eucalyptus: tangy and sweet, warm and spicy—like the smells of love.

"Lovely," she said, looking back into his eyes.

The luscious herb and blooms looked charming near her crystal blue eyes.

"Rosemary—an herb of love," she said, caressing the tip of the sprig on his cheek. She giggled, then took his hand softly and placed the stem in his palm. "Now you must be faithful to me." She teased him, smiling her beautiful smile again. "Legend has it that any person who is touched by a flowering sprig of rosemary by another, is to be faithful to them," she smiled brightly, giggling.

"Should the touch of rosemary bind me to my lady?" he asked, smiling. His young heart pounded in his chest.

"If one wishes it," she teased again.

Tairren came closer to her, wanting to kiss her then. He wanted to tell her how he felt about her. He wanted to show her how much he cared for her. His young body wanted to kiss her like lovers did. They stood so close to each other, looking into each other's eyes. She didn't move, seeming to wait for that kiss—for something to happen. He didn't kiss her though, for the fear of rejection and anxiety of him being a common boy germinated inside of him. Instead he held up the rosemary to her, giving her back the flowering herb.

"Add this to your bouquet, for I will always be faithful to you," he said, smiling, caught up in the innocent moment.

She gave him a warm smile, taking the rosemary from him and adding it amongst her wild flowers. She turned away from him, beginning to sing again. He walked with her through the beautiful forest, listening to her enchanting voice. She stopped singing, staring off as if in deep thought. Breezes came and went, playing with her long hair.

"…Does your suitor have to do those impossible things, in which you sing of—to have your love?" Tairren asked, looking towards the ground, then at her.

"Hmmm?" Marrisa came out of her daydream.

"Must he make you a golden crown made of fine feathers, or find a castle of lace?" He smiled, teasing her of the song she always sung.

"Am I not sweet enough for such a challenge?" She asked, teasing back. Her eyes gazed into his, mesmerizing him like deep clear spring water.

"Oh, yes—you are, princess," he said, blushing. "You are sweeter than nectar—and one would be lucky to win such a sweet love…"

They stood before each other, staring into one another's eyes again. She brought her lips close to his ear, nearly touching his skin.

"Then sprinkle the halls with sprigs of heather…," she whispered, reciting the last line of the song.

She smiled again, then ran off through the forest, giggling. Playfully, he ran after her, just smiling, blushing the whole time with a rapidly beating heart…

†††

Tairren came out of his daydream as he walked out of the forest and into the Great Field of Minslethrate. The long way in which he went seemed to be quick as he was lost in thought. He smiled at his daydream, wishing that he could have relived it. He wished they were still in the Forest Provence together. But at the same time, he regretted not telling Marrisa of his feelings for her that day… He wished he would have told her then how he felt. He began to hum the song that he remembered Marrisa singing as he continued through the field.

✝

CHAPTER 4
The Lady Natalia Ducre'

"Lady Natalia! It's time to get out; you've been in there all morning!" Sora hollered as she rushed into Natalia's large chamber.

Natalia was in her bathing room with the door shut, and had been in there ever since the sun came up—two hours prior.

"The Lord and Lady Ducre' are waiting for your appearance for dinner! Don't keep your father and mother waiting, child!" Sora hollered as she barged into Natalia's bathroom.

The candles were lit, nearly melted down to the core and Natalia lay in her tub, covered in stale bubbles.

"Sora! Leave me alone! I'm not coming down yet! I'm still— soaking," Natalia fussed as she sat up in her tub.

"Don't you mean sulking? I know that water isn't hot anymore and you should be a wrinkled prune by now. Come out and air out that soggy body of yours," Sora said, motioning her dark hands for Natalia to stand up.

Sora was a middle-aged woman with dark skin, and hair and eyes that were as black as the night sky. She was a large woman with a personality to match, that could keep anyone in line, except Natalia, who did whatever she pleased. Sora was loud and voice-tress and blunt and possessed an islander accent like Natalia's mother, but her's seemed to be much stronger.

The Ducre' family was the only family that Sora had patience for. Sora was like a mother to Natalia, and had been Natalia's handmaiden ever since she was born sixteen years ago. But even though Natalia put up her guard and acted like she didn't care what Sora said, she still loved her, and seemed to be closer to Sora than her own mother and father.

Natalia's mother and father were always so busy, just like any other noble couple of Minslethrate. With her father being a Marquis and her mother a Marchioness, her family was one of the most powerful families in Minslethrate. Lord Fernund seemed to always be off with business; and Lady Christianne was always shopping, having tea with other courtiers and noble-women, or locked in her personal study room of their huge home, reading or writing.

Lady Ducre' would bring Natalia along sometimes to have tea, only if other courtiers her age were there, or if she wanted her to meet someone else involving the aristocrats of Minslethrate. But most of the time Natalia would be with Marrisa anyways, doing their own shopping, having their own tea gatherings, or just stopping by Tairren's shop to say hello.

"Sora, let me be," Natalia said as she reclined back into the tub. Stale bubbles fluffed out over the edges of the tub, looking like soft dried out clouds. "Just inform my father and mother that I am skipping dinner—I feel ill," she said as she hit some bubbles off the side of the tub.

"Child, I already did that, I know you like the back of my hand and I knew you wouldn't get out anyway. I just told you that they're waiting so you would get out of that tub!" Sora said, sternly. "And you are not ill, if I told the Lord and Lady that you were ill, they'd have those physicians up here faster than I could tell them—we don't need your pretty blood drained for no reason. You know how the physicians do—one word of being ill and they'll drain you like a milked cow!"

Natalia just acted like she didn't hear her. Natalia never cared that Sora always got stern with her, or that she didn't address her by saying *your ladyship* during every conversation they had. Considering that she was her servant; she was used to it and it didn't bother her.

"Sora—don't be so *sore*," Natalia mocked, smiling.

She knew that Sora hated when she said that. She hated when Natalia mocked her name.

"Child, get out of that tub!" Sora yelled again as she scooped Natalia's small and naked frame out of the almost cold water.

Sora's large body seemed to easily lift her out of it, getting bubbles and water everywhere, including her apron and dress.

"Sora!" Natalia whined as she wiggled away from her grasp, trying to cover herself, "why do you do such things?!" Sora just shook her head as she grabbed Natalia's robe, then put it on her. "I am not a child!" Natalia fussed as she snugly wrapped the robe around her.

"Then stop acting like one! You know I have to clean that tub of yours, you making me behind on my chores. And you know you have your afternoon lessons! A noble lady must be well educated!" Sora fussed as she directed Natalia out of the bathing room and into her room, nearly pushing her over. "Now I have to clean up that mess," she said as she grabbed an undergarment from Natalia's large wardrobe. "How do you take a bath for two hours? And what are you pouting for anyway? You knew this day would come for a couple of years now. It is a sad thing that we'll be losing our princess, but you need to keep your pretty little head up. Cheer up my lady, okay?" Sora said, now smiling, patting Natalia on the shoulder.

Sora's mood always switched from irritated to sincere within seconds. Natalia always thought she was kind of unstable and stressed out and needed to just relax sometimes.

"But I will be losing my companion, my sister, and I'll have no one to talk to or be with every day," Natalia said, frowning.

"Child—you are so dramatic. You got your mother," Sora said as she took the robe off of Natalia, and then helped slip her undergarment down over her head.

Natalia laughed at her comment.

"You expect me to talk with The Lady Ducre'—or should I say, *the most honorable Marchioness of Ducre'*, every day?" Natalia said sarcastically as she rolled her eyes, mocking the way her mother and father would be announced and addressed when they would first arrive at any royal function.

"Don't you mock your mother child, and what about that handsome young shop keeper named Tairren? He's one of your friends and you and Marrisa are always chatting with him at his little shop," Sora said as she walked back over to Natalia's wardrobe, pulling out a red gown, her favorite red gown.

"Yes, well," Natalia said with a shy smile as she looked away from Sora. "I am very fond of Tairren—and he is and always will be a great companion to me... And even though we are friends...," Natalia stopped speaking, as if she were too shy to continue. "... It just won't be the same without Marrisa here. And Sora you know, as well as I do, that my mother has been wanting me to socialize with other courtiers and nobles now that Marrisa is leaving Minslethrate," Natalia said as she sat on a small chair next to her bed. "I know every lady and every eligible bachelor and lord in Minslethrate, but I choose not to associate with snobbish people. Every courtier and noble in Minslethrate carries themselves as high and mighty. I cannot stand that," Natalia fussed as she pushed herself off of the small chair and walked over to her wooden vanity to brush out her long brown hair. Sora smiled, as if amused at what Natalia was ranting on about. "And my mother is always setting up tea dates with The Lady Daleasa Vaughn and The Lord Fredrick Vaughn for me—I can't stand those twins, they annoy me so, Sora. I don't know why my mother wants me to associate with condescending, annoying people.

"But after today it seems as if that will be the only people I will be able to affiliate with, besides Tairren. But my mother does not want me to socialize with Tairren, she actually forbids it. I can just imagine my parent's bellowing out, *"what impropriety is this?!"* Natalia mocked in a voice she thought her parents sounded like. "Tairren is loving and kind—and I will always want him in my life...," Natalia said as she brushed her hair, irritably.

"Calm down child, before you brush your hair straight out of your pretty little head," Sora said as she fiddled through Natalia's small jewelry box, picking out the usual brooch and hairpiece that she usually wore with her red dress.

"Child, you know you act like them too. Don't go casting stones or it will come back and hit you square in the nose!"

"Sora! That's not fair!" Natalia fussed back as she smacked her hairbrush back on her vanity.

"Child, you sound like your mother when she gets spoiled milk for breakfast—fussing over things that don't matter... Come, get dressed. You have lessons in an hour."

Natalia giggled at Sora's comment. She then stood up to get dressed.

"I'm skipping my lessons this afternoon and meeting Marrisa in the Marketplace instead. This is the last time I will be meeting with my sister before she leaves... I hate how it will be our last outing, ever," Natalia said, staring out the window into the open field which surrounded their massive castle-like home. "It's a lovely day as well, maybe today will be a beautiful ending for Marrisa," Natalia said with a frown.

"Oh yes, it will be! Especially with that grand feast and ball that is tonight," Sora said as she helped Natalia dress. "How lovely everything will be with the dancing and beautiful young ladies and those handsome young men! And I can only imagine the beautiful decorations and all of that wine! I am so excited for you all. Oh, how I wish I could go!" Sora exclaimed. "It would be in my wildest dreams to ever participate in such a royal function," Sora said, chuckling, "I would probably spoil everything!"

"Oh hush, Sora," Natalia said, pulling her long hair to one side, over her shoulder. "They are indeed beautiful and enjoyable, but I'm not as excited about this one. I do hope that it goes well for Marrisa's sake, and I hope Marrisa has a splendid time as well. Maybe tonight will help release some stress that she has been carrying around about her. But only God knows," Natalia said as she looked into her mirror that stood next to her vanity.

Sora tightened Natalia's laced up bodice that fit snugly around her torso. She looked beautiful in her elegant red dress. The sunlight from the window reflected off of the small red jewels that were sown onto her beautifully embroidered bodice. Sora clasped a gold chain around her neck that had a red jewel that dangled from it. The round jewel sparkled as the sunlight played off of it.

"You always look so lovely," Sora said with a big smile. She looked at her like a proud mother would at her child.

Natalia studied herself in the mirror, appearing surprised, as if she had never seen herself in the red dress before. Her vibrant green eyes and light brown skin looked beautiful against the expensive red fabric.

There was an urgent knock at the door. Natalia turned quickly to open it, wondering who would be knocking so boldly at her door. She opened the door to find that it was just Alexa, another servant of the house. She was a short young chubby girl about the same age as Natalia. She had curly blond hair that was back in a frazzled bun and rosy red cheeks that had splotches of acne on them. Natalia wrinkled up her nose as she got a whiff of some of Alexa's body odor; she always smelled of roasted poultry.

"Excuse me, your ladyship," she said nervously as she peered into the room, "but is Sora at hand? The Lady Ducre' has asked for her."

Natalia rolled her eyes as she opened the door all the way. She walked over to the window, annoyed by Alexa's request.

"What is it Alexa?" Sora asked with an aggravated look on her face as she hung Natalia's robe back into the wardrobe.

"I'm so very sorry for bothering you both, I'm just the messenger," Alexa exclaimed nervously.

She was right. But Natalia never understood why her mother needed Sora so much. The Marchioness had three other personal handmaidens, as well as random servants like smelly Alexa who also worked in the household, to get whatever she wanted. Natalia thought that her mother would purposely do that because she was jealous of the relationship that she and Sora possessed.

"It's quite alright, Sora," Natalia said as she leaned over onto the ledge of her opened window, her head propped up in her hands. "The Lady Ducre' *desperately* needs you," she said with an annoyed tone.

After a minute or two, Natalia heard the heavy door close behind her. "So, this is how it will be for now on," Natalia thought as she still peered out of the window. She knew everything would be so different after that night was over, after Marrisa left. She wouldn't really have anyone to talk to about her problems anymore. Her mother would slowly steal Sora away from her and replace her with someone like bland Alexa, and Marrisa would be miles away as a queen over the land of Ishkar. "What kind of name is *Ishkar* for a kingdom anyway?" Natalia thought.

Natalia closed her eyes as the cool air of the bright mid-morning brushed at her face and hair. The mixture of the cool air and warm sun seemed to clear her thoughts, comforting her. She opened her eyes, looking down. She was on the second floor, but seemed higher than that. She could see their rather large vegetable garden below, and that a couple of servants were on their knees, pulling at lettuces and other vegetables. Fields of tall grasses and flowers waved back and forth in the breeze just beyond the garden. Natalia would never forget all of the times when Marrisa and she would ride their horses, Lilly and Orchid, through those fields and pastures and through the apple orchards.

Natalia looked down noticing that between the garden and fields were tall bushes with white flowers all over them, which looked like white dots from her point of view. And just beyond the fields was a small forest, and just beyond that Natalia could see the tall standing castle of Minslethrate. She always thought her bedroom window had the best view in all of the kingdom. And just to the right of her, Natalia could see the far-off Mountains of Minslethrate, which looked like gray mounds of dirt painted on the horizon.

Natalia had actually never gone that far off into the wilderness of Minslethrate, but Tairren has. He used to always tell his stories of how he and his father used to venture off deep into the beautiful lands, discovering things that weren't even looked upon by any other human during their time. Even though the far-off lands were forbidden, they went into them anyways.

Natalia caught the scent of wood and leaves burning as another breeze floated past her nose. The gardeners must've been burning some old dead leaves and random rotten branches that fell from the trees. The scent of the warm and spicy fire triggered a memory that she had forgotten. Natalia smiled softly as nostalgia came over her. She thought of the times when Tairren would tell her and Marrisa different legends and myths about the land and all that inhabited it.

"How I wish I could go back in time," Natalia thought as she gazed off into the seemingly magical land of Minslethrate. She thought of a moment during the summer that had just passed, when Tairren made a small fire in the woods one evening…

†††

The fire crackled and popped as Tairren threw some dried leaves into it.

"Tairren, don't let the fire burn too greatly, for my sake, please." Marrisa said as she sat down onto a log that lay a couple of feet from the small fire.

Even though the fire was tiny, Marrisa still didn't like it, she never did…

"I won't, Marrisa," Tairren said as he sat next to her, who sat next to Natalia. "This fire will stay just as it is."

Tairren knew that Marrisa was not fond of fire, but he never knew why. He thought maybe it was that she might have gotten burned by it at some point in her life. But he had gotten burned plenty of times in his life and never thought anything of the orange light.

"It seems as if the sun was just going down," Natalia said, "and now it's absolutely dark out here."

The forest seemed as dark as a cave because of the heavy overhang of the tree tops and the thick timber and grass that surrounded them. That summer night was enchanting as fireflies danced in and out through the dark trees of the woods. The chirps of crickets made a soft melody as a hoot of an owl echoed through the darkness every now and then, creating a soft and relaxing tune.

They had just left Tairren's house where they ate some hearty vegetable soup that Moral had cooked for supper, and decided to go for an evening stroll through the woods. Then it was Tairren's idea to make a little fire. The sun was just going down as Tairren finished getting the fire going.

"I probably shouldn't have started this fire. We should get going. Your parents will have the royal soldiers out looking for you both," Tairren said as he poked the crackling light with a long stick.

"No, we should be alright," Marrisa said as she pulled her long red hair over her shoulder, "My father doesn't even know I am gone and Lilith thinks I'm resting. I told Lilith that I was going to bed early, but I'm actually surprised that she hasn't discovered that I'm not in bed," Marrisa said with a smile. "I would have already been bombarded with soldiers by now if she knew—I actually wouldn't be surprised if she was lurking through the woods right now looking for me!" Marrisa said as they began to laugh.

"Well, my mother and father never know where I'm at and Sora probably is wondering what I'm up to, but she knows that I am with you both," Natalia said as she swatted at a small bug that kept swooping in front of her face.

"Marrisa, if you don't mind me asking; don't you think that Lilith is a little strange? I don't want to offend you because she is your head handmaiden, but she's very deviant. And I don't think she's fond of me," Tairren said, looking into the cozy little fire.

"Yes, I'm very well aware," Marrisa said as she giggled a little. "She is very different and of course I don't know why she keeps her distance away from you, but she has been my servant since I can remember… But actually, over this past week it seems as if she hasn't really been caring about how I feel lately. I may be acting like a child, but I feel like I need more emotional support from her because of me having to leave in the upcoming early spring," Marrisa said, and then she went silent for a second or two.

Natalia and Tairren stayed quiet as well because of the thought of Marrisa leaving, and didn't want to talk about it. And even though it was her special sixteenth birthday coming up in the spring season, none of them were as excited about it as they should have been.

"But what I'm trying to say is that I think she has been doing things on purpose to upset me," Marrisa continued as she fiddled with the curled ends of her long red hair.

"What do you mean?" Tairren asked as he looked at her. She still kept her gaze on the tiny fire.

"Well, for one thing, you both know how I feel about fire, and she knows this as well, but I find that she lights the fire place in my room more often now, just to taunt me. It's not cold outside, and we're in the middle of summer for God's sake!" Marrisa fussed as she twisted her hair into one thick lock.

"Have you said something to her about it?" asked Natalia.

"Actually yes, I have. And she just says that she thought that I might have wanted it lit. And then she always says that she forgets that she lit it and didn't mean to," Marrisa said as she shook her head and rolled her pretty blue eyes at the same time.

"You just have to be mean to her to make her get the point," Natalia said with a big smile, "that's what *I* would do."

"Yes, we know that," Tairren said as he laughed a little.

"Well maybe so, but I just can't be mean to someone. I don't think I've ever raised my voice at any of my handmaidens. I think I would feel bad about it afterwards. Besides, she says she doesn't mean it. Maybe it's all in my head about her doing it on purpose to upset me. I guess I need to get over this fire nonsense, I am about to be considered a woman and a queen soon enough—but I just can't help it." There was silence for a moment, then the flickers of the firelight reminded Tairren of something.

"Can I ask you another question?" Tairren asked, still looking at Marrisa. "If you don't mind me wondering, what is it about fire that frightens you?"

Marrisa was quiet, still gazing into the small fire that illuminated with a soft orange glow, painting spots of gold on everything that it touched. It crackled softly and seemed to add another melody to the music of the crickets and owls.

Natalia glanced at Marrisa, and knew that she didn't like to talk about her fears; but Natalia wondered about the same thing as well. Of course she knew that Marrisa didn't like fire, but she never knew why. And every time that subject came up, she would always ignore it or change what they were talking about. Natalia felt bad for not changing the subject herself, but she wanted to know as well and knew that it would be good for Marrisa to talk about it anyways.

A small tear began to roll down Marrisa's cheek as the fire's soft light danced on her beautiful face. Anxiety began to build up inside of her. She was still quiet as more tears swelled up in her crystal blue eyes, making them sparkle.

"I'm so very sorry," Tairren said, breaking the awkward silence, "I should've never been so bold as to ask such a question…"

"No," Marrisa said, cutting him off, "I need to stop acting like a child… But to tell you the truth…I really don't know why I get so emotional or why I'm so terrified of blazing fires. This small fire is fine and could be stomped out in a second, and doesn't make me feel so uncomfortable. But it's the big fires, the uncontrollable ones that terrify me so," Marrisa said, wiping the tears from her eyes. "I just get this sad, horrible feeling when I come near fire. And I feel as if I have just lost someone I love or someone I am close to. My heart starts pounding in my chest and I begin to become terrified… I just get this horrifying feeling that someone I love has been tortured in it…and I don't know why. And I hate the way it feels, and I hate that I have no idea why I feel like this. But When I look into the flames, I get these flashes of someone being—burned and burned and burned and screaming out and no one will stop to help!" Marrisa started to cry as she covered her face with her hands.

Natalia and Tairren were shocked, not expecting anything that came from her mouth. They both rubbed her back, trying to calm her down.

"It's okay," Natalia said as she put her arm around her friend, pulling Marrisa closer to her.

"No, it's really not," Marrisa said, wiping her eyes again, "I feel that it's not okay. There has to be some reason why I feel this way!"

They were quiet for a while, giving Marrisa time to calm down.

Tairren thought to himself, wondering what he could say next without offending her. "I'm sorry, Marrisa, I never meant to get you upset. I didn't know," Tairren said quietly as he wiped a tear drop from her chin.

She looked at Tairren and smiled her beautiful smile again as her eyes twinkled in the firelight.

"It's okay, Tairren," Marrisa said, not sounding as upset, "I think I'm happy that you've asked, I kind of feel relieved that I've told someone, and that it was you both and not anyone else. I've never told anybody about this, because of the fear of someone thinking that I may be mad." Marrisa laughed a little, still hugged up against Natalia.

"We don't think that of you," Natalia said, kissing her head.

"Thank you," Marrisa said, sniffling.

"Well, on the other hand—*you are stranger than an old noblewoman with a bucket of brew*!" Natalia said in a loud voice, mocking her beloved Sora and her islander accent.

They all laughed, breaking the intense feeling of angst that had developed among them.

A huge smile crept across Marrisa's face. She quickly grabbed a huge wad of dead leaves and threw them at Natalia.

"Marrisa! That wasn't at all lady-like!" Natalia snapped as she pushed Marrisa off of the log.

They both laughed again, including Tairren. Marrisa just lay on her back on the crisp leaves and fresh earth, pulling Natalia down with her.

"Marrisa, I don't want to be associated with the filthy ground and dead leaves!" Natalia fussed as she got up quickly, dusting the leaves and dirt off of her deep-blue colored gown.

"Well, you already have when I threw them at your face! What's the difference?" Marrisa laughed as she just lay there, putting her hands beneath her head.

"Come on Natalia, don't be a ninny," Tairren said with a big smile as he lay down next to Marrisa.

Natalia just rolled her eyes as she crossed her arms, sitting back down on the log. "I am a *lady*," she said as a smile appeared on her face.

"You know Natalia, you look like Fiara with those flames glowing behind you like that," Tairren said with another one of his teasing smiles.

"Who is Fiara?" Natalia asked, picking a leaf out of her long brown hair, "and don't insult me."

"Isn't she an ancient Minslethratian goddess?" Marrisa asked, propping her feet up on top of the log, next to Natalia. "The elders of Minslethrate say that she is a seductress, a promiscuous woman of beauty who knows the secrets of any man whom she gazes upon," Marrisa said with a low voice, trying to sound mysterious.

"She sounds like a trollop," Natalia said, nonchalantly, making Marrisa giggle.

"Well, legend has it that she is a goddess, a lady of fire, and the sister of Haifen and Dolsia. They are the goddesses of water and earth. Fiara dwells far off in the south, deep in this land towards the mountains. She lives with other women who wait on her hand and foot, serving her as if she were the creator of fire. Haifen dwells behind the Great Falls and Dolsia dwells deep in the heart of the Black Forest." Tairren spoke as if he were telling a ghost story, speaking low and mysteriously. "And obviously that's where we get our great landmark names from, like Mount Fiara, Haifen Springs and the Dark Lands of Dolsia.

"Do you believe it, that there really are goddess-like women out there who live to be worshiped as the creators of fire, water and earth?" Marrisa asked, sitting up, pulling her long red curls over her shoulder as she combed through it.

"Well, I only believe in one God, who is the creator of this earth and of the sun and the moon and heavens. These legends of Fiara and her sisters are just old beliefs of our pagan ancestors, long ago before the Great King from the past brought his mighty words to the land of Minslethrate, which were later written down in a book. I don't believe in the goddesses; they are just interesting stories that are told and passed on from generation to generation. But I do believe that there are monsters and evil beings out there that live to spread false prophecies. And I believe that these beings want to be worshiped as a god, to live on and rule as a great god, and to crush every believer and follower of our true God. My father used to tell me stories of the old legends of Minslethrate, and of the ancient pagan goddesses that some elders believe in, still to this day. They make great bed time stories though," Tairren said, sitting up as well.

"But do you think there are really women out there deep in these lands, who live that way still, to be worshiped?" Natalia asked, interested in the conversation.

"Well, I will tell you that when I was a young boy, my father and I went on a journey deep into these lands to fetch some things to sell in our shop, things like special herbs and flowers to make oils with. I remember that we had a compass and a drawn-out map of Minslethrate. I know that we went really far because I remember that it took us a couple of days by horse. And I remember one of those afternoons we set up camp in the Black Forest because my father was tired. He fell asleep quickly. Shortly after we set up camp, I decided to look around a bit, just to see what was around.

"And then I heard the voice of a woman, singing. It seemed to echo through the woods, and I still remember to this day how beautiful and sad it sounded, full of melancholic mystery. So of course I followed the voice and it led me to a small temple, covered in the nature that grew all around it. You could tell that it was ancient because of the way the trees took over it. I remember how vines and other greenery seemed to grow all over the place, inside and out of the old temple. Then once I stepped inside of the temple, the singing seemed to fade away. Then I remember seeing a figure walk past one of the many columns towards the back of the temple. I really couldn't tell who it was because I stayed glued in the great threshold of the entrance. Then I ran back to our camp, which was about a twenty-minute walk away from the temple. I woke my father up; I remember how alarmed he looked. So, I told him what I saw and led him to the ancient temple. And as soon as he saw it, he knew exactly what it was because of a symbol that was etched in the stone above the doorway. Apparently, it was the symbol of Dolsia. But we didn't go into the temple. I remember my father said that it could be dangerous and infested with evil spirits. But I wish we would have because to this day I always wonder who it was that I saw, and whose voice it was that I heard." Marrisa and Natalia were quiet, as if in awe by what they had just heard.

"I would like to see it," Marrisa said, smiling. "All my life, I have never gone beyond the great fields of the kingdom. I have never seen what's out there in these lands."

"Well, that was the only temple that I've ever seen. After my father died, I've never went that far into the lands again. It's far too dangerous, and forbidden. But apparently there are three other temples out there that were built many years ago, to honor the other two, Fiara and Haifen."

"*Three* other temples?" Marrisa asked, looking confused. "But I thought you said that there were only three goddesses total."

"But there is a fourth great temple far off in the south. It sits just before the Great Mountains on the edges of its shadowed cliffs. This temple was built many years ago, subsequent to the other three temples. Legend has it that once a year, there would be a great celebration at that temple, commemorating the three goddesses and their work that they had done for the land that year.

"Every adult consisting of the upper-class of the kingdom traveled to the temple, leaving their children at home with their servants. The people brought with them one young virgin woman against her will, usually a very beautiful one. These people would stay up all night, drinking, laughing, dancing—celebrating the prosperous harvest of that year. Then at the peak of twilight, they would bring the beautiful and pure young woman up to the top of the temple, dress her in a black gown, then they would sacrifice her to the goddesses in return for the great year that the goddesses allowed the land to have." Tairren's blue eyes seemed to glow in the fire light as the girls sat, awestruck.

"Oh my," Natalia said, with wide green eyes, "how disgusting and horrifying. Our ancestors were brutal."

"Yes, things were very different a long time ago, and more treacherous," Marrisa said as she sat on the log next to Natalia. "Animosity was a lover to our land."

Tairren stayed where he was at, sitting still on the ground beneath them.

"We are now in a period of grace. Thank God for the ancient king who brought the truth and the word of light to Minslethrate," Tairren said, looking up to them. "I think Minslethrate would still be a pagan country today if it wasn't for him. God brought him to this country long ago to take the blindfold from our ancestor's eyes. But like I said, there are still people today in Minslethrate who choose to practice the old ways and worship the false gods Fiara, Haifen, and Dolsia."

"That is so strange…," Marrisa said with a yawn, "and as much as I think this conversation is interesting, I think it's about time I go back to the castle, I'm getting awfully tired."

"I agree," Natalia said, standing up.

"I'll walk you two to the edge of the forest where Lilly and Orchid are," Tairren said, standing up as well. "Because I wouldn't want either of you to become snatched and *sacrificed*," he said facetiously.

Marrisa laughed as Natalia shoved him.

The firelight got dimmer as it was very close to dying, making the crackle die down as well. But the crickets still chirped and the owls still hooted as Tairren stomped out the fire before they left to go home…

✝✝✝

"Lady Natalia, get your precious little head out of that window before you fall straight to the ground like a sack of potatoes," Sora said, startling Natalia.

"Oh Sora, you frightened me," Natalia said, turning around to find Sora in the doorway. Natalia glanced at her, then turned back to the beautiful scenery of Minslethrate. "That was a quick errand."

"Well, I was gone for a while," Sora said as she walked over to where Natalia was standing. "Your mother wanted me to fix her hair up; she says I do it best."

"Yes, well you've had plenty of practice on mine," Natalia said, looking back at Sora with a friendly smile.

"That's the truth," Sora said, smiling back, "well I got to finish my chores, I have a lot to do today before tonight."

"Yes, don't we all," Natalia said, looking back out of the window towards the castle.

†

CHAPTER 5
A Royal Surprise

Marrisa looked despondently into her mirror. She had to at least make sure that she looked her best before leaving her room for the day. It didn't matter to her that she wasn't as kept up as she normally would've been, but she wasn't in good spirits and had to cover up how she was truly feeling some how.

She wore a light-blue gown that set off her crystal blue eyes. Her long red locks fell over her shoulders and she wore a jeweled diadem around her forehead that looked like a crystal halo as it sparkled in the sunlight. A teardrop shaped jewel, the color of her eyes, fell in the middle of her forehead, dangling from the diadem. Taking one last solemn glance at the mirror, she left her room.

She started her journey through the castle to where her father usually was, which was in the grand study hall. She wanted to tell her father good morning. She wanted to actually chat with him for a moment before leaving the castle for the day. So, she walked down the hallway, down the stairwell and through another small hallway which led to the main hall of the castle.

Walking into the main hall was like walking into a room of chaos. Many Servants of the castle worked like bees, rushing here and there as they hung veils of sheer fabric, placed bundles of trimmed roses, put out vases of lilies everywhere, and set up many tables and chairs for the grand ball that was going to take place that night. Some servants were cleaning and dusting the windows, some were sweeping the halls, and others were rushing about to their next project. It was strange to Marrisa how all of this was for her, and she didn't feel even an ounce of excitement or happiness.

Marrisa walked into the grand hall, looking to see if she could spot Lilith anywhere. Amongst the bustle of all the servants, she spotted all of her handmaidens, except for Lilith and Katrinka. She didn't see them anywhere, which was an odd thing. But on the other hand, she didn't want Lilith to spot her and try to talk to her. But it was definitely strange that Katrinka was not there, she was usually the first one to start setting up things for any special event that happened in the castle. As a matter of fact, Marrisa didn't remember seeing Katrinka that whole week. She had so many handmaidens that it didn't even occur to her that Katrinka had been absent all week long. "I wonder if she is sick," Marrisa thought to herself, "I'll have to ask Lilith about that, if I ever see Lilith today."

Marrisa walked swiftly through the hall, trying not to be seen by anyone; she didn't feel up to talking to anyone at that moment. Normally Marrisa would stop to talk with everyone, but that day she felt different, she didn't want to spend too much time in the castle knowing that she had too little time to see the important people in her life. No one seemed to notice her, they were too focused on what they were doing that they missed the blur of red hair that hurried through the great hall. She made it to the other side, passing two royal soldiers that guarded the entrance to the hall. Marrisa passed them with a gentle smile.

She walked into her father's great study hall and began to make her way across it. The hall was huge with many shelves of books and globes everywhere. There were many paintings on the huge walls, of Marrisa and of her mother and father. Huge brightly lit candelabrums lit up the room, as well as many torches on the walls. Many tall windows covered the left side of the room, adding more light to it. Large tapestries and the royal family crest above a shield in a coat of arms also hung on the gray stone walls. She finally made it to the other side, finding her father standing at a large table that was covered with papers, maps and other things that looked really important. She realized that her father was in a meeting, accompanied by two other men. She recognized the older man who was her father's royal advisor, Master Odwa, but she didn't know who the young man was.

"Oh daughter, it's so good of you to grace us with your presence," King Julpen said as he reached out his hand to her, signaling that it was okay for her to approach them.

"Good morning, father," Marrisa said with a smile as she gave him a hug. She appreciated that hug, which rarely happened.

"It is a wonderful day to celebrate the day of my only daughter's birth," he said with a small smile, then kissed her on the forehead. She smiled a little as she shyly nodded her head. "Marrisa there is someone I would love for you to meet," he said, with that same small smile, "this is Prince Phillip—from Ishkar, he just arrived this morning."

At that moment Marrisa's heart dropped as she realized that her father had just said Prince Phillip and Ishkar in the same sentence. Her heart began to pound rapidly as it dawned on her that she was meeting the person she had to marry. She felt sick all of the sudden as her heart seemed to move up into her head, pounding its way into her ears. She was speechless as he took her hand, gently kissing it.

"It's a pleasure to have finally met you," he said in a low voice that held an accent she had never heard before.

She nervously bowed to him.

"So, you can speak the same language as I," Marrisa thought to herself.

She could only smile a little.

"I am Princess Marrisa of Minlsethrate," she finally said, realizing that he obviously already knew that.

He bowed his head to her, then smiled. She realized that she thought he was handsome. He had dark brown eyes and black wavy hair that came down to his shoulders. He looked about twenty-five or so and his smile was nice and looked bright against his tan skin.

"My princess, I've been anticipating you all morning. May we go for a walk?" Prince Phillip asked, then turned towards King Julpen. "Your majesty—if that is okay with you," the prince said with a smile.

"Certainly, prince," the king said, then escorted them through the great hall. "Dinner will be served within the hour—Alexander and the kitchen staff is getting a wonderful meal ready for us filled with the finest Minslethratian foods," the king said as he patted the prince's back.

Marrisa heard her father talking to them as he walked them out, sounding slightly excited as he spoke, but she only heard energized gibberish. She was too deep in thought, wishing that none of this was happening. She had never seen her father act that way before. She wondered why her father seemed much happier than usual, cheerier; but she had an idea why. He had never showed that much excitement before, or even smiled. He didn't seem too sad that he was losing his only offspring and daughter, but more excited that he would be associated with the powerful Kingdom of Ishkar. Of course, now that she would be queen of another kingdom, especially a mighty one, Minslethrate would have access to many goods from Ishkar, and both of the kingdoms would form an alliance with one another.

Marrisa wished that she would've never even walked down there to see her father. She should have just left the castle. But at the same time, she knew that she just couldn't keep on ignoring the situation. Prince Phillip seemed nice and charming, and someone it would be worth getting to know, but she didn't want to get to know him, she liked the life that she had already.

"Your kingdom is very beautiful—one of the most attractive I've seen yet," the prince said with a smile as he motioned for her to walk through the great arched threshold and into the fresh air and bright colors of Minslethrate.

Marrisa realized that they were now outside in the gardens of the castle. The bright sun felt good against her skin and it smelled wonderful outside, like fresh sweet earth. The garden was amazing and beautiful, with majestic statues, decretive columns and arches everywhere; and not to mention there were thousands of brightly colored flowers and rose bushes that adorned the earth. Servants every now and then could be seen as they walked here and there, working in the garden, carrying baskets of fresh clippings and unwanted weeds. A large fountain sat in the middle of the garden, surrounded by violet and cream-colored irises. In the center of the fountain was a marble statue of a great king, standing tall and proud, pointing his sword to the heavens with one hand and holding a large opened book in the other hand.

"This is a beautiful piece of art," Prince Phillip said as they dawdled past the great fountain, "very inspiring."

"Thank you," Marrisa said with a gentle smile, "it is based off the original statue that used to stand there. It has been with my family for many years. It's a reflection of one of the ancient and mighty kings of Minslethrate. My ancestors had the original carved from marble many generations ago, to commemorate the belief of the mighty King of Light who saved Minslethrate as well as many kingdoms, from more insidious beliefs. It was destroyed somehow and during the reign of my father, it was created again. It is said that the Great King went on many crusades during his reign, spreading the word of light to many kingdoms and leading his men in battle to fight for truth… I love everything about it."

"What a stirring story—Legend has it that the Great King of Light was the mightiest of all kings," the prince said, looking at Marrisa as if waiting for a reaction.

"You know the legend?" Marrisa asked, surprised.

"Indeed, I do—the Great King was a very controversial king. The legend of the king was simply created so people could have something to believe in," the prince said nonchalantly.

"Controversial? Those who are offended by good works do not know good works," Marrisa said, peering back up to him. "History is always turned into legend over time when one simply does not understand it, my dear prince. the Great King brought his good words to Minslethrate so long ago, when the earth was much younger. His words were so inspirational that they were written in a book many years ago after his death, along with many chronicles written by his knights and followers. That book resides in the palace... Only a few copies now remain—most had been burned many years ago by the hands of corrupted people..."

The prince was quiet for a moment. "I see you believe strongly in the Great King and his word," he said finally.

"The idea of him is what keeps my sanity in a good place... I've had to study countless pages about him...," Marrisa said with a faint smile. "And how does a prince like yourself come about the legend of the Great King?"

"I've studied about your culture and history for a very long time it seems, preparing for this day," the prince said with a smile. "The legend of the king is very different from Ishkarian beliefs—but I have come to be more receptive of the legend of the Great King... I've been learning about Minslethrate's customs and rich lands since I was a young boy."

"That explains why you speak Minslish so well," Marrisa said, astonished.

Marrisa became quiet and embarrassed, feeling dim-witted for not even knowing nearly as much about Ishkar as Phillip did about Minslethrate. In the past instead of studying the Ishkarian language and customs, she was off with her beloved friends, swimming in the lakes and going on thrilling horse-back rides.

"Yes, your language is not as challenging as others I come to know, but it is very ancient and the root of many languages. Your language dates back to the beginning—it's very special," the prince said with a smile. "But Ishkar and Minslethrate are on two opposite ends of the spectrum—we are two opposite kinds of people put together by an arranged marriage," he said, looking off into the distance. "And I know of Minslethrate, but not of its princess," Phillip said as he smiled at her, "tell me about yourself."

Marrisa was quiet for a moment, thinking of everything he had said about them being different.

"What do you want to know, your Highness?" Marrisa asked shyly as he finally stuck out his elbow for her to put her arm around it. She did, so not to offend him.

"Call me Phillip, my lady. I know your beliefs, so tell me what you're fond of—your hobbies, passions," he said.

She was quiet for a second, then cleared her throat as if she were about to recite something.

"Well, I do want you to know that I am like no other princess, or lady for that matter. I ride my own horse everywhere I go, or walk. I don't ride in carriages like the usual ladies do, accept when going to Sunday church, or when my father requests it, which is unusual. My horse's name is Lilly, whom I love dearly. I admire poetry and melodies, reading and writing—I love to sing. I've sung for the nobles of Minslethrate many times. I like to talk to and befriend everyone in my kingdom, along with the peasants, who don't get enough respect—from anyone. I don't get caught up in dainty things and I'm a rather good swordswoman and practice almost every day, which I've learned from my father as well—who is excellent. I have no mother, and learned everything from my father, whom I barely see now these days. And I don't like that this is my last day in Minslethrate...," Marrisa stopped abruptly, realizing that she had been ranting on, which was not lady like either. "Do you have any questions?" Marrisa said with a pretty smile.

"Well, you are a different kind of princess, aren't you," Phillip said, then laughed.

"Don't insult me," she said jokingly, "and what about you, Phillip?"

"Well, to begin, I have never seen any lady as beautiful as you," he said, smiling at her. "The women of Ishkar will be jealous of their queen." Marrisa's smile faded away when she heard those words. "The ladies in Ishkar are lovely but all of them carry the same features, and are not as fair as you. Your red hair, crystal blue eyes and fair skin are fine features to behold. And for me, I think I will be a great leader, one who will lead my future kingdom into the right direction, continuing in excellence. And I will make sure that we will have the greatest kingdom in the entire world—a fine example of leadership," he said with an excited look on his face. "And many ladies of my kingdom think that I am very pleasing to look at, so I think with your beautiful face and my handsome appearance, you and I will appear physically stunning to everyone, not to mention we will have the best-looking children in all of Ishkar. We will have many children, all boys of course—to carry on my legacy," he said with a big smile. She just returned his smile with one as well, but a forced weak one. "And I love riding my horse as well, which I brought with me, and his name is Sable because he is as quick and black as the night's sky. And my kingdom is not as beautiful as Minslethrate but it is a great city—but lately it is always raining. There are beautiful days like this one every once in a while, though…"

The more Phillip spoke, the more Marrisa's heart sunk lower and lower. She would be married to a man who boasted with his snobbery, and would be queen over a kingdom where it rained every day.

She looked off into the horizon, over the beautiful garden of the castle. She could see the amazing mountains and the miles and miles of greenery. She would miss her evening strolls through the garden, and the scenery of that beautiful land. Phillip kept talking, about himself and everything in Ishkar, which bore Marrisa. After a while of listening to Phillip's repetitive boasting, Marrisa began to accidentally tune him out.

"Can I ask you a question, Phillip?" Marrisa asked as they made their way to the other end of the garden. Marrisa cut Phillip off, but she didn't care. "What if…," she stalled as they sat on a bench beneath a cherry blossom tree. The pink petals of the flowers floated away with the breezes that passed them every now and them. "What if I told you that—that I think…"

Marrisa stopped what she was saying again, thinking that she would offend him if she were to tell him that she thought that she would be unhappy in Ishkar and that she didn't want to go. She could see him getting upset, confronting her father about it and then calling off the wedding and the alliance that Ishkar would have with Minslethrate, and then there would be a war between the two countries. Marrisa could see this happening and did not want any ill feelings to stir, so she decided to change the subject.

The sun was up in the center of the blue sky which meant that it was noon. The golden orb burned through the cerulean sky and the billowy white clouds passed its mighty face every now and then.

"Phillip, I have to go," she said, standing up quickly, "I've forgotten that I—have an appointment at mid-day—which is now. It was a pleasure." Just as fast as she said it, she was off through the gardens.

"What about dinner!?—I will see you this evening then at the festivities!" Phillip hollered to her as he watched her run back to the castle.

✝✝✝

Marrisa hurried through the great hall where the castle servants were still putting things together for the grand ball that evening. One of her handmaidens spotted her and tried to ask her something, something probably dealing with that night, but Marrisa ignored her and continued to rush through the hall. She had to get out of the castle; she couldn't take the pressure anymore. "So, what if I miss dinner today—I've had plenty of dinners in my lifetime," she thought. She finally made her way to the castle entrance, running out and through the courtyard. Her long blue gown fluttered behind her as she rushed towards the town square.

✝

CHAPTER 6
Mid-Day

Tairren sat in his shop, reclining back in his wooden chair. He was reading a book and eating a bright red apple as random shoppers would walk by every once in a while, taking a look at what was on the tables or hanging around the top of the small tent-like shop. The marketplace was actually not that busy as he thought it would've been. Most of the shoppers on a random day were usually courtiers or servants of courtiers, or maybe the random commoner; but that day there were actually just a handful of servants shopping for their lords.

Tairren thought it being slow probably had something to do with that night's big event. The servant people walked here and there to each shop, mainly for fruits, vegetables and live poultry. Every now and then a random chicken would escape out of its cage, flapping its overexcited wings as it flailed away with feathers flying. Tairren laughed a little to himself as an overweight man went running after the chicken. After a while, the man finally caught his chicken, grabbing it by the neck and tossing it in its cage with curses and grunts. Tairren got back to his book, taking another bite of his apple.

A carriage came into the marketplace and parked a couple of yards away from his shop. Tairren recognized the carriage to be Natalia's. He watched as the coachman silently got off his seat and went to open the door. But in a quick second, the door flung open and bashed the poor coachman square in the nose. His head flung back as if it were weightless. Tairren tried not to laugh as the man straightened his back and put his hand over his nose.

Tairren could hear arguing coming from the inside of the carriage. The louder voice came from Sora who was fussing at Natalia for opening the door herself. Then he could hear Natalia fuss back. He watched as Natalia poked her head out of the carriage, making sure that no one had notice what was going on before she stepped out.

Natalia let herself out of the carriage anyway, fussed at Sora once more as she yanked a basket out of the carriage, then slammed the door shut. Sora's muffled voice could still be heard as she put in her last words. The coachman finally got the horses going, flying off towards the gate.

64

Tairren acted like he didn't notice her approaching him as he continued to read.

"Excuse me kind sir," she said, smiling at him as if nothing had happened.

Tairren looked up at her from his chair, "oh, it's just you," he said, facetiously.

Natalia stood there with one hand on her hip and the other one holding a large basket.

"Can you believe Sora? She ruined my entrance," she fussed as she put her basket down on the ground. "She is so dramatic sometimes… But look at you," she said in a now playful tone, "don't you look bored to tears."

"Yes, I am, it's so slow today and barely any one is out; I think it has something to do with the celebration tonight," Tairren said, taking the last bite of his apple. "It's a good thing the entertainment has just arrived," he said, trying not to laugh.

"Tairren…" Natalia said in a tone that implied that she wasn't in any kind of mood for jokes. She said nothing else but fiddled around with some trinkets that were on the table.

"Are you meeting Marrisa this afternoon?" Tairren asked.

"Yes, but she's late for some reason. She's probably walking as usual, I don't know why she doesn't ride in a carriage like a normal princess," Natalia said, smelling different candles that were on the table.

One candle smelled of rosemary and lemongrass, another of rose petals, and the last one smelled like—mushrooms? Natalia made a funny face as she put down the last candle.

"She loves her strolls, you know that," Tairren said, watching as she waved her hand in front of her pretty face with a scrunched nose.

He didn't like that last candle either, it was supposed to smell like the sweet earth.

"I know, I rode in my carriage today, *obviously*," Natalia said as she looked back down at her basket. "Oh—Sora packed us a small meal," she said smiling as she held up the basket. "I thought maybe we could have a small picnic dinner together by the creek, hopefully."

"Oh, that sounds great, my mother should be here soon, she usually comes around noon and she won't mind if I left with you both for lunch. But I think we will close up shop early today anyway. I'll definitely come, you know that I will never pass up food," Tairren said, smiling as he stood up to stretch.

A large carriage pulled up across the way on the other side of the large oak tree and fountain that sat in the middle of the marketplace. The old coachman hopped off of the brown horse that pulled the carriage, opening up the small door. He helped out a blonde-haired girl about the same age as Natalia and then a blonde-haired boy, looking the same age as her. They both resembled each other and looked as if they came from a high-class family. The girl looked around, fanning herself with a red fan that was the same color as her dress and the boy wore a white tunic and hat to match with a red feather that stuck straight out of it.

"Oh, no," Natalia said in a stressed voice as she quickly turned towards Tairren, turning her backside towards them.

"What's wrong?" Tairren asked, looking at the two courtiers that had just arrived. "Their entrance was quieter, but at least yours was interesting…"

"No, no Tairren!" she cut him off, "It's the annoying twins, The Lady Daleasa Vaughn and The Lord Fredrick Vaughn, give me that fan, and do it quickly!" Natalia said, pointing to a fan that was on the table behind Tairren. It was a smooth wooden fan that had bright colors painted all over it. The flamboyant fan was bright blue with blotches of red, yellow, and green all over it. Moral must have painted it after drinking too much Minsleberry wine. Tairren quickly handed her the fan, "I don't want them to notice me, and I can't stand talking to them!" Natalia said as she put the brightly colored fan in front of her face, fanning it. "They are the nobles that my mother wants me to become companions with… What are they doing?"

"Well, actually the girl is looking this way, and now they are walking in this direction with an older woman following them—she must be their servant."

"Maybe they won't recognize me," Natalia said in a low voice, fanning herself cantankerously.

"I don't think so, they are definitely coming this way," Tairren said, trying not to laugh. He had never seen Natalia act that way before, and thought it hilarious.

"Oh, look Fredrick, isn't it The Lady Natalia Ducre'? How quaint…," Daleasa said as they walked up right behind Natalia.

She put the fan down by her side, took a deep breath, then turned around to see two insincere looking, smiling faces. They both reminded her of two stupid-looking members of the bard that would travel to the kingdom to perform in their flamboyant clothing.

"Hello Lady Daleasa, Lord Fredrick," Natalia said, forcing a smile as Fredrick took her hand to kiss it, "how are you both doing today?"

"We're lovely, and it is a beautiful day for shopping," Daleasa said. "I see that you're shopping for a fan, is it for tonight? Interesting choice," she said condescendingly, glaring at the brightly painted fan that Natalia held.

"Oh, well thank you, I do try to stand out," Natalia said, still smiling as she put the fan back on the table, "and look at you, I just love that red gown on you Daleasa—have you been in my wardrobe again?" Natalia said, looking up and down at Daleasa, who was wearing a very similar gown as she did.

Natalia raised her left eyebrow as she smirked. Tairren walked to the other side of the shop to another table, covering his mouth while trying not to laugh.

"I wouldn't say that—I never wear cheap material…," she said defensively, glaring at Natalia's obviously nicer attire.

"The last time I checked, Lady Daleasa, the *Marquis* of Ducre' purchases the *finest* gowns of the *finest* fabrics of the *latest* fashion for his daughter," Natalia said, cutting her off.

Daleasa glared at her, then quickly changed the subject.

"So how is our Princess Marrisa? Is she excited about this evening? We're actually shopping for a new brooch for me for tonight and Fredrick a new hat," Daleasa said, with her same old arrogant smile.

"Oh, you were invited? How lovely. Her Royal Highness is wonderful as expected and can't wait for tonight to begin," Natalia lied as she tightened her jaw, but kept smiling at some effort.

"Oh, that is wonderful—well I better be off Natalia," she said, "I have so much more important things to do than to be standing around fiddling with a revolting painted fan. I'm sure I will see you this evening," Daleasa said as she waved her fan at Natalia, as if she was dismissing her.

She turned around quickly and was off, with Fredrick and their servant right behind her. Natalia had her hands behind her back, clenching them as well as her teeth as they walked away.

"Okay, well I hope you have a horrific day, and I pray not to see you tonight," Natalia said to herself, still smiling as they kept walking.

When the cost was clear, Tairren let out a huge laugh as he bent over, holding his stomach.

"Stop!" Natalia fussed as she crossed her arms.

"Well, they seem very nice," Tairren said, jokingly, still laughing.

"You see what I have to go through with these snobbish people? I'm so terrified that Marrisa is leaving, I'll have to associate with people like them!" Natalia said as she shook her head. "I guess it'll be just you and I then, friend."

"I must think so," Tairren teased, still trying not to laugh. "Just don't let them bother you Natalia. I think they are just envious of you. But I'm actually surprised that you didn't throw that fan at them."

"They walk around as if they rule Minslethrate," Natalia said, irritably. "Their father is just a *Baron*," Natalia said, still crossing her arms.

"Baron?" Tairren said, confused.

"Oh Tairren," Natalia said with a sigh as she raised her left eyebrow again. "A Baron is of the lowest status of nobility—everyone knows that."

"I didn't know that there were different statuses of nobility. A noble is just a noble in the peasant world—someone of power and wealth."

"Yes well, in the world of aristocrats, status is everything," Natalia said with another sigh. "A rose is a flower and so is the bloom of a *weed*—but they are both flowers—understand?"

"I see…   Well then, if you are of higher status than she is, you should've just thrown that fan at her anyhow," Tairren said, jokingly."

"If I wasn't a lady I would have! Why are you selling such an appalling thing anyway, Moral has better style than that," Natalia fussed as she picked the fan back up, inspecting it.

"I painted it, actually," Tairren said, "I think it looks attractive."

"Oh, it is indeed," Natalia said sarcastically as she began to fan herself with it again.

"Why, lady Natalia, that is an interesting choice," a familiar voice said from behind them. Natalia turned around to find Marrisa walking up to them with a big smile.

"Where have you been!?" Natalia demanded, giving her a hug as she tossed the unwanted fan back onto the table.

"I'm dreadfully sorry; I got myself caught up with some things at the palace. That I will tell you about later," Marrisa said, then turned to Tairren. "Why, hello Tairren, I'm happy to see you as well," she said with a beautiful smile.

"Hello princess," Tairren said nervously, smiling back at her. His heart began to beat rapidly as his cheeks turned a rosy shade of red. Even though they've known each other for years, he still felt weak in the knees when she came around him. "If you don't mind me saying it, you look beautiful in that blue gown."

"Thank you, and you look very handsome today yourself," she said with another smile.

He just smiled at her, wondering if she really meant it or if she was just returning the compliment.

"I brought us dinner," Natalia said as she held up the large basket. It was covered in a white piece of cloth. "Something small, yet delightful."

"Oh, how lovely," Marrisa said excitedly as she put her hands together, "you're such a sweet friend to me, and I was just beginning to get hungry."

"I figured we could all eat a picnic lunch by the creek and talk for a while, spend time with each other, you know, before you leave Minslethrate," Natalia said in a not so happy voice.

"Yes, well, that sounds great," Marrisa said, smiling a little.

"Oh, here comes mother, just in time," Tairren said as he nodded towards Moral.

She was wearing a gray shawl around her head, and was carrying a small basket that contained a couple of apples and something else that was wrapped in white cloth. She walked up to them, having a big smile on her round face. Her cheeks were rosy colored and wisps of black and gray hair fell from her shawl.

"Hello, dears," she said, giving each one of them a kiss on the cheek.

"Hello, mother," Tairren said, returning the kiss on her round cheek, "as you can see it has been very slow today." They all looked around, noticing only a handful of people that mingled here and there.

"It probably has something to do with the big affair tonight, the whole kingdom has been talking about it," Moral said as she smiled again, making her gray eyes look squinty. "You would have to be deaf not to hear about it. Oh, princess, your heart must be racing with excitement," she said, turning to Marrisa who didn't look excited at all."

"Yes, tonight is an important night for me," she said, looking down towards the gray bricked ground. She was quiet for a second as she fiddled around with a small stone with her foot, pushing it here and there.

"Oh my," Moral said, breaking the silence, "Isn't that your father, dear?" She pointed her round finger to a group of men that entered the marketplace on horses.

It was King Julpen leading the group, and right beside him was Prince Phillip, riding his great black horse. They were followed by three soldiers who also rode on horses. The king would point here and there while talking, looking as if he were telling a story of some sort as the prince would take a glimpse at whatever the king would point to.

"Oh—no!" Marrisa said with wide eyes, "I have to hide—I can't let them see me! I will tell you why later, please help me hide!"

"Must this whole afternoon be like this?!" Natalia fussed as she rolled her eyes.

They glanced everywhere quickly, realizing that there was really nowhere to hide without being seen. She could quickly run into one of the bigger shops, but she would definitely be seen with her red hair.

"Here my lady, put this on," Moral said, taking off her shawl and wrapping it around Marrisa's head, covering the long locks of bright red hair. Tairren grabbed a blanket that was folded neatly on one of the tables and handed it over to Natalia. It was white with embroidered designs of flowers all over it. Moral helped Natalia swathe the blanket around Marrisa's body, covering every bit of her elegant blue gown.

"Here, take this and act like you are shopping at the other table behind Tairren," Natalia said as she handed her the notorious brightly painted fan that was on the table beside them. "Oh my, Marrisa you look like a poor tramp," she said with one eyebrow lifted. "Well, at least a fancy tramp. Anyways, hurry, they'll see me and come this way," Natalia said as she pushed Marrisa towards the other end of the little shop.

Marrisa put the fan in front of her beautiful face, fanning as if she were hot. Tairren acted like he was helping her shop as he held up a hand painted pot, talking about it as if she were interested in it.

Natalia was right, King Julpen happened to glance over in their direction and spotted Natalia standing next to Moral. He nodded towards her and the group of men made their way over to her.

"Moral, act like I just said something humorous!" Natalia whispered to her.

Just then Moral let out a loud disturbing laugh, seeming to startle everyone in the marketplace, even Natalia herself. She threw her head back acting as if Natalia had said the most hilarious thing she had ever heard.

"Hello Lady Natalia," the king said with a big smile as they stopped their horses right before them.

She smiled back and bowed to him. She cleared her throat as she took a glimpse at Moral, who bowed quickly then immediately began to fiddle around with random things on the table.

The king made an odd face as he watched the excitable-looking shopper.

"Why, your majesty, what a surprise, what can I do for you?" Natalia said in a surprised voice, getting the king's attention again.

"Lady Natalia, I want you to meet Prince Phillip of Ishkar—Marrisa's fiancé," the king said, sounding as if he was so proud of the prince.

Natalia was quiet for a second, realizing why Marrisa was hiding.

Tairren looked at Marrisa with wide eyes, then turned his head to look behind him towards the prince as a surge of jealousy shot through his body.

"Oh, well, it's wonderful to finally meet you, Your Royal Highness," she said, bowing her head to him as well.

"The Lady Natalia Ducre' has been a dear companion to my daughter as long as I could remember," the king said to Phillip who kept gazing at her from head to foot.

"Lovely to meet you, my lady," the prince said as he smiled at her.

"I was showing the prince around the kingdom, and noticed you standing here, thinking that Marrisa would be with you," the king said, looking around. "Phillip says that she left so abruptly during their meeting this afternoon. I hope she is well with everything—I wanted her to accompany us. I was hoping to find her here but I don't see her, she may be still at the palace," he said, continuing to look around. "Well, we must go; I'll see you tonight, my lady."

"It was a pleasure to have met you," the prince said with his Ishkarian accent, smiling at her again.

Then they left, going towards the great arched entrance to the town square.

After watching them for a moment, Marrisa walked over to stand next to Natalia.

"That is why I was hiding," Marrisa said as she began to take off the unsightly shrouds.

"You might want to keep that on," Tairren said. "They may come back this way."

"Oh, you're right," Marrisa said as she tightened the shawl back around her head. "I hope no one recognizes me, I feel revolting."

"It's okay princess, you look a beauty in that get-up anyhow," Moral said with another tender smile. "It's a good thing Tairren wanted to keep that retched thing of a fan here at the shop. It was good for something." They all laughed.

"We should leave," Natalia said, picking up her basket.

"Mother," Tairren said, "do you mind if I left with them, I want to have some lunch with Marrisa and Natalia. Natalia brought a charming picnic basket."

"Oh yes, indeed," Moral said, sounding excited all of a sudden, "I want you three to spend as much time with each other as possible. You go along and I'll be alright here, I think I can manage this shop by myself today, as slow as it is. And you should go quickly; the king may come back this way."

"Thank you, mother," he said, kissing her on the cheek again.

"You all go, take your time, I think I want to close the shop down early today anyway," Moral said as she made her way behind the table, sitting her little basket down beside the wooden chair.

"Thank you Moral, you are sweet," Marrisa said, kissing her on the cheek as well. "I will make sure that I see you one last time before I go back to the palace this evening." She held Morals hand as she said this.

After they said their goodbyes, they left the little shop, going towards the main entrance of the marketplace. Moral watched until she could no longer see them as they left through the opened entrance, off into the wide-open land of Minslethrate.

†††

They laughed as they crossed the field of Minslethrate, towards the forest. The grass was bright green with patches of clovers and little violet colored flowers growing sporadically all over the place. Random small trees, hills and patches of timber could be seen here and there, looking peaceful far off in the distance. The sun exposed its dazzling face brightly as they made their way into the forest. Large puffy clouds passed over the sun every now and then, casting large shadows over the land. It was fascinating to see how the field ended so abruptly, just before the forest.

Entering the forest was like entering a new world. The sun trickled in between the trees, playing off the tall grass and flowers, appearing golden and burnished and enthralling. Butterflies and dragonflies, as well as other flying creatures, bounced here and there in the air from one plant to another. The trees were large and stretched their large arms here and there as it created a leafy green ceiling. Everything felt cooler and appeared dimmer beneath the canopy up above. Rays of sunlight came in through breaks in the canopy, giving them a relaxed feeling as they strolled through the enchanted forest.

Eventually they walked past Tairren's quaint little home, which looked even more delightful during the day. The cottage was small and pleasing to the eye, surrounded by flowering trees and bushes. The roof was covered with bright-green colored ivy, which bloomed violet colored flowers and hung off the edges of the roof like ice-sickles.

After passing the small abode, they continued to stroll through the forest, chatting of the odd things that happened that afternoon. They talked about Natalia's dramatic arrival at the marketplace, the comical repartee between Natalia and Daleasa, the witty decision to disguise Marrisa in the peculiar shrouds, and even the visit from King Julpen and Prince Phillip.

"Prince Phillip from Ishkar—*Issshhhkarr*," Natalia said, making fun of its pronunciation.

"I wonder if all the people of Ishkar will be as condescending as he is," Marrisa said as she raised her left eyebrow. "He's such a lofty, stuffed shirt, imbecile!" Marrisa fussed as she pulled her long red hair to one side, over her shoulder.

"A handsome imbecile at that!" Natalia added.

Tairren rolled his eyes, aggravated that they were talking about Prince Phillip. Even though he didn't know the prince, he didn't like him.

"I can't believe this, I just can't—I hate everything about my *soon-to-be* life! Oh God of light, why me?!" Marrisa screamed out as she dramatically raised her hands into the air.

"Marrisa—stop shouting!" Natalia fussed as she pulled her hands back down.

"What if you were to sit down and talk to your father and Prince Phillip about how you feel?" Tairren's face was concerned and his voice was low.

"I could, but if I do that, I would be jeopardizing not only my father's reputation, but the relationship between Minslethrate and Ishkar. It's not that easy, I just can't say I won't go through with it. I've been betrothed to Phillip since I was an infant. It's odd but it's the way things have always been." Marrisa's voice was serious but still friendly. "There has to be an agreement between the prince, my father, and the king of Ishkar to stop everything in peace. But I know they wouldn't just decide to impede the marriage and negotiate to stop it, because they have too much at hand to end everything." Marrisa's voice became shaky, as if the conversation was upsetting her, then she became quiet for a second to contain herself. After a moment, her face lit up as a peculiar idea popped into her head. "Since I know that they won't end it, maybe I could stop it from happening. Maybe I could throw everything off!" Marrisa said, with wide blue eyes as she seemed to get a little excited.

"What do you mean?" Tairren asked.

"What if I didn't show up tonight, to any of the events? What if I just run away?" A smile crept upon her beautiful face. "I've been thinking about this all morning..."

"I don't know, Marrisa," Natalia said, slowly shaking her head. "Where would you go? Where would you live? And you know your father would send out an army of soldiers to look for you."

Marrisa became quiet, realizing that there would be no way that she would be able to get away with it.

"I could come with you," Tairren said, looking into Marrisa's sad blue eyes.

She smiled at him, noticing how serious his face was.

"We could hide out at the cottage, then we could make a plan about what we would do and where we would go off to."

"What?! This conversation is absurd... Where would you go?!" Natalia demanded.

"I've been all over this land, except far, far south. We could go there. We could build a small home and live off of the land far, far away!" Tairren's face was glowing, as if convinced that this would be a good plan.

"You're mad!" Natalia exclaimed. "The Forbidden Lands! You can't be serious, Tairren. That would be so dangerous—and besides, you would never be able to pass the Great Wall of Division without being seen... And what about me, I just can't live my life knowing that you two have run away to the southern parts of Minslethrate. They are *forbidden* for a reason!"

"That is but a name to keep people out of the south. Come with us— Tairren knows a secret way through the wall." Marrisa's face was serious when she said this, looking straight into Natalia's eyes.

Natalia looked back, waiting for a chuckle or something indicating that she was being facetious. But there was no laughter, not even a smile. Only the quietness between them and the sounds of nature were present.

"It sounds ridiculous," Natalia said as shook her head.

The sound of running water could be heard from where they were at, so they walked faster. They finally came to a pleasant, shaded creek right beyond a small hill. The creek looked lovely with tall yellow and white flowers all around it. The water was crystal clear and small round rocks could be seen beneath the water. Tiny silver fish swam about the water, appearing like small bolts of lightning as they dashed to and fro.

They spread the blanket out that Marrisa had used as a cloak in the marketplace earlier that afternoon. They sat on it in a circle, facing each other. Natalia unpacked the basket, spreading everything out. She neatly put the plates, cups and silverware out in front of each one of them. She pulled out some cheeses, a small pouch that contained some herbed bread and flat biscuits, a couple of apples and pears, and a large glass jug that contained some kind of dark-red juice of some sort which was stopped with a large cork.

"As much as you think this is a good idea, I just think it may end up in a disaster. I just feel apprehensive about it." Natalia was serious as she finished putting everything on the blanket. "Oh my, where's the meat?!" she said, panicked as she looked into her basket, going from serious to silly. "You can never have an appropriate dinner without any kind of meat," she quickly said as Tairren and Marrisa began to giggle at their dramatic and scatter-brained companion. "Anyways, I can just see hundreds of soldiers everywhere, looking high and low for us, mainly you Marrisa. I have a hunch that they would probably search for months, until you are found. Then I could see them arresting Moral, making her talk because everyone in the kingdom knows that we all associate with one another. Then they might think that it was a kidnapping. It would be treason in the eyes of the court." They began to eat quietly as she spoke.

"Yes, I think you are right, Natalia," Marrisa said, quietly. "It's a brainless idea, and I don't know if I could live out in the middle of nowhere without having any clothing or going without any meals, and wondering if we would make it, especially through the winter seasons." She fiddled around with her plate of food. "And I would never want anything to happen to Moral or any of you."

Tairren was quiet as well; he knew that it wouldn't be a good idea after all. And he would worry about his mother every day. But he would jump at the idea again if Marrisa wanted him to.

"This is lovely, Natalia," Marrisa said. She changed the subject, trying to make herself feel better. "The juice is delicious—what is it?"

"Sora made it," Natalia said, taking a bite of her biscuit. "It's a mixture of freshly squeezed oranges, crushed mint and juiced Minsleberry and cherry. I love it," she said smiling as she went to sip her juice. "I would've snuck a bottle of wine from the cellar but Sora forbids it. She said the last time I brought wine to one of our picnics, I went home soaking wet because of jumping into the stream…"

They all laughed, remembering that picnic very well.

They continued to eat quietly, talking every now and then about how beautiful everything was around them. After eating all of the fruit, biscuits, cheeses and drinking all of their orange, Minsleberry and cherry juice, they packed everything back up into the large basket. Then they rested on the blanket, enjoying the weather and each other's company.

"You know, I won't let this bother me anymore, I'll think of the positive side of it all," Marrisa said, putting her hands beneath her head. "Even though I don't like it, I'll deal with it—like a responsible princess should. Everything will be okay…"

"We'll miss you so much though," Natalia said turning on her side towards Marrisa, putting her arm around her waist.

"I don't know what I'll do without you," Tairren added in a low voice, turning his head towards Marrisa to make sure that she could only hear him.

Marrisa smiled back at Tairren, wondering what she would do without him, and Natalia as well. She lied when she told them that she wouldn't let the situation bother her anymore. It bothered her tremendously, and she couldn't stop thinking about it. Even though she smiled at her friends and said that everything would be okay, she was depressed on the inside, and felt as if her heart would literally break any minute. It wasn't okay, and she continued to hide her miserable feelings from them. Marrisa didn't want them to see how depressed she really was, and she didn't want them to worry about her.

As she lay on her back, staring into the great white clouds up above, she fought back her tears, refusing to cry. She knew that crying wouldn't help the situation.

They laid there quietly as the sounds of the creek trickled on, and the cool breezes blew the white flower petals of the dogwood trees everywhere all around them. They all fell asleep as the sun slowly passed over the sky.

†

CHAPTER 7
A Blue Heart

Tairren woke up, lying on his side. He just lay silent and still, watching Marrisa as she peacefully slept. She was lying on her side as well, facing him. She looked so beautiful, even with her eyes closed. He never noticed how long her eye lashes were, or that she had faint freckles on her pink cheeks. He imagined what it would be like waking up to her beautiful face every day of his life.

A soft breeze drifted by, moving a lock of red hair onto her face.

"I love you," Tairren thought as he moved the curly red lock from her face with his fingers, caressing her cheek.

Marrisa woke up, slowly opening her eyes. She smiled as she looked into his. Tairren's heart sped up as he realized that she must have felt his touch.

"Hi," she said as she rolled onto her back. "We must have fallen asleep. I wonder what time of day it is." She sat up, stretching her back and arms

"I don't know, but I think we may have been napping for a while, the sun looks like it might be on its way down." Tairren sat up as well, pointing his knees up and resting his elbows on them.

They looked up into the sky above the creek. By the way the sunlight hit the trees, it looked like it must have been in the early evening.

"I can't believe that I've fallen asleep outside." Natalia sat up, stretching her neck. "What if a bug would've crawled in my ear?" She said as she pulled her long hair to one side.

Tairren smirked at her. "We better get going," he said.

They stood up, folding the blanket. Then they shoved it into the large basket.

Walking to Tairren's house went by much quicker than they had anticipated. Tairren opened the door, allowing Marrisa and Natalia to walk in first. The small house was filled with the scent of something sweet baking in the oven. They found Moral moving about in the kitchen area of the small house, appearing busy as usual.

"Mother, you're home." Tairren sat the basket that he was holding for Natalia down on the floor as he walked in.

"Oh, hello!" she said, excitedly, rushing over quickly to kiss each one of them on the cheek. "Oh, yes dear, I decided to come home early today. I closed the shop down a couple of hours after you all left. Can you believe that no one at all came over to the shop?" Moral rushed back over to the oven, pulling out a batch of sweet biscuits. "You've arrived just in time."

Marrisa sat down at the table, not really saying anything; Natalia stood at the door with Tairren.

"Oh, have some tea," Moral said as she placed a tea pot and some cups down on the table. She hurried to fetch the basket of biscuits, placing it onto the table as well.

"I would love to but I must be going," Natalia said. "I told Sora before I left to have the carriage ready for me at the marketplace when the sun begins to go down. I have a walk ahead of me as well."

"I'll walk you to the marketplace." Tairren picked the basket back up, opening the door.

"I'll see you tonight," Natalia said as she hugged Marrisa goodbye.

Tairren held the door open for her as they left the small cottage.

Moral sat across from Marrisa at the small table, pouring them both a cup of tea.

"The sun is on its way down, which means it will be dark in a couple of hours," Marrisa said, taking a sip of her tea. "I have to leave soon..." She took a bite of the flat, sweet biscuit. It tasted like warm cinnamon and sugar. "I feel like my heart is slowly breaking as the sun goes down... I don't want to leave..."

Marrisa put her elbows on the table, resting her chin on her hands. It was quiet and warm in the little house; and it smelled of dried flowers and sweet things. The small house always smelled that way, and Marrisa knew that she would miss it. She would miss everything about it.

"Oh, Princess," Moral said as she fixed up her tea, "I look at you as if you were my very own child... And if I may be bold enough to say this to you—I think it's time you begin acting like royalty. You are the daughter of kings—not a maiden that should be around peasants like myself." Her voice was kind and sweet. "You will be a queen tomorrow—The Lady of Ishkar. You don't need to be socializing here with us common folk."

Marrisa was quiet for a moment as she looked down at her tea, then back up to Morals kind face.

"No, Moral, you don't understand..." Marrisa put down her biscuit, looking into Moral's grayish-blue eyes. "This place, here in the forest amongst you and Tairren's presence, is more enchanting to me than any kingdom, or prince in the entire world. I would love to live the life you have. To be free to make my own choices, to love whomever I choose. You don't know it, but you live a very affluent life, Moral. You may not have power, or wealth to purchase material things for pleasure, but you do have freedom and happiness. That's the most important thing anyone could posses. That is what fascinates me so, why I love to be in your presence." Marrisa's face was glowing with zeal. She never looked so beautifully ardent before; and she never came across as inducing as she did during that moment. "I would choose your life and this atmosphere over any prince or king, land or riches."

Moral was quiet as she sipped her tea. She never realized how Marrisa truly felt about her own life.

"Oh, you are sweet, Marrisa." Moral reached across the small table and caressed Marrisa's cheek. "You are like your mother, child, strong hearted and caring. If I didn't know it, I would have thought that I was sitting here with your mother, having tea with her majesty."

Marrisa smiled as her eyes became glossy with tears. Hearing things like that touched her heart, giving her a warm feeling in her chest.

"Really?" Marrisa said as a small tear rolled down her cheek.

"Oh yes, child." Moral smiled her warm smile as she wiped the glistening tear from her cheek. "There is something about you that attracts people. You have a heart of gold and a beautiful presence that can light up a darkened room—like your mother. Your mother was the most loving queen that has ever walked these lands. She loved the Holy Father with all of her heart, spreading his joy and love to everyone in the kingdom. When she passed it was such a sad day. There seemed to be no joy, no love in all of Minslethrate."

"Tell me Moral, what happened in the palace when I was a child? You have to know... You are the same age as my mother would have been. This is a small kingdom, and everybody knows everything about everyone. I just feel in my heart that something must have happened to my mother, something more than illness. All I know is that she died from being Ill... But she was the only one around that time who died from an illness. Usually if one becomes ill, many do. My father told me...he said that it was such a mystery. Not even the royal physician could figure out my mother's illness."

Marrisa's eyes went from happy to anxious in a matter of minutes.

"Princess, it was such a long time ago, almost fifteen years at least." Moral spoke quietly, sipping her tea every now and then. Her face was calm and endearing as she looked down at the warm biscuit on her plate, crumbs sprinkled here and there. "I remember there was so much gossip and talk about strange things that went on in that castle. You know how everyone is in that marketplace and town square; everyone gets together and talks, talks, talks... Gossip is a lover to the people of Minslethrate.

"I remember the odd gossip about a strange woman who resided in the royal palace, as your mother's servant. She was an odd one." Moral's eyes became wide as she spoke. "I don't remember her name, but shortly after the death of your mother, she mysteriously disappeared. Your mother was as healthy as an ox, and a week before that woman disappeared—God bless her soul... I don't know what happened, but I do know your mother was deathly Ill that week—delusional and hallucinating. Some say that a cold wind from the Forbidden Lands of the South blew an evil curse upon her; others say that it was just a bad case of some kind of sickness caught by eating something rancid. But most say..." Moral became quiet, stopping herself, looking sad all of the sudden. "Just know child, that your mother was a beautiful woman and a gift from God."

She sipped her tea, not saying anything else.

"What?" Marrisa asked with those anxious eyes again. "What was it that most people said?"

"Just know that this was just gossip in the marketplace." Moral took another sip, taking her time. "They say—that she was—poisoned..." Moral grew quiet after that.

Marrisa sat back in her chair, not saying anything. She had a look of disbelief on her face, shaking her head slowly.

"My mother—was poisoned? ...Possibly, murdered?!" Marrisa brought her hands to her mouth as tears built back up in her eyes again.

"Oh, honey, I really didn't want to say it, but you have the right to know what was said about your mother's death. But that was only gossip, mind you." Moral stood up, walking over to give her a hug.

"There would've been a great possibility that my mother would still be alive today, with me, helping me get through this appalling time in my life. I hate everything about my life right now, everything." Marrisa held onto Moral, crying on her shoulder.

That was the first time that she showed her emotions in front of anyone other than Natalia and Tairren. She couldn't keep it in any longer. Her tears flowed like an unending vessel as the weight of great stress slowly lifted from her.

"I want my mother so badly," Marrisa cried out, holding onto Moral.

Moral just hugged her, doing her best to comfort her.

†††

The sun was going down, making the field of Minslethrate glow a soft orange color. Dark-blue clouds, miles away to the south could be seen, looking very strange and ominous. The air became a little cooler as the breezes picked up, rolling over the grass and flowers in the field.

"It looks as if strange weather is coming our way," Natalia said, moving her long brown hair that blew in front of her face. "Thank you so much for walking me." She smiled at him, but noticed a look of pensive sadness on his face.

"Oh—you're welcome." He looked up towards the sky taking note of the weather, then back down towards the grassy field.

They both strolled through the field, not saying anything. The kingdom slowly got closer, getting larger as they approached its splendor. The castle peered over the large gray brick walls of the kingdom, revealing large red flags with the golden Minslethratian symbol on them. The flags rippled around fiercely as the winds began to pick up in the sky.

"Tairren—how does it feel?" Natalia looked at him again, her green eyes reflecting the vibrant orange sunlight that contrasted against the edge of the dark clouds.

He looked back at her, revealing a look of confusion on his face. His blue eyes gazed into hers for a second.

"What do you mean?" He moved his long black bangs from his face.

She was quiet for a moment, looking off into the distance. "How does it feel—to be in love?" She was quiet for a moment longer, looking back into his eyes, and waiting for an answer. "I see the way you look at her, how you smile at her, how you become so nervous around her sometimes." Natalia smiled, looking away from his surprised face. "Tairren, she is my best friend, and so are you. I know what is going on; I can see it in your eyes. You fancy Marrisa," she said with a smirk. "You can't hide these things from me, it shows on the outside." She noticed that a smile crept upon his face as he blushed. "You need to talk about how you feel—and a boy as handsome and loving as you can always talk to me."

Tairren smiled as he glanced back down at the ground. He could feel himself becoming nervous as Natalia smiled her soft smile at him.

"I do have feelings for Marrisa, and always have…," he finally said. "I—I fell in love with her the first time that I saw her. I just haven't told her; I've never had the courage to tell her before—until today. Unfortunately, it seems like time with her is almost over. However, I feel like she should know how I've been feeling." His voice sounded a little nervous as he spoke.

Natalia giggled, thinking that the situation was sweet. She grabbed his arm as they walked together.

"Tairren, you are lovely," she said as she rested her cheek on his shoulder. "I think you need to tell her how you feel, and unfortunately this evening is your last chance." Her tone was low and faded away.

"I know—and I will. I'm just—nervous." He felt asinine talking about it. He could feel his face turn red as warm blood rushed upon it.

"I wish I could be in love with someone, I feel so—green with envy," Natalia said as her voice drifted away.

She truly was envious of Marrisa. She always wanted to be loved and desirable. Sometimes she wished that even Tairren was attracted to her the way he was to Marrisa.

Natalia just looked up at Tairren and gave him a sweet smile.

Tairren smiled and returned the affection with a tender hug as they walked.

"And why haven't you said anything about this over these last four years?!" Natalia fussed. "Four years is a long time to be keeping something like that a secret."

"I.." he paused. "I didn't think that she could ever love a commoner. And she is so beautiful—I just didn't want to ruin what we have, which is our friendship."

"Oh Tairren, you are sweet. But you do know that Marrisa is a different kind of princess," she said with a chuckle. "You should know that having royal blood and being a commoner has nothing to do with loving someone. You know how our princess is. And you are a really handsome fellow with a loving personality." She smiled at him. "I think if she was able to stay here in Minslethrate—I think something could have happened between you both…"

"I wish that was something that could possibly come true," Tairren said. His smile faded away as he thought some more. "But it would not be acceptable."

"Tairren… There are many maidens out there whom crave that love in which you give…," Natalia said in a low tone, seeming to say it to herself. "Marrisa is lucky to be loved by you…"

They approached the gate, walking past swaying trees that released their blossoms into the crisp air. They walked across a bridge that went over the moat below them. The water was clear and flowed from the rivulets that branched off of the Great Mislethratian River.

"Thank you, Natalia." He gave her a hug. "I hope tonight will be an astonishing night that you all will never forget." He smiled at her as she began to walk through the gateway.

"Farewell Tairren!" She waved as she proceeded inside the marketplace.

†††

The sky was a bright orange with yellow and pink clouds; it seemed as if it were painted onto the heavens. The dark-blue, billowy clouds in the southern part of Minslethrate slowly made its journey towards the castle. The forest got darker, evolving from an enchanted forest into a gloomy woodland. The animals of the forest wandered about, looking for grainy food before the night's sky wrapped its arms around Minslethrate.

Moral lit some candles here and there before it got so dark that they wouldn't be able to see anything. She lit a lantern that hung above the small table, spreading its dim light everywhere in the small home.

Marrisa lay on Moral's small bed, looking out of the low, small window that was right next to the bed. She could see that the sun would be down soon. The forest grew dimmer and the leaves in the trees moved about as the breezes picked up. She felt as if the sun was counting down to her fate. Her eyes were red and they burned from her crying.

After having her talk with Moral about everything, including her mother, she didn't feel like talking anymore. But she did feel a little bit better, kind of happy that she and Moral were able to talk. Moral recommended that she lie down before she left, to calm herself down. She wanted to wait for Tairren to get back anyway, to say goodbye to him before she left. She knew it would be the hardest part of that evening for her. She couldn't stand to leave such a beautiful and loyal friend.

She noticed a small blue bird that landed in a patch of flowers. She watched as the bird picked up something in its beak then flew off into the thick shrubbery of the forest. She wished she could be that bird, free to fly around, away from everything…

The door squeaked as Tairren walked in.

"Hello son," Moral said as she stirred a pot of something hot and delicious smelling.

"Hello ladies," Tairren said, closing the door behind him. "It smells wonderful as usual in here."

Marrisa turned her head, looking towards Tairren as he walked to her. She sat up, placing her feet onto the wooden floor. He sat next to her on the bed and looked into her crystal blue eyes.

"Hello," he said with a half smile. "Are you okay?" He noticed how red her eyes looked. Her cheek bones and the area around her eyes were red as well. He could see a blue light in her eyes, a sadness that he had never before seen in them.

"To tell you the truth, no—I'm not," she said, trying to smile a little. "I wanted to see you before I left, of course. But I have to leave now; the sun will be down soon... Will you walk me through the forest?"

"You know I will," he stood up, offering his hand out to help her up. She placed her small hand into his. He noticed how soft and fragile her hand still was as he pulled her up.

Marrisa said her goodbyes to Moral, hugging her for what felt like hours. She couldn't stand to leave the only mother figure she had in her life.

"I love you, child. Be strong," she said as she wiped away a small tear that rolled down Marrisa's cheek.

"I shall try—and I love you too." She held Moral's hand as she began to walk away. Tairren opened the door for her as she let go of Moral's warm hand, turning quickly to leave.

The cool air swept across their bodies as they walked through the forest. Marrisa walked silently with her arms wrapped around herself. She glanced everywhere, taking in everything for the last time. She wanted to remember Minslethrate as beautiful and enchanting.

Tairren looked over at her, becoming nervous, feeling as if butterflies were fluttering around in his stomach. His insides were flustered and quivering, making him become slightly nauseous. He decided that he didn't have butterflies fluttering around in his stomach at all, but large buzzards—that were pecking at their supper in his intestines.

He reached beneath the loosely laced up collar of his tunic, grasping the blue heart pendant that he had saved for her.

"Marrisa—I have something for you," he said as he took off the necklace from around his neck. "It's your birthday present from me... Happy birthday." He placed the rough blue pendant into the palm of her hand.

"Oh Tairren," she said as she lifted up the necklace to take a better look at it. "It's beautiful!" she exclaimed as she hugged him.

She put the necklace around her neck, holding the pendant to look at it closer as they walked.

"Do you like it?" Tairren's heart fluttered with excitement as she smiled her beautiful smile, indicating that she was happy.

The buzzards in his stomach flew off as his nervousness deceased.

"I love it. Did you make it yourself?" she asked as she rubbed her fingers on the smoother side of the heart shaped crystal.

"Yes—especially for you. Do you remember when I showed you a blue crystal and told you about how I found it with my father as a child?"

She nodded her head yes as she looked into his eyes.

"That was it. I wanted to give you something that was so special to me." He stopped walking and held her hands. "I want you to know that when you are sad, and feel alone, that you can hold this in your hand and know that I will always be thinking of you. That way you will never feel alone." His heartbeat pounded in his chest as he looked into her beautiful eyes; he thought that she could see it straight through his chest.

He touched her cheek and hair, not able to resist himself. He could see her eyes becoming glossy again, hoping that she wouldn't cry. She was quiet as she looked up into his passionate eyes.

"Marrisa, I want to tell you something that I have been longing to tell you since I first met you—ever since the first time I laid my young eyes on your beautiful face. You're dearest to me than life itself. I can't stand that you will be married to another man, I can't stand that you have to move to another country. You can't fall in love with anyone else..." He breathed heavily as his emotions began to stir. "Every time I look into your eyes, my heart skips a beat. Every time I know you're looking into mine, my mind goes blank... And—I want you to know that I—I love you, with all of my heart, with all that is in me. I love you more than a friend should love a friend. I love you like the earth loves the rain, and like the honey bees love the flowers that grow from the earth. I love everything about you. Marrisa, my life has been enchanted with you in it—and I know we were meant for each other, I feel it, I know it."

Marrisa was quiet as tears began to flow down her flushed cheeks. She brought her hand to her mouth and slowly shook her head.

Tairren touched her face, wiping the tears from them. He could feel her tremble as his nervous hands touched her smooth skin.

"Tairren, why do you tell me this now?" she softly asked as more tears flowed. "Why haven't you told me these beautiful things years ago?" She squeezed his hands as she pressed her chest to his. She felt confused and numb, and wished with all of her heart that she would have known how he felt for her years ago…

They could feel the heart pendant between them as they came so close to each other.

"Remember the day when I found you singing in this very forest?" he asked, touching her cheek. She shook her head yes, still quiet, stunned. "I wanted to tell you then, but was frightened, insecure, I wanted to kiss you then like lovers do, because that's the way I felt and still feel for you. I'm sorry I never told you, I never meant to upset you," he whispered as his face came closer to hers, "I love you…"

They kissed, their first and seemingly last kiss, ever so gently, feeling the smoothness of each other's lips. They gently touched each other's bodies as their gentle kisses evolved into passionate ones. They could feel it, the passion emitting from each other's mouths and hands. It seemed as if electricity flowed through their fingertips and bodies. It felt right, perfect, like beholding a sunrise on a fresh spring morning or lying in a clover field with the breeze upon their bodies. They wrapped each other in love, a love that seemed to be locked away and set free for the first time.

Tairren laid her down upon the cool, soft grass, gently laying upon her as they still melted in each other's kisses. He touched her face and her neck tenderly.

"Wait, Tairren," Marrisa said as she stopped kissing him. She sat up quickly, stunned and quiet.

He looked into her eyes as his heart pounded ferociously.

"What is it, my love?" Tairren asked, caressing her face.

"I can't do this knowing that I will never see you again after today." Marrisa's face looked sad and beautiful at the same time. "I cannot, knowing that I will be married to another man… We must stay pure… Our innocence must not be tarnished! I feel as if my heart shall burst and I don't know if I'm happy or that I want to cry with sadness… We shouldn't be doing this…when we don't belong to each other…"

Her body wanted Tairren's so badly, but she knew that her heart would not be able to withstand the mental outcome. Her heart was breaking, and she didn't want Tairren's heart to end up like hers.

"I'm sorry, Tairren… I have to go," Marrisa said as she stood up. She put her hand to her forehead as tears began to stir.

Tairren stood up quickly, grabbing her waist.

"Please," he said as he touched her face. "Please don't go." Passion burned in his blue eyes as he gazed into hers. "Let's run away! Let's do something to get away from here! I know in my heart, that you are for me—and I know you feel it deep within yours. Please tell me you do."

He didn't want her to ever leave his side. He wanted her forever. He craved her touch already as she backed away. And if he couldn't have her—he still wanted her to say that she loved him too. He wanted to hear those words from her sweet lips.

She grabbed the blue heart that dangled on her chest, fighting back more tears. She didn't know what she could possibly do to change the ultimate outcome of her future. She didn't understand anything at that moment and just wanted to run away from everything. She wanted to just disappear—on her own.

She gave him one last hug, followed by one last passionate kiss. Then she tore herself away from him.

"I will never forget you, Tairren." Her face was emotionless now as tears began to flow again.

She turned quickly, running off into the pastel colored sunlight, through the forest—leaving him like fallen petals from a wilted rose…

Tairren watched, stunned, as she ran away towards the field. He wanted to run after her so badly, to come up with an escape plan, to run away with each other—somewhere far, far away. But this time he couldn't run after her like he did once before in the forest. He knew he wouldn't be able to say or do anything to change the situation, or her future. "Why do you leave me crushed and torn?" Tairren thought to himself. He could literally feel his heart breaking as she disappeared into the brush of the forest; cracking and crumbling one piece at a time. He stood there for what seemed like hours. His heart ached badly as he realized that he may not ever kiss her full, beautiful lips ever again or see her charming face. He would never be able to touch her, or feel her body against his. He would never love another woman the way he loved Marrisa. Tears formed in his eyes as his heart felt as if it were ripping from his chest.

He couldn't take it anymore. At that moment he ran to his home, which felt as if it were miles away.

Moral was startled as he burst through the door, breathless.

"What in God's name is wrong, Tairren?!" she fussed as she stood up.

Her eyes were wide with worrisome curiosity.

"Mother, I have to go tonight, I have to see Marrisa again. I don't care if she is a princess or not, I have to be close to her. I love her." His face was anxious and filled with emotion as he walked back and forth, running his hands through his black hair. He breathed heavily as Moral walked to him with that same worried face. "I have to see her, to change her mind—to get her to run away with me—something! She is the woman for me, I feel it in my heart—she is the one. God created her for me."

"My son, sit down, calm yourself. You can't go running around saying such things." She walked him to the wooden chair that was next to the table, sitting him down. "I have something for you."

She walked over to her little room area, pulling something out from beneath her bed that was wrapped in a white cloth.

"I've worked on this for a while now, trying to make it as elegant as possible," she said as she sat it on the table, unfolding the white cloth. "I was going to give it to you later on this evening, but I think now is best."

Tairren stood up, unfolding the expensive looking light-blue fabric that was revealed from beneath the white cloth.

"Blue, like your eyes," Moral said with a smile. "It suits you."

He lifted it up, letting the rest of the blue fabric unfold itself. It was a tunic, and a really beautifully sewn tunic that looked like it belonged to a courtier. It was adorned with exquisite embroidery with golden trim around the collar and the bottom edges.

"Mother, it's fantastic," Tairren exclaimed with a big smile. "You are a true artisan."

"There are new trousers and a new black belt for you as well."

"This must have cost a fortune," Tairren said, picking up the belt and trousers.

"I've been saving some money here and there; and I bought the best fabric in Minslethrate. I've been sewing every morning after you left to open the shop."

He gave her a hug and kissed her on the cheek. His face glowed with zeal as he looked back at the splendid tunic.

"I know this may be risky, but you should go tonight—I do feel it in my old heart. And you will be the most handsome young man at the ball. I want you to experience this with a beautiful young woman whom you care about most. You'll fit right in splendidly, looking more stylish than the courtiers themselves." Moral had a smile on her face that went from ear to ear. "Now take them dirty boots off and let me clean and shine them up for you."

Tairren was happy that he was given a chance to see Marrisa again. He had to see her one last time before the night was up. He knew that him going to the celebration wouldn't change Marrisa leaving, but at least he would see her one last time.

†††

The dark-blue clouds from the South finally made its way to the kingdom. They stretched their long billowy arms out across the land, making the land look dark and haunting as the wind picked up.

Marrisa ran through the woods, making it to the edge of the darkened forest and out into the opened fields. The wind blew her hair and gown around as she ran up a grassy slope. She stumbled to the ground, falling on her hands and knees. Small drops of rain began to fall, turning into bigger drops. Marrisa began to cry again.

Many thoughts whirled through her head as she stayed on her knees. She was so confused, more than ever as she thought about Tairren, and him kissing her, and what could've happened if she stayed with him in the forest. She wished none of it had happened, because it was making it so much harder for her to say goodbye, to everything. But at the same time, she wished that she would've stayed longer with him in the woods.

So many things had happened to her emotionally that day and she felt as if her heart and feelings were an unending storm. She never cried so much in one day as she did that day. She didn't know what to do, her body felt numb, frozen from the chilling rain and her broken heart. She wanted to go back to Tairren, but she knew that it would make things harder on both of them. She realized that she did love Tairren, and that he was the only man on earth that made her feel like she wanted to feel, safe and loved—and free. She wished that he would've told her those things years ago; but she didn't blame him though. They could've had plenty of time to come up with the perfect get-a-way plan, to run away with each other. But she knew that everything happened for a reason.

At that moment she wished that the wet ground beneath her would just devour her, allowing her to be part of the earth. The rain came down harder now, pouring on Marrisa as she lay down on her back. The rain felt refreshing but cruel simultaneously. It felt as if it were washing her misery away, but adding to it at the same time. She laid there for a while, wishing that the rain would just drown her...

Marrisa finally stood up, wrapping her trembling arms around her bosoms. After what seemed like hours of lying on the wet earth beneath the rain, she slowly made her way towards the castle through the relentless weather.

"Happy Birthday," Marrisa thought as she walked through the main gates of the castle. She walked along the huge wall of the courtyard. Cherry blossom trees lined the inside of the wall, creating more concealment for Marrisa as she continued to saunter along the brick.

She finally made her way through the courtyard to the side door of the castle. She walked through the servant's quarters of the castle, rushing past bustling servants as she hurried to a back hallway. The servants stopped what they were doing, gazing upon the very soggy and depressed looking princess. She didn't stop to even look at them. She knew that there would be a lot of gossip amongst the servants about her rushing through that back door, looking the way she did. She didn't care though, she felt as if she didn't really care about a lot of things lately anymore.

She rushed through the back hallway, running up a flight of cold stairs and through her main hallway. Her cold wet gown clung to her skin, sending goose bumps through her flesh as the air hit it. Marrisa ran into her room, slamming the door shut behind her. She was surprised that no candles were lit, not even the fire place was lit; and for the first time she wished that they were. The room was dark and cold and she could barely see anything. Any minute, she thought, Lilith would come knocking on the door. But there was no knock, not even one of her handmaidens came in to see if everything was okay.

Marrisa sat against the door of her room, sitting in the light that crept beneath the door. The light seemed to want to touch her cold and darkened body, but it couldn't. She began to cry as she felt so alone, so sad. She held the blue crystal pendant that hung on her chest, squeezing it in her hands until they began to tingle. She began to think about Tairren and everything he said to her, everything she loved about him. She wished that he was by her side, putting his arms around her. But she knew none of it was going to happen—ever again.

Marrisa sat alone in the dark, wondering if the rest of her life would be this way. She wondered if it was even worth living. She wondered how she could even be a great queen and a dedicated wife to Phillip if she didn't even love him, or her future life. She continued to cry as she put her hands to her face. She hated being alone, she hated crying so much and at that moment, she realized that she hated herself…

✝✝✝

…There was a Loud Silence…

The dark chamber was cold and dreary, filled with the strong presence of something that held only madness and darkness. Lilith sat there in the loneliness of her small chamber, with no light or no warm feelings of love or existence, in the wet air that came in through her small opened window. The weather outside was horrendous, exploding with lightning every so often. The excited flickers of the lightning bounced off her skin and glassy eyes.

During every strike of powerful light, black shadows appearing like slithering creatures and horned things could be seen creeping across the stone walls, emitting from her seated silhouette. Those were the dark spirits within her—and they were anxious. Her eyes were large and unblinking, not moving except for a sporadic twitch. The room was silent except for the crashes of lightning…and the noises in her head. The sound of a thousand treacherous voices bombarded her mind, crushing every sane thought that tried to trickle through. The taunting voices never stopped, never. She never slept, ever, but her body and mind seemed to be energized by the thousand wicked souls, making her cold heart pump. She never ate, and her body didn't seem to care.

The small room began to stink of death the night before last and still continued to linger, but that didn't bother her because the stench didn't make it out of the room yet. Her bloody sacrifice began to finally fester and rot, still laying on the stone floor where she cut the innocent young woman open to steal her heart...and left her corpse there for the flies and maggots. The corpse's eyes stared at the ceiling, foggy and grayish looking, unblinking as young flies developed on them. Lilith had devoured the heart the night before last as well, when everyone in the castle lay fast asleep in their beds.

She did as the dark father wished. The blood of the innocent filled her empty heart, which pleased him. Her mouth had only tasted blood within the last ten years, which she consumed on the strange nights when the moon was the fullest. Usually it would have been an animal deep in the forest, for the simple fact that it was not as risky. She tried to keep the missing numbers of people down to a minimum, and that's why she went for servant blood first. Missing nobles would have put the people in a state of panic. But it was time for human blood now, a much worthier sacrifice to the Lord of Darkness...

There was another crash of lightning, a loud one, which made her head twitch to the left a little. Even though her body was energized, it seemed to be drifting away, as well as the last little bit of her heart she had left. It was like a small flame burned inside of her...and it was slowly going out...

"Do it and live forever... Do it... Live forever... Do it... YOU ARE MINE... I WILL NEVER LET YOU GO... Do it and live forever... DO IT FOR ME... You are a god... do it... Do it... DO IT! ..."

The constant voices were strong in her head, never leaving her, never. Her large black eyes stared off into the blackness of the room as she spoke to herself, the voices within her mind and soul...

"I know she is home now; I do. I know where she went... YES, WE KNOW YOU KNOW, THAT'S WHY YOU WILL DO IT. She was with the disgusting ones, I hate them, I do... We know, we do too, father hates them too, there's so many of us, that's why you will do it. I long for her blood, you do too, you do, but they will get in the way, the disgusting ones will, I know they will! Father, they will! They will! YES, I KNOW— THAT'S WHY YOU WILL STOP THEM, WE WILL HELP YOU.

"I've been sensing that the light in Marrisa's heart is weakening, I have... Yes, it is, time draws near, her heart is as feeble and as vulnerable as most, we will shroud her heart with ourselves, we will. I feel the disgusting light strongest in the boy who is called Tairren, father… YES, I KNOW, WE ALL KNOW, YOU WILL NOT LET HIM INTERRUPT, YOU WILL NOT! WE WILL HELP YOU DO IT… Yes, I will do it, we all will, I will wait in the shadows for her like I usually do… Yes, we will be lurking in the black shadows—the celebration grows near. This is the night we have all been waiting for, this night. Do it… Do it… DO IT—TAKE HOLD OF HER HEART AND SMITE THE LIGHT WITHIN!"

Every night Lilith's body always sat that way, talking to the dark ones and staring off into a black abyss of insanity as the many taunting spirits crept about her—until the morning sun came over the mountains in the south. Ever since she first met father, her heart progressively hardened like a black lump of coal. But this seemed to be the last night she would ever sit this way—because the great celebration drew near, marking the time of great change and the beginnings of a reign of terror…

†

CHAPTER 8
I Am Called Natas

The castle began to fill with many courtiers, nobles and many other important people of Minslethrate, each family being announced as they graced the hall with their presence. The halls echoed with laughter and loud chatter as it came closer to the time of the royal feast. Everyone was so dapper, dressed in their finest eveningwear. Many people talked of how beautiful everything was, and how excited and happy their princess must have been.

Natalia walked into the great hall with her mother and father, being announced properly by one of the high servants of the castle who welcomed the new arrivals. Natalia glanced here and there, looking for Marrisa. She looked around, noticing how beautiful everything was. She thought it must have taken them since morning to get everything looking the way it did. Long veils of white and light-blue fabric hung everywhere, along with long streamers made of white cambric, roses and lilies, which were twined together. Every chair and table were adorned with the same fabrics and flowers, making everything look so whimsical. Tall candles were lit on every table, as well as the great candelabras that dangled from the tall ceiling. Servants were dressed in plane, but nice dresses and tunics that were the same shade of blue as the decorations. They all stood up against the walls of the main hall, waiting to be summoned.

Natalia stood there as her parents began to chat with other nobles in the hall. They were always the center of attention everywhere they went. Natalia left her parent's side, beginning to get annoyed as they began to laugh about whatever they were talking about. Natalia couldn't stand being ignored by the swaggering peacocks that flocked over to her parents anyway. She always thought that some of the aristocratic people of Minslethrate looked like peacocks, embellished birds, with their large and feathery hats and fans, and their bright gowns and tunics, squawking around and pecking at everyone. She thought of how comical it would be if she were to start tossing corn at them.

Natalia strolled along, smiling and making small conversation with people as she passed them. She looked to see if she could find Marrisa anywhere, walking with her future husband or chatting with any of the courtiers. She didn't see her, not even Lilith, who should've been all over the place.

Natalia walked through a great doorway that led into another great hall. There were long tables lined up everywhere, running vertical ways against the length of the great room. The tables were covered with the same decorations as the other hall. At the head of the room was another long table that sat horizontal before the other tables. That table was obviously for the royal family, because the chairs were bigger and more elaborate. The long tables were also covered with plates and silverware and beautiful golden goblets. The goblets on the head table had red jewels adorned all over them. That room was obviously where the grand feast would be held.

She could see servants quickly walking in and out of a doorway that led to the kitchen. She knew it was the kitchen because she remembered running around in the kitchen with Marrisa as a child. Natalia smiled as she remembered how the royal cooks would always get so upset with them.

Natalia walked out of the dining hall, noticing Prince Phillip standing next to King Julpen, without Marrisa. The king was talking with courtiers and lords, introducing them to the prince. The prince had a great smile on his face, chatting with everyone as if he had known them for years. He looked as if enjoyed all of the attention. He noticed Natalia and smiled at her, waving to her without anyone noticing. Natalia just smiled a little and continued to walk. By the way Phillip kept looking at her, she felt like Phillip had more interest in her than onyone else.

She decided that she needed some fresh air and thought it would be a good idea since the harsh rain seemed to stop for a while. The rain was really horrendous earlier that evening and luckily stopped an hour before she arrived. But it still looked as if it was going to rain later on that night. The moon and stars were hiding behind thick black clouds and soft rumbles of thunder could be heard far off in the distance.

As Natalia came closer to the entrance, she passed a young man that seemed to be looking at her; she could see him out of the corner of her eye. She glanced at him quickly and smiled, then stopped in her tracks.

"Tairren?!" Natalia said, astounded, as she came to him.

He was dressed up in very beautifully sown, light-blue tunic and trousers, which brought out the vibrant blue hue of his eyes. He wore a shiny black belt and shiny black boots as well. His black hair was pulled back out of his blue eyes, showing off his handsome face. He looked very dapper and looked like he belonged amongst many of the aristocrats of Minslethrate.

"I hardly recognized you!" she said, giving him a big hug.

She looked around noticing that some other young women who were chatting in a corner, glared at them. She knew they were gossiping about her; it wasn't lady like to hug a man so boldly like that in public. A kiss on the hand was socially acceptable, but of course Natalia didn't care what other courtiers thought of her.

"You look very handsome," she said, smiling. "How did you come about such a beautiful tunic?" Natalia spoke lower this time so that no one could hear their conversation. She didn't want to expose Tairren.

"My mother made it for me, and she did a wonderful job. Do I look like nobility?" he said with a huge smile.

"Oh yes, I'd say so!" she said as she put her arm around his. "Let's walk somewhere—we're being stared at by a pack of *ravaging* wolves," Natalia said facetiously. She pulled his arm. "Now you guide me or there will be more for them to gossip about," she said in a low tone.

They slowly strolled across the great hall to where there weren't too many people—smiling and nodding as they went.

They walked across a wide-open space, which was obviously room for dancing. To the right of the great space, up on a balcony, was a large group of people who were fiddling around with their instruments. They were the royal musicians who played at every royal function.

"This is splendid," Tairren said as they sat down on some chairs that stood against the wall. "I was really apprehensive about showing up on my way over here. I didn't want to be recognized by anyone."

"I don't think you will," she giggled, "you look very different." She smiled at him lovingly.

"And so do you, you look very beautiful," he said, smiling back. "I've never seen you dressed up this way. I mean, you usually do, but tonight you look exquisite."

Natalia was quite stunning. She had on an emerald colored gown that had gold trimming and embroidery on it. Her hair was up and adorned with small jewels and a small golden hair piece that was in the shape of a butterfly. Right below her chest was a beautiful golden brooch that sparkled with little jewels on it. The brooch was very showy, and would bring anyone's eyes down in that direction, right below her exposed cleavage.

Her light brown skin and her green eyes looked very luscious adjacent to the emerald color of her long gown.

"Thank you." She smiled her pretty smile again, but this time she looked as if she were becoming shy.

"Have you seen Marrisa? I had to see her one last time; that's why I risked coming here."

"Oh?" Natalia said in low tone, disappointed that the conversation was directed away from her and back to Marrisa as it usually did. "Well—I was wondering the same thing earlier. I haven't seen her yet, and I did see Prince Phillip, but not Marrisa. It's so strange though, and I haven't even seen Lilith anywhere either." She looked around as she spoke.

"I hope she is alright. She's had a strange day today. I really want to see her, I wanted to surprise her," Tairren said, also glancing around.

At that moment, a tall, snooty looking servant man walked into the great hall, ringing a bell. Natalia recognized him to be Alexander, one of the head servants who had been working for the royal family ever since she was a young girl. He was in charge of many of the servants and the one who made sure that every royal event in the castle went accordingly. He announced that dinner was served and welcomed everyone into the dining hall.

Everyone began to make their way into the hall, carrying their conversation and laughter with them. Tairren escorted Natalia, nervous as ever as they passed many courtiers and noblemen and women. Everything was so different to him. Everyone was so spectacular looking, and proper. Tairren was worried that he might say or do something that would offend somebody. He watched the other men and their body language, trying to come off the same way as they did.

As they walked to their seats, Natalia gave Tairren a quick whispered overview of everyone around them, telling him who they were and their social status in the kingdom. They spotted Lady Daleasa and Lord Fredrick at another table, mingling with other courtiers the same age as them. Natalia gossiped about them, making fun of the ridiculously showy clothing they were wearing and the immaculate headdresses that adorned their heads. She also talked of her parents and how she didn't want to sit next to them that evening.

Every seat had a covered plate waiting for them at the table, along with many utensils and goblets. Along the center of the tables were platters and baskets containing a nice selection of cheeses, herbed breads, fruits, different kinds of sauces with roasted meats, crisped fish and all sorts of other different kinds of foods that Tairren had never seen before. The goblets were already filled, one with water and the other with Minsleberry wine. Everyone sat, still talking all at once.

King Julpen, Prince Phillip and other important people found their seats at the head table. King Julpen sat in the largest thrown-like chair in the center, and the prince to his left. There was an empty chair to the king's right, which obviously was meant for Marrisa.

Just then Marrisa walked into the dining hall, being followed by three of her handmaidens. She looked beautiful as ever as she walked to her seat. She wore a long white gown that dragged behind her as she walked. The material was embroidered with small clear crystals, making her gown sparkle as she passed the torches that hung on the brick walls. Her long red hair was made up, showing off her long, elegant neck. She wore a meshed looking elegant headdress on her head that consisted of diamonds, and a diadem that dangled from it and pointed downwards on her forehead. She was absolutely beautiful.

Tairren's heart-beat began to quicken as he watched her walk to her seat. She looked so sad but beautiful at the same time as she sat down. Tairren wanted to get up out of his seat to go to her, but he knew that would be a ridiculous move.

"She looks so beautiful," Tairren said softly, still watching her.

Natalia responded to his comment and began to talk about something else, but he didn't hear anything that she was saying. He didn't even seem to be hearing any of the loud conversation of anyone in the dining hall at all. He heard no one as he gazed upon Marrisa across the room. He couldn't help himself; he couldn't keep his eyes off of her. He noticed how sad she looked, and how she didn't seem to be making conversation with anyone at her table, not even her father. She just sat there, looking as if she was in deep thought…

Just then, King Julpen stood up, holding his goblet of Minsleberry wine. He got everyone's attention as they all quieted down. He made a toast to Marrisa and the prince and went off with a long speech about that night and it being a special day for Marrisa. Marrisa seemed not to be paying attention to any of it as she sat there with an emotionless face. After what seemed like an hour of the king ranting on, everyone lifted their goblets in the air as the king said the final words of his toast. The clink of metal could be heard as everyone toasted, tapping their goblets together and then taking a sip of the sweet and tart wine afterwards.

†††

Marrisa sat there, not hearing anything her father was going on about— she didn't even realize that he was toasting to her and Prince Phillip. She was too lost in her thoughts and emotions. She felt as if her heart was screaming out to everyone, and no one cared to listen. She felt as if she were all alone in the massive dining hall. Everyone in the room had great smiles on their painted faces as her father spoke, except her. She seemed to be the only one in the castle that didn't care to be there; everyone was celebrating her last night in Minslethrate, and she loathed it.

Marrisa nibbled at her food, and it was quite delicious, but she wasn't hungry. She stared at her plate as the reddish-brown juices from her roast ran across it, mingling with the bitter herbs and sweet potatoes.

After looking at her colorful meal, she picked up her goblet. She needed something to chase her anxiety away. She didn't sip on her wine like the ladies in the castle did, but drank it down quickly, not caring when Prince Phillip took a glance over at her. She beckoned to a nearby servant who carried a large decanter of Minsleberry wine around. The servant poured her more, and she downed that one as well.

"One more, kind sir," she said as she smiled at the stunned looking servant. "Fill it to the rim please."

King Julpen noticed how absurd his daughter was acting and signaled for the confused looking servant to go away.

"Daughter, pace yourself, the night is young and that is no way for a princess to act." He glanced around, looking to see if anyone was looking.

"Why father, do you wish to spoil your daughter's fun on her *last* night?" she said facetiously. She just smiled at him as she began to sip on her wine now.

Prince Phillip kept looking over at Marrisa as he took large bites of his roast.

She glared at him as she sipped on her goblet, then smiled as she wiped a small drop of wine from her full lips. She hoped that he would think she was disgusting, so un-lady like that he wouldn't want to have anything to do with her. But instead, he winked at her, following his wink with a bright smile. Marrisa turned away from his gaze quickly, not trying to engage in anymore eye contact.

"Daughter, I know this is the wrong time for this, but I want you to have this. I meant to give this to you earlier but didn't get the chance," he said as he took the red jewel necklace from around his neck. He smiled as he put it over her head. It was a long golden necklace that had a deep-red pendant embedded in gold, hanging from it. The pendant was a deep blood-red, and sparkled as the firelight from the tall candles on the table glistened off of it.

"Oh father, your necklace," she said with a small smile. She looked into the pendant, rubbing the smooth stone with her thumb. "Thank you." She looked into his dark eyes, then gave him a kiss on the cheek.

"My father, King James, gave it to my mother when she first became queen of Minslethrate… I took it from my mother before she died…" He paused for a moment as his mind seemed to drift off, as if heavy thoughts began to burden him. He had that same look on his face whenever Marrisa would ask him about his childhood. "…I knew my father really wished me to have it… I gave it to your mother long ago, and before she died, she made me promise that I would give this to you on your sixteenth birthday, the eve of your wedding." He became quiet, sipping his wine. His face was serious and sad looking, as if he were giving away a piece of his heart.

Marrisa didn't know whether it was the sadness of him losing his only daughter and child, or the fact that he gave her the only thing that seemed so dear to him.

"This is truly special to me," she said with another small smile as her crystal blue eyes became glossy. Her smile was a mixture of sadness and happiness all meshed together. "But you didn't want to keep it here, amongst the royal family of Minslethrate?"

"I would rather my only daughter obtain such a precious keepsake— and it was your mother's request." He sipped on his wine, gazing off into the large room. "I don't have an heir to the throne yet, my daughter." He paused as Marrisa continued to look into his saddened face. "But it's time I remarried—to continue my legacy. I can't reign forever you know." He smiled a little, watching the feasting crowd of courtiers.

Marrisa was quiet, starting to feel the after affects of drinking down her Minsleberry wine too quickly. Her mind drifted off, beginning to think of Tairren, and how she would never see him again and how she was going to hate her soon-to-be sad life. She was startled by the laughter of Prince

Phillip, who was chatting with her father now. She looked off into the large room, watching the laughing and cheerful courtiers. They all ate and drank and laughed merrily—which provoked Marrisa.

She took another sip of her wine, then decided to drink her whole goblet of wine down again. She didn't eat much of the delicious food on her plate, she wasn't hungry anymore. Her head began to swirl a little as she glanced at her glistening necklace, then back up to the scene of the happy courtiers. The wine didn't seem to be helping with her anxiety much.

"Excuse me, father," she said as she slowly stood up.

She grabbed her goblet, signaling to the nearest servant to bring over another decanter of Minsleberry wine. It was a young servant girl this time. She poured it, filling the sparkling goblet until Marrisa signaled for her to stop.

The king acknowledged her and just smiled, looking around to see if anyone had noticed her odd behavior yet. Marrisa left quickly, trying to do so discreetly. She tried her best to not fall over as she rushed along the gray brick wall, carrying her goblet of wine with her. Her handmaidens rushed over to her, following her out of the large dining room.

Marrisa rushed off to her chamber. She couldn't stand being around the dining hall any longer. She detested how everyone was so happy when she herself hated every waking second of what was taking place. She didn't care that the ball would begin soon; all she wanted to do was to get out of there. She hurried down the hall and up the stare case into the main hallway that led to her room.

"My Lady, are you ill? The ball in your honor will begin soon," one of her handmaidens said as they walked up to her door.

"I am not *ill*," Marrisa responded irritably as she pushed open the large door. "I think I just need to rest a while," Marrisa said, bringing her hand up to her head.

"My Lady!" a foreign voice called out from behind her as she began to proceed into her room.

She looked over to see who it was. She recognized the voice right away because it was the voice of her future husband.

"My *dear* Prince Phillip," Marrisa said with an annoyed look on her face. "How may I assist you?" she said as she stopped, standing halfway in the threshold.

"My dear Lady, I just need to know that my future queen is well," Prince Phillip said as he approached her.

"I'm quite well, *actually*, and why are you approaching me when there is a whole crowd of courtiers waiting to meet you down in the dining hall?" Marrisa demanded as she signaled for her handmaidens to give them some privacy.

"I'm quite annoyed—I only wonder why my future wife runs from me so. When I am king, I want nothing of this matter to take place. I want nothing more than respect from my queen!" Prince Phillip said with a more dangerous look on his face. He appeared more aggressive as he approached Marrisa. He came so close to her that his chest was barely touching hers. He looked into her crystal blue eyes, lifting his hands to her face. "Oh Marrisa, you are truly the most beautiful woman whom I ever laid my eyes upon." He caressed her face as he said this.

She looked away from his dark eyes. His eyes appeared passionate, burning with fire. It scared her that a man whom she didn't even know grew passionate for her. She tried to think of something quickly to change the subject.

"I mean no harm, I only need time to myself," Marrisa said as she continued into her room.

He pulled at her arm, yanking her to him. Some of the wine in the goblet she was carrying splashed out onto her white gown, dripping down as a slow-moving red stain.

"You've had ample time to yourself, and soon you will be on my time. I will have none of this childishness in Ishkar. You are my future wife and queen, and I expect you to act like it. You will surrender to my requests— submitting to me like a flower to the sun," the prince said as he pulled her closer to him. Their chests were pressing against each other now as he said this.

He went to kiss her but she turned her head quickly. His lips caught her cheek. He looked at her, not saying anything as he peered into her crystal blue eyes.

The tension in the hallway was so thick that it seemed as if one could cut it with even a dull knife.

"You are like a rose—beautiful to gaze upon but painful to the touch...," he said with a grimaced look upon his face.

After what seemed like hours, he left as quickly as he came.

Marrisa felt every emotion creep upon her except for happiness. She raised her hand to her mouth as she slowly walked into her room. Her head and emotions whirled as she began to cry.

"Is everything well with you, my lady?" one of her handmaidens asked with a concerned look on her face.

"Leave me," Marrisa said in a low and trembling voice, "I don't need your assistance—anymore this evening. Go away... Take the rest of the evening off."

"But, my lady..." The servant girl looked worried.

"Did you hear what I told you to do?! Can you not hear?! Leave! Me!" Marrisa shouted out, releasing her anger. Her voice echoed down the stone hallway as she turned to the surprised looking handmaidens.

Marrisa had never shouted at her servants or showed any kind of anger before. She never shouted at anyone else for that matter.

The handmaidens quickly glanced at each other, speechless, then left quickly, shutting the door behind them.

Marrisa was alone again, and she began to feel an overwhelming wave of anger and depression wrap around her trembling body like taunting hands. She walked slowly to the center of her room, feeling as if the floor would fall from beneath her. She still carried her half full goblet of wine and slowly brought the goblet to her lips, drinking the rest of the wine down as tears swelled up in her eyes.

The wine was getting to her—and her emotions were like a storm. She had to sit down. She slowly made her way to her vanity which sat beside her bed, allowing herself to fall into the chair. Marrisa looked around her lonely room, realizing that a bright fire was ablaze in the large fireplace. The curtains of the arched threshold that led to the balcony was open, letting the cool breezes from the night come in. She hadn't seen Lilith all day, and knew it was her who lit the fireplace and unfastened the balcony curtains.

Marrisa looked into the mirror that sat on top of the beautifully carved vanity. She sat and stared for a while, which seemed to her like hours. She noticed that her eyes were puffy; and even though she couldn't see that they were red, she knew they were because they burned. Marrisa stared more into the mirror, noticing how pathetic and imprudent she looked. She didn't like her reflection at that moment. She despised the person she was looking at, the person she was becoming. An overpowering feeling of anger shot through her body as she began to cry harder. She didn't want to look at herself anymore and wished that her face could be erased at that moment.

"I hate you," a strange voice came into her head like an uninvited guest...

Disturbed by the silent voice, Marrisa began to quickly look all around her. She thought she saw movement in the shadows of her dark chamber. Tears continued to trickle down her flushed cheeks as paranoia came over her. Her reflection in the mirror caught her attention again. She looked again at her pale face. She whispered, "I hate you", to herself unknowingly. She didn't realize she did as she watched her lips move.

"I hate you!" Marrisa screamed at her reflection as her fist tightened around the stem of her goblet.

She let out another frustrated scream as she smashed the goblet into the mirror. She pounded the glass with her goblet a couple of times, releasing the anger that built up inside of her. Pieces of glass flew everywhere, looking like twinkling stars as they sparkled in the fire light. Some cut her face and hand, allowing small drops of deep-red blood to emit from her fair skin.

She stood up quickly then pushed over her vanity and chair. She breathed rapidly as her gaze fell upon the old family portrait that hung above the fire place. The smiles of her parents seemed to tease her. "Fake smiles... Unloving smiles..." Marrisa thought. Anger began to fill her heart again as she let out another scream—throwing the goblet at the painting with all of her might. The portrait fell onto the ground, and without any kind of pause or guilt, she quickly grabbed the large painting and shoved it into the fire place...

Marrisa walked to the middle of her chamber without looking at the burning and crackling painting. She fell to her knees, allowing herself to fall the rest of the way to the ground. She lay there for a moment as she pounded her fist against the cold stone floor. She then slowly sat up, realizing that her hands were covered with blood. Negative thoughts ran through her head as she looked to the glass-stricken ground. She thought it would do not only her good, but Prince Phillip good as well if she were to just end it all... He didn't need her and she didn't need him. She felt worthless. She began to understand that her existence was pointless...

Small voices in her head made her think that ending her life would be the right thing to do, that she would never be a good queen, and that she would hate her life and her husband that she didn't even know. She believed the thoughts that came into her mind—and she didn't think of anything else.

Marrisa's bloody hand slowly crept across the floor to a piece of the broken mirror. It was large and sharp like a knife and appeared as a shiny blade, reflecting the movement of the fire light. More tears flowed down her cheeks as her head continued to whirl. No thoughts of her father, Tairren or even Natalia came across her mind. All she knew was that the bitter sweet feeling of wanting to die came across her shaken body like the brisk crash of ocean waves into jagged rocks.

Marrisa held up her white wrist as she slowly tilted her head. Her breathing pattern began to slow as her heart calmed down somewhat. But her heartbeat was loud in her ears. She could feel the blood in her veins rush towards her pulsating wrist. She began to hear her blood like a pounding hammer. It seemed to beg to be cut as her seemingly loud heartbeat pumped through her chest. She slowly brought the sliver of glass to her wrist, holding it tightly in her other hand. Blood poured from the palm of her trembling hand, which slowly dripped down the white sleeve of her gown and onto her lap.

"Why me, God?!" Marrisa screamed out to the darkness around her. "I know you can see my beating heart! They say your blood was spilled for mine! You know what I've been through! Why me?! I have no one who truly loves me. I have no mother—my father doesn't value me… Why was I chosen?! What value am I—what is my worth?! How am I to love a kingdom or anybody else if I do not love myself?! There are so many people much wiser than I…" She began to sob again as she shook her head. "Say something!"

Marrisa continued to cry as she lowered her aching head. She closed her watery eyes tightly, holding her breath as she attempted to put pressure down onto her wrist with the ice-cold glass dagger. She could feel the sharp edge of the glass slowly cut into her wrist. She could end it all with one deep slit—and she decided that she was going to…

"Is He really listening?" a low and familiar voice said from behind her.

"Oh, God!" Marrisa gasped, startled. She turned her head quickly, stopping the attempt of her bitter-sweet suicide.

"No God—just me… But I see you—I see your beating heart…," the voice said.

Marrisa's surprised face found a dark silhouetted figure slowly creeping upon her. The figure skulked out of the dark shadows of the room and into the light of the fire. It was Lilith, appearing as a ghost as she made her way to Marrisa.

"Lilith!" Marrisa shrieked as she tried to stand up without falling over. She still held the bloody piece of glass in her hand.

"Oh my... How surprising," Lilith said in a low and teasing voice. Her face was as white as snow and her eyes were as black as the night's sky. "We have a very serious problem here... What would come of your father? Another death in his life would drive him to darkness... And who would help rule Ishkar? It would be devastating to waist such innocent and royal blood all over this cold, stone floor... Yes, it would..."

She came face to face with Marrisa, slowly running her ice-cold hand down Marrisa's arm. She took Marrisa's bloody hand still holding the glass, and brought it up to her face.

Marrisa was shocked, not realizing that Lilith had been in the room that whole time.

"How dare you! Spying on me—watching me from the shadows!" Marrisa fussed nervously as she tried to pull her hand away from Lilith's grasp. She was stronger than Marrisa had expected.

Lilith began to laugh, throwing her head back. Her breath was grotesque, smelling of something dead.

"If only there was *something* I could do..." Lilith said teasingly. "Oh, but there is *something*... It's not your time to die—I need you." Her face turned emotionless and deviant all of a sudden.

Marrisa was quiet, confused as ever. Instead of being a worried and tender handmaiden, Lilith was threatening and furtive.

"What do you mean, Lilith?" Marrisa asked in a low voice as Lilith continued to stare into her eyes, as if she was trying to peer into her soul.

Lilith was still quiet, filling the atmosphere with a strange feeling of fear and darkness. She squeezed Marrisa's wrist tightly, making her drop the bloody sliver of glass.

Marrisa winced in pain as Lilith squeezed harder, not letting go.

"You're hurting me!" Marrisa shouted as Lilith brought her bloody hand to her mouth.

Lilith let out a wicked chuckle as she stuck out her long tongue, licking the blood from her palm in one long stroke.

Marrisa's eyes widened with fear as she began to breathe harder. She was so shocked at what had just happened that she didn't know what to say.

"The taste of crimson innocence feels so good in my mouth," Lilith said with that same wicked face.

Lilith's eyes were larger than normal and shiny and black as coal, with no sign of life behind them. She wiped her mouth with her white wrist, smearing the blood that was on her pale lips across her cheeks and chin.

"Lilith, what has come over you?!" Marrisa asked in a shaky voice as she yanked her hand from Lilith's now not so tight grip. Fear spread across her body as she walked backwards, away from the disturbed looking Lilith.

"Lilith is no longer here…," she said, walking slowly towards her. "I have blown out her puny flame of a soul. Her rancid *flesh* is here with you, but her heart and soul are *lost*, forever. Father has finally taken her soul in full. Father has received her."

Marrisa was frightened and confused, and had no idea what she was talking about. Just then she heard the low rumbles of thunder as another great storm seemed to grow nearer. The soft flicker of lighting lit up the room for a quick second, making Lilith appear frightening. Her heart pounded rapidly as she raised her hands to her stomach. She felt as if she was going to get sick at any minute.

"Have you gone mad?! What do you mean?" Marrisa couldn't hide her fear as her voice shook.

"I am not Lilith—she has been drifting away ever since I first beheld her disgusting body ten years ago. I am called Natas. But I am one of many. I am Friend of darkness, and lover of fear and uncertainty. I am servant to my dark lord, and stealer of souls. And I have been in your family from the beginning, snatching bodies, doing rituals, and drinking blood to please my father. But I've learned that I've been doing things wrong, ruining our quest for my great lord, not able to go through with his plans. I was sent here many ages ago, spawned by the old ways of Minslethrate; the old ways that your ancestors followed before that *pig* of a king tainted the ancient spiritual beliefs of the Minslethratian people many decades ago. He thought he could end the reign of the dark lord by bringing that putrid Book of Light into our world! But darkness will triumph again! The dark lord promised that I would become a god, *if* I complete my quest."

Marrisa couldn't believe what she was hearing and didn't know whether it was the consequences of drinking too much wine, or that Lilith's strange mind had truly deteriorated.

Lilith ran her cold hand up Marrisa's arm and caressed her neck and cheek. Marrisa closed her eyes, wincing in disgust as tears flowed down her cheeks.

"Your innocent face is so—deliciously lovely," the monster in Lilith's body said, bringing its caressing fingers down her throat and over her chest. Lilith's wondering fingers stopped at the red jewel necklace that her father had given her earlier. She held the blood-colored pendant away from Marrisa's chest, staring into it with large black eyes.

"Aaah, the undying symbol of royalty—filled with your family's blood-line." Lilith's large black eyes slowly drifted up to Marrisa's, penetrating her heart with a surge of fear. "I wore this necklace many years ago—in your grandmother's skin—the *queen* of *carnage*," it mocked, then smiled a huge demonic smile, appearing impossibly wide. "She, the exotic Queen Karnidge, your father's mother, was from far, far away—and scared to death when I captured and dragged her to the Dark Temple—she was a perfect fit... But her black hair wasn't nearly as lovely as your red hair—the color of blood..." Lilith's cold, white hand caressed the top of her jewel adorned head. "We all played a little game of chase before we became one with her." Another disturbing smile crept upon its face again. "She came back to this kingdom, and ruled with a lust for blood—burning every drop of it in great screaming fires!" Another frightening laugh emitted from its mouth as Marrisa slowly walked backwards away from the thing.

"You see—I was sent to make your life a living hell—to take all goodness away from you and your family. I was there, one of many, in your grandmother's skin, making false and grotesque love to your grandfather, finally giving birth to your father; and by your grandfather's side when I shoved a poisoned dagger into his wretched heart!" Marrisa placed her trembling bloody hand over her mouth, shaking her head in disbelief. "After I left your grandmother's sickly body and became one with a brainless servant, I was there when your father, young and determined, stole this necklace from his mother's dying body. Years later when your father married your mother, he gave the jewel to her. You see, I was here in this castle, fixing your mother's hair and telling her how beautiful she looked—I wanted to vomit the whole time. I was there at your birth, assisting, and cleaning you off. And I was there, putting crushed deadly night-shade into your mother's food and tea, watching her blissfully as she lay in a state of delirium, and waiting for that joyous day when her disgusting light-loving soul would leave this earth!"

Large tears swelled up in Marrisa's eyes as she shook frantically. She put her bloody hand to her chest, thinking that her heart would explode any minute now.

"Your mouth stinks of cruelty... You are a liar!" Marrisa screamed, trying not to cry at some effort.

"Yes, *I* am a deceiver," she said with that wicked chuckle again. "But not this time, I think you need to know the *truth*," she mocked. "You are part of me and I am part of you. Your soul is destined to be with us, to be with Lucif, Father... And if I'm lying, then how would I know that your beloved *swine*, Moira, was innocent ten years ago before your father burned her at the stake!" She let out a terrible laugh as Marrisa's knees went out, making her fall to the ground.

Marrisa held herself up with her trembling hands—face down as she gasped for air. She was so overwhelmed with emotion that it was taking her breath away. The name Moira shot through her head like a lightning bolt as the memory of her being burned on the stake replayed over and over in her mind. She had never thought of Moira till that moment, and realized that she had blocked her out of her memory all these years, ever since she was a child watching the horrid scene.

"Aww, you do *remember* Moira after all," the thing in Lilith's skin teased. "I didn't think you'd ever remember that wretched woman. I took over Moira's puny heart and continued to sacrifice for father, waiting for this day. It's too bad she had to take the blame for my works—and was punished, burned to death. And it's no wonder you aren't fond of *fires*!" Lilith let out a teasing chuckle, followed by a half smile. "It was a memorable day when you watched as Moira screamed out, with her flesh burning away."

"Your disgusting words are wicked! What do you want from me?!" Marrisa screamed, between sobs.

"I want your body—you are our master plan, the key to our triumph! I've been waiting all of these years for this day, for this night—father has been waiting a very long time—we cannot make him wait any longer. We have been longing for this day, your sixteenth birthday, the day you rightfully become a woman and the evening you become engaged, the time when you will reign as queen of Ishkar.

"You see, Minslethrate is but a small kingdom, corrupted by man and too concerned with worldly goods and irrelevant things. But Ishkar is a great influential kingdom with a massive army, a strong hand and many absent-minded inhabitants that will do whatever they are commanded. Ishkar will be the kingdom of many, the king of the world. And I will rule in your body as a great queen, and you will kill your husband who is named Phillip—we will not need him. You will do great things to deceive your people, the followers. Your words will be like water to their souls and will set fire to their hands. Then they will worship you! We will live as a god and father's words and power will spread all across this world as poisoned and great water. The waters of the people will spread and their fiery hands will destroy. Light will be broken like a flame beneath that water. the Great King of light will fail—falling down into nothingness—forgotten forever. We will live for eternity in a world of darkness!" Lilith's body appeared mad as she lifted her hands into the sky.

Just then thunder could be heard, followed by lightning that bounced off the walls in the room. Marrisa's mind worked quickly, even though she was in a state of shock. She scanned the floor with her moist eyes, looking for something to protect herself with. Just then she spotted the bloody shard of glass next to her. She frantically picked it up and held it out in front of her like a knife. It seemed so ironic to her, that the dirty bloody piece of glass that she was going to use to take her own life with; was the weapon of her choice to protect herself.

"I will take you with me far to the south of Minslethrate, deep into the Forbidden Lands to the Dark Temple of sacrifice; where your ancestors gave blood to the goddesses and to Lucif, my great lord. Your father will send his brainless soldiers to come looking for you—but by that time you will show up back to the castle, unharmed and beautiful as ever. And they will never know that it isn't really you that they will be looking at… I will live on this earth forever!" The evil being in Lilith's ugly and decrepit body seemed excitable and terrifying as it raised its arms into the air again. The flash of the lightning glistened off of its black eyes as it looked quickly back at Marrisa. "We have been waiting for this night. Everything has been according to plan over the years, except for your disgusting mother! She would have been my first choice but her heart was too full of light! I could not go near it! So I did what the dark lord wanted me to do—poison it until it pumped no more." Its face was frightening as a wicked smile crept upon it. The dried blood from earlier still stained her white skin as her hideous smile grinned from ear to ear.

"You disgust me!" Marrisa screamed, then spat at her.

"My lady, you will never know the feeling of disgust until I get inside your skin," the thing called Natas said in a low and terrifying voice.

Just then, Natas turned its face quickly towards the door, pointing its nose into the air with a squinted face, as if it smelled something putrid.

"I sense a presence in the air—coming near, a presence that I hate and have almost forgotten… I smell a foe!" The thing slowly walked backwards, away from the door. Its wide, unblinking black eyes were locked onto the closed door, as if waiting for something to come bursting through it.

Just then there was a light knock at the door, followed by the muffled voice of a male.

"Marrisa, it's me, Tairren, I know I am a surprise, but I had to see you one last time."

"Tairren!" Marrisa screamed, but didn't get his whole name out before Natas quickly yanked her up, pressing its cold, white hand tightly across her mouth.

"Hush your pretty little mouth or he will meet his doom like everyone else in your pathetic life!" Natas whispered a putrid smelling whisper as it pressed its mouth to her ear.

"Marrisa?!" Tairren yelled from the other side of the door, banging on it as he tried to yank it open, it was locked.

Marrisa bit down hard on the dying flesh of Lilith, tasting a small bit of coagulated blood in her mouth.

A horrifying growl emitted from its mouth as it loosened its tight grip on her.

Marrisa yanked herself away, screaming. Panicked, she realized that she was still holding the large sliver of glass. And then with a quick raise of her arms, she shoved the large glass dagger down, hard into Lilith's shoulder. A loud scream echoed through the room, as it grabbed at the shard quickly, yanking it out.

Marrisa ran quickly to the door where Tairren and now Natalia were banging from the other side. She yanked at the door, realizing that it was locked somehow. Natas turned towards Marrisa, walking slowly towards her while chuckling.

"Oh, the *mayhem* of it all! A stab in the shoulder will never defeat me!" it laughed, throwing the bloody shard down at the ground. It shattered into many small, shiny pieces. "Do you need these?" It laughed again as it shook the ring of many keys that hung around its waist. "Did you forget that Lilith held the keys to every door in this castle? I locked it while you were too busy sulking in front of your beloved mirror!"

Just then as if energy ran through its veins, it ran full force at Marrisa, banging its hands on either side of Marrisa's head as it stopped right in front of her.

"Be prepared to meet the ugly!" It raised its hand up high, hitting her clear in the face with the back side of its hand. The force was so strong that Marrisa flew a couple of feet away, landing unconsciously to the ground…

†††

…Some time ago…

Tairren sat and ate his deliciously royal food as Natalia chatted with everyone who sat around her at the table. Tairren didn't speak much, worried that he would be asked a question that he wouldn't know how to answer. The courtiers who sat around him were older and by the way that they smiled and looked, they appeared gentle and caring. Some of the women who sat around him looked very odd, with their eyebrows and hair-lines shaved off, making them look like they had a very large fore-head beneath their headdresses. It was obviously a fashionable thing amongst the noble women since more than one appeared that way; it just appeared odd to him.

Tairren didn't hear much of what they were talking about amongst each other because he was too busy watching Marrisa. She looked dreadfully sad and uncomfortable, but still beautiful. He noticed that Marrisa drank down too many glasses of Minsleberry wine, which was very unusual. He could tell that she was becoming influenced by the wine. He watched King Julpen give her his beautiful red pendant necklace. She put it on, fiddling around with the red jewel. He noticed that she still wore the necklace that he gave her earlier that evening; it was tucked in the lace of her gown. It made him feel good to know that she seemed to care for him.

Some of the courtiers left the dining hall, making their way into the grand hall or out into the gardens for some fresh air. Goblets were refreshed with wine and laughter and conversation echoed through the hall as the night carried on. Soft thunder could be heard in the distance, making it known that another storm was approaching the castle. Tairren sipped on his wine, noticing that Marrisa had left quickly with her handmaidens following close behind her.

"What's happening? Where is she going?" Natalia asked Tairren, softly.

112

"I don't know, maybe she just needs some fresh air." Tairren took another sip of his wine. He noticed that Prince Phillip was excusing himself from the royal table and slowly went off in the same direction as Marrisa.

Tairren didn't like how the situation was looking and decided to go find out what was wrong with Marrisa. After a couple of minutes of waiting for nearby courtiers to quit staring, Tairren left his table, casually walking towards the entrance of the dining hall. No one seemed to notice, except for Natalia who was glaring at him from the table with a *"what are you doing*?!" look on her face. He made his way through the entrance that led to the great hall, looking back towards Natalia. She stood up, excused herself, then smiled as she made her way to him. She discreetly motioned her hands for him to stop as she walked toward him.

"What are you doing?!" Natalia demanded as she took his arm.

"I have to see Marrisa, something is wrong," he said as he looked around for red hair.

Courtiers were walking around, mingling with each other and sitting down at the smaller tables in the great hall. The musicians on the balcony above the wide-open space of the dance floor began to play music.

"The ball is about to begin, Marrisa should be down here," Natalia said as she pulled away from Tairren.

He watched as she approached a servant boy who was walking around with a golden tray that held filled goblets of wine. Natalia smiled and chatted with him for a minute, then he pointed towards a small hallway that was across the great hall. Natalia said something else with a smile, as he offered her a goblet of wine. She took one, then made her way back to Tairren.

"She went through that small hallway over there, which will eventually lead to her room," Natalia said as she put her arm around his again, escorting him towards that direction.

"Lady Natalia, how are you?" a familiar voice said from behind them.

Natalia cringed.

It was Lady Daleasa, who was accompanied by a group of young courtier women that she had been sitting with during the feast.

Natalia rolled her green eyes as the group of fashionable young women approached them. Natalia took a large sip of her wine as she looked at Tairren, who raised his eyebrows.

"Oh—Lady Daleasa, how *quaint*," Natalia said, with a cunning smile.

"I hope your evening has been well," Daleasa said as she fanned herself with a dark-blue fan. She looked at Tairren with a flirtatious smile. "Natalia, I believe I haven't met your companion yet." She kept smiling at him, making him blush.

"This is my—companion, Lord—Smithington, from—far away," Natalia lied, hoping that Daleasa would believe her.

But Natalia knew Daleasa would fall for such lies—she wasn't as sharp as Natalia was.

"Hello, Lord Smithington, I am The Lady Daleasa of Vaughn." She brought her ringed hand to his lips.

He glanced at Natalia as he took Daleasa's hand. He kissed her hand lightly, then smiled at her.

Natalia made a noise as if she were clearing her throat. "What can we do for *you*, Lady Daleasa?" Natalia raised her left eyebrow, crossing her arms.

"Why Lady Natalia, aren't we annoyed this evening," Daleasa looked at the other courtier girls as she said this, making them giggle and whisper amongst each other. "I just wanted to make a comment that I heard that our princess hasn't been doing so well today," she said condescendingly as she looked at her ringed hand, moving her fingers so that the hall light would catch the facets of the decedent jewels. "After I left you and your *odd* fan this afternoon in the marketplace, I bought this beautiful trinket." Daleasa stuck out her chest, showing off a jeweled necklace that dangled upon her ridiculous amount of cleavage. "After I left the luxurious shop, Lilith stopped to speak with me, telling me that Marrisa seemed to be—*jaded*—with her life. Lilith spoke of how worried she was about her, and that Her Royal Majesty even spoke of *running* away... Oh—my..."

"And what makes you so special that Lilith would tell you such things?" Natalia demanded with one eyebrow still raised. She took a sip of her wine, peering over the rim of her goblet.

"I think it's because Lilith can clearly see that Marrisa and I are so fond of each other. She is just concerned about our princess and she said that I am a *better* friend to her." Daleasa continued to fan herself. "Are you envious, Lady Natalia?"

"I'm not one to be patronized, Lady Daleasa. I think you were strongly misinformed. I think it may be that she knows that you have the ugliest and most rancid mouth in all of Minslethrate, and that you would tell everyone any little lie and gossip just to get attention." Natalia raised her eyebrows, and then smiled.

The other courtier girls covered their mouths with their hands, trying not to giggle.

"How dare you!" Daleasa scolded. Her face turned bright red with embarrassment.

She glanced at Tairren, and then at the other girls. She glared at Natalia then turned quickly to leave. With the sounds of their gowns gliding across the smooth, elegantly tiled floor, her entourage followed right behind her like a litter of lost puppies.

Tairren and Natalia watched as they made their way across the hall, their outrageous evening ware appearing like a blob of colors that were meshed together.

"I can't stand that little harlot," Natalia said as she took another sip of her wine, then sat it down on the empty table next to where they were standing.

"Do you really think that Lilith told her those things?" Tairren asked as they turned back towards the hallway.

"I don't know, but I believe it's a lie. I don't trust Lady Daleasa or Lilith. But even though Lady Daleasa is conniving and as worthless as vermin, I don't think she made that up—she's not that bright," Natalia smiled at her own remark again. "Lilith probably did tell her those things, but I don't know the intentions behind it.

"Well, let us go ask her ourselves," Tairren said as he motioned his hand towards the hallway.

"Yes, we shall." Natalia pulled Tairren's hand as they went through the small hall.

The hallway was small and dark, only lit by a couple of torches that were scattered here and there along the stone walls. The faint sound of rain against stone could be heard down the cool hallway.

"I can't believe she had the nerve to say those things; and even if Marrisa loathed her own life and had the intentions of running away by herself, she would've spoken to *us* about it first." Natalia's low voice echoed down the hall as they came to a twisted stair case. It was just as dim as the hallway. "Marrisa would never keep such secrets. I can't stand Lady Daleasa—that conniving little..."

"Shhhhh," Tairren put his finger to Natalia's ranting mouth, cutting her off. "Someone is coming; I hear heavy footsteps."

They stopped in the middle of the twisted stair case, right below a torch. The sound of footsteps came quickly down the stairwell, echoing off the steps. The flicker of lightning bounced off the stone walls, coming from a small window just a foot above their heads. The rain was still falling from the black sky, spitting some drops in through the opened window.

"It'll be okay, just act natural," Natalia whispered as she began to walk up the steps slowly, motioning Tairren to follow her.

Lightning flickered again, sending a rolling thunder clap behind it. Natalia jumped a little, and then leaned against the moist stone wall. Just then a large dark figure came quickly around the curve of the stairwell. Natalia let out a scream, startling not only Tairren but the dark figure that came quickly down the stairs. The dark figure let out a startled gasp as it came into the dim light.

"Oh my, Prince Phillip!" Natalia said in a surprised voice as she placed her hand over her chest. "You frightened us."

Both Natalia and Tairren bowed their heads to him.

"You gave me a fright as well," the prince said.

"We were just going up to check on Princess Marrisa." Natalia took a quick glance at Tairren as she said this.

Tairren was leaning against the wall, emotionlessly looking up at Phillip.

"What a coincidence, I've just spoken to her highness a while ago. I don't think she is up for company."

They were quiet for a second, and noticed that the ball must have begun already. The sound of music echoed up the stair well, as well as the repetitive sound of the rain which emitted from the window.

"I think it will be okay, you know I am her best companion, your royal highness." Natalia smiled her soft smile as she began to go up the stairs.

"Yes, well, I better go, I don't want to come off as *rude* for missing the festivities," the prince said as he glanced up the stairwell, insinuating that their unsocial princess was being just that.

He started down the stairs, glancing at Tairren as he passed him. Tairren didn't say anything or even smile as he passed. After a moment of awkward silence between both the prince and Tairren, he quickly went off into the shadows of the stair well, carrying his echoing footsteps behind him.

"Let's go," Tairren said, breaking the silence.

They rushed up the stairwell, which led them to a silent and dim hallway. It was quiet and much larger. They hurried past many paintings of the royal family, nicely carved chairs and small tables with vases of flowers on them.

"This is Marrisa's pleasant little quarters," Natalia said, motioning around with one hand and holding her gown with the other. "Just down the hall is Marrisa's private library and study—it is quaint and quite charming. Odd Lilith resides at the very end of the hall—her chamber is, well, let's just say that it suits her. Just beyond that is a back staircase, which leads down to the servant's quarters and a back exit. When we were children, we used to sneak through there to go outside. The servants used to get irritated with us on many occasions," Natalia giggled a little as she said this. "Speaking of servants, I'm actually surprised that there isn't any of her many handmaidens going in and out of her room right now."

They kept walking until they came to a large door on the left side of the hallway, which had a red banner hanging above it with the royal family's coat of arms embroidered on it with gold thread. Small tables also sat on both sides of the door, with a small vase of red roses on each one.

"Here we are," Natalia said, smiling. "You do the honors." She motioned towards the door as if presenting something. Tairren stood there, not saying anything. "Well, come on," Natalia said in a low voice, pulling him towards the door.

Tairren slowly came to the door, bringing his hand up to the heavy wood with a fist ready to knock. His heart began to pound in his chest as he began to realize that he was going to see the girl he had always loved, again, for the last time. After a minute or so, he lightly knocked on the door, bringing his mouth closer to it.

"Marrisa, it's me, Tairren, I know I am a surprise, but I had to see you one last time."

Just then Tairren could hear Marrisa scream out his name! Tairren quickly glanced at Natalia, noticing that she heard the scream as well as her eyes widened.

"Marrisa!?" Tairren yelled, realizing that something wasn't right.

His heart sped up as he yanked on the locked door. A surge of worried fear shot through his body as he now knew that something horrible was going on.

They rushed to the door, beginning to bang on it, as well as Tairren. They both yelled out her name as Tairren yanked on the door. Strange screams could be heard from the inside. Just then a loud thump from the other side of the door could be heard, as if something was slammed against the door.

"Go get help! Call the guards!" Tairren yelled as he pulled Natalia away from the door. He started to strike at the door with powerful kicks, trying to knock it in.

Natalia ran off down the hall, looking back one more time before she entered the stairwell.

Tairren rushed to the other side of the hall across from the door, getting himself ready for a hard hit. After a second of bouncing, he ran hard at the door, hitting it with all of his strength. The door crashed in, making him fall to the ground. Tairren stood up quickly, automatically reaching for his dagger. It was not there! He quickly picked up a piece of broken wood for protection. It was the first time that he had left his dagger at home and the first time he actually needed it.

Not knowing what to expect, he looked around quickly as he continued into the room. He found a dark figure, leaning over a body that lay lifelessly on the ground. He was surprised to see that it was Lilith and the unconscious body belonged to Marrisa.

"What has happened?! Tairren yelled, breathlessly, as he looked around the room.

Broken glass was everywhere, as well as furniture and also what appeared to be a knocked over vanity stand. A large painting, hanging half way out of the fire place, was ablaze. The chamber was a wreck.

Lilith still stayed where she was at. She was quietly hunched over Marrisa. Behind them was a dramatic background of the weather upon the opened balcony. The thunder and lightning crashed in as the wind blew at the red curtains that fluttered on each side of the balcony doorway.

"What has happened, Lilith?!" Tairren quickly rushed to Marrisa's side.

His heart dropped as he noticed the blood stains on her white gown and the gash on the palm of her bloody hand. After quickly inspecting Marrisa, he checked her pulse, which revealed that she was alive.

He realized that Lilith still hadn't moved or said anything yet. He slowly looked up at Lilith who was a silent dark shadow with her face at his eye level. The dim light from the hallway came into the room, mingling with the blazing fire that danced in the large fireplace. Tairren looked into Lilith's eyes as she just stared at him. She was emotionless and appeared haunting. Chills went up his spine as he studied her wicked looking face. Her eyes were as black as coal and her white skin was like that of a dead person's. Dried blood was smeared across the lower half of her face and the odor of death emanated from her mouth. He noticed that she had a wound on her right shoulder, leaking a thick, black-colored fluid.

"Lilith?" Tairren said in a low voice as he slowly backed away, reaching for his piece of wood that he had grabbed earlier.

She was still silent, staring her large black eyes at him.

"GET AWAY!" she roared out in an inhuman voice. It was so loud that it made Tairren's ears ring.

Her voice was that of a vicious animal! Tairren moved back quickly as his eyes widened. A feeling of terror surged through his body as he watched Lilith quickly stand up and toss Marrisa over her shoulder like a sack of potatoes. Her strength was shocking. Lilith then moved quickly and quietly like a cat, towards the balcony. The crude storm crashed outside of the balcony as Lilith stopped short right before the cement balustrade.

Tairren stood up quickly, running after Lilith who began to climb over the left side of the balcony. Before Tairren could get to the balcony, Lilith disappeared into the harsh gray rain that fell so intensely. "Where did she go?! There is nowhere else to run!" Tairren thought as he ran into the rain. He became alarmed as he looked over the balcony.

"Marrisa!" Tairren yelled out, hoping that she would call out to him.

Horror ripped through his body as he looked to the left of the balcony. He was taken aback at what he had just witnessed, wondering if it was all really happening. His vision was so obscured by the rain and night sky that he thought he was just seeing things. Then there came another crash of lightning, enabling him to get a glimpse of it again. It was Lilith, quickly climbing down the stone wall of the castle appearing like some kind of crab or spider, with Marrisa dangling from her mouth! Lilith was biting down on the back of Marrisa's gown, holding her by a huge wad of the fine fabric in her retched jaws; appearing as a puppy hanging by its scruff from its mother's mouth. Just then Marrisa seemed to come to. Her dangling lifeless body began to thrash around as if she just realized what was going on.

"Marrisa!" Tairren cried out as his heart raced.

His heart pounded against his ribs as he seemed to be frozen, not knowing what to do.

He could now hear Marrisa's faint screams through the harsh rain. Just then, as Lilith got closer to the ground, Marrisa fell from Lilith's jaws, landing onto the soggy earth of the courtyard. Tairren could see Lilith's body leap at Marrisa from the wall, like a panther pouncing on its prey. He frantically looked down beneath him, wondering if he could resist a long jump and if his bones would brake if he attempted to do so from the balcony. But he knew it was much too high.

Tairren ran quickly, taking his soaking wet body and stunned brain through Marrisa's wrecked room and out into the dimly lit hallway. He took a left, remembering that Natalia had said that there was a back stairwell which led to the servant's quarters, along with an exit. Tairren didn't hesitate as he ran as fast as his legs could go through the seemingly long hallway and down the stairwell.

He ran through the servant's quarters, startling a group of servant women who were talking and eating amongst one another at a large long table that sat in the middle of the large room. He ran over to the only door that led to the outside which was between two windows. He burst through the door running out into the harsh rain, wondering if he would ever see Marrisa again.

†

CHAPTER 9
A Night of Fear

The small hallway went from total silence to noisome in a matter of minutes as the king and a handful of soldiers, as well as Prince Phillip, crowded Marrisa's quarters. Their shadows danced on the dim light of the stone walls as the torches of the hall crackled and popped.

"What has happened, Natalia?!" King Julpen demanded as he and his soldiers rushed upon the opened doorway of Marrisa's dark chamber.

"I don't know, your majesty, but Marrisa is in danger. I heard her screams from behind her locked door!" Natalia's voice trembled as she spoke.

She felt terrified and tried to stay calm as tears kept trying to swell up in her eyes. Many thoughts ran through her mind as she followed behind Phillip. Her heart began to pound as she approached the doorway, wondering what horrific scene she would behold.

The soldiers went in first, their swords ready to strike at any moment. King Julpen followed behind them, his hand on the hilt of his sword. They looked serious and nervous at the same time, appearing as if they were anticipating an ambush.

Natalia tried to rush into the room but Phillip held out his hand, abruptly stopping her. She stopped for a moment, surprised at his gesture. She looked into his eyes as her face went from worried to appearing irritated in a split second. She shoved past his arm, forcing her way into the room. She didn't care that he was a prince; she wasn't going to let him stop her from seeing if her companion was safe just because of her being a lady.

The room was dimly lit by the massive fireplace that stood at the far end of the room. She didn't see Marrisa anywhere—just a wooden vanity-stand which lay on its side with broken glass all around it. She noticed that a large painting sat halfway out of the massive fire place; it burned and crackled as heavy smoke came from it. There was also a tipped over chair, lying in front of the opened archway which led to the balcony. The wind blew at the curtains which resided on either side of the archway, making them appear as scarlet apparitions.

Natalia put her hand over her mouth, surprised by the mess in the room. She knew something bad had happened, and that Marrisa was in grave danger. "What horrible situation has taken place?!" she thought as she scanned the room for Tairren, expecting him to walk out of the shadows at any minute now with a broken Marrisa.

The soldiers as well as King Julpen and Prince Phillip, rushed about the room, looking onto the balcony and here and there in the shadows of the room.

Natalia watched with tears in her eyes as the royal guards searched the chamber. She noticed that one of them had picked up the goblet Marrisa had been drinking from earlier that evening.

"Tell me again what you heard," the king said in a serious tone as he approached her.

"Like I said before, your majesty, I was coming to check up on Marrisa and I heard a scream from the other side of the door, so...," she paused, catching herself before she revealed that she wasn't alone, but with Tairren. "So I ran down the stairwell to fetch a guard. I don't know what happened, but I think Marrisa is in some kind of danger."

She looked at the prince who was standing beside the king. She knew that the prince had seen her with Tairren on the way up the stairwell, and hoped that he wouldn't say anything.

Phillip just stared at her with his dark eyes, bringing his fingers to his lips. By the look on his face he seemed to be thinking of something, which made Natalia nervous.

"The door appears as if it was busted in by some force," the king said, looking around. His serious face showed no other sign of emotion. "You said the door was locked?" he asked as he looked at Natalia for a second, then back at the broken-in doorway.

She nodded her head, wondering why it mattered that the door was locked.

The king became quiet as if his mind was rushed with a billion thoughts all at once.

With anxious looks on their faces, the soldiers gathered near the king after rummaging around the chamber, waiting for an order.

"Call the other soldiers and search everywhere!" the king shouted. "No one is to leave this castle until everyone is questioned?!"

The soldiers rushed through the doorway, carrying the clanging sounds of their armor with them.

"Go fetch Lilith and bring her to me!" The king pointed to a nearby soldier who was just about to exit the room.

The soldier bowed his head and left quickly out of the room.

"Where is that woman!?" the king mumbled to himself in an irritated manner, then shook his head in disappointment as he looked around the dim chamber. "She should have been by Marrisa's side at every waking moment! She will be chastised for this!"

The room became quiet all of a sudden, except for the rain that still poured outside onto the balcony. The king walked slowly to the opened archway of the balcony, staying silent as he seemed to daze off. He leaned against the cold stone threshold of the archway, looking out into the dark rainy night's sky.

"Lady Natalia—come to me," the king said in a less demanding fashion as he still stared upon the rain.

A soft rumble of thunder rolled into the room as Natalia approached the silent king. He rubbed his face and forehead, trying to relieve the stress that rushed upon his body. Phillip stayed glued in his spot, watching the awkward scene as Natalia slowly crept upon the king. She did not say anything; she just stood there, becoming oddly nervous as the king did not even turn to look at her.

"This room is colder than I remembered—just like my daughter... I don't know what has become of my daughter, Natalia," the king said, now turning towards her.

His face went from sad to angry as he stood up straight.

"What is meant by that, your majesty?" Natalia asked as she rubbed her left arm.

She was confused now. How could he react this way? He was irritated and then nonchalant when something terrible seemed to have happened to Marrisa.

"This was supposed to be a great night, a night that would be the spectacular beginning for our kingdom. Marrisa would become Queen of Ishkar, giving Minslethrate a strong stable hand." Suddenly the king was silent as he looked back into the rainy darkness. "I know Marrisa has run away," he now said with an annoyed tone. "I know she is not fond of her future—I can tell by the way she has been acting, by her deportment, by her aloofness towards her royal obligations." He glanced at Phillip as he said this, making sure that he was not listening. Instead Phillip was talking with a guard outside of the doorway. "She will not taint the future of my kingdom—she will not yield to her emotions! And it is best if I know the truth from you, Natalia. You are the closest companion she has—tell me where Marrisa has run off to! Tell me how you've come up with such a ridiculous plan, making her appear as if she has gotten captured!"

Natalia was shocked by his accusations and was offended that he thought such things.

"My king, I have told you what has happened, and I don't know where Marrisa is." She tried to stay calm but her anger started to show around the edges.

He stared his dark eyes into hers, trying to find a sign of deception.

"So she has *not* run away," the king confirmed arrogantly as he began to walk to the middle of the room.

"No! She hasn't! Something has happened to her!" Natalia only slightly raised her voice, tying not to sound too disrespectful.

"Natalia, hold your tongue! The Lady Daleasa approached me earlier this evening and has told me what Marrisa's intensions were. She has informed me of what Lilith has revealed to her—about Marrisa acting strange and wanting to run away. I did not believe Marrisa would go through with such a ridiculous plan, so I did not pay any mind to it. But by the looks of this situation, I've made a mistake by trusting my daughter." The king turned to Natalia.

Her mind raced, thinking about what Daleasa had told her as well. As conniving as Daleasa was, she would never be so bold as to lie to his majesty.

"She has been deceived," Natalia said quickly, walking towards the king.

"I beg your pardon?" The king's eyebrows went up, surprised.

"My king, Lilith has lied to Lady Daleasa, I know she has. And as you know, I am Marrisa's best friend, her sister, I would never let her do something as stupid as to run away." Her eyes began to water as she said this. "I would never allow her to put her life in danger. I've told you and I am telling you again—Marrisa is in danger!"

The king became quiet as he looked down to the ground then back up to Natalia. He inhaled then exhaled as he slowly shook his head. Suddenly the soldier who was sent for Lilith frantically came into the room, followed by Phillip.

"Your majesty, you must come quickly!" the soldier said with a shaken voice.

The king looked at Natalia once more then left the room quickly, following the young soldier.

Phillip glanced at Natalia, then followed the king.

"What has happened?" Natalia asked with wide eyes as she caught up with him. She could tell by the look on his face and by the flustered soldiers that something terrible was going on.

"They found a woman," he said as they quickly continued down the long hallway.

Natalia watched as the soldier and the king stopped at Lilith's room, standing in the doorway. Natalia came up behind them, trying to peer in between the large bodies of the men. The king turned around quickly, lightly backing her away from the doorway.

"My Lady, why don't you go to the grand hall and mingle with the other courtiers?" He looked at her with dark, anxious eyes and a crooked smile, as if forcing it. "You go dance, have fun. Don't you worry about Marrisa, we will find her..."

Incredulous, Natalia stood there for a second or two, then shook her head as she began to take a couple of steps backwards. She was irritated that the king hadn't believed her and was shooting accusations at her, then he was acting as if it all had never happened.

The king watched her for a moment, then motioned for the prince to follow him into the room. Something strange was going on, and Natalia wanted to know.

She walked a little, then turned her head to see if she was still being watched. She stopped walking then turned around. No one was in the hallway anymore, so she silently walked back to Lilith's room, hoping to catch a quick glimpse at what the king was acting so queer about. She tip-toed to the doorway then pressed her back to the stone wall, bending her neck to take a quick peek. She peered into the room, noticing how dim it was. A half-lit candelabrum dangled from the ceiling, barely producing any light. A putrid odor began to creep upon her. She quickly covered her nose, wondering what was giving off that horrid smell.

Both Prince Phillip's and the king's back were towards her, with the young soldier squatting over something. Just then the soldier stood up, revealing feet which lay lifelessly on the dirty stone floor! Natalia's heart raced as she leaned further into the room, trying to catch a glimpse at who was laying on the floor. Natalia's eyes widened as she realized who was on the ground. It was Katrinka, one of Marrisa's handmaidens! She was lying in the center of a ring of unlit, melted candles! Her face and arms were a grotesque greenish-white color with dark gray blotches all over them. She obviously had been dead for a while, lying in a pool of black, coagulated blood that stained the ground. Her torso was ripped open and her neck had a large gash across it, revealing more black blood.

Natalia turned quickly, covering her mouth and leaning her back against the wall. Her heart raced as tears began to flood her eyes. Her stomach began to churn as she started to breathe heavily. She felt sick. She felt as if a panic attack was coming upon her. She started to walk slowly down the hallway, trying to understand what was going on. "What if the same thing has happened to Marrisa?! Was it Lilith who was doing this? And poor Katrinka—she was the sweetest of all Marrisa's handmaidens. How could anyone want to murder the poor darling?" Natalia's thoughts raced around and around in her head.

More tears swelled up in her eyes, as she thought about Marrisa and what could have happened to her. She wrapped her arms tightly around herself as her confused head whirled. She felt so lost and terrified all of a sudden as she began to cry. She didn't know what to do as she continued slowly down the hall.

"Please don't let her be dead—great father of the heavens... Watch over Marrisa... Please... What do I do?" Natalia softly prayed, lowering her head while squeezing her arms tighter.

Natalia opened her eyes, wiping the tears from them. Just then she stopped walking, noticing that the stone floor of the hallway had random splotches of water on it. She followed it with her eyes, noticing that it was a path of wet footsteps and spattered water that led from Marrisa's room and down the hallway. The faint watery footsteps led right past Lilith's room and towards the back stairwell. She followed them quickly, stopping before she passed Lilith's room. She peered in, making sure that the men wouldn't see her pass the opened doorway. She noticed that they covered Katrinka's dead body with a blanket and seemed to be searching the chamber. Swiftly, Natalia rushed past the doorway, nearly running as she made her way to the stairwell.

Natalia ran quickly down the twisted stairs while holding up her gown. Thoughts of Katrinka's dead body flashed through her mind as she made her way into the servant's quarters, still following the small puddles of water. A group of startled handmaidens sat around a long table, sipping on tea and nibbling on what seemed to be leftovers from the feast. Some of the women were Marrisa's servants, and were obviously off for the night.

"Who came through here?!" Natalia demanded, breathlessly.

The servants appeared surprised at Natalia's visit. They were quiet for a moment as Natalia searched them with anxious eyes.

"It was a frantic young nobleman, my ladyship," the youngest out of the women said, putting down her cup of tea.

"A very wet one at that," an old woman mumbled, making the others giggle.

"Tairren…," Natalia said under her breath as she ran to the door, opening it to a very dark and drizzly night.

She hurried out, not even closing the door behind her. The night was cool and the dying rain made it colder than normal. The wind blew harshly, making Natalia's gown blow up over her knees. The rain seemed to let down to a mist as Natalia ran along the stone wall of the castle. Locks of wet hair that fell from her intricate hairstyle clung to her cheeks and neck.

"Tairren!" Natalia screamed out, hoping that he could hear her now that the harsh part of the storm had passed by. "Tairren, where are you?!"

There was a soft glow of lightning that lit up a portion of the dark sky, flickering like a massive lightning bug in the black clouds. A low rumble followed, sounding distant and calm. Natalia ran around the corner of the castle wall, not caring when she splashed through a large mud puddle. The castle stable was just around the corner and the faint sound of startled horses could be heard.

"Lilly!" Natalia said to herself, having the idea that she could take Lilly to find Tairren quicker.

"Tairren had to have seen something, or knew where Marrisa was. Why else would he leave so quickly? But why was he soaking wet?" All of these thoughts ran through Natalia's head as she ran towards the stable.

She held up her gown as she made her way through some bushes and through the stable gate. The stable was dimly lit by two lamps that were lit on either side of the massive entrance. The sound of horse grunts and hooves on hay could be heard from the dark shadows of the stable, as well as other animals like pigs, cows and chickens. The only light in the stable illuminated from two torches that were tied to two large posts in the middle of the building. The first post had no torch on it, as if someone had taken it.

Natalia walked in slowly, cautiously peering around as she wrapped her arms around her bosoms. The thought of Katrinka's rotten body shot through her mind again as a surge of fear came over her body. "What if the murderer was hiding in the shadows of this very stable?!" She thought as she stopped in her place, beginning to panic. She looked around for some kind of weapon—just in case. Directly on the right side of the entrance, hanging on the wall, were a bunch of tools of some sort. Instead of going for the smaller objects she went for the biggest weapon she could find. There was a pitch fork that leaned up against the wall, sticking out of a small pile of hay. Natalia grabbed the rusted pitch fork and pointed it up towards the ceiling, holding the long wooden handle tightly.

Even though she was a petite, young noblewoman, she still had some strength. Natalia and Marrisa had always practiced sword fighting with each other, taught by the king himself.

Just then a strong gush of wind raced in, knocking over some other gardening tools that lay against the wall on the other side of the entrance. Natalia jumped, expecting to find someone coming after her. Her heart pounded wildly. She closed her eyes, breathing in and out slowly, trying to calm herself. "Take hold of yourself," Natalia thought as she turned towards the stable again, walking in deeper. The stable was huge, it went straight back, making room for other random animals; and after a couple of yards in, it turned to the left allowing more pen room for all the other horses.

Natalia walked quicker as the thought of Marrisa, Tairren and even Lilith ripped into her mind. "What if it was Lilith who was doing all of this?" she frantically thought, "I always knew that Lilith was strange... But if it was Lilith and she was hiding in this very stable, the horses would be going crazy right about now. The horses never liked Lilith for some odd reason."

"Lilly!" Natalia whispered loudly as she looked around again, searching each pen with her eyes.

She saw many different colored horses except for a white one. Lilly was the only pure white horse in the whole kingdom, and the most beautiful for that matter.

"Lilly! Make a horse noise—or something!" She whispered loudly again, as if a horse could understand her.

She didn't see Lilly or any empty pens where she was at. She gripped the pitch fork tighter as she turned the left corner. It went further back having five pens on each side, and at the very end in the center was a large pen—a large empty pen!

"Tairren must have taken Lilly," Natalia thought as she turned quickly to leave.

Just then, as if out of nowhere, a dark figure came quickly a few feet in front of her!

Natalia let out a loud scream as she swung the pitch fork as hard as she could at the dark figure. It ducked, barely missing the sharp points of the fork, falling down in the process.

"Stop! It's me—Prince Phillip!" He yelled out, having a startled edge in his voice. "I've only come to ensure that you are okay."

"What?! Prince Phillip forgive me, I could have impaired you!" Natalia exclaimed breathlessly as she threw down the old pitch fork to help the prince up. "I've been a little uneasy this very night," She said as she pulled some hay from his dark hair.

He stood up quickly, staggering while pulling at his tunic and dusting off his velvet robe, making sure he didn't appear so queer.

"My lady, I was just a little surprised is all—I assure you, you couldn't have hurt me," he said with an awkward chuckle. He cleared his throat as he stood up straight, then began to escort Natalia out of the dim stable. "Why is a young lady like yourself creeping in the wet night and hanging about in a dark stable?" he asked with a smile that looked as if he were mocking her.

"Have you been following me?! Where is his majesty?" Natalia demanded as she pulled away from the prince, walking quicker to the entrance of the stable.

"I saw you pass by Lilith's door-way quickly so I just excused myself and followed you," he exclaimed as he hurried by her side.

"How dare you spy on me! You nearly frightened me to death!" Natalia fussed as she crossed her arms over her chest, making her way out of the stable and into the chilled air of the night.

The rain still drizzled on softly and the thunder was down to a very low rumble.

"I beg your pardon, I only wanted to see if everything was okay," he said as he moved his wet hair from his face. "As we all know, tonight has been a very odd night, and now with a dead body in the castle and the princess missing—I don't know what to think." He glanced at Natalia who stopped in her place. "She acted very strange with me earlier this evening, so I left her abruptly, and when we came into Marrisa's wrecked chamber I thought of the moment when I stumbled upon you and the other gentleman in the stair-well. That's when I thought maybe…," he hesitated, looking off into their dark surroundings. "Maybe a quarrel went on between you, the gentleman and Marrisa…"

"How dare you insinuate such things!" she snapped with wide eyes. "Yes, Marrisa is missing and *no* I do not know what is going on either! We heard screams from behind the door. I did not see her, much less quarrel with her!" Tears once again began to stir in Natalia's eyes. "That other gentleman is a very close friend to Marrisa and I, and when I went to fetch the guards for help, something happened in that room. And that is why I am looking in the stable," she wiped her eyes then motioned to the dark stable house. "I was looking to see if Lilly, Marrisa's horse, was still in her pin so I could go looking for them. She's not! Someone has taken her and I think Tairren did to catch up with whoever was attacking and has taken Marrisa!"

There was another low rumble of thunder as they stood in awkward silence for a moment.

"I'm truly sorry, my lady…"

"Marrisa is my best friend! My sister!" Natalia cried out, cutting him off, "And I'm dreadfully worried that something horrible has happened to her! And you should too since she is the future queen of your country!"

The prince was quiet for a moment, then put both of his hands on her arms, looking into her scared eyes.

"Truly, I will help, whatever is within me—to find Marrisa," he said with reassurance.

Phillip just looked into her green eyes, which comforted her. She looked back into his dark eyes for a moment, smiling a half smile a little and nodding her head.

"Alright then…," she finally said with sniffles, "where is your horse?"

†††

The town square was dark and quiet as Tairren rode through the dark streets on steadfast Lilly. The only light in the area came from the random, dim candle-lit windows of the small buildings and that of the torch that Tairren held.

He had taken the torch from the stable. Luckily there were no guards or anyone watching the stable to stop him from taking both Lilly and the torch—they must've all been in the castle. Lilly was actually excited to see him and put up no kind of fight when he pulled the saddle upon her back. Besides Marrisa, he and Natalia were the only ones she trusted.

The clap of Lilly's hooves on the brick ground echoed through the dark air as the constant trickle of the rain continued to make puddles here and there. He had seen Lilith riding on a carriage, splashing through the puddles of the streets and going as fast as she could get the horse to go. He had lost her when he went down an alleyway. He began to look frantically through the dark streets, listening as hard as he could through the rain. Tairren stopped Lilly for a moment to try to figure out which way the small carriage went.

The sound of distant screams could be heard now over the echo of rain slapping on the stone streets.

"Marrisa! I'm coming for you!" Tairren hollered out as he got Lilly going in the direction of the screams.

Lilly obeyed as usual, splashing through the rain puddles as she dashed off. She seemed to love Tairren's company and the thrill of running through the soft rain.

Of all the nights, this had to be the night that there were no soldiers standing guard around the marketplace or town square, or anywhere for that matter. Because of the strange weather, they must have been around the castle or in their quarters.

Tairren followed Marrisa's screams through the town square and out into the dark fields of Minslethrate. Tairren could see a soft orange glow off in the black distance of the field, appearing haunting in the chilled night. It was the pulsating flame of a torch, revealing the direction in which Lilith was taking Marrisa.

"Let's go Lilly! Run like the wind!" Tairren hollered as he softly hit her sides with the heels of his boots, encouraging her to go even faster. He remembered how Marrisa would always yell that to Lilly when she took him for thrilling rides through those fields.

Tairren held on tightly to the reins with his left hand, making sure he didn't let go of the torch in his right. Lilly's speed was intense and powerful and Tairren held onto the horse with every muscle in his body, moving with the flow of Lilly's gallops as a massive surge of adrenaline pumped through his veins.

They made their way closer to the small carriage, gaining speed as they went. He caught up to the carriage easily. Tairren directed Lilly to dash on the side of the carriage, going with the speed of the dark horse that was pulling the carriage. As they caught up with them, Tairren noticed that the small carriage was the one in which the castle warden used to lock up the criminals caught in Minslethrate. It had a small door and was locked with a large lock-pad which bounced up and down against the door. Lilith must have stolen the carriage, because there was no sign of the warden.

"Tairren?!" Marrisa shrieked out from the carriage, surprised and waving her hand outside the window of the small door. The opened window was small and square shaped, only allowing the passenger to look out. "Tairren, Help me! Lilith is possessed and has gone mad! She is taking me to the south to the dark temple!" She cried as loud as she could out of the small window. "The curse is upon me!"

Tairren maneuvered Lilly closer to the carriage, taking a glance at the shadowed driver holding the torch. It was Lilith, looking even more wicked in the night with the torch light playing off her unpleasant face. The thought of Lilith bellowing out like a wild creature popped into his head as he got nearer to the carriage. All of a sudden Lilith quickly turned her head towards Tairren, as if realizing that he was creeping upon them. Her face crinkled up as she showed her teeth and gaping mouth, and growled like a vicious animal. Tairren was startled by Lilith's repulsive, pale face, noticing how black her eyes and mouth were.

"Be with me my Lord!" Tairren shouted as he came so close to the carriage that lilly's side nearly touched it.

He threw the torch down then quickly grabbed hold of the top of the carriage, pulling himself on top of it. He could here Marrisa call out his name, giving him a surge of energy as he used all of the upper body strength he had to pull the rest of himself up. He held on tightly to the roof of the carriage with his belly touching the roof. Small rain drops continued to pelt his face and body, making it harder to hang on without slipping off.

"Father! Protect me with your black embrace! Send me your defense!" Lilith screamed out to the darkness of the night. She then continued to snarl and shriek as Tairren came closer to her. "You will be punished!" she sneered as she began to thrash her torch at him, dropping the reins to the horse in the process.

The horse still continued with its speed, pulling the carriage and making its way to the ends of the field and closer to the beginnings to the Forest of Old. Tairren tried to knock the torch from her hand as she still thrashed about. He began to slip but grabbed both sides of the carriage's roof.

All of a sudden distant shriek could be heard. It sounded like a mixture of howling, growling and high-pitched screams of women. Lilith stopped thrashing about and became still as she pointed her face towards the night's sky like a creature catching a strange and familiar scent. All of a sudden, a raspy chuckle came from Lilith's mouth, turning into a wicked laugh.

"Abaddon!" she yelled out to the flying things. "Yes! Father has sent them like flies! Fly down you black winged destroyers, tormentors from the depths of Hell!"

The shrieks began to get louder as Lilith let out another loud and wicked laugh. Tairren looked up, noticing that a group of rather large birds came flying down towards him. He couldn't clearly see them because of the rain and the black sky but he knew that they came closer because of the loudness of their ear-piercing shrieks.

Lilith continued to laugh her wicked and putrid laugh as she raised one of her white hands into the air, as if she were welcoming them. While she was diverted, Tairren hurried towards her with all of his strength and grabbed her arm, twisting and pulling, trying to fling her to the ground. She did not falter; her strength was far more powerful than he had expected. Her black mouth gaped open as she let out a crackled shriek, elbowing him hard in the face. Ignoring the pain, he yanked the torch from her, slipping off the roof of the carriage and crashing down to the soggy ground.

He landed on his side, the still lit torch beside him. Before he could even get up, a mighty gust of air blew down upon him, followed by one of the large shrieking birds. Tairren quickly grabbed the torch and looked up, realizing that the screeching birds were not birds at all, but some kind of creatures that had human faces and forms with massive wings! They were as black as night and two large twisted horns jutted from the tops of their deformed heads! A long bony tail protruded from their backsides with a very sharp looking hook-like stinger on the tip.

Tairren inhaled sharply as the creature pounced on him, clawing at his chest and grazing his face with its massive hands. Its claws upon his flesh felt incredibly hot, like a poker straight out of a fire. Tairren blocked most of its strikes with his arm, having more damage on his arm and his chest than his face. The screeches of the creature rung in his ears and the burnt smell of its breath stained his nostrils. He cried out as he jabbed the fiery end of the torch into the monster's chest, making it let out another ear-piercing shriek. The thing leaped into the air, escaping the hot flame of the torch.

Tairren stood up quickly, wide eyed and shocked at what was going on. It was hard for him to believe everything that was happening that night. It was as if he was lost in a dreadful nightmare and couldn't wake up. He franticly looked every which way, holding the torch in the air as the screams of the creatures scattered into the black sky, indicating that the creatures had quickly dispersed. But why did they all leave so abruptly?

Now he was alone in the middle of the dark field. His eyes searched for the carriage but could not find it. His heart pounded fiercely in his chest as he tried to listen for Marrisa's screams, but couldn't hear anything but the nature around him. It was as if he imagined everything and within a blink of an eye, it stopped.

The rain had stopped completely, leaving everything chilled and quiet. Everything seemed eerily tranquil as the chirps of crickets and frogs sang on. He felt lost and anxious for a moment, not knowing what to do. His emotions were numb but his heart felt as if it was about to burst.

But those strong feelings oddly vanished as he caught the glimpse of a large white bird which gracefully glided above him, giving him a warm feeling of hope. The bird glided elegantly and calmly and seemed to peer into Tairren's heart. A small moment went by and he felt warm and at peace.

"Marrisa!" he finally called out, determined now, wanting to hear her call back to him, "I will come for you!"

All of a sudden, he heard the sounds of something running behind him. Something was charging at him! Panicked, he turned quickly, but was stopped short by a vigorous blow to the head. A sharp pain surged through his head as everything became dark as he fell unconscious, crashing down upon the wet earth below him.

Quiet and full of malice, Lilith stood over him for a moment, staring her eccentric black eyes upon his calm and bloody face. She raised the large stone that she had hit him with high above his head, ready to heave it down to crush his handsome countenance.

"Let the dark powers of hell smite your heart!" Lilith shouted with a sneer. The uncontrollable urge of wanting to kill shrouded her body as the muscles in her ugly face quivered.

Just then there was a soothing call of an owl as the large white bird swooped down at her, charging her as if she were its prey. Fearful, Lilith let the stone fall to the ground, making a deep thud sound as it hit the earth. She hissed at the bird, then quickly and quietly vanished into the blackness of the silent night and towards the beginnings of the Forest of Old…

†††

There was darkness, everywhere, shrouding Tairren's body like a thick black cloak. The air around him was still and quiet, undisturbed. His unconscious thoughts were of nothing, of no one... But there came a small light in the black shroud, like that of a gleaming pinhole. The small shimmering spot became larger, shining like a massive star.

"Tairren..." a low and clear voice said from the light, resonating beautifully like the sounds of chimes, leaves and feathers fluttering in a soft breeze. "Tairren, son of Timotheus, awaken your mind to me."

Tairren's eyes opened to the beautiful light, looking upon the great lustrous orb of many colors. Two great gleaming wings came from either side of the light, revealing their splendor.

"Who are you?" Tairren asked, intimidated.

"Do not be afraid, for I am Malakh, messenger of the Great King of light," he said. His serene voice exuded assurance and radiated with warmth and harmony. "The time of great tribulation has begun. Stay true to the Lord of light, steadfast and full of faith... your destiny will unfold itself in time."

"I don't understand," Tairren said.

"Heed my warning young Tairren son of Timotheus, the powers of Lucif are amongst your people and this golden land. Depart these familiar lands of Minslethrate and venture off into the south with your companions—when the sun breaks through the night. You will face many things you have not seen... Following the night when the moon glows like blood, during twilight when the morning star shines the brightest, evil will prevail and take on a new form... The time draws near when you will witness the true face of evil. Stay true to Him and the ones you love—you are the golden key in this quest..."

"My thoughts are incredulous," Tairren responded. "I do not know of what you speak, but I will do as you say. Lilith has captured Marrisa and my love for her is strong. I will go to the ends of Minslethrate to find her."

"You will do what I say because it is the Great King's will, you are the chosen one..." the light seemed to get brighter as Malakh spoke. "The light in you is strong and unwavering. Lilith and Marrisa, whom you mention, are merely an apparatus to Lucif. He will not have pity on them when he completes what he came here to do. Lilith is now a nomed of the night, temple to the fallen Archlegna, Lucif. Lilith must spare Marrisa—until it is done... Lilith's soul is lost and now rests in the hands of Lucif. Find

Marrisa and you will find the prince of Hell, for Marrisa is as precious to him as gold is to the earthly king."

"I have only heard of these names in legends and in lore... I do not know of what you speak," Tairren said, timidly.

"Know this, what I have spoken of will come to pass... Amen...," Malakh's voice seemed to fall away from him, like a disappearing whisper. "Awaken... Tairren..."

The magnificent colors and light slowly diminished with the dissipating voice of Malakh. Just as Malakh had commanded, he came to, slowly opening his eyes to the night's sky. A rush of cold air covered his wet body as the frightened voice of Natalia echoed in his ears.

✝✝✝

"Oh Tairren, thank God!" Natalia squealed as tears flowed from her eyes. She was on her knees and hovering over him. She threw herself upon him, hugging him as if she hadn't seen him for years. "I was so worried, I thought I lost you! What happened and where is Marrisa?! I'm so relieved you are alright!" She sat up quickly as Tairren began to groan out in pain, realizing she was probably making things more uncomfortable for him. "We have been here for a little while by your side, I didn't know what had come of you!"

He slowly sat up, placing his hand on the back of his head as it began to throb. He pulled his hand away to find a small amount of blood on his fingers.

"I was attacked," he said, his voice shook a little. He put his hand on his brow. "A pack of some kind of wild flying—creatures came out of nowhere... They were human-like and repulsive, with wings the length of my body and they smelled of—burning things. The shrieks that they made were horrible..."

Tairren stared into the black horizon as he spoke. Natalia and Phillip both glanced at each other, then back at Tairren.

There was an awkward silence, then Phillip cleared his throat. "Do you need a physician?" he asked, now kneeling over him.

Tairren looked at him, then back at Natalia.

"No, I'm fine," Tairren scoffed, wiping blood from his lips and nose.

Even though it was a kind gesture with Phillip wanting to help, Tairren only saw it as his way of trying to take over the situation.

"You are a battered mess," Natalia said, panicked as she moved his long, wet bangs from his face. "What you say is frightening and incredulous. And your face is bleeding and it looks as if the wild animals have gotten the best of you."

Tairren began to get up, both Natalia and Phillip helping him the rest of the way.

His handsome light-blue tunic was no longer vibrant and clean, but dirty and blood-stained. The fabric on his arms as well as his torso was ripped, revealing bloody lacerations. They were bad enough to leak blood but not too bad where he would need them to be stitched. He was muddy and wet, and looked pale. The lower half of his face was covered in blood from the powerful blow of Lilith's elbow smashing into his face.

"Lilly and I chased Lilith into the fields," Tairren said, motioning his hand around him. "She drove the warden's carriage, in which Marrisa was locked. I found the way because of the torch Lilith held." Tairren looked around, noticing that Lilly and another horse stood next to each other, grazing in the wet field. "Lilith has evil in her, and is taking Marrisa far off to the south—to the Dark Tower of Sacrifice. Something horrible is going to happen," Tairren said with a serious voice as he began to walk towards the horses.

"What do you mean Lilith is evil, and that something horrible is going to happen?" Natalia asked, following him, with Phillip right behind her. "I knew she was strange—but evil?!"

"I know this may sound mad, Natalia—but I've been…," he paused, looking at both Natalia and Phillip, wondering how all of this madness had come about.

"What?" Natalia said, raising both her eyebrows.

"I've been called by a being of light… Before I was struck from behind, I saw a great white owl flying above me, making me feel at peace. Then I was attacked from behind and darkness came over me. And as I was unconscious—a spirit of light came to me, annunciating what I should do and foretold things that would come to pass." Tairren stroked Lilly's long mane, then hugged up against her, resting his cheek on her wet fur. He felt anxious and lost on the inside, wanting to go right away to save Marrisa, but he knew going without weapons and food would be useless. He thought of what Malakh had told him; to wait until the sun broke through the night— dawn. "I must do what He says and I will find her, Marrisa will be saved," he said, as if talking to Lilly.

Natalia was speechless, not knowing what to think or say about what Tairren spoke of. Everything was happening so fast, and felt as if she was stuck in a night terror. She glanced at Phillip, wondering what was going through his head and if he was having second thoughts about Minslethrate and of marrying Marrisa. "This night was supposed to be a grand celebration, a night to remember," she thought, taking a deep breath. "Tonight, will definitely be remembered... Pity it will be a dreadful memory... And how could he marry a missing princess anyway?!"

"Let's get you home and mended," Natalia said, her voice sounded nervous. She was confused and frightened and didn't know what Tairren was talking about. She didn't know what was true, whether he got hit on the head too hard—making him delusional, or that he really was visited by a spirit of light. "We'll discuss a plan when we get you home," she said, apprehensive.

"How did you know I was in the fields?" Tairren asked, glancing at them both.

"We saw the light of this torch," Phillip said as he walked over to the dying light, picking up the torch. It now gave off a soft orange glow, indicating that it would die soon. "It was brighter when we first saw it. It must have been dowsed heavily in oil—the drizzle of rain didn't even kill it."

"Not to mention we saw Lilly frantically running through the fields by herself," Natalia said as she climbed onto Lilly's back. Tairren climbed up behind her, knowing that he was in no shape to direct Lilly through the night. "Now let us go before those creatures come back...," Natalia said, gripping Lilly's reins.

"My lady can maneuver such a powerful beast?" Phillip asked with a teasing smile as he climbed onto his horse's back.

She glowered at him, then yanked the reins to turn her around.

"Hold on, Tairren," she said, still having a fixed stare on Phillip.

He smirked as they went off into the night.

The frogs and crickets chirped on as the bright moon had begun to come out from behind the dark clouds, giving them a glowing light as they made their way towards Tairren's abode.

†

CHAPTER 10
The Night Is Late

They all sat and listened to Tairren's quick brush with death, and of Malakh. Wide eyed and minds wondering, Moral and Natalia sat across the small table from Tairren and Phillip stood on the side, leaning against the rough wooden wall on one shoulder while having his arms crossed. They sipped on hot chamomile tea and nibbled on warm sweet bread, to help comfort their soggy bodies. The cozy house was warm from a small fire burning in the stone oven and Moral had given each one of them a woolen mantle to help dry them and to keep the chill off their backs.

"This is horrible news! I don't know what will come of Minslethrate, but you must go and rescue Marrisa, you must!" Moral said, her voice beginning to shake. "The poor dear must be awfully frightened."

Moral sat in a state of melancholy, shaking her head slowly and looking down every once in a while, to hide her emotions. She didn't want to look like a blubbering fool in front of her guests.

"I know mother, and I will," he said, placing his hand on hers. "I will, as soon as the sun comes up, breaking through the night." He glanced over at Natalia who looked distraught. "Malakh said to venture off to the south with my comrades, when the sun breaks through the night." He looked out the black window, quiet for a moment, "Lilith and those things in the night will be waiting, and it is much safer in the day light."

"I will go with you," Natalia interrupted. "I cannot believe this is happening, but I will go with you." She happened to glance at Phillip who seemed to be very surprised at what was happening.

Tairren was quiet as he nodded his head in approval. "And I will not stop you," he said, putting his hand on hers as well.

"This is unheard of! It's—it's absurd!" Phillip bellowed out, shaking his head in disbelief. "No weapons, no armor, no plan, creatures attacking in the night and a courtier boy who is really a commoner, is summoned to save the captured princess, accompanied by a lady?!" He paced back and forth, shaking his head.

Tairren bit his bottom lip, containing himself, trying his best not to lunge over the table at him. He glanced at Natalia as he took a deep breath, who also looked irritated, as if she wanted to slap him.

"If this is so ludicrous to you, prince, then go back to your mighty kingdom of riches and pleasantries and have nothing to do with us," he said in a low tone, trying to maintain his composure at some effort.

The prince stopped pacing, looking at Tairren with a sneer. "What impropriety is this?! I am prince of Ishkar and the son and descendant of powerful kings—I will not be told to do anything from anyone," he said in a stern voice, "especially from a peasant!"

"Stop it! Both of you!" Natalia yelled out. They all looked at her, surprised. "We are not ourselves tonight. Prince Phillip, I know you are a man of your word. You told me at the castle stable that you would do anything to help Marrisa. Did you not?!" She said sternly, looking up at him from the table.

He nodded his head, looking back at her. "Yes, my lady—I did," he said in a low voice.

"Then you must!" she looked back at Tairren who was quiet now, slowly shaking his head in disapproval. She could tell Tairren was not fond of Phillip, but she knew Phillip would be of great help. "We must do this, we have to, and Tairren has even said that Malakh has foretold this… If this is all true—if we don't do this, not only will Marrisa and Minslethrate be damned, but our whole world will be and all that dwells upon it. We are all in grave danger…"

Moral sat quiet and wide eyed at everything that was going on. It was hard to believe that one day would be normal and grand and the next would be ill-fated.

"Then you must go—all of you…" Moral said in a low tone.

She stood up, now quiet, walking away from the table and beginning to dig in her small pantry.

"Tonight, I will go to the castle and write King Julpen a letter of what my intensions are: that I will be off to look for the princess…" Phillip said, putting his fingers to his chin.

He looked at Natalia with a soft smile, trying to show her that he cared.

"He will not want you to without an army or such," Tairren said, taking another sip of his tea. "And what of your families' expectations of you getting married in Ishkar?" Tairren asked, seeming to test him.

"I will write that I must go alone, and if he wants to send an army behind me, he can do so—the more the merrier—but not with me because I know he will want an explanation and a plan of action. He will think that I was mad if I told him everything that has happened. And if his men catch up with us, we will simply tell them that this Lilith woman and a group of mad men have captured Marrisa—that way they will see for themselves, the madness of the creatures and of Lilith, when and if they arrive. But by the time your king reads the letter we will already have been off." He grabbed a piece of bread as he spoke, eating it while speaking. Wet pieces of the bread sprinkled out of his mouth as if he was blowing dust as he ate. He spoke ardently and excitably, as if he had an awakening. "And as for Ishkar, I will send a letter back with my servants and assistant this very night, they will do as I say. I will write to my father telling him that I will not be coming back to Ishkar for a while and that I will stay for a holiday here in Minslethrate before I get married. He will be surprised—but my father accepts everything I do."

They were all quiet for a moment, taking in everything that he spoke of. It was all so surreal—like a dream.

"It sounds like we have a plan then," Tairren broke the silence, shrugging his shoulders and wishing Phillip had no part in it. But he seemed to have everything all figured out already.

"Go now, the night is late," Moral said, in a low and worried tone.

"Yes, we must," Natalia agreed, standing up.

She hugged Moral goodbye, kissing her on the cheek, and thanked her for her hospitalities. Prince Phillip thanked her as well, and she bowed her head to him politely.

"I will see you tomorrow morning then, at twilight," Natalia said, kissing Tairren on the cheek. He nodded his head yes.

"Look for me at the edge of the forest, I will be waiting with Lilly by firelight," he said.

They nodded their heads. Tairren watched as both Natalia and the prince left the small house.

Tairren watched his bothered mother. She was still quiet, fiddling around in the kitchen area and packing food into a satchel. She seemed to be doing busy work. Tairren knew that his mother was fretful, he knew she didn't like anything that was going on—but he didn't either.

"Mother, what are doing?" he asked softly, placing his hands on her shoulders.

He knew very well what she was doing; he just wanted to break the silence. She was quiet for a moment, staring out of the small window. The window was a small black square, and their dim reflections could be seen on the glass.

"You will be hungry on your journey..." she said, stopping her progress. She exhaled, as she placed her hand on his, then turned around. Her gray eyes sparkled with saddened tears, bordered with the signs of weeping crow's feet. Tairren never realized how greatly his mother's face had changed over the years, until then. "Promise me that you will be safe, Tairren... Promise me!" Moral pleaded, her eyes releasing their tears. "The wilderness has once taken my love away from me—I will not lose my only son, the only person in my life!" She put her face against his chest, beginning to sob. "I'm frightened and worried for your life, my son."

Tairren was quiet for a moment, saddened by her emotions. He rubbed her back, trying to comfort her.

"I promise...," he said softly, hoping that it wasn't a lie. "The God of light will be by my side..."

She looked up at him as tears rolled down her pink cheeks. He wiped them away, giving his mother a tender hug.

"And I will pray for you," Moral said as she tried not to cry. "I know you will bring Marrisa home and stop these evil works, I know you will. You are brave and passionate like your father. You will do great things— you will." She smiled at him and caressed his cheek. Tairren nodded his head, responding to her encouragement. "Now you must go to sleep, off with you now," she said, patting his back. "Enough of this sniveling, the night is late and the morning comes soon. You need your rest."

He gave her a kiss on the cheek then walked towards the ladder to his loft.

"Goodnight, mother," he said as he began to climb up the ladder, "and do not fret..."

"Goodnight, my son," she said, turning towards the satchel she was packing earlier.

She turned her head towards Tairren one last time and watched as he entered up into his room. She smiled as the thought of Tairren as a young boy popped into her mind: when she used to turn to see his small feet dangling from that hatch doorway. Those thoughts were so vivid, as if it happened just the day before. Her small smile faded while tears formed in her gray eyes once again. She turned back to her work, refraining from sobbing...

✝✝✝

The moon peeked in and out of the black clouds as Phillip and Natalia arrived at the manor. The huge house was dark except for her window, which strangely glowed with a soft orange. It reminded Natalia of the soft orange torch they had seen that led them to an unconscious Tairren. Chills went up her spine as frightening thoughts of that night crept through her head.

"Thank you, prince," Natalia said, sliding off of the horse with ease.

"You're welcome, my lady, and do call me Phillip," he said, smiling down at her.

She could see that he was smiling by the moon's bright glow which now came out from the clouds.

"And you can call me Natalia," she said, moving the long lock of hair that fell in front of her face. She began to walk towards the front door, looking back as Phillip still sat there.

"Should I come to get you at dawn?" he asked, still watching her.

"Orchid, my horse, and I will meet you at the edge of the forest where Tairren wishes," she said, giggling at his chivalry.

He still sat there, watching her as she walked the rest of the way to her front door. She waved to him as she rolled her eyes, letting him know that it was okay to leave. She smiled softly, shaking her head as she walked into the great, dark house.

She thought the door would have been locked, which meant she would have to go through the back. She was relieved. Sora must have left it unlocked for her. She made her way up to her chamber, walking into the dim light which emitted from a bunch of candles that were lit on her night stand. She walked over to her vanity, pulling the hairpieces from her damp and now matted hair.

"You must've had a big night," a voice said from the corner of the room.

Natalia turned quickly, startled. It was Sora, sitting in a rocking chair and obviously waiting up for her. Her large body was in the shadow, and her dark skin mingled well with it.

"Oh, Sora you frightened me!" Natalia fussed, trying to keep her voice low.

"Where have you been, your ladyship?! I've been worried sick!" Sora fussed back, coming over to her to help her change out of her soiled gown. "And you are soaking wet. Oh my, look at that soiled gown, and you smell like a wet horse. Have you been horse-back riding through the rain again?!

Oh, you young ones and that sly Minsleberry wine. You always come home late, sopping wet when you've been drinking. What has happened?!"

"Everything is well with me. I didn't let the wine get the best of me," she said, pulling her damp hair to one side and beginning to brush it. "But something terrible is happening Sora, and I don't know what."

"I know, I know," Sora said, then she shook her round head while clicking her tongue. Natalia glanced at her, surprised that she already had known. "A servant was found dead in the castle, I heard from Alexa who heard from Tella, saying that she heard from…"

"Sora!" Natalia cut her off, "Yes I know—but I'm talking about Marrisa." She rolled her eyes, placing her brush back on the vanity.

"Oh yes, my lady," Sora said, and then clicked her tongue again. "The poor princess has run away," she said in a saddened voice, fetching her night gown.

"No, no!" Natalia fussed, irritated. "Who said that? Never mind—you all gossip more than the courtier women of Minslethrate."

She quickly put her night gown on, trying to get to bed; she knew she had a long journey the very next morning.

"Well, what is it? What has happened?" Sora asked, pulling down the soft goose-feather stuffed blankets of her bed.

Natalia wanted to tell her of everything that had happened that night. Besides Marrisa and Tairren, she was the only one she could really talk to and trust. But she decided not to burden her with any of it. She knew that Sora would never allow her to venture off into the wild—to search for Marrisa. She didn't want Sora to have a heart attack anyway.

Instead she decided she would write a letter to Sora and have it waiting for her on the bed. She thought it was a brilliant idea, thanks to Phillip. So in the morning when Sora would come into the room to draw her morning bath, she would find it. Natalia thought it was the only way that made any sense.

"Don't fret over it, Sora," She said, yawning. "I'm going to bed, I'm tired."

She lay down, covering herself as she melted into her soft bed.

"You should be," Sora said as she went to blow out the candles.

"Leave them lit—please, and good night," Natalia said as she rolled on her side, watching her. She wanted to see Sora's face before she went to sleep, before she would have to leave on their perilous quest. Sora nodded at her request, having a puzzled look on her face. "Oh, and please don't wake me until early noon, please, I am awfully tired," she lied, feeling bad about it in the process.

"Goodnight then, my lady," she said with a nod.

Sora left the room, slowly closing the door behind her. Natalia rolled on her back, thinking about the strange night and about what she would write to Sora. She decided to get it over with and write it just then. After waiting a moment, making sure that Sora wouldn't come barging back into the room, she got out of bed and walked over to her writing desk, beginning her letter.

My Dearest Sora,

I am writing you this letter because I couldn't tell you of what my intentions were last night. I knew you would not agree and I did not want you to become frightened. By the time you read this letter, I will already have been hours deep into the Southern parts of Minslethrate, the Forbidden Lands. Something terrible is happening in Minslethrate this very night, as I write. I can not tell you of what right now, but it is concerning Marrisa's life, as well as others. I ask of you not to fret, for I will be in safe hands. When I return, I will tell you everything. You may show this letter to mother and father if you wish, but it may not impact their thoughts of me. I only wish to be prayed for.

Best Regards,
~~Lady~~ Natalia

When she finished her letter, she waited for the ink to dry, then folded and sealed it with hot wax that she dripped from a candle. She drew a small flower on the outside of the folded letter, writing Sora's name next to it. She stared at it for a while as it sat on the desk, hoping everything would be alright and that she would return safely.

She was worried and scared, wondering what would come of Marrisa and of Minslethrate. She trusted everything that Tairren had told them, but at the same time, she had her doubts. She still couldn't believe everything that had happened that night. She wondered how and what they would do to make the situation dealing with everything better. She wondered if everything would ever be the same again. It felt as if it were the end of life itself. Everything felt lost and out of control, chaotic. Nothing was the way it should've been, and that was the worst feeling of all.

Natalia climbed back into bed and lay there, closing her eyes. She felt herself slowly sinking into the thick blankets of the bed. She wished that she could bring her bed with her in the morning. The thought of Orchid pulling her bed through the fields with her still laying on it amused her, making her feel slightly better. She giggled a little to herself then closed her eyes.

She had to go to sleep, but couldn't. She imagined what Sora's reaction would be like to the letter. She pictured Sora being overdramatic and emotional, with her eyes wide open like that of an owl's and her nostrils flaring, which made Natalia smirk for some odd reason. She loved Sora and her personality, and thinking of her and her rambunctiousness always made her smile. Then she imagined Sora giving the letter to her mother with tears in her big dark eyes, and… and she really didn't know what would happen next. She never really saw her mother or father in any kind of emotional state—much less see them at all… Natalia laid there for a while, then finally fell asleep as the moonlight continued to creep in through the window.

✝✝✝

"Know this, what I have spoken of will come to pass…" Those frightful words that Malakh had spoken upon Tairren earlier that night kept repeating through his sore head.

He couldn't sleep, the anxiety of the night and the smoky thought of his fate lingered on his heart and brain, pulsating and rushing about like swollen cockroaches swarming over a raw piece of meat. He kept thinking of everything: of Marrisa, Lilith, and the frightening creatures, and of Malakh and his message.

His head pounded and the wounds on his arm and chest burned. Moral tried her best to treat the wounds earlier that night when they first arrived. She was taken aback by everything, and ran around, boiling hot water in the fireplace and fetching herbs and clean cloths, appearing like a chicken with its head cut off. She cleaned the wounds as best as she could with the hot water and a healing elixir she had created and kept in the house, then slathered the wounds with some kind of ointment made from crushed anise and lard, for the pain. Then she dressed them with strips of clean linen.

His small room was dark and cool, and the moonlight, which slowly came in and out from behind the black clouds, sprinkled some of its luster in through the small window. Tairren folded his arms behind his head, looking up and out towards the window. He could smell the light scent of the ointment Moral had slathered on his wounds, smelling warm and sweet. The moon was persistent. He could see bits of silver through the dancing leaves and stems of the trees. It reminded him of large fireflies, dancing around in the dark wind-blown branches.

His arm continued to throb. He pulled his bandaged arm from behind his head, laying it on his bare chest. His head ached like a tree against an axe. He closed his eyes, almost able to fall asleep. His muscles began to relax finally, seeming to melt in his skin, releasing the tension of that day. His eyes kept opening and closing, feeling heavier every time they opened again. They finally closed, allowing the cool darkness of sleep to take over…

"Tairren…" There came a reverberating whisper.

Tairren quickly opened his eyes, wondering who it was and why the ethereal whisper sounded so familiar. He sat up, listening carefully. He heard a melody, a soft hum that seemed to echo in his confused ears. The voice was light and delicate, seeming to belong to the air and the dark sky. His heart began to quicken as the melody became familiar, striking a chord in his brain, releasing the memory of Marrisa, when he saw her in the forest for the first time. It was the song that the bards would sing at festivals and in the marketplace, and the song that Marrisa loved.

He quickly got up, walking over to his small and dark window. Looking out, startled, he saw the form of a female. She wore a long white gown that seemed to glow in the dark atmosphere of the forest. Her long wavy hair fell over her shoulders and her face was blackened by shadows. She stood still in the night, motionless, staring up at him through the window.

"Marrisa?" Tairren said in a low and confused tone.

She giggled in the cool and dark air. Tairren could strangely hear her haunting giggles through the dusty window as they echoed in his ears. He hastily pulled on his trousers, not caring to put on his tunic or his boots. He quickly left his room, rushing outside as quietly as he could. He opened the door to a stale and cool night. The air rushed upon his body, sending goose bumps up his chest and abdomen. He rushed outside, looking frantically around the dark shadows of the night.

"Marrisa?!" he called out, but only silence answered.

He stood for a moment, listening to the sounds of the night. He heard only nature: the whispering of the soft breezes, the chattering of the trees and dead leaves upon the earth, and the sounds of small claws on crisp leaves as the night animals crept about. Then there came a swift breeze, brushing leaves and chilling air upon his skin. The strange breeze also carried the light and echoing sounds of the haunting melody again.

"Marrisa!" Tairren called out as he began to run through the dark forest.

The singing voice began to giggle, reverberating and sounding eerie through the dark night. He followed the voice, jumping over black roots and fallen trees and dodging sharp limbs and naked branches that came at him.

"Come to the South…," the beckoning voice of Marrisa whispered again, piercing into his racing heart.

Tairren followed the voice and the intuition of his spirit upon a clearing in the forest, and a spot he knew very well. He stopped short, looking around. The strong, spicy-sweet scent of rosemary filled his nostrils as the soft breezes continued to play with his bare back. The moon revealed its face brightly this time, flooding the clearing with silvery-blue light. The massive rosemary bush that grew in the center of the clearing seemed to twinkle as the moon's light sprung from its breeze-blown branches. The air was quiet, dead. There was no sound, not even of the whispering winds or of the chattering night sounds. He only heard the deep breaths that came from deep within his burning chest and the loud thumping of his heart. He slowly walked to the middle of the clearing, looking up into the night sky. The sky was clear all of the sudden, having every twinkling star out. The moon and the stars looked beautiful together, staring at him from the quiet kingdom above him.

He looked around at the dark edges of the forest. The darkened edges of the forest looked as if a black curtain had been drawn about it, dark and thick. His heart continued to race as he approached the luscious and aromatic bush. His numb body felt distant and hypnotized, enchanted and taken over by the pure quietness of the clearing. He broke off a flowering sprig of the rosemary, feeling its crisp snap through the thin wooden branch. He brought the aromatic herb to his nose, sniffing softly as he closed his eyes, thinking of Marrisa's beautiful face and blue eyes.

Strangely, his bandaged arm began to throb as a burning pain scraped at it…

Then there came the haunting giggle again... It seemed to emit from the darkness of the wood and bounced off his ears, and heart...

"What are you doing?" Marrisa's soft voice asked from behind him.

He turned quickly to find her standing there in the pool of moonlight. Tairren was speechless and taken away by her beauty. Her elegant face was fresh and sweet and her eyes glistened like two small pools of deep, deep water. Her long red hair fell over her shoulders in moon-kissed locks, hanging below her breasts. She wore a long white gown, with cascading sleeves and lace that was speckled with clear rhinestones, glistening in the pale light. Her head was adorned with a diadem that sparkled with more rhinestones upon her brow. She looked like a being of light.

"I've come looking for your companionship," she smiled softly. "Are you picking herbs for your mother?" Her voice still echoed in his ears, and sounded odd but beautiful against the dead silence.

Tairren shook his head no, slowly, having an incredulous look on his face as he was fixated on hers.

"What has happened? I...I don't understand," he said in a low tone.

She just looked down at his hand, softly taking the rosemary from his hand and caressing it in the process. Tairren watched, numb, with a booming heart, as she softly sniffed the flowering herb. She smiled flirtatiously, keeping her intense gaze upon him.

"You cannot read it in the stars?" She asked, her intense eyes gazing into his.

The burning pain still lingered in his arm, but he ignored it...

"But... Marrisa... What is a princess like yourself doing out in the forest at night?" Tairren asked, softly.

He was oddly in a silent state of euphoria, dazed and confused, but thrilled. The thought of Marrisa being captured by Lilith didn't even come to his mind, for he only dwelled on that present moment. She didn't answer at first, but came closer to him.

"Tell him to find me a castle of lace," she began to sing in a light and soft tone. "Rosemary, love, and sunshine," she sang as she caressed the tip of the sprig against Tairren's cheek, bringing it slowly down his neck and bare chest. He closed his eyes, his breath becoming deeper. "Between the saltwater—on a mountain's face—then he'll be a lover of mine." His heart pounded madly as she rubbed his chest softly with her teasing hands, leaving a fingertip trail down his abdomen. She brought her lingering hands back up, then softly placed her hands on his chilled cheeks, bringing her face to his. "And sprinkle the halls with sprigs of heather—then he'll be a true love of mine," her voice sang softer now, almost whispering. The fiery smell of the rosemary and the brisk touch of the breezes engulfed their bodies, beginning to become icy hot. Their lips barely touched, feeling the warmth of each other's breath.

Tairren quickly opened his eyes. Startled by her appearance, he cringed. Her face looked different all of a sudden. Her face appeared paler, sickly, no longer having a lustrous or dewy look. The curves of her face were no longer elegant, but angular and ugly. She had dark rings under her eyes, and her glossy red hair was not glossy at all, but dull and lifeless. He stood looking at her for a moment, feeling unsure and lost all of a sudden.

"Am I not sweet?" she asked in a soft and teasing voice.

There was silence between them for a moment as Tairren looked upon her.

"Sweeter than nectar," Tairren finally said in a timid voice.

"Sweeter than the honeysuckle that embraces it?" She appeared coy, speaking in a low tone.

She then pressed her body against his again, her eyes appearing dark now, black like the sky.

Tairren backed away again, having a strange and cold feeling come over his body. The burning sensation in his arm became more intense just then. He rubbed his bandaged arm, looking into her now darkened face. He couldn't see her features anymore as she took a step back. Her body seemed to become silhouetted, shrouded in blackness. As she stood still and silent for a moment, a soft whimper began to emit from her blackened face, a soft cry that seemed to reverberate in his ears.

Everything around him became dim, as a soft red glow shrouded the moon. The once silver disc now looked like a dying sun, or a circular pendant that was dipped in translucent blood.

An eerie sense of being lost and darkened came over Tairren's body, as if his heart was being scribbled on by thick charred wood. His arm throbbed now as if his skin was being pulled open. He winced in pain as he grasped his arm. The once white bandages were now sopped in blood, as if a red faucet was opened from beneath his wound and bandages. Warm blood trickled down his cold skin, falling down to the black grass. The soft pat of the blood hitting the grass seemed to echo in the darkness.

"Following the night when the moon glows like blood, during the twilight when the morning star shines the brightest—evil will prevail and take on a new form…," Marrisa said quickly from the darkness, her voice went from a soft whimper to a low and evil growl as she spoke.

Tairren stepped back slowly as his confused eyes became large with fear.

"Marrisa?" Tairren said, not knowing what to think now as he became colder.

"GET AWAY!" a terrifying voice exploded from her mouth as her now shockingly ugly face came from the black shadows.

The smell of death emitted from her dark form and her white face twisted into an ugly snarl. Her mouth gaped open revealing nothing but a black abyss—like her wild, black eyes.

†

CHAPTER 11
The Wing Pendant

Tairren sat up quickly. His heart raced and his body was drenched in a cold sweat. He breathed in and out sharply, sucking in the cool air. He looked around, realizing that he was in the comfort of his cool room. It was just a dream—just a dream… He lay back down, waiting for his heart to slow its beat. The light outside of the window was a dim dark-blue, indicating that the sun was on its way up. He realized he must have fallen asleep, which was good. But he didn't understand his dream. The thought of Marrisa whirled in his head as he sat back up. He remembered the blood in his dream and quickly grasped his bandaged arm. The bandage was clean and white but he still had the strange pulsating pain beneath it. Reality took hold of him as he touched the scratches on his chest and face. Marrisa was still gone, and his once pleasant world was still flipped upside down. The day had begun and his quest was coming—whether he was ready or not.

Nervous and filled with anxiety, Tairren got up quickly as he realized he was supposed to meet Natalia and Prince Phillip at the edge of the forest when the sun broke through the night. His body and mind were tired already and his journey hadn't even begun. "Battered before I begin," he mumbled to himself has he pulled his tunic over his head. He softly touched the back of his head, remembering his attack in the night. The hair on the back of his head was still matted with some coagulated blood. Moral had cleaned it as best as she could but it still bled a little. His head-ache had nearly ceased, finally, and the pains in his arm were not as intense, but still lingered with relentless agitation.

"Mother," Tairren thought as he quickly got dressed. He had remembered how upset she was. He had to see her. He finished dressing himself and collected his things and put them in a leather satchel. He opened his hatch door to darkness. Usually he would wake up to a warm and lovely smelling home, inviting him for something sweet for breakfast. But there was no light coming from the lantern above the table. There wasn't even a warm cozy fire in the brick oven indicating that breakfast was being made. There was only a small faltering orange fire burning in the fireplace, barely lighting the dark home. Besides the tiny fire there was just early morning darkness.

"Mother?" Tairren called out in a low tone as he crept down the small wooden ladder.

He softly walked towards her bed. Maybe she is still sleeping, it was still rather early. But he could see by the flatness of her bed that she was not in it. The small window above the bed poured in the dim, dark-blue glow of the early morning, revealing an empty bed.

He walked outside, thinking that she must've been out in the garden. It was cool and moist outside, and there was a mist that strangely covered the earth's atmosphere. He could see through the branches that the early-morning sky was cloudy. It was still dim outside, and the sounds of crickets chirped softly in the deviant mists. He grabbed the dead torch that he placed outside the door in the night. He quickly went inside to light it with the small fire in the fire-place. As he lit the head of the torch, he noticed that the satchel Moral had packed was sitting on the table, with a small piece of paper laying on it. After lighting the torch, Tairren grabbed the piece of paper which read:

Good morning to you, my dearest son,

Come to the rosemary bush.

-mother

He read the letter out loud and slowly, wondering what she would be doing out there. The images of his dream ran through his head, reminding him of how frightening it was. He then placed the letter on the table and grabbed the satchel, throwing it over his shoulder. He grabbed his bow that hung on the wall next to the door and his arrows that sat in its quiver, leaning against the wall.

Before he left his small home, he stood in the doorway, looking over his abode for the last time before leaving. He pressed his lips together as he peered into the only place which made him feel safe. He didn't know whether this would be the last time he would ever see his home or not.

"Watch over my sweet mother and my father's home," Tairren prayed softly as he slowly shut the door.

He heard Lilly's grunts as he quickly went around the house. Lilly was grazing on some tall onion grasses as he greeted her. She turned her head towards Tairren as she chewed the sweet grass. Her large friendly black eyes greeted Tairren.

"Here you are, this will be a much ample breakfast," he said as he dug into his satchel Moral had packed for him.

He pulled out a large red apple and gave it to Lilly. She gobbled up the glossy fruit from his hand as small droplets of sweet juice speckled his palm.

"Mother is always so considerate of me," he said with a smile as he glanced into his bag. It was filled with different fruit as well as bread, nuts and berries, and left-over pastries wrapped in white cloth.

He caressed Lilly's long white mane then got his bag and bow and arrows situated on the saddle. He quickly pulled himself onto Lilly's back, balancing himself with the reins in one hand and the torch in the other. Luckily, he had plenty of practice in the past with riding Lilly while holding something in his other hand.

Anxiety and nervousness clouded his heart and stomach as his quest was almost upon him. He closed his eyes for a quick second and took in a deep breath, then exhaled.

"Ride on Lilly," Tairren said as he nudged her sides, maneuvering her towards the direction of the rosemary bush.

With the help of the torch, they went through the darkened forest. They maintained adequate speed to get to the rosemary bush quickly, but slow enough to dodge trees and low hanging branches if needed. The mist blanketed the forest and was even quite dense in some areas. But even though the mist was discouraging, it was still refreshing upon Tairren's tense skin. The forest was not as it usually was: fresh, colorful and filled with serene enchantment. Instead, the mists had turned the wood into a gray and cold place, clammy and quiet. Their ride to the rosemary bush wasn't as long as he anticipated.

He came upon the clearing in the forest, which was veiled with mist as well. Bringing Lilly to a halt, he hopped off her back. His heavy black boots hit the wet grass making a thud sound upon the earth. He jabbed the torch into the soft earth, making it stand up right. Tairren looked around the clearing as the memory of his dream made its way into his head again. But instead of the image of a starry and clear night, it was a gloomy and misty early morning.

He could see the dark-gray silhouette of the massive rosemary bush through the dark-blue glow of the early morning atmosphere as they came into the clearing. The bush must have been six feet tall at least, equaling the width. He'd forgotten how overgrown and massive the bush had gotten.

Tairren had picked from the bush at least once a month, but hadn't visited the bush in the last couple of months.

He and his mother usually maintained the bush by clipping at it once a year. She took over the cultivation of the bush after his father had died six years prior. The rosemary bush was at least twelve years old. He remembered the day when his father returned home from the trade fair with the small herb plant, as well as other interesting things. He was about six, and his father strategically planted the push along the side of the small cliff in the middle of the clearing.

He remembered that his father always said that it needed to grow in well-drained sandy soil with plenty of sunlight and care. This memory stayed so fresh with him in his mind because his father planted and kept up the bush with him, teaching him everything. Growing up, Tairren was always excited to help his father, taking every opportunity to be with him. Even though they were just chores, Tairren's young eyes looked at it as valued time with his father.

"Mother," Tairren softly called as he crept through the mist. "Mother I am here."

As Tairren came closer he could see the dark-gray silhouette of his mother. Moral was kneeling over something with her back towards him. Her head was down and by the way she trembled softly, she seemed to be crying. Tairren rushed upon her, realizing that she had been digging for some reason. There was a pile of wet over-turned dirt by her side with a small dirty and beautiful chest sitting amongst the dirt, which was opened. Tairren went down on one knee by her side, putting his hand on her back.

"Mother, what is this?" She looked up at him. Her eyes were red and puffy and her pink cheeks were smudged with dirt where she had been wiping. "What are you doing?"

"Tairren, my son," she said with sniffles, "these were your father's things."

She was hugging some kind of cloak. She slowly handed it to Tairren. It was a deep blue color and was folded nicely, feeling very soft to the touch and appearing old but elegant.

"Your father wore it on his travels," she said as she grabbed the small chest, pulling it closer to herself.

"Thank you," Tairren said with a small smile, still holding it.

"I buried these things after your father died," she said as she took the rest of the things out of the chest. She pulled out a rolled-up piece of paper, a beautiful and shiny compass, and a small velvet pouch tied with string. "I remembered where I had buried it because I marked the spot with this rock," she said as she placed the things on the large stone that was sitting on the right side of her, which was in front of Tairren.

Tairren's eyes lit up as he looked upon the things. He remembered the compass, and how he always wanted to play with it as a child. He picked it up as a small smile came and went upon his face. He rubbed his thumb on the face of the compass, noticing the small scratches on the glass face.

"Why do you show me this now?" Tairren asked as he placed the compass back on the rock.

He looked into his mother's saddened gray eyes. They sparkled as tears began to come back up. She was quiet for a moment as she looked down at her soiled hands, white, callused and fingernails caked with dirt.

"I couldn't bare the pain of seeing these things again after he died," she said as tears flowed down her cheeks. "And something told me in my heart to never throw them away—so I buried them. These things were so special to him." She tried to smile as she gave the rolled-up paper to him.

"What is this?" Tairren asked as he unrolled it.

"It's a map of Minslethrate," Moral said as she sniffed.

"I remember this," Tairren said quietly as he looked over the worn map.

Tairren remembered how his father used to take it with them on their small adventures when he was a child, adding more to it every time. The map was made of thick paper and drawn with great detail, with everything labeled.

"Your father actually drew this out when he first came to Minslethrate—he loved the thrill of finding new things." Moral tried to smile a little again as she dusted some of the dirt from her lap.

"What do you mean he drew it when he *first* came to Minslethrate?" Tairren asked as he rolled it back up, tied it and placed it back on the rock.

Moral was quiet again as she took the small pouch and held it to her bosom.

"Son, I have to tell you something—that I've been hiding from you… Something I've made your father promise, not to tell you until you were old enough… But he did not get the chance." Moral looked up at him with those same saddened eyes.

"What is it, Mother?"

"…Your father is not from here, but from a small kingdom far east from here, the Kingdom of Hanon, along the great river of Minslethrate. He isn't from common blood…," Moral had a nervous edge as she spoke.

She looked into Tairren's confused eyes.

"What do you mean?" Tairren asked, having a confused look on his face.

"Your father is a descendant of royal blood—raised by nobility, and came here to find his roots, to learn more of his ancestry. Haven't you always wondered why he knew so much? How he knew how to read and write so well and how he came across the Book of Light? Your father was brilliant. He taught me how to read and write and I taught you. You see, I met your father in the small town of Prat, which sits between Hanon and Minslethrate. Your father's eye caught me when he was traveling through town." Moral began to smile a little.

"He was staying at the Inn and went out for a walk. He spotted me walking through town with my sisters. We were shopping for fruit for our mother—you could not merely go and pick fruit like you can here in Minslethrate. Hanon is not abundant in goods, and purchases fruit and such from Minslethrate." Moral became quiet for a moment with that same soft smile, as she looked back up at Tairren. "It was love at first sight, truly. Your father asked for my hand in marriage only after a couple of days of knowing me. Such a gentleman he was. How much in love we were. But my father wouldn't have his eldest daughter marrying for nothing. You see we were a very common family and my father was a blacksmith, who made very little money in Prat. So, for a fine price, your father took me away from Prat—he saved me. It did not matter to me that my father sold me, for I was in love." Tairren smiled after a moment, trying to cover his confused and shocked feelings.

"So, his journey ended here in Minslethrate. We stayed at the Inn here until he produced us a home… Your father was in love with the forest. So, he found a wonderful spot not far from the stream and beneath some beautiful oaks. And he built our lovely home… He went off on many occasions to learn more of Minslethrate, to discover the land, culture and its history. He was very charming and gregarious and made many acquaintances. And then he blessed me with a beautiful baby boy—my son." She smiled as she caressed his face.

Tairren was quiet for a moment, taking in all the surprising information.

"But, mother, you said my father came from royal blood? Raised by nobility? Why did he come to Minslethrate to find out more of his ancestry?" Tairren asked, still confused.

"Your father was raised by nobility, but possessed very ancient blood; an ancient royal blood that flowed with knowledge, power, and love—and still does. Your father once told me that he found an old chest in his grandfather's home, filled with ancient journals and documents, knowledge of his ancestors. He read them all and asked his grandfather about its existence. His grandfather told him the legend of their family, how he was the direct descendant of a king who gave his crown to a savior king who ruled here in Minslethrate generations ago. Your ancestor king loved this savior king so much he entrusted his children, your ancestors, to him. This great king was a miracle maker—and your ancestor king venerated him. This man who was pronounced as a great king did many unbelievable things like heal people and raise dead souls from death! The people did not like this and years later— slew the Great King. Your ancestor avenged his death by rising up against these evil men in war, and killed them. But he was ultimately succumbed to death by the bloody hand of the great war.

But Legend has it that the Great King was a prince born into poverty, and rose up to become a great leader as a man. He led your ancestor king and the people and fought for them. He did many miracles and enlightened hundreds of people. He had many followers and did things a normal person could not. This great king declared himself as the one great king—the King of kings and Lord of lords. Your ancestor who was king, your royal bloodline, handed the crown over to this miracle-maker man. But this man was hated by unbelievers… As time passed, some of the people did not like how the Great King ruled and rose up against him, eventually storming the castle. The king knew of the great danger that augmented in some of the people before hand, so he sent his young adopted son and daughter, who are your ancestors, and a couple of servants away to the small Kingdom of Hanon in secrecy, before he was seized.

Along the Weeping Road, adjacent to the Great River of Minslethrate, their carriage was attacked in the gloominess of the wood. You see, the evilness of the people wanted everything to be as it was before the mighty king ruled—even if that meant to rid of the young prince himself. For they knew that the king would bequeath his knowledge upon that prince and he would be influenced by the king's words and would reign one day in the same manner, if not more powerful and influential…

The side road was no protection to the travels of the young prince and princess—for many knew of the shaded path… Amongst their attack, the princess took her younger brother and escaped into the brush of the forest as their coachman and servants were killed. They hid and waited in the thickness of the wood until the evil men left. Strangely, those men did not look very long for the children, for something had happened, but that I do not know. In the writing—it was said that the children saw a mighty white bird of some kind fly away… The mighty bird must have frightened those evil men.

The children found their coachman's horse, unharmed, so the children made their own way to the Kingdom of Hanon. The poor children were fatigued and starved. Something must have been watching over them for the journey to Hanon was too long and perilous for children. Luckily, they came across a manor on the outskirts of Hanon. Forced to forget about their past, they lived at that manor in Hanon for the rest of their lives."

Moral became quiet, watching the fascinated look on her son's face. Tairren looked at his father's things for a moment, then back at Moral.

"…Do you think that is true—the legend of my ancestors?" Tairren asked with an incredulous look on his face.

"Your father has told many stories and legends—but this legend is history—he read it in an ancient diary that was kept by the princess… along with this…"

Moral didn't say anything else as she went to take one last thing out of the chest. It was a piece of paper that was folded in half. She slowly handed it to Tairren, who accepted it mindfully. He slowly opened it with care. It looked very worn and was the color of grass in the winter time. It was a letter. The edges of the paper were tattered and the crease of the fold in the paper was thin and delicate, as if it might easily rip apart. The letter was still readable.

Tairren read it with admiration.

To the obedient one,

 Out of importance, this urgent letter was prepared and sent from myself, king and servant of Minslethrate. To whomever receives this, I have great veneration for. I do not know you, nor do you know me. But I know in my heart that everything will be okay with you.

With all of my heart, I plea, accept these children as your own. I am forced to out of love for them. The children are in grave danger. The south of my kingdom has risen up against me. Filled with malice, they have revolted, trying to rid of me and what I stand for. By day they shout and scream, while breaking the castle windows and catching the gardens ablaze. By night they relentlessly do this by the light of torches and the fires they have produced. There is not a hint of peace nor tranquility in my kingdom any longer. It is in their hearts to destroy me and my beliefs, the word of my father—the truth of life. Soon my soldiers will no longer be able to contain them. But I still love my people and humanity. So I am sending the children, the heir of Minslethrate, away to the safe haven of Hanon. I do not wish to be relieved by the Hanonnites, nor do I want a strong hand from the soldiers of Hanon. Not all of my people are against me, and they can not withstand another war. I know the madness will come to a halt if I yield to them. I want the utmost safety for the children, the future. The lunacy will not stop until my reign and the heirs to the throne of Minslethrate come to an end. I love my kingdom and people so much that I will die for them, even if it is them who wants me dead. They know not what they do… I must risk the lives of these children by sending them to Hanon. Their lives are better secured away from Minslethrate. Verily I say unto you, never repeat this to anyone, nor reveal the children's true identities—and by doing so you will be in the favor of God. Keeping the children in secrecy will not only secure their safety, but your own as well, as well as the future of the world. You will be blessed beyond measure… Teach them your culture and the ways of Hanon. Keep this letter in solitude, away from strangers' eyes but close to the children's hearts. In time this shall unfold itself. Let them forget their past but never let them lose the knowledge of their roots. The children were instructed to present this to you upon arrival. You will know them when you see them, for the prince will be wearing a royal family heirloom I have given him, a necklace with a wing shaped pendant. Truly I thank you with all of my heart. Truly, I thank you.

May the Lord of light, my father, bless you and the children of time,

King Yehoshua

After reading the letter, Tairren slowly folded the letter and placed it on the rock. With his ardent face and small tears in his eyes, he slowly looked back up to his mother.

"Your father found this letter folded in half and wedged in the princess' old diary. He took it, as well as the Book of Light, which he found amongst the many old documents in his grandfather's home. He brought it with him on his journey from Hanon long ago." Moral spoke softly, placing her hand upon his.

"It is an incredible story… And I feel honored to know this. I just only wish to know why you failed to ever tell me, mother." Tairren's face was serious now, but his eyes were still glossy.

After a quiet moment, Moral's chin and bottom lip began to quiver as she held back tears.

"I'm sorry, my son, truly I am… I feel so ashamed of myself… I didn't tell you because I never wanted to lose you," she said as small tears fell for her gray eyes. "I thought you would leave Minslethrate like how your father left his home town; to learn more of your past. I thought you would leave me like how your father did…"

Moral held back her emotions, not wanting to upset her son anymore. "But I have been foolish, Tairren. After all of these years of me trying to protect you—you must leave. I thought that I could hide this from you, son. I thought the past would not matter, that it was just history—but I've learned that history happens for a reason and unlocks the unstoppable future. Just as the letter says, in time this shall unfold itself. I—I thought that I could keep you safe with me—in our small home by the creek.

"But I have been wrong, in so many ways. This letter came to you for a reason. This is happening for a reason. I now know in my heart that this is fate, everything is happening because it has to—and will not stop. You are not just a young poor boy—you are a man with rich blood. You were put on this earth for a reason. God has great plans for you," Moral said with a smile. "You are—a chosen one. Your life reflects the legend of the king…" Moral became quiet as she wiped her eyes. "You are the direct descendent of royalty who honored King Yehoshua. In your own right, you are the prince of Minslethrate." She slowly handed Tairren the small velvet pouch that she had been grasping to her bosom.

Tairren accepted the pouch as he looked at his mother incredulously. He was speechless and bewildered. The pouch was slightly heavy. He untied it and tipped it upside down against his palm. He felt a cool tingle hit his palm as something slid out upon it. Tairren looked at it in amazement as he picked it out of his hand. It was a beautiful golden necklace. The chain was thick and elegant and the pendant that dangled from it was in the shape of a wing. The wing was beautifully crafted with small jewels embedded in it. The necklace sparkled as Tairren held it out from himself, letting it dangle.

"This is the necklace the young prince wore in the letter. This is the heirloom of my family—the heart of my ancestors," Tairren said in amazement as he looked at the necklace in awe. After admiring it, he put the necklace on. It hung to the middle of his chest. Tairren felt inundated but proud at the same time. He was so overwhelmed with nervousness and happiness that he didn't know what else to say. After a moment, the thought of Marrisa came into his head. "But mother, if I am a direct descendant of a king—who is Marrisa to me?"

"Tairren, when a king no longer can rule, his son or brother or a male figure in his blood-line must reign on. If there is no one in line then the commander-in-chief of the king's legion or one of his most trusted and eligible subjects must rule... Marrisa is born from another line of kings. Marrisa's ancestors could've been one of the followers of the Great King."

Tairren nodded his head then looked off into the mist as if thinking. They sat for a moment admiring the necklace, then Moral looked around, noticing that it was not as dark outside. The atmosphere was still misty but was no longer deep-blue, but a soft gray.

"The sun rises this deviant morning," she said as she stood up, dusting the dirt from her apron, "you must go."

He put his father's cloak on. It had a large hood and came down past his knees. It was a cape and would come in great handy on his journey— protecting him from the sun, rain, and chill of the night. His mother fastened the neck of the cape with the gold pendant that was sewn on it.

"You are the spitting image of your father," she said as she patted his chest, then stepped back to catch a look at him. Tairren smiled as he hugged his mother goodbye. "This is not the end, only the beginning," she said as she tightly hugged him back.

After a moment of embracing, Moral bent over the large rock to fetch her husband's things.

"These are now your things," she said giving them to Tairren. "These will come in great handy. These were meant to be yours." Tairren took them from her as he nodded. "Go to the south my son—begin your quest— fight for the one you love..."

They walked together back to Lilly. Tairren was still in deep thought as he put the things into his satchel and pulled his torch from the damp earth. With an aura of solicitousness, he climbed onto Lilly's back, then looked down to his mother one last time.

"Thank you, mother, for everything… I am happy and thankful that you've shared this with me." Tairren smiled at his mother, which seemed like the last smile he would ever give her. "I love you mother—be strong."

"I love you too my son—and please forgive me…" She placed her hand on Tairren's boot, then looked up at her son lovingly.

"I do forgive you mother… I must go, the sun is rising and Natalia and the prince will be waiting."

She nodded, patting his boot.

"I am proud of you—and I will be praying for you," she said, placing her hand upon her face, her voice beginning to shake with emotion.

Tairren gave his mother one last smile, then he was off…

Moral watched her son as Lilly galloped away into the forest. She stood there in the gray dew, wondering if it was the last time she would ever see her son. Tears rolled down her round cheeks as she still stood in the silence amongst the mist…

†

CHAPTER 12
A Moment in Time

Lilly dashed through the forest as Tairren encouraged her to keep up the speed. He was ready to take on his quest. With the sun coming up, the forest was not as dark—but the mist still lingered on.

The thought of his family's bloodline and the legend of his ancestors whirled through his head. He felt secure and empowered by what his mother revealed to him. The feeling of the ancient necklace he wore upon his neck, bouncing against his chest, exhilarated him. He felt like a new man and that he could take on anything and everything. He felt blessed to know such an inspirational story of his ancestors. He was proud to know that his ancestors died for what they believed in and fought for such a king as the legendary King Yehoshua. He was also proud to be wearing the family heirloom and having his father's things in his possession. Tairren was excited to carry on what his father strived to. As he was vigorous and alive, he still wasn't sure of him being a prince in his own right—being raised poor, it was hard for him to comprehend and accept that he had royal blood running through his veins. He believed everything his mother had revealed to him, but at the same time, a small doubt ran through his head.

After a short while they finally made it to the outskirts of the forest. Tairren pulled on Lilly's reins, slowing her down as they came into the field. The field was wet looking and gray as the mist stretched as far as the eye could see. Tairren Looked around for Natalia and even Phillip, but could not see neither of them anywhere, but only the silhouettes of some nearby trees and shrubbery. Even if they were in the fields, Tairren would not be able to see them anyway because of the mist.

"They'll be here soon," Tairren said to Lilly as he pat the side of her neck, hoping that they would show up at any minute.

After a moment of sitting and looking, Tairren noticed that Lilly began to graze upon the wet grass, reminding him to eat something.

Tairren's stomach began to squirm as the hunger pains began. He had forgotten to eat something before leaving his home. He pulled up his satchel and dug in, pulling out a beautiful red and shiny apple. The red color of the apple reminded him of Marrisa's red hair. He began to think of her and her beautiful face, her smile and laugh. It was strange to be sitting upon Lilly without her. He began to think of how they used to go horseback riding together through the fields. Still holding the torch, he took a big bite of the juicy apple as the silence of the early morning was broken by its crunch.

He thought of the time he and Marrisa rested beneath an apple tree after a thrilling ride through the apple orchard…

✝✝✝

Tairren remembered how beautiful and cool that crisp day was, and how the sunlight sparkled through the branches amid a clean and fresh atmosphere. The serene orchard was interrupted with laughter—happiness he had almost forgotten. Startled, a bunch of blue birds that were pecking at the earth, flew up into the dancing branches of the trees. Marrisa and Tairren were lying beneath an apple tree, talking and laughing together. Apples were scattered about them on the cool and soft grass and earth, indicating the tree's abundance.

"Forgive me, Tairren," Marrisa said still laughing as she turned on her side towards him, patting his head.

She had been tossing an apple up and down while laying and missed as it came down, crashing into Tairren's forehead.

"My lady can be brutal," Tairren said jokingly as he rubbed his forehead, "striking my head with an apple."

"Oh Tairren, stop whining," Marrisa said with giggles as she pushed his head.

"I'm not whining," he said, still rubbing his brow.

"You were whining when I clobbered you this morning during our little game of swordplay," Marrisa teased as she sat up against the tree.

She took a bite of the apple she had been playing with.

"Yes well, *princess*, I only allowed you to," he said, stressing the label "princess" as he spoke. He sat up against the tree as well. "And besides, you've been practicing swordplay since you were a young maiden. I remember my father was an expert, and taught me some before he died…"

"I know Tairren," she said, smiling at him. "Being raised with only a father has brought out the vigor in me. I feel everyone, including women, should be trained to swing a sword," she said. "Most royalty and nobility would not approve of me—or any woman for that matter with sword fighting. But I feel that knowing how to fight can save one's life," she said as she finger-combed her long hair over one shoulder. "I had gotten Natalia involved with swordplay when we were younger. My father had swords made especially for us," Marrisa said with giggles. "You should have seen Natalia when she was first trained with a sword, so petite and swinging that small blade as if her life depended on it. And I have never seen anyone fall so much." They both laughed. "But now she is vigorous with a sword in her hand."

"That is very true," Tairren said as he played with a patch of green grass that grew beside him. "I am very lucky she is having tea with her mother right now or I would have another bruise on my arm," he said jokingly as he rubbed his right arm.

"Tairren," she said, gawking at him, "we dueled with sticks, I hit you with a *stick*—a small branch from a tree. You should've been blocking," she said, teasing him. "I told you I clobbered you."

"Alright then," Tairren said, smiling as he shook his head, blushing. "You clobbered me with a stick. I'm not as talented as you. Your father should be proud," he said as he nudged her with his shoulder.

"And your father has taught you well," Marrisa said, nudging him back. "The basics are what everyone should know." She took another bite of her apple, softly wiping the juice from her bottom lip.

"Thank you, I just wish I could've had longer time with my father," Tairren looked away from Marrisa, propping his elbows on his knees.

Marrisa took another bite, silenced for a moment. "You know Tairren," she then stalled, looking away for a second. "If you don't mind me saying it—a peasant with a sword and knowing how to fight with it is a very rare thing, indeed. You will not witness that anywhere in all of Minslethrate." She looked back up at him and smiled. "You are blessed, Tairren."

"Thank you, and you are as well," Tairren said as his face turned a light shade of red again.

"Where is your father's sword, if you don't mind me asking? It wasn't left for you?" she asked, knowing that she was prying too much on a sensitive subject.

"When my father died—we buried him not too far from the creek— where we found him that day... We did not have enough money to get a nice stone made, so I took up my father's sword and drove it deep into the earth at the head of the mound, marking his grave. Only the hilt is seen. But both the grave and the sword are now covered with white lilies—my mother had planted years ago. I dare not pull the sword from the earth—I feel it is a part of my father, and should not be disturbed—only left near his body."

"Tairren, as long as I've known you—you have never shared that with me."

"I don't speak of my father too often," he said looking back down at the patch of grass, picking one long blade at a time and tossing it into the breeze. "I know I should—because he was a great man and father." He became quiet.

The grass moved in the breezes that fluttered by, and the tree limbs swayed and creaked while the leaves chattered above their heads and all around them.

"What happened?" Marrisa finally asked in a low tone, tossing her half-eaten apple away from the tree. The apple bounced on the earth a couple of times, catching Lilly's attention who was a couple of yards away, eating random apples on the ground, even the rotten ones. "How did he pass?"

Tairren was still quiet for a moment. The noises of the trees and the song of the birds covered the silence.

"Forgive me, Tairren. I'm too bold sometimes," Marrisa said as she wrapped her arms around her knees.

"No, my lady, everything is well," he looked up at her. "I am thankful you take much interest in my life." She smiled at his comment. He smiled back, then looked out upon the tranquil orchard. "I remember mother wanted me to go look for my father because it would've been dark soon and he said he would be back hours earlier. He was hunting some conies for supper that night," Tairren said with a small smile. "He was a great hunter. I remember I wanted to go with him—and how angry I was with him because he told me to stay home. I was twelve then and thought I was a man. But mother needed my help with some chores.

"We thought it was strange that he did not come home because rabbits were the easiest for him to hunt… I was out chopping some firewood when my mother came to me, asking if he had come home yet. She began to get worried, but I wasn't—my father was brave and strong. I thought he might have gone too far out into the forest, losing track of what time of day it was. Mother insisted that I go call for him—so I did. I called and called—no answer… I went a little deeper into the wood, looking into the spots where we normally hunted. He was not at any of those spots. So, I continued to call for him, even louder because by then I was becoming a little alarmed...,"

Tairren became quiet as tears began to swell up and twinkle in his deep-blue eyes. Marrisa was still quiet as a look of pity formed on her beautiful face.

"I—I found him not too far from the creek. He was lying on his back, quiet and peaceful looking. At first—I thought he was sleeping... But I knew in my heart that something was wrong—because he looked—he looked different..."

Marrisa placed her hand upon his shoulder as tears rolled down his cheeks.

"I thought he may have taken a nap after a long day of hunting, so I tried to wake him... But he would not budge. His peaceful face was ice cold and his lips were the same shade of his skin...pale, white."

Tairrens chin began to quiver as he held back his emotions. Marrisa immediately hugged up against him, rubbing his back and arm. The beautiful weather still lingered on, comforting them as they sat in silence amongst the shaded grove, seeming to contradict their emotions. Tairren rubbed his face and forehead. It felt good as the tense muscles in his face released some stress.

"I remember I ran and ran, but seemed not to run fast enough—my feet were heavy and my chest was throbbing. I felt so scared and lost. I burst through the door, scaring mother nearly to death. I remember I could hardly speak as I was in shock and so emotional. She was frantic. Then we were off into the forest. I remember me thinking that I had never seen her run as fast as she did that evening... I remember it was the darkest hour of my young life—watching helplessly as my mother feverishly screamed and cried over my father's lifeless body..."

Marrisa wiped the tears that went down his cheeks with her long sleeve. Her eyes became glossy as sympathy arose in her heart.

"When my mother went to clean his body, before anointing it with oils, herbs and flower petals, she found the wound on his upper back. It was bloody and deep—really deep—appearing as if he was stabbed straight through with a long blade. His heart must have been punctured because there was a lot of blood beneath him when he was lying upon the earth, his blood sopped up by it. I know if it was just an ordinary wound, he would have made it back to us... His sword was by his side, still in its scabbard, clean and gleaming and that way still when I thrust it upon his grave."

Tairren put his hand upon his forehead, as if it ached. He partially covered his eyes, embarrassed because of him becoming emotional in front of Marrisa.

"He didn't even have the chance to fight back… What happened when he was alone in the forest? I do not know. But I do know that someone murdered him," he said with an angry edge. "Someone smote my father with an evil hand and heart! Who, you may wonder? That I do not know! But I do know that he did not deserve to die—especially in that manner. He did not deserve to die…"

Marrisa began to rub his back again, trying to calm and comfort him. He began to become quiet again, not saying anything as he held his head down. After a moment, he looked back to her.

"The thing, Marrisa, that eats my heart up like a pack of ravaging wolves—is that I never told my father goodbye," he said, looking into her eyes. "I never told my father goodbye or that I loved him when he told me first before he left the house that day—leaving forever…"

Marrisa was quiet with tears in her eyes, not knowing how to respond. All she could do was listen to him.

"I still remember to this day how he waited for a moment at the door, for my response… I never responded. I was too childish—angry, because he was leaving without me… I was acting selfish… And the worst feeling of all—is the feeling of penitence in my heart—for dishonoring my father— for not telling my father goodbye and that I loved him before he died, for being angry at him and resenting him at that moment… And if I was with him, I could have done something to protect him. I could have seen who it was that took my father's life."

Tairren tried to hold back his tears with an angry brow as the soft breezes of the day touched his face. The sun still sparkled through the branches while Marrisa looked lovingly upon her friend, wiping away the tears that flowed down his cheeks.

"Tairren…" Marrisa finally said, placing her hand on his cheek while turning his face towards hers. His eyes were sad and full of remorse, glistening like two deep-blue jewels. "Your father knew that you loved him. At that moment when you were angry, he knew that you were just simply angry… You were just a young boy—who loved his father very much, and he you," Marrisa said with a smile. "It only matters that your father knew that you loved him—very much. He smiles tenderly as he watches over his family from the Great Kingdom in the sky…

"And there is a reason why you didn't go with your father that day… You don't know what could have happened—to you," she said with a now serious face. "This world is full of wicked people—anyone who can kill an innocent man can kill an innocent child… What would have happened if your mother lost you both? It is fate—you being alive—you and I speaking together right now… Everything happens for a reason…"

"…Thank you," Tairren said with a half smile as his emotions softened; feeling better as he always did when he was with Marrisa. "The God of Light has put you in my life—for a reason…"

She smiled a tender smile at him, still looking into his eyes. A lock of red hair blew in front of her face, caught by the breezes. Tairren lovingly moved it from her beautiful face.

"…You are welcome, my dearest friend…," she said with another tender smile. "You know, when I am sad—and feeling alone—I just walk into the deepest parts of the castle gardens and just lay there in its quietness and seclusion—my dwelling place. I close my eyes and think of what paradise might be like," Marrisa then said shyly, as if embarrassed. "I imagine it would be like walking through the most beautiful forests and hills, with healing breezes on my back and consoling flowers beneath my feet…

"And then I walk into the courts of the great castle in the sky—and I see my mother, smiling at me… And she tells me that she was so proud to be my mother… And then after I rest in this great kingdom, I then open my eyes to reality and somehow—I feel better." Marrisa just smiled and looked into his eyes. "I know it is just part of my imagination—but it helps… I am truly sorry Tairren…," she said as she laid her head upon his shoulder. "I probably should not have asked about your father…"

"I am happy I've told you," Tairren responded truthfully. "You are the only person now who knows—besides mother and I of course."

She looked up at him and smiled, patting his chest.

"And I am happy you've told me," she said, still looking into his melancholy-filled eyes. "Tairren, you have a mighty heart of gold. If your father was alive today, he would be so proud of you—the man you've become… Any girl who captures your heart will be proud to say that she belongs to you…"

His cheeks turned that light rosy-red shade again as a smile crept upon his face. He thought what a great compliment it was—but at the same time he wished that she was that girl whom was proud of him. He wanted her…

✝✝✝

"Tairren!" a familiar call broke his bitter-sweet daydream.

Marrisa floated away from his mind like a lost wind in the fields.

"Tairren!"

He looked through the mists towards the call as a soft silhouette of someone on a horse galloped towards him. Tairren couldn't help but to smile, waving his torch as Natalia approached him on a light-brown colored horse, who was called Orchid. She rode up with a smile, wearing a wine-red colored hooded cloak, and a gown to match.

"Good morning Tairren, I apologize for my tardiness," she hollered as she came near him, parking Orchid right beside Lilly.

"Good morning Natalia," he said as he tossed the apple core he ate from to the ground. Lilly ate it up in one gulp. "Don't worry, the prince hasn't even arrived." He smirked.

"I would have found you sooner, but I ran into one of our servants, Alexa," she said.

"She saw you?" Tairren asked, alarmed. "Do you think she will tell anyone?"

"No, she is such a fool... I threatened her anyways," she said nonchalantly.

"Threatened? What do you mean?" Tairren asked with a curious smile.

"Sora tells me everything, Tairren. Even what goes on between the servants," she said, smiling. "Sora once told me that Alexa had been taking food from the pantry. It didn't affect me then because I didn't care. But now I do and I had to use it against her—it was urgent that I did! So, I simply told her that I knew it was her who had been stealing from the pantry, and that I would reveal to my mother and father that she is an insolent thief—if she ever told anyone of me leaving. Because I would find out if she did tell. And for every missing piece of food that was ever questioned and every slice of cake that went missing—would be taken from her pay, meanwhile one of her hands would be cut off and thrown to the dogs and then she would get sold—to a tyrant. But of course, she would not be sold for that much... Who wants a one-handed servant girl who steals anyway?"

"You are malicious," Tairren said, facetiously, "threatening that poor girl."

"I had to; she would've told!" Natalia said with wide green eyes. "I wouldn't have told my parents, really Tairren, who do you take me for? Even though Alexa annoys me, I wouldn't want her to get sold—or have one of her meaty little hands removed. At least she now knows that she has been discovered as a thief, and she will most likely never take from the pantry or stealing one of my delicious cakes again."

Tairren shook his head with a smile, crossing his arms.

"That is true," Tairren said, snickering at her. "But even if anyone was on to us, it would be hard to find someone in this heavy mist without knowing where to look first."

"That is very true," Natalia said, looking off into the mist. "Tairren, I was so relieved when I found you. The mist is strange and thick this morning. I saw the soft glow of your torch," she said, pulling the hood from her head.

She pulled her long mane of dark-brown hair out over her shoulder. Her hair was partially up in braids that went around the crown of her head, with a small golden dragonfly-shaped clip in her hair.

"Must you always look your best? Even with a long journey ahead of you?" he smirked.

"Indeed, I do," she said, smiling. "I've also come prepared," she said as she pulled open her cape to reveal a small sword in its scabbard, hanging from a thin belt around her waist. The hilt of the sword was very feminine looking and the sword itself looked like a very long dagger more than a sword.

"Is that your sword?" Tairren chuckled, "It's fit for a child."

"I have you know I've had this since I was a young maiden—Marrisa has one identical to it," Natalia said defensively, "It is a *fine* sword and the blade is still sharp." Natalia hastily pulled her cape back over her sword.

"That incredible dagger will come in handy," Tairren stopped chuckling. "I've only a dagger myself."

Natalia just scoffed at him. "Even though it's a small sword, it will work fine. It's better than nothing," she said, as if trying to convince herself that it was a good weapon. "I don't believe we will be in any kind of *real* danger... We will rescue Marrisa from that Lilith and easily come back home."

"...I hope that is true," Tairren said in a lower tone, looking off into the mist and wondering if she had forgotten about his attack the night before. After experiencing the things he did that night—he didn't know what to expect. He didn't know what kinds of horrifying things awaited them. "I hope it's just that easy," he thought to himself.

They became quiet for a moment as Natalia slid off of Orchid and began to rummage through one of her saddle bags.

Tairren began to become nervous as the thought of the quest before him entered into his mind. He didn't know what to expect, but he had a feeling their journey would be a perilous one. He remembered what Malakh had spoken of, and the horrifying evil that emitted from Lilith. Natalia didn't experience what Tairren did. Even worse, he thought of what Marrisa would be experiencing, how much in distress she probably was. He knew he had to be patient, but he did not know how much time they had, or what kind of condition Marrisa was in. He didn't even know how the world could possibly be in any kind of danger. According to Malakh they all were—which left an unsettling feeling in his stomach.

His heart began to quicken and he became worried as he thought of Marrisa. He clutched the wing pendant in his clammy palm as he closed his eyes, thinking of Marrisa's beautiful eyes and smile—and the kiss they shared together. The pendant was cool to the touch. He became more at ease somehow—and somehow, in his heart, he felt that everything would be okay…

"Hello there!" Phillip hollered as he galloped toward them on his black horse, which was apparently named Sable.

Tairren came out of his thoughts, looking towards Phillip. He felt relieved, seeing that the prince had finally arrived. He was not happy to see the prince, but he was happy to finally be off on their quest—one step more in their journey and one step closer to Marrisa.

"Forgive me, for I am late," Phillip said, pulling up to them. "I had a time sneaking out of the castle unseen."

He tossed the part of his cape over his shoulder that was covering his chest, showing off his gear. He wore a leather vest over his tunic and other protective equipment on his arms and legs. His cape was made of thick black velvet, and his tunic was a deep-gray. Instead of the usual coronet a prince would've worn, he had a thick golden circlet on around his head with red jewels embedded on the front. His sword dangled by his side, contained snugly in its scabbard.

"It shouldn't have been that hard for a crafty prince like yourself," Natalia said, smiling up at him.

"And good morning to you, my lady," he said with a big smile.

Natalia easily pulled herself back onto Orchid, straddling the horse with no sign of embarrassment, showing the prince that she was not the usual lady he might have been used to. And even though she was not fond of coming into contact with nature, she was ready for an adventure. She smiled a witty smile at him as she grabbed the leather reins.

"Everything is well with the letter written to King Julpen?" Tairren asked Phillip with a serious face.

Everything had to happen according to the plan.

"Indeed, Master Tairren," Phillip said, nodding his head, "I never fail."

"Are you both ready then?" Tairren asked them, wanting to get going.

They nodded their heads.

"You know where Marrisa was taken, Master Tairren?" Phillip asked.

"In that direction is the southern parts of Minslethrate," he said, pointing to the left from where they were gathered. "Lilith is taking her to the south to the Dark Tower of Sacrifice, which rests on the outer edges of the Fiara Mountains. Just beyond these fields of Minslethrate are the Forest of Old and then the Great Wall of Division, which is the half way point to the Dark Tower. Beyond that point is the Black Forest, which is the beginnings of the Forbidden Lands—anything can happen," Tairren said in a serious manner.

"I trust you all slept well." They both looked at each other. Phillip nodded his head while Natalia just shrugged her soldiers. "Good—because we have a long journey ahead of us—a couple of days at least." Tairren knew they didn't sleep well; he could tell by the look in their eyes. He didn't sleep well at all either, but he wasn't going to tell them. "But we will make stops of course. I think we can set up camp at Lake Iris—we should get there by early evening."

"I hope you are a fine guide, Master Tairren," the prince said with a half smile, which had a hint of mockery.

Tairren pressed his lips together, not impressed by Phillip's smart remarks. He tightly held the wing pendant in his hand, acknowledging the smoothness of the gold and roughness of the small jewels. He didn't want to start an argument before the journey even began.

"Just follow me, I know those parts," he said.

Natalia noticed the necklace that Tairren wore and the fine cape he had on. She decided she wouldn't ask him about it just then. But she knew they were fresh in his possession, especially the necklace he was wearing, which was rather beautiful, she thought.

"Well, show the way great leader," she said, smiling her "I trust you" smile at him.

Tairren smiled back, then with the nudge of his heels and the sound of his command, Lilly took off.

Phillip glanced at Natalia, having a childish grin on his rugged face.

"Will you be able to keep up?" he asked, rather facetiously.

"Eat my dust," she said with a scoff, then as quick as a wink of an eye, she was off in Tairren's direction.

"Looks like we have some tough ones on our hands old boy," Phillip said with a grin as Sable grunted.

With a nudge and a smile on his face he got Sable going, swiftly making his way towards the determined Tairren and a loyal Natalia.

The mists had thinned out only a bit, giving way to the three adventurers. With their hearts beating with zeal and adrenaline running with determination, the young comrades rode on through the mists, with Tairren as their guide. Not knowing what to expect, their main goal first and foremost was to save their companion and loved one, Princess Marrisa.

Even though they were the most peculiar guild: a peasant with a secret, a lady with a reputation, and a prince with a pretentious heart; they were ready for whatever came at them. With the winds on their backs and the chill on their faces, they were headed towards the Forbidden Lands, and into the valley of shadows.

†††

There was a mighty voice that reverberated in the kingdom of light called Nevaeh, which was set in the deepest parts of the great veil. All that dwelled amongst the kingdom listened and yielded to the beautiful voice that rose up like a great trumpet. The voice which was heard, said to them:

"…I hear my children crying out from their broken hearts… The time is now that light will arise in the darkness like a great fire in the night. Arise, children of light—all that was to come is now. Arise and make forth the Kingdom of Minslethrate, which was my first settlement of light. Three keys must be awakened—for something dark which I have not forgotten still stirs in its being. Its heart has become lost and darkened. Verily I say unto you, the time of my coming and a mighty awakening is on the horizon…"

Darkness was becoming thicker and stronger, like an antagonized heart of a man, on the earth and upon the lands of Minlsethrate which was the first settlement of light. Man on earth was becoming week and submitted to the darkness that augmented so strongly.

In all of their luster, the legion of light which was summoned, journeyed afar to the Kingdom of Minslethrate in search for three gleaming keys—obeying the mighty words of the Great King of Light...

†††

†

CHAPTER 13
Darker Times

The kitchen of the Ducre' Manor possessed everything but silence as many female servants of the household filled it with the sounds of gossip, melodious ballads and cooking. Dinner was being prepared in the warm kitchen for the lord and lady of the house, as well as the many servants of the household, which was always a big deal. Many of the servants, including the lord when he was at the manor, only ate twice a day; dinner was the bigger meal which was eaten at mid-day and supper was lighter and eaten six or eight hours later at mid-evening.

The servants went about getting dinner ready for the lord and lady of the manor while Sora fetched fruit, bread and hot porridge for Natalia's very late breakfast, making sure it looked pleasing to the eye on a shiny silver platter.

"Alexa, I need your hand, child!" Sora called out as she took a hot kettle of tea from a hook that hung in the large fireplace, which was boiling amongst a large pot of beef and vegetables that had been braising all morning.

Alexa looked up from her work towards Sora and then glanced at her pudgy hands. As anxiety developed, she began drying her hands off with her soiled apron. Her sleeves were rolled up to her dimpled elbows and her frazzled curls were up in the same old bun hairstyle she always had. She had been scrubbing a large crusted pot and seemed to be happy to stop what she was doing.

"Take this kettle and have a platter ready for tea with its crockery and fixings," Sora said as Alexa rushed over to her, grabbing the handle with her water spotted apron.

Alexa quietly fetched everything she needed as Sora kept glancing up suspiciously at her.

"You've been really quiet this morning, Alexa. What's on your mind, child?" Sora wiped the sweat from her dark brow, waiting for an answer.

"Nothing—I'm fine, just—keeping busy is all," she mumbled evasively with a nervous smile on her round face. She began rubbing her wrist.

Wisps of curls fell along her forehead, sticking to her sweaty skin and small dimples appeared on her cheeks, which made her face resemble a basket of speckled apples.

"I've never seen you so dedicated to your chores—you just seem different today is all," Sora said as she shrugged her round shoulders.

Alexa just smiled a little as she brought the platter of tea over to the table where Sora was working.

"I don't know why that child has to sleep the day away, she's been acting strange lately," Sora fussed as she placed a small vase of flowers and a dish of softened butter onto her platter.

"The Lady Natalia?" Alexa asked in a nervous manner as she looked over at Sora by the corners of her squinty eyes.

"Of course, child, who else would I be talking of? She asked me to wake her up at noon. I don't even know how anyone could sleep till mid-day! She's been skipping her lessons too much. It's about that time of day. I need to get this upstairs," Sora rattled on as she gently picked up the platter. "Child, give me a hand and carry that tea platter up after me."

With shaken hands, Alexa placed a small dish of cream onto her platter, nearly spilling it over when Sora asked her to carry the platter up.

"Wake up child," Sora fussed.

"I—I have to get on with…," Alexa coyly murmured.

"With what," Sora interrupted, "more scrubbing? Those hands of yours must be tired of scrubbing anyhow—looking like two rough prunes. They're better to be chopped off! The dogs would enjoy such a treat. Now, follow me up with that tea, and don't you drop it. My chores are already in over my head. I swear child, you are stranger than a cow in a poppy field," she said, then shook her round head.

Alexa just quietly nodded her head and picked up the platter, anxiously following behind Sora to Natalia's chamber. She knew Natalia was not there, but far off somewhere, which made her feel nauseous to even think of it. She would have just told Sora that she saw Natalia sneaking off somewhere early in the morning at dawn, but she was too frightened by Natalia's threats.

She did have a bad habit of eating too much, which led her to take food from the cupboards; and she was highly embarrassed that Natalia was even aware of her bad habits. Ever since the uncomfortable confrontation Lady Natalia had with her that early morning, she felt that she wouldn't even be able look Lady Natalia in the eye anymore. Even though they were about the same age, Natalia always intimidated her. Her striking looks and strong personality always made Alexa feel like an anxious piglet amongst an abrasive and exotic cat.

They finally made it up the stairs and into the west wing, which were Natalia's quarters. Red carpet covered almost every inch of the cold stone floors and beautiful candelabras lit the decadent halls. Vases and pots of flowers sat everywhere on beautifully carved tables, which softened up the dim halls; Natalia demanded that fresh flowers grace her halls at all times.

"Hurry up child, you are slower than a worm during the hot seasons," Sora fussed as she made it to Natalia's door.

Alexa quietly crept behind Sora, who was gawking at her with large owl-like eyes.

"Here we are," Sora said with a smile as she placed her platter down on the table next to Natalia's door. "Lady Natalia always wishes her door to be locked while she rests—she has a twin key."

She pulled a bundle of keys out that hung from her leather belt and picked out Natalia's chamber key, unlocking the heavy door. Grabbing her platter, Sora walked into the dark and cool room with Alexa following right behind her like a scared puppy. The dull afternoon light leaked in through the cracks of the heavy curtains, giving them little light. They placed the platters down on a table that sat in the middle of the room.

"Good morning, my lady," Sora said in a cheerful voice as she went to open the curtains. "You've been sleeping far too long, child."

She flung open the curtains, letting the gray light of the day come in. She unlatched the windows and opened them out, allowing the cool breezes to come into the stuffy room. A light-gray blanket of clouds covered the sky, making the Golden Lands appear depressing and drab.

"Such a gray day, but at least the mists have pasted. Natalia...," Sora said as she turned, stopping her sentence as she was surprised to see that the bed was empty. The blankets were turned down and a mess. "Child, I am in no mood for games," Sora fussed as her mood quickly changed. She walked quickly over to the large bed, pulling the covers and looking under them.

Alexa continued to stand quietly and off to the side, her lips pressed together and her arms folded as she noticed the letter on the bed. The letter glided off the bed and onto the floor as Sora pulled the blankets down to the foot of the bed.

"I beg your pardon, Sora...," Alexa said as she picked up the letter.

"Don't beg to me right now, Alexa," Sora fussed as she quickly walked to the bath chamber, peering into the darkened room.

"But I found this on the floor," Alexa said, walking over to her.

Sora looked confusingly at the letter then snatched it from Alexa. She opened and read it to herself, her dark eyes wide and nostrils flaring. She wasn't sure if she read it correctly, given that she wasn't too good at writing, so she quickly reread it a couple more times. All the times she sat near Natalia during her lessons paid off. Her heart began to quicken with every word she recognized.

"Oh my," Sora exclaimed with a surprised tone after deciding that the letter was an emergency, "She's gone to the south!"

Sora quickly rushed out of the room and down the stairs, with Alexa right behind her with a look of guilt on her face. Alexa hadn't been taught how to read at all, but she could tell by Sora's reaction that it wasn't a good letter.

Sora didn't want to disturb the lord's dinner, but she had to. She rushed past two servants who were waiting outside the dining room hall and talking quietly amongst each other. They gawked crazily at Sora who was obviously in panic mode. Sora burst through the dining room hall doors with tears in her eyes. Alexa stayed behind by the other two women.

"I beg your pardon, Lord Ducre', Lady Ducre'," Sora said, nearly running while trying to cover her emotions.

The servants waiting in the dining hall looked shocked. The lord and lady looked up from their plates, having a surprised look on their faces as well.

"What is the meaning of this, Sora?" the marquis barked as he wiped his mouth and the scruffy hair around it.

"Forgive me for disturbing you, my lordship," Sora said as she quickly bowed her head, "but Lady Natalia has run away to the Forbidden Lands!"

The lady dropped the goblet she was drinking from; it fell onto her plate as the deep-red wine from it splashed out all over the white table linens. The surprised servants who stood nearby quickly rushed over to tend to the mess.

Lord Ducre' quickly took the letter Sora held out to him. He read it quietly to himself as a worried look came over his face, which then faded into anger.

"What is it, Fernund?" the marchioness asked in her islander accent as she stood behind her husband and placed her elegant, dark hands on his shoulders. The expression on her face revealed disapproval.

"She writes to Sora—that the princess and Minslethrate are in grave danger and that she has ventured off to the Forbidden Lands to help?! What kind of a fraudulent hoax is this? I've just arrived a couple of days ago and this comes about?!" He barked as he slammed his fist on the table. Startled, the servants flinched as they continued to clean up the dining hall table. "Our daughter has certainly acted out in a manner of impropriety before but this time she has gone too far! I worry for our daughter, Christianne… King Julpen must know about this—if his daughter and land is in jeopardy—if it is true."

The Marchioness took the letter from her husband, inhaling before she read it.

"Have the coach ready, Sora," Lord Ducre' said in a low tone as he put his ringed hand to his forehead. "We must deliver some news to his majesty."

Sora softly nodded her head and started towards the hall doors.

"And Sora," Lord Ducre' called as she quickly turned to him, "I am pleased my daughter confides in you over her own parents…," he said as he peered at her with a serious face beneath his large eyebrows.

The Marchioness just glared at her from the letter, which struck Sora.

Sora was quiet as she nodded her head again, glancing at both of them. As small tears built up in her dark-brown eyes, she turned to walk away, thinking that somehow the lord of the manor did not mean what he said, that Lady Christianne would hold a grudge over her even more, and that Natalia, the only person she had ever loved and cared for as her own daughter, was in real danger.

✝✝✝

The dull, gray light of the late afternoon leaked into the giant hall, flooding the dim chamber with a melancholy ambiance. The castle was dark and dreary, and seemed to reflect the mannerism of everyone within it. With the concerns of the missing princess and possessing the knowledge that a slaughtered servant was found in Lilith's chamber casted upon them, every servant walked about the castle like foggy minded lost souls.

The gossip amongst the servants had spread like a ravaging disease, causing great stress and sadness to come about the servants and courtiers of the castle. The insidious news poured throughout the kingdom within hours. The kingdom had once seen darker times—and now it was happening again... Over the years the faith of Minslethrate seemed to diminish, leaving Marrisa as the positive symbol within the kingdom, and now that she and her kindness and love was missing and seemingly in grave danger, the happiness of Minslethrate seemed to be smothered like a rose to thick smoke.

The head servant, Alexander, walked through the great hall of the castle carrying a golden platter. The platter contained a folded letter, an empty goblet and a full golden vessel of wine. Alexander made his way to the king's study hall, passing curious servants who were still taking down the decorations and cleaning from last night's festivities. With his head held high and having a patronizing demeanor, Alexander found himself at king Julpen's unorganized table, quietly sitting the platter down upon it.

The king sat at the table in his large throne-like chair, not acknowledging Alexander's presence. He sat with his head down and his ringed hand at his forehead. His long dark hair fell over his shoulders, obscuring his extravagant tunic. The whole chamber was quiet and still, except for the roaring fire in the large fireplace that crackled behind him.

"I've brought you a correspondence, sire," Alexander said in an emotionless tone, as he poured some wine into the empty goblet. "The prince of Ishkar has requested that you receive it at noon."

King Julpen looked up, not saying anything. He took the letter from the platter and broke the wax seal. He read it quietly, sipping the goblet of wine Alexander had produced for him. After reading the letter, he tossed it onto a pile of documents, then rubbed the left side of his bearded face.

"When did you receive this, Alexander?" the king asked as he irritably rubbed his eyes with his thumb and pointer finger.

"Jasper, his assistant, gave it to me last night and instructed that the prince had demanded it be presented to you at noon, Sire," Alexander said quickly.

"Must there always be unsettling news," the king said in an aggravated tone.

"My apology, sire," Alexander said as he bowed his head then picked up the platter. "Does my lord need anything else?" he asked

"Fetch me my advisor and my commander-in-chief... There is something ominous abroad...once again..."

"As you wish," Alexander said as he bowed his head. "Dinner will be served within the hour, sire." Alexander turned to leave, leaving the king with his wine.

The king sat for a while, sipping at his wine, thinking of everything that was going on—and of his daughter. He felt emotional and scared for his daughter, but dared not show it upon his face. He had not cried in many years—and had barely shed a tear when his loving wife passed away nearly thirteen years earlier... He thought of Marrisa and wondered where she was at, if she was in jeopardy, if she was frightened—if she ran away—or if the letter that Prince Phillip had addressed to him was accurate... The king put his hand to his head again, squeezing his eyes shut and pressing his dried lips together. He drank down the rest of the bitter sweet wine, then poured himself another goblet full.

"Something is not right," he thought. He knew something was wrong as soon as he heard the news that Prince Phillip's servants had left late last night in a hurry. The king's advisor told him as soon as he heard about the news at dawn. They seemed to leave in a hurry, packing everything up and sailing away back to Ishkar hours after the festivities. Rumor had it that the prince had strangely stayed behind, and his letter confirmed that very rumor.

He read the letter again, studying it this time, noticing small errors of random misspelled Minslethratian words. He drank down his goblet of wine, then got up from his chair. With the letter still in his hand he walked over to one of the many great windows on the left side of the chamber. He looked out of the clean and clear window, taking in a deep breath as he looked out over his stunning gardens. Usually he would see Marrisa reading or writing in the gardens, or strolling around with Natalia. He sighed as the thought of Marrisa came into his mind again. He thought Marrisa should turn up at any time of the day, at any moment now. He had sent out many soldiers all over the kingdom to locate Marrisa and to seize Lilith—some news was bound to come up to the king.

He searched the gardens with his weary eyes, noticing how beautiful it was even in the gloominess of the cloudy day. He noticed how even in the darkest of hour, the beauty of nature still lifted his spirit somewhat. His eyes caught the magnificent fountain that graced the garden. It still poured out the purest of waters, still working like the many servants who tended to the garden. He looked upon the grand statue of the Great King that stood tall and mighty amongst the fountain: his sword pointing up to the heavens in his right hand and a large opened book in his left, his large shield leaning against his armored leg. The beautifully sculpted statue was always a beacon of hope to the king. The statue of the legendary king seemed to lift his spirit even more and reminded him of why humanity was even put upon the earth.

The original marble statue was carved generations ago, after the reign of the Great King. Inspired, the lord who took the legendary king's place upon the throne had it carved out of marble and placed upon the beautiful fountain, to always remind him of the glory of the Great King. During the reign of King Julpen's mother, Queen Karnidge—it was destroyed... But king Julpen had an identical statue produced at the beginning of his reign when he was a young boy.

"Please help me, father of kings and lord of lords," King Julpen prayed in a low tone to himself as he looked upon the beautiful monument through the window. "Show me what to do..."

The statue looked exactly the way it did when he was a young boy, before his mother had it destroyed after his father, King James, died.

Nostalgia came over him. His thoughts went back years earlier to his childhood. He remembered how he used to play in the gardens as a young boy, admiring the mighty statue when he crossed its path... On one particular day, a couple of months after his father passed, he sat out in the garden—just thinking of his father—and his dreadful mother...

†††

Being young, at the tender age of seven, Prince Julpen didn't understand death—or even the death of his father. He didn't understand anything that was happening to his family really. All he knew was that he was angry at his father for leaving him—alone with his cruel mother. His mother had told him that the earth was a far much better place without his father on it. But Julpen didn't believe her. Even though he was angry at him, he missed his father, greatly. He missed everything about him, and didn't understand the fact that he was never coming back. His mother was now the only one in his life. One would think it was a wonderful thing for him to be left with his mother, the one who gave birth to him—but that would only be thought by one whom did not know of her evil ways. His mother frightened him...

He was never close with his mother—finding any kind of way to stay clear of her wicked path and black shadows. He didn't even know if he loved her or not. His mother was bitter and cold and abusive—and he resented her for it. She never showed any kind of love towards him, only aloofness and pain—and anger. Julpen was the only child and heir to the throne to Minslethrate, and being the only child and receiving no real love and kindness from his mother, he didn't know how to show love. There was once love that his father had showed him—but now there was no more. He was alone in the darkness—alone and lost.

Over the duration of their royal marriage, King James with the succumbing of Queen Karnidge, tried numerous times to create an heir to the throne, and after the grotesque proceedings of two miscarriages and one still-born, a baby boy was finally born. Prince Julpen brought much happiness to the castle, especially to his father—who appreciated everything about him. The heir to the throne was always the special child, being respected greatly. The prince was the smile to the king's face and the happiness to his heart. But on the other hand, his mother looked upon him as if he was a disgusting unwanted creature, vermin which needed to be rid of. It was said by her handmaidens that even on the day of his birth, his mother refused to hold him, nearly knocking the newborn to the cold stone floor.

When Julpen's father had strangely passed when he was seven years old, his mother took over the throne. Like the weather, the queen changed from cold to brutally freezing, as if a terrible flood of ice-cold anger was released from her. She ruled over Minslethrate aggressively and demanded that great change take place—and that's when the terror began to erupt in Minslethrate... The people of the Golden Lands began to only know fear and sadness...

Beginning with a huge bonfire—every copy of the Book of Light was burned, including anyone who refused to yield to the queen's demands. But the young prince was crafty, determined to keep the one special thing in which his father treasured—the Book of Light. His father's advisor, Master Odwa, instructed him to hide the original Book of Light from his mother by putting it in a chest and burying it in the furthest and thickest part of the gardens, unnoticed. His father spent the majority of his reign in Minslethrate having copies of the Book of Light made and distributed out amongst the kingdom—and now they were being burned... Frightened and anxious, the young prince prayed that she would never find out about him taking and hiding the book—and she never did...

She demanded that there would be no talk of the legendary King of Light, and if there was, the ones who spoke it would be burned at the stake. Everyone was to submit to their queen, and if they refused—they knew what was to become of them. The whole kingdom was put into shock, going from the benevolence reign of King James to the terror of Queen Karnidge. From nobility to the poor, everyone was punished—anyone who offended the queen in any kind of way. The people of Minslethrate began to only know fear, terrified that their death would come to them quickly—by the slow cooking of a great fire.

At first there was a burning at the stake almost every day, covering the kingdom in rancid smoke. Then there was a burning at least once a week, sometimes a couple of times a week including more than one terrified person. One who would be burned would pray that they would be suffocated by the thick smoke first.

The kingdom was always dull and gray and saddened because of the heavy, rotten smoke, which spread like foul waters. The horrible sounds of the screaming victims could be heard anywhere around the kingdom, startling anyone who would listen to or watch the burnings. The kingdom always smelled of burnt flesh, sickening the stomachs of everyone who walked through the castle town. One walk through the marketplace would make the shoppers smell like the heavy and putrid scent of burning fat and flesh. The stench of the smoke and the anguish that burned in their hearts kept their eyes dripping with tears and their souls scorched by fear.

Prince Julpen was always frightened by his mother—even her appearance startled him. As he grew, so did his mother's fashions. She always had a magnificent red gown on, elaborate and beautiful and the color of blood upon a rose petal. She would also have on his father's family heirloom every day, which was a beautiful ruby that was large and embedded in gold and hung from a long sparkling chain. The pendant represented power and his family's bloodline.

But the thing that startled the young prince most of all was her face. Her skin was white as snow and her eyebrows, hairline and sideburns were always shaved off, revealing a great white, smooth fore-head. Her long black hair was always up beneath an elaborate headdress, having a red jeweled diadem, which hung from it and dangled on her massive forehead. Her face was always plain, revealing the natural wrinkles and lines of her skin, and her eyes were always horrifyingly—black. Even with the light of the day shining in her eyes, one could never find a pupil.

One day after a lesson in Pell-training, which consisted of hours of crafty and strengthfull sword technique, Prince Julpen had decided to go out into the gardens for a break. He had just started his sword training and his seven-year-old arms had begun to become sore and achy from the long lessons.

The weather was actually slightly nice that day, having the sun come in and out of the gray sky every so often, revealing its missed and beautiful face. There had been no burnings in almost a whole week, allowing the smoky atmosphere to relent.

Prince Julpen was walking about, sniffing the red roses as he passed them. Nature always made him feel better when he was down, and now with his father gone, he wanted to be in the gardens all of the time. His father always taught him to look to the sky to the God of light when he was sad and feeling alone, but now after the death of his father, there seemed to never be light—always gray and smokiness, and coldness. "How could I look to the sky, not seeing the great God of light but only gray clouds and black smoke, and feel happy?" he thought. And that's why he looked to the beauty of the gardens, it was the closest thing to God that he could look at and touch—he thought.

The prince had walked amongst a rose bush, stopping to snap a rose from its thin branch. He flinched as he pricked his finger in the process. He looked upon the small dot of blood that accumulated on the tip of his finger. He put his finger to his mouth, stopping the small flow of blood, then he looked upon the rose, smiling a little. The flower was opened, full and beautiful with dark-green leaves and large thorns on the stem. He sniffed the rose, closing his eyes and thinking of happy thoughts. He thought of his father and his warm smile—that was the only happy thought he had, and he never wanted to forget his father's face.

He walked to the great fountain, peering into the clear water, noticing how clean the bottom was. He looked at the empty space where the marble statue of the Great King once stood. The only thing left of the once beautiful monument was the base on which it was mounted.

His mother had it pulled down and broken into a thousand pieces right after his father died. The day his mother had it destroyed, he cried uncontrollably at her feet, pleading for it to be salvaged for it had been in his family's possession for many generations. The queen had the prince punished for sniveling—after the statue was crushed into a thousand sharp pieces, she made him kneel on it all day while having a large bag of sand rest on his back.

But his punishments weren't as nearly as vicious as some of those that were bestowed upon the servants... The prince had witnessed their servants being brutally punished many times, leading to some of them being burned at the stake... Some even came up missing, seeming to just vanish. There was even a horrifying rumor that stated that the queen had even hired on young servant girls—to use them in rituals...

The prince went to his knees before the fountain, remembering that day when his knees bled amongst the shards of the broken statue. He laid the rose on the fountain's ledge, then closed his eyes.

"Dear King of Kings—please help me," he prayed, remembering when his father had prayed that same prayer for help during his uncertain times.

Just then he opened his eyes, and cringed. His heart began to pound ferociously as he saw a familiar shadow looming over him, which cascaded over the waters of the fountain before him. The shadow was tall and dark, and had two large horns jutting from the top of its head. Startled, he turned around, quickly standing up and bowing to his mother.

She stood before him, tall and intimidating, daunting and cold. She had her usual garment on that was the color of blood, with a headdress that had two large dragon-like horns which stuck out from the top with a lacey fabric that cascaded over it and down her back. His father's pendant dangled from her neck, catching the light of the day. The sun that came in and out of the clouds gleamed off of her high, jewel-adorned fore-head.

"Who are you talking to, Julpen?" She asked in her smooth voice which still had a hint of her home-land accent.

The tone of her voice was always low and decorous at first, smooth and inviting, which frightened the young prince. He never knew when she was going to lash out at him.

"I—I am talking to no one, mother," the prince said, trying to cover his nervousness.

She peered down at him with her cold, black stare as he just helplessly looked back up to her.

"Why are you in the gardens? You should be at Pell-training with your sword," she said in a more forceful voice.

"I—I came to take a rest, mother. Does this displease you?"

There was a terrible silence between them, making the prince shyly look down to the ground every so often.

"A prince should be studying about mighty laws and training with his blade to become a great king," she said, still looking down upon him. "A great king does not wander around gardens like that of a princess and go about talking to himself... What is that behind you?!" she demanded, pointing her long white finger to the rose that sat on the ledge of the fountain.

The prince became frightened, his young mind going blank. He just looked up at the ill-tempered queen.

"Are you hard at hearing? Did you hear what I asked of you?!"

"No, ma'am—I mean, yes ma'am," he stuttered—his heart racing.

"What is it then?! Do not jabber like some kind of fool."

"I meant—yes ma'am, as always, I hear you mother," he quickly said, turning around to pluck up the rose with his eyes still on her. "It is a rose—for you—mother," he said nervously as he offered her the attractive flower.

He didn't intentionally pick the rose for her—his seven-year-old mind just didn't know what else to do.

She still looked down upon him, emotionless, as his small and slightly shaken hand continued to offer her the rose. After a moment of silence, she accepted it, snatching it from him without a smile. The many thorns on the flower stung her hand just then, piercing the white skin on the inside of her finger and making her bleed. She cringed with a gnashing jaw as she quickly looked at her bleeding finger, wiping the drops of blood off with the other hand.

"YOU MONGREL!" She roared out angrily as she sneered down at him.

She slapped the thorny rose harshly with all her might across the prince's young and frightened face. It happened so fast that shock hit his body first before the pain settled in.

"Do-not-pick-my-roses!" she yelled as the rose petals and some leaves from the destroyed flower glided to the ground like autumn leaves, as well as a couple of blood drops. "Give me a thorny flower will you!" she grunted with a tightened jaw as she threw the thorny and bald rose-stem at him.

The swipe from the rose's thorns had pierced his cheek, tearing the skin across it and making it ooze blood. The prince quickly put his hand to his bloody cheek as tears began to swell up in his dark-brown eyes. His chin and bottom lip began to quiver.

"If you cry—even the sound of mighty lashing will not cover your screams," the queen said in a now low and threatening voice.

The prince didn't say anything as he tried so strongly to hold onto his tears. The last time he had cried in front of his mother, he had been whipped so badly upon his back that he couldn't sit or lay comfortably for a whole week. She would say: "Sniveling is for the weak and pathetic...spare the rod and spoil the child...," before she would have him harshly punished.

"I won't cry for you! I do not pity you! You will never see me shed a tear for your pathetic being! Never! You will never be compassionate," she said as she bent over to look closer at him—his father's blood-red pendant dangling from her neck before him. "Do you understand me?! You will never have compassion for anyone! It is for the weak! Compassion is weakness!"

Her eyes were wild and searching into his—and were circled with a red-purple color. The muscles in her pale face were tense with anger, revealing prominent lines in her ghostly-white skin. The main veins in her neck bulged out of the sides as her face began to turn scarlet. Her breath smelled foul and her teeth were stained yellow.

The young and frightened prince just nodded his head as he still covered his bloody cheek—that's all he could do.

"Stupid, fatherless child. Bastard you will always be. Queer you are...but weak you will not be! I forbid it! Do not ever cry—appearing like that of a sniveling princess. When you become king, you will rule like your mother—you will show no mercy. No mercy! Your father was weak—nothing comes from weakness! Do you see where weakness has brought him? Rotting bones in a grave of silence! And if I catch you picking my roses again—there will be more than just a couple drops of blood you will see. The shade of red will be in your eyes."

She continued to stare her cold, black eyes upon him. Then, after what seemed like one torturous hour of many, she pointed her long finger at his nose, pocking the tip of his nose with her long yellow fingernail. She then stood up straight—still looking down at him.

"Now go—get out of my presence you worthless ingrate," she said in a lower tone, motioning for him to go away with her hand like one would to a dog.

The prince nodded, obediently hurrying away, still holding his bloody cheek. He ran through the gardens, relieved to get away from his mother but saddened at the same time. He ran until he came upon the thicker part of the garden, a lovely shaded grove and his favorite spot, and the spot where he had buried his father's Book of Light months ago. The prince fell upon the shaded spot and began to cry as he buried his face into the cool grass, making sure that the sounds of his cry would not float back to the castle and to his mother's ears. He released all of his sadness and anxiety amongst the earth, above the buried book.

For many moments he lay there in the shadow of the forest, wrapped in the cool serenity of the nature all around him. But then he heard the soft call of an owl. It was calming and resonating, seeming to comfort and sooth his saddened heart. He had heard it before when he was in the gardens, but never regarded it till then. He sat up against the tree, wiping the blood and tears from his face. He heard the call of the owl again. He looked up into the tall shaded trees where the calls emanated from and noticed a large and beautiful white owl. The owl was the purest of white with flecks of gold in its feathers. Its eyes were large and dark, but mysterious and inviting. He had never seen such a beautiful owl like that one. It sat quietly, and seemed to be peering inside of his heart. Just then the sadness seemed to lift from his pensive heart as his tears dried.

"Hello," the prince said with a small and shy smile…

He would see the wonderful bird every now and then in the garden, when he would be in the lowest state in the darkest hour of his young life. He didn't know whether he had made it up in his mind—the things he heard from the owl's calls, or that he really heard them from the owl itself. But he heard things he longed to hear and felt it in his inner being. The calls of the owl would send him loving messages to his heart, telling him that he was not worthless and even in the midst of the coldest and darkest moments— light would mend his heart and he would still be loved—everything was going be okay in the end…

…After the death of his mother five years later he never saw the strange and beautiful bird again. He began to think that the bird was just a figment of his young imagination, and was just a symbol of happiness his mind had only created…

†††

The king came out of his daydream—one of the many memories of his childhood. He rubbed the faint scar on his cheek that his mother had left on him. That was the first time he had thought of his mother and childhood or the mysterious owl in a very long time… His mother had tormented for five years, five short years that felt like a reign of eternity when he was a young boy—then she strangely became ill and died. Julpen wasn't sad when his mother had died, but relieved and thankful.

He couldn't help it, but he loathed his mother, and shuddered every time she came into his mind. He resented her and never spoke of her to anyone, not even to Marrisa. Marrisa knew nothing of her grandmother and the things she had done almost forty some odd years ago. He kept his mother locked away in his mind, a dark secret, never wanting to let her out or speak of her. On a rare occasion she would sneak into the crevasses of his mind—and he would have nightmares, seeing her frightening face looming over him…

After the death of his mother, when he was twelve, he took over the throne and demanded that her name should never be said by any mouth. The five years that Queen Karnidge had ruled, severely wounded the Kingdom of Minslethrate, and he wanted to mend those wounds.

He was advised by Master Odwa, who was an old friend of his father. Master Odwa had helped his father with the production of the many copies of The Book of Light—turning the one book into many books. With the help of Master Odwa, King Julpen tried to restore Minslethrate, trying to make the kingdom how it was when his father had ruled.

He swore to himself and to his people that he would never treat his family and kingdom so dishonorably, the way his mother did. He stopped the burnings and restored the kingdom and ruled with a characteristic his mother had hated and denied—compassion.

But it was hard for the king to show any kind of physical love, so he did it in a way by trying to help the people who were less fortunate and making sure that nature was being taken care of. Once a year he would hold a celebration for his people, rich and poor, to commemorate the day he became king and to celebrate the beauty of the earth and the gifts of God. They celebrated the earth and gave praise and thanks to the God of Light. The people of Minslethrate looked forward to it every year and called it the Spring Celebration.

The celebration was held on the anniversary of his notorious mother's death. The spring celebration would be held in a couple of days, during the spring equinox. The spring quinox happened when both the day and night were equally the same length. That was the time when the king wanted everyone to be equal. No matter the class, whether rich or poor—everyone was welcome to attend. Growing up, the beauty of nature was the only thing he could escape to, that kept him sane. And that beauty of nature was shared by everyone—and made for everyone.

Even though he wanted to show happiness and love—it was hard for him to. It was especially hard for his people to see him as loving, especially after the incident of the burning ten years ago. For the first time the king had ordered a burning ten years ago, hoping to rid of the evil that began to augment in the kingdom once again. Like his mother who burned everything that was good in his life, he wanted the evil to be burned. He felt like it was revenge towards his mother—to burn all evil. But that was the first and the last time he would ever order someone to be burned—and he never had anyone burned at the stake ever again…

That day ten years ago when Moira was accused of being a witch and blamed for doing works of evil, he saw his mother in her. He wanted to rid of her—of the evil that tried to bring him back down. That ominous day in the town square, he had gotten a flashback of his childhood and began to see his mother in himself. After that day the king had dreamt about his mother and the numerous people she had killed. That's when he swore to himself that he would never cast anyone into the fire again.

Till that very present day the king still felt uneasy about the burning of Moira ten years ago, thinking that something wasn't right when he had her burned at the stake. He remembered how her face looked so innocent and frightened the night when she was convicted and sentenced to death by the court… With the situation that Moira was in, there was no proof that she was innocent… And now with the evil works that were done in Lilith's chamber, he knew something dark had made its way back into his life once again. It didn't matter if he burned evil or not, it still found its way back to him. With the experiences of his mother, the rumors of Moira, and the dead body in Lilith's room with his daughter coming up missing, there was no doubt in his mind that something negative and evil was still lurking around Minslethrate—but what?

He thought of his daughter again, and how badly he wanted her to be safe. He thought of all the times he had not been around for his daughter. Being raised, physically and mentally abused by an unloving mother, and not really remembering his father—he had become hardened. And then with the death of the only woman he had ever loved, his late wife, his skin had become thicker and his emotions were now absent. "Forgive me, my daughter," he thought. "I pray that your husband will show you love—for I have failed you." Just then he thought of Prince Phillip and his letter.

His mind quickly switched back to the present situation.

He looked back down to the letter. The prince wrote that he went off into the southern parts of Minslethrate, to rescue Marrisa from a guild of mad men—and that he, the king, could send an army if he wished.

The king wondered how he would find his way to the south—and even if he knew his way, how would he get past the great wall without being stopped by the many soldiers who guarded the wall. By the decree of the king, no one was allowed to pass the Great Wall of Division, into the forbidden lands; and whoever tried without a letter from the king would be arrested and brought back to the kingdom. It would take about two days to get to the great wall from the kingdom anyways, passing through many great sloping fields and forests. By the time Phillip got to the great wall, he would be forced to come back.

"I beg your pardon, Sire." It was Alexander again, this time followed by the Lord and Lady Ducre'. "The honorable Lord and Lady of Ducre' has come to bare news to your majesty," he said, welcoming them into the room with a polite arm gesture.

The lord and lady bowed, then made their way to the king. The marquis was an average height man in his early fifties, having long dark hair with gray highlights and pale skin. His eyes were dark beneath two large, thick eyebrows and his face was thin having a small and well trimmed beard. His pale skin stood out more because of the dark-colored garbs he wore. His wife, the marchioness who looked much younger than he, stood by his side, petite and beautiful, with smooth dark skin and black hair that was up and beneath an elegant headdress. Her vibrant green eyes sparkled upon her stern face, looking exotic adjacent to her golden-brown skin. She wore a vibrant green gown of the latest fashion that pulled the color of her eyes out even more.

"Ah, Fernund, it is good to see an old friend amongst these troubling times," the king said with a weak smile as they came forward. They greeted each other, then the king kissed the Marchioness on the hand. "Come, sit— Do you wish to have a goblet of wine?"

"No thank you," The Marquis said as they followed the king to his table. "As always, I enjoy your majesty's hospitality—But I come to bare some disconcerting news. You must read this first," he said, handing him the letter that his daughter had left for Sora.

The king read it quietly, then looked up at The Marquis.

"Something in the south stirs," he said, then looked out of the window. "I'm afraid something malicious is happening again—like that of ten years ago, Fernund. And your daughter knows something that I do not... She defies the behaviors of a lady."

"Yes, I know my daughter can be bold—but she has a good heart," Lord Ducre' said, then looked at his wife.

"Yes, Fernund, your daughter is a mighty companion to Marrisa—and as long as I've known her, she has been dedicated to my daughter when I was not..." he said with an honest face. "I spoke with Natalia last night and she was convinced that something terrible has happened to my daughter," the king had a look of guilt on his face all of the sudden as he continued to look out of the massive windows. "She tried to tell me—but I did not believe her warnings—till now. There is something insidious in the air that keeps trying to pull this kingdom apart and I need to find out what it is," King Julpen said as he looked into the Marquis' bewildered eyes.

"If our daughters are in danger—I suggest sending out a legion of soldiers." Lord Fernund said as he placed his hand on his wife's back.

"That has already been done, Fernund. I believe Natalia is being accompanied by his royal highness, Prince Phillip. She will be protected from the wilderness."

"This is certain?" asked Lord Ducre'

"Prince Phillip has left me a correspondence stating that he has ventured off to the south as well, to find Marrisa. According to Phillip—my daughter has been abducted... The captors will want ransom. There will be great anguish upon these men if my daughter is harmed in any way—they will be vanquished...," the king said with a tightened jaw. "But your daughter is with the prince, it is too much of a coincidence that both Natalia and the Prince have written correspondences and are both going to the Forbidden Lands to look for Marrisa. But what bewilders me greatly is that they've chosen to go off on their own... But by the time anyone gets to the Great Wall of Division, they will be seized by my soldiers who line the great wall. Natalia will be fine. There are many soldiers looking for them as we speak. But I will bring up an army and we will head to the southern parts of Minslethrate..."

"I am truly sorry, your majesty, about your daughter—I pray they all will be found," Lord Ducre' said in a low tone. "I will go to the south as well..."

Lady Ducre' had a serious face as he spoke. She glanced at her husband, then at the king Julpen.

"No, my old friend," the king said in a low tone as he placed his hand on his shoulder. "I am appreciative of your dedication to our kingdom and daughters. But I need you here by your wife's side—in Minslethrate. You are no warlord, Marquis. I have no son or Duke to my throne—I need you to keep my people feeling safe while I am gone. You are highly respected in Minslethrate. The people need to feel safe, and will feel so by a respected man like yourself residing before them in the palace."

The Marquis nodded, having a solemn look on his face.

Lady Ducre' looked up at her husband, holding onto his arm. She knew he was going to leave their home for the cause, which she was not pleased with.

"I am honored," Lord Ducre' said.

"Good," the king said as he nodded his head, then sat back down in his throne-like chair. "My advisor, Master Odwa, will be with you while I am away."

Just then Alexander came into the hall again, followed by two men.

"Your royal highness, I have commander in chief, Sir Hawkington and The Royal Advisor, Master Odwa.

The two men came before the king and bowed their heads. Sir Hawkington was a tall and intimidating looking middle-aged man with a shaved head and a black beard, having a scar on the left side of his face. Master Odwa was an older man with a long white beard and a slender physic, appearing wise and able. He was adorned in elegant robes which wiped the tiled floor as he made his way towards the king.

"My men, my cohorts—there is darkness upon us which has been an old friend of Minslethrate. It must be rid of—I will not tolerate such evil that has once again enveloped Minslethrate in darkness..." King Julpen said as he stood up. "Strange things are abroad. We shall put our heads together, and then hold a quick court meeting to notify the people of our actions..."

Huddled around the king's table, they spoke of a plan of action as the Marchioness despondently left the hall, following Alexander.

†

CHAPTER 14
The Watchers and The Guardian

The sun was beginning to set as it was mid-evening. The sky was still cloudy and gray, but looked as if it were on fire in the northern parts where the sun was slowly making its way down upon the lands of Minslethrate. The Forest of Old was dark and dreary and had a totally different feeling than that of the Forest Provence where Tairren lived. After passing many opened and sloping fields and thick forests, they finally had made it to Lake Iris—many hours away from home. Tairren, Natalia, and Phillip began to set up a little camp, making sure it was near the water and comfortable for sleeping. As soon as they found the perfect spot next to the beautiful Lake Iris, Tairren had gotten a nice little fire going as Natalia and Phillip went to fetch some sticks to feed the fire with. After making their quaint little spot of fiery light, they sat around it and ate their small meal of bread, fruit and water.

"I'm starving," Natalia said she nibbled on a small loaf of barley bread she had brought with her. "Missing dinner really put some pains in my stomach—I thank the lord for this bread and pity the ones without a meal."

"I'm okay, I'm used to having small meals," Tairren said as he shrugged his shoulders while eating an apple. "And I thank God every day for it."

"Give me a royal meal. I would love to have a nice piece of beef with some potatoes to go with this bread, along with a golden goblet of wine," Phillip said to himself, while eating a piece of bread that Natalia had shared with him.

Both Tairren and Natalia just looked at Phillip, having an unimpressed look on their faces.

"I could've gone hunting for rabbit or duck, but it'll be getting dark soon," Tairren said, looking up into the sky. "And this strange weather is not helping either."

They sat in a small opening in the forest, next to the beautiful lake— tired, irritated and hungry. With the dark-gray sky, the forest made it appear darker all around them than it really was. Amongst the sounds of falling water and the crackling fire, the crickets and the frogs chirped excitedly, sending a resonating melody over the lake and small clearing. The hoot of a forest owl could be heard every once in a while, sounding low and haunting. The lake had many patches of blue, purple and yellow colored irises all around it and in the shallow parts of the clear water, for this reason it was called Lake Iris. Small waterfalls that flowed from creeks and rivulets from the Minslethratian River, along with flowering vines, cascaded all around the back side of the lake, falling from small cliffs that loomed over some parts of the lake. The trees that circled around the lake were tall, dark and mysterious, reflecting off of the glistening waters of the lake and appearing like a painting. Everything about the lake was serene and beautiful.

They finished eating their small supper as it got darker outside. The air around them became cooler and the trees above swayed in the faint breezes. The massive tree they sat beneath stretched out its knotted and twisted branches above them, seeming to protect them with its eerie arms.

"I don't like this forest," Natalia said as she sat still amongst the cozy fire, pulling her cape tightly around her arms. "During the day it must be beautiful—but it seems it is much too dark and old of a forest to be beautiful."

"And that is why, my lady, it is called the Forest of Old." Tairren teased as he poked the fire with a stick. "These parts of Minslethrate are strange and mysterious—this dark forest is a very ancient forest and filled with things one can only imagine," he said in a low voice.

"Do not frighten the lady," Phillip said as he sipped some water from a flask which was wrapped in dark-brown leather.

"I do not frighten, I inform, prince," Tairren said defensively.

"Yes, you know all, Master Tairren," Phillip quickly said, mocking him. He propped up his knee, leaning on his right side and elbow upon the grass.

"Tairren, please continue," Natalia interrupted as she glared at the prince. She sensed an argument that was ready to erupt between Phillip and Tairren.

Tairren was quiet for a moment. The day was long and the lack of sleep and not having an ample meal was starting to get to him. Besides all of that, he had been having a strange feeling ever since they first came into the Forest of Old. He felt like something was following them—or even watching them. Sometimes it was a good feeling, and other times the feeling was—bad. But he did not want to alarm Natalia or the prince with what he was feeling. He knew their minds must be at rest if they were going to have a good night's sleep.

He just peered at Phillip, then began to speak again. "It has been many years since I've come this far to the south. This ancient forest expands throughout the middle lands of Minslethrate and becomes the Black Forest right on the other side of the Great Wall. But I do know that it is not as safe as the Forest Provence amongst the castle. There are many creatures abroad, things like wolves and bears who rule these parts of the woods. But they say there are even worse things than any wolf or bear—like Banshees and dark spirits that lurk through the darkness of the thick wood, snatching up any weak soul that passes through.

Natalia looked upon the darkened forest, which was becoming even darker as the sun went down. The light of the fire bounced off nearby trees and bushes, playing with her eyes and sending dancing shadows everywhere. She slowly scooted towards Phillip, trying to make it not so obvious that she was becoming a little uneasy.

"What are these dark spirits you speak of?" Phillip asked, slightly smirking.

"They are followers of the fallen Archlegna, Lucif. Legend has it that they are monsters of darkness that will do anything to make a person's life miserable—filling one's life with misfortunes and troubles."

"Do you believe that, Tairren?" Natalia asked, scooting even closer to Phillip.

Tairren was quiet, looking off into the darkness of the forest. The forest around them became almost black.

"Most of everything I speak of has been passed down in legend and in lore—but some are real and written in the Book of Light. Yes, I do believe—and last night was a prime example," he said in a more serious manner as he looked back at both of them. "Last night when I was amongst Lilith and those horrid, screaming creatures, I felt an evilness in the atmosphere—one that I do not want to feel again. It put fear in my heart and bumps upon my flesh… But I know there is nothing fear can hurt if your heart is lit by His flame."

Tairren became quiet as he rubbed his bandaged arm, noticing the throbbing pain that had been bothering him all day, became stronger. Natalia was quiet as well as she noticed him rubbing his arm—and the healed scratches on his face.

"Let us hope we do not run into your creatures," Phillip said, sitting up and smirking.

"I'm afraid, Phillip, that they are not my creatures. Beyond the Wall of Division there will be many things which lurk with evilness soaked upon them," Tairren said, slightly aggravated that Phillip seemed to be making a mockery out of everything he was saying.

"What is this great wall you speak of? Is it to keep everyone from traveling to the south?" the prince asked.

"Long ago, the wall was built out of love for his people, by the legendary King of Light—to keep the evil out. It is said that the Great King had the wall built before he and his men went off on his last crusade. He wished it to be built many miles long and many cubits high, separating the north of Minslethrate from the south. The wall's purpose was to keep the ones who love darkness and live the ways of the old ages of Minslethrate, on the other side…

"After his last crusade, and before he had the wall built, there was a mighty war in Minslethrate between the people of light and the people of darkness who served Minlsethrate's ancient pagan goddesses, Fiara, Dolsia, and Haifen. With their hearts drunken by dark spirits, an evil tyrant leader from the south rose up against the king with all of his followers. You see, legend has it, and also it is written in the Book of Light, that Minslethrate was the first settlement of light, planted by our God of Light in the beginning of time and of the earth.

"His fallen Archlegna, Lucif, fell upon the earth, and infiltrated the beautiful lands of this divine settlement of light. And generations later, Minslethrate became a pagan country—as the ancient goddesses, Fiara, Dolsia, and Haifen were born. And so, the many lost people of Minslethrate who were blinded by the beliefs of the false gods, rose up against the king, wanting Minslethrate to be as it was when everyone worshiped the goddesses—like in the old days of yore.

"But the Great King of light led his people into battle—and won. He restored the lands of Minslethrate and spread the truth of the word of light, and during that time, he had the great wall built—to keep evil out. The temples of fire, earth and water were soon forgotten, as well as The Dark Tower of Sacrifice, on the other side of the wall.

The southern parts of Minslethrate are protected by a mountain range, Mount Fiara, which borders the southern parts, and the ends of the Great Wall of Division meet with the mountains. So, you see, no one, not even the bravest of travelers can easily get into the southern parts of Minslethrate from the outside—unless they are allowed by the king of Minslethrate. The southern parts of Minslethrate are forbidden to walk upon, receiving its name, the Forbidden Lands… Cursed, only the ones with a heart of darkness dwell on the other side—and only the one's with a protected heart can walk through such dark madness."

Tairren became quiet as he glanced at Natalia who was looking into the now blackened forest. The chirps of frogs and crickets could be heard now, going along with the atmosphere of the early night.

"That is an amazing story, Master Tairren," Phillip said, "but how does a wall keep evil out?"

"The wall is massive, and is guarded by many soldiers at all times. There is only one main gate through the wall which is always shut, and only one with a letter from the king of Minslethrate can pass through it… When early morning comes, if we continue to go straight in a southern direction, we should be at the doors of the wall before the day is finish."

"How will we pass through these gates of the wall when a letter from the king is needed? Which, we do not possess." The prince seemed to test Tairren.

Both Natalia and the prince looked at Tairren, waiting for an answer.

"There is a way through the massive wall where the forest grows the thickest, right outside of the left side of the field that sits before the great doors of the wall. My father and I went through it only one time when we went into the beginning parts of the Black Forest, to look for interesting things to sell at the shop. We did not get caught, but we never went past the wall ever again. The way is through a tunnel, where a rivulet from the Minslethratian River flows through. The water was low at that time so we were able to get our horse we had at that time, through. It is risky, and we could get caught if we do it all wrong."

"Oh, I hope this is all as easy as it sounds," Natalia said in a low tone as nervousness began to come over her petite body.

"You had mentioned that Marrisa was being taken to The Dark Tower of Sacrifice. How long do you suppose it will take to get from the great wall to this southern temple?" Phillip asked as he rubbed his lightly bearded chin.

"This temple is in the furthest area away from the castle of the southern parts of Minslethrate. It sits at the bottom of Mount Fiara, on a cliff, so it won't take too much time getting up the mountain. I believe it may take a couple of days from the great wall to get there."

"Oh my," Natalia said with a stressed tone. "That may not even give us enough time to get to Marrisa—it may be too late when we get there." Natalia's voice began to shake a little as her emotions began to stir.

Phillip stood quietly with his arms crossed and his head now lowered. He seemed irritated and anxious.

"Lilith is probably still on her way to the south. She will probably get there many hours before we do. But if we hurry, we may get there in the nick of time... Have faith, Natalia—everything will be okay..."

"Have faith?!" Phillip barked, interrupting him. "How do we possess any kind of faith when we don't even know what is going on?!" Phillip stood up quickly. "You talk with such an assuring edge—as if you know all! Marrisa could be dead as we speak! Tell me this, Master Tairren—how can I even have faith in what you are saying—if what you are saying is just legend?"

Tairren got up quickly, looking Phillip in the eyes—aggravated even at Phillip's temper. Tairren felt attacked and goaded by the prince, which set his feelings on fire.

Natalia stood up as well, quickly standing before them. For the first time she felt nervous by Tairren and Phillip's sudden anger.

"Because that is all we can do!" Tairren raised his voice in anger for the first time. He was tired of Phillip's pretentious disposition and was running out of patience for him. "I have faith in the God of Light—that everything will happen as it should—I have faith. Without faith we are nothing but lost wanderers!"

"We are nothing but lost! You are a dreamer, Master Tairren," Phillip said, looking Tairren back in the eyes as they were almost face to face. "You make up plans to go and rescue Marrisa from some evil woman, with no back up men, barely any weapons, and you told us that you have not even gone that far south before! This is all so dim and lies on the brink of dreams—irrational dreams!"

"Gentlemen...," Natalia said, panicked, trying to stop them from arguing and yelling.

"The greatest men dream! Even you cannot be so dim to not believe that! But I do this because the being of light, called Malakh, told me of what I need to do—it is God's will and I have faith in it!" Tairren shouted back, coming closer to Phillip. "Through the God of Light, we can do any and all things. You don't have to believe me but I promise you—this is more than a legend; this is all real—as real as this very night!"

Tairren was a couple inches shorter than Phillip, even having a smaller build then him, but he was not intimidated by him. He had fire in his soul and passion in his heart and wasn't going to yield to just anyone—especially the prince.

"I love God and will do whatever I am asked of him—especially when it comes to the woman I love!"

The prince was quiet as he pressed his lips together, folding his arms and standing up straight so that he could look down at him.

Natalia stood quiet as well, surprised by the burning zeal and anger that rose up in Tairren.

"The woman you love?" Phillip said as a smirk came across his face. "How can a princess even love a lonesome peasant boy?" Phillip mocked, looking down in disgust at him.

Tairren stood for a moment while feeling antagonized by Phillip. Unwanted anger and rivalry built up in his chest, making his heart begin to pump rapidly.

"Like I said, you are a dreamer, Master Tairren—the poorest of dreamers who depend on something called faith that is not even tangible, just to get through the day because you don't have anything else. Your faith wouldn't even have come about if it wasn't for the silliness of that woman whom you love. If she would've stayed by my side last night during the festivities, I wouldn't be here speaking to a peasant boy in the middle of the woods in the darkness! I would be on my ship with Marrisa on our way back to Ishkar... Don't forget, Master Tairren, that silly woman whom you love—will be my wife..."

Not being able to contain his anger any longer, Tairren lunged at Phillip, punching him square in the face with one hard blow as they began to fight.

"Stop it!" Natalia screamed out, becoming angry as she tried to pull them away from each other by yanking on Tairren's tunic.

They fell to the ground and rolled amongst the leaves and grass as they fought, swinging and grunting. Natalia fell to the ground and landed on her behind. Frantic and irritated, she quickly stood up and picked up dead leaves and sticks and began to throw it at them.

"Tairren!" she yelled again, "stop it both of you!"

Finally, after a while of rolling and yelling on the ground, Tairren pinned Phillip down by sitting on his chest and holding down his arms.

"You are not even worth this!" Tairren grunted with a clenched jaw, spitting as he talked. He shoved Phillip one last time into the ground, then got up.

Breathless, he continued to look down upon Phillip. He walked over to Natalia as he combed his hand through his hair that fell upon his face. Natalia glared at him as she crossed her arms, pressing her lips together.

"You need to know your place!" Phillip spat out, staggering as he stood up. He had blood running from his nose while leaves stuck out form his wavy black locks. "I don't need this," he said, breathless.

"This is my place! Fighting for the ones I love! If you don't want to be here then you can leave! I have the light on my side," Tairren yelled as he placed his hand on his chest. "And when you leave, make sure you come back for my bones because I will not yield! I will die for my quest if that is what it takes!"

Tairren gave Phillip one last glare, who was now silenced with a grimaced look on his face and still wiping blood from his nose. Tairren walked off into the darkness towards the lake, wanting to be alone for a moment.

"Tairren…" Natalia said softly, starting to walk towards him. She began to feel emotional as she lowered her hands in disappointment. "Where are you going?"

He didn't acknowledge her or even turn towards her—so she stopped in her place. She got the hint that he wanted to be alone. She was startled by Tairren—never seeing him like that before. She stood for a moment as she watched Tairren walk into the darkness of the wood, then turned towards Phillip who was now sitting by the fire again—sulking and appearing like that of a large child. She slowly walked towards him, not knowing what to say at first. She stood for a moment in the awkward silence, watching as Phillip noticeably ignored her. She slowly sat next to him and wrapped her cape around her arms again.

Cooling down from the heated fight, they sat in silence for a moment as the fire continued to crackle and the frogs and crickets continued to chirp. The air between them seemed thick at first, but then slowly thinned out as they sat for a while. Natalia would look up at Phillip every once in a while, who randomly would wipe the blood that trickled from his nose.

"I don't like feeling like this," he finally said, looking up at Natalia. "Feeling lost and defeated is a sign of weakness…"

"Weakness is saying things out of spite... You shouldn't have said those things to Tairren," she said quietly, then pulled a white handkerchief from her satchel that sat next to her. She tenderly wiped the blood from his top lip. "Take this and hold it to your nose."

He took the linen from her and did as he was told.

"Thank you," he said, quietly.

He sat for a moment, staring into the fire.

"Why are you kind to me when I have insulted your companions?"

"...I know you are kind—I saw it in your eyes last night at the castle stable, and then when you brought me home...," she said with a soft and pretty smile. "And I know you didn't mean what you said to Tairren."

They were quiet again as Phillip looked into her green eyes. The fire light sparkled off her eyes and made her skin appear like burnished honey.

"And bold you are—but sweet you will always be," he said as he smiled at her. "...I did not mean what I said to Tairren... I said it out of anger—out of spite," he said, then looked back into the fire. "I must be weak then... When I feel like I am backed into a corner, I belittle people—I want them to feel smaller than I," he said in a low tone. "Everything I've learned has come from my father. I don't like being this way sometimes— it's just embedded deep within my heart."

"If you declare such things upon your life, your future will keep them. To you it seems embedded—but it can be dug up and become as a shining jewel," Natalia said softly with a tender smile.

Phillip sat quietly for a moment while he stared off into the night infested forest, then looked up at her.

"Jewel?" Phillip asked with confusion. His face was serious but then a small smile crept upon his face. "My Lady is a poet of many words."

"My words come to me suddenly when I least expect them," she said while gazing into his eyes.

"How is my ill-temper and seemingly foul disposition a jewel?" Phillip asked, pulling his eyes away from Natalia's and into the crackling fire.

"I am very familiar with jewels—there are all types... Jewels are what my mother loves best...," Natalia said as she pulled her long dark hair over her shoulder.

She became quiet for a moment as she thought of her very vain mother. She was not only vain, but selfish. She thought this of her mother more than anything else and she knew it was a shame, but it was the only notion she had of her.

"I've seen my mother silently worshiping jewels in her own silent and pathetic way—many times… So, they are the first of many images that come to my mind when you mention that your ill-temper and foul disposition are embedded deep within your heart. A jewel, uncut and dirty, has a foul appearance when it is dug out of the rock of the mountain. But when it is cut into precise facets and polished, it shines like the ripples upon a gleaming lake. And it is then full of wealth and wanted by many— particularly when its luster is like that of the sun or the caps of mountain tops. I know once you are ready, you will find that light within you—and your heart will gleam like that jewel…"

"You, my lady, are full of surprises," Phillip said with raised eyebrows.

He thought that Natalia was not only enchantingly beautiful, but she seemed to be deep and fervent and more heart-felt than any lady he had ever met within his twenty-five years of living. Everything about her tantalized him and he loved every bit of it. Everything from her vibrant green eyes to the lusciousness of her light-brown skin; from her bold and abrupt attitude to her tender heart, captivated him. Ever since they left the kingdom to retrieve Marrisa, he never thought of the captured princess once—not even for one split second. And when he mentioned Marrisa to Tairren during their fight, it was only because he wanted to antagonize him.

"So, if I may ask, my dear Lady Natalia of Ducre', how bright is your jewel?" he said facetiously.

Natalia just stared at him for a quick moment, then rolled her eyes.

"You are nothing but a child," Natalia said with a giggle.

They both sat for a moment in silence, just looking at each other. The presence they held between their bodies began to become thick with intensity. Natalia just cleared her throat as the thought of Tairren popped into her mind. She wanted to direct the conversation back to the fight that happened between Phillip and Tairren.

"Well, my dear Prince Phillip, I am not your superior and I know I am only a lady to you, but I think you need to apologize to Tairren… Think about what will happen before you decide to say something foolish out of anger."

Phillip looked back up to her with an impressed look on his face because of her speaking so boldly to him. He just laughed.

"My, you speak so valiantly. Now I say things that are foolish? It is hard for me to believe the situation I am in… If I was in Ishkar and was to be struck or talked to so disrespectfully by anyone, it would be treason. That person would be…"

"Hung, burned, beheaded—exiled unto unknown lands?" Natalia said quickly, cutting him off. "Treason is just a term used to have a reason to punish someone. Doesn't any man deserve to use the word treason if they are offended? I think not. It is okay for royalty or nobility to say or do what pleases them—but God forbid if anyone lower than they even look upon them wrong… Tairren has not struck anyone in his whole life. He is the most loving man I have ever known. So, it is you that has antagonized him first… We are all the same, Phillip, with a heart that pumps life and feeds on emotions. We are all only flesh and blood upon this earth. If only the hearts of man could see that. Just think about that the next time you let your foolishness get the best of you."

The prince was quiet for a moment. He was speechless and didn't know what to say. He had never been corrected by a woman before—or by anyone. For the first time in his life he felt bad for the way he acted out. And for the first time in his life—he felt he was beginning to fall in love…

"I—I am sorry," he said as he softly looked upon Natalia. "I do owe Tairren an apology… I suppose I am the cause of all this… It's funny how you have impacted me so since I have been in Minslethrate. A lady has never spoken to me like the way you do…"

Natalia giggled a little, moving a lock of black hair from his face.

"I am a different kind of lady," she said as she picked a leaf out of his hair. "I have been threatened many times by my father that he would send me away for a year to serve under a queen so that I could learn from her—how to be a respectable lady. My father would do anything to be away from me, even though I am his only daughter and flesh and blood…" She rolled her eyes than laughed a little. "I know my mouth is bold but my thoughts are always good… I can't help that I am different."

"That you are…," he said with another warm smile. "I don't think any queen would be able to change you—you have a heart of an inspirer." He took the cloth from his nose which had now stopped bleeding. "You know—that is exactly what Marrisa told me about herself when I first met her… That she was a different kind of princess…"

They became quiet for a moment as they looked back into the fire.

"We are just alike—except that she is fairer and sweeter than I…," Natalia said with a faint smile—but it faded away like a soft sunset. "I hope there is still time Phillip," she said in a low tone as her emotions seemed to stir. Soft tears swelled up in her eyes as she lowered her face. "She must be safe in the end… She must… My biggest worry is that her life will not be spared… This is the most frightened I have ever been in my whole life…"

"Don't be, my lady… What is that word Tairren used? Faith," he said as he put his hand to her chin, raising her face back up to look at his.

A small crystal-like tear rolled down her cheek as she looked into his dark eyes. They sat in silence and looked into each other's face for what seemed like a while. The soft light of the fire played off of their skin, making it appear polished and warm to the touch. Not controlling their intensions, they slowly brought each other's faces together. Their lips slowly touched as their eyes closed, feeling each other's breath.

Just then there came noises form the blackened and threatening woods. Startled, they quickly looked over to the area of the woods where the noises were coming from. The noises sounded like someone or something was skulking through dead leaves and branches and moving past pushes.

"Is that Tairren?" Natalia asked as they slowly stood up.

As they went to their feet, Phillip grabbed his sword that was resting next to him. Natalia noticed what he was doing and grabbed her own small sword just in case.

"Nice sword," Phillip teased as he smirked a little.

With wide green eyes, Natalia just ignored him and focused on the sounds that came from the blackened forest.

Just then there came more crunching and brushing noises, like many feet scurrying over leaves and moving through bushes. Just then there came growling sounds, sounding low and rough—all around them.

Their hearts quickened as the unexpected growls became more persistent.

"If that is Tairren—he is very angry," Phillip said as he looked all around the small clearing.

"Phillip…," Natalia said in a low and now frightened voice as she moved closer to him. "This is no time to be facetious."

They both stood, uneasy with their swords tightly gripped in their hands and their backs facing each other. Just then Natalia let out a squeal as a wolf crept into the firelight. The wolf was dark gray with a black face and had its lips curled up with its teeth showing. Then there came another wolf, then another. Soon they were faced by a pack of intimidating and hungry looking wolves—all of them growling and snarling with gnashing and foamy mouths.

"Oh my," Natalia said with a low and shaken voice as her breathing pattern and heart quickened. "I think I am going to faint."

"Don't—because if you do you are giving up your life to them," Phillip said with wide eyes, still keeping his keen eyes on the wolves.

"Tairren!" Natalia squealed between clenched teeth as the wolves came nearer. "I have faith, I have faith," she repeated, reassuring herself, "Oh God—be with us."

Just then one of the wolves that were the closest to them charged at Natalia with a loud and wet growl, saliva sailing to the ground in syrupy-like drops. She let out a loud scream as another came running. The wolf snarled loudly as it lunged at her, jumping at her face with a wide jaw and sharp teeth. She swung her sword at it as hard as she could and penetrated its side with one deep, red slit. The wolf cried out with a dog-like yelp as it fell to the ground.

The other wolf charged Phillip as his sword was ready to strike. He swung his sword at its neck as hard as he could, slicing its head clean off. Blood splashed everywhere appearing as red, thrown water—falling and spraying to the ground and on Phillip's face with warm sprinkles.

The wolf that Natalia had wounded wiggled up, then lunged at her again, knocking her over as her sword went smoothly into its chest. Just then a couple of other wolves began to attack them, growling with anger. Natalia got to her feet as quickly as she could then pulled her bloody sword out of the wolf's chest.

Just as quickly as they attacked, the wolves fell to the ground with squeals as two arrows, one after another, quickly pierced through their matted fur and deep into their flesh. It was Tairren with his bow and arrow, who then came running to back up his companions. The persistent wolves kept on, eager to kill. They growled with sneered snouts and chomped with sharp yellow teeth.

Just then there came loud howls that echoed through the trees, making the wolves stop attacking. Surprised and confused, Tairren, Natalia and Phillip looked around franticly as they came closer to each other. The startled wolves began to whimper, as if they were worried or frightened—then they all ran off into the darkness of the wood.

All of a sudden it was quiet—too quiet.

"What is happening?!" Natalia said, frantically, as she looked around the dark clearing, glancing at the four bloody wolves that laid about them.

"I think I'm going to become ill," she said in a shaky voice as she looked upon the head of the wolf that had been wacked off.

The grotesque head stared at Natalia with black eyes while its tongue hung out of its toothy jaws—blood oozing out of the wet part that was attached to the neck…

Then there came the terrifying howl again, this time it was closer and joined with other howls. The howls did not sound like that of a normal wolf or any kind of animal for that matter. The howls were loud and raspy, high-pitched—reverberating in their ears. The howls sounded like a mixture of gurgling growls and raspy screams.

"What is that?!" Natalia squealed as the three of them came closer together.

Natalia and Phillip grasped their swords tightly while Tairren stood tall with his bow and arrow, ready for whatever was about to come out of the threatening woods.

"I don't know—but whatever it is—it comes with others," Tairren said courageously, pulling his arrow tightly back, ready to release it.

Just then, there came the same noises that they heard earlier when the wolves surrounded them—it was the sounds of leaves being crushed and moved about as if something heavy lurked around in the brush.

"Let's run to the horses and get away from here," Natalia said in a low and quick voice, still staring into the dark woods with her sword up.

"No—do not move," Tairren said in an assertive tone. "Whatever is in the wood is closer than we know—and you will surely die if you turn your back on whatever it is."

Low, deep growls came—sounding like nothing they had ever heard before. They sounded louder and more frightening than the growls that came from the wolves that attacked them earlier. Loud snaps of breaking branches could be heard as whatever was in the woods came nearer.

Just then a large black creature slowly crept out of the darkness of the wood and into the dim light of the fire. It walked on all fours and its head was hunched over with its back curved up. Its hunched backs had notches all down them as their bones could be seen beneath their black skin. Glistening eyes could be seen as the light of the fire reflected off of them— appearing green with flecks of red like that of a feline's eyes at night. But the thing that was frightening most of all was that there were four glistening eyes instead of two coming from the large creature. Then another black thing skulked out of the darkness, appearing just like the other one.

"God be with us," Tairren said to himself, not believing what he was seeing.

The creatures growled and snarled like monsters as they slowly came closer to them—the fire light playing off of their features. Now they understood why there were four glistening eyes instead of two—both of the grotesque creatures had two heads! Four deformed heads, two on each creature, threatened them as they barked and growled viciously, snapping their massive jaws. The creatures looked like large, ugly hunchback wolves or dogs, having large ears that were cocked back, a thick flat snout and a massive flat and deformed head. Two black horns on each head curved up, reminding Tairren of the horned flying monsters. The creatures were also totally black like the flying ones, like shadows, and hairless with long thin, bony tails. Their mouths seemed larger than their heads with many sharp and jagged, wet teeth. They looked as if they could tear one's whole head off with one quick bite.

Tairren, Natalia, and Phillip stared at the two-headed creatures in disbelief—not thinking of anything but their own lives. With a pounding heart, Tairren began to get that same feeling upon him as he did the night he saw the evilness come out of Lilith and of the flying things. The feeling became more intense as the black creatures seemed to look into his eyes and heart with their gleaming eyes.

"We see you—Tairren… So, the eyes of the Lord of Darkness also see you…," dark voices whispered in Tairren's head as the things came nearer to them.

The voices seemed to be coming from the creatures… Tairren was shocked that these creatures knew him and seemed to be speaking only to him.

"You have no power over us!" Tairren yelled out in a forceful voice as his bow and arrows still threatened the creatures.

Just then the large creatures seemed to become enraged and aggressively charged at them, squealing and blowing out frightening and ferocious barks from all four heads. Tairren shot one of the creatures in one of its faces with his arrows, then immediately shot it again, doing the same to the other monster.

During the chaos, something flew down from the sky in a white blur, viciously landing on the back of one of the creatures. The other black creature noticed the white thing and yelped like a frightened beast, backing away. The white thing was a massive white owl—the same owl that had flown over Tairren the night of the attack by the flying things. The owl grabbed onto the grotesque creature's back with its massive talons, lifting it off the ground as its glorious wings spread to fly away. The creature's determined heads snapped at the owl constantly, trying to bite its talons as it flew into the night sky. The owl tossed the creature harshly against the side of a tree, shaking it and making leaves fall to the earth, then the thing fell to the ground like a sack of heavy rocks. The other creature ran away into the woods as the owl came down upon it as well. Both of the black two-headed things ran off into the dark forest, disappearing into the foliage as quick as they came.

Quiet and staring with awe and wonder, Tairren, Natalia, and Phillip lowered their weapons as they watched the massive bird fly into the top of the tree that loomed over their little camp. It rested on a large branch and just silently looked down upon them. The owl was beautiful—purest of white with golden flecks in its feathers. For a while, the three of them just stared at the bird as a sense of peace and grace came over them—chasing away the shock and terror that the black creatures had brought to them.

"This is the bird that saved my life last night," Tairren said in a low and breathless voice, slightly shaken. "He has come to save my life again..."

"Your life must be of great importance," Phillip said in a low voice as he glanced at Tairren, then back up to the bird."

"No—our lives... We are a chosen generation..." Tairren said, still watching the bird with wonder.

They became quiet and did not say anything as they became numb from all of the chaos and wonder that had just happened to them one after another. Tairren bowed his head to the bird, wanting to show his respect after it had just saved his life for the second time—as well as the lives of his companions.

Phillip and Natalia noticed what he was doing and did the same thing.

"Thank you—friend," Tairren said softly.

Tairren felt in his heart that this owl wasn't just a normal owl. But some kind of divine guardian, sent to them. Not only was this owl the most beautiful and purest of white, massive owl he had ever seen—but it seemed to speak to his heart, comforting him with loving messages.

"Do you feel that?" Tairren asked in a low and shaken voice, still looking up at the owl that sat in the quietness of the dark branches. "Do you hear words in your heart? Please tell me you do..."

"...I—feel a presence—all around me," Natalia said in a low tone, also still looking up at the angelic creature. "I feel peace all around me—like a sweet whirlwind of affection... It tells me that I must be strong—that I am strong... That I am loved—more than I could ever fathom..." Natalia's voice was low and soft with emotion.

After a moment of what seemed like hours of dwelling in the comforting presence of the overwhelming passion that lay so thickly amongst the air, the mighty bird flew off into the darkened sky. Its large white wings stretched and sailed off into the black sky, flapping in comforting pulses. They watched until they could see the white bird no more—disappearing quickly into the night sky. All three of them were left in a state of euphoria—seeming to not be worried about anything. The stress of going through such great trauma from the attacks, were not even present amongst them.

Natalia glanced at Tairren with a smile, then at Phillip who seemed to be lost in his thoughts.

"Phillip?" Natalia said in a quiet voice, awakening him from his thoughts.

His eyes were watered with small tears. He quickly wiped them away when he realized a small tear had started to fall down his cheek. He cleared his throat then looked around, tying to cover his emotion. He felt ashamed for getting somewhat emotional in front of Natalia.

"We should get some sleep," Phillip said quickly as he walked towards the fire to get his things.

Natalia looked at him strangely, wondering why his tears flowed a little and why he became so dismissive.

"I agree," Tairren said, also fetching his things while not noticing Phillip's emotions.

"What if the wolves or those things come back?" Natalia asked, following Tairren.

"They won't," Tairren said as he squatted over his satchel. "I feel we will be protected as we sleep this very night. But we will smite the fire just in case."

"Did the owl reveal to you these things?" Natalia asked, picking up her satchel as well.

"Yes," Tairren said, slightly smiling. He then walked over to the tree and put his things beneath it.

Phillip and Natalia followed, fixing up a grassy area and pallet to sleep upon.

"Tairren," Phillip finally said, breaking the silence. "Forgive me for doubting you... I now believe... It's just that everything that has been happening has never happened to me before. Forgive me for everything I have done or said that has angered you..."

Tairren was taken aback by Phillip's consideration and was somewhat touched by it. He smiled a little, then nodded his head, excepting his apology while patting his shoulder. "I too believe... If someone would've told me of these happenings a couple of days ago—I wouldn't have believed them myself."

Natalia smiled at their kind gestures as she sat down upon the cool grass beneath the tree.

"I will go to smite the fire," Tairren said as he spread his cape upon the ground.

They both nodded.

"Tairren," Phillip said again as he sat down next to Natalia, "thank you for earlier—if you would not have come with your bow and arrow—we might have been mulled to death by those wolves."

Tairren was quiet for a moment then smiled at him again. He squatted down, looking at both of them.

"You're welcome," he said while nodding his head. "I'm glad I listened to that voice in my heart... You know that still small voice—the one that will keep stirring up deep inside of you if you do not listen to it at first? I took a walk along the lake—when a voice in my heart told me to go with haste and get my bow and arrow from where I left it hanging from the saddlebag on Lilly's back. All three horses were acting strange and uneasy so that's when I rushed to the clearing—I knew something threatening was coming. Animals can sense evil... I just had this feeling of impending doom come over me..."

Tairren emptied out his leather satchel on the ground next to where he was going to sleep, then stood up.

"I'm going to the lake to fill this with water to put out the fire," he said.

"Do you want my help?" Phillip asked, beginning to get back up.

"No, stay here with Natalia. The fire is getting low and this satchel is pretty sturdy—just one satchel full will flush out the fire. I'll be safe—we'll be safe this very night. The words spoken to me by the owl revealed this to my heart..."

Phillip sat comfortably next to Natalia, watching Tairren as he disappeared into the darkness towards the lake. Phillip leaned against the tree than turned to Natalia who was now lying amongst the grass close to him. He also lay down. He placed his sword right next to him and his hands beneath his head.

"Phillip," Natalia said as she looked up into the blackness of the tree with tired eyes. "What did the owl reveal to you?"

He was quiet for a moment, then cleared his throat.

"At first I thought it was just my thoughts trying to comfort myself after everything that had just happened... But then I knew it wasn't just me—because I felt I was touched by something and it overwhelmed me... I can't really explain everything that was said—but I got this vision of a hand that was made of light—it came down and it touched my heart with tender fingers... And a voice came over me, saying, "Phillip—open up your heart unto me... For my kingdom is great and my plan for you is immense...""

Phillip became quiet for a while, laying amongst the quietness of the forest and thinking about what he had just said. A passion bubbled up in his heart that he had never felt before. His thoughts began to become clear as if he was on the brink of an awakening...

He didn't realize that Natalia had not responded to anything he had said yet, for his mind only thought of the vision he had.

"Was this light that touched me the hand of God? ...And this owl—is it not just an owl, but is it a divine creature of light that Tairren has been talking about?" he said, looking beside him at Natalia who had now fallen asleep. "This is all so unreal. I did not believe Tairren at first—but I do now—I believe... Something great is happening deep within my soul—I have never experienced before..." Phillip became quiet as a tear ran down the side of his face.

After a moment, Tairren came back with the water and put out the fire. They fell asleep quickly in the darkness as the crickets continued to chirp on. Their minds were at rest and their spirits were made whole that night. Something great watched over them as they slept that night, protecting them with a comforting wing of love. As they slept deeply amongst the quietness of the darkness, awful things lurked moments away about them, yearning to take hold of any one of them whose heart was unprotected—for the three companion's quest was great and the creatures of darkness wanted it stopped... The darkness that lurked around in the dark forest could not touch them—for they were protected by a mighty presence of light.

†

CHAPTER 15
The Whisperers in The Forest

The dull gray light of the morning seemed incredibly bright as Marrisa slowly opened her eyes. Her eyes squinted to tree tops amongst a gray sky looming over her. She sat up slowly and looked around the forest she was shrouded in. She began to become panicked as she realized where she was at. She did not see Lilith anywhere, which also frightened her. She had come to learn that not seeing Lilith was even more terrifying than seeing her all together—she didn't know where she was or what she was going to do. Marrisa stood up slowly, nervously looking around the dreary and misty forest. It was cool and moist in the forest, which sent chills up her spine. The trees were twisted and dark with massive gnarling branches hanging beneath them and the earth was littered with knotted roots, old dead leaves and large bulbous mushrooms. Random patches of grass grew here and there amongst the ground, showing the signs that very little sunlight touched the ground.

This was the way the entire south of Minslethrate appeared—dreary, cold and dark. They had come past the Great Wall of Division the day before, and ever since then Marrisa could see how drastically different everything was compared to her homeland in the northern parts. She never knew how dreadful the southern parts of Minslethrate was, and how much she missed her home and the life it possessed in the Golden Lands of Minslethrate.

Ever since Lilith had forced her into the Forbidden Lands, a strange and haunting presence had been following her. Sometimes the horrible feelings around her would be weak, and other times it would be so strong that she would just curl up into a ball upon the ground and hide her face—just crying. The insidious presence would come with whispers, shrouding her like a thick garment—and it contained no warmth. The haunting whispers would whirl through her ears like stale breezes, spreading goose-bumps across her cold skin. It would be terrifying and morbid—and felt as if she were stuck in a world of pandemonium and miles away from love or light, alone and lost amongst something full of malice and terror...

She hugged herself and rubbed her arms as she began to walk through the forest. Her long red hair hung down along her back and chest in knots with small crumbled pieces of dried leaves clinging to the frazzled strands. Her once beautiful gown was now dirty and stained with old blood and the ends were tattered and torn and soiled. Her face was smudged with grime and her cheeks were striped with dirt where she had been crying. Her right cheek bone had a green bruise on it and her bottom lip had been busted and dried blood stained it. And even though she was in a pitiful state, she was still beautiful.

They had been traveling the whole day before and her body was exhausted and terribly hungry. As they went deeper into the grim and dark Forest, the terrain became more extreme as it was bumpy and small cliffs and steep slopes and hills lay here and there. The trees grew thicker and larger further into the forest, having their massive roots and knots randomly grow everywhere, which protruded from the earth. So, with an attempt of trying to get through when they first came into the forest, the wheel of the small carriage in which Marrisa was contained in, broke, and they had to trek the rest of the way. She had plenty of times to escape from Lilith, and when she did, Lilith was always there—Lilith would always find her.

Marrisa continued to walk through the forest, wondering where Lilith had gone and thinking about everything that had been happening. She thought of Tairren and Natalia and wondered what they were doing—if they were worried about her or if they had ventured off to find her. She wondered if her father had set off to look for her, or if he even knew of what was going on. Whatever the case, Marrisa hoped someone would find her soon. She was terrified of what was going to happen and terrified of the things Lilith had told her. The things she had seen and felt within the last couple of days frightened her—and she never wanted to see or feel them again. But she knew she would have to face the unknown again, and that's what scared her most of all—knowing that she would see and feel the evil things again.

"Marrisa…," a frightening and whispering voice emanated from the shadows of the forest.

Marrisa grew frightened as she stopped in her tracks, her heart dropped in her chest and she began to breathe harder and whimper as tears built up in her weary eyes. Even though her legs ached and burned because of walking and running so much, she began to run through the forest anyways, as she knew something bad was going to happen.

"Marrisa…," the whispers came again, haunting and wicked.

"Leave me alone!" she cried out as she began to run faster, her tattered gown trailing behind her.

Marrisa began to cry as she ran. She knew that voice, and it frightened her. The dark voice came not only in her head, but it resonated from the darkness of the forest and seemed to echo in her lost heart... When the voice came many horrific whispers followed it, and then that heavy and terrifying presence came upon her.

She tripped over a large knotted root that stuck out from the dirt and fell onto her stomach, bashing her face into the ground. Grime stuck to her lips as she lifted her throbbing head. She became inundated with fear as a heavy presence came over her.

She tried to get up but something seemed to push her back down to the earth. It felt like something was sitting on her back! The heavy presence came all around her as she began to panic, choking her like thick smoke. She pushed with all of her might as she got to her knees, making the force on her back relent. She began to run again. She was afraid to look behind her, but she couldn't resist. She quickly turned her head to see what was behind her. She let out a scream as her heart dropped once again into her stomach. Chills ravaged her skin as she kept screaming. Something was chasing her and it was only a couple of feet away behind her!

It was a black creature, a little shorter than her with spiraling horns sticking out from the sides of its head. Its legs were structured like that of the hind legs of a goat and they were covered with thick black hair and it had hooves where the feet should have been. It had a bare chest, arms and hands like that of a man but a head like a goat. Its eyes were red and horrifying and it made grunting and squealing sounds as it chased after her.

Not paying any attention to where she was running, she ran right down a steep hill, and fell the rest of the way down. She tumbled down the leaf-matted slope, falling on her side in a pile of leaves at the bottom, barely missing a tree. With heavy breaths she turned to look up at the top of the steep hill, looking for the dark creature that was chasing her. She could see nothing but mist, trees and shadows. Panicking, she quickly stood up and looked all around her. She held her side as a pain shot through it, indicating that she had pulled a muscle or bruised it badly.

She tried her best to run again while holding her side, dodging low hanging branches, going through bushes and hopping over fallen, dead trees. The heavy presence relented around her so she stood still to take a breath, leaning over and holding on to her knees. The forest was now quiet and still—opposite of her heart and soul. After a quick rest and breath of cool air, she began to run again. She had no idea where she was going, but running was all she could do. She would do anything to run right into the great fields of Minslethrate, right before the castle.

Just then she felt something staring at her from her right side, so she stopped, breathing hard and slowly turning her head to where the feeling emitted from. The dark whisper came to her again, chanting her name. She began to panic once again as she could see a tall, black form standing yards away from her. It was still and cloaked in a black hooded robe, standing amongst the darkness and mist of the forest. It was completely black where the face should've been and the long sleeves and train of the robe covered the form completely. All of a sudden fear sprung up in her heart as the air around her became heavy again. She began to scream with horror as she began to run.

She ran until she could run no more, falling upon the ground and grasping for air. She began to sob as her body became numb as she looked all around herself, becoming nauseous. The black robed silhouette was gone now… She went on her hands and knees, not knowing what to do. Her mind was so afraid that she didn't even think to pray—for the light in her heart was dwindling, and she was not strong. Everything that was happening to her was driving her mad and she couldn't stand to even live anymore…

She noticed that the blue-heart pendant necklace Tairren had given her for her birthday still hung from her neck. She no longer had the necklace her father had given her—Lilith had taken it. She grabbed the blue stone that hung from the thin leather strap as she sat upon the earth. She held the blue stone tightly and began to cry. She remembered what Tairren had told her: when she felt all alone—to just grasp the pendant and just think of him… She wanted Tairren by her side more than anything, but she knew he would not be there. She seemed to have given up hope—and her faith ran very thin… She sat in the silence of the dark forest for a while, just waiting for something to happen.

"Still holding on to love?" A familiar voice said from behind her, which she loathed.

She turned around quickly to find Lilith standing over her. Marrisa quickly crawled away and sat against a tree. She put her knees up to her chest, then held onto the heart shaped pendant again, not saying anything as she looked up at Lilith with red, teary eyes.

"I am one of many," Lilith said as she slowly walked over to her. "The others just wanted to meet you," she said as a large ugly smile crept upon her white face. "…But they do not like you…"

Lilith looked dead. Her skin was white as snow, with greenish-blue rings around her large black eyes. When she smiled, her gray lips stretched and cracked and her rotting gums and teeth were revealed. Her long hair that fell upon her face was thin and lifeless and straggly. Not only did she look like death—but she smelled of it.

"Father wishes to meet you—but it appears that you won't stop running…," Lilith said in a low voice as she stood right over Marrisa, glaring down at her with those cold, black eyes.

Marrisa did not say anything as she looked up at her with her hands almost covering her eyes. She was terrified of Lilith now and everything that seemed to follow her. She couldn't take looking into her eyes anymore but she had to keep her eyes on her to see what she was going to do.

All of a sudden Marrisa began to feel as if she were having a panic attack as that heavy and terrifying presence came over her. She began to become paranoid, looking to her right, then to her left as she felt something coming upon her. Her heart began to flutter and ache and her head began to become numb. She wanted to cry but felt that she couldn't at the same time. Instead she tried to hold it in as Lilith still stared down at her.

"I give you—The Lord of Darkness," Lilith said as she stepped to the side.

Marrisa screamed a loud, blood curdling cry as the tall, black hooded thing now stood before her. It quickly came over her like a malevolence and foul-smelling black cloud as she continued to scream. She wiped and scratched at her arms and face as she could feel its tormenting presence crawl all over her like millions of relentless and cruel insects. Her body could not take it any more as she quickly leaned over to vomit. Her heart continued to beat rapidly in her ears as her body became numb. She then fell over onto her vomit, passing out with darkness upon her eyes… Then there came a loud silence.

✝✝✝

Tairren shot open his eyes—frantically awakening to another gray day. He inhaled the forest's air into his lungs and licked his dried lips as he quickly sat up, with his heart racing. The forest smelled of moist soil and fresh greens and the sounds of small running waterfalls and rustling leaves filled his ears. Slightly confused, he glanced all around him as his heart still pounded in his chest. He looked up into the dreary sky, wondering if the mysterious owl still lingered around in the forest. His eyes caught the many moving leaves that danced high above him in the darkened tree tops instead. A scream from a maiden had awakened him. He had dreamt about Marrisa that night, but he did not remember his dream—except that she was screaming...

He looked all around him again, realizing that there were no signs of Natalia or Phillip anywhere. Their belongings were gone and he was alone with only his things. He thought of the prior night and wondered if it were all another bad dream. He wondered until his eyes met the dead corpses of the slaughtered wolves. He saw the dark-gray, almost black fur from a distance and noticed that flies and bugs had begun to swarm about them. He stood up, stretched his back and legs, then bent over to gather his things. Catching the foul scent of the dead wolves, he hurried through the clearing than into the woods towards the lake.

Natalia and Phillip couldn't have left without him—they wouldn't dare do such a thing; they didn't even know the way. Tairren began to walk faster as the thought of the wolves and the strange creatures from the night came into his head once again. Chills ran through his skin as he thought of how the massive and grotesque malformed wolves had spoken to his mind— and how frightening their voices were. But the fear diminished as he knew something far greater was on his side.

He didn't know if anything horrible had happened to Natalia or Phillip. He became nervous as he thought about them—then became alarmed when screams could be heard echoing through the woods, coming from the lake. It was the scream of the maiden again, which must've awoken him earlier. Tairren ran the rest of the way to the lake with his satchel bouncing on his back and his bow and arrows in hand.

He made it to the lake, only to find Natalia screaming, then laughing as she was playfully trying to get away from Phillip. They both had their swords in hand and were out of breath. They stopped in their tracks as Tairren walked over to them.

"Good morning, my friend!" Natalia said as she lowered her small sword to her side.

"You frightened me," Tairren said with an aggravated edge, "and why didn't you waken me?"

"Forgive us, Master Tairren," Phillip said as he put his long sword into his sheath, "we only meant for you to catch up on your sleep. It is still early. The light of the day came less than an hour ago."

Tairren just nodded his head as he got his things situated on Lilly's saddle. He seemed irritated as he pulled out an apple from his satchel and took a big bite. He rubbed his arm that was still wrapped with bandages and began to scratch at it.

"Does it bother you?" Natalia asked as she walked over to him while putting her sword into her sheath.

"Yes, slightly," Tairren said, still rubbing his arm. "It's starting to itch; the pain comes and goes—but I fear it is no normal wound. Infection would be the last thing I need right now."

They grew quiet for a moment

"Tairren, what do you think those creatures were last night? Have you ever seen anything like that before?" Natalia asked.

"No," Tairren said, "I have never seen anything like those things—but they carried the same presence as those flying creatures did. They are evil and born from darkness…"

"I thought you said that the Great Wall of Division kept the evil out," Phillip said.

"Yes—it did. But I fear something far more evil is spreading upon the lands," Tairren said as he looked off onto the lake. "When the being of light came to me—it said I will see things that I have never seen before… We must be strong and vigilant."

"That frightens me," Natalia said as she looked back at his wounded arm. "I hope we will be safe—and I hope your health is well.

Tairren began to dig in his satchel again, then pulled out a large rolled up piece of paper.

"If God is for us—who could be against us?" Tairren smiled at Natalia, reassuring her. "And my arm is the least of my worries," he said as he squatted down, unrolling the paper upon the grass.

Phillip and Natalia looked down at him curiously, then squatted down as well to take a look at what he was looking at. It was a hand-drawn map of Minslethrate. Every inch of the map was detailed and labeled. It appeared old and worn but looked magnificent.

"Where did you get this?" Natalia asked in a surprised tone as she pulled her long hair out of the way, which fell onto the map as she peered closer at it.

"It was my father's," Tairren said as he took another bite of his apple, then threw the rest of it to Lilly who was grazing at the grass. "I didn't need to pull it out till now—I need to refresh my memory of the lands. It is of Minslethrate and shows every aspect of it."

"Oh look, there's my family's provence," Natalia said excitedly as she pointed at the area of the map that was labeled, "Ducre' Provence", which was accompanied by a little drawing of a manor surrounded by fields, then trees. "And look, the Forest Provence."

Amongst the Forest Provence was a small square, which had the label "Cottage of Timotheus" right next to it. Then a couple inches away from it was a little drawing of a clearing with a rosemary bush right in the center of it. Then many inches to the right was the small town of Prat, then many inches away from that was the small Kingdom of Hanon. A thin line connected the outsides of the provences which was labeled, "Weeping Road". There were also small dotted lines separating the different regions, and a drawing of a wall which separated the northern parts of Minslethrate from the southern parts.

Tairren smiled at the great detail his father had laid out on the map and became happy to find out what an explorer his father was.

"Your father was quite an adventurer," Phillip said as he leaned back on his haunches with his arms folded.

"That he was," Tairren said as he grasped the wing pendant that dangled before the map. He had almost forgotten about it until it had slipped out of his tunic.

He pointed to each part of the map, correctly pronouncing the names of each provence and briefly revealed what he knew about them.

"We are here," he said, pointing to a small area on the map that said, "Lake Iris", which was drawn out as well and sitting amongst a forest which was labeled "Forest of Old". "We need to get here, The Dark Tower of Sacrifice," he said as he led his finger to the bottom part of the map. "So, as you can see, we have a little journey ahead of us—past some random fields and woods, across the Great Wall of Division and into the Forbidden Lands, through the Black Forest, across the Black Field of Old Blood, and to the Dark Temple of Sacrifice."

Quietness came over them as the realization of how strenuous their quest was going to be, settled in their minds.

"Looks easy enough," Phillip finally said, smirking.

Both Tairren and Natalia just looked at him, while Natalia slowly shook her head. Phillip's grin slowly faded from his face as he just cleared his throat.

"Well we must get going," Tairren said as he rolled the map back up, "like I said before—it'll take us a couple of days."

Tairren threw on his cape as Natalia and Phillip did the same thing. They quickly got all of their things together, situated and fastened to their saddles—getting ready for another long horse ride. Natalia walked over to Tairren as he was digging in his satchel which now sat in one of the saddle bags.

"Tairren," Natalia said in a low tone, not wanting to catch Phillip's attention.

She had been waiting to ask Tairren about his necklace he was wearing, which seemed to be of great importance to him. She noticed his cape was new as well but she figured Moral probably had produced it for him.

"Forgive me," she said after a moment, "—but where did you get such a beautiful necklace? The pendant is wondrous. It is far more intriguing than any piece of jewelry I've ever seen."

He smiled a little as he grasped the wing shaped pendant.

"It was passed down from generation to generation in my father's family—and my mother gave it to me before I left, along with my father's traveling things." he said as he looked upon it.

"Wonderful," Natalia said as a pretty smile came across her face. "I'm thrilled you've come about these things. To hold such keepsakes are truly amazing," she said as she held the wing-shaped pendant in her hand, analyzing all of the sparkling jewels which studded the fine gold. "You must've had some wealthy ancestors somewhere up in your family tree," she said, teasingly. "And they must've been extraordinary—like this very pendant. A golden wing to mark a golden heart...," she said as she still smiled at him, looking into his dark-blue eyes. "A free soul is like a bird that flies on high with no limits," she said, letting the pendant fall back onto his chest.

Tairren wanted to share with her then of what his mother had revealed to him, about his father and his ancestors. He wanted to share everything with her and how proud and overwhelmed he was with knowing about his ancestors—that he was more than just a peasant boy. But he knew then wasn't a good time.

"Thank you," Tairren said, instead.

He tenderly took her hand to kiss it.

"You need not act that way with me, Tairren," Natalia said as she giggled.

She came near him and gave him a kiss on the side of his mouth, barely touching his lips with hers.

"I only kiss the one's I love," she said as she placed her hand on his cheek, still smiling at him.

They looked into each other's eyes for a moment, as two young companions did who truly cared for each other.

"Shouldn't we be off?" Phillip asked, appearing slightly irritated as he sat still and upright on his horse.

Natalia glanced up at Phillip then quickly went to her horse. Her cheeks turned red with embarrassment as she realized that Phillip must've been watching.

"Let's go," Tairren said as he pulled himself onto Lilly's back.

Tairren gave Lilly a quick nudge and signal with his voice, then he was off. Phillip just glanced at Natalia who didn't make eye contact with him at first. Then she glanced at him, feeling guilty for some reason. Without waiting for Natalia, Phillip got Sable to speed off right behind Tairren. Taking in a deep breath, Natalia followed.

✝

CHAPTER 16
Heavy Burdens

The marketplace was quiet and subdued as only a hand-full of shoppers walked here and there about the shops. Many shades of gray blanketed the kingdom, making the marketplace appear as a dark dream. The sky was still morbid and dreary with dark-gray clouds, and the stale breezes of the early day continued to carry on. Instead of early spring, it looked as if they were in the winter season. The kingdom seemed as if every living color was sucked from it, as well as every inch of happiness and love.

Moral sat still on her chair in the quaint little shop, just thinking. She appeared as a silent statue. People past by the shop just to take a glance at what was in it, then carried on with their business. Moral sat quietly and just softly smiled at them as they passed by every once in a while. She thought of Tairren and Marrisa, Natalia and the prince, and wondered where they were and if they were okay. But she tried not to worry about them too much, because she knew everything would be okay. Her faith was the only thing that was keeping her away from having a nervous breakdown. The strange being that came to her in the night said not to fret, not to worry...

She had a strange dream the night before, or at least she thought it was a dream. It was too unreal for it to have really happened, but at the same time, it felt so real that it had to have really happened. Everything about it felt alive: the sounds she heard, the adoration she felt, and even the smells that came all around her in her dream. It all felt so real.

Moral sat up in her chair and rested her elbow on the wooden arm rest, propping her cheek on top of her round fist. She watched the people pass by, appearing like solemn shadows in the gray breezes. She closed her eyes and thought of her dream—or maybe, the glorious visit from an angelic and mysterious creature...

✝✝✝

That night Moral was sitting at her table and drinking a hot cup of chamomile and lavender tea, drowning in a deep sadness as she thought of her son, her only son. She was overwhelmed and worried and could not sleep ever since her son had left for the Forbidden Lands. She couldn't help but think that something horrible was happening to the young adventurers. She worried that her son would get hurt out in the wilderness, or sick or even fall into the hands of death. Anything could happen to any one of them out there beyond the kingdom and she couldn't stand the thought of it.

Tears collected in her eyes and rolled down her cheeks as her mind continued to whirl with horrible thoughts of what might become of Tairren and the others. She buried her face in her hands and began to sob. Her emotions flowed out like rivers of sadness as she let them go for the first time since Tairren had left. All of a sudden, she heard a soft call of an owl as she felt a loving hand touch the top of her head.

Startled, Moira lifted her head, looking all around the small cottage. Her tears stopped flowing as her heart quickened. No one was there, but a presence could be felt upon her—a good presence. Movement in the window caught her attention. She could tell that it was something large and white. Her heart began to pound as the thought of her house being surrounded by spirits burst into her mind. She looked closer, realizing that the movement was not from any kind of frightening spirit, but from an owl that had perched on a low hanging branch right outside of the small window.

She sat still, mesmerized by the large white owl. The mighty bird was beautiful and mysterious like a dream. Messages of comfort surrounded her body and touched her heart, which seemed to emit from the owl…

"…Do not be afraid. Though they walk in the midst of trouble—He will revive them. He shall stretch forth His hand against the wrath of the enemy—and His right hand shall save them…"

All of a sudden, her sadness melted away. Right then she knew her son was okay.

✝✝✝

A slight smile came across Moral's face as she came out of her thoughts. She sat up in her chair as she noticed a woman approaching the shop. The woman was lugging around a large basket which was filled with all kinds of different things. The woman was kind of on the heavy side and she wore a red dress with a long white apron that was tied around her waist, below her great bosoms. Her hair was up and unseen beneath a white veil and her round dark face was circled by the cloth and pinned beneath her chin. By the looks of the apron and the keys that dangled by her side; she was obviously a servant and Moral recognized her to be Sora, Natalia's handmaiden. She put her basket down beside one of the tables of the little shop then exhaled, as if she had been lugging a ton of bricks.

"Hello," Moral said, greeting her frazzled customer with a smile.

"Oh, hello there," Sora said in her mild islander accent, which was filled with anxiety and sadness.

Moral noticed that she was not accompanied by a lady or lord. Sora would usually be seen following the Marchioness of Minslethrate around the marketplace, chatting and giggling with her ladyship. She usually looked happy, but that day she had a worried and saddened expression on her face. Her black eyes were like two deep wells filled with a dark sadness.

"How may I assist you ma'am?" Moral said as she stood up.

"I only need a couple jars of your wonderful sweet-spice apple preserves," Sora said in a low tone as she pulled out a pouch of coins, "the Marchioness loves it on her morning tarts."

Sora silently paid for the preserves, then placed the jars in her already filled basket. Moral watched as Sora picked up her basket with a sigh. As she went to thank Moral, the basket slipped out of her hand and everything fell out and all over the ground. The jars of preserves rolled out of the basket as the other things tumbled out.

"Oh my," Sora said in a stressed tone as she hurried to her knees to pick up the goods.

Moral rushed out from behind her table to help the frazzled woman.

"Thank you, ma'am, you are kind," Sora said as she dusted off the things before she placed them back in her basket. "Oh!" Sora grunted as she went to pick up one of the jars of preserves. The jar was broken, allowing the sweet apple to ooze out onto the ground. Sora appeared as if she were about to cry as she lowered her head, slowly shaking it with closed eyes. "Nothing good happens for me," she said.

Moral could read the stress all over her face and had a feeling it was because of Lady Natalia going off to the Forbidden Lands. Sora was always seen in the marketplace with Natalia or the Marchioness, or sometimes both; but this time she was alone.

"Don't worry yourself," Moral said as she helped pick up the rest of her things. "There is enough stress in this world to be bothered by a broken jar of preserves."

Sora didn't say anything as she still sat back on her haunches. She brought her hands to her face and began to cry.

Moral's eyes widened as she placed her hand over her mouth.

"Please don't cry madam," she said as she placed her hand on Sora's round shoulder.

"You don't understand!" Sora said in a much louder tone, "Do not tell me not to cry."

Moral became quiet for a moment. She did understand, and knew clearly how she felt.

"Ma'am… I know how you feel…" Moral finally said "And you should know that Natalia is safe…"

Sora stopped crying that instant as she looked up at Moral. Her eyes were wide as a shocked look came across her wet face.

"What did you say?" Sora said with a trembling voice, then wiped her eyes with her apron.

"I know that Natalia is okay," Moral said with a soft smile. "My name is Moral—and my son is a dear companion to The Lady Natalia—and the princess."

Sora sat for a moment, sniffling every once in a while.

"How do you know she is okay?" she finally asked.

"Well… I… I just know in my heart that she is okay; I feel it right now… The other evening, I was in a deep hour of darkness, just as you are now. My heart was aching and laden with heavy burdens because I was worried for my son—Tairren. You see, they are together, deep in the southern parts of Minstlethrate and looking for Marrisa…"

Sora was confused about everything, but realized who Tairren was and remembered that Natalia wrote that she was "in good hands" in her letter. Natalia mentioned Tairren on many occasions, and Sora knew she was really fond of him.

"But you see, something wonderful came to me in the night, and told me that they are safe. We must always know that—if we who are weary and carry heavy burdens go to Him—He will give us rest… God will sustain us…" Moral became quiet as she noticed the incredulous look on Sora's face. "Just know that Natalia is safe—she is with my son and Prince Phillip—God watches over them like a shepherd who watches over his sheep at night. When the wolves come prowling, he will be there to protect them…"

"Your faith is something we all need," Sora said as she gave Moral a smile.

She became quiet for a moment, and then stood up. Moral stood up as well, then dusted off the front of her dress.

"It's beginning to make sense. The night of the ball Natalia was acting strange, and I could tell that she wanted to tell me something. I didn't think anything of it until I found a letter from her the next afternoon," Sora said. "I've been so worried…"

"Yes, I understand," Moral said with another soft smile. "Here, take this."

Moral hurried behind her table and held out another jar of preserves.

"Oh no—I couldn't," Sora said with a look of guilt on her face.

"Go on, I insist, from one worried woman to another," Moral said with a chuckle.

"Oh, you are so kind, no wonder Natalia loves to be around you and your son—I'm sure your son is just as loving as you are."

They continued to chat for a few more minutes, which seemed to cheer up Sora. Their laughter and smiles looked to be the only sign of happiness on that gloomy day in the market-place.

"Oh, do come over for some tea and biscuits whenever you have the time," Moral said, cheerily. "I live just beyond the field—in the Forest Provence. My home is the small cottage near the creek… I'm sure I'll see you at The Spring Celebration as well—it is in a couple of days."

Sora smiled her big-toothed smile then nodded her head.

"Yes—it will be different this year, but I will be there. I must be going, the Marchioness is waiting for me and these linens," Sora said as she glanced down at her filled basket.

"If you don't mind me asking—how is the Marchioness doing? She must be a worried mess with her daughter gone and all. And I know the Marquis has been spending much time at the castle since his majesty as left for the south… She must feel so alone."

Sora glanced down at her basket again, then back up towards the scenery of the marketplace.

"She—The Lady Christianne is well, the Marchioness is strong and always has been—that's where Natalia gets it from…"

Moral just nodded as silence fell between them. She could tell that Sora wanted to say something else about the Marchioness, but chose not to.

"It was nice chatting with you, but I must go," Sora finally said as she picked up her basket. "And again, thank you so much."

Moral just smiled and nodded her head, watching as Sora quickly scurried away.

✝✝✝

Sora quickly made her way through the marketplace and past the main gate that opened to the great fields of Minslethrate. A coach was waiting for her outside the gate, with the Marchioness in it and peering out of the small window. The coachman hopped off his seat then opened the small door for Sora, allowing her to put the large basket of things into the coach.

Lady Christianne sat silently as she watched Sora get situated in the coach—she appeared like a sly cat watching its prey's every movement... The interior of the coach smelled like the pricey oils that the Marchioness practically bathed herself in, smelling of citrus and sweet basil. The oils smelled wonderful but powerful at the same time, irritating Sora's sinuses.

Sora sat across from her but did not look at her at first. After a moment Sora glanced up at her and gave her a quick smile as she nodded her head. The marchioness looked beautiful and exotic as she sat upright and proper-like. She wore a deep-blue colored gown made from the finest of fabrics and her hair was up and beneath a headdress made of pearls and sparkling blue jewels. Her light-green eyes appeared cat-like and her brown skin seemed to glow in the pale-gray light that came in through the small curtained windows.

"What took you?" The Marchioness finally asked in her islander accent as she fanned herself irritably. "I knew I should have gone with you—But I just can't stand the site of people today."

"I beg your pardon your ladyship, I was chatting with...," Sora stopped in mid-sentence, catching what she was about to say. Lady Christianne had forbid not only Natalia, but even the handmaidens from "chatting" with anyone possessing a low social status.

"With who, Sora?" Lady Christianne asked as she stopped fanning herself.

At that moment the coach gave a quick jolt as the horses pulled them off into the fields and towards the Ducre' Provence.

"With the Baron's wife's servant, of course," Sora quickly lied, looking out of the small window and watching the passing trees and the far-off slopes of the fields.

Normally she would feel bad for lying, but that day it didn't bother her at all. The marchioness had been in one of those moods that upset Sora.

Lady Christianne just rolled her vibrant-green eyes at Sora's answer.

"The Baroness and her servants are *drier* than the stale biscuits that Alexa makes," the Marchioness teased with a small chuckle. Sora chuckled as well, but it was a weak one and not the usual loud one that she would normally let out when they gossiped about someone. "Truthfully, Alexa couldn't bake well even if her life depended on it," the Marchioness added, condescendingly.

Awkward quietness came over them as Sora continued to look out of the window. The marchioness just looked at Sora who appeared as if something was bothering her.

Sora normally would be chatting with the Marchioness in a loud manner, which would be filled with laughter and mockery. But their relationship seemed to dwindle within the last couple of days. Even though Sora served the Ducre' family for many years, her feelings of Lady Christianne were back and forth. One day she would love talking with her, but the next, she couldn't bear being around her. The Marchioness was short tempered and seemed to turn on anyone whom she felt betrayed by, including Sora. Lady Christianne had changed over the years and became acquisitive, inconsiderate and greedy—loving any materialistic thing that the world had to offer and forgetting about the things that should truly be important in one's life. But the main thing that upset Sora the most was the fact that the Marchioness seemed to worry more about her wardrobe and spending money than her own daughter.

"Something is bothering you, Sora—you can not fool me," The Marchioness said quickly, becoming irritated by Sora's aloofness. She slapped her fan shut with her hand and began to tap it on her lap. "Your deportment reveals everything."

After a moment of silence and staring out of the small window, Sora finally made eye contact with The Marchioness.

"Nothing is wrong with me, my lady," Sora said, beginning to become annoyed herself.

"I can see straight through you, Sora," she said, staring coldly into her eyes now. "You know Sora—you have always been like a piece of glass—dusty, but transparent."

Sora clenched her teeth and looked out of the window again. The Marchioness was beginning to patronize her and it was hard for Sora to hold her tongue when she became greatly annoyed.

"Oh, my poor *sister*—I know something bothers you," Lady Christianne said in a much lower and teasing tone, which really got under Sora's skin.

Sora quickly looked at her, glaring her dark eyes into the lady's bright green ones.

"I am your sister when you want something but just a simple servant to you any other time!" Sora raised her voice.

"Do not use that tone with me, Sora," The Lady said, trying to control her temper. "You work for me—remember that! You will respect me! I will not have you speaking to me in that tone!"

"Your husband bought me to be your help—but then he wanted me to strictly "raise" Natalia," Sora said, emphasizing the word raise. "I don't owe you any of my respect. I owe you nothing but my tone!"

"That's right, The Marquis purchased you to be "*my* help" first—then raise my daughter! So, if you disrespect me, you disrespect my husband— you offend *me*, you offend *my* husband!" The Marchioness yelled with wide eyes. "And you know what can happen if you offend my husband!"

"Your threats don't frighten me, sister. It's been seventeen years that I have been serving under you and all these years I've been holding back— refraining from telling you what kind of person you have become! Your heart has become a cold stone. You use The Marquis to build yourself up, as if you are a queen on a golden thrown with precious jewels stuck all over you! Remember where you came from Zorrina!" Sora yelled. She couldn't contain herself anymore.

"Do not *ever* address me in that manner, servant!" The marchioness yelled as she sat on the edge of her seat, coming closer to Sora.

"*Zorrina* is your real name isn't it?! You even changed your name like you changed your heart! You seem to forget that you are not even of noble blood! You come from the same home-land as I—the same blood! We are the same, but in different clothing. Have you forgotten your father? Your father, Chief of our home island, is my father too. We are family, sisters, and you are just the daughter of a chief. The Marquis bought us both. Your beautiful face is the reason why you are his wife."

The Marchioness bit her bottom lip as her eyes watered up. Her chin began to quiver as she slowly shook her head.

"If it wasn't for me you would not be here right now—living in a beautiful manor and walking upon these beautiful lands! I wanted you with me..."

"To make my life miserable!" Sora shouted, taking her by surprise. "I am the older one and ever since we were children, I was always there taking care of you—and you still act as if you are greater than I! From the daughter of a chief to the Marchioness of Minlsethrate, you still act like you are some kind of goddess. If it wasn't for my beautiful niece, I would absolutely hate it here, working for you! I may have been poor at home, but I had my freedom!" Sora began to become emotional. "My own niece does not even know that I am her aunt! No one knows that you and I are sisters, family—and I have kept quiet all these years just for you—just to protect you and your social status! The day we left the island seventeen years ago I promised our father that I would protect you—and I have kept that promise! But you take me for granted, little sister—and always have."

The Marchioness sneered at Sora in disgust, as if she were some kind of repulsive animal—threatening her in every kind of way.

"Yes *sister*, we are family—but in everybody's eyes, including Natalia's—you are nothing but a servant...," The Marchioness said in her low and patronizing tone again as she raised her left eyebrow. "You are the smallest of all beings in all of Minslethrate. And I-do-not-pity you..."

Sora was quiet for a moment as her eyes began to become glossy with tears. It was always a rare situation when Sora became emotional—but with everything that was going on in Minslethrate, it was so easy too. She never took anything her sister said seriously—but this time her cold words slashed her heart like a knife.

"Yes Zorrina, I may be but a servant—but I will always be a far better mother to Natalia than you will ever be."

Just as soon as Sora finished her comment, The Marchioness swiftly slapped her face so hard that it seemed to echo in the small space of the coach. The Marchioness' eyes were wide and her face was tense with anger.

Surprised, Sora placed her hand on her cheek—having nothing else to say. After what seemed like hours of awkward silence, without making eye contact with the Marchioness, Sora banged on the wall of the coach behind her to signal to the coachman to stop the horses. The coach stopped suddenly, then without the help from the coachman, Sora pushed open the door to let herself out.

Lady Christianne watched as Sora began to walk away from the coach and through the grass of the wind-blown field. Her chest swelled as she breathed quickly with anger. She irritably pulled open her fan to cool herself down.

"Is everything alright my lady? We are only half-way to the manor," the coachman said with a confused look on his face as he glanced at Sora.

"Let's go," she said in a low tone as she still watched her sister trek her way towards the manor.

"But my lady…"

"Have you no ears to hear?! I said, let's-go!" she shouted as she glared at the helpless coachman.

The speechless coachman went to close the door of the coach but the lady pulled the door shut the rest of the way, slamming it. The small carriage was closed and silent now as Lady Christianne realized that she was by herself in the dim light of the coach. She was alone like she always was when Natalia or her servants weren't around. She was alone like she always was when her husband left her for weeks on end. She sat for a moment, just staring.

After a few moments, the coach gave a quick jolt as the horses began to pull it. She stared at the empty seat across from her and thought about all the things Sora had said to her. She grew angrier as she thought of the details of their argument. But then after a moment of calming down, she began to become saddened and felt somewhat regretful of everything she had said. She knew everything her sister had said was true, but she loathed hearing it. Tears swelled up in her beautiful green eyes as her bottom lip quivered. The warm tears began to become cold as they rolled down her cheeks. She cried—something she hadn't done since she left her home-lands. She buried her face into her hands as uncontrollable sobs came from deep within her belly. She refused to look out of the window towards Sora as the coach hastily flew by her.

†††

Sora stopped walking as the coach hurried past her like a harsh wind. She watched helplessly as Lady Christianne abandoned her in the middle of the massive field of Minslethrate. She began to shed tears as she stared helplessly.   She fell to her knees, burying her round face into her hands. Every emotion shrouded her body as she began to tremble uncontrollably. Strong feelings of unwanted hate towards her sister began to cover her heart like a black shroud. So many thoughts crowded her mind like fog.

Every thought of when she and her sister were young came to her. She thought of that day before her mother died from sickness—she promised her mother that she would always take care of her baby sister. She thought of all the times when they were children, she would run to pick her little sister up when she would fall and scrape up her knees. She would hold Zorrina in her arms and comfort her like a mother would. She thought of all the times when she, herself was hurt—and her sister never came... Zorrina never came to her side. She thought of that day when her father sold them to Lord Fernund—how she promised her father that she would always look after her younger sister.

It seemed to her that she gave up everything for her sister—like she had always done. She thought of Natalia, and how beautiful she looked when she was born—how then she vowed to always look after Natalia—to protect her and look after her like she was her own daughter. And she kept her promises, all those times—giving up everything for her mother, her younger sister, and her niece. But she was never thanked for giving everything up for her family. She was taken for granted like she always had been. Sora was a strong person—but sacrificed herself for the ones she loved—even when they didn't appreciate her or love her back... She truly loved her sister but it was so hard to feel it sometimes when she treated her like the dirt she walked on.

Sora looked up to the coach as it quickly made its way further from her, appearing smaller and smaller as it went up and down the rolling slopes of the field. Soon she was all alone, and felt like the only person on the earth. The sky taunted her with its dark-gray clouds and the breezes brushed at the tall grassy slopes which reached miles around her in all directions. Everything around her seemed so sad, so vulnerable, and so miserable—and had been that way since the princess was taken. It seemed as if something morbid and evil was slowly creeping upon Minslethrate, overruling the kingdom, leaving everyone in a state of sadness and anger. Those dark feelings felt like uninvited guests—silent but bold.

Sora looked down at her knees, noticing small flowers all around her. One would never notice the small flowers right away because of the persistent, morbid weather. The small white blooms seemed to reach out to her amongst the thick grass which choked them. She picked one, analyzing it, noticing how beautiful it was even amongst the darkness. Just then she remembered what Moral had told her earlier that day in the market-place.

"...If we who are weary and carry heavy burdens go to Him... He will give us rest..."

It repeated in her head like rippling waters—soothing and rhythmic. She began to think of herself as if she were that small bloom, being choked by everything and everyone around her. She knew that she was a strong person, like that small bloom against the thick weeds around it. She had to stay strong and continue to live strong. She felt that if she were to fall victim to darkness, she would never be able to care for her younger sister or her niece at all. It would be better to lift up the fallen after being knocked down then to just stay fallen. Sora lifted the bloom into the air and let the soft winds carry it away—like her burdens. She imagined all of the hardships that she had ever went through in her life—was in that bloom, and she let them all go.

She lowered her head and began to pray—doing something she had never done before. She remembered the times when Natalia brought the subject of God up to her, telling her many things that Tairren had revealed to her about the God of Light. She even thought of the things Moral had told her earlier that afternoon. She cried out to that God whom was revealed to her—and she lifted her arms to the dark sky and poured out her heart to him. After many moments, her cold and sad heart began to lighten up, feeling like the warm barley bread she would bake for Natalia—coming right out of the oven. Even though the cold darkness augmented so strongly around her, her heart began to beat with a soft, warm glow... But it was the darkness around her that made her warm skin crawl.

†††

At that same moment, across the vast lands of Minslethrate, in the southern parts, King Julpen and his men had finally made their way to the clearing of Lake Iris. They looked closely around the lake and its clearing in search of any clue that would lead them to the missing princess or the where-a-bouts of the prince and lady.

"Its head was knocked clean off," Sir Hawkington said as he held up a decapitated wolf's head. "No doubt by a well-sharpened sword—the edge of its flesh is smooth and not tattered."

The wolf-head's eyes were large and black and its tongue hung out like a limp piece of body tissue. The head was swarming with flies and stunk unbearably. Sir Hawkington gave it one last look then tossed the ghastly head towards its stinking body.

"They must've come past here," King Julpen said with an unsettling look on his face as he swatted at some flies. "By the looks of that charred spot upon the earth, they must've made a fire—then got attacked by a pack of wolves."

"Yes, Sire," Sir Hawkington said as he brought his large and callused hand to his bearded chin. "And the blood upon these wolves don't look too old. It seems they must've gotten away unharmed—and it had to be more than one person here—it is unlikely that one soul could have taken on a pack of wolves... Even if he had a bit of luck, the chances of survival are low—but it seems as if luck is all they have..."

They continued to look around the small clearing and near the banks of Lake Iris. They noticed horse-tracks upon the sandy bank of the lake, indicating that more than one person was accompanied by a horse. They then decided to take a short rest, refilling their canisters with the fresh lake water and stretching their limbs.

"We must make a camp soon, Sire, the night comes soon," Sir Hawkington said as he took a swig of some water."

"We'll continue south for a little while longer, then make a camp. The wolves may come back here in the night," King Julpen said as his eyes wondered across the rippling lake. The lake was calm and dark.

"Yes, Sire," Sir Hawkington said as he rubbed his hand over his bald head.

He made his way to the other men who were sitting and talking amongst each other. They all appeared weary and insensible, like drained shadows. Sir Hawkington announced to them what their plan was and to get themselves ready. The men got up to get their things together, then they were off to make their way further towards the south.

✝

CHAPTER 17

The Book, The Tree and The King

As the hidden sun made its slow path across the sky, Lord Fernund paced back and forth in the dimly lit study-chamber of the castle. Many thoughts passed through his head as he dwelled on the kingdom's current state. He hoped that his daughter and the princess were safe and found—and that King Julpen would return back to the kingdom safely. Lord Fernund already held the stress of the kingdom on his shoulders while the king was away, and he didn't think he was mentally ready for anymore bewildering uncertainty.

He had just come home from a long journey of selling and buying goods a couple of days prior and was now in a precarious situation. He was the Marquis of Minslethrate by noble blood and a very wealthy business man—he had no idea how to rule a kingdom… The people of Minslethrate respected him greatly because of his blood-line and the large amount of money and land he possessed.

The Ducre' family was very powerful and wealthy and one of the richest families in Minslethrate. But even though he was just a wealthy business man and traveler, he wanted to do something to help the king and the Kingdom of Minslethrate—even if that was to be a temporary sovereign. But impermanent is what Lord Fernund hoped it was.

"Anxiety in a man's heart weighs it down—but encouraging words makes it glad," a low and kind voice said from behind Lord Fernund. It was Master Odwa.

The old man smiled lightly amongst his long white beard. He was hunched over slightly and walked with his hands behind his back. His long white beard went to his waist and his glistening white hair was topped with a chaperon hat. The dark-blue fabric of the hat was piled high on his head which shadowed his face. His long dark robes dragged on the tiled floor and seemed to just hang from his small frame.

"And what would those words be, Master Odwa," The Marquis said as he turned towards the old man.

"…Strength. I see strength in your eyes. Love—I see love in your heart. Love is light—light is God." The old man said as he walked towards Lord Fernund.

Master Odwa was old and frail and kind. His words were always filled with knowledge and uplifting kindness. And even though he was ancient, his senses were like that of a young man.

Lord Fernund nodded at his answer, then looked out of the massive windows which looked out to the castle gardens.

"It is strange how during these troubling and dark times—that even the smallest glimpse of light yearns to exists—like a small flame in the darkest of night," Lord Fernund said, still looking out into the gardens.

"He uncovers deep things out of darkness, and brings the shadow of death to light...," Master Odwa said as he placed his frail white hand on Lord Fernunds shoulder.

Lord Fernund turned to the old man, looking into his old gray eyes.

"How do you stay so positive amongst these uncertain times—as if no bad can happen? Your tenacious words never falter. The clouds out there in the sky grow thicker and darker at every growing moment and it is as if you do not see it," Fernund said, looking away from the light-filled old man. "Can you not see what is going on in this kingdom—in this world? Can you not see the state of darkness that we all are in? What do you know that I do not?"

Master Odwa was quiet for a moment, then looked out of the great windows beside Lord Fernund. The view of the garden was grim, but beautiful—like a winter's afternoon. They both stood for a moment, viewing the nature like a mysterious painting.

"Such a man will not be overthrown by evil circumstances. God's constant care of him will make a deep impression on all who see it. He does not fear bad news nor live in dread of what may happen, for he is settled in his mind that the God of Light will take care of him. That is why he is not afraid—but can calmly face his foes," the old man said in a low and peaceful tone.

Just then a blue bird perched on a marble statue that stood near the window. The vibrant blue color of the bird stood out amongst the gray atmosphere like a blotch of blue color on a shadowy painting.

"Do you understand Lord Fernund?" the old man asked, watching the bird.

Lord Fernund was just quiet.

"Do you see that blue bird perched on the statue?" Master Odwa asked, standing still with his hands placed behind his back.

The bird flew from the statue to the ground, pecking at something in a twitching motion. It hopped around the earth a couple of times, pecked at it some more, then flew off into the sky—free spirited with no worries of that gray day.

"This bird—it does not sow, nor reap, nor gather into barns and yet the Father of Light feeds it… Are you not of more value than it?" Master Odwa glanced at him; his countenance did not seem as stern and anxious as it did when Master Odwa first arrived into the room. "The stress that you carry on your shoulders, Marquis, should not destroy you… Do you think that the God that takes care of that blue bird cannot take care of your worries? Do you think that our God of light that cares for that small blue bird, will not take care of our kingdom—or us?"

Lord Fernund glanced at Master Odwa again, pursing his lips.

"True faith is so strong," the old man said, "like a mighty river. Nothing can stand in its way—not even the highest mountain or deepest ocean… Faith is that small flame you mentioned—that yearns to burn even in the darkest of night… Faith is my secret. That is why those dark clouds do not fluster me—that is why I am not frightened by the current situation that the kingdom is in… Come with me Marquis," the old man said as he silently began to walk away with his hands still behind his curved back. "I shall show you something that should never be kept a secret."

The Marquis watched the old man as he walked away, but then began to follow him. They walked quietly through the dim halls of the castle to the great library. There was no one around the dark and gloomy halls. Usually the castle would be bursting with busy servants but that day the castle was dead. The stained-glass windows did not pour in the colorful light of the day and even the stones of the castle were not as bright as they would be on a normal day; the gloominess of the castle colored them dark. Everything seemed dead, as if the world and everything upon it had changed. But the old man seemed to be the only light in the dark castle. Dead and silent was the atmosphere all around them. The only noises were that of the sounds of their footsteps bouncing off of the cold stone walls and the crackle of the torches they passed.

They entered into the grand library, passing through a great archway. The magnificent archway was guarded by two statues which stood on both sides of the library entrance. The marble statues were tall and elegant and appeared to be scribes, looking intensely into the large books that they held. Walking into the library was like walking into a whole other world in the castle. The ceiling of the massive chamber was tall and constructed of beautiful arches. The arches went so high that they almost vanished into the tops of the now darkened chamber. Many different sorts of books consisting of many different sizes lined the walls and rested on tall ornamental book shelves. The massive walls contained beautiful balconies which were lined with many more books and finely crafted book shelves. The large candelabrums that hung from the ceiling were not lit, and silently dangled like giant spiders from thick cords.

The only sources of light were that from random lit torches that stuck out from the walls and from the soft gray light that was filtered in through the massive stain-glassed windows. They stood tall, the beautifully crafted windows, directly across from the entryway of the library, consisting of many warm-colors. The image of a great leafless tree was crafted in the central window. The span between the entryway and the windows was vast, seeming to go on forever. Lord Fernund silently followed Master Odwa towards the attractive windows, seeming to be transfixed by its colors—especially the magnificent tree that stretched out its jagged limbs. The tree stretched its leafless branches all throughout the glass, sectioning off the many different colored pieces. The tree had two main arms that stretched out from both sides and a central trunk that went from the roots of the tree to the tops of the window. If the sun-light were to shine through it, one would be blown away by the image of a great jagged tree with mighty arms, shrouded by the colors of warm amber and golden light. The colors would have shown through brightly, flooding the library with a soft orange glow and would pour onto a small table which held a large book.

"Do you know what this is?" Master Odwa said in a low voice as they approached the small, tall standing table.

The table sat in the center of the large central window and had a large book sitting on the top of it. The book appeared to be ancient and worn. The book's cover was blank and the old pages were bound in old brown leather.

"It is a book," Lord Fernund said, staring down at the unattractive thing.

He did not look impressed or interested.

Master Odwa was quiet as he placed his frail white hand on the dark-brown cover.

"This, Marquis, is not just any book. This relic contains the secrets of life... This book contains words of truth—these words are what makes faith grow and the flame of the heart to become a great fire—if you allow it to do so. This fire will become stronger than any light." The old man began to become slightly excited as he spoke. "This is the Legendary Book of

Light," he said as his slanted, old gray eyes sparked open as if he had electricity running behind them.

Lord Fernund quietly came closer to the book, examining it as if he was in disbelief. The book did not look exquisite or important at all, and looked rather unsightly compared to the more attractive books that sat on the shelves all around them.

"I do not know much about this book—but I imagined it to appear more powerful than this," Lord Fernund said as he slowly opened it.

The opened book released the scent of ancient, stale pages. The book creaked slightly as he split the book in the center. The pages were thin and of the color of golden wheat and the words were old and hand-written. The writing was not blotchy or poorly written, but neat and perfectly spaced out, perfectly aligned.

"Power is not in its appearance—but in its message," Master Odwa said as he pointed to the ancient Minslethratian writing that covered the old pages. "Power is not the book—but rather what will happen when you dwell on its words. This mysterious book was written in two parts by many great men. The first half is called the Ancient Light and the second half is called the New Light. The Ancient Light was written by many great prophets and leaders about their righteous walk in life and the laws of light that they followed. The New Light was written about the Great King of Light and his existence and walk upon this earth—it teaches how to live a righteous life—and how the blood of Christ, the Great King of Light, saves us…"

The words in the book were old and unrecognizable, used by the ancient ancestors of Minslethrate.

"Many years ago, during the rule of the late King James, I assisted his majesty, as well as many eager scribes, in the production of the numerous copies of this book," Master Odwa said as he gently rubbed his old hand across its smooth old pages. He then slowly closed it, doing the same thing to the rough leather cover. "It took the scribes many years to translate this book—and after it was done, the copies of the book were built." Master Odwa paced a little as he spoke, with his hands clasped once again behind his curved back. "You may have been too young to remember this, but these glorious copies were burnt in great angry fires—by the late King James' wife—Queen Karnidge, after he died."

Master Odwa glanced at the Marquis every now and then as he spoke.

"I vaguely remember... I spent most of my young life at the manor—my father had me sheltered most of my life," Lord Fernund said in a low tone, as if he were ashamed.

"Aye, Marquis," he said with raised eye-brows, "you would have been the same age as his majesty, King Julpen. I was a young man, about the same age as King James, and was there assisting his majesty every step of the way... I was here in the castle when King James died... He was a mighty king and friend. And I was here, when her majesty, Queen Karnidge, took the crown... She had me imprisoned and beaten during her reign. My life began to hang on by a thread during those times—but my faith and heart beat fierce and free. She tried to smite the light within my heart—her majesty wished to suffocate my soul... So, during her short five years of her reign, I was imprisoned for my strong beliefs. You see, Marquis, she could not break me—the light within me was too strong and I was protected. I had faith in my God, the great God of Light who could move mountains—and still does...

"I still assisted the young prince Julpen as he snuck deep within the jail-cell chambers of the castle to see me—to give me a drink of water and bread to eat." As Master Odwa spoke, he looked up into the beautiful stain-glass window. "God put it in my heart—I wanted so strongly for the prince to be influenced by His words—and that he did...

"When King James died, I instructed the young prince to bury this book deep within the castle gardens—and he did—to hide the book from the wicked queen. I remember so vividly how a being of light came to me the eve of King James' death—and informed me that Queen Karnidge would begin the burnings of the books that following morning. The being of light told me to instruct young Julpen to put the original book into a small chest and bury it beneath a certain tree deep in the castle gardens. For five years this book rested beneath the earth, and after the death of Queen Karnidge, we dug it up—and had it restored..." A small smile crept over the old man's face.

"It is an intriguing story indeed—but why do you tell me this?" the Marquis asked, looking at the old man.

"I tell you this so that you can see how strong faith is. This book has been through many periods of devastation—and still you see it here, right before your eyes. This book is meant to be spread—like fresh and living water amongst a dry field. These fields are so thirsty for a drink—and dying. These fields are men and this living water is God...," the old man said with passion in his eyes. "This book is the very word of God. This book is a constant reminder that the Great King of Light is the light of the world...

"During those black days when Queen Karnidge burned the many copies of this book, as well as innocent light-loving people—she was fooled. You see, many hidden copies traveled out, away from Minslethrate and her evil grasp... Those copies were carried by mighty men who traveled to great cities like Troaaz and Masedonnia, which lay on the boundaries of far off lands—also to nearby kingdoms like Hanon. Those copies are planting seeds in the hearts of man...

"And strangely I was fortunate, only imprisoned and beaten and not burned to death like the many innocent people of those days... My life was spared—by the mighty hands of God! I was sentenced to death after I was imprisoned for those many years. I still remember how the queen told me that she wanted me to know that I helped kill the innocent people by helping in the production of this book. That is why she only had me imprisoned—so that I would be constantly told by her every day, how many people were burned, how many people died because of me. Then after five years of this emotional torment, I would be burned myself. She told me that she had won... But you see—she has not. My God has won! Yes, people died—but the faith they dwelled on opened a door for them to live in constant light... Queen Karnidge strangely became deathly ill after five years and died.

"So, you see, this faith is so strong, that even the darkest hands of evil cannot smite it... The God of light is so magnanimous that even in the midst of darkness—he will reveal something that must be made known—just to remind us of his greatness..." Master Odwa grew quiet for a moment as he watched Lord Fernund go into subtle thoughts.

Lord Fernund was still quiet, turning to the old man. "I understand," Lord Fernund said as he continued to peer down at the old book. After a moment of silence, he looked back up to the stain-glass and gazed at the mighty tree. "You, Master Odwa, are a great man... And I am pleased to know that our king has been influenced by such a mighty man of our God of Light."

"It is the God of Light—who influences me," Master Odwa said, looking back at the old book.

"There have been many insidious acts that have attacked this castle and our kingdom," Lord Fernund said in a low tone, "they are relentless and yearn the day when all of man will submit to darkness... There have been so many attacks by shadowed spirits that it seems that his majesty should have gone mad. But now I know why—because our king is blessed."

"His majesty is truly blessed, but his heart still continues to become shrouded by sadness and silent anger," Master Odwa said. "Darkness still continues to cover his heart. The darkness will try to devour what it is intimidated by. Over the years I have consoled him—but his faith is still growing and his spirit is still mending from his devastating childhood. One must be vigilant and steadfast—strong-hearted and true. One must have total faith in the God of Light. Because you see, darkness and evil can become so strong, that it will deceive you and inundate you. One must be strong… The light in your heart must be strong and must be kept full of His precious oil…"

Master Odwa walked to the window, placing his old hand upon the base of the tree on the stained glass. The pieces of glass were colored brown and black, imitating the colors of tree bark.

"But there is good news amongst all of this darkness," Master Odwa said, glancing at Lord Fernund. "Do you know the legend of the Great King of Light?" the old man asked. Lord Fernund stayed quiet, just watching Master Odwa.

"Many ages ago, before the ancestors of King Julpen ruled, before King James and his ancestors—there was a great king. This king is the Great King of Light who is mentioned in the book of light. His name was, and still is, King Yehoshua…"

Master Odwa's eyes lit up again, sparkling with zeal. The mention of his name seemed to brighten the room somehow even though it was still dull. Lord Fernund became strangely enthralled, awestruck by the mention of the ancient king's name.

"Yes, such a holy and grand mystery—his name is filled with power and living water!" Master Odwa smiled as he slowly raised his hands into the air, looking upwards. "King Yehoshua was a mighty king—born from light and made flesh. It is the greatest legend of all mankind—born from truth. It is the greatest story and the most brilliant of light. This king was not a king of wealth or born into royalty—or a king of land or precious metals and jewels. This king was a king of men, sent down from the Great Kingdom of Light, to save men. This king was made flesh by the words spoken by the God of Light. This king named Yehoshua was God made flesh, and still is God. He was born into poverty by a young common maiden whose womb was blessed by the God of Light. As a young boy he was a prodigy, speaking influentially to wise men.

"He grew up to be a mighty man. He led people by the hundreds, casting mighty words amongst them and healing them out of sickness and casted out unclean spirits. He was so influential that he became king. He was good and still is and endures our sins and burdens forever. His love for the people was so strong that one day he died for them. You see, where there is good, there is also evil. There was a band of old believers who worshiped Minslethrate's ancient pagan goddesses—there were many who still followed the old ways of darkness. They did not want Yehoshua to be proclaimed as king, for they loathed him.

"They rose up against the king to rid of him and the light, yearning for the darkness of the old ways. You see, the king saved the ancient people of Minslethrate from evil and deception. But the followers of the old ways came against him and forbid him from being king. There was a great war and the king was betrayed by one of his twelve nights—one of his brethren, then taken by the band of bad men. The king gave up his life for the people so that they would all be forgiven—so that everything evil would be forgiven, if asked to be.

"We are all forgiven, every one of us—by the blood that poured from his body when the evil men had him killed. We are forgiven of the darkness that men are doomed to keep, the sin that dwells in our hearts and the destruction that we create. We are forgiven by the shed of his innocent blood—for the God of light loves us so much, that he gave up his only son, the Great King Yehoshua, to die on that lonely tree for our evil ways. Darkness thought that he had won—but light won the moment King Yehoshua had been born. You see, Yehoshua was placed upon the earth just to save us all—and that's what the New Light of the book is about."

"This mighty tree on this glass is so important because it represents the tree that the Great King of Light was sacrificed on... The people who condemned him brought him to the south where people were brought to be killed as a punishment long ago—to endure the greatest of all punishment. This place was called Skull Hill—which lies before the Black Field of Ancient Blood. On top of Skull Hill is a great tree with stretched out limbs. The king was nailed to it and hung there to die."

Lord Fernund sat in a state of awe, listening to one of the greatest legends he had ever heard.

"But there is life…" Master Odwa said with another small smile. "King Yehoshua rose from the grave his people had produced for him—and lives in the light-soaked hearts of his people. Legend has it—that if your heart is soaked with his light—you will become part of his kingdom in that Great Kingdom of Light in the sky…"

Lord Fernund looked saddened, as if he was ashamed of himself. He did not know how to comment to this mighty legend.

Master Odwa studied his face, and felt as if he should ask the Marquis a bold question. "Let me ask you something, Marquis… In your heart, deep inside your soul, deep inside the crevasses of your being—can you find peace there? Do you feel the light I have been talking about, within you? Do you know the legend of which I speak?"

The Marquis looked back at the old man, slightly shocked and somewhat embarrassed. No one has ever been so bold to ask him of his inner thoughts or questioned his faith. But he knew this question was important to be asked. He did not have faith—in anything but himself. He only knew his wealth and the importance of it in not only in his life, but his family's. He was taught to love wealth by his father, he was taught always that respect was given to the wealthy—and that wealth was power… The Marquis was quiet for a moment, then slowly shook his head.

"No," Lord Fernund said with a somber look on his face.

"Will you allow me to bless you?" Master Odwa asked in his kind old voice.

Lord Fernund was quiet for another moment, then finally shook his head yes. He wasn't sure at first, but he saw the passion in the old man's eyes and the kindness and holiness that poured from him—and he wanted to become more like that. Anger and sadness always filled his heart more than anything else—and he only knew greed. He was the wealthiest man in all the lands of Minslethrate, but still the knowledge of this didn't seem to fill his heart. He was not happy. He loved his family but didn't really acknowledge them. He didn't know his daughter anymore because he barely saw her. His wife, the beautiful Christianne, was almost non-existent in his life as well. He felt ashamed of himself as he realized that he had taught her unknowingly to only love wealth and idols—to only love herself.

At that moment Master Odwa placed his warm hand on the Marquis' head as he closed his eyes. He spoke mighty words over him and prayed a prayer that would change his life—forever.

†

CHAPTER 18
Silver Stones and Dead Bones

The three young travelers had been riding all day and assumed it was about noon, but still didn't truly know the time of the day because of the relentless dark-gray clouds. They rode over many hills and rivulets, through small forests which would have been beautiful in the sunlight, and amongst thick, tall grasses that erupted with small birds and insects as their horses galloped through it. The things to see were lovely and never been seen before by Natalia or Phillip.

The ride had become strenuous and uncomfortable and they were ready for a break. They soon stopped in another small forest that consisted of small ponds and tall, thin pines. The forest was dark and gloomy like everything else because of the ebony clouds above them. They found a perfect resting spot near an inviting pond which was among many full minsleberry bushes and flowering trees. They filled their water-pouches to the brim and let the horses become refreshed by the pond's clear, cold water. They snacked on the foods they brought with them. Their small supply of food was becoming slim, so they mainly ate from the luscious minsleberries and from the nuts and herbs they found amongst the earth.

"Look through there," Tairren said as he drank from his water-pouch, pointing.

Both Natalia and Phillip glanced through the trees to where Tairren had pointed. They barely noticed the structure. Far off in the distance, through the forest, between some trees and over a vast field, they could see the Great Wall of Division. The wall seemed small from where they looked, but they could tell that it was mighty.

"We are almost to the half-way point!" Natalia squealed as she stood up.

She squeezed the berries she was holding as excitement got the best of her.

Phillip stood up as well, peering through the forest and at the great wall.

"You might want to sit and rest yourself—we still have much of a ride," Tairren said, then popped a dark-purple berry into his mouth. "We are resting in the ends of the Forest of Old—but it is the Black Forest which comes next..."

They sat for a moment quietly, thinking of the stress that would soon come to them again.

"So that is the great wall," Phillip said, breaking the silence. "Very impressive; I can tell from here that it is a mighty structure.

Phillip sat down against a rock, stretching his legs upon a bed of dead leaves.

"I am very happy to see it," Natalia said as she sat down as well, noticing the squished berries on the palm of her hand. Her face turned sour as she wiped the dark-blue juices of the berries from her hand with some dried leaves.

"Yes, we are near the half-way point towards the south. That great wall is the line that splits the north from the south in Minslethrate—dividing the Golden Lands from the Forbidden Lands. The legendary Great King of our ancestors built that wall to keep evil away. The wall is ancient, but like an old mountain—strong and majestic, just like its creator." Tairren became quiet for a moment. His emotions slightly changed when he mentioned the legendary Great King. "But danger lies ahead of us. Right past that wall is the Black Forest and the beginnings of the Forbidden Lands, which is full of dark spirits and evil creatures that should not even exist. The Forbidden Lands are forbidden because it consists of everything that defies the God of Light's laws."

"Like the creatures we were attacked by last night," Phillip added.

"Yes—and those creatures should not have been on this side of the wall. Darkness seems to be spreading towards the North, slowly but surely allowing evil to infiltrate these parts. Those creatures we have seen are but a taste of what we will witness."

Natalia sat quietly, wondering how they were going to get through the uncertain quest that lay before them. They were running out of food and they were becoming weary and anxious. They were becoming tired and their bodies ached and their stomachs squirmed with hunger. Their spirits seemed as if they were stretched thin, ready to brake. There weaponry was not only inadequate but very light and not fit for any kind of mighty fight. Their weapons were fine for the rescuing of Marrisa from Lilith, if that was the only thing their quest consisted of, but with all of the dark surprises that they were running into, they were beginning to doubt them.

"What are we to do if we are attacked again by many of those black creatures?" Natalia asked, worried.

"Fight like you've never fought before," Phillip said, looking deep into her eyes.

"Natalia—we will fight, with all of our might, we will fight—with the thought of our purpose in the back of our minds," Tairren said with an uplifting smile. "Never forget our purpose—never forget about Marrisa and these lands—the ones we love. That is our purpose. We have something powerful on our side... Do not forget Malakh's words."

Natalia slowly nodded her head as she pressed her lips together. She did not get upset but she felt like crying—especially when Marrisa's name was mentioned.

"I will," she said with a soft smile, "and from here the wall looks manageable, but I know it will probably be somewhat of a stressful task," Natalia said, continuing to look at the wall far off in the distance, wishing that they were already on the other side.

"If we take the path my father and I took many years ago, we should be unseen by the guards."

"Let's hope so, Master Tairren," Phillip said, looking back towards the wall.

After a short rest, they were off again. They rode until they hit the edge of the forest, which ended abruptly right before a vast and clear field. The field had nothing but grass and stone upon it. There were no trees, hills, or large bushes—nowhere to hide even if they wanted to go straight across to the wall. The wall was becoming more and more massive the closer they got to it. They could now see that the wall had towers upon it that were spread out across the top of the wall, which must have been watch towers; and straight below the towers on the base of the wall were doors, which must have been entrances to them. And between every tower stood a tall statue that resembled a guard, stretching his right arm towards the north as if they were signaling any oncoming person to stop. The wall was actually beautifully built and magnificent and intimidating, it stretched far from east to west. The bottom of the wall became lost in the forests beyond the field, but the top of the wall loomed over the trees.

"We will follow along the outskirt of the field on the edge of the forest but behind the shrubbery and trees," Tairren reminded them as he continued to stare towards the wall, looking for any kind of movement. "Do not go into the field for anything, the field is too clear and will reveal us, even from afar. If one of the many guards spot us, our journey will grind to an abrupt halt."

"How strange though, I don't see any one," Natalia said. "Not even anyone patrolling the field or the edge of the forest."

"Are you sure the wall is guarded?" Phillip asked, in a low tone.

"Yes—it is one of the many laws of Minslethrate—no one is to pass without a marked letter from the king himself. Whoever passes unlawfully or attempts to pass will be ceased and arrested for treason."

"Look," Natalia interrupted, pointing to a seemingly small pillar of smoke that came from the top of one of the towers.

"Curious," Tairren said in a low tone.

"And the smoke is hard to see because it mingles with the dark clouds," Phillip said. "There is another tower smoking as well."

The prince was right. They spotted at least three smoking towers. The smoke would be hard to see at first glance among the morbid clouds; but after looking for a while, they could tell that the pillars of smoke were rather large.

"I don't like the look of this—where there are strange fires, there is always a fire starter." Tairren said as he got Lilly going in the direction towards the great wall.

Phillip and Natalia followed Tairren on Orchid and Sable, nervously watching the wall for even the slightest of movement.

As they got closer to the wall, creeping along the edges of the forest, they noticed that there were fires in the windows of the smoking towers. And as they came closer, the wall got taller. Soon they were yards away from the massive wall. They could now see how nothing would be able to get across the wall—it seemed even taller than the castle in the Golden Lands. They sat for a moment on their horses, just listening and watching and taking in the magnificence of the wall. They still didn't hear or see anyone though. As great as the wall was, it seemed that it should have had hundreds of soldiers standing guard. It seemed that there should be guards rushing to get the fires out or guards patrolling the grounds of the wall. They saw nothing but the stillness of the uncertain structure. Everything was too quiet and dead. They noticed that not only were there the tall statues that stood on top of the wall, but there were winged gargoyles that sat still and hauntingly on random spots of the wall between the massive stone guards. The winged statues were frightening and would make any traveler uncomfortable.

"What is that?" Natalia asked, startled.

She pointed to something way off in the field that looked like a heap of shiny large stones. The stones looked smooth and gleamed a little. They soon spotted other piles of the same shiny substance that lay before the great wall in the field.

"I don't know," Tairren said. "You stay here, Natalia, on the edge of the wood, Phillip and I will go see. There doesn't seem to be anyone around this area of the wall."

They quickly rode off towards the mounds that lay in the grass. Natalia shook her head a little, annoyed that she was left alone in the safe haven of the trees like a child. She got Orchid going a couple of yards into the field so that she could get a better look at what they were going to do. Tairren and Phillip slowly and vigilantly made their way towards the silver mounds, searching on top of the wall and around them with their eyes for anything suspicious.

"I feel like we are being watched—something does not feel right in the air," Tairren said in a low tone as they got closer. "It is far too quiet."

The clouds in the sky seemed to become darker, and the winds picked up. It looked as if it were about to storm.

"It seems as if those statues are watching us," Phillip said, looking up towards the top of the massive wall.

Chills went up Tairrens spine and across his skin as his heart began to race. He hopped off Lilly's back as soon as he noticed that the mounds were not shiny silver rocks at all—but armored bodies! Both Tairren and Phillip ran towards the nearest body, realizing why it was so quiet and why there were no signs of guards anywhere—they were all dead. There were many dead guards lying sporadically around the field, along with their horses. It looked as if there was some kind of battle—and the guards of the wall were defeated horribly. It seemed as if some of the guard's armor was torn off—with their bloody chests revealed—and looked as if their hearts were torn out!

They both huddled over the dead guard. Tairren pulled off the guard's helmet as a plethora of flies came flying out. The man seemed to be dead for a while but not that long, maybe a day at the most. His face was pale with small signs of decay and his eyes were a haunting, pale-blue—wide and staring. Tairren wondered what the last thing that helpless soul had witnessed was.

"We have to get away from here," Tairren said looking all around them and up towards the top of the wall.

He noticed that the gargoyle statues were—gone!

All of a sudden, the familiar sounds of loud, blood-curdling screeches could be heard. Panic shot through Tairren's body as he remembered the flying black creatures from the first night Marrisa had gotten captured. Tairren quickly pulled out one of his arrows and Phillip pulled his sword from its sheath, both ready for whatever was going to come at them.

"What's happening!?" Natalia yelled from her spot near the forest.

They all looked up into the sky where the screeches were coming from. They could hear the blood-curdling screeches and growls but they could not see anything but dark clouds above them.

"Run," Tairren said, still watching the sky.

They both ran back towards their horses. But as soon as they got on their horse's backs, Natalia let out a loud scream. Tairren and Phillip watched in horror as Natalia was yanked from her horse and up into the dark air. A large flying creature came out of the forest and swooped down, grabbing her like how a hawk grabs its prey.

"Natalia!" Tairren screamed out as they both raced their horses towards her.

Tairren got a flash-back of the night Marrisa was taken from him right before his very own eyes. Seeing his companions in danger tore at his heart. Anger flashed through him as he heard Natalia's cries for help.

Natalia screamed and fought, trying to swing her sword at the flying, black creature. All she could do was blindly swing the small sword, trying to get the fiend to drop her before they were too high up into the air. The creature would not relent and its grasp on her only got tighter. She kicked her legs, but the creature stopped her by wrapping its long bony tail around her legs tightly. The smell of burnt flesh emitted from the thing, burning her nostrils. Her heart raced as she was taken up into the sky with the repulsive creature above her. Its grotesque arms were wrapped tightly around her chest while its serpent-like tail swathed firmly around her squirming legs. The pulses of its clawed wings against the air thudded in her ears as it flapped away.

"Tairren! Please help me, Tairren!" Natalia screamed out as she was taken towards the top of the great wall and towards the Forbidden Lands.

She was terrified of the thought that it might have been the end of her.

All of a sudden more screaming and evil looking creatures came from the forest, and even more came from over the top of the wall, from the Black Forest. The black winged creatures looked like a cross between a monstrous bat and a deformed human with a long bony tail that had a sharp hook-like point at the end. Their mouths were opened wide, releasing their terrifying screams and their large black eyes were wild, searching into their souls. Their horns were sharp and pointed like their massive black claws and they left the foul scent of burning death in the air. They were like nightmares that had escaped from the deepest pits of hell.

They swooped down at Tairren and Phillip, trying to grab any part of them to bring them into the air and into the Forbidden Lands like one of the creatures was doing to Natalia. Phillip swung his sword violently at the frenzied creatures as they attacked. He knocked off one of their legs and another's tail. Their blood was like thick, black fluid as it sprayed out into the air and on their faces and tunics. He also got the best of one as he sliced off half of its wing and another by knocking off its head. They flapped and screamed madly as they crashed to the ground.

Tairren shot some with his bow and arrows. His arrows pierced their chests and necks, but seemed to not affect them but only get them angrier— until he shot an arrow through one of their heads. The black fluid squirted out of the thing's hideous head like a thick stream of water from a fountain. The creatures that were wounded crashed to the ground with heavy thuds, curling and thrashing about like wild, hurt animals.

Tairren kept his eyes on Natalia during the chaos, waiting for the right moment to shoot the creature down, who would not relent. The creature was taking Natalia to the top of the wall, which was really high up. If Natalia fell from the monster then, she would surely die from the fall.

"You are my strength—God of light," Tairren whispered to himself with his heart pounding as he pointed his arrow directly at the creature who held on so tightly to Natalia. He raced Lilly as close as he could to the wall, to get a good shot at the creature. "Direct my hand," Tairren prayed.

Then as soon as the creature took Natalia right above the wall, Tairren shot his arrow, right at the creature's head. The arrow, with full force, pierced right through the creature's deformed and horned head, jutting straight out of the other side. The thing let out a blood-curdling and raspy cry as it released Natalia, dropping her. She awkwardly flung her legs and arms as she fell on top of the wall. The creature fell onto the top of the wall as well, making some kind of splat noise as it hit. Tairren's heart jumped with excitement as he saw that Natalia was safe and away from the creature and that his shot was perfect.

✝✝✝

Natalia got up from her bruised knees, quickly standing to look down from the wall. She grabbed her sword that fell to the stone top of the wall and leaned over a short stone barrier that protected her from falling off. She was really high up—everything below her looked so small. Her heart seemed to be pounding in her head now as she watched in horror at the pandemonium below her. The many creatures swarmed around Tairren and Phillip below as they tried so hard to fight them off and get away from them on their horses. She noticed her poor Orchid was trying her best to get away from the attacking creatures as well, running here and there and jumping up to use her hooves to hit them. The creatures were relentless and tried so hard to get to their hearts.

"What should I do!?" Natalia yelled out as she brought her shaking hands to her head while looking for a way back down again.

The top of the wall was really wide as well and could fit at least ten large men standing shoulder to shoulder, all the way across. She looked around, feeling sick as she noticed many more dead men on the wall around her—some were torn open and others lay with their eyes locked open. She passed the limp and lifeless creature that had attacked her, slowly. She didn't know for sure if it was dead, but once she saw the black liquid that oozed from its head and surround it like a rain puddle, she knew it was.

The creature was bigger and longer than she thought and looked about six feet tall. It was really repulsive looking and still frightened her even though it was dead. Its massive wings lay broken and crinkled on the stone and its body lay in an awkward-looking position. If its wings were spread open from tip to tip, the wing span probably would have been twice as long as its height. Its large black eyes and gaping mouth were quite jarring and stayed open, even when it was dead.

She hurried to the other side of the wall, looking for a way down. The wind whipped at her hair and gown as she nearly fell over one of the dead guards. There was no way down, anywhere. Her heart sunk like a stone in the ocean as she realized that there seemed to be no way off of the wall to help her companions. She began to become frantic.

She looked off into the distance and noticed how vast, dark, and gloomy the other side of the wall was.
The Black Forest went on for miles. Farthest to the south she could see the mountains and something that looked like a great tower. She quickly wondered if Marrisa was in that tower and if she was scared or safe—or

even alive. She glanced around the view. Her heart raced as she got the full outlook of the Forbidden Lands—and she loathed it already. She could see that the farthest parts of the south were the darkest and appeared as if no life really existed there—no light. The clouds were black, the forests were dark, and the lands were dead. It appeared like something straight out of a nightmare.

All of a sudden more shrieks erupted from the Black Forest. Her heart skipped a beat as she frantically looked everywhere. She looked towards the tops of the shadowy and twisted trees and noticed many more creatures coming from them. They were like shadows with mighty wings. Dozens began to swarm in the distance, looking sinister and hectic as they flew about in a whirling black cloud.

"No," Natalia groaned to herself as she began to become upset and sickened, watching as many swarms of the wicked things came flying towards her and the wall—screaming and growling, whirling and flapping.

Panicked and feeling helpless and terrified, Natalia went running towards the nearest tower, wanting to get down from the top of the wall as quick as she could. Her heart sunk even lower as she realized that she was between two of the towers that roared with fires. There was no way down! She ran to the short wall again, peering over—wishing that she could just jump off with no pain afterwards. She saw that Tairren and Phillip were struggling, fighting for their lives while she was trapped on the mountain of a wall…

✝✝✝

Tairren had just run out of arrows and was beginning to become nervous, all he could do was try to get away from the creatures as quickly as he could. He searched the grounds for some kind of weapon with his quick eyes—something that could be useful to him. His heart thudded rapidly and the adrenaline flowed through him like mighty waters as sweat dripped from his brow.

He finally saw the perfect chance to retrieve an adequate weapon. He saw a sword lying next to one of the many dead guards. His only way to get it was to jump from lilly who was dashing like the wind. He could not stop because the creatures were gaining on him. He refused to look behind him because he knew that they were right on his back—the shrieks from the things rang through his ears like lightning, making him cringe.

The time was upon him that he had to fall from Lilly's back. Not doubting himself in any kind of way, he let go and crashed to the ground, rolling and tumbling, then stopped abruptly against one of the dead guards. He quickly went to his knees, frantically searching for the sword. He spotted it within seconds and as soon as he grabbed the sword, one of the creatures dove down at him—missing in the process and crashing head first into the earth. The snap of the winged creature's neck sounded disturbing but the thought of one of them dying was invigorating. Tairren fought the creatures with all of his might as they attacked in a whirling and angry wind.

Phillip saw that Tairren was in distress and made his way back to him, swinging his sword at the wild flying things in the process. He wouldn't be of any help if he stayed on his horse, so he jumped from Sable's back. He swiftly tumbled to the ground with his sword in his hand and got up as quickly as he fell. He was by Tairren's side swinging, making sure their backs were facing each other so that the creatures would not get the best of them. The fiends began to circle them like a massive twister, screeching and taunting with gnashing jaws and swinging claws.

"Glance up towards the wall!" Phillip yelled.

Tairren quickly looked up towards the top of the wall, realizing what Phillip was yelling about. Natalia seemed to be screaming out something and pointed behind her in the southern direction. She looked terrified and the wind blew at her.

"There are too many! We must get out of here for the sake of our lives!" Phillip yelled.

Phillip was right, there were too many and the swarms seemed to multiply by the second. They had no chance and the fight was too big for them.

"Run towards the nearest tower door, now!" Tairren yelled back as he took one last swing.

Just then, they sprinted as fast as they could, dodging oncoming creatures and jumping over dead guards and horses. The tower entrance on the closest part of the wall didn't look so far away from them, but as they ran it felt like they were never going to make it there alive.

✝✝✝

Natalia noticed that they began to run. She felt relieved but she knew the worst was coming as the screams from the looming creatures became louder. The oncoming beasts were swarming around her now, circling around her in a whirlwind of screams. The smell of burning flesh and death began to surround her, filling her nostrils with the stench. Her heart felt as if it were about to explode as the terror and stress of the situation lay thick on her mind and body. Natalia began to scream out as she dropped her small sword. The now useless sword made a clank sound as it hit the stone. The many taunting screams and growls were too much for her ears to handle all at once. She began to cry as she frantically covered her ears with her hands, pressing hard as she screamed at the taunting creatures. Through the screams she heard many threatening things in her heart. They were speaking to her spirit, and told her many wicked things—and they yearned for her beating heart and the blood it was soaked with.

Natalia backed away towards the short wall-barrier, pressing her lower back against it as she continued to scream and hold her ears. The flying beasts came in on her, whirling around her like a mighty tornado. The wind from their wings was too powerful and hard to stand up against. One of the creatures swooped strongly down at her, bringing a wind like that of an evil storm. The wicked creature went to grab her but she fought it as much as her petite body could. She remembered what Phillip and Tairren had said to her earlier about protecting herself—and she fought like she never fought before.

She panicked as she realized that she was falling over the edge of the wall! One minute her feet were on solid ground and the next, they were up in the air! In a quick second her heart felt like it dropped into her stomach as her body flung over the wall-barrier. She screamed as she flung her arms and legs frantically, speeding down to the earth in a mighty and terrifying pull of gravity…

✝✝✝

Tairren and Phillip saw the attack of the dozens of creatures upon Natalia. And just as they almost made it to the entry-way of the lowest part of one of the watch-towers—they saw her fall. They screamed out her name as the creatures continued to attack them. She looked so frantic and helpless as she hurtled down to the ground at full-force. Tears swelled up in Tairren's eyes as he continued to scream, not realizing that the tormenting creatures were coming in on him and covering him, like a black blanket. All he could see was darkness now. All he could hear were screams in his ears and taunting voices in his heart—trying to get into his soul as he was taken down to the ground… "Bring forth your hand—my God!" his heart cried out—thinking that death had taken hold of him…

†††

Something happened so quickly then—like the blinking of an eye, or the flashing of lightning during a thunder storm. As it seemed to them that it was all over, like there was no way out—like darkness had won and suffocated every source of light out of them, and like their lives were over, defeated and gone—something miraculous happened… It came as quick as the wind or as quick as the flashing of light—and each and every one of them felt a pull within their hearts. A mighty strength of power seemed to come over them as they were on the threshold of death.

Natalia's life flashed before her eyes as the wind rushed over her body. She saw the faces of everyone she loved, she saw her childhood—and she saw Marrisa… And then—a strong hand reached out and grabbed her. She didn't know what happened and she didn't know what was going on—because it happened so fast—but as she was falling to her death, something swooped down and caught her. She felt as if she were caught into the air, as if a mighty wind became solid beneath her body. At first, she thought it was one of the flying tormentors who caught her, but the grasp of the rescuer was too gentle, too considerate and loving—and she felt it through its touch. The next thing she knew, she was sitting in the lap of someone, but she was still in the air because she felt the wind in her hair and the coolness of it on her face.

She realized she was now sitting on the back of some kind of flying animal—an animal she had never seen before. It had the whitest of white fur with golden flecks in it and it had mighty wings that were the color of snow in the sun-light. And it had the sweet smell of fresh air—it smelled like nature on a cold bright morning or like the crisp winds that would blow down from the north. She could see below her now as she felt that she was in peace. She was confused for moment, going from a state of frantic terror as she was crashing down to the ground in a chaotic whirlwind of death, to graceful peace—soaring through the air. And for the first time since she left her home, she felt safe and sound, protected, and wanted to stay that way.

She looked up behind her at the being that saved her, the one who held on to her securely as they soared through the brisk atmosphere. And she was shocked when she got a good look at him. He was beautiful but strange-looking at the same time. His long hair was like the color of the flying animal's wings—the color of the snow in the sunlight. His skin was white like his hair and looked as if light glowed beneath it, as if every cell of blood in his body was made of soft light. His eyes were kind and beautiful, and had a light-golden hue in them, deep within them—like the color of the sky in the early morning which reflected off of rippling waters or mountain tops. She felt as if she were at home, safe and sound. She felt a strange connection with the being of light, as if she had known him her whole life. Natalia couldn't take her eyes off of the beautiful strangeness of his face; and when she finally did, she snapped back into reality and realized that they were gliding safely down to the ground.

✝✝✝

Like Natalia, Tairren and Phillip were also forced into a radical change of scenario. It was like a dream of some sort, the way they went from a horrifying state of panic and back into the presence of life. It began with a loud sound, like the sound of a trumpet—and there were many of them. The sounds of the trumpets were beautiful and seemed to rip through the screams that came from the black creatures like a burning blade. The shrieks of the creatures diminished beneath the sounds of the trumpets and they began to disperse like a swarm of hornets beneath a heavy rain.

It happened so quickly. Golden arrows shot through the black creatures like beams of light. They began to drop like flies as the golden arrows defeated them. As soon as the creatures relented and fell from Tairren and Phillip—they witnessed a powerful and heroic scene. They could see many creatures of light coming down from the sky, quick like the wind and beautiful like a sunrise. There were dozens of them; beautiful people who seemed to glow even though the sky was thick and black like shadows.

They rode on great white beasts which looked like a cross between an exotic cat and an owl, which had great white wings that thudded through the wind. The beasts had great talons like that of a mighty owl, and the faces and body shapes like mighty white lynx cats. The beings of light shot golden arrows down at the black monsters, appearing like fire raining down from the sky, piercing through the evil things. And in the lead of all of the wonder—there was the great white owl...

Shaken, Tairren slowly stood up as the beasts gracefully landed upon the ground. He looked with wonder and somewhat disbelief. Some of the golden beings hopped off of the backs of the beasts while shooting their arrows. The beasts attacked the remaining black creatures that lingered around the ground—ripping off their black wings with great white jaws. Tairren watched with amazement and shock as some of the beings pulled out their golden swords from their jeweled scabbards and smote the rest of the low flying tormentors. The rest of the swarms of the black creatures quickly dispersed throughout the blackened sky, squealing and growling as they seemed to disappear into the shadows.

Within seconds it was all over, and Tairren and Phillip stood quietly together, surrounded by the wonderful beings. Tairren quickly glanced at each one of them. They all resembled each other, but each one had their own look. All of them looked striking and they all seemed to have a soft glow about them. There were women amongst them as well, appearing just like the men did but they had feminine features. They were all tall, having many different body types. Some were bulky and muscular in build and others were lean and thin. Some looked at least nine and twelve feet tall while others looked even taller. They looked as if they were sculpted from glowing marble. They all had glorious long manes of sun-kissed hair that looked as if air and light lived within each strand. Each one had a large feather braided into their hair, looking like the feathers that adorned the flying beast's wings. They all wore white tunics trimmed with gold and all wore golden circlets around their heads. Their armor was light and their weaponry consisted of bows and arrows and glorious swords.

But out of all their appearances, there was one thing that stood out to Tairren the most. He noticed that they all wore the same wing pendant as he did, except their pendants were a solid yellow-gold and weren't encrusted with jewels like his was. Tairren held his pendant in his hand as his heart pounded in his chest. He wanted to say something about them having similar necklaces, but decided not to.

Tairren was distracted as he noticed that the great white owl gracefully glided around them, then landed on a boulder that sat a small distance from them. It sat still and silent, just watching.

Natalia quickly ran over to them with teary eyes, hugging Phillip first then Tairren. She stayed where she was at, holding onto Tairren and resting her head against his chest. She was relieved and thankful that she was standing on solid ground and by his side again.

One of the beings came to them through the crowd of light-people, quickly bowed his head, then looked into Tairren's eyes. He seemed to be one of the captains amongst the large group. He was dressed in different garbs and the golden circlet around his head was slightly larger, embedded with small, sparkling stones of many colors.

"You must be weary, Tairren, son of Timotheus," he said in a tone that held no anxiety or fear but held only assurance and confidence.

Tairren was surprised, wondering how he knew not only his name, but his father's name as well.

"My body is tired, but rest will not stop me while my quest is still at hand," he said nervously, glancing back and forth from the captain to the others who seemed to have their eyes locked on him. "…Who are you and how do you know my name?" Tairren finally asked.

"We are legna," he said proudly. "We are the Legion of Light from the kingdom of Nevaeh. Our Lord is the Great King of light—the king of all kings—whom we serve. I am one of the Archlegna—I am called Mikhal. We were summoned to these lands by our king and given the quest to find three keys and to stop the darkness that is consuming all of these lands—for it is spreading like evil waters across this very earth. As you can see—it has already begun," he said in saddened voice as he motioned his hand towards all of the dead men and horses that lay upon the field. "Some will not have a chance… Minslethrate sits on the boundaries of death. As we speak, this darkness is making its way towards the northern parts where your kingdom resides—and you are all in grave danger."

As Mikhal spoke, the three of them glanced at each other. Everything Mikhal said just confirmed everything Tairren had been talking about. They began to worry as they thought of their families and the ones they loved.

"I thought this great wall was supposed to keep all evil out," Tairren said as he looked up at the mighty wall.

"Yes, Tairren, this wall was built many ages ago to keep evil people out. But there is an ancient evil one who has been living on these lands for many generations and has now called upon the forbidden dark lord to make all evil rise. The presence of evil itself has taken physical form. These dead creatures you see all around you were summoned from the deepest parts of hell. They have escaped from the depths to torment—they are called Abaddon."

The three of them looked around at the ugly black creatures which lay dead all around them. They still sent chills up their spines, even when they were not living.

"There are many more. All of these beings of darkness are called nomed—and they come in many shapes and forms—they are the followers of darkness—servants to the great evil, sent to kill, steal and destroy. You will know when you see them for they are as black as shadows and carry an evil presence about them. They will look into your spirit and try to find a way in—and torment you. They will speak evil things to you, but you must not listen or yield to them. The stronger they get—the stronger their lust for blood comes upon them. The nomed yearn for your heart and soul..."

Just then Mikhal pointed over to the massive gate that sat right in the middle of the wall, directly in the center of the field. The gate seemed a great way away and looked like a haunting door-way to the unknown. They never noticed before, but the gate was raised half-way open...

"The gate has been opened, allowing these creeping things of darkness to escape towards the northern parts of Minslethrate—towards your people. Someone has opened and destroyed the gate. But it is useless now to fix and close it—for the powers of evil are stronger than ever and are already spreading."

"That explains the great two-headed dogs that attacked us last night," Tairren said to Phillip and Natalia.

"You have seen some of the nomed—only a taste of the evil that is now lurking upon these lands. But do not be fearful—for if you believe in Him, you and your family will be saved... Tairren, son of Timotheus," Mikhal looked back into his anxious eyes. "Malakh was sent to you by the Great King of light and has revealed everything I have spoken unto you—has he not?"

Tairren nodded his head as he glanced at the mysterious owl. It sat there in the beautiful silence and peace that surrounded them, just staring its dark eyes at him. Tairren wondered if the owl was the one called Malakh...

"Yes, he has," Tairren said.

"Then you know that your quest is as much as an importance as our own," Mikhal said, looking at each one of them.

"Yes, and it is why we nearly died today... Thank you so much for saving our lives," Tairren said as he bowed his head to them.

"Yes, thank you," Natalia spoke up, "Those black creatures would have gotten the best of me if it wasn't for you and your people—my life would have been over... I owe you my being."

"No—we only do what our king commands us to do. You owe your life to Him—for he loves you and these lands so much that he died for you and your ancestors and now, sends us here to these lands to stop the darkness that is augmenting so strongly around you." Mikhal spoke with a stern voice, but never sounded cruel.

With that said, Mikhal spoke out in another language that they had never heard before. He seemed to be giving the other legna a command, for they began to get on their beast's backs. Mikhal motioned for another legna to come to him. The legna came to Mikhal's side and stood before the three of them.

"This is the Archlegna Gaibriul," Mikhal said as Gaibriul bowed his head. "He will guide you to the camp—you need rest."

Natalia looked at Gaibriul in awe as she realized that he was the one who rescued her in the midst of her fall of death—and she began to have the sensation within her that she was connected to him. He looked at her and nodded his head with a slight smile.

All of a sudden Mikhal and his fellow legna were up in the air on their beasts in a mighty whoosh of air. It was interesting to see how the grand beasts pushed their hind legs into the earth and then leaped up into the air as their magnificent wings opened up. They soared up into the dark sky and over the wall towards the south. After the thuds of their wings quieted in the air, they were gone.

Tairren felt anxious and worried and did not want to follow Gaibriul to their camp—and wanted to continue towards the south. Every second seemed to matter—and it seemed as if they were running out of time. He thought of Marrisa and her beautiful face and worried that they would be too late... He trusted the legna and their knowledge—he just didn't trust Lilith and didn't know what she was capable of.

"Do not be afraid," a soothing voice said from within his heart. He instantly looked at the owl who still sat there. The voice seemed to come from the owl, but it seemed that he was the only one who heard it.

The owl pushed himself up into the air and spread its wings and glorious feathers, going in the same direction as the legna.

"We must go," Gaibriul said as he walked towards his beast.

"Where are we going?" Tairren asked, watching as Gaibriul stood on the side of his great beast.

"I will lead you to our camp—it is set up about a mile from here, in a clearing in the Black Forest."

They nodded, then looked around, realizing that their horses were not by their sides.

"The horses," Tairren said as he quickly looked around, "I fear they met their end by the tormentor's wrath."

Gaibriul just looked at Tairren with his golden eyes, then stared towards the forests, as if listening to something. He stood still as his eyes intensely gazed across the field.

"Never declare the workings of evil... Your horses are strong," Gaibriul said as he held out his hand towards the forest.

Relief fell over their bodies as they looked over to where Gaibriul's hand had reached out to. The three horses came running towards them, safe and unharmed.

"How did you know?" Tairren asked, shocked.

Gaibriul was quiet for a moment, as he looked back into Tairren's eyes. His gaze was intense and his golden-yellow eyes were welcoming and beautiful like the morning sun.

"I hear their spirits," he said in a low tone, almost whispering. "They are fast and free, innocent and loyal like that of a new-born child."

As the three horses approached, each owner greeted them with smiles, petting their faces and manes. The horses were excited from the action of that early evening and happy to see their owners once again. Gaibriul caressed each one of the horses' faces while looking into their big, dark eyes—as if he were speaking to them with his own. They seemed to calm down and began to act as if they've known him their whole life. Tairren, Phillip and Natalia watched curiously, amazed at how receptive the horses were to Gaibriul. They weren't afraid of Gaibriul's mighty beast either, and seemed to like its company. After a moment he went to the beast and did the same thing to it: tenderly petted its face while looking into its eyes.

They were intrigued at how peaceful and loving the beast was but it was so intimidating at the same time. The beast was beautiful and mind-blowing. It was massive and even when it sat on its haunches it was almost as tall as Gaibriul. Its fur was thick and white with golden-beige streaks on it and its wings were mighty and strong looking. Its talons were mighty and strong looking as well. Its eyes were of the same color as the legna's—beautiful and looked like golden-yellow raindrops.

"Come, Serafim," he said as he petted the mighty beasts head, then pulled himself onto its back.

The three companions pulled themselves onto their horse's backs as well, but still watched Gaibriul and his beast. They could not take their eyes off of the strange and beautiful creatures of light.

"This forest is filled with sadness and anger and will pull you into its madness if you allow it to. Keep your eyes on me and your mind on your quest if you begin to feel that you are being drawn into the darkness. Follow me closely and you will be safe. Serafim will not fly, but I will have him run upon the grounds as horses do so that you may follow me easily. Do not stray from the path or straggle behind me. The darkness is thick and the evil that lurks upon it is hungry."

They all glanced at each other, then took deep breaths. Gaibriul swiftly got his mighty beast going towards the gate. They didn't get a chance to talk or make quick comments to each other before they went into the forest's gloom, for the beast was swift and quick even upon the ground, but it never went too fast. The three companions rode steadfastly behind Gaibriul and made sure to never take their weary eyes off of Gaibriul or Serafim for more than a long minute.

✝

CHAPTER 19
The Black Forest

Within moments they entered into the treacherous Black Forest—the threshold to the Forbidden Lands. Gaibriul entered in first of course, then Tairren followed with Natalia following behind him and Phillip last, after Natalia. It was strange how quickly their surroundings changed. The atmosphere became darker all around them as they went further into the forest.

The forest looked and smelled really old, and had the appearance that there hadn't been any new life within it. There wasn't any sight of new growth or anything green within the black clutches of the forest. The feelings of sadness and anger lay heavy upon them now as the forest loomed over them. They did not feel anguish internally but they could literally feel it all around them. The haunting trees began to close in behind them, stretching their dark and knurly branches all around them.

The forest was cold and dreary, and the smell of decaying earth lay thick all around them. The trees had dark leaves on them but most of the wood looked dead and appeared as monstrous hands with arthritic, long fingers. Large, black crows sat on random branches, and spider-webs stretched here and there amongst the thick trees and shrubbery. The ground was dark and matted with dead leaves and branches and heavy roots. Mushrooms of many sizes and mildew of many shades of brown, gray, and black also covered the dark ground. There was nothing green or colorful within the forest and if there was any color at all, it was brown and the dark-green shade of some leaves. They could not go too fast anymore because the path was overgrown and had many holes, cracks and dips about it.

They remembered what Gaibriul said and tried their best to keep their eyes on them so that their minds wouldn't drift too deeply into the darkness. Gaibriul and Serafim looked beautiful even in the darkness of the wood, giving off a pale-silver glow like the moon, soft and illuminating. It was strange because they never glowed intensely like burning light, but they seemed to always have a soft light on them even in the blackness.

"I do not like it in here—one bit," Natalia said with shivers as she timidly looked all around her. "I feel as if I walked into a cold nightmare. I feel—sadness and anger—all around me…"

"The sight of this forest makes my body feel sickened in the inside," Phillip said in a low tone, looking all around him as well.

They wished to be anywhere but there and longed to sit by a great, hot orange fire and eat and drink and lay down for more than twenty minutes. Even the thought of lying in a nice grassy green field below the sun comforted them. They missed their homes greatly and the familiar lands of it, but they knew it would not be the same if they stopped their quest.

Shivers matted their skin as the temperature seemed to drop, going deep into their bones. The feelings of sadness and anger lay thick all around them—as if the forest itself felt that way. Their exhausted bodies became even more overwhelmed as the uncomfortable presence of darkness came around them. One would surely go mad if they were to get lost in that black labyrinth of trees and earth. Any soul lost in that forest would yearn for death to just take them, swift and painless.

"Do not tremble—do not be afraid... Did He not proclaim his purposes for you?" Gaibriul said in an uplifting voice. "Always keep your eyes on the light, even in the darkest of hour."

They became quiet again, understanding the words that he spoke. But the quietness of the cold air and the feeling of anguish all around them were unbearable.

Tairren noticed something lurking in the distance. It was quiet and black and looked like a shadow amongst the dark trees. At first, he thought it was just a shadow because there were many of them in the thick wood. But when it began to move in different spots—he knew it wasn't just a shadow. It was something sinister—and it seemed to be stalking them. It slowly crept behind the trees and bushes and seemed to fade in and out of the darkness. There was more than one. They appeared like black phantoms and they sent shivers through his skin.

"I see something in the shadow of the wood, through the trees," Tairren said in a quiet voice, not wanting to panic anyone.

"They have been following us since we first stepped into this forest," Gaibriul said in a calm voice. It did not seem to frighten him at all, but just make him more alert as ever. "Those lurkers will not come near you—but they will have you come to them if you allow them to..."

They looked around, feeling slightly panicked but not terrified. They trusted everything Gaibriul said. The black shadows did not come near them, but they slowly followed in the distance, lurking quietly. When they stopped the shadows stopped—when they quickened the shadows did as well.

It was really quiet all around them, except for the noises of the horses. The mighty beast called Serafim whom they followed did not make any noises and was as quiet as the cold air around them. But they did hear random squawks of the crows that randomly perched around them, or the sounds of branches breaking or leaves moving in the darkest parts of the forest. The thought of something moving in the blackness of the forest made them nervous. Gaibriul could have been nervous, but they would never know it because of his intense and serious mannerism. But his calmness and peace he carried about him comforted them, and that was something they needed most of all in the forest.

There were strange whispers in the distance, sounding haunting and familiar. The whispers seemed to call their names but each one of them only heard their own name. Each call sounded different in their ears and sounded like a companion each one of them had possessed in their lives.

"Do you hear that?" Natalia finally asked, breaking the uncomfortable silence. She began to look around frantically. She wasn't sure if she was hearing things in the forest or hearing her thoughts in the terrible silence. "A familiar voice is calling me…"

"I hear it too…," Tairren said in a low tone, "they are calls for help."

"Do not listen to them," Gaibriul said, intensely looking into the forest. He appeared as a cat that sensed something threatening around him, alert and cautious. "There is no one here whom you would know…"

It became quiet again as they continued through the forest. The haunting calls Tairren heard reminded him of the day he and his father came into the Black Forest…

"Many years ago, when I was young," Tairren said, breaking the haunted silence, "we rode through this forest, my father and I, to search for things to sell in our shop—ingredients for my mother's elixirs and ointments and things such as that. But I remember it being more alive and the presence it held was not as terrifying as it is now. I remember being nervous, because my father appeared as if he knew that something was following us, but he did not say anything. I remember when we took a quick rest my father fell asleep, and I heard the voice of a woman…

"The woman was singing, and I remember how beautiful but sad, and haunting her voice was. The melody of her voice seemed to pull me. I remember how her voice echoed through the trees like a faint breeze—and that I couldn't understand it because it was in another tongue. But I knew it was a song of sadness.

"I followed the voice to an old ruined temple. I remember that the temple was taken over by the forest and I thought it appeared so intriguing. I did not go into the mysterious temple and only stood in its massive threshold. I saw something in the temple move—something swift like a shadow but it did not linger. I looked again and it was gone…

"I was disturbed, so I ran back to our small camp and woke my father. I brought him there. My father took my hand and we left quickly when he saw the temple. It had a symbol above the once grand post and lintel and he recognized it to be the symbol of Dolsia. He told me that it was dangerous around there and we left abruptly, never returning to these southern parts ever again…" He became quiet again as they slowly and vigilantly made their way through the morbid forest.

Natalia sat silently as well and remembered when Tairren had told that story to her and Marrisa one summer's evening. Her mind drifted off… It seemed so long ago and the thought of it put a strange sadness upon her. She wished so badly that she could turn back time to those innocent moments of her past. Those moments were filled with freedom and happiness…

Just then that whispering call came again to her from the darkness of the forest. The voice was familiar and seemed to bring back more memories. The whispering voice caught her attention. She quickly looked towards the darkness where the voice was coming from. The voice sounded like Marrisa's! It whispered her name and called out to her for help, trying to draw her into the darkness…

Natalia saw someone in the darkness of the wood, someone who looked like Marrisa but wasn't sure if it was her. She whispered her name and urged Natalia to come to her—to go with her into the darkness. Natalia's heart raced as she could clearly see that it was something that looked exactly like Marrisa. That someone stood still and silent in the shadows of the forest. She could see its long red hair and white gown, and fair complexion but she could not see the face—it was covered in black shadows. She quickly became frightened for some reason.

Natalia squeezed her eyes shut then brought them back to Gaibriul. She remembered what Gaibriul had said and brought her mind back to their quest, just like he told them to do when they felt that they were being drawn into the darkness of the forest. She brought her gaze back to the thing that looked like Marrisa—but it was now gone… It all seemed to go on forever to Natalia, but it happened in a matter of seconds. Nobody else seemed to even notice any of it.

"Do you know the story of Dolsia?" Gaibriul asked, breaking the silence once more. "The singing voice that fills this black forest is the haunting cries of Dolsia..."

"Yes. Dolsia is one of the many ancient legends of Minslethrate," Tairren said, seeming to perk up a bit. Stories and legends intrigued him, and he liked to reveal what he knew about his homelands. "Dolsia was one of the pagan goddesses to the ancestors of this land, ages ago when the beliefs of Minslethrate were dark. The ancestors of Minslethrate blindly worshiped Dolsia as the goddess of earth and life. But she deceived our ancestors—as you can see these parts of Minslethrate are full of sadness, anger, and death and is far from living and her temple is in ruins, just as is she...

"After the great war, which was led by one of our great ancestral kings, between the north and South parts of Minslethrate, her temple was stormed and destroyed... Dolsia was never recognized as the goddess of earth and life hence forth..."

Gaibriul was quiet for a moment, as if in a deep thought and seemed to be reminiscing on something that was far in his past. His face was fierce but kind, but the quietness that emitted from him revealed that something nostalgic came over him.

"There is some history that is turned into legend...," Gaibriul said mysteriously. "As the earth ages, so does its stories. And over time, the men that had witnessed such great things, told them many times as stories—and then died, and fell away from the earth and from the minds of every living man. The stories of these dead men turned into legend, and merely become an age-old tale, a story written on a page—something that may have not happened... But I speak the truth. The men of Minslethrate see Dolsia as an ancient goddess, the creator of earth and life... She was worshiped as so—indeed Tairren, those men were blind. The legend is this..."

Gaibriul began the legend of Dolsia—a story he knew very well... The time Dolsia first stepped upon the earth was many ages ago, around the birthing era of Minslethrate, but seemed to Gaibriul that it had just happened. Gaibriul knew their journey to the camp would be a little longer than expected, so an intriguing story seemed appropriate. With the story beginning, they continued to pass through the frightening forest, anticipating the moment when they would leave the forest and see the opened field again.

"Long ago, during the beginnings of Minslethrate, when these lands were new and vibrant and this very forest was full of life and beauty—my king began the first Settlement of Light. And the very beginning of his grand Settlement of Light was called the Garden of Nede. This garden resided in the very location of the ruins of the earth temple, the temple known by man as the Temple of Dolsia. the Great King of light created the Garden of Nede for the very first son and daughter of light, which are your earthly ancestors. Everything they needed was in that garden—it was to be the most perfect dwelling place for a human. the Great King knew it was good and adored his first children of light very much.

"But these first children of light disobeyed the Great King and they were casted out of the garden, exiled unto the wild of the new and young lands of Minslethrate and forced to fend for them-selves. the Great King wished us to close up the Garden of Nede, never to be seen ever again by human eyes. So, my king chose Dolsia and I to come to Minslethrate to do just that. You see, my comrades, Dolsia is a legna; she was a very respectable and beautiful being of light in the kingdom of Nevaeh and my very close companion. This was so very long ago. She is fallen now, lost and dull and the light she had once upon her is now gone... A fallen legna is what we call her—because she has fallen away from light... This very forest was once beautiful, and now reflects the curse of Dolsia...

"In the beginning, she was the first lady of song and was blessed with the most beautiful voice. the Great King of light gifted her with a voice that could soften anyone's heart. She sang for the king of light and worshiped him every morning in the kingdom of Nevaeh... She sang for him amongst the royal court of light during every feast and celebration. So out of great love and delight, my king chose us to be his trusted ones to come to Minslethrate and close up the Garden of Nede.

"The garden was beautiful—even more beautiful than any man-made garden. Every color in the garden was even more vibrant than a sunset and there was an abundance of fruit and living things that could be eaten. The animals and plants that resided there would never be seen again upon this earth. Tranquility was the feeling of it.

"But amongst all of this beautiful nature, there was a tree that was forbidden to eat upon, and sat in the center of the garden. This tree produced fruit unlike any other—but it was the only fruit in the garden that

was not to be eaten of." Gaibriul stopped talking for a moment, as if going into thought, but then began again. "When Dolsia entered into the garden, she admired it with all of her heart. Her eyes began to become of the world. The beauty of the garden caught her heart and she began to see how much the Great King loved your ancestors, the first children of light.
His love for them is the reason why he produced such a beautiful, serene safe-haven—why these lands were created, why this earth was created.

"Dolsia began to become tempted by it—she longed to feel what humans felt. Her eyes caught the splendid tree and she was also tempted by the luscious fruit that dangled from the tree—and ate from it... Dolsia's actions reflected that of the first son and daughter of light, for they did the same thing—ate from the forbidden fruit when the Great King of light had forbid it.

"Dolsia revealed to me then that a being in a black cloak said she would live forever in love if she just ate from the fruit and simply lie to his majesty. She said that the being in the cloak was dark but beautiful and its voice was pleasing to her ears... He told her that he once loved the Great King of light and once followed him—but now he stands on his own and lives forever... He said that if she ate from the fruit, her life would be complete and she would live an immortal life filled with everlasting love... I told her that she had been deceived by darkness... And she was deceived by darkness...

"My king came back to the garden, but he already knew of what she had done and what her intensions were. He knew that she dishonored him by disobeying him—and dishonored him by having lust in her heart for eternal love, which was not through him... He asked her three times of what she had done—she tried to deceive him all three times... But you see—my king knows all... And he punished her by not allowing her to come back to Nevaeh, the Great Kingdom of light—but if she were to simply ask for forgiveness, she would be blessed and able to come back. But because her heart was not pure anymore, her heart did not desire the Great King anymore... It is a sad thing, a cursed thing...

"You see, over time a curse fell upon her. This curse of eternal life on earth came from the being that walked with her in dark robes. Her heart became hardened as it fell upon this being in dark robes. Dolsia was condemned to that garden forever... She would live in the spot where the Garden of Nede once flourished, for eternity—even when everything around her dies and decays. She would dwell in darkness even when all man passes away and she would become but a faint light of sadness.

"The Garden of Nede was no longer a garden, but a memory of the past. The area where the garden once sat was no longer a beautiful garden anymore, but a wilderness of shadow and death. She would witness many deaths and seasons and phases of the earth—but she would never die with the many years that would pass by her... Her life shall be like a sorrowful breeze, passing through the shadowed trees like a dark spirit. Even when she yearns for death to take her—it would never come..."

They were silent as the story settled in their hearts—and it began to become as a burden to them. The sadness of the wood that lurked around them reflected the story. That sadness began to try to overtake them. But they would not let it.

Natalia sat quietly on Orchid, swaying side to side on the bumpy ride as they continued through the darkness. Her eyes began to swell with warm tears. Thinking of the story brought tears to her eyes and her heart broke for Dolsia. "She only wanted to be loved—like that of humans...," Natalia thought to herself as a tear trailed down her cheek. "She only wanted to feel love..."

She thought of herself and felt that she could strangely relate to Dolsia. With her being the daughter of a Marquis, she had everything a lady of noble blood could ever want—but she felt that she had nothing. Being wealthy and having a large social stature cannot fill the human heart. She thought of how badly she wanted someone to love her own self as well. She wanted so badly to be in love. She wanted so badly to feel some kind of love, even from her own parents—whom she may never see again...

"She did not understand that the Great King of light did care for her, just like everything else he created," Gaibriul continued. "But she wanted more and wanted to be loved like that of the first son and daughter of light— like a human...

"You see, the forbidden fruit that was eaten upon was the fruit of knowledge—the knowledge of human-nature, the imperfections that all human beings share. Once it was consumed, the doors of transgression would be opened wide upon the eater—and would be ravaged by not only human behavior, but impurity...

"Dolsia knew of this—and yearned for those human feelings. So, she ate from the fruit—and her innocence was broken. But once the presence of the mighty king came upon her in the garden, she felt ashamed and dirty and felt the sins of man well upon the inside of her heart—and for the first time, she lied, three times to him..." Gaibriul was not angry when he spoke, but he had a sense of agitation about him, as if he cared for Dolsia but was very disappointed by her.

Gaibriul ended his story and began to become quiet. The darkness around them was still thick and the emotion that came from the Black Forest was even thicker. The story that was told by Gaibriul lay on their hearts as they began to think of the people they possessed in their lives.

Natalia thought of her mother and father, and how they never showed her any kind of love or appreciation—and then her thoughts went to Sora, who always appreciated her, and then to Tairren, because he was the only man in her life who did.

Tairren thought of his mother and how she always showed him love, he thought of his father and how he was the most inspirational father one could ever have, even though he only knew him in childhood, then he thought of Marrisa—for she was the only love in his life...

Phillip thought of his father, and how much he appreciated him even though his majesty was really hard on him and looked down upon him. Phillip thought of how sickly his father was and how greatly he pushed him to marry the princess of Minslethrate, but he seemed to realize that his love was not and would never be for Princess Marrisa...

Strange voices that they only heard came to them again from the shadows of the forest. Phillip began to hear a voice coming from the darkness of the murky wood that brought back childhood memories. The voice sounded like his father. He looked over to where the haunting voice was coming from and he could see his father standing in the shadows! He stood off the path and further back in the blackened forest. His father seemed to be calling to him. He was dressed in the same garbs as his majesty and wore the same crown. His face was blackened by shadows. But Phillip knew it was him—it had to have been him. The voice that emanated from it was that of his father's—it was deep and of older age and was in the Ishkarian language. Phillip wondered why and how he could've gotten there.

"Father... Father!" Phillip yelled, startling the travelers and the eerie quietness around them.

They quickly looked back at Phillip who was behind them all. Phillip appeared surprised and worried and was frantically peering into the forest.

They looked over in the same direction he was, but only saw the black shadows that had been lurking quietly!

"I need to get to him!" Phillip yelled out as he hopped off of Sable. "The darkness will have him!"

They began to panic as a state of shock and confusion came over them. They did not know what was going on and wondered why he shouted out to his father who was not even there.

"Stop him!" Gaibriul shouted as he hopped off of Serafim. "The forest is taking hold of his mind!"

They got off their horses as quickly as they could, to get to Phillip who had already rushed off of the path and into the shadow of the forest. They would have quickly ridden their horses through the trees, but that part of the forest was too thick and was filled with many small trees, large nettles and poisonous bramble bushes.

"Phillip! Stop!" Tairren yelled out as he quickly rushed behind him. "Your father is not there!"

Phillip rushed through the forest to where his father stood in the darkness. As he came closer his father's shape seemed to change and become darker. Phillip slowed down as the old man became a solid black shadow. His father was now nothing more than a morbid shadow! The shadow's eyes became a red-green glare that flashed like that of a cat's eye at night. A strong presence came over Phillip. The presence that came quickly over him went from a deep sadness to a sharp feeling of wrath. It was thick and seemed to take his breath away.

It all seemed to happen in slow motion—the way he came upon the shadow and the way it seemed to leap out of the blackness at him. The shadow raised its long fingers at him and let out an ear-piercing shriek. Phillip winced in pain as the shadow quickly came upon him in a shrieking and thick whirlwind of angry darkness. The blackness of the shadow appeared as a shrieking woman—with her twisted mouth wide open and her naked body appearing as a black mass of absolute terror. The screaming woman wrapped her shadowy hands around his neck and seemed to transform into a thick black and swirling mist, trying to make its way into Phillip's screaming mouth!

Tairren and Natalia tried to help him but other black shadows began to take over them in the same manner as it did Phillip.

"Go back to the stinking pits of darkness you lurkers of the shadow!" Gaibriul yelled out as he began to shoot his golden arrows at the shrieking forms of darkness. The arrows glowed in the darkness and pierced it like lightning. "You have no power over these children of light!"

Just then they began to shriek even louder, as if Gaibriul's words and presence angered and offended them. They gave one last threat and howl, then they rushed off into the blackness of the forest again, vanishing quickly into the distance.

Phillip just lay there on his back and looked as if he was dazed and confused. He tried to speak to them but began to slur instead. They hunched over him, panicking as they looked into his dazed eyes. His dark eyes gazed up into the thick, dark canopy of the forest. Even in the darkness of the wood they could tell that the blood had rushed away from his face, making him pale and sickly looking.

"Phillip! Are you okay?! Phillip are you hurt?!" Tairren spoke loudly to him. He felt fear and anxiety rush upon him as he watched Phillip's silent face.

Phillip did not respond and looked as if he was slowly slipping away.

"What is wrong with him?!" Natalia shrieked.

She quickly looked up at Gaibriul who stood above them. His face was serious and concerned.

"I fear he allowed some of the nomed's darkness come inside of him. Those nomed are called Banshee—spirits of sorrow and wrath who shriek when they yearn for death… We must get to the camp, quickly!"

Just then Gaibriul bent over and grabbed Phillip, picking him up. Gaibriul's build appeared slim and lean, but he had great strength and picked Phillip up as if he were as light as a feather.

"Come away with me—we must go quickly! I feel Phillip's life slowly slipping away from his body. He will soon be headed into darkness—the small light in him is slowly going out. When your guard is down and weak, evil will attack and prevail if you allow it to. You must always have the armor of light upon your heart—filled with oil to burn always. The nomed around us in the blackness of the forest are growing angrier and there will be great numbers of them soon if we linger."

They quickly went to their horses, glancing everywhere as they went, worried and shocked at what was happening. Gaibriul placed Phillip on Serafim's back then spoke to it in that strange, foreign tongue. As Tairren and Natalia quickly got onto their horses, Gaibriul went to Sable and caressed his face and looked into the horse's dark eyes again, as if speaking to him, then he quickly got onto his back. Just then he shouted and gave a loud signal to Serafim in that strange language again, then Serafim ran and leapt into the air. The mighty beast spread its wings and crashed through the dark canopy of leaves and limbs as it flew into the dark-gray sky with Phillip on his back.

"Phillip will fall—he is not himself and has no strength to hold on!" Natalia shrieked as she covered her mouth.

"Serafim will protect him and will not let him fall—he is headed quickly to the camp so that Phillip can be cleansed of the darkness that is eating his heart! This must be done or he will surely fall into the clutches of evil hands. Follow me and ride with haste and vigilance!"

Just then Gaibriul got Sable going quickly before them. They rode like the wind through the Black Forest. They flew through the forest as quick as the wind upon the fields. They leapt over deep cracks and ditches in the earth and over fallen trees and through black and cold streams. They flew by outstretched branches and massive thorn bushes and over-grown nettles. Their hearts raced as their minds worried for Phillip.

As they hurried through the forest, more black shadowy figures of all different shapes and sizes began to chase after them. Some of them looked like shadowy figures of mist and others looked like wild black beasts with eyes that gleamed. Loud shrieks and groans became loud all around them. Treacherous whispers came from the black forms, trying to pierce their racing hearts. It seemed as if the whole forest was infested with the evil beings. They could hear the whispers and screams as if they were right by their ears!

Gaibriul fought off the advancing nomed with his glorious arrows, as both Natalia and Tairren hurried behind him, gripping on tightly to their horses with sweaty palms and throbbing hearts. Long shadowy arms reached for them as many more chased right behind them, over them and all around them!

"The camp draws near!" Gaibriul yelled back to them, catching a glimpse of their terrified faces.

After a few more intense moments which seemed like hours of being in the forest and chased by black sinister beings, they were suddenly out and upon a massive opening in the forest. They burst into the field as if they were being carried away by the wind. The dark blue-gray clouds of the sky and the breezes from it were suddenly upon them, and the heavy smell of rotten wood and moist earth was away from their nostrils. They could see the glow of the camp before them, consisting of torches and tents that glowed with light within them. The glowing camp was a fine sight, and their hearts jumped with joy as they realized that they were no longer in the forest but amongst an opened field filled with cool winds.

Tairren quickly turned his head to see if the nomed were still advancing upon them, and to his surprise they weren't. He could see the many forms of blackness fall back into the dark forest, seeming to disappear into the shadows of the trees.

✝

CHAPTER 20
The Awakening of The Three Keys

Bursting out of the morbid and black forest and catching the iridescent glow of the camp of the legna was like being in a dream—and the nightmare part of it seemed to be almost over. They were relieved as they came closer to the warm glow of the camp, which was much larger than they anticipated. Tairren and Natalia followed Gaibriul as they quickly came upon the camp.

There were legna everywhere, by the hundreds. All of them appeared to be relaxing and going about their business. Some were eating, drinking, and laughing—talking amongst each other; some were playing music and others were sword-fighting. It was as if they entered into a small kingdom of light. They all appeared pleasant and beautiful and peaceful and seemed to make the camp glow with even more warm light. A sudden feeling of peace came over both Tairren and Natalia as they came into the camp. Tairren was overwhelmed by serenity and by the amount of legna and wondered why there were so many of them.

Many of the legna looked up from their business and watched them as they continued to follow Gaibriul through the camp. They quickly made their way towards the center of it and within seconds they were off of their horses and walking swiftly towards a large tent. A group of legna stood by the tent, and one of the legna, particularly a taller one out of the bunch, kept watching Tairren as if he knew him. Tairren felt a strange connection to him, as if he did know him.

They quickly burst into the tent to see that a group of legna were standing over a convulsing Phillip. Gaibriul hurried to the chaos as Mikhal, the Archlegna, came out of nowhere and hurried to the side of the bed as well. Phillip shook uncontrollably as his eyes rolled in the back of his head. He was soaking wet with sweat and his once light-brown skin was nearly white.

"Phillip! Natalia cried out as she took hold of Tairren tightly, she began to cry as she buried her face into his chest.

The legna stood around the bed and placed their hands on his head and chest and began to command things at Phillip in that strange tongue. Phillip began to thrash his head around and let out a loud roar! His eyes quickly tightened shut as if the words that the legna spoke were hurting him. After a few intense moments, his eyes shot open wide. His eyes were fully black having no white in them at all! They looked like two frightening pools of black water and gleamed as the fire-light bounced off them, like how the moon would on a lake at night.

Tairren watched in shock with wide-open eyes as he held Natalia tightly. He became nervous as the thought of Lilith flashed into his mind. Phillip appeared as Lilith did that night Marrisa was taken.

"Following the night when the moon glows like blood, during the twilight when the morning star shines the brightest—evil will prevail and take on a new form!" Phillip quickly roared out in a terrifying voice that wasn't his. The wicked voice that came out of him began to laugh as Phillip quickly looked at Tairren. "That is what was spoken to you—Tairren, son of Timotheus!" Phillip roared out. The voice that came out of him seemed to tease Tairren. "Evil will prevail and take on a new form!"

Tairren's heart skipped a beat as the dream he had of Marrisa popped into his head. It was the dream he had the night before they left on their quest, when Marrisa stood by the rosemary bush. The images of his dream rushed upon him and felt so real. In the dream he remembered Marrisa's face and how it had turned horrid and terrifying as she growled the same words which Phillip spoke. It was also the same words that Malakh had spoken to him when the being of light came to him in a dream; the night when he was knocked unconscious by Lilith in the fields.

"Leave this child of light, you rancid spirit of darkness, in the powerful name of King Yehoshua!" Mikhal yelled out in a powerful voice that seemed to shake the tent.

All of the sudden Phillip's back arched up as he screamed out, then in a quick second, he lay silent with closed eyes.

More legna rushed into the tent carrying golden vessels of precious oils and bowls of some kind of dried herbs and flower petals. They covered Tairren's view of the bed and he could no longer see Phillip.

Tairren watched nervously, the chaos all around them, as he still held tightly onto Natalia. He had never witnessed such a thing and was confused and frightened by it. He worried for Phillip and wondered if he was now dead.

"Come with me," a kind voice said from behind them. The voice was comforting in the midst of all of the frightening drama. Tairren turned to see who it was as Natalia looked up as well.

The voice came from a female legna. She resembled all the other legna and smiled softly at them. She stood calmly and seemed to not be shaken by anything that was going on. She led them out of the tent and into the cool air of the dark atmosphere around them. The sky was nearly black, giving a hint that night was falling upon them.

"Will Phillip be okay? What is wrong with him?" Natalia asked frantically as she wiped her moist green eyes.

The legna looked deeply into Natalia's eyes and could feel the fear and anxiousness that dwelled so deeply within her.

"He will be fine, Natalia," The legna said softly. Natalia was shocked that she knew her name. "The darkness that made its way inside of Phillip grew strong within him, which opened up a door-way upon his heart. This threshold allowed a dark spirit to take hold of him… But the darkness upon him is gone now and will not come back—he is being cleansed. Phillip is fine and no harm will overtake him. He will just be a little weak—so rest, a sufficient meal, and blessings spoken upon him will bring Phillip back."

Natalia just nodded her head as she glanced up at Tairren, who looked worried as well.

"Do not be perplexed and frightened… The fear of man brings a snare—but whoever puts their trust in the mighty king of light shall be safe," the legna said in a low tone, looking into Tairren's eyes with her yellow-gold stare.

After a moment of silence, she smiled a beautiful glowing smile that even the sun and moon would envy.

"I am called Uriel," she said.

It was strange to Tairren that Uriel looked much like Gaibriul and Mikhal and felt as if he were looking at a twin. But Uriel looked slightly different and just as beautiful. Her features were more delicate and she wore a long white gown, and had on the same wing-pendant around her neck and jeweled diadem around her smooth forehead. Her long white-blonde hair also had a feather woven into it.

"We have been waiting for you here… Follow me so that you may be cleansed as well—so that we can feast and celebrate our mighty king—then we shall rest, for tomorrow's challenges will come with haste…"

"Cleansed? But we do not possess any kind of darkness," Tairren said, confused.

"Tairren, son of Timotheus, the light upon your heart is strong, but an infection of darkness lingers on your skin," Uriel said as she went to place her hand on his bandaged wound. She was quiet as she caressed her delicate hand upon his arm. "I feel it beneath your bandages right now as I touch you."

His arm was still wrapped tightly from when Moral had bandaged it the night he was first attacked by the flying nomed. The bandage was almost completely black because of it being dirty and when she touched it, he could feel the burning sensation swell up deep inside of his flesh. His arm had been bothering him that whole time but he did not want to fret about it and felt it was the least of his worries.

"And you Natalia," she said, setting her gaze on a deep cut that marked the side of her neck. Natalia felt a tingle in her neck as Uriel placed her hand on it.

"Rafiul," Uriel called out in a voice that was soft and pleasant. She beckoned a nearby legna. Tairren noticed that it was the same tall legna who was taking many glances at him when they first arrived at the tent.

The legna came to her call. He was standing and talking with a group of other legna. They stood outside of the door-way of the tent where Phillip rested. As Rafiul came closer, Tairren felt the connection he had with Rafiul become stronger, feeling as if they were brothers or old friends.

"Rafiul, please show Tairren to his dwelling spot, he must be cleansed—and I shall show Natalia to hers."

Rafiul nodded his head then began to escort Tairren through the camp. Tairren gave Natalia a reassuring smile, then turned to leave with the legna.

"I'll see you at the feast then," she said as she smiled back. She occasionally turned her head back to watch Tairren as he followed Rafiul.

†††

Tairren watched the many legna as he passed them by. Some would glance up at him and give him a nod of the head or a small smile, welcoming him. All of the legna appeared intriguing to him; they were all different heights and seemed to glow even though there was no physical light coming from them.

Even the camp was intriguing. All of the tents were perfectly standing up straight and had beautiful golden designs and embroidery on them. The craftsmanship reminded him of his mother's talent in sewing and embroidery. As the tents glowed, there was soft music in the air all around them. The many sounds of stringed instruments, airy flutes, soft drums, and bells filled the atmosphere around him.

The smell of delicious things lingered in the air as well. The air was sweet all around him. The legna carried a scent about them, which smelled sweet and fresh like the clean breezes from mountain tops or the smell of an early ice-cold spring morning. The camp also carried the savory scents of succulent herbed meats roasting and oiled vegetables cooking over smoky fires—which took over his nostrils. They had not eaten an ample meal in two days and the wonderful smells were making his hunger pains worsen.

"Why are there so many of you?" Tairren finally asked Rafiul as he continued to follow him, keeping his eyes on the many beautiful beings of light.

"We are warriors of light, Tairren, and do whatever the Great King commands of us. We are many. We were sent here to protect you and your companions and the kingdom of this land. There will be great struggle and tribulation—and that of Phillip is but a touch of what will come of your people in the Kingdom of Minslethrate. Lucif has become stronger, and he and his followers are feeding off of these lands—off of the darkened hearts of man. The threshold of darkness has been opened by a being which has been living upon these lands for many ages..."

"Lilith," Tairren said in a low tone to himself.

"Yes, this Lilith whom you speak of is a carrier of many vile nomed and is a doorway in which Lucif, the father of evil, uses... Like Phillip, once darkness takes hold of one's heart, a door is opened and Lucif has his way upon that person. This doorway is called the passage of the spirits, and is a threshold which leads to two extremely different kingdoms... Depending on the heart—it can be a passage to the kingdom of light, or a passage to the kingdom of darkness."

Tairren's mind began to become overwhelmed with thought. He realized that they were now walking into another tent. Rafiul held open the doorway as he let Tairren walk inside. The tent was warm and cozy and quiet. It had a sleeping area which was piled high with white linens and feather-filled quilts and a sitting area with a chair and table. There were large candles lit inside of it which filled the tent with a serene ambience. There was a large wooden tub which was filled with hot, steamy water and next to it was a small table which contained small vessels of liquids and oils and bowls of dried herbs and flower petals. Sitting next to that was a chair which held fresh, clean garments which were folded nicely and looked like the ones the legna wore.

As Tairren looked around what seemed to be his very own tent, Rafiul continued to speak.

"Lilith is a domicile of darkness and merely a tool in Lucif's grand scheme," Rafiul said with his hands clasped behind his back.

"I've been hearing the name, Lucif, mentioned many times. I've read of him in ancient writings and heard of him in old lore—but still I do not understand where he comes from," Tairren said as he rubbed his bandaged arm. His arm throbbed a little at the mention of Lucif.

"Lucif was once a legna, long ago in the very beginnings of time. Before this very earth was created, Lucif was an Archlegna and servant to the Great King of light and the commander of the Legion of Light. Out of jealousy and spite, he tried to deceive the Great King, but could not—for the Great King knows all. Lucif yearned to become ruler of Nevaeh and everything that the Great King created. He rose up against the Great King with his followers, to try to rule the Great Kingdom of Light.

"There was a great war. Then when it was all finished, the Great King had won and exiled him and his followers out of Nevaeh and unto the darkness. Lucif, a fallen legna, and his followers, other fallen legna also known as nomed, infested the Great King's creations—like that of the earth and everyone upon it.

"You see Tairren, Lucif and his nomed loathe the Great King with all of their might, and will do anything to stop his great works. They, known as darkness, will do anything to destroy the creations of God and the children of light. They yearn to destroy light. The creations of God and the children of light consists of you, and everyone else who follows Him—everyone and everything which was created by the Great King of light—every living soul upon this earth.

"Over the many years and ages and phases of the world, Lucif traveled upon these lands as a wicked nomad and soul snatcher. He prowled around like a roaring lion—looking for anyone to devour.

"Lucif continued to lurk upon these lands for many years until he crept his way into the royal family by the overtaking of the beautiful Queen Karnidge of Minslethrate, Marrisa's grandmother. The doors of darkness began to open as the royal family fell prisoner to Lucif and his powers. Princess Marrisa is Lucif's ultimate piece and prize in this insidious scheme and will stop at nothing to snatch her soul and overpower her body.

"If Marrisa's body is taken in full—that means a nightmare, which is the end of light upon this earth and human freedom, will become a reality. If Marrisa is overtaken, Lucif will have his way with whomever Marrisa comes in contact with… The Kingdom of Ishkar is a great kingdom of this world and by far the strongest—and this kingdom is the one place in which Lucif will infiltrate next, after Minlsethrate has fallen… The kingdom of Ishkar is anticipating Marrisa's arrival as queen, along with Phillip as king...

"False prophets will rise in her name like foul winds, wickedness will become normality, and the mighty laws of the God of Light will be taken for granted and forgotten. And because of Ishkar's greatness and influence, this very world will fall into the shadow of darkness for many years. Lucif reigns over the world as a deceiving prince and will do anything to become king…"

"How will Lucif reign in Marrisa's body without a king? Marrisa is betrothed to Phillip, but Phillip knows of Lucif's plan and will not be so blind to become deceived by Lucif. He will not bring Marrisa to his kingdom knowing that she is filled with unclean spirits. The light within Phillip grows stronger every day," Tairren said.

"Tairren, Lucif will stop at nothing, and will force the power of darkness upon all men of this earth. Men will be deceived and brainwashed and a blindfold will be pulled tightly upon their eyes. They will submit to him, they will worship him, they will want to become like him. Sin of man is so powerful when one is weak…

"But among all of the darkness there will be guilds of people who follow the light—and they will continue to build the light within them until they die… But only physical death will come upon them—for they will live an eternal life even after death. It is so important to keep the reign of darkness from happening. So many people will become lost—so many people will fall into the clutches of Lucif and his nomed, and those fallen people will become darkened. Their souls will die and everything good in mankind will fall. They will be tormented in the ruthless lake of fire if their soul is not awakened by light… So many people will be deceived and will die—physically and spiritually… That is why it is so important to spread the light of God."

Rafiul looked saddened for a moment as he looked away.

"We cannot let this happen! Mankind must be delivered! Marrisa must be saved—she must. I love her dearly. I long for her to be my prize at the end of this quest," Tairren said as his face lit up.

"I understand your determination, Tairren, but I will never understand the love of a human—for I am in love with the light which the mighty king keeps and gives—my passion is to do what my king commands," Rafiul said with intense eyes. "To save mankind, we must stop the darkness and continue to plant seeds of light into their souls. Those seeds should be planted by the passion of light and the mighty words of God."

"Marrisa is my love and the King of Light is my passion—so I will have this quest and I will not fail!" Tairren said with a shaken voice.

Rafiul nodded and smiled at his zealous mannerism. The dim light of the fire sparkled in his eyes, and through that sparkle, Rafiul could see that Tairren's heart consisted of golden-light. Rafiul knew right then and there that Tairren was the key to this mighty quest, not because he could see a strong burning light deep inside of him, but because he was chosen by the Great King of light himself.

"Lilith will not have Princess Marrisa—Lilith will not defeat us...," Tairren said in a low tone with emotion beginning to stir. "...Lilith has been in Marrisa's life since she was young—I do not understand the change that has taken place in her."

"Lilith was once a typical maiden of Minslethrate. But she came from a very broken past. Many years ago, somewhere in her life, she submitted to the darkness and was seduced by its deception. A seed of iniquity was planted inside of her soul by the darkness—and over the years it grew, and her body was taken over till the very breath of her soul was suffocated. This seed could have taken root by deep anguish, wrath, great sin, or even by closing the windows of light.

"Your companion Phillip could have been in the same state of torment if he was not saved by the light—for Phillip's heart is new upon the covenant of light. Lilith is not a threat—but the army of darkness inside of her is... This army of darkness will spread across these lands like a wild plague."

Rafiul placed his hand upon Tairren's shoulder, then brought his hands to his dirty bandaged arm. His arm continued to tingle a little and pulsated with an uncomfortable pain.

"Darkness is like an infectious disease—and will slowly but surely take over one piece of your body at a time till it contains it in full, if you allow it to," Rafiul said as he unwrapped Tairren's wounded arm. The almost black bandage became whiter as the untouched ends of the cloth were unraveled.

"And sometimes what seems like nothing—is ravaged with something dreadful and unstoppable," Rafiul said as he unraveled the last bit of cloth.

Tairren was taken aback at what dwelled on his arm. He cringed at the sight of it. The deep gashes that the flying creatures left on his arm were infected and seemed to become larger. The wounds covered his arm, and oozed out small amounts of pus. The skin between the lacerations was red and the edges of each wound had black and green around it. He never noticed that his hand was red as well because of it being stained with dirt. Rafiul raised Tairren's sleeve to reveal red vein-like streaks which ran up his arm.

"Your arm is badly infected which is releasing a poison into your blood... When penetrated by a nomed, infectivity and corruption slowly take over the body tissue until it dies..."

A worried look came over Tairren as he pulled open the collar of his tunic. He found more red streaks on his chest, so he pulled his tunic off. The red streaks went up his arm, over his shoulder and across his chest, appearing like a web of dark-red veins that reached for his heart.

"The infection of the wound is trying to make its way to your heart. It must be stopped before your heart becomes poisoned."

"What must I do?" Tairren asked as he looked into Rafiul's golden eyes.

Rafiul was quiet for a moment, then looked at the beautiful wing pendant that hung on Tairren's bare chest. The many jewels of the pendant sparkled in the fire light of the candles.

"Like us, I see that you wear a symbol of light upon your breast. And if you wear this symbol as we do, it must not be an idol, but merely a symbol which is meant to show other eyes whom you follow—for our lord is the King of Light who is with us, inside us, and all around us. So, you must keep the lord, who is the Great King of light, upon your heart. Meaning, like us, you must be a follower of the Great King of light"

Tairren nodded his head slowly. He noticed that he was still looking at his pendant. He held it up to get a better look at it, then left it alone.

Rafiul continued in a low tone, "Because you have made the Lord, which is my refuge and king, even the most high, your habitation, there shall no evil befall upon you—even shall any plague come nigh thy dwelling... Our Lord the most high says that he will restore health upon you, and will heal you of your wounds—if you would just believe and declare this in your heart... And I see the belief in your eyes and I feel the faith in your beating heart…," Rafiul said as he placed his hand on Tairren's arm. "Accept healing and believe it deep within your soul," Rafiul said as he closed his eyes. I shall bless you with the song of healing. Close your eyes and call out to the Great King with your heart, as you once did."

After a moment of silence, Rafiul began to softly sing out in the divine tongue again. He sang out a peaceful prayer and even though Tairren could not understand it, he felt that it was good. The prayer song was soft and lovely and seemed to sooth his wound, even his soul.

After he was done singing, Tairren opened his eyes. He was amazed that his wounds did not tingle and throb anymore as they did before and looked much better. The skin around his wounds was no longer red and the wounds themselves looked much better. The skin on his arm no longer looked sick and grotesque, but alive.

"Thank you," Tairren said in a low tone, still looking at his arm.

"Thank the lord of light," the legna responded. "For healing does not come from the song, but from the lord of the most high.

Rafiul smiled then walked over to the wooden tub. He took the small vessels of liquids and oils from the table and poured them into the hot water, and then sprinkled the dried herbs and flower petals out onto the steaming water as well. He pulled his sword from its jeweled sheath. The sword was of pure gold and the hilt was embedded with jewels. The glow from the soft candle light flickered off of it. He stirred the hot tub water with the grand sword, then looked up at Tairren with his piercing, yellow-golden eyes.

"Come, Tairren, you must finish the cleansing." Rafiul walked over to the entrance of the tent, and then looked back. "Make rest in the lord and he will calm your weary soul—his yoke is easy and his burden is light. Come—find your peace and be made whole. Rest your aching muscles and wounds in the water. There are clean garbs ready for you. You must be famished and exhausted after a long journey. When you are ready, come to the great fire in the center of the camp—we will feast and celebrate all of the great things the God of Light has done for us."

After Rafiul left, the calm and ambient atmosphere came over Tairren. He looked at his dirty hands and torn and soiled garments. He thought he must've looked filthy standing amongst the legna and their clean and orderly provisions. He glanced at the pile of fresh garbs they had ready for him and smiled at the thought of becoming new again. He stripped off his clothing and got into the hot water. Goosebumps that felt like rays of sunlight went through his skin as he settled down in the soft, hot water.

He thought of all the things Rafiul had said as he melted into the water. Every tense muscle and burning cut seemed to diminish as he thanked the God of Light for everything. He felt very blessed and thankful for the legna and their kind hospitality and words of wisdom. He was thankful for healing and protection. He was thankful that even in the times of the most intense situations, he seemed to be in God's favor.

He couldn't get over how one day he was worried about their lives and not having food and the next he was being taken care of. He knew this was by the grace of the Great King. He then thought of Marrisa and wondered if she was okay and if she was in good health. He began to feel great pity for the woman he loved; because while he was relaxing in hot, sweet-smelling herbal cleansing water, he knew that Marrisa wouldn't be.

After a long while of resting and washing in the hot water, Tairren slipped on the soft garbs that the legna had ready for him. He strapped on the sturdy belt they left for him and attached his dagger and its sheath to it. He pulled on the boots that sat on the floor next to his new provisions, realizing that it was like putting each one of his feet into a perfectly molded cloud.

He was anxious to see the legna and if Phillip was well. He wondered if both Phillip and Natalia were being treated as wonderfully as he was— and he hoped that they were.

Tairren walked out into the cool, open air of the camp. He was surprised by the quietness of his area of the camp. There were no legna anywhere around him, and everything was still around him. He could hear the soft sounds of music and laughter coming from the distance. The soft sounds of the drums and flutes made him feel happy and the smells of the food made him hungrier. The legna must've begun their celebration without him. He thought he must've been in his tent too long, but he couldn't resist the lengthy time he was allowed to have in the hot, cleansing water.

Tairren walked to the large tent where he last saw Phillip. He became nervous for Phillip as he walked into the soft glow of candle light which filled the tent. He didn't know what state of mind he would be in. Tairren looked around, noticing that the tent was empty as well, and quiet. He could tell that the tent must've been used for mending and healing because of all the bottles of liquids, herbs, and strange looking devices that sat on shelves all around the tent walls. There were many other beds in the tent, each one having a large wooden tub sitting by its side.

There was a doorway in the back of the tent which led to another section of it. Tairren didn't notice the door-way before because of all the commotion that filled the tent earlier. It was strange how calm and quiet it was compared to when they first arrived to the camp. Someone came out of the doorway, startling Tairren. It was Phillip, appearing refreshed and almost back to normal. He was wearing the same new garbs as Tairren, appearing not as a prince, but a born-again man. Tairren walked over to him, not saying anything, but only having a small smile on his face.

"I was worried, for your sake, prince," Tairren said, placing his hand on his shoulder. "It is nice to see that a familiar face is doing so well."

Phillip stood quiet for a moment, placing his hand on Tairren's shoulder as well.

"I have been saved and made new," Phillip said, then pulled Tairren to him and gave him a warm hug. "We are brothers now."

They both chuckled a little bit at the situation they were in, going from disliking each other and fighting one day to embracing each other the next.

"That is strange to hear," Tairren said, with a smirk.

"Everything is strange now, Master Tairren, or should I call you— brother Tairren," Phillip said with a large smile.

Tairren laughed a little, then cleared his throat.

"So, tell me—how are you feeling? You were not in a good state of health or mind at all when I last saw you," Tairren said. "The state of you was not welcoming, but very uncomfortable and somewhat jarring."

"Well—I do not know much of what happened to me," Phillip said as he walked over to his things. He inspected his sword and other weaponry. "All I remember is darkness. I remember I was in the Black Forest with you all, then I remember falling into darkness, down, down—then I opened my eyes and I saw that hand of light again. The hand was loving and glowing and made of bright fiery light—and I reached out and touched it... Then I opened my eyes again and I was lying on this bed and looking up at the many wonderful faces of the legna...

"But I am well now and feel as if I've been reborn! I feel as if I am a new person! I feel as if my eyes had been closed all of this time and now, I can finally see. I feel as if I've been awakened somehow—as if I have been sleeping my whole life and now, I am full of life..."

Tairren nodded and smiled at his enthusiasm. The words that came out of his mouth were wonderful to hear.

"Welcome back," Tairren said, then patted him on the shoulder. "You have surely been spared and saved…"

After a moment of appreciation, Tairren gave Phillip one last brotherly hug. "I suppose we should be off to find Natalia and the others."

With that being said, they left the tent and walked out into the still darkness of the night. They passed through the camp, walking past many tents, torches and small fires that glowed with soft orange hues. There was no motion around them, except for the dancing fires that crackled here and there around them.

Something caught their eyes in the stillness of the tents. It looked as if someone was watching them. They saw something rush past one of the tents. They thought they saw someone in a dark cloak with a hood that shadowed its face. They rushed over to where they thought they saw it to find that there was no one there. They thought it could've been a legna rushing by, but it was too dark to be a being of light. They thought it must've been a trick of the dancing shadows which came from the fire light. Instead, eager to get to the celebration, they continued through the hall made by the tents.

As they came closer to the center of the camp, the music got louder, as well as the laughter. The closer they got, the more their hearts began to fill with joy. Soon they made it to the center, walking out of the wall of tents and into a very large space and an atmosphere filled with excitement and companionship. The area of the center of the camp was one large circle with a huge bonfire which sat in the very center of it. All of the tents circled around the center, giving the space the appearance of some sort of courtyard.

There were decorated tables and benches everywhere. The long tables were topped with many different kinds of lavish food, drink and beautiful candelabras and the benches were filled with cheerful legna. Even the horses seemed excited as they grazed upon the cool grass. Many of the horses fed on the outside of the circle, flicking their tales and standing with each other like cohorts.

They noticed many beasts sitting here and there, resembling Serafim greatly. Some of the mighty, beautiful beasts were the color of a pale-gold sunrise and others were white as snow. The beasts were not like the horses that stood and grazed upon the earth, but they seemed to mingle with the other legna, as if they were a part of the legna and not just a means of traveling.

The beings of light were everywhere; some were dancing, some were standing and talking while others were sitting at the tables eating and drinking merrily with one another. Some of the legna were playing wonderful music while others were lounging on the soft grass and on large embellished pillows and cushions that sat sporadically upon the soft green grass. The whole sight of it was the true meaning of fellowship, and every single one of them appeared very happy and true to each other.

They made their way through the crowd, enjoying everything they beheld. As they walked, they caught the attention of many legna who looked on them with friendly smiles. As they walked, they began to feel somewhat important, as if the legna knew something grand and spectacular about them that they did not.

"You appear very refreshed and uplifted," a soft and kind voice said from behind them. They turned to see that the kind voice came from Uriel. She stood tall and beautiful and looked as if she had just come down from the stars and moon. She appeared like a celestial queen. "You must be looking for your companion, Natalia," she said with a soft smile.

She looked at Phillip who never took his eyes away from her fair countenance and striking eyes.

"I am called Uriel, my dear Prince Phillip," she said, looking into his eyes with her golden-yellow stare. "I am very pleased to see that you have been made whole."

Phillip felt as if he were connected to Uriel somehow. He didn't know why but, in his mind, he saw a shiny golden cord connecting both Uriel and himself together. Just by standing in her presence, he felt safe—as if he was at home. He felt a strong bond between them, as a friend would for another, or as a relationship between a brother and sister.

"Thank you, my lady," he finally said with a slow nod of the head.

"Follow me," she said as she walked towards the great bonfire.

They gladly followed beside her and took in the sights and sounds of everything and everyone.

"Lady Uriel," Tairren said, watching the legna. There seemed to be hundreds of them. "Where did you come from? I mean—where are you and your people from? I know you are from a kingdom called Nevaeh—but, where is this kingdom?"

Uriel looked at Tairren with a smile. Tairren thought he saw stars in her golden eyes as she smiled. She then looked over all of the joyful legna, smiling proudly.

"You know where this kingdom is. But it is impossible to find this kingdom if you do not know the God of Light. He is the way, the truth and the life—no one can come into the Kingdom of Light, except through Him. Only the ones, whose names are written in the Great King's Book of Life, are welcome—only the ones who know Him, are written in this book. Nevaeh is where the God of Light is—and where the God of Light is, that is where Nevaeh dwells. When you believe in Him, and know Him in your heart—that is where He is. And if He is in your heart—that is where the Kingdom of Light is." Uriel looked into his dark-blue eyes, then smiled. "Do you understand, young Tairren?"

Tairren looked confused and looked away from Uriel, not wanting to appear daft.

"That means that the Kingdom of Nevaeh is—within me?" he said.

"The Kingdom of Light is near you, within you and all around you… Do not fret—do not feel ashamed that you do not understand the full mysteries of God—but He will reveal them to you in time… The God of Light and His is kingdom are so vast and the human mind can only configure what it has experienced—so I will explain it in such a way that you will understand.

"The Kingdom of Nevaeh is a great kingdom—further away than even the ends of this earth. It sits north from here, on the edge of the sparkling black veil, away from the eyes of men. Here in this kingdom, the Great King of Light has made a splendid home for every soul that invites Him into their lives... Every heart that contains light—contains Him… He will wipe away every tear in their eyes, and there will be no more death or sorrow or pain… For all these things will be gone forever… And you will live forever in a peace that you have never felt before… And He waits for you—and has been doing so since you were born…"

Uriel stopped speaking, then smiled again at them. They just looked at her with wonder. Every word that came out of her mouth was mind-blowing to them, and they wanted to see this Great Kingdom of Light, they wanted to follow this king of light even more. They continued to walk through the crowd, making their way to the massive fire that gleamed brightly before them. Tairren and Phillip thought of everything that she revealed to them, and they dwelled on it as they watched the beings of light around them. They did not see any sorrowful or burden-laden person around them, and they wondered if their surroundings were similar to that of Nevaeh.

As they came closer to the fire, they spotted Natalia who was sitting with a group of legna on some lavish pillows, listening to the music that was being played by a group of legna. The music was very soothing and beautiful and Natalia looked very relaxed and pleased as she listened, randomly making conversation with the legna who were sitting around her. They looked as if they were family or old friends, just spending time together.

"There she is," Uriel said, motioning towards her with a graceful movement of her arm.

Natalia noticed them right away and got up excitedly. She looked as if she were an eager child who had just found her long lost pet.

"Tairren! Phillip!" she said as she hurried to them. She gave them both a huge hug as if she hadn't seen them for some time. The legna around them chuckled a little as they watched, having great smiles on their faces.

Natalia pulled them to the group of legna she had been conversing with and introduced them all to each other. They were all pleased to finally get to meet them in person. They all ate and laughed together for some time, enjoying each other's company and stories. Other legna served them wonderful food and drink, while the others sang for them and entertained them with dances and special light-filled music ballads. They had forgotten all about the stressful state that they were in. They felt full of peace and happy again for the first time in days as they listened to the beautiful ballads...

They all sang joyfully together in a song of worship.

You are the light that burns within us,
Burning like the stars!
You are the winds that whirl about us,
Brushing upon our scars!
You are the fire that grows around us,
Burning up every darkened thing!
You sculpted the mountains and the oceans deep,
Every beautiful thing for our eyes to keep!
You are the passion that ignites a flame within us,
That is why we sing!
We sing you a song of praise, a song of adoration,
Because you pour your light upon every nation!
Oh, how we love you!

Oh, how we smile,
Even when we know that trials and tribulations go
On for miles!
You are the light that burns within us,
Burning like the stars!
You are the shield that always defends us,
Even when we are mulled and scarred!
We dance for you like the flowers do in your
Whirling and twirling wind!
We shout for you like the men do when their hearts
Begin to mend!
Hand in hand and feet jumping up on high,
We will always be dancing children of Light!

Through the words of the song, they could feel the happiness from it that the legna felt. They felt peace and joy and love. They enjoyed watching the legna dance and sing for the God of Light. And even among the darkness and hard times, it was thrilling to see joy and love—it was good to see the legna loving and worshiping their king. After a while of enjoying everything all around them, they noticed that the group of dancing legna began to settle down. The legna still continued to sing a little as they sat. Tairren, Natalia, and Phillip still laughed and talked amongst each other, beginning to feel comfortable where they were at. They felt that they could stay and fellowship all night if they were allowed to.

Just then, the legna around them became quiet as Mikhal, Gaibriul, Rafiul, and Uriel walked into everyone's view right before the great fire. They were followed by other important-looking legna whom they hadn't met yet. Tairren, Natalia, and Phillip glanced at each other as they looked towards the large group of Archlegna. They admired their mannerism and appearance as they stood tall and beautiful like living statues. They all looked so grand and beautiful and created a soft glow around them. Mikhal came first with his hand raised in the air, and the others right behind him. Some of the mighty beasts walked with them as well. They noticed Serafim who perched quietly next to Gaibriul—his mighty head came up to Gaibriul's shoulder. The quietness spread amongst the whole camp like a wave of silent peace. The only noise was that of the great bonfire that crackled behind them.

Tairren noticed that the great white owl appeared in the sky, but not where everyone could see it. He seemed to be the only one who noticed it as it glided through the night sky. It flapped its large, beautiful wings upon the black velvet canopy above them, leaving the sounds of deep heart-beats trailing behind it. It gracefully fluttered down to the ground, then perched on a large boulder that sat far off on the outside of the clearing. Tairren admired the owl, and somehow, its mysterious presence seemed to make him feel at peace.

"My fellow brothers and sisters of light—I come to announce joyful news!" Mikhal spoke aloud to the whole camp with his powerful voice. "As you all know, we have been sent here by our great king—the almighty King of Light—to rid of the darkness which is augmenting so strongly upon the earth! And it starts here in Minslethrate. During our quest upon Minslethrate, which is the first settlement of light, we were called to find three keys upon the lands first. These three keys are to unlock three quests upon our one mighty quest. Without these three keys, our mighty quest to save these lands will come to an abrupt halt.

"And by the grace of our God we have found them!" All of a sudden, the whole camp began to cheer and clap. The legna who sat around Tairren, Natalia, and Phillip cheered for them and patted their backs. They were confused and clapped along with them, not knowing exactly what they were clapping for. "Yes, we have found them!" Mikhal continued with a kind face. "Come forth—Tairren, son of Timotheus, The Lady Natalia of Ducre', and Prince Phillip of Ishkar!"

All three of them glanced at each other, appearing confused and surprised. They slowly stood up and walked towards the Archlegna as everyone around them continued to cheer and clap. They glanced at all of the legna who cheered zealously all around them, then to the tall Archlegna who stood before them. Their hearts fluttered with excitement and their minds were flooded with wonder. They had no idea what Mikhal spoke of or what was going on, but all three of them knew it was good. They felt that they were walking in a dream, and strangely did not want to awaken from it. They walked towards the beautifully intimidating Archlegna and humbly stood before them.

"You are the keys in which I speak," Mikhal said to them with passion in his eyes. "You are the keys in this journey—to this quest! From the very beginning, when you were first born, God had a plan for you. You are all part of a grand design which was created by the Great King of Light. All three of you, who are very different and from different back grounds, were put together in each other's lives for a reason.

"If it wasn't for each one of you—you would not be standing here right now. You are the pieces to a mighty puzzle—and fitting together perfectly. Hear me when I say this, God has a plan for you, and it is happening as I speak this very moment. Every person you have ever touched, and every soul you have ever spoken to are part of that plan. This earth is a grand scheme, designed by our almighty God—who is the King of Light and all that is good and all that is of love.

"You all have great things happening within you!" All three of them had a twinkle of a tear in their eyes, and that twinkle was from the light that sparkled within them.

"Each one of you is to be sent on your own quest—sent to a dark place which has stolen the righteous armor of the Great King of light. Without this armor, our hero will not be able to withstand the evils which are coming like a mighty black dragon. Then, on the eve of war, when darkness is as thick as fog, evil will take on a new form... But do not fret—for light always breaks through the darkness. Just as the sun rises upon the night sky; just as the moon and stars shine through the black veil and like the burning of a great fire amongst the darkest of dark—so will the children of light— burn and shine bright!" Mikhal looked at each one of them in the eyes. They felt nervous and slightly frightened by all of the abrupt information— but empowered at the same time. "But first a test—a personal quest... One of you will face fallen earth, one of you will face deceitful water, and the other will feel the fervor of false fire... Then all of you will face the beings of darkness..."

Everything that Mikhal spoke of was like an intriguing poem or riddle. They did not understand everything he was speaking of right then, but they knew it would become unraveled later on in their quest.

"Let me ask you something," Mikhal said, looking at each one of them. "Do you believe what I am speaking of? Do you want to know what I speak of? Do you want to know the king of all kings—Yehoshua?"

All three of them were quiet. Their hearts beat so loudly that they could hear it in their ears. They began to think that Mikhal could even hear their heart-beats. Happiness swelled up within them and came out as more twinkling tears. They felt an urge within them that felt like a mighty tug from a great hand. They felt the same tug before, when they were rescued at the Great Wall of Division. They felt empowered and nervous and inundated with something they were beginning to become familiar with—passion for light. All three of them shook their heads yes, and meant it.

Mikhal came to them and bunched them together before him. They looked up at him as he stood a foot or so taller than them. He smiled at them.

"He is proud of your decision," he said. "Declare this sacred prayer out loud and within your very being," Mikhal said in a now low tone. "This sacred prayer is a declaration of your faith." After every line he spoke, they repeated it after him.

"Father of Lights, I believe everything you reveal to me… Great King of Light I want to live for you and no longer for the darkness of this world… I know I am part of your divine plan… Show me your plan… Make me new… Come into my heart and soul and fill my heart with your precious oil… I believe your blood was shed long ago for me, King Yehoshua… Burn within me a light of unending zeal…"

After they were finished reciting the sacred prayer, they looked at each other with tears in their eyes as smiles crept across their faces. They started to laugh a little as happiness flooded their hearts.

"Now—do you accept this quest?" Mikhal asked in a low tone that only they heard. They shook their heads to accept and meant that as well.

"Then it has begun! Welcome our new family members of light with joyful noise!" Mikhal shouted out loud to the on looking legna with raised hands.

All of the legna shouted and clapped with joy again, and they could feel the love all round them.

"Phillip, our strong and brave prince—you are like the mighty beasts that roam the earth, and will do great things because of your dedication and bravery, accept this as symbol of light—for those who see it will know that you serve our mighty king of light—the one true God." Mikhal motioned for Uriel to step forward. She smiled at him as she put a beautiful golden chain around his neck. A wing-shaped pendant dangled from it and twinkled in the fire-light.

"Natalia, our witty and compassionate Lady, you are like the furtive cat that strikes and loves. You will help a lost soul because of your love and wit." Just then Mikhal motioned for Gaibriul to come forth. He also placed a wing-shaped pendant around her neck. She felt very thankful for Mikhal's words and very proud to wear such a symbol.

"And Tairren, our true hero—you are the main piece to this grand design. You held this group together by your words, you protected them with all you had, and you kept the light so strongly within your heart. You know what must be done… You are a true hero—and wear a wing-pendant which was passed down from a true hero…," Mikhal said as he came closer to Tairren. He pulled Tairren's beautiful jeweled wing-pendant away from his chest so that they both could see it clearly.

Both Phillip and Natalia peered over curiously, wondering where he got his pendant from. Natalia remembered that he had told her it was passed down from Moral; but where did she get it?

"You already wear the symbol of light upon your breast—but more importantly you always wore your faith upon yourself…," Mikhal continued. "You know that wearing this pendant does not make you righteous, for that is idolism, and idolism is a seed of darkness—you know that your heart and faith makes you righteous and true. For the Lord thy God is upon us, within us and all around us." Mikhal placed his hand on Tairren's chest, then motioned out over the crowd as he said this. "And the pendant which you wear—was passed down from generation to generation and ended up in your grasp. This is the very pendant which was created in King Yehoshua's honor—to always remind the onlookers, whom the keeper of it followed. This great man who created it was one of your ancestors and was one of the ancient earthly kings of Minlsethrate."

Natalia and Phillip quickly glanced at each other, amazed at what they were hearing. They were shocked to know that the one they knew as a humble peasant boy, was the descendant of a king.

"Your ancestor was awakened by a legna long ago and he was advised by the legna to create this wing-shaped pendant. Your ancestor who wore this pendant worshiped King Yehoshua and announced and declared that King Yehoshua was the one true king. Yehoshua reigned as king and did many miracles and led his children of light against darkness. After it was all over, the darkness fell—and became silent for some time. But evil was not dead and waited for the right opportunity to attack again. This opportunity came, and the darkness crept into the life of one of King Yehoshua's twelve trusted knights—and this trusted knight betrayed Yehoshua. The king was captured and killed deep in the southern parts of Minslethrate—upon Skull Hill, amongst the Black Field of Old Blood."

Tairren had a tear in his eye as he took in the powerful story. Mikhal wiped his tear away like a care-giver would to a child.

"You see Tairren, your ancestral king created this necklace and wore it so that everyone could see who he believed in. He stood up for the Great King Yehoshua and was not afraid. He did everything he could to follow Him and the word He taught. You see Tairren, son of Timotheus, you are the rightful descendant of a king who ruled Minslethrate—you are the true prince of Minslethrate from a very ancient and royal bloodline... And the pendant has found its way to you to reveal this... Long ago, a legna was instructed by the Great King of Light to tell your ancestor to create this pendant. Like I revealed before, everything happens for a reason. And many years ago, the pendant was created so this moment could happen. You see—you are the chosen one..."

Tairren smiled, beginning to think of everything his mother had revealed to him before he left Minslethrate. That great moment with the legna had confirmed everything his mother had told him. He felt so proud of his family, his mother and father, and knew that even if he did not find out the information of his true bloodline, he would still love himself and would continue to live strong. He thought of King Yehoshua and wanted to do everything he could to follow his path and word, to honor him.

Everyone continued to cheer. Tairren glanced at Phillip and Natalia who had great smiles on their faces. Phillip respectfully nodded at Tairren as Natalia continued to wipe the tears from her eyes.

"All three of you now stand before me as children of light. Yesterday you were dying. Yesterday you were merely a peasant boy, a lady, and a prince of the world. Right now, as I speak, you are all the same—you are all children of light! All three of you are reborn and the same in the Great King of Light's eyes. So now you have it!" Mikhal spoke out loud again. "You are the three keys of Minslethrate and the Union of Light! So, with that said, let all bitterness, and wrath, and anger, and clamor, and evil speaking be put away from you, along with all malice. And be kind to one another, tenderhearted, forgiving one another, even as God for Christ's sake has forgiven you," Mikhal said proudly. "For you were sometimes darkness, but now you are light in the lord! So, continue to walk as children of light."

The three keys, the union of light, stood with smiles on their faces and looked so proud. For that quick moment they had left the full amount of stress and severity of that day, behind them. The feeling of death and uncertainty did not sit on their shoulders as it did before they arrived at the camp. Tairren looked into the great fire that crackled and roared behind the group of Archlegna.

The fire reminded him of Marrisa and that one summer night when she shared her fear of fire. He began to miss her terribly and wondered what was happening to her that very night. He began to not understand why they weren't leaving that very night to rescue her. He began to wonder if she was even still alive. But all of a sudden as the darkened thoughts of Marrisa began to creep into his mind, he caught the glimpse of the great white owl who sat very still and quietly upon the boulder far off in the background. He was somehow reminded to be patient—that everything happens for a reason. He heard the still small voice in his heart say this. Then all of a sudden, the great white owl opened its wings as if flew into the air. Tairren watched as it flew off into the night sky—going towards the south...

"But do not be frightened of your quests," Mikhal continued aloud. "For each one of you will be accompanied by a guardian. Your guardian is the one who has given you your pendant," Mikhal said, motioning his hand towards, Giabriul, Uriel, and Rafiul. "These are your Guardian legna and will be with you and will help you and protect you. Phillip your guardian is Uriel; Natalia your guardian is Gaibriul, and Tairren, your guardian is Rafiul." Mikhal then looked at Tairren and spoke softly, "Tairren, do not feel forgotten. You did not receive a pendant from Rafiul for he knew that you already had one and that you already contained the light of God within you... Your bond with Rafiul began when he laid his hands upon you to heal and cleanse you of the sickness that grew upon you..."

Each one of the Guardian Archlegna walked over to their comrade. Tairren, Natalia, and Phillip understood why they felt at peace and why each one of them felt a silent connection with them. Rafiul, Gaibriul, and Uriel were their guardians and their spirits knew of this as soon as they saw them.

"Now—my brethren! Come and let was worship Him in song! Praise the Great King of Light for everything he has done for us! Love him because he has loved us first! Let all who has breath—praise his holy name!" Mikhal shouted out with passion.

All of the legna jumped up to their feet, cheering as the group of musicians began a song of bliss. The legna held hands and skipped and danced through the field. They swayed their clasped hands back and forth and glided merrily along the earth as the breezes played through their long hair. The sounds of drums, flutes, bells and stringed instruments filled the air. A beautiful female legna that was dressed in gold began to sing. Her voice rang out in beautiful wisps, rolling across the camp in ripples of serenity. The whole atmosphere seemed to worship the Great God of Light, and everyone within it gave Him glory.

The other Archlegna and the beasts joined the many dancing legna as well. The Archlegna held hands and danced and sang while the beasts leaped from the ground and flew into the air with opened wings, twirling and flying and roaring with one another. But Tairren, Natalia and Phillip stood near Mikhal, wanting to know more information about many things. None of their guardians moved yet, and still stood by their sides.

"Mikhal," Tairren said, catching the Archlegna's attention, "What are the quests in which you spoke of and what is the armor that you have mentioned? Why should we wait to begin the quests if they are ours? Marrisa needs our help!"

Mikhal was quiet for a moment, looking into Tairren's eyes with his golden stare. He smiled at Tairren and placed his hands on his shoulders.

"My brother Tairren," he spoke softly but seriously, "You know the answers to those questions. With time, they will be answered again unto you. Tairren, remember, everything that happens—happens because it has to… And if whatever happens comes from darkness—God uses it to test, uplift, and make you stronger upon this world. God uses things that happen out of darkness—for good, unto light. This world you walk on is but a test. This test is to prepare you for the Great Kingdom of light that awaits you after your time on earth is finished. You will receive great rewards from the God of Light when you do what he asks of you on this earth…

"Do you understand what I have revealed to you?" Mikhal's face was kind and full of passion. Tairren did not know what else to say so he just nodded his head as he always did. "I know that you want answers now, young Tairren, but all of your questions will be answered in time. Trust in the lord with all of your heart—and do not lean on your own understanding."

Mikhal stood up straight, then motion his hands out to the scene of the dancing and joyful legna. The guardian Archlegna smiled at them and placed their hands on their shoulders, slowly pulling them away.

"Go brethren—Celebrate with the legna and worship Him! Know that for those who love God all things will work together for good, for those who are called according to his purpose!"

Just then the Archlegna grabbed their hands and began to dance with one another. Tairren, Natalia and Phillip submitted to their pulls and danced with them. It was like a release of stress as they danced with the legna—

letting themselves go into the light-filled presence that lay thickly amongst them. They all had smiles on their faces and laughed with joy as they danced in bows and in circles throughout the clearing of the camp.

They danced around the great fire and sang the light-filled ballad again with all of their hearts…

We dance for you like the flowers do in your
Whirling and twirling winds!
We shout for you like no others do because our
Hearts are filled with you!
Hand in hand and feet up on high we will always
Be dancing children of Light!

While the legna continued to celebrate, Tairren walked off to the side of the clearing. He couldn't help but think about Marrisa. He wanted to know if she was safe or not. If he could he would leave right then and there to pull Marrisa from the darkness. He couldn't understand that, if danger and darkness was so thick around them—why were they resting so much?

Tairren sat on the outside of the clearing on one of the lavish pillows and next to a small fire. He watched everyone for a while. They all had smiles on their lovely faces. He spotted Natalia and Phillip smiling and laughing together, holding hands while dancing. They seemed to enjoy each other's company and seemed really fond of each other.

He seemed to be the only one that felt stress upon his shoulders. He felt as if he had the weight of the whole world upon him. He knew deep down that he should give that stress up, because King Yehoshua took the weight of the world and died for it… But he just couldn't help it. He knew this quest was for him. He knew what he had to do. He just wanted to know what would happen, he wanted to know that everything would be okay; he wanted to know that Marrisa would come back to the kingdom with him, safe and sound. He looked into the small fire, watching how the flames moved and how the wood crackled and popped beneath it, turning into glowing embers.

"Why do you sit alone?" a kind voice said from behind him. It was Rafiul. "May I sit with you?"

Tairren looked up to the tall legna, then just nodded his head. Rafiul sat near him, glancing at him every once in a while.

"I feel overwhelmed," Tairren finally said. "I am just a peasant boy who is in love with a princess. I am just a poor boy. I only want to know that Marrisa is safe—and will be safe…"

They both sat still, staring into the soft, dancing flames.

"Tairren—I will tell you what you are… You are not just a peasant boy—you are a son of kings. You are the son of the king of kings. You are a key to this quest. You are a human…you worry because you don't know what will happen. I don't understand human emotions but I do know that you must trust in God with all of your heart—do not lean on your own understandings…" Rafiul continued to look at him as he stared into the fire. "Tairren, the God of Light is so immense and so grand… You are but a sparkle of dust upon his hand. You are like a star among his great countenance—which is the heavens… When a human tries so hard to understand things on his own—he tends to fall away from God. He will know when this happens because the burdens of the world will come over his body like a heavy thunderstorm. But sometimes that's what it will take to remind him that God is greater. Always remember that God is greater than any problem you face. Always remember that you are that one star upon his heavens… If he takes you to these problems—he will get you through it…"

Tairren understood what he was trying to tell him and knew that he was right. Everything a legna said was always important and a message from the Great God of Light. Like Rafiul had said, he was just a human and had the propensity to feel that way. He thought of the Legend of the first children of light, his ancient ancestors, who were the first to set foot upon the lands of Minslethrate—and the first to fall… Just as Gaibriul had said that they disobeyed the Great King of light, leaning on their own understandings—he was doing the same thing. Tairren understood that he had the natural tendency to feel that way—he just needed to lean more on God.

"I needed to hear that," Tairren said, turning to Rafiul with a small smile.

"You are humble and silent… When you feel that no one understands what is going on within you—know that God does. God knows every detail of your heart. He knows how much stress you can take. It is a test—and it will strengthen you… And you must be strong for what awaits you beyond this camp. You must be strong and know that whatever happens, God will use it."

"What else is there? I know the legends and I know that darkness is upon us—but what must I do for my own quest that was prophesied by Mikhal?"

Rafiul looked into his eyes with his golden stare. The firelight mingled with his skin, making him look as if he were glowing.

"Your quest was decided for you by the Great God of Light. Each one of you has learned something great that has touched your hearts during this journey. Only you know what it is. This is your own personal quest. You may not know what I speak of now, but in time you will know. You have fire in your heart Tairren—and fire is what you must face. Do you understand, Tairren?"

Tairren stared into the fire. It continued to dance, sending small shadows here and there.

"Fire," Tairren said to himself. "I must face fire…"

"Yes, brother Tairren," Rafiul said. "Deep within the Forbidden Lands, there is a temple that rests on the west side of Fiara Mountains. This temple is your quest…"

Tairren's heart skipped a beat when Rafuil said this. He knew of the temple and heard many legends and lore about it.

"I've heard of this temple—I have it marked on my map," Tairren said with an excited edge.

"This temple holds a piece of weaponry, which is needed for a much greater task. You must retrieve the weaponry with what you have learned—that is your quest. It will all make sense when the time comes."

"I must go then—now." Tairren said, standing up.

He felt as if the fire inside of him sparked up, giving him a surge of energy.

"No Tairren, you must rest first—for the journey is long," Rafiul said, now standing before him. He put his hands on his shoulders and looked into his eyes again. "Morning would be wise."

Tairren felt as if he didn't need any rest then—he didn't want to rest.

"I should go…," Tairren said with a serious face.

Rafiul just studied his face as he stepped back.

"There is a small clearing, just past a small wooded area," Rafiul said, pointing in that direction. "There is a mighty cliff which looks out upon the whole southern part of Minslethrate. Walk a couple yards straight through that small wooded area and you will find it. It is safe—a single nomed will not be so bold to creep upon this camp. It is secluded and quiet. I suggest you wait on the lord there in the stillness of the night—you will know what to do then."

Rafiul patted Tairren's shoulder and gave him a reassuring smile. Tairren softly smiled back, and then nodded his head. He glanced in the direction in which Rafiul had pointed. Tairren left towards the spot by the cliff. He was beginning to feel better—but he still kept getting an urge within him to go. He just wanted to get on with his quest. He just wanted Marrisa by his side.

†

CHAPTER 21
Revelations

All through the night a cursed, dark figure watched the fellowship of the legna and their new brethren. The skulking figure crept on the outside of the clearing, hiding behind the tents and hurrying past the small open spaces which the tents made. It seemed to be stalking the legna and was curious of everything that was going on. The figure wore long dark garbs that consisted of a large hood that shadowed its face and long sleeves that covered its arms. The thing seemed timid but menacing as it crept about, just watching—unnoticed...

†††

It seemed that the legna danced all night, being enveloped in a presence that felt as if light had become alive upon them. They worshiped and fellowshipped for some time, not realizing how late it was getting. Then, it seemed that many of the legna had retired for their tents. The clearing of the camp was not melodic or crowded as it was before and even Serafim and his beastly comrades seemed to depart somewhere. Natalia and Phillip had been holding hands and danced for a while, laughing and engaging with one another; then they began to mingle with the legna in cheerful conversation.

Natalia looked around, realizing that Tairren was nowhere in sight. She realized that she actually hadn't seen him for a while. She left Phillip's side, parting him as he stayed in deep conversation with the some of the legna. She noticed Rafiul walking away from the clearing, wondering if he knew where Tairren had gone. He was walking by himself and looked as if he were beginning to retire for the night.

"Rafiul," Natalia called out softly as she rushed upon him, catching his attention. "Have you seen Tairren? I haven't seen him for some time and— was beginning to worry."

Rafiul nodded, then pointed to the southern area of the camp. The southern parts of the camp looked off a tall cliff which loomed over another vast sea of darkened forest.

"Yes, my lady, he is resting among the cliff with his thoughts—just beyond the small forested area. He came to me with anxiousness upon him so I advised him to wait upon the lord—to be still."

Natalia looked in the direction he in which pointed to. It wasn't too far from where they stood. She could see more of the darkened background through the tents. There weren't too many tents in that area because of it being close to a wooded area, which sat right before the cliff.

"Thank you, Rafiul," she said, then turned to leave.

"Natalia…," Rafiul said, catching her attention.

She turned to him quickly but walked to him slowly. He was quiet for a moment as he studied her mannerism. She appeared anxious and nervous for some reason.

"There are three things that amaze me," Rafiul said, "no…four things in which I don't understand… How an eagle glides through the sky, how a snake slithers on a rock, how a ship navigates the ocean—and how a man loves a woman…"

She looked at him for a moment, confused. Her countenance had an expression of perplexity upon it.

"I'm afraid I don't understand…" she finally said.

"Many waters cannot quench love, and rivers cannot wash it away… If one were to give all of the wealth of his house away for love—one would be utterly scorned… That is why Tairren waits for Marrisa—why he becomes broken at the thought of her being lost… And that is why you run to him so…"

Natalia stood silently, shocked at what he had said to her. She felt offended at his insinuation—not because he was implying that she loved Tairren, but because he was saying things boldly to her about her own business. She didn't know what to say at first and wondered how deeply he could see into her heart and mind.

"I am not one to reveal my inner most feelings to anyone, and I am certainly not an open book to be read…" Natalia said in a low tone. Her voice shook as emotion crept upon her.

"Natalia, only God knows the very details of your life," Rafiul said. "I cannot read your inner feelings but I can read your mannerism. Forgive me for I do not tell you this in harm—everything I say is through the Great King's will. I do not understand love between the man and woman—but I do understand love because the Great King speaks of love. Just know that love is patient, love is kind. It does not envy, it does not boast, it is not proud. It is not rude and it is not self-seeking, it is not easily angered and it does not keep a record of wrongs. Love does not delight in evil but rejoices with the truth. It always protects, trusts, hopes, and perseveres—love never fails..."

They stood for a moment in awkward silence. Natalia just politely nodded to the Archlegna then gave him a subtle smile. She took a couple of steps backwards then turned and left quickly. She did not even turn to see if he was still watching her.

She didn't want to be rude, but she also didn't want to speak of that topic anymore. She felt terribly embarrassed and wondered how he even knew she felt that way about Tairren. She wondered if she appeared like the young immature girl who fancied the local boy. She wondered if she appeared asinine in the eyes of other people when she was with Tairren. She shook her head and tightened her fists on her gown as she quickly made her way towards where Tairren was apparently at. She was angry at herself for even allowing Rafiul, whom she didn't even know, make her feel irritated. She did have feelings for Tairren, but it was a secret that she only knew. She didn't have feelings for anyone, and that's why Tairren was so important to her because she secretly began to love him. Natalia was confused because she loved Tairren—but Tairren loved her closest friend, Marrisa...

Natalia made her way to the small patch of forest which lay right behind some glowing tents. The wooded area was not as thick and there was no path. She could see faint light from a fire through the black trees. She slowly crept into the wood, cautiously looking around. It got darker the further she went from the camp, so she just continued in a straight path which was directly ahead of the fire light. The last thing she wanted to do was to get lost in the Black Forest at night.

Then there came noise in the dark woods. She stopped quickly, silently listening for more noises. It sounded like someone or something was creeping through the forest in the distance. The noises were from the rustling of leaves and the breaking of branches.

"Tairren...," Natalia said in a low tone as she peered into the direction from where she heard the noises.

Her heart pounded in her chest as she thought of the dreadful nomed. The noises that came from afar in the forest reminded her of the night they had gotten attacked by the wolves. She began to quickly make her way faster towards the fire light, which was a couple of yards away. After a few intense moments, she made it to the fire light. The light was from a torch that stuck out of the ground, with Tairren sitting right beside it.

He rested a couple of yards away from the forest, sitting upon a clearing which was right before a steep precipice. She stayed quiet for a moment, just watching him as he sat quietly upon the darkness. He had his knees up and rested his arms upon them. He looked as if he were in deep thought. She slowly walked towards him, not wanting to disturb him.

He turned to look up at her, then motioned for her to sit next to him. He smiled at her as she came to him.

"It's amazing even without the moon," Tairren said as she sat right beside him.

The view was beautiful, even when the stars and moonlight weren't out. They sat on a high cliff which looked out over the southern parts of Minslethrate. The small area of the woods opened up to it, which then drastically jutted down into a valley of black trees. There seemed to be a river way down below, and many more small openings in the forest. Beyond the forest was more sloping fields and hills—the beginnings of the Fiara Mountain Range. Then they could see the Great Mountains. The sky was black but the moon tried its best to leak through the thick clouds. They could tell where the moon was because the sky became a vibrant gray hue in that area.

"It's strange how you can find beauty in such a dreadful place," Natalia said, glancing over at Tairren. "This view really gives a sense of hope."

"Yes... And we still have a way ahead of us," he said as his voice trailed away.

They sat for a moment in silence, listening to the sounds of crickets and nearby bats. The tiny squeaks of the flying bats seemed to echo through the empty air above the valley, which was below them.

"Natalia," he said in a low tone, "I've decided that I'm leaving this very night to the Fire Temple."

"What?! Fire Temple? Why?" Natalia grew frantic. The silent ambience around them went from peaceful to stressful in a matter of seconds. "I mean, how will you find your way in the dark? Why there? What about the nomed? What about—us?"

"Natalia, I will be fine... Rafiul revealed to me that the fire temple is my own personal quest. I must go there. And you and Phillip will be okay with the legna. I've been sitting here for some time and I feel that I should leave before anyone else. The fire temple is the furthest away and I feel that we don't have much time. All I keep thinking about is getting to the fire temple. I'm just worried about Marrisa. I know Mikhal says to wait—that everything will happen when it should. But when it seems we've gotten so close—there is something else that we must do which pushes us back. Now we must each go on our own quest. It seems we will never make it in time. What if she is hurt or sick or—dead?"

"Don't say that! Don't you *dare* say that!" Natalia raised her voice as her emotions began to stir. "You said she will be okay! Where is your faith now? You shouldn't go when you are not ready—anything could happen to you."

"I know but I must take a risk," Tairren said, becoming irritated. "I must know that Marrisa is okay. I must know! I can't stand not knowing what will happen—what will happen to her. I feel horrible knowing that we are well and she may not be. She is somewhere out there, lost upon this blackened land! She is alone and probably frightened." He paused for a moment as he rubbed his forehead. "I don't understand anything that is taking place… All I know now is that I must go to the Fire Temple. I don't even know how long we have!

"The only thing that comes to my mind is what Malakh said to me when Marrisa was first taken. It's the same thing that I've heard in a dream—then Phillip yelled it out when he was taken over by darkness… Following the night when the moon glows like blood, during the twilight when the morning star shines the brightest—evil will take on a new form…" Tairren stopped talking abruptly as he looked over at Natalia. He appeared as if he had a sudden epiphany. "Wait…," he said as his eyes became large. "When the moon glows like blood! Natalia, do you understand what that means?!" Tairren became excited all of a sudden.

She shook her head slowly as tears went down her cheeks.

"When the moon glows like blood… The spring equinox! The Spring Celebration… The moon glows red during the eve of our spring festival. The spring equinox is tomorrow night—the eve of the Spring Celebration!" Tairren spoke with wide eyes, excited as if he figured out the answer to a riddle.

"I see, Tairren," Natalia said, reluctantly. "The spring festival would be in a couple of days…"

"Yes, that's when the kingdom would usually celebrate the Great King of light and all the gifts of nature he provides for us. The legna said that Lucif will stop at nothing to rid of everything good—because darkness wants to smite light. Lucif is taking the day in which we celebrate the God of light, and turning it into a day of darkness. That is when Lucif chose to take over Marrisa. Do you understand? That's when Lucif will take on a new form! Marrisa is the new form! That's why she was taken and being brought to the Dark Tower of Sacrifice."

Natalia put her hand to her mouth, realizing the grave danger that Marrisa was in—realizing the grave danger they were all in. Everything was making sense now. Before they could not see the full scale of the situation, but now that it was coming to them, they felt overwhelmed. It was as if a massive wave of stress was inundating their bodies.

"Lilith is using Marrisa as a living sacrifice—to offer to Lucif! Natalia said. "Lilith is doing what the ancient pagan ancestors of Minslethrate did many generations ago before the Great King of light came to Minslethrate!"

"Yes, in those days they gave human sacrifices to the goddesses and The Dark Lord once a year. That is what is meant when it is said that Lucif was looking for the right timing and the perfect human sacrifice. During the twilight when the morning star shines the brightest—that is the moment when the moon goes down and the sun comes up. In legend, the morning star represents The God of Light; Lucif wants to deceive the world by making it known that he is the true morning star. The morning star is the dawn of a new day!

"Tomorrow night the moon will glow red which is the spring equinox and the eve of darkness. Darkness is the war between light and darkness— darkness is the death that will come that day. Then that night during the twilight, just before the sun comes up when the morning star shines the brightest—Lucif will take Marrisa in full! The following day will be another new day and the day Marrisa will go to the kingdom like nothing has happened, putting an end to Minlsethrate. Then Marrisa will make her way to Ishkar, which is known as the most powerful kingdom of all kingdoms. Lucif is the Lord of Darkness and will rule Ishkar in Marrisa's body in power and in full darkness. Lucif's powers will spread across the world like rapid waters as other kingdom's and nations yield to Marrisa who is really the Lord of Darkness!"

"My poor, dear Marrisa," Natalia said in a shaken voice. "Our poor, dear kingdom…"

"But we can stop it just as the Archlegna said—we must stop darkness from eating up man and our world," Tairren said as he quickly stood up. "I must go…"

"No—wait, Tairren!" Natalia said, rushing up to grab him. "Please don't leave now. Please don't leave without me." Natalia came upon him with tears in her eyes. She wrapped her arms around him, keeping her eyes on his.

"Natalia," Tairren said in a much softer and calmer voice. He wiped the tears that rolled down her cheeks. "Each one of us must do this—we gave our word. You have a task of your own. You have always been so strong and independent. You do not need me. Be the brave lady I know you are."

Natalia started to cry as she slowly shook her head. Tairren felt shocked and didn't know what to say. He had never seen her cry before. He had always seen her in high-spirits with a bold and blunt attitude. He felt really sad for her all of a sudden as she looked up to him with beautiful and weeping eyes.

"Tairren... I... I..." She stopped herself, not wanting reveal anything to him. She wanted to tell him so badly that she loved him—that she wanted to be with him. She thought of Marrisa and became ashamed of the feelings that grew for Tairren. She did not want him to hear those words from her mouth—and she didn't want to hear them either. But she yearned for those words to be said to her.

"What is it, Natalia," he said, just looking into her eyes.

After a moment of touching his face and a lock of hair that fell upon his cheek, Natalia just threw herself on him and wrapped her arms around his neck. She pressed her lips to his and kissed him passionately. She couldn't contain herself in that moment and surprised even herself. Finally, she pulled herself away as tears continued to trickle down her face. She looked up into his confused eyes, wondering what he thought just then.

"Go," Natalia said as she softly put her fingers upon his lips.

Tairren stood for a moment, feeling greatly surprised and some-what numb. He slowly backed away, then turned and left quickly. He stopped before he entered into the woods, turning to look back at her. She stood quietly amongst the stillness of the night with tears in her eyes. He left quickly, running back towards the camp.

Natalia fell to her knees and began to cry. She covered her face, feeling humiliated and broken. She truly loved Tairren, but did not want to tell him. She knew that he loved Marrisa with all of his heart—and she didn't want to take that from him. She felt alone as she looked up to see

Tairren make his way back to the camp. She thought that Tairren was perfect in every way, and always knew that. He was just not perfect for her.

She thought of what Rafiul had said to her right before she came to Tairren. She raised her dewy face to the sky and looked to the horizon. Everything made sense now. She understood what he was trying to tell her. He was trying to tell her that love is patient—that all she needed was God's love. No man could quench her heart like God does. She understood now how great Tairren's love was for Marrisa, and that he would not see any other woman's heart. She just wanted someone to love her, the way Tairren loved Marrisa. But she was finally starting to understand that God, who chose her, could fill her heart unconditionally if she were to open up to Him and not man. She would never understand such a love. But that love that she didn't understand was slowly planting a small seed in her heart, like a mustard seed that was set amongst soft soil. She didn't realize it but she was slowly changing and growing like the new herb upon the earth. Before her journey, she didn't care about anyone's feelings but her own. And now, she was beginning to care for others…

Natalia just sat in the dim light of the torch with tears drying on her cheeks. She thought of everything that had happened to her on her journey—and somehow, she knew she was growing from it. Quietness enveloped her body and stillness lay all around her…

✝✝✝

Natalia didn't realize that someone was watching her in the woods. Someone she didn't know crept through the darkness, stalking her through the shadows of the trees and behind thick brushes. It was that same cursed, cloaked figure who timidly crept through the camp like a silent breeze…

✝✝✝

Phillip walked to his tent, feeling irritated and betrayed… The image of Natalia and Tairren kissing kept popping into his head. For the first time his heart ached, and he was angry that it did. He was upset at himself for allowing a female to make him feel that way. He never had feelings for a woman the way he did for Natalia. He wasn't used to not having the upper hand in everything. He felt he was changing ever since he came to Minslethrate and he wasn't sure if he liked it or not.

317

Phillip finally made it to his tent. He paced back and forth for a minute as the thought of Natalia went through is head again. Frustrated, he grabbed a nearby chair and flung it across his tent. It crashed into a small table, knocking it over and spilling everything that was on it. He felt out of control so he decided to lie down. He let his body fall onto the many layers of feathered cushions that was spread out upon the ground. He placed his hands behind his head as he took a couple of deep breaths. The thought of his comrades kissing came in his mind again. He didn't understand why, if Tairren loved Marrisa so much, was he kissing Natalia? Then he thought of himself—he was supposed to be marrying Marrisa, and Natalia was all he thought off.

He thought that he shouldn't have ever gone off to look for her earlier that night. He would have rather not known that they were together in the woods alone. But when he realized that Natalia was no longer beside him, he wondered where she had gone. He thought he shouldn't have ever asked a legna where she had gone to. If he wouldn't have asked, he wouldn't have seen Tairren and Natalia kissing in the woods. When he saw them, a wave of jealousy came over his body, and he left. He felt angry towards Tairren—but he didn't want to feel that way. He was tired of being angry at people. He knew that there were much more serious things to worry about than a heart break.

Phillip stared at the tent-ceiling above him, watching the shadows dance and move about like soft gray clouds. Some of the large candles were still lit, giving off a small glow. The dim light around him seemed to calm him down. He thought of all the conversations he and Natalia had over the duration of their journey together. He thought of when she awakened his mind to an opened way of thinking—letting him know that they were all the same, no matter their social stature. He thought of the conversation they had after he and Tairren had gotten into a fight. He never had anyone try to cheer him up before—and she did. He thought it was brilliant how she compared him to a diamond in the rough—letting him know that through time, he will become what God put him on this earth to become.

He knew because of her words, he wanted to change. He never knew how damaging words could be until he met her. He only cared about himself and his needs when he first arrived to Minslethrate, and now he realized that he cared for other people and their needs. He truly cared for both Natalia and Tairren. And even though his heart was broken—he still loved Natalia. He knew he probably would never let her know that—but he still loved her.

Phillip's eyes opened and closed as sleep was coming upon him. He felt peace all around him now. Everyone must have been sleeping—because it was quiet outside of his tent. The serenity reminded him of the vision he had that night when they were attacked by the two-headed nomed. He thought of the peace that came with the vision—and the mighty hand of light that seemed to reach out for him. And the words he heard, saying, "My Kingdom is great—and you are destined for greatness…"

Phillip's heart seemed to smile a little, now feeling content. His eyes closed for good as his mind drifted away. His body was finally feeling the strain from the long day and it began to shut down. His muscles relaxed and his breath slowed and deepened—dreams beginning to stir as he fell fast asleep.

✝✝✝

Tairren felt numb as he rushed to his quarters to quickly grab his things. He was shocked at Natalia's advances on him, but he also had an idea that Natalia had begun to create feelings for him during their journey. He thought then that Natalia just wanted to be close to him because of her being out in the dark wild—but now he knew why. Tairren began to feel bad for his very close friend, but he knew that beginning his new quest was the most important thing at that moment. He felt that he was even closer to rescuing Marrisa.

Tairren burst into his tent, quickly looking around for his things. He found his dagger and strapped it on his belt. He grabbed his bag and made sure his provisions were ample, then he looked for his bow and arrows. He realized that the legna had filled his bag with some type of food and other things he may need. His quiver was also filled with plenty of golden arrows. He noticed that the legna had left him a sword which looked just like their swords. It was a grand gift. Tairren held it up, examining it. The sword was made of a strange metal. It looked like pure gold and had a luster that shown like the sun. The sword was light as a feather but it was tough and hard like steel, and the blade was sharper than any blade he had ever seen. His dagger was dull compared to the fine edges of the sword. The hilt had jewels speckled upon it—much like the wing pendant he wore. It looked so beautiful and grand that he didn't feel right using it as a weapon.

He was pleased with his new things and felt strengthened and zealous as he put them on.

He began to think of his father as he pulled his seemingly clean cloak on. The deep-blue fabric looked good as new and the golden clasp on it shined like his new sword. He smiled to himself as he held the wing pendant that hung from his neck. He felt so blessed and comforted. And even though he was about to begin a whole new journey—he had peace about it. All of the stress and aggravation and doubt seemed to leave him. He thought about nothing but his quest now. He forgot about Natalia and Phillip and even the dark nomed then. He began to understand that if he focused too much on things that were not of God—that he would have no peace. And he needed much peace before he was about to travel further towards the south.

"Thank you so much—my God of Light... You have put a crown of favor upon my head and a burning fire deep inside my heart..." Tairren said in a low tone—knowing that his God was listening.

After a few more moments of preparing for his departure, he quickly left his tent. He put his hood on and furtively rushed through the camp to where Lilly rested. The camp was silent and no one was out and about. The fires around him burned with a soft glow and the tents were dark. He finally made it to Lilly who seemed excited to see him again. He calmed her down then got his things situated in the saddle bags. He climbed onto her back, then looked around. He wished he could have thanked all of the legna for all of their kindness and hospitality, but he knew he couldn't. He silently got Lilly going. She calmly galloped through the camp, seeming really happy to get going. They made it to the edge of the camp, which faced south. Tairren pulled his compass out, making sure they were faced in the right direction, which would be in a southeastern direction. They had to go around the cliff, so they had to go in a much easterly direction.

They quickly went through a small forest which eventually thinned out, opening to a full view of the south. All Tairren could see was forest, hills, brushes and beyond that the great Fiara Mountains and a night sky that looked gloomy and haunting above him. He began to become nervous, wondering if it really was a good idea to go off by himself, at night. He knew that there were many nomed abroad and that the forest was thick and cruel. But by his map and the view he had from the cliff, he saw that ne was near the end of the Black Forest. He began to think of Mikhal's word about his quest and how he was to have his guardian legna, Rafiul, by his side to guide him. But then he became comforted by the thought of him having his map, compass, new weaponry and a torch with him.

He sat on Lilly's back for a moment, thinking of his journey and how much he had strengthened and grown spiritually since he left Minslethrate. When he first left the kingdom, he was clueless, his provisions were low and his weaponry was weak. His strength was feeble and his health was slowly declining because of the infected lacerations the flying nomed left on his arm. He had fire in his heart but he also was scared. He knew this quest was his, but he didn't know exactly what he was getting himself into. All he knew was that he loved Marrisa with all of his heart, and that the God of Light who was his strength—was also his passion… Now he felt as if he was a new man—the power of light had changed him. He knew deep down inside that he was changed. He felt saved, sanctified and that he could take on anything that darkness had to give.

He felt so thankful—for everything. He thought of his mother and deceased father again. He thought of his comrades. He thought of the legna and the great owl. He thought of the Great God of Light and the legend of King Yehoshua… He thought of his quest and Minslethrate—the world. And he thought of princess Marrisa. He knew he had to get going, for the night was late and a new day would come soon—closer to the night of a blood-red moon…

Tairren grabbed his wing-pendant as he pressed his lips together. He patted Lilly's neck, then he was off. With a pounding heart, he rode off into the night, ready for whatever was to come at him.

†

CHAPTER 22
Full Circle

The night was silent and still and very late. It seemed that all should have been sleeping upon Minslethrate. All through the south was hushed as dark shadows and insidious things lurked about the lands. Much deeper into the south lay a dark and dreadful tower, sitting upon jagged cliffs at the base of Fiara Mountain. Inside the tower a dark and evil presence rested quietly, waiting for a new day to approach. There was no light within the frightful place except for a couple of randomly lit torches. Rats and chattering bugs skittered upon the stone floors, looking for anything to fill their mouths. Dried bones and whole skeletons lie here and there, covered in dust and cobwebs. Spiders dwelled in the corners of the dark chambers and bats made their homes in the darkest parts of the massive halls that inhabited the insidious temple. The air smelled heavy of mildew and mold, and the stone walls were covered with different types of growth. The heavy presence of something dark and mad filled the air, seeming to grow angrier every day that went by.

In a chamber at the top of the tower, Marrisa sat, cowering in a dimly lit corner. She had her back against the cold stone walls, her body balled up upon a bed of straw. Her knees were up against her chest and her face was buried into her dirty hands. A torch crackled above her, allowing a soft light to touch her head. All around her was dark, and the thick feeling of terror grew thick upon her frail body. She trembled with fear and from the chilled night. Her emotions were like the jagged tops of mountains—going up and down. One moment she would be so depressed and become self-loathing, and the next she would feel wrath come upon her—then terror.

She grew angry that no one had come for her, and that everything good seemed to have abandoned her. She was angry at God for seeming to turn his back upon her, she was depressed that even Tairren had not come for her, and she was terrified at what was happening to her. She was alone, and wished so badly that she would be pulled away from everything. She wished that she could sprout wings so she could take flight right out of the window.

Her skin crawled and she didn't know whether it was from the dreadful atmosphere or from the small bugs that dwelled inside of the hay she sat on.

322

There was a large opened window to the right of her, above her head. She would randomly look up out the window, catching only darkness upon her eyes. There were no stars or moon in the sky, and a strong wind came in every now and then—pushing the stale smell of the chamber away from her nostrils. She had no idea how far she was from home, or exactly where she was at. She knew she was in the Dark Tower of Sacrifice, but she didn't know where that tower was.

After they had left the Black Forest, Lilith blind folded her and bound her wrists so that she had no idea where she was at, and if she knew she couldn't get too far. She was forced into the temple and pulled up a stairwell of a dark tower. Finally, her hands were unbound and eyes set free before she was pushed into the small chamber. Lilith had told her that she wasn't even going to bother putting her in shackles yet because there was no way she could escape, unless she took her own life. There were many times she tried to end her life when escaping from Lilith—but Lilith would not let her… She kept telling her that her flesh was wanted by the Dark Lord and needed to stay fresh and alive as long as possible.

Marrisa had been in the chamber for hours on end. She knew it was really late because the sun had gone down what seemed like ages ago to her. She told her to rest her body, "flesh" Lilith would say, but she couldn't. Her eyes were tired and her body ached but her mind was wide awake.

Sporadically, she would quickly glance in the dark space across from her. On the other side of the small chamber, where it was the blackest— Lilith sat quietly. Marrisa could not see her, but she knew she was there; she could hear her breathing. She could feel Lilith staring at her from the darkness of the chamber even though she could not see her black eyes.

"You do not want to rest your lovely countenance?" Lilith finally asked from the darkness, after hours of silence. Her voice was low and threatening.

Marrisa just sat silently, staring at the blackened side of the chamber across from her. She began to breathe heavily as fear welled up in her heart.

"It is strange how time flies—soaring like destructive winds on high… Time kills, and destroys—but yet it lives forever…" Lilith let out a low raspy chuckle. "…Do you want to hear a story?"

Marrisa continued to stay silent, staring into the darkness where Lilith perched.

"Once upon a time—there was a glorious kingdom. And this kingdom was called—Minslethrate," Lilith mocked as she spoke. "This kingdom was so lovely and filled with things that despised darkness... This kingdom despised darkness so much that a king came—and banished it! But darkness is so powerful, so fierce, that the people of it killed that *pig* of a king—stripping him of his armor and crown and dividing it out amongst four leaders of darkness... His shield was given to water, his armor was given to earth, his sword was given to fire, and his crown to darkness... The Dark Lord was so pleased, but still had grand plans to punish all who denied him—all those who followed this king of light.

"So, he elected many powers, advocate followers of darkness, to continue on with his great plans... And do you know who those chosen ones were?" Lilith became quiet for a moment, watching Marrisa as tears fell from her eyes. "Us... Yes us, my princess. Lilith is filled with many of us, but I Natas, am the high power over Lilith—and I have many followers of darkness... And soon you will have us and even a higher power among you—the Dark Lord yearns for you!" Lilith gave out another chuckle. "Oh, but don't fret—it will be soon...

"Now back to our story... It is the best part for your ancestors are about to be added unto it... Many years went by. Many people died. People became heavy with burdens—and darkness became stronger. We nomed became stronger. The Dark Lord called upon us—and we were spawned by the pagan worship that dwelled amongst the old ways of Minslethrate. And we ascended out of the darkest parts of Minslethrate... So long ago I sat with a lost maiden in this very chamber. Our full circle begins with a fair maiden... Her face was pale like the moon and her hair was long and like that of a raven's tail. She was young and beautiful—and terrified."

Lilith grew quiet as Marrisa continued to weep. The madness was thick around them and Lilith enjoyed every moment of it.

"Do not cry, my princess," Lilith said in a mocking tone, "for that maiden was your fair grandmother—the grand queen of Minslethrate—Queen Karnidge... The Dark Lord followed her through the halls of this temple while we played a game of hide and seek...

"Do you know that game? As I can recall, you used to play that many a time with Moira... I hope you haven't forgotten that bond that you and Moira possessed when you were a child. It should not matter though—she is lost in the fiery pits of hell..." Lilith let out another chuckle, taking pleasure in tormenting Marrisa. "But we should not stray from our story...

The beautiful Queen Karnidge ran through these very halls, screaming like a Banshee. She was taken by the Dark Lord, and he became one with her.

"She went back to the Kingdom of Minslethrate, carrying many of us along with her. Just like Lilith—she was a doorway to the kingdom of Lucif—just as you will be… We influenced her during her rule—and she killed and burned and killed and burned—many people…" Lilith let out a laugh this time. Her croaky sounds echoed through the chamber. "But the story is not finished yet…

"Queen Karnidge died and I Natas, along with many other followers of the Dark Lord, stayed planted among your family and your kingdom. Many servants died—many innocent souls were killed because of us… Your grandparents, Moira—your mother… And the story continues as I sit here and look upon you. You are the next chapter… But our story will not end until the Lord of Darkness has taken his crown—and rules over all the kingdoms of this earth with light trampled beneath his feat!"

Marrisa covered her face and shook her head, still crying.

Lilith let out another revolting laugh—making Marrisa cringe. Lilith became quiet and an uncomfortable feeling came over the chamber. Silence was the most terrifying sound when Lilith could not be seen. The thick silence lingered on for some time.

"Do you want to play a game?" Lilith finally asked in her wicked voice.

Marrisa slowly looked up into the darkness as she stopped crying a little. Her heart quickened. Her eyes became wide while large tears continued to fall from them. She shook her head frantically, looking intensely into the blackness before her. That question frightened her, sending goose bumps across her cold skin.

"I will count to three—and when I get to three… I am going to—get—you…" Lilith said in a terrifying and teasing voice.

Marrisa began to cry frantically again as she brought her shaken hands to her mouth. Her heart began to pound in her chest and she felt as if her breath was leaving her.

"One… Two…" Lilith's voice grew louder with every word.

She slowly crept out of the darkest area of the chamber, making her way towards Marrisa. She crawled on her hands and knees, appearing like a threatening animal. She looked like a menacing fiend with black eyes and dying skin. She had a large black smile on her face that stretched from ear to ear—appearing wicked.

"THREE!" Lilith roared out as she quickly crawled towards Marrisa, having an angry look on her ugly face all of the sudden. She pounced at her—appearing like an unruly beast. Her white and knurly fingers were spread out like claws. Her black mouth stretched wide open as she roared out an inhuman sound.

Marrisa let out a blood-curdling scream as she flung herself on her side, dodging Lilith's thrashing hands. She got up to her feet as quick as she could. She hastily ran, flying through the threshold and past the heavy chamber door. Her feeble and exhausted body kicked into action as panic and adrenaline sprung up inside of her. She grabbed and pushed the door close as hard as she could. The door was solid and heavy and the rusted hinges made it difficult to close, but the strength and energy that came upon her allowed her to do so. Lilith forced her hand through the doorway with a shriek as the heavy door quickly closed. It slammed onto her hand, making her squeal like a hurt wild animal.

Without knowing where to go, Marrisa ran down the dark hallway. She never looked back. A few torches were lit throughout the hall so she had very little light to see anything in front of her. She continued down the hall and down a stair-well. She breathed loudly as her feat patted against the bitter stone. She could hear Lilith behind her somewhere, shrieking and laughing as the taunts from the unclean spirits emitted from her mouth. They echoed down the halls, seeming to come from every which way. Marrisa ran down another hall as quick as she could. Her chest burned as she sucked in the stale air around her. She tried all the doors but they were either locked or stuck shut! Her shaken hands barely had the ability to hold on to the door-latches. She screamed with frustration as she yanked at the latches as hard as she could. Nothing would budge! She pressed her hands on her ears as Lilith's advancing voice echoed all around her.

"Leave me alone!" Marrisa screamed out as she tightened her fists.

She began to cry frantically as hope seemed to get smaller and smaller. She felt so lost and helpless. There seemed to be no way out! She looked down the hall and could see two curtains which barely hung from the threshold of a doorway. The curtains moved in the air, indicating that wind was coming through the massive doorway. Her terrified heart fluttered as she flew down the exceedingly long hall and through the massive door-way.

A gust of wind pushed at her as she ran out into the open air. She realized she was now standing outside. She frantically looked around. Her heart sunk as she realized that she was standing on a large balcony. The wind blew at her long red hair and tattered and soiled gown. She began to cry as she looked up into the night veil. The moon tried to peek through the thick clouds, making the sky around it all different shades of gray. All around her was darkness—she couldn't even really see the lands around her. The only things she could see were the trees and hills that sat below the balcony. Marrisa placed her frail, shaken hands on her chest, upon her pounding heart. She closed her eyes, thinking of the people she loved—her father, Natalia, and most of all—Tairren. She thought of her home and how beautiful it always was. She thought of all her fondest memories. All of these thoughts trickled through her mind in quick images. She knew her life was coming to end. She knew her spirit was going to die—and she wanted to remember the things she loved before it did.

All of a sudden, she heard the deep thudding sound of wings upon the air. She turned to see a large white blur rush upon the stone railing of the balcony. At first, she thought it was a spirit and it frightened her. It was a massive white owl. It perched upon the balcony, now silently sitting and staring at her. Marrisa stood for a moment with her hands upon her chest, looking back at the mysterious and intimidating creature. The wind blew at her hair and caressed her face, making her look hauntingly beautiful. Her gaze was like a long thought. The mighty bird never took its eyes off of her and she couldn't look away. A feeling of peace came over her like a wave of water. She didn't feel out of control and terrified as she did before. Even though she stood trapped on a balcony with Lilith after her—she felt calm. She felt transfixed by the beautiful creature, mesmerized by its large, black eyes. The owl's eyes weren't the kind of black like Lilith's, which were terrifying and wicked—but a black that was deep and beautiful. It was like looking into a dark, shining pool, making one wonder what lied beneath it.

Marrisa slowly walked over to the creature, bringing her hand out to touch it. She stood before the owl, which seemed to be half her size but appeared mightier as it sat upon the stone balustrade of the balcony. Her finger tips slowly reached out upon the dark, wind-blown air. She touched the pure white feathers of the owl, slowly running her hand upon them. Her cold hand felt the warmth from the creature, sending chills down her arm and through her body. Just as she touched the soft feathers, Marrisa heard a voice upon her. She did not know where it came from—but she felt it in her feeble heart...

"May it be that your castle has crumbled...and that the shadows have taken you... It is so that you are far from home—and have become lost...

Verily it is so, that the fire within in you has been blown out by the shadows... Always know that I love you... When you seek me, then will you find me... And your castle will rise like the sun and your crown will be added unto you..."

Tears flooded Marrisa's eyes and streamed down her frozen cheeks as she heard those words... Her icy-blue eyes sparkled as the wind blew locks of scarlet hair upon her pale face. She slowly pulled her hand away, placing it back onto her chest again. She did not believe... Her heart became like stone all of a sudden.

Just then, the mighty owl opened its breathtaking wings and flew off into the windy darkness of the night. A feather from one of the owl's wings fluttered into the air, getting caught in her long red tresses. She listened to the thud of its massive wings as she watched it disappear into the darkness. The thuds of its wings went with the beat of her heart.

She picked the large feather out of her hair as she heard the howls and shrieks of Lilith echo down the hallway behind her. She stood still as Lilith's noises became louder and louder, indicating that she was almost upon her... There was madness behind her—but silence before her. Instead of running or crying—Marrisa gave up... The white owl was like a glimpse of hope to her, and it warmed her heart. But as she pulled her hand away from it, doubt and fear came over her again. The owl let her know that there was a second chance, somehow—but in her heart, she didn't believe it. And as she watched the owl fly off into the darkness, a frightening numbness came over her.

She gave up—surrendering to darkness... She slowly brought her hand into the cold wind with the feather dancing upon it. She released the golden-tipped feather into the black sky, watching it as sadness began to slowly creep upon her cold body again.

The feather twirled and sailed amongst the wind, and disappeared into the sky's gloom.

*But if a man walk in the night, he stumbleth, because
there is no light in him.*
John 11:10 KJV

Heard a carol, mournful, holy,

Chanted loudly, chanted lowly,

Till her blood was frozen slowly,

And her eyes were darken'd wholly,

Turn'd to tower'd Camelot.

For ere she reach'd upon the tide

The first house by the water-side,

Singing in her song she died,

The Lady of Shalott.

-Alfred, Lord Tennyson

*Put on the whole armor of God, that ye may be able to
stand against the wiles of the devil...*
Ephesians 6:11

Time is the present that passes by like a faint breeze… If one does not care to catch it—it will pass and become forgotten—and return as something new… Only time will tell if that something new is good…or bad.

In the beginning, time was created and scattered about unto the creations of Earth. The heavens and earth were created by the Great God of Light. But during the course of time upon the earth—things such as nature, fire, and water had flourished—and then became sacred…for it was life... The dwellers of the earth craved the mysterious powers of the world and forgot their creator…

During the reign of man in the beginning, after the fall of the first son and daughter of light, the purity of light had diminished, and darkness came to be. As time passed, the people upon the Kingdom of Minslethrate had forgotten the laws of the Great God of Light—and the Kingdom of Nevaeh became but a legend. And the men of Minslethrate put the legends of the God of Light and the Kingdom of Nevaeh in the back of their minds, forgetting them. Men began to create their own legends and lore—and darkness began to grow like thick clouds do before a storm.

Long ago the Father of Darkness, Lucif the fallen Archlegna, ascended from the deepest chasm of Minslethrate in which he had been sleeping. He then called upon false prophets and gods. These false gods came in the forms of women and the false prophets who were filled with unclean spirits, worshiped them. The false gods ruled in the southern parts of Minslethrate as goddesses. Earth, fire, and water, which were the mysterious powers of the Earth, were stolen by the goddesses so that they could rule over them. And they did exceedingly. The men of Minslethrate were deceived and they worshiped these false gods. They had names and everyone upon Minslethrate knew who they were: Dolsia, the goddess of earth; Haifen, the goddess of water; and Fiara, the goddess of fire…

Many generations had passed and the land of Minslethrate was nothing but a pagan country, and much blood and souls were lost because of it. The Father of Darkness, Lucif, ruled over Minslethrate through Fiara, Haifen, and Dolsia…and once a year upon the Dark Tower of Sacrifice, innocent blood was shed and given to them. The people of Minslethrate who followed the pagan beliefs, traveled to the south and sacrificed a virgin maiden on top of the Dark Tower of Sacrifice. The deceived people would celebrate and thank the goddesses by marrying the night—feasting and becoming drunk—dancing all throughout the nightfall. During the twilight, when the morning star shown the brightest, they gave the innocent virgin to Fiara, Haifen, and Dolsia—unknowingly worshiping the Lord of Darkness…

But even when darkness seems so thick—there is still a glimpse of light…

There were many small guilds of light who worshiped the one true God, who was the Great God of Light, in secret. And among the guilds of light a great king was born…who was sent by the Great God of Light. This great king was called Yehoshua, and he saved the kingdom and banished darkness and the pagan rituals and built a great wall to divide the south from the north. Minslethrate was separated into two parts: the north being the Golden Lands, and the south being the Forbidden Lands. Minslethrate began to become whole as the followers of light yielded to King Yehoshua.

Out of spite and wrath, the pagan followers of the goddesses rose up against King Yehoshua, in the shadow of a foul king called Baffmit. The dark king of the south who followed the Dark Lord rose up against King Yehoshua and his people and took him and smote him with death. His armor, sword, and crown were stolen by King Baffmit and the followers of darkness… the Great King Yehoshua's armor was given to Dolsia, his shield to Haifen, his sword to Fiara, and his crown—to the father of all darkness… The Father of Darkness, Lucif, thought that he had won—until King Yehoshua rose from his grave as light, and ascended into the Kingdom of Nevaeh and unto his people…

The people of darkness were trampled beneath the followers of light— and the goddesses and their followers faded away.

And after the passing of much time, a new line of earthly kings was born who followed the light—they were the fair Princess Marrisa's ancestors.

Time had passed and generations had died and the goddesses and the Dark Lord were seemingly forgotten… And the new line of kings carried on King Yehoshua's laws and light.

But even though the evil darkness was banished and had been forgotten long ago—it was not dead… Darkness rose up in deceitful forms and attacked the Kingdom of Minslethrate many times thereafter, weakening the royal kings which were Princess Marrisa's blood-line.

As king after king weakened—so did their people. Time continued to pass by like the faint breezes of earth….

The time is now that the forgotten legends of light and the powers of darkness are rising…

†

PROLOGUE
Born into Darkness

A young girl with golden hair stood in the corner of a carriage. She held on tightly to the iron mesh wall of the carriage and watched as they passed through the marketplace of Minslethrate. There wasn't any room to move. The space in the carriage was limited and crowded with other poor-looking people. The carriage wasn't the usual carriage that one would be used to seeing. It was in a square shape and looked more like a prison on wheels with its cage-like appearance and iron structure. Chains and shackles hung from the ceiling and there were no seats or benches. It was the same carriage that was used to bring criminals to court. The rhythm of the horse's hooves against the stone was the only thing that soothed their poor souls.

Everyone in the carriage stood together, almost pressed against each other. The smell about them was horrid and their clothes were soiled. They stood in silence, holding onto the cage-like walls and chains and shackles that hung from the ceiling, while some who were tall enough, held onto the mesh ceiling of the cage-like carriage. Their dirty faces hung with depression and they swayed silently with the motion of the carriage.

"You be too dainty to be a servant," an older woman said who was standing next to the young girl.

The woman's face appeared haggardly and her skin looked like brown leather boots. She looked as if she had worked out in the sun her whole life.

The girl didn't say anything and continued to stare at the shoppers of the marketplace as they slowly passed by them.

"You don't talk much," the woman said, just staring down at her. "But, no one really does when they is sold... No one knows where they be goin. Your parents needed the money probably—or maybe you be a lazy servant and your master didn't want you anymore..."

The girl slowly looked up at the woman with her dark-brown eyes and just gave her a cold look.

"Oh well," the woman said again as she dug into her ear, ignoring the girl's cold look. "All's I know is that I been prayin to be a servant to a good home... We be headed to the castle, you know. Your dainty face is probably gonna be the face of one of the newest servants of the royal family. You know that new princess was born? I heard my old masters talkin bout it… Such a big deal it's been. The royal family is gonna need more servants. I know I be just what they need," the woman said, then made a wide smile. Her teeth were rotten and looked like they were made of curdled milk and dirt. "They will look right over me…I knows it. Ha! I be too ugly—but I got a strong back and a tough will… But you—you got a dainty face!"

The young girl just looked at her, then looked back to the random shops and buildings as they passed them.

"What be your name?" the woman asked as she looked down at the girl with another crooked smile.

The girl was quiet for a moment, then finally looked back at the haggardly woman.

"Lilith…," she finally said without any kind of emotion.

The woman was quiet then slowly shook her head, surprised that the young girl even spoke. She then continued to talk about other things, but Lilith just ignored her.

The young girl just watched the passing scenery of the town and its people as they made their way to the castle. Her mind kept drifting back and forth going from her past to her present state. She thought of how all of the woman's guesses about her were all wrong. She was sold, but her parents didn't sell her, and she wasn't sold from her master either. She wasn't only sold, but she was traded off within the year from three different homes, but not because she was a lazy servant, but because she was unwanted. At least that's what she thought… She was an orphan servant— and a very disturbed one…

✝✝✝

Lilith was twelve years old and very intelligent and mature for her age, but she was extremely quiet and odd. She wasn't like the usual girls who would go running about picking flowers, singing or playing games; instead she would sit solemnly by herself and dwelled on her thoughts. She would just watch people. She observed everything: the way people walked and ran, the way they became sad or frightened. Her favorite thing to observe was people's emotions: their faces when they cried or when they looked like death was coming over them…

But no one took her seriously with anything and assumed she was easy to walk all over. She was thin and plain looking with pale skin and blonde hair, and had eyes that were dark and cold. She was small and mousey-like and even her voice was faint. She was a deviant girl…but had witnessed many things a young child shouldn't have.

Lilith's parents were a pair of eccentric gypsies who had been deceased a year prior to her being a servant. Her parents and their clan were nomadic people who entertained by performing magical acts, music, dances, palm readings, and told fortunes for fine payments. They also sold charms and interesting trinkets and jewelry. But they had to work quickly in many kingdoms—their work was considered witch-craft and was forbidden in most lands, Minslethrate being one of them. They weren't respected by any of the people of Minslethrate, but it didn't stop them from paying for their interesting services.

Lilith always thought that the people of Minslethrate were fools and hypocrites. She would observe everyone from the shadows of her clan when they went into town. She could see in their eyes that they adored the magic acts and thrilling fortune telling sessions. She thought that the people acted high and mighty, but were really just disgusting pigs.

During their travels, she saw many people—and disliked every one of them. They traveled all around Minslethrate and nearby kingdoms and towns, and everybody was completely different. She learned that not everyone followed the old beliefs of Minslethrate, and that there were very few people who did. Her family and fellow gypsies were worshipers of the pagan fire goddess, Fiara, and were the offspring of the ancient followers of Fiara. Pagan beliefs were all she knew—and despised everything else.

Lilith had never been in a stable environment before she became a servant. The average person would've thought that she had an adventurous life—a thrilling life; but little did they know that she lived a disturbing life revolved around darkness and abuse. Her father worshiped wine and brew and was in a drunken state almost every waking moment of her young life. She never heard a pleasant word come from her father's mouth, or saw any act of kindness or love from him. She only heard his corrupted words and only felt the bruises he left on her. She came to realize that he didn't care that he neglected his family or put scars upon their bodies, but only cared for the drinks that sent him into a state of oblivion.

She watched her parents from the outside of their tent on many occasions. Her father beat her mother almost every day in the peaks of his drunkenness, and then he would pass out in the muck of the campground afterwards.

After her mother would calm down some, she would coat many colors on her face to cover the bruises and then would smoke strong herbs for countless hours from their glorious hookah pipe—to ease the pain and suffering of her emotions. She would pet Lilith's head while she whispered, "Everything is okay...," as her eyes glazed over and eyelids became heavy. She came to realize that her mother didn't care about anything either, and only longed for that ease of pain... Her mother even slept with many members of the clan just for a tender touch, and it didn't even matter to her that she was diseased and filthy.

Lilith's concerns for her parents slowly slipped away, and she emotionally detached herself from them the moment she saw that they didn't care. She stopped crying when she was a very young child—and hadn't cried ever since then.

Lilith became distant and numb towards everybody the night she saw her father murder her mother. It was the same night she ran away... She saw her father grab his dagger—and slit her mother's throat with it—and then he killed himself by shoving the dagger into his stomach. Lilith watched from the crack of the tent doorway.

It was the first time that her father had any kind of facial expression on his face, besides a look of rage or drunkenness. Lilith noticed that he looked afraid after he killed her—and that look on his face intrigued her... She knew he wasn't frightened because of him killing her mother—but scared of what the clan would do to punish him. They probably would've cut his hands off and let him bleed to death. She had witnessed it before as it was done to another clan member.

Lilith was also intrigued by the way the blood looked in their tent abode. Her father just stared at her when she silently walked into the tent. He tried to speak a little but blood came out of his mouth instead of words. It was strange to her that she didn't hear angry or foul screams erupt from his filthy mouth. After a few moments of silence and bloody gurgles, he fell to his knees and landed on his back. Red was everywhere and the whole inside of the tent was heavy with the strange scent of blood. She thought that the dagger he had used was so beautiful—the way the jewels of the hilt glistened in the fire light and how some of the jewels were covered with blood. Only the hilt of the dagger could be seen, because the rest was deep inside of her father's stomach.

She stood in what she called her home for a while, just staring and observing the scene. It was the first time that she had ever seen her parents with peaceful looks upon their faces. It was the first time that she thought they looked beautiful—pale and silent, soaked in the shade of red.

She was very curious by what blood tasted like… She saw blood all the time—when her people slaughtered the animals for food or when they gave them up as sacrifices to Fiara. She knew it was a bad idea to do it, to taste it—but she couldn't help herself…

"Do it…," a heavy, strange voice said from inside of her head. "Taste of your father's blood before it dies…"

The voice didn't frighten her—because she had heard it before. That voice in her head was the only voice that comforted her...

She obeyed the strange voice inside of her head and grabbed the wet, jeweled hilt of the dagger. It took her a couple of tugs, but she pulled the dagger from her father's belly and held it up. The warm blood dripped down her hand as she just watched it flow. She licked the dagger, tasting the rancid blood of her father. Her face was emotionless and did not change when she wiped her mouth. She knew she must've looked terrifying with smeared blood on her mouth and with her dead parents lying before her. But she felt exhilarated…

But she knew her life was about to change the moment one of the clan members walked into the tent. It was one of the men her mother laid with. A look of terror came over his face when he took in the scene before him. Just as quick as he popped in, he was gone.

Lilith knew right then and there that she had to leave. She knew they were going to blame her for the death of her parents and were going to condemn her. They were going to punish her horribly. Her people weren't kind and contained no feelings of remorse or sympathy within them. She knew there was no other way around her situation—so she ran. She left the camp quickly before her people could get to her, and just like that—she was gone forever from what she only knew. She never even looked back to see if her people were running after her…

When Lilith finally stopped running, she noticed that she was in a thin forest. The night was dark but the moon was bright. She knew she was on the outer boundary of the Kingdom of Minslethrate—so that was her destination. She began her trek across a field towards the kingdom, then stopped in the moonlight. The grasses were tall and swayed back and forth among the breezes. Something in her head influenced her to stop… It was that voice again… She looked around herself, realizing how alone she was—but it seemed not to bother her because she was always alone. The swaying grasses formed many dark shapes around her. She looked at her white hands in the bright moonlight and noticed that her hands were covered in dry blood. She stared at them for a while and then tightened her fists.

"Lilith…," a low whisper said from the darkness.

It was the same heavy voice that she had heard in her head, but this time the voice seemed to be all around her now. She looked around again— then noticed a tall, dark figure standing a couple of yards away from her. She wasn't frightened and seemed to be drawn to the quiet, dark figure. She knew the dark person was not one of the gypsies, because it was still and quiet like a shadow as it just watched her.

Lilith blinked her eyes, then strangely the shadow person was gone. It had vanished quickly…

All of a sudden, as if out of nowhere, something came flying down towards her. It was a massive white bird which had a great wingspan. It was a majestic white owl. Lilith fell on her backside and just watched as the bird silently glided back up into the starlit sky and then back down to perch upon a nearby tree. The bird just sat on the branch of the tree and watched her. The moon's light touched its white feathers, making them glow.

Lilith tried not to look at the massive bird. She began to feel nervous as she fixed her eyes on the darkness around her. Any normal person would've been in a state of wonder because of the beautiful appearance of the great bird. But Lilith wasn't, and was in a state of panic. She thought the bird was ugly and threatening—and she didn't like it one bit. She could feel something from the bird—something she had never felt before. She was repelled by it… It was something new, something strange to her—she didn't understand it and she was frightened by that feeling…

She turned her gaze back towards the direction of Minslethrate. She quickly made her way across the field, running past the tree as fast as she could. She didn't look up at the bird as she flew past it and didn't even turn around to see if it was still there when she got further away from it…

She never wanted to see the great white owl again or feel the presence that came from it…

She made her way to the nearest manor on the outskirts of the kingdom. The lord of the manor pitied her and welcomed her into his home. That was when she became a servant. But she was sold and traded off by three different aristocratic homes throughout that year because of her erratic and disturbing behavior. She was sold to the authorities of Minslethrate all together when the last family she worked for found their dead chickens beneath her bed. They were headless and gutted.

Everyone was frightened by her and nobody wanted her…

†††

"I have my own daughter, she be bout your age I suppose," the woman said as she continued to rant on. "She be in a good home now… You need to talk more deary—you be like a ghost... Ah! There be the castle now," she said excitedly as they came upon the beautiful structure.

Lilith just continued to ignore her as she looked upon the exquisitely dressed noble people and courtiers of Minslethrate who walked about.

The people just glared at them with their awkward looking expressions, as if they were offended by the people in the carriage or by the carriage itself.

The horses pulled the cage-like carriage around the grand castle to the back of it. The area where they pulled up to looked to be the servant's quarters. There was a woman and a man standing tall and quiet, waiting for their arrival.

"You all stay still!" the large coachman said in a rough voice, then hopped off his seat. "They might not want any of you rats."

The coachman hobbled over to the man and woman. They were much taller than him and looked as if they were high-ranking servants. Their appearance made the coachman look like a dirty pile of trash. They looked too clean and proper to even be servants. Their clothes weren't even soiled and had no wrinkles or patches on them.

Lilith had never seen a castle servant before and thought they must've been like any other type of person that wasn't a peasant in Minslethrate—arrogant. She watched as they talked among each other. The man was doing most of the talking while the woman just kept looking over at them. They were only a couple of feet away and Lilith heard every word they were saying…

"Are there any clean ones? They look as if they may carry diseases," the man said as he looked over at them, having an unpleasant look on his face. "The king doesn't need any filth in the castle."

The man was older than the woman and looked very presumptuous and rude. He was obviously one of the head-servants of the castle. He stood with his back very strait and his nose up.

"There are some that have been servants in noble households—there are some youngins too," the coachman said as he scratched his bald head. "The young usually ain't diseased anyhow."

"I may have to turn this plethora of vermin away," the servant man said as he looked at the woman.

"Oh please, Alexander," the woman finally spoke up," calm yourself before you have another nose bleed. I see some that look promising..."

She made her way over to the carriage with her hands clasped in front of her. She slowly walked around them, eyeing everyone from head to toe. Every now and then she would keep glancing over at Lilith. She made her way right over to her and stood right in front of Lilith, and just stared her dark eyes into hers for a moment. After many seconds, a small smile crept over her face.

"Coachman," the woman called out. "I want her..."

The short, round dirty man hobbled over to her, seeming to be somewhat excited. But his mannerism changed when he noticed who she was talking about. A look of concern came over his face as his awkward smile faded away. He usually would care less about what servant he sold to the castle, but the young girl made him nervous. He knew something was not right with her because of the gossip that followed her...

"Well—madam—she ain't a good one...," he stuttered. "There be somethin wrong with that one...," he said in a much lower tone, trying to hide his words from Lilith who just stared at him. "I have other young pretty girls...that one on the other side of the cage. Oh—and I have a young lad that looks strong and healthy..."

"What's wrong with her?" she said quickly, cutting him off.

"Well—she be a little—sick in the head," he said, almost whispering to the woman.

The woman didn't look the least bit worried. She just kept staring at the young girl. She looked as if she knew something about the young girl that even the coachman did not...

"I want her...and the other two you've mentioned, sir. No one else— that will due," she quickly said, then turned to walk over to the man named Alexander.

The coachman did what he was told without saying anything else.

"I've chosen, Alexander—I hope this pleases you," she said.

"Yes, Moira," he said, looking as if he didn't really care. "I always did trust you with hiring our servants," he said as the coachman pulled the children out of the carriage. "The two girls do look promising as you say. Our new Princess Marrisa will be well with them—with you there of course… The young boy will be fine for work around the castle."

Alexander paid the coachman as the three children now stood before them.

"Are you sure you don't need anymore?" the coachman quickly asked. "The rest will be auctioned off and the ones still lingerin will be sold to other kingdoms.

"That will due, sir," Alexander said as he motioned for him to go away. "I don't want to look at them anymore."

The coachman just nodded his head, then hobbled over to his carriage. He got the horses going and left quickly down the dirt road.

"Young man, you come with me," Alexander said, leaving without hesitating. "You two girls go with Moira."

The boy left quickly, following behind Alexander like a lost puppy. The two girls just looked up at the tall, beautiful woman named Moira. Lilith just remained silent while the other girl began to cry.

"Oh, come now—you are in good hands…," Moira said to them, but was looking at Lilith while she said it...

†††

Over the duration of her living in the castle, Lilith learned many things. She learned everything from Moira—who seemed to be a kind person. She understood that Princess Marrisa was just a baby and that she was going to help take care of her. She learned that the princess had many servants but Moira was her head-servant and main care-giver. She also learned that the princess' servants were called handmaidens, and that they seemed to be of a higher rank than any ordinary servant of a random household.

Moira taught Lilith and the other young handmaiden she was chosen with, castle etiquette and how to behave and perform in front of royalty and nobility. Lilith learned that the other girl servant was a couple of years older than her and went by the name, Katrinka. She also learned that she was the youngest handmaiden out of all of Princess Marrisa's servants. Moira had told her this, and also told her that she was a very special girl…

Lilith also learned many things about Moira. She figured out that Moira was a completely different person than she portrayed herself to be. She seemed to have two personalities and only showed her caring and loving personality to the royal family. She learned that Moira kept many dark secrets—from everyone…

Moira was beautiful and would smile in the presence of other people, but when she was alone—she changed. Just as Lilith used to watch her parents from the shadows—she would watch Moira. Lilith saw that when Moira sat by herself in the quietness of her dark chamber—she would talk to someone… But she could never see who that someone was. Moira was always all alone when she talked to the person in the darkness. She would hear her say things like, "…I will do it…," or, "…she will be perfect…" Lilith began to understand that the silent person who she talked to was called "father"… Lilith learned that Moira never slept. Moira would sometimes leave in the still darkness of the night, when everyone slept, and wouldn't come back till right before the sun came up. Sometimes she would go off into the forests at night—she knew this because she would follow her and watch her as she disappeared into the foliage of the forest. But most of the nights—she would creep down into the deep dark chambers of the castle…

On one particular night, Lilith followed Moira down to the darkest cavities of the castle—to the ones that seemed to take forever to get to. She silently followed her down many steps and through long halls to get to the deepest chamber of the castle. Lilith stood in the shadows as she watched Moira unlock a heavy-looking door that had a small barred window in it. The chamber must have been a place where criminals were contained long ago. Moira closed the door behind her. Lilith quietly came to the door and peeked through the barred window. She watched Moira light some candles with the torch she had been carrying.

If any other person would have seen what Lilith saw, they would have uncontrollably screamed out in terror and then ran away. But Lilith stood quietly, drawn to what Moira was doing. Lilith was intrigued by what she saw and began to understand Moira's secrets… The chamber had not been used by the royal family in many years and stunk of rotting things. It was filled with dust and cobwebs and rats ran about the stone ground. There were many skeletons in the cold chamber and bones laid about piles of stone, mud, and dead animals. Lilith even noticed a fleshy hand protruding from the pile of stones. Whoever the hand belonged to was dead… There were many black stains upon the stone ground, looking like old blood. There were many candles in the chamber sitting upon an old-looking table, and on wooden shelves that lined the walls. There was a large wooden vat that stood in the middle of the room that looked like one of the tubs in the castle. The vat contained a black liquid of some sort...

Lilith watched as Moira walked over to the corner of the now dim chamber. There was some kind of animal cowering in the corner—or at least she thought it was an animal. Lilith noticed that the animal was tied up with a rope and shook with fear. The animal began to whimper as she untied it. She now noticed that it wasn't an animal at all—but a girl! She was wrapped in a wool mantle and looked to be sixteen or so. Lilith noticed her to be the same girl whom Moira had hired on recently that month, to help around the castle. The girl began to cry as Moira petted her head, as if she were an animal.

"Hush, my sweet pet," Moira said with a tender voice as she walked the girl over to the vat. "The moon is new and covered in red. The time has come for father to receive a much acceptable sacrifice..."

Moira pressed her up to the vat and pulled the wool mantle off of her. She was bare and trembled in the cold air. Moira just continued to softly hush her as she petted her long hair.

Then with a quick, startling motion, Moira sliced the girl's throat with a dagger with one hand as she used her other arm to hold on tightly to the girl's head. She leaned the girl over the vat to let her blood drain into it. After a few moments of holding onto the girl, Moira let her go. The girl's arms fell limp as her head fell into the black fluid.

Moira unfastened the robe she was wearing then let it fall to the ground. She was naked and just stared into the tub of blood.

"Let this be acceptable to you, father. I have done what you have asked of me—I have continued the rituals of the ancient ways... Now fulfill your promise unto me, father. Show me eternal life—that I shall live forever and stay beautiful... I have done everything you have asked of me..."

She then lowered herself into the tub. She reclined into the tub, laying down into the blood until her whole head was beneath it, and after a few moments, she slowly stood up. She appeared like a dark-red statue as the blood covered her whole entire body.

Lilith watched Moira's whole ritual silently through the barred window of the door, never allowing herself to be seen. She continued to watch as Moira washed the blood off of her body in another vat, filled with cold-looking water. She got back into her long robe, then dragged the girl's dead body over to the large pile of stone, mud, and bones and pushed her over it onto the other side. Lilith understood everything now—Moira was a follower of this "father" and worshiped him, and the chamber was her temple. Lilith was exhilarated by the whole ritual and wanted to know more about it. She wanted to know all of the secrets Moira had known and wanted to know the relationship she had with "father". The dagger Moira held and the blood that lay all around the chamber reminded her of her parents. She felt she never had a true father, and wanted to know Moira's "father"…

Lilith continued to watch Moira. After Moira had fastened her robe, she walked over to a large ring of candles and sat in the center of it. She sat quietly for what seemed like hours. Lilith noticed that Moira was whispering to herself while she stared off into the shadows of the chamber. Lilith finally crept into the chamber, slowly making her way over to Moira. Moira seemed not to notice her as she stood right before her. Moira's eyes were large and black like coal and looked glassy. She never blinked as she continued to whisper.

"Moira…," Lilith finally said as she stood before her.

Moira stopped whispering, then slowly turned her head towards Lilith. Her eyes looked like glossy, black pools of frightening water.

"No… I am called Natas…"

†††

After that night, Lilith had joined Moira for every ritual. Moira had revealed every dark secret to her and taught her the ways of "father". She told Lilith to never tell anyone and that only a few chosen ones were allowed to know. Moira told her that they were the ways of the ancient times and were taught to her when she was young, by her mother. She revealed to her that her mother was the servant to Princess Marrisa's grandmother—a woman by the name of Queen Karnidge. She said that the chamber they did the rituals in was the very chamber that Queen Karnidge used, to do the very same thing…

Lilith learned that Moira and Natas were two completely different beings. Moira was kind and a loving handmaiden—Princess Marrisa's caregiver. But Natas was the thing that lived inside of Moira, making her become cold and aloof. Natas did not reveal itself all of the time. When Moira was doing the rituals, it was as if Natas came over her, making her forget about her life, and she wouldn't even remember doing any of them when it was all done with. Lilith could always tell when Natas took over her body because her eyes would become large and black and shiny like glass.

Over the years Moira became colder as if Natas, who lived inside of her, was slowly changing her. Moira had told Lilith on one particular night that there were more beings like Natas—that Natas was one of many... She said that they wanted to meet Lilith… So, on Lilith's sixteenth birthday, she was given to "father". During their ritual Moira had cut Lilith's hand to drain some of her blood into the vat, then she dunked her whole body into it. Lilith was made new that night—and "father" revealed himself to her. She was awakened unto darkness. Lilith was received by father—and was lost in darkness forever…

†††

Two years had passed by as they continued to follow darkness in secret…

On one particular night, Natas spoke to Lilith through Moira, and told her that she must not continue to sacrifice with Moira any longer. Natas revealed to her that Moira was no longer acceptable to participate in the rituals. Lilith was told that Moira was going to be condemned and it was time for Moira's body to die...she was no longer needed… Lilith found out that a time of great change was drawing nearer and that she must tell someone of Moira's actions.

Lilith didn't understand, but only listened to what the dark beings told her. She did what she was told—and revealed to Katrinka, the handmaiden, that Moira told her that she had been sneaking off in the middle of the night to go down into the dungeons of the castle. Lilith was a liar just like "father", and told Katrinka that Moira had revealed to her that she was a witch.

On one particular night, Katrinka had followed Moira down into the dark halls and chambers of the castle. She witnessed Moira and her disturbing acts, and told many of her fellow handmaidens.

The following day the disturbing news made its way to Alexander. Alexander and King Julpen saw for themselves, the gruesome chamber that lay deep beneath the castle. They were shocked and disgusted. That same day the chamber was cleaned out and Moira was sent to court for witchcraft. She pleaded for mercy and said she was innocent and that she knew nothing of it. She was telling the truth, but only half of it was true. Moira was a murderer and did evil-craft, but didn't remember doing it. She had no memory of the bloody, dark chambers. When Moira was convicted of witch-craft—father had left her completely. She was of no use to him any longer. She had become herself again and had no knowledge of the rituals and sacrifices. But Lilith had told the court that Moira had said she wanted to be beautiful and live forever—that is why she killed many servant girls and animals. She said that is why she bathed in their blood. The court believed every word that came from Lilith's mouth and condemned Moira to the stake—and she was burned to death…

Lilith continued to follow the dark being, father, but was very careful and hid her secrets very well. She continued her duty to take care of Princess Marrisa, but only because that is what father told her to do…

When Lilith closed her eyes—all she saw was darkness. She had no images or dreams within her mind. She had no light within her. She was cold and dark and deceived everyone. She was born into darkness—and darkness was where she continued to go. She became a silent monster and was blinded by father. She understood that her business was only to lie, steal, kill, and destroy… Father eventually revealed to Lilith that he was the Lord of Darkness—that he was father of the world… He told her that he had many names… He told her many things she would become and come to have… They were all lies—and she believed all of it. Just like the lies father had told Moira and Moira's mother—he told them to Lilith. Lilith became a domicile of wickedness—a temple to darkness and a doorway to a very dark world.

Over the years Lilith's body slowly faded away. Just like that of Queen Karnidge, Moira, and many other innocent souls who fell victim to the Dark Lord, Lilith's flesh died and her spirit was stolen by darkness.

Death had taken her flesh. It was already done—and the Great King of Light never knew her…

Just like in the old days and many days to come, the Dark Lord feasted on lost people—the ones who did not love the Great King of Light. The ones who did not know the light, contained nothing to protect themselves from darkness. They had no armor of light to protect themselves…

The Dark Lord loathed the Great King of Light and ate up every soul who did not contain any light at all.

Because Lilith was born into darkness—she only knew darkness. Because she loved everything dark—she did not know the Great King of Light. She was lost. Legend has it that everyone is given a chance to ignite their souls with burning light. Lilith was given this chance the moment the great owl, a being of light, flew upon her the night she ran away from her clan. But she rejected the light that tried to touch her cold heart…

A part of the legend is this: Pity to those who do not heed it—for they are cursed…

Natas had taken hold of Lilith's body in full and craved to be part of a new temple. Many nomed came and went through Lilith. She was infested with darkness.

…But the time is now…

Just like how Lilith was once a temple of darkness, and how Moira was before Lilith, and Queen Karnidge before Moira—Marrisa was the new temple to behold…   She was forced upon the Forbidden Lands of Minslethrate and dragged into the Dark Temple of Sacrifice. The ancestors of Minslethrate who were of the Old Ways had used that temple to sacrifice to the goddesses many ages ago, unknowingly giving to father, the Dark Lord—who had deceived them all.

The Dark Temple of Sacrifice was where the Lord of Darkness wished Marrisa to be confined until the Blood Red Moon was to appear.

Legend was prophesied as so… Following the night when the moon glows like blood, during the twilight when the morning star shines the brightest—evil will prevail and take on a new form…

Legend stated that the Legendary Great King of Light's earthly crown was stolen when the Great King gave up his life—and placed in the Dark Tower of Sacrifice by an evil man named Baffmit. That crown still sat in a dark and dusty chamber of the tower.

The Dark Lord waits in the darkness for his new form, craving the moment when that crown would be placed upon Marrisa's head, his new head....

Book Two
Unto The End

†

CHAPTER 1
Be My Armor

Tairren sat up slowly and rubbed the back of his head. His body ached from sleeping upon the rock-hard ground of the valley. He stood up and stretched his arms and aching back. The sky was a deep gray-blue, indicating that the sun was coming up, and was still covered with dark clouds. It looked even darker ever since he had been in the Forbidden Lands. He looked around, noticing the terrain of the south. He was standing in the middle of a great valley that was adorned with random trees and large boulders. The grass was thin and the earth was hard like rock. Small stones were littered throughout the field and there seemed to be no life around him. He hadn't seen one bird in the sky or rodent among the earth. He looked off into the distance and shuttered. He noticed that the sky got really black where the mountains were. He could see in the early morning light that the south before him was filled with rugged hills, massive boulders and cliffs, and even more dark forests. He became nervous all of a sudden as he took in the morbid path before him.

He decided that he would eat something before he began his journey towards the Fire Temple. He sat on a nearby rock and dug into his bag, pulling out some bread the legna had given him and a couple of apples. The bread Moral had given him before his journey became stale, so he gave it to Lilly along with an apple. The strange bread from the legna was white and smelled like coriander, felt like a crispy wafer, and tasted like honey. It seemed to give him a boost of energy and made him feel full and new.

As he ate his bread he looked out into the mysterious valley. The dark shadows of the distant forests reminded him of his dream… The thought of his dream startled him as its strange images flashed through his head. He began to wonder what it all meant... His father was in his dream—and so was Marrisa… The forest in the distance seemed to pull him into it. His mind slipped away into deep thought as his dream came back to him…

†††

He was a timid child again and was running through a wind-blown forest. The trees around him swayed and creaked and the branches seemed to reach at him, scaring him. Leaves blew all around him as he ran. His heart pounded beneath his young chest. He was terrified and felt lost. He was looking for something—or someone. And then he remembered that he was looking for his father. His father had left him in the forest and he felt terrified, and cried. He thought that his father had forgotten him… He kept running as he called out to him. He wanted to hear his father's voice call back to him—but he never did. He kept running until he fell upon the leaf-matted earth. He cried and covered his ears as the wind and trees around him became louder.

The wind whistled loudly and the trees groaned. It began to sound as if a treacherous storm was brewing all around him... And then—it all stopped… It became quiet all around him. He heard the sweet song of the birds and the now soft breezes that crept through the tree tops. Even though he still covered his ears and had his face buried in the leaves, he could feel that it was now peaceful. He slowly sat up, still covering his eyes out of nervousness. He could see through the cracks of his fingers that it was bright and sunny now, and he could feel the warmth on his skin. He could hear the trickle of water from a nearby creek and the noises of calm forest animals now—and he felt safe and at peace.

"Don't be frightened, my son," a kind voice said to him, "for I will always be with you—even in the darkest hour…"

He didn't recognize the man's voice—but he knew deep down in his heart that it was from someone who only held love and kindness. His voice somehow reminded him of soothing chimes and feathers brushing across the air—or the sun when it first rises over a mountain… The man's voice was like life itself. It was beautiful.

He slowly took his hands from his eyes. He could now see why it was so bright all around him and why he felt warmth upon his skin. The man before him seemed to be made of pure light. Tairren had to partially cover and squint his eyes just to look upon the man. He could see that the man wore a crown, and had the most beautiful garbs on which were white as snow. But he couldn't see who it was. Tairren knew that the man was a king—and he knew it must've been the Legendary King of Light... His heart told him so. He stood among vibrant green grass and colorful flowers that seemed to literally be alive and breathing. The earth looked happy beneath his feet. Everything seemed to be filled with life now.

Then the glowing being of light reached his hand out to Tairren. Tairren slowly took his hand as the light pulled him up. He felt as if he never wanted to leave the king's side. He felt as if he were enveloped in total peace and protection. But then the light around him seemed to go down. It faded like the sun in the evening. Everything around him became dim and dull and the warmth and peace that he had felt, slowly diminished.

Tairren could now see that the hand he held was now made of flesh. He looked into the man's face even harder now that he could see clearly. Tairren realized that he recognized his face now. He wasn't holding the king's hand anymore, but he was now holding his father's hand... Tears flooded his eyes as he hugged the man who was now his father. Tairren could smell his father's scent that he had never forgotten: the smell of fire wood and the outside air. He felt as if he hadn't seen his father in years. He held on tightly to him, never wanting him to leave him again. His father didn't speak but just hugged him back and caressed the back of Tairren's head.

After what seemed like hours, Tairren let go of his father's embrace and slowly stepped back to look at him again. As he stepped back, everything around him became even darker, as if the light all around him was fading away. His father's smile also seemed to fade with the light...

Tairren looked all around him as they now stood in complete darkness. Black was all around them and there was no sign of light or life. His father's face continued to change as he stepped away from him. He looked as if he were in pain now. His father made a grunt noise as his mouth partially opened. Blood came from his mouth, trickling down his chin like thick red water. Tairren watched in horror as his father grabbed at his chest. A long bloody blade now stuck strait out of his heart. He appeared dead now as he noticed someone staring at him from behind his father's shoulder. It was Marrisa. Her face slowly came out of the shadows and became more visible as a large, wicked smile came across her face. Her eyes became black as a disturbing chuckle emitted from her pale lips. She pulled the long blade from his father's chest in one quick motion as he fell away. She let out a loud, deep, roar as Tairren now stood a ways away from her in the darkness.

He felt alone again as fear came over him. But the fear left quickly as the words of the king echoed in his heart, "Do not be afraid—for I am always with you..."

He realized that he was no longer a child but an adult now. He watched as Marrisa now sat upon a massive throne made of flesh, human parts, and weaponry. Her throne sat upon a mountain of dead bodies. She held a long scepter in one hand and a massive sword in the other. She was now dressed in a royal, black gown and wore a black crown.

Her mouth stretched wide open as another loud roar erupted from deep within her. Blood began to come from the dead bodies she sat upon, slowly flowing up the fleshy mountain and up the black lace of Marrisa's gown. The blood went into her mouth and she was now covered in it. Dark shadows began to come from Marrisa's blood-soaked body by the thousands and began to make their way towards Tairren.

Tairren stood tall and unwavering now. His heart pulsated with light which seemed to come from his chest and race through his veins and limbs. He had a glowing sword of light in his hand while a courageous look was set on his face. He wasn't afraid as the shadows, which were now an army of darkness, rushed upon him like a black wave of wickedness...

✝✝✝

The sound of shrieks in the distance shook Tairren from his day dream. His heart sped up as he quickly glanced all around him. He swallowed down the rest of his breakfast as he reached for his sword. He backed nearer to Lilly, who seemed nervous. Everything became silent again. He lowered his sword as his eyes searched the dark-blue sky and the strange valley around him.

Tairren learned that nothing was to be taken for granted in the Forbidden Lands. The night he had traveled deeper into the Forbidden Lands by himself, he realized that he was always being hunted. That night when he left the camp of the legna, he was filled with determination and felt as if he could take on anything. But the further he went from the camp, the more noises and treacherous shrieks he heard, and the more anxious he became. He traveled most of that night, running from insidious creatures and lurking monsters. He realized that the forests were good for hiding, but seemed to be infested by the creatures of darkness more than the fields. So that night he decided to sleep in the middle of the valley. But now that the unseen sun was coming up, he could see that he still had a way ahead of him.

After a couple of moments of searching his silent surroundings, he put his sword into its sheath. The sound of the smooth sword sliding into the beautiful sheath reminded him of the legna, and he became thankful for the golden sword and ample provisions they supplied him with. Tairren threw the saddle bags over Lilly's back and got everything situated. He noticed that Lilly still seemed a little nervous so he worked quickly. He knew that when Lilly became anxious, that meant she sensed something near that she didn't like.

Tairren quickly pulled himself onto Lilly's back. He looked over his map and compared his surroundings to it, then took out his compass. He saw that the Fire Temple was in a southeast direction and looked only a couple of hours away. Proud of himself for not becoming lost, he put his things back into his bag, gave Lilly a pat on the back of her neck, then got her going.

Tairren thought of his journey as they dashed across the valley. He wondered how he was going to fulfill his quest on his own. He became worried as he thought of what the Archlegna, Mikhal, told him: that he was to go with his guardian legna, Rafiul. He knew it would've been best if he went with him, but he was impatient and wanted so badly to begin his quest to save Marrisa. Tairren thought of his beloved companions, Natalia and Phillip, and wondered if they were waking for their very own mission.

Tairren could see in the distance that another forest was before him. The forest didn't look as massive and appeared thin. Just after the small forest, there seemed to be more hills and mountains.

"Tairren!" came a shrieking voice.

Tairren stopped Lilly as he looked all around again. The voice sounded like Marrisa's!

It was strange because it sounded like Marrisa was right behind him…but no one was there.

"…Marrisa!" he shouted as he sat still.

The atmosphere was quiet again as he frantically searched with his eyes. He strained to listen as his heart pounded in his chest.

"Tairren!" the voice shrieked again.

Tairren noticed that the shrieks were coming from behind him, far off in the distance.

"Tairren…," the voice said. But this time the voice wasn't that of Marrisa's. The voice was low and threatening and reminded him of when the two-headed dog nomed spoke to him.

Tairren could see that some kind of dark shadow began to stir and grow. The shadow became thick and slowly began to expand where the voice was coming from. The shadow looked like thick mist, but it appeared very dream-like and unnatural. The whole area of the valley where the shadow grew became dark, appearing like a starless night.

The shadow took the form of seven creatures of some kind. Tairren thought he was imagining it and had to shut his eyes tight then open them again just to make sure. A large, tall creature stood in the middle of the darkness and was circled by the smaller animal-like creatures. The tall being was frightening, having the head of a goat with large spiraling horns that twisted then pointed up into the sky. It had large black eyes and its torso and arms were that of a man. It wore a long garb from the waist on down and large hooves could be seen protruding from its black mantle. It had two large wings that spread out in both directions and looked like massive bat wings covered with shiny black feathers.

The smaller creatures were half its size and crouched down like ferocious tigers. The animal-like creatures were black as night like all of the other nomed, and had a body and head like a massive lion. Tairren could see that the smaller creatures also looked as if they had other strange heads and great tails that squirmed around like snakes. They seemed to be waiting for the approval to attack. They looked eager to kill with growls and gnashing teeth.

"Tairren… Go back to the north… You are not wanted here… Be wise and go back…" Marrisa's voice came again from the dark figure.

Tairren's heart skipped a beat as confusion came over him. It was surely Marrisa's lovely voice, but the grotesque body it emitted from was not hers… And even though the creatures seemed far away from him, Tairren could hear them clearly as if they were right before him.

"Your trickery will not fool me. My quest is at hand and I will not falter!" Tairren yelled out to the nomed who stood still and silent. "Who are you to tell me what I should do!? You are not my master and have no power over me!"

The dark figure stood quietly and menacingly for a moment. They were ever so still but the darkness that grew all around them seemed to pulsate and swirl as if it were alive.

"I am called Baffmit…," it finally said in a low voice that wasn't Marrisa's. "I am King and Warlord over the Legion of Darkness and conqueror of light and man…who bow down to me under my lord's hand."
Its voice seemed angry now and more threatening. "Go back to the north… The Dark Lord does not want your putrid soul here. Go back. Your kingdom will fall… Your loved ones will die… Do you not want to see

them before their hearts become ripped from them? Do you not want to see your kingdom before it is trampled beneath the Dark Lord's feet?" King Baffmit asked.

"Your deception and wicked words do not frighten me. There is only one king...King Yehoshua!" Tairren yelled out as he became flustered by King Baffmit's words. "He is the Great King of Light. And he has conquered darkness long ago!" Tairren said forcefully.

"King Yehoshua?!" King Baffmit grunted in disgust. "Foolish boy...your king is DEAD! He is dead as your people will be!"

"No! King Yehoshua is alive and his people will live forever—fierce and free! You go back to the stinking pits of darkness with your deceiving lord where you belong!" Tairren shouted. His voice was strong and unwavering. "No weapon formed against me shall prosper! You have no power over any of us! I will leave when the King of Light commands me to do so! In the name of Yehoshua, I stand!"

King Baffmit became angered by Tairren's passion and strength and by Yehoshua's name in which he boldly spoke. He roared like a beast as the darkness around him began to pulsate even more.

The thick black mists began to move all around King Baffmit like a storm. The atmosphere steadily began to become darker all around them, making all of the creature's eyes gleam and flash even more.

"THEN YOU WILL DIE!" King Baffmit roared out as he lifted his arms into the black sky. His long, pointed fingers spread out among the mists. "This is but a taste of things to come. Your skin will tear and your bones will break! Smash and rip, crack and split for the Dark Lord's sake! Blood will flow until it runs no more; light will fade on Father's door. Your people will cry; your loved ones will die! Marrisa will become darkness in the Dark Lord's eye!"

It gave out another loud roar as its wings pounded against the stale air, then twisted around its body. And then as if the darkness dissolved into the earth's air, it vanished, taking the darkness and stinking black mists with him. The sky became its usual shade of dark-gray again. The only entities that threatened Tairren were the six black beasts that came hurtling towards him now with immense speed!

"My God...be my armor...," Tairren said to himself. "Run like the wind, Lilly!" he shouted as he nudged the horse's sides with his boots.

Even though the nomed were a good distance away from Tairren, they caught up with him quickly, growling and roaring the whole way. As they came closer to Tairren, he could see that the beasts were just as big as Lilly! They were ferocious and their eyes gleamed just like all of the other nomed's: like that of a cat's eye at night. Each one of the black creatures had a thick neck that protruded from their muscular backs, having an ugly goat's head on top with large spiraling horns. Tairren realized that their tails appeared like squirming snakes because—they were snakes! Their tails were thick, scaly serpents that had large heads with sharp fangs.

As Tairren went as quickly as he could, the ugly beasts caught up with him, surrounding him on all sides. They rushed through the valley in one quick wind. The goat heads tried to ram Lilly with their massive horns and the snake tales snapped and hissed at him. Grunts and growls echoed in Tairren's ears as he pulled out his golden bow and arrows. He was quick and agile, vigilant with every move the nomed made. He shot at the goat heads and the sides of the beasts as they relentlessly attacked. His hand was steady and his eyes were keen even though the ride was rough. His shots didn't fail him as they penetrated the black flesh of the nomed. Some of the injured goat heads dangled lifelessly at the beast's side now as the arrows stuck straight out of them. The ugly goat heads thrashed around as the rest of its body ran upon the bumpy terrain of the dark valley. Tairren then pulled out his sword and swung at the snake tails that kept snapping at him. A black substance sprayed from them as he quickly cut them off like branches from a tree. The writhing snakes flailed in the air as they went hurtling towards the ground.

Before he knew it, they burst into the forest like a mad wind. The trees were tall and thin and the terrain was filled with slopes and cliffs. He noticed that three of the beasts kept advancing on him. The other three beasts were probably too injured to carry on, Tairren thought. The main lion head of the beasts continued to bite at them. One of the nomed's massive jaws took hold of Tairren's boot, nearly pulling him down to the grown. Tairren swung his sword as hard as he could, cutting deep into its side in the process. He swung again, aiming for the Lion's neck, but instead got its ear and half of its face. They raced along a slope that jutted down into a dark abyss, which was filled with jagged rocks amidst a dark rivulet. Tairren swung his sword at the beast with one more quick motion, knocking the snarling thing off the edge of the slope and down into the jagged rocks. The nomed tumbled down, slamming into the jagged rocks with black fluid bursting from its head as it hit.

Tairren's heart raced in his chest as his head pounded. Adrenaline pulsated through his body as sweat poured from his brow. Lilly raced through the forest, jumping over jagged stones and large crevasses that shrouded the earth. Tairren's heart skipped a beat as they lunged towards a steep slope! The earth took a steep dip down. Surprised, Tairren grabbed tightly onto Lilly's reins as they flew over and down the cliff-like slope. Lilly cried out as her knees buckled, sending Tairren soaring over her head and down the side of the slope. Tairren tumbled down the leaf matted earth, nearly bashing into the large rocks that stuck out of the ground. Leaves flew and tall wispy trees that stuck out the side of the slope broke as Lilly and the other two beasts crashed down as well. One of the beasts slammed into one of the jagged rocks which pierced through its black flesh like a blade.

Tairren tumbled to the ground, landing on his back and hitting his head on the side of a tree in the process. He stood up as quickly as he could. His head whirled and his vision became blurry. He stumbled, nearly falling over as he looked around for any one of the threatening creatures. There came a ringing in his ears. He could only hear the pounding of his heart and the pulsating of blood in his burning ears. After a moment his head became quiet and silence came all around him now. He wiped the sweat and blood from his brow. As he reached for his sword, he realized that it wasn't in its sheath!

He panicked as his eyes searched the ground. As quickly as he spotted his sword lying upon some dead sticks and leaves, a loud roar echoed down at him. In a dark flash an ugly beast seemed to come out of nowhere! The creature leapt into the air with claws spread and jaws wide open. It came down at him in a rush of angry energy. Tairren was quick and grabbed his sword. He swung with all of his might. The muscles in his arms became rushed with powerful blood as he swung. His blade cut through the air and the nomed's neck, slicing its ugly lion-like head off with one quick motion. The head tumbled and rolled upon the ground with a spray of black blood. The rest of the creature's large body fell to the ground, but its snake tail caught him. It wrapped its thick body around Tairren's leg tightly, pulling him down to the ground. Tairren took his sword and swung at the snake as it opened its large jaws to snap at his face. He swung his sword as hard as he could in the position he was in, cutting the snake off of the beast's backside. The snake still held on tightly to Tairren's leg as it wiggled and lashed around with opened jaws, then finally died.

Tairren was out of breath and his heart still pounded in his ears. It was quiet once again all around him but he was oblivious to it. He just lay there, looking up into the tops of the forest's trees. His head pounded and he felt a wave of nausea from the intense battle. He closed his eyes as he placed his hand over his aching chest. It seemed that he had won, but he was stuck. One of his legs was pinned beneath the nomed's heavy, lifeless body and his free leg was still wrapped tightly by the dead snake-tale. He was out of breath and felt weak.

Then after a couple of breaths, he heard another growl. He began to feel wet drops on his face. Startled, he quickly opened his eyes to find that a nomed was standing right over him! He went to cover his face as the nomed let out an ear-piercing roar. Its massive jaws were wide open, ready to attack with its many jagged teeth. He closed his eyes tightly and clenched his jaw shut, ready for the beast to tear his arm off. But it didn't. Instead, Tairren heard a swoosh sound of something quick flying past him and then heard the sound of something pelting the creature. The sounds were quick and repetitive. The creature let out grunting and squealing noises, followed by the sound of something heavy falling onto the earth. Then there was just silence.

Tairren slowly moved his arm from his face and opened his eyes. The creature was no longer standing over him and he could see the tops of the trees again. He sat up quickly, turning to find that the nomed was dead and had multiple golden arrows sticking out from its black flesh. Tairren was confused and looked quickly all around him. The arrows were golden and Tairren knew that golden arrows were rare, and only came from a certain group of people—legna.

"Master Tairren!" a familiar voice shouted. "Tairren are you well?!"

Tairren looked up to see a familiar person rushing down the side of the slope towards him. The person was tall and appeared as soft light among the dark atmosphere. It was a legna! And Tairren recognized him to be his guardian!

"Rafiul!" Tairren shouted out in a semi-weak voice. "Rafiul! It is so good to see you!"

"Are you injured?" Rafiul asked as he rushed over to Tairren's side.

"A little but I'm okay. I'm pinned beneath this nomed though. You came in the nick of time…that nomed would've taken my head off… Thank You."

"Thank the Lord, Tairren," Rafiul said as he moved the heavy nomed from Tairren's body and pulled the massive snake-tail from his leg. "I felt uneasy all through the night…then the Great King spoke to me and told me of your doing. I should've known that something was not right when my spirit felt uneasy. I am your guardian and my spirit knows when you are astray… That is how I found you—my spirit and senses, which comes from our king, led me here."

Tairren grew quiet as Rafiul helped him up. He felt ashamed of himself for leaving on his own and disobeying Mikhal's words. Tairren knew he was supposed to leave with Rafiul, but he ignored the Archlegna's wishes.

"Forgive me for leaving on my own," Tairren said.

"You have already been forgiven. The steps of a good man are directed by the Lord. the Great King knew that this would happen. You felt directed to go because God put it in your heart to go. His voice spoke to me late in the night. I followed his voice and told Mikhal of your doing."

"Everyone knows?" Tairren asked, becoming more ashamed. He rubbed his head as he looked away from Rafiul's golden stare.

"Yes, Master Tairren. But you are forgiven. I am here now and will guide you to the Fire Temple. But you must always know that it is not good for a man to be alone… It is far better to be wounded with someone else than to die alone. Remember that when more than one comes together in His name, He will be there in their midst."

Rafiul's eyes were serious but caring. The yellow-gold of his stare seemed as if warm light was glowing from beneath it.

"I understand Rafiul," Tairren said as he wiped a trickle of blood from his brow again.

"What of Natalia and Phillip? Are they on their way upon their own quest?" Tairren asked.

"Do not worry about your companions; they are safe with their guardians… The laceration upon your head needs to be mended. Come, let us sit down and rest for a moment. But not for too long; those nomed will be back with others."

Rafiul led Tairren over to a large stone and sat him down. He gave him some water to drink from a leather flask. He then pulled out a small container and a clean linen from his satchel. He spoke in the foreign tongue in which Tairren didn't understand as he cleaned his wound. Some kind of herbal ointment was in the small container and he slathered it on Tairren's wound.

Rafiul then called out in the unfamiliar tongue. His voice echoed through the tall trees and strange spaces of the forest. After a couple of silent moments of him staring off into the distance, Lilly and a beautiful winged beast came to them. Lilly nudged at Tairren's back and the winged beast sat next to Rafiul.

"This is my companion, Cherbim," Rafiul said as he patted its great head.

The winged beast was beautiful and looked much like the other flying legna. It was mighty and looked like a cross between a white Lynx and an owl. It had bright golden eyes and its beautiful wings were white as snow. It had golden flecks in its fur and its wings had a luster to them. Cherbim was about the same size as Lilly but appeared larger because of its bulkiness.

"Cherbim found Lilly running off in the darkness of the forest. She was frightened," Rafiul said as he ran his hand over Lilly's long mane. He looked into Lilly's eyes, which seemed to calm her.

"The nomed gave her a fright…as well as that nomed king." Tairren said

"Nomed king?" Rafiul sat next to Tairren.

"A nomed of large size appeared from a growing shadow and said that his name was King Baffmit."

Rafiul grew quiet for a moment as a concerned look came over his face.

"Yes…we legna know Baffmit very well," Rafiul said as he looked off into the forest. "I have not heard that name in many years… King Baffmit ruled these southern parts long ago. He was a tyrant—a foul king who followed the ways of Lucif. King Baffmit fell into Lucif's dark grasp long ago, before King Yehoshua was born upon this earth. Baffmit was not born of earthly kings and became the ruler of the south, only because of the fear he casted over the southern people was very strong. The south feared him and followed him. He was a being of evil and was filled with many dark things. He led the people of the south against King Yehoshua in a great war long ago… King Baffmit's earthly body was taken over by one of Lucif's ancient followers. The creature you saw today is the nomed who took his body long ago… The real body of King Baffmit is lost forever—covered by the earth in the Black Field of Old Blood…"

Tairren thought of Marrisa as Rafiul spoke. Marrisa was in the same situation that Baffmit was in a long time ago. He shuttered to think that Marrisa was part of something so terrible… He even thought of Lilith and how her flesh was being used by darkness.

"Was King Baffmit a part of King Yehoshua's death?" Tairren asked.

"King Yehoshua gave up his life for your ancestors, you, and everyone else who walks upon this world. King Baffmit thinks that darkness won when King Yehoshua was taken and killed. But you see, King Yehoshua could have easily gotten himself out of the situation he was in…but he chose not to. He knew that him dying, was his quest. King Baffmit did orchestrate his death…but the Great King knew everything before it was going to happen. King Yehoshua was and still is the God of Light!

"Long ago my fellow legna and I, along with the earthly king and his men, rose up against King Baffmit and his followers. King Baffmit was defeated, slayed upon the south. After King Yehoshua's death, the northern kingdom rose up against King Baffmit's body and his people and defeated them all… Everything became silent after King Baffmit's body died and after King Yehoshua rose as light from the grave. But now that darkness has been unleashed, King Baffmit roams free upon these lands," he said.

Rafiul stood up and helped Tairren to his feet. "We must get going," he said. "The Fire Temple rests a couple of hours from here."

Tairren nodded his head then went to pull himself up onto Lilly's back. But something caught his eye just then. He paused, fixing his eyes on something blue that was peeking out from the dead leaves. Curious, he went to see what it was. The blue object was the only colorful thing in the whole dreary forest. It was small and about the same size as a large pendant. Tairren kneeled down to get a better look, then realized what the blue object was. He picked it out of the pile of dead leaves and held it upon his face. It was the blue heart-shaped pendent! It was the same pendent that he had given Marrisa on her birthday. It was still attached to its thin leather necklace.

Tairren slowly stood up as he put the necklace around his neck. He grew anxious at the thought of Marrisa coming through those woods. Marrisa's beautiful face came into his mind like a fresh breath of air. Tears began to collect in his eyes as he looked at it more. He squeezed the stone in his hand until the inside of his palm began to burn.

Marrisa had it that whole time… Marrisa held on that whole time… Something happened, he thought. Somehow it came off. Maybe Lilith took it from her and discarded it? Or maybe Marrisa herself took it off? But why would she do that? Did she lose all hope?   All of these questions went through Tairren's head as small tears fell from his dark-blue eyes.

"We must go, Tairren," Rafiul said, sitting still on Cherbim's back as he just watched him.

Tairren quickly wiped his face, then tucked the blue heart-shaped pendant beneath the collar of his tunic. He was silent as he pulled himself onto Lilly's back.

Rafiul saw the sadness in Tairren's eyes and knew why. "Tairren, let not your heart be troubled…believe in God," he said.   "He is near the brokenhearted, and will relieve your crushed spirit…"

Tairren nodded his head a little and felt somewhat better. He didn't want to talk about the blue heart-shaped pendant. He knew Rafiul could feel the sadness that came upon him, and just by knowing that, Tairren felt better.

Tairren and Rafiul rode through the forest quickly. Rafiul knew that time was important to Tairren and Tairren was glad that they went with haste.

†

CHAPTER 2
Broken Dreams & Blessed Things

"Tairren…oh, Tairren… Where are you?" Natalia thought as she walked into a grand and strange hall.

The hall was great and had tall ceilings that seemed to disappear into the darkness above her. Chandeliers of all shapes and sizes hung from the ceiling, dangling from the darkened arches like luminous crystal stars. Even though the massive chamber had many lights hanging all around like a starry night, it was still very dim in the hall. Long sheer streamers and wisps of dainty fabric also draped from the ceiling, cascading down the walls like still waterfalls. Music filled the strange air, grand music with stringed instruments and airy flutes. The music was beautiful and filled the place with a magical ambiance. Many people danced all around the hall, twirling and gliding around together in one motion. The dancing people looked like nobility and royalty and they were dressed in exquisite evening-wear. Their hair and headdresses sat high atop their heads, adorned with dark jewels and black pearls; and they all wore beautiful but haunting masks which hid their faces.

Natalia realized that she was at a masquerade ball…and everything was like a dream. She slowly walked past everyone as they danced. She watched them with curiosity. She was in the middle of the grand ballroom and seemed to be the only one without a mask. She felt alone and out of place as she always did when she attended royal functions. She noticed that the over-the-top dancers were dressed in dark-colored tunics and ball gowns. Not only was she the only one without a mask, but she was the only one dressed in white. Her elegant ball gown was white as snow and had tiny crystals sown into its fabric that sparkled from it. She looked beautiful and stood out in the dark crowd like a light.

"Lady Natalia," a voice said from behind her.

Natalia turned to find a man. He was wearing a magnificent black tunic and had on a mask that covered the top part of his face. She couldn't see his eyes because they were two dark shadows. His mask was strange though. It was white and looked like it was created from one solid pearl and had two large horns that spiraled and jutted up into the air. The mask was enchanting but alarming.

The man smiled at her and Natalia could tell that he was charming. He took her hand and kissed it gently.

"I've been longing to know you…," he said in a low tone. "May I have this dance?" he asked.

She didn't say anything as she seemed to become lost in his voice and handsome smile. Her green eyes stared upon his lips and face. She was transfixed by him and didn't want to take her eyes from him.

He then gently took her other hand and came closer to her. He put his arms around her as they began to dance. They became one with the dancing crowd as the masked man led her gracefully around the ballroom floor. As they danced Natalia looked into his shadowed eyes, trying to find a glimpse of who it was behind the mask.

She was swept up in the magic of her surroundings and didn't even realize why she was there or where she was at exactly. "Where am I?" she asked finally.

"You are in Father's court…," he said with a soft smile.

She didn't say anything else as she tried to remember where she came from and how she got to "Father's court".

They twirled through the crowd in a graceful motion. Everyone seemed to be watching them now for some reason. Natalia realized that everyone's masks looked like some kind of strange creature. Some masks had great horns while others had snarling mouths. Some masks looked like decorous goat heads while others looked like a mixture of different kinds of ferocious animals. There were even some masks that looked like skulls that were black but sparkled like a starry night. The masks were covered in lustrous but dark colors. The masked dancers had on beautiful headdresses that were the shape of dragon's horns, and hats that had long black feathers coming from them. They began to look frightening to Natalia as the lights around them became dimmer. Natalia began to become nervous as the man's grip on her became tighter. She felt like a nightmare was becoming alive all around her.

She looked through the dancing crowd and noticed that a king sat on a large thrown at the head of the ballroom, who just watched everyone. The king was hard to see because of all the dancing people and the dim lights. All Natalia could see was a dark form...

She brought her eyes back up to the man who continued to smile at her softly. "Who are you?" she asked.

The man was quiet for a moment. "...If you wish to know...you must love me first," he said.

A confused look came over her face. "How can I love someone whom I do not know?" she asked.

"I thought you longed for someone to love you...," he said as his smile faded away.

Natalia then noticed a dancing couple, and recognized them very well. "Tairren...Marrisa?" she said as her thoughts began to collect.

The thought of her companions crashed through her head with a sudden rush of emotion. She realized that she was supposed to be doing something...something that was important. She realized that she had a purpose, and seeing Tairren and Marrisa reminded her of it.

Tairren and Marrisa danced beautifully as they gazed into each other's eyes. They danced slowly with each other as everyone seemed to be watching. Natalia realized that something was not right though. Tairren had no mask on either and seemed to be in a trance. His face was emotionless and his blue eyes were lifeless. Marrisa had on a mask that covered her whole face. Her mask was plain and looked like her own face—except it was black. Her long red hair fell over her shoulders and her head was adorned with a large black crown. She was dressed in a long gown that was black as night.

"Do you not want my love?" the man asked, catching her attention again.

Natalia was silent as she became worried. She looked around her as the darkness seemed to grow thicker all around them.

"...I know someone else who wants your love... Father wants you," he said as a wicked smile slowly crept over his face.

Natalia stopped dancing as a look of disgust came over her.

"My heart belongs to no one—no man! There is only one father who has my heart and that is the Father of Lights. You and your "father" can go sit in the lonesome darkness," she said as she went to walk away.

The man pulled her back to him as his grip got tighter around her arm. "Get your filthy hands off of me!" Natalia said as she became angry.

She started to push the man away but his grip was too tight. Natalia grabbed the horn of his mask and pulled it off, jerking his head to the side. Her eyes widened with fear as her heart began to pound.

His eyes scared her. They were large and black and had no white in them at all.

Natalia beat his chest with her fists and pushed him off of her with all the strength she had. She got away from his grasp. She went to run towards Tairren and Marrisa but the other dancing people began to grab at her, trying to stop her! They pulled at her gown and crowded her in a black rush of air.

"Get your hands off of me!" Natalia screamed out. "Tairren! Help me, Tairren!"

Tairren didn't hear her screams as he continued to dance with Marrisa…

The people began to make shrieking noises and beastly grunts and squeals as they grabbed and pulled at Natalia, covering her like a black shroud…

✝✝✝

"Tairren!" Natalia screamed out as her eyes shot open.

She sat up quickly as she breathed in and out sharply. She looked all around her, realizing that she was in a tent. She placed her hand over her damp forehead and closed her eyes. She was relieved that it was just a dream.

She quickly got out of bed. Her dim tent reminded her of the strange dream. Her dream didn't make any sense to her and she wondered what it meant…or if it meant anything at all. Tairren seemed to be the first thing on her mind and she wondered if that's why she was looking for him in her dream. Then she thought of the nobleman with the black eyes and white horned mask. She thought of Marrisa and the frightening black mask she wore, which gave her the chills. She knew what the black mask meant and she didn't like it.

Everything was coming back to her as she looked around the sleeping quarters the legna had prepared for her. She quickly got dressed, anxious about what she had to do that day. She placed her hand over the wing pendant that still hung around her neck. She felt safe knowing that she had the light within her, and her dream didn't seem to bother her anymore at the thought of the legend of King Yehoshua.

Tairren came into her mind again. She was worried about him leaving by himself and thought about him that whole passing night. She couldn't sleep during the night and thought of what Tairren had told her about his quest and that she had her own to worry about. She also thought about the kiss she shared with him… She felt asinine all of the sudden as the thought of her throwing herself at Tairren came into her mind. She wished she would've never shared her feelings with him in the forest on that small cliff, but at the same time, she was glad she did…

Natalia then thought of Phillip and wondered what he was up to. She hadn't seen him since they had danced with the legna that night. She wondered what his quest was about and if he was ready.

Natalia hurried out of her tent and into the pale-gray light of the morning. The camp didn't appear as magical as it did during the night. Smoke came up from all the spots where the torches and fires had burned and the gray light of the dreary sky lay thick upon the camp. She didn't see anybody. She made her way to the opening where the great bonfire was.

She walked out into the massive clearing of the camp. The great fire that once burned in the night was gone, revealing a massive charred spot among the earth. Wisps of smoke came from the burnt earth which got caught up in the morning breezes. All of the legna sat all around, eating and talking among each other. Even during the gloomy daylight, the legna had smiles on their faces as if nothing was wrong. They seemed to glow softly even in the day and still looked beautiful.

Natalia walked past the feasting legna. They looked up at her and greeted her with smiles. Some legna raised their glasses while nodding their heads, while others told her "good morning". Natalia smiled at the legna, then began to look out over all of the bright faces to see if she could get a glimpse of Phillip.

She spotted the prince easily. Phillip stuck out like a sore thumb because of his dark hair and skin. She made her way over to him with a smile. She noticed that he sat next to Uriel who seemed to be in deep conversation with Phillip. Phillip sat solemnly at the table as Uriel spoke to him.

"Good morning," Natalia said with a smile, then sat next to Phillip.

Uriel and the other legna smiled at her and nodded their heads, greeting her.

"Good morning, Lady Natalia," Phillip said with a serious edge. His face was straight and he didn't give his usual bright smile. "I hope you slept well," he said, not even looking at her.

Phillip began to eat his breakfast silently.

She gazed at him quietly. Natalia was confused for a moment. She sensed that he was being aloof and wondered why. He hadn't called her

"Lady Natalia" since they first met. He seemed irritated, and she didn't like it.

"Not too well—but thank you," she said with a smile that faded away.

A legna who was serving them put a plate of food down in front of her. Steam came up from the sweet bread and savory bacon that sat before her. Natalia began to eat silently as she looked all around the table. Natalia noticed that the legna talked amongst each other as she and Phillip only sat quietly.

"How did you sleep, Phillip?" Natalia finally asked, breaking the silence between them.

"I slept fine," he said. He became quiet again.

"Phillip…what's wrong?" Natalia asked in a low voice.

He set his eyes on her. "Does it really matter to you what's wrong with me? It seems as if you would be more worried about someone else… I saw you and Tairren in the forest last night," he said quickly, not hesitating before he spoke.

Natalia became quiet as she felt blood rush upon her cheeks. She knew what he meant—that he saw her kissing Tairren. She was embarrassed and quickly looked around to see if anyone was looking at her. She glanced back at Phillip, speechless. She now understood why he was acting so distant and irritated.

Phillip just looked into her surprised eyes. He then wiped his mouth with a cloth and stood up to leave the table. He left silently, not trying to catch anyone's attention.

Natalia watched as he walked away. She looked up from her plate and realized that Uriel had been watching them. Thankfully none of the other legna seemed to know what was going on, and continued to talk cheerfully among each other.

"Natalia," Uriel said in a kind voice. "Phillip's spirit is saddened. There is a tear in his heart…I can see it. Human love is strange, Natalia. I do not understand it—but I do know that love is a powerful, powerful thing. Love is stronger than even the weaponry of man…it conquers all... King Yehoshua's love for the people of this world is so strong that he laid his life down for it, for everyone…and even his mortal body cried tears that stung… Love comes in many forms—and tears are one of them. But where there is love…there is light, you see. And in that light—love is filled with joy, peace, and passion…"

Uriel then smiled softly at her. Her golden eyes looked like honey mixed with sunshine.

Natalia nodded a little as she moved her food around on her plate with her fork. The bacon looked crispy and delicious, but she wasn't hungry anymore. She was in deep thought. Her mind kept drifting back and forth from Tairren to Phillip. She loved Tairren and couldn't help it—and her feelings for Phillip were strong as well. Then she thought of King Yehoshua and how his love mended her heart when she was all alone... Then she thought of Tairren and how much he loved Marrisa, how he would risk his own life to save her.

"Love bears all things, believes all things, hopes all things, and endures all things," Uriel said with a kind smile. "Go and talk with him... Let there be no ill feelings between you and Phillip... He that is slow to anger is better than the mighty. Sometimes the difference that is made in someone's life is determined by the tone of the voice. Speak boldly when the time is needed, and speak lovingly all of the time...because words and love together can change a life..."

Uriel smiled again and placed her hand on Natalia's shoulder.

Natalia inhaled a deep breath then nodded her head again. In the past if she were in that awkward situation, she would've said something blunt and cheeky and then left dramatically from the table. But now, things were different—she felt different and wanted to do the right thing. She wanted to make things better during her walk upon the earth.

She took her gaze from her plate to look for Phillip. She spotted his dark hair beneath a tree. She silently stood up, excused herself, then made her way across the clearing.

There were a couple of trees off to the side of the clearing, away from all of the feasting legna. Natalia watched Phillip as she moved towards him. He was sitting alone beneath the trees and seemed to be shining his sword and shield with a cloth. Him sitting alone reminded her of the night when he pouted by himself by the fire, after he and Tairren had gotten into a fight. She walked up to him and stood in silence for a moment and then sat next to him.

Phillip took a glance at her then continued to rub the white linen against his artillery in a circular motion.

"It's just going get dirty again," Natalia said, breaking the silence.

Phillip just ignored her as he continued to work.

"Phillip," Natalia said. She placed her hand over his to get him to stop. "Ignoring me is not going to make things better. We must be free of any ill feelings if we are to go on our quests... What's ahead of us is more important."

"So, my feelings are not important?" he quickly asked, looking into her green eyes.

Natalia didn't know what to say as she looked back at his dark-brown eyes. His eyes weren't as they usually were—and had a sad light to them.

"You've stolen my heart, Natalia," Phillip said in a low tone. "Can't you see that? I've never felt this way before... When I saw you and Tairren kissing in the woods—I became enraged. Anger became real upon my body... I actually didn't sleep well last night because—I only thought of you every moment my eyes opened. Every moment my heart beat—I seemed to only think of you... Because of you I've changed, Natalia. Because of you I've met something bigger... There's a light inside of me that is consuming my heart...and I wouldn't have known it if it wasn't for you... When my eyes fall upon you—I know that God exists in this dark world. I know, because he loves me enough to place you in my life... You are the reason why I agreed to accompany Tairren. If it wasn't for you—I would've left Minslethrate and sailed back to Ishkar that night the dead maid was found in the castle... I would've ended it all and gave up on this kingdom. But I wanted to make sure that you were safe...

"I would've left because—because I do not love Marrisa... I went with the motions of courtship with her only because my father demanded it... Remember that night by the castle stable when I promised to help you rescue Marrisa? Well, I've kept my promise and will continue to do so—for you. The first time that I saw your beautiful green eyes in the marketplace that day when King Julpen was showing me around the kingdom...something sparked inside of me. And that spark ignited when we talked together the other night by the fire. You made me feel something. That night when we fought the nomed by the campfire—I only wanted you to be safe and alive... And when we won our battle, the white owl made my heart explode with fire... If it wasn't for you, my heart would still be cold. You don't know how much I appreciate you—how much I've changed because of you. I feel different. I feel like a new man...and I know it's because of the Great God of Light—and you..."

Natalia sat silently as she continued to search his eyes. She was flattered by his words and felt paralyzed because of them. She was thrilled

that he had changed because of her—but she was sad that he loved her...
She knew how he felt because he seemed to love her the way she loved
Tairren. Everything was confusing to her and her heart ached because of it.

Phillip sat quietly for a moment, just waiting for her to say something.
But she never did. He noticed that tears formed in her eyes as she looked
away from him. She looked off into the camp as the silent breezes went by
them.

"Natalia, I just want—well, I just want to say—thank you. For
everything," Phillip said, breaking the silence.

He wished he wouldn't have told her that he loved her and needed her.
He had never shared his love with anyone. And he had never shared
passionate words with anyone either. She made his hands shake and his
heart pound. Somehow, she made him do things he would've never done
before he met her. He did love Natalia and meant everything he said to her.
He knew she cared for him, but he also knew that she didn't love him the
way he loved her.

Natalia looked up at him as a small tear fell down her cheek. "You are
welcome...," she finally said, then smiled.

She thought it was very strange to hear those words come from him.
She also thought it was strange that he said them to her. All throughout her
life she dreamt of the day when a man would sweep her off of her feet and
tell her how much he loved her. She realized that life would never happen
the way she dreamt it would. Phillip's words touched her heart, and she
loved hearing them. And deep down, she wanted to feel the same way—but
didn't. She truly cared for Phillip, and she was so glad that she impacted his
life in such a powerful way.

Just then they heard a horn sound out from across the clearing. The
sound of the horn echoed across the field, breaking the moment between
them. It was a low and smooth sound which meant for everyone to come
together. Breakfast must've been over, and their day was about to begin.

Natalia and Phillip looked at one another again. They knew that it was
the last chance that they would have to speak privately among each other.
They knew that their own quest was about to begin and that they would be
on their own after they departed.

Phillip knew that moment was the last chance to share his feelings with
Natalia, and he did. And when she didn't say anything to him—he knew
how she felt. Her silence revealed everything, and he understood. He knew
that their companionship was more important than anything else they

shared. No matter what happened, he would always be there for Natalia—and would fight by her side.

Phillip tenderly wiped the tears from her cheek, smiled a caring smile at her, then stood up to leave. He began to leave Natalia by herself. But he stopped in his tracks and turned with another soft smile. In the past he would've just left a girl all by herself if she didn't do what he wanted. But everything had changed...he had changed. And he decided that he was leaving his past behind him. Instead of leaving Natalia, he stuck out his hand to help her up.

Natalia smiled back and accepted his gesture.

He pulled her up and they walked back together across the clearing to the legna. They didn't say anything to each other, but they still respected each other. Their silence was kind and understanding.

As they walked up to the legna, they noticed that Mikhal, Uriel, and Gaibriul stood before everyone. Mikhal had his hands raised to silence everyone. Phillip and Natalia made their way through the crowd to get a better look at what was going on.

"Brethren of light, listen well!" Mikhal said in a loud voice that echoed across the clearing. "Time is going and coming quickly and we must be ready for what draws near! We must take this day boldly! Tairren, son of Timotheus, has left for the Fire Temple in the night." Everyone glanced at each other with small whispers, and worried looks. Phillip glanced at Natalia with a surprised look on his face. "But do not fret!" Mikhal shouted, "for the lord thy God knows of what has happened because *He* put it in Tairren's heart to leave. He is safe with Rafiul now. The three keys are not tarnished and will press on to unlock what needs to be opened!" The legna began to cheer.

Then after he spoke, he looked at Natalia and Phillip and gestured for them to come before him. They walked up to him together, looking up at his tall stature.

"Children of light you now are...," he said in a quieter tone, as if only speaking to them. "You have been cleansed of darkness and saved upon the light. You have accepted light into your hearts and you now believe... Your faith is growing and will continue to grow day by day. You have been anointed...but now you must be washed—baptized and dedicated to the God of Light before you begin your quest."

Natalia and Phillip looked at each other, then back up to Mikhal. They didn't quite understand what he was talking about but they trusted him. Everything the legna did and spoke of was always good.

"The King you follow now, the King of Light, was brought upon the water long ago before he began his quest upon this earth. He was baptized unto the water and the God of Light ascended upon him like a glowing dove and filled him with the power of light…and He was glad and is always glad by it." Mikhal smiled warmly at them. "Now allow me to ask you this… Do you want to become purified and cleansed, baptized upon the water?"

Natalia and Phillip smiled. "Yes," they said together, then glanced at one another tenderly.

"Then it shall be done," Mikhal said.

The other Archlegna looked at Natalia and Phillip and smiled, as if proud of them.

"The light within them will be completed!" Mikhal said in a loud voice to the crowd of legna who watched silently.

The silent onlookers burst with excitement. They began to cheer as Mikhal gestured for Phillip and Natalia to walk with him.

Natalia giggled and Phillip smiled at the reaction of the legna. They seemed so excited for them and proud of them for agreeing to become baptized. They followed the Archlegna to a large vat of water that sat beneath a large oak tree. They watched as Uriel sprinkled the water with flower petals.

Two legna led them into their own small tent nearby and had them dress into a white robe. After changing, they walked back out upon the legna where they waited. Mikhal was already in the water and waited for them with a smile. They were both led up wooden steps that sat beside the vat and down into the water. The water was warm and the smell of aromatic spices and sweet flowers came from it. Small flowers and petals floated upon the water, bobbing around in the dim morning light.

"This is the last step before you begin your quest," Mikhal said to them. "This is a public testimony. It signifies the washing away of the darkness of your past. As I lower you back into the water, it is a reflection of the death, burial, and resurrection of the King of Light, King Yehoshua… Come, Phillip," Mikhal said.

Phillip came to Mikhal, and the Archlegna lowered him down into the water in one quick motion. The warm water came over him like a blanket and he felt inundated with happiness. When he came back up and out of the water, he felt new again. All of the legna cheered and shouted as he stood up.

Mikhal did the same thing with Natalia, and afterwards she smiled. Natalia looked out to the cheering legna after she came back out of the water and noticed how happy they were, and she felt the same. She raised her hands up to her mouth as she became overwhelmed by their love and joy.

Both Phillip and Natalia stood together in the water with great smiles on their faces. They both knew that they had done something special, and they were happy that they had done it.

"I am well-pleased... You are my children of light...," a voice said in their hearts.

They both heard the voice. The voice was clear and they even heard it above the roar of the crowd. They quickly looked around as the voice took them by surprise. They glanced at each other with giggles, realizing that they both had the same thought and wonder in their minds.

They didn't notice but the great white owl sat above them in the oak tree that hung its large branches all around them. It watched them with its dark gaze. It perched quietly in the shadow of the oak. It spread its massive wings and flew off into the gray sky with the sound of its grand feathers upon the air. Then, above the heads of all the tall legna, both Phillip and Natalia saw the splendid owl as it flew off into the distance.

The rest of the morning went by quickly. They departed one another and went into their tents to dress properly for their journey. The legna equipped them with their own sword and shield. Their new weaponry was not heavy and looked beautiful and strong. The legna had them dress in garbs that looked similar to their own. They put a braid in their hair with a feather that dangled from it. They looked like beings of light and felt ready for anything that was to come upon them.

Phillip and Natalia met Mikhal one last time before they left the camp. He explained to them that he and the legna were going to move their camp further south, upon the cliffs, right before Skull Hill and the Black Field of Old Blood. He then said a blessing over them and then told them of their quests and what it involved. Then, just as quick as it all seemed to have happened, they rode off into the Forbidden Lands.

Phillip rode upon Sable towards the ancient Water Temple with Uriel by his side—who rode on her mighty beast named Eralim. Natalia rode upon Orchid towards the Earth Temple with Gaibriul by her side, who rode upon his beast named Serafim. They went in opposite directions, away from the legna's camp, who watched them with admiration.

†

CHAPTER 3
Smoldering Heart

The water was clear and cold because of the persistent gray clouds. King Julpen sat upon the rocks by a river and stared into it. He could see small fish darting here and there and rocks which were covered in green. The river was calm and the noises of the clear water rushing past the rocks soothed him. The trees from the small forest they were in loomed over the river, creating more shadows and cold spots.

They had traveled across the lands of Minslethrate the whole day before and ended up in another small forest. The map he carried showed that they were almost to the Great Wall of Division. He was glad they were making it across the lands quickly, but he was worried that time was going by too fast. He was also worried that something much greater was going on in his kingdom. The sun had not come out in days and the clouds seemed to get darker as they made their way deeper into the lands. There was even a disturbing presence that seemed to follow them. He remembered feeling that same presence when he was a young boy…when he stood in his mother's shadow…

He had no idea what kind of state his daughter, Lady Natalia, or even Prince Phillip was in. He was tired and worried but did not tell any of his men that, not even Sir Hawkington. So instead of having breakfast with his men, he decided to sit alone with his thoughts. Sitting by himself upon the nature of the forest somewhat calmed his spirit.

The shadows of the trees and the dark clouds reminded him of his dream he had that night. He couldn't sleep that night, not only because of his current situation, but because of the strange images that kept shrouding is mind. He dreamt of Marrisa, O'nessa, and…his mother. It had been some time since his beloved, deceased wife or his mother had come into his dreams.

He began to think of his vision-like dream. His mind began to drift away again as he became inundated by his thoughts. The dream of his daughter and deceased wife and mother was nothing but quick images, but the thought of them sent chills across his skin.

†††

King Julpen was walking upon his garden at the castle as he always did when something bothered him. The sun was out and the cool breezes of the day went by. But even though everything was beautiful, the feeling of sadness crept over his body. He was thinking of his daughter. He was worried about her and wondered if she was okay.

Then he heard a noise… He stopped in the shaded pathway of the garden so that he could hear it better. It sounded like soft cries that were being consoled and hushed by another, like whimpers from that of a young girl and hushes from a worried mother. He rushed to where he heard the cries. He made his way through the bushes and tall grasses. The cries came more clearly to him now as he seemed to get closer.

He came upon a small shaded grove that had a lovely fountain in the center of it. Small trees and flowers surrounded the fountain with their many colors. He noticed that a woman sat upon the edge of the fountain. She was a beautiful woman who was consoling a young maiden. He noticed she had red hair and a loving face. Her face had features that he had nearly forgotten and had not seen in many years. Her face brought tears to his eyes as he began to become broken. His heart began to pound as he realized who the woman was.

"O'nessa?" he said as he watched from the bushes.

She looked just as she did the last time Julpen had seen her, before she died. She was caressing Marrisa's head as she cried upon her lap.

He tried to go to them but he couldn't move. So, he continued to watch the woman, who looked very sad.

The woman slowly looked up at Julpen as tears rolled down her cheeks. She knew he was watching but wasn't disturbed by him.

"Please don't cry," Julpen tried to say, but no words came out of his mouth.

All around them became dark as the woman slowly began to fade away.

"O'nessa! Please don't leave, O'nessa!" Julpen tried to call out to her, but only silent words came from his mouth. "Don't leave Marrisa…she needs you! I need you!" Julpen cried out as more tears built in his eyes.

She gave him a soft smile as she began to slowly fade away, leaving Marrisa crying alone in the darkness upon the fountain.

He held onto his emotions as something caught his eye. Someone was watching Marrisa from the darkness that grew all around her.

King Julpen noticed that he was no longer outside in the gardens, but in a dark throne room. Marrisa was no longer crying among a fountain but upon a throne. He realized that the dark person who was watching her was now sitting upon the throne, and Marrisa was whimpering upon that person's lap.

Julpen came closer to the throne as all around him became black. The person upon the throne was his mother! She was pale and ugly and had two large horns that came from her headdress. She was caressing Marrisa's head while staring her black eyes at him. A large, wicked smile came over her face as she just chuckled at him. Large flames rose all around the throne as she began to laugh. Her ugly face slowly turned completely black with shadows as her eyes glistened with a terrifying red light.

"They are mine—they are all mine," she said with a low growl.

✝✝✝

"They are all ready, my lord," a voice said from behind him.

King Julpen jumped a little as Sir Hawkington disturbed him from his deep thoughts. The commander noticed that the king appeared very tired and not himself.

"Then we must go with haste, commander," King Julpen said as he quickly stood up.

He noticed that the commander was looking at him strangely, as if he wanted to tell him something but was holding back. King Julpen just ignored him and started towards the camp.

The king never told anyone of his deepest thoughts and dreams—and he was surely not going to tell any of his men, not even Sir Hawkington. He kept everything to himself. To him it was a sign of weakness to become emotional or speak on emotions. Ever since his childhood, he never wanted anyone to pity him. His mother, whom he never wanted to speak or think of, left a lasting impression on him. Whether or not he admitted it, he was becoming cold like his mother.

"Forgive me, but I'm afraid my king needs more rest," Sir Hawkington said as he noticed the drained look upon the king's face. "You have never been unprepared for any kind of surprise. If I were an enemy, I could have caught you off guard..."

The king was silent for a moment as he stopped in his tracks. He knew his commander was right and he was not alert like he usually would've been. His thoughts were heavy and he felt lost. But instead of continuing to think of his dream or any of his heavy burdens, he pushed them in the back of his mind as he always had done.

"That lets me know that my commander is well rested and cunning—which is why you are highly favored," King Julpen said as he patted the commander's shoulder. "I will not rest until the darkness that haunts us is put away. When I see my daughter—then I will rest. Until then we must press on."

Sir Hawkington nodded his head with a grunt, then pulled out his map. "We are nearly to the Great Wall of Division, which is an hour or so from here. We are at the ends of the Forest of Old. As my king is already aware, the great wall has many guards on duty and many forts to rest in for a while. We can take one last break before we make our way into the Forbidden Lands if you like, sire," the commander said as he pointed to the map.

The king responded with just a nod of his head.

They made their way into the camp where the men were finishing packing up and getting ready for another ride. King Julpen made an announcement of their plans to go to the Great Wall and how they were nearer to the Forbidden Lands.

The men seemed somewhat excited as they hopped onto their horses. No one had ever been into the Forbidden Lands and seeing something different was much better than riding for hours through hills and forests that all looked the same. King Julpen pulled himself onto his horse, along-side Sir Hawkington, and rode off towards the wall with his men behind him.

They rode through the rest of the Forest of Old and across some fields as they came closer to the wall. The ride seemed to go on for hours; so, when they saw the Great Wall through another small forest, they became relieved.

They stopped at the edges of the forest, just before the clearing of the wall. King Julpen raised his hand as he peered out over the clearing. Everyone obeyed his command and came to a halt.

"Something is not right," the king said in a low tone to the commander.

"Aye, sire," Sir Hawkington said as he looked over the clearing with his cunning eyes. "I fear there has been some kind of battle."

The clearing was littered with dead bodies and horses and the towers of the wall were charred. Wisps of smoke could be seen coming from the watchtowers where fires must've been ablaze.

"Stay alert men!" King Julpen said out loud to his soldiers, who looked on behind him.

They slowly came into the clearing, looking all around them. They became overwhelmed as their eyes fell upon the poor bodies of the men. Their hearts sunk for their kingdom's loss. Bodies of dead soldiers lay here and there. Some of the dead men had their armor ripped from them, revealing opened chests that exposed their insides. Horses lay dead as well. Swarms of flies hung about the dead bodies and the air smelled of decay.

"What in God's name has happened here?" King Julpen said to himself.

"Sire, look!" Sir Hawkington shouted as he pointed to a large black creature which lay dead upon the earth.

They quickly made their way over to the massive thing to inspect it. It was sprawled out on its back and a plethora of golden arrows stuck out from its bony chest. Its wings stretched out upon the ground and its mouth was twisted open. It was terrifying to gaze upon.

"It's something I've never seen before!" Sir Hawkington grunted. He was amazed but nervous. "This thing is bigger than even a large man."

"There are more of them," a nearby soldier gasped as he pointed towards the wall.

They looked with wide eyes at the other dead creatures who laid lifeless and twisted upon the earth in pools of black fluid.

"What evil doing is this? These things must've attacked the stronghold of the wall. There must've been a battle…but it appears there is no one alive…," the commander said as he glanced all around the premises. He then yanked one of the arrows from the dead creature's chest and held it up. "This arrow is nothing like I've ever seen and was crafted magnificently," he said, inspecting it. "It seems to be made out of pure gold…but it is not bent or broken and appears very strong."

The King took the arrow from the commander to get a better look at it. The arrow was very sharp and looked beautiful with even the black fluid caked on it from the creature. The arrow was indeed made out of some kind of gold, and it seemed to have been constructed as one solid piece. There were even some small jewels embedded into it. "Strange—it is. What kind of craftsman would use such precious metals and jewels for artillery? Not even a king possesses such beautiful weaponry."

"There are more of them," Sir Hawkington said as he motioned his hand towards the other dead creatures.

Many golden arrows stuck out from the grotesque creatures and glistened among their black flesh.

"I fear we are heading into something that is much greater than any kind of manmade warfare," Sir Hawkington said to the king in a low tone. "It is as if these things were released from the deepest pits of hell...they even smell and look as if their flesh had been burning..."

"We must find some answers. There could be more of these creatures. Search the stronghold of the wall for any survivors, anything that could help us!" the king said to the commander but loud enough where everyone heard him. "My God...what is this madness?" he then said to himself as he looked back at the lifeless creatures. "It seems as if darkness has come alive before my eyes..."

The commander shouted orders to the men and directed them in different areas of the wall to search. They all spread out among the area of the wall and then made their way into the towers which led to the top. They searched eagerly and vigilantly for any survivors or clues to what had happened.

The commander followed the king into one of the towers. The tower they went into was smoky and smelled heavy of burnt things. The stone walls and steps were black and the smoke lay thick the further they went up the tower. Every sporadic window they passed by let in fresh air, allowing them to breath better. They quickly made their way up the spiraling stairs and into the lookout which was at the top of the wall. Dead, burned men lay upon the ground of the watchtower as smoke still lingered all around them.

The smells that lay thick around him and the gruesome sight of the scorched men opened a door in King Julpen's mind. He was pulled into his past when his mother, Queen Karnidge, ruled. He began to feel those same feelings of sadness and fear come over him as if he were a child again. Images of when he was a young prince came crashing into his thoughts. The death, burned smells, and char around him reminded him of when his mother had many innocent people burned at the stake. He could still hear the people's screams and the smells of their burning flesh as if it had just happened.

"Sire?" Sir Hawkington said, catching the king's attention. "Are you alright?"

King Julpen shook his head as he hurried out of the watchtower and out onto the top of the wall for fresher air. "Death seems to be everywhere... What has happened?! Where did these great fires come from?! It seems as if every watchtower and everyone within it has been burned. These men suffered greatly," the king said in a loud voice. "Someone must pay for this!" he growled through clenched teeth.

He became angry. Death seemed to be around every corner. There was no one left alive and everything, including their maps, food, and weaponry, was burned in the towers.

They walked upon the top of the wall to only find more dead men and a couple of crumpled creatures. The king shook his head as he brought his hand to his forehead.

Something shiny caught King Julpen's eye. It was a small blade, which was fit for a child. He crouched down to pick up the blade. "Why would a child's blade be upon this wall? There are no children here," he said as he picked up the small sword, inspecting it.

The blade looked familiar to him and reminded him of Marrisa. Then he realized that it was very similar to a blade he had made for Marrisa when she was a child. He looked at it more, finding a small "$\mathcal{N}$", which was etched into the bottom of the blade, above the hilt. Just then more long forgotten memories flooded his mind.

"Natalia was here," he said to Sir Hawkington who was looking over his shoulder. "This was Lady Natalia's…"

He remembered when he had made a blade for Natalia too when she was child, which was identical to Marrisa's except Natalia's hilt was red and Marrisa's was blue. He remembered he had the first letter of their name etched onto their swords.

"Lady Natalia and the prince must've come past the wall… They must be safe because their bodies were not found," the king said as they stood up.

"Look over there, off towards the Black Forest," Sir Hawkington said.

Over miles of forest, they could see wisps of smoke coming up from it.

"It looks like smoke from a fire of some sort…maybe a campfire," King Julpen said, looking into the Forbidden Lands.

"Those wisps of smoke coming up must be large, which is why we can see it from here," Sir Hawkington said. "If it is a campfire, it must be a massive one."

"That is our next destination," King Julpen said, still gazing upon the Black Forest. "I have seen enough of this wall. It has failed us…all of us," he said as he looked back over the other side at the many dead soldiers.

They quickly left the top of the wall and back towards the clearing. Sir Hawkington blew a horn to catch everyone's attention. All of the soldiers met them at the center of the clearing, awaiting orders of what to do next. Both the king and the commander sat in the middle of the crowd on their horses as King Julpen raised his hand into the air.

"I fear no one has been found alive—but we have found something that belongs to Lady Natalia!" King Julpen announced to everyone. "She is alive and she must be found, along with my daughter and Prince Phillip! We will continue to make our way south through the Black Forest! ...As for our lost men," Julpen said in a lower tone that held a hint of remorse, "they will be revenged!" Just then the men began to roar as they lifted their fists and swords into the air. "These men gave up their lives for the Great Wall of Division—for our kingdom! They will be revenged! Evil men who do evil works will be punished!"

The crowd continued to roar as the king lifted his sword into the air. But the cheers of the crowd began to diminish as the sky quickly became darker. A strange mist began to appear all around them as an even thicker mist began to swirl in the air above them. The mists became black in the air and churned all around, forming a black orb in the dark sky.

King Julpen looked into the sky and slowly lowered his sword. Everyone became quiet as all eyes stared at the strange mist that pulsated around the black orb.

"What in God's name is happening?" King Julpen said to himself.

Just then two glistening eyes could be seen in the darkness of the orb, and a form slowly began to become visible around the eyes...

†

CHAPTER 4
The Dark King

The soldiers became nervous and frightened as the large form came out of the black opening in the sky. A silhouette of a being with large horns and mighty wings could be seen through the threatening mists. Just then out of nowhere, the creature appeared on the ground upon everyone. It was at least twelve feet tall and had the fleshy head of a goat, the bare chest and arms of a man, and animal legs with massive hooves. It wore a long black garb that was wrapped around its waist, revealing only one of its legs. Large horns spiraled out from the sides of its head and its mighty wings were matted with black feathers that looked like that of a raven. Its eyes glistened in the black mists that lay thick upon the clearing. It stood tall and menacingly over the men as they trembled with fear.

"…Who is your leader?" the creature finally asked.

The men stood quietly as they glanced at one another, speechless. They were shocked at what they were seeing and thought that their eyes were deceiving them.

"I am!" the king shouted, making his presence known. "I am King Julpen of Minslethrate—king of these lands!" he shouted as he held on tightly to his sword.

The creature was quiet for a moment as it continued to gaze at them.

"We have traveled far in search of my daughter, a young noblewoman, and a prince," King Julpen added. He spoke boldly, but nervousness could be sensed around the edges of his tone.

"…Who do you follow?" the menacing thing asked.

"I follow no one!" King Julpen shouted.

The creature stood silently again, which made the king even more nervous. "You do not follow a king called Yehoshua?" it finally asked.

King Julpen grew quiet for a moment, wondering why the creature was bringing up an ancient king from the old legends of Minslethrate. "Why does it matter to you whom I follow?" he asked.

"A pathetic boy named Tairren spoke of Yehoshua… He was traveling deep in the south in search for your daughter. I sent the biters after him to rip his heart out… You see, if you walk in the dead King Yehoshua's name…you will die. Follow me and I will take you to your daughter…"

"I do not know anyone called Tairren," King Julpen said with a stern voice. "But my daughter is loved by many! There are more people in search for her than what you know of!"

"Follow me, King Julpen," the dark creature said straight away. "You and your army are great and will be favored significantly by my master. Follow me if you wish to see your precious daughter again."

King Julpen looked over at Sir Hawkington who slowly shook his head. Even though the strange creature appeared terrifying, he began to wonder if he should allow him to lead them to Marrisa anyways.

"You can not trust that thing," the commander said in a low tone, where only the king could hear him. "You must resist it... Something giving off an evil presence as that does can not be trusted..."

King Julpen looked back at the tall creature. The monster was indeed frightening but it didn't seem to want to hurt the king or his men. For some strange reason it was only trying to know them. King Julpen wondered why the creature kept pressing for them to follow him.

"That is correct, human," he said towards Sir Hawkington. It must've heard the commander's whispers. "You can not trust...anyone. Not even your own people. Tell me, King Julpen," the great creature then turned his gaze back on Julpen, "didn't one of your own people take your daughter? One of your own has kidnapped your daughter and has put her life in danger... So, who then can you trust? I am all powerful. I can give you things you never thought you could have. I can give you your heart's desires... I can bring you to your daughter if that is your desire," he said in a low tone that was not threatening at all, but strangely inviting. "You can be a hero and a legendary king—if you just follow me..."

King Julpen glanced at the commander and then back at the creature who just watched him with its glistening eyes.

"Who are you and where do you come from?" the king finally asked.

"I am King Baffmit, ruler of the lands in which you are trying to infiltrate. I come from darkness..."

"I will not follow darkness!" the king yelled.

"You unknowingly have followed darkness everyday of your life, King Julpen... Long ago, before you or this world was created—there was darkness...and it dwelled heavy and beautifully like a dark star. You follow darkness when you sleep... You follow darkness when you become angry and depressed, when you allow your emotions to take you down into a deep oblivion... You follow darkness when you yield to sin, which is why you are walking upon this world now… What is life without darkness? When you were created, darkness became part of you all. What is this world without darkness? Why does the night fall and why do the lights go out if darkness was not meant to be? Why is this world filled with so much darkness if no one is to yield to it? You were destined for it the day you were born, King Julpen… You live in it. What has light alone done for you except sting your eyes? What has light done for you? Nothing… It does nothing but burn and scar you, deceive and blind you!"

King Julpen just stared back at the creature. He began to think of his life and the world he grew up in. King Baffmit's words brought him to a thought-realm that he had always pushed to the back of his mind. He thought of his kingdom and its uncertain fate. He began to realize that he lived in darkness every day. When his father died and left him when he was only a child—he was left all alone with pain and suffering.

He thought of his evil mother and the darkness she spread over the land during her reign. He thought of the pain she had inflicted upon him every day. He would never forget her dark, black eyes… He thought of his physical and emotional scars… He thought of the multitude of innocent people she had put to death by fire. Images of people burning and calling out to be saved flashed through his mind. So much pain, he thought.

He closed his eyes tightly as one of the crying voices in his head sounded like his deceased wife. He then thought of the death of his beloved O'nessa. He would never forget her face and the tears that fell when she passed away. She completed him so long ago…but when she died—she left him broken… Her beautiful face fell away from his thoughts, just as she did years ago when Marrisa was very young. He then thought of his beautiful, missing daughter… Moira also began to rip through his head—and how Marrisa screamed out for her as she burned to death on the stake ten years ago. Why is this world filled with so much pain and suffering? Why is this world filled with so much darkness?!

His thoughts were becoming so real upon him that he wanted to just scream out.

King Julpen just looked back up at the menacing creature. His head ached and his heart pounded in his ears. He realized that everything about the creature reminded him of his pain and suffering. The creature reminded him of everything he was trying to get away from, everything that was killing him spiritually and emotionally. And at that moment, he no longer wanted to listen to its provoking words. At that moment he began to loath King Baffmit.

"I will not converse with darkness… Darkness has torn my family and kingdom apart! Darkness has killed my father and has only taught me to know fear and sadness as a child! Darkness has driven my mother to madness where she only knew to kill and destroy! Darkness has taken my wife and now my only flesh and blood, my daughter! I will not stand for it any longer! You are death before me! I will not follow something that relentlessly tries to tear my life apart!" King Julpen shouted angrily as his emotions stirred.

All of the burdens and strife that he had suffered throughout his life seemed to crash upon him like a dark wave. He had never told anyone of his inner darkness, his feelings and burdens. But during that moment, he revealed everything because of the provocative creature that stood before him, and it was more than he had intended.

"Darkness is coming upon you now! Why push something away in which you've always known? Give into it and follow me, King Julpen," Baffmit said in a more forceful tone. "What has light ever done for you? Nothing!"

"You are filled with deceit and I will not yield to it! You asked me of whom I follow, and I shall tell you…I follow the one who harbors light! I would much rather follow the legendary King Yehoshua in darkness than walk upon this world with you and your dark lord! Free Marrisa or your head will become my prize!" the king shouted.

King Baffmit began to become enraged as the darkness around it became even darker, beginning to pulsate. "You fool! You will die then, just as your precious legendary king did long ago! Do not underestimate the powers of darkness! Light is dead—trampled beneath the Dark Lord's feet! I will crush you like the vermin you are and leave your feeble body for darkness to eat! Your bones will break and your skin will burn for darkness' sake! Meet your doom like these dead men's fate!" King Baffmit then gestured his hands out over the clearing towards all of the dead soldiers. "Your daughter will not be spared and your kingdom will fall like the rotting flesh of these men. The powers of darkness shall rise and will not bend."

King Julpen became angry. He let out a shout as he thrust his sword into the dark air. "Destroy this monster!" he shouted. "Bring its tongue to me that I may shut its mouth forever!"

The king, followed by Sir Hawkington and his other soldiers who were on their horses, began to shout as they pulled out their swords. Sir Hawkington blew his horn as he motioned with his sword to attack. The other soldiers quickly pulled themselves onto their horses and began to shoot King Baffmit with their bows and arrows.

King Baffmit let out a loud roar to the sky as he opened his massive wings. He twirled like a powerful whirl-wind as his black wings knocked the cloud of arrows away. He leapt into the sky and flew over them like a monstrous bird. The soldiers did not relent and continued to shoot arrows at the creature. Many of the arrows hit his chest and legs but King Baffmit did not falter.

"Cut my tongue out if you dare to! My fiery wrath will consume and snare you!" King Baffmit then let out another roar as a large cloud of fire erupted from out of his large mouth!

The wicked fire spread out over the clearing in one big explosion. The massive heat-wave knocked them over with a powerful blow. Most of the soldiers blocked the fire with their shields, but some were caught off guard and became ablaze in the burning flames. The soldiers shot more arrows at the creature, this time making him fall to the ground with a crash. Nearby soldiers swiftly swung at Baffmit with their swords, but the creature opened its massive wings again and flew up into the air with a mighty wind. The power of his wings sent them flying across the clearing as if they weighed nothing.

"Father! Send your darkness with haste! Fill them all with your black embrace!" King Baffmit roared out as he hovered above King Julpen and his men. "Come alive you dead, pathetic men—with your rotting flesh and blackened sin!" the creature continued to shout as he stretched his long fingers into the sky.

As King Baffmit spoke, more black mists began to rise from the earth. The mists swirled out over the clearing and flew around the creature in a putrid smelling wind. The strange wind crashed back down to the earth and made a noise like thunder, making everyone fall to the ground. The mists began to growl and moan as they took the forms of creeping shadows! The shadows thrashed around like hungry animals as they eagerly searched for dead flesh. They quickly crawled upon the bodies of the dead soldiers, becoming one with their rotting flesh.

King Julpen and his men watched with fear as the dead soldiers began to stir and rise from the ground like spiritless corpses! They moaned and growled in the frightening air that mingled around the living. The dead bodies of the soldiers picked up nearby weapons and began to attack as they howled and squealed like ferocious animals.

The clearing became a battle ground in a matter of moments as the dead army attacked. The sound of metal clanking filled the air as swords flew and shields clashed.

Nearby dead soldiers attacked the king like quick phantoms. Even though the soldiers were dead, the darkness within them gave them inhuman speed and strength! King Julpen blocked their blows as they growled and moaned. With a quick swing of his sword, King Julpen decapitated one of the corpses. The motion was fast and the sound was gruesome. Its head flung off and tumbled upon the earth. Julpen became shocked as the corpse kept swinging and attacking even without a head! The king quickly realized that the soldiers conjured up by King Baffmit would not falter. They were already dead! Even with no head or arm, they were still fighting and attacking. The corpses were going to fight until they all were dead!

Julpen quickly looked up into the black sky and noticed that King Baffmit was not fighting at all. The monster seemed to be locked in some kind of trance as it hovered in the air above the clearing. Its arms were stretched out and its fingers were spread. King Baffmit seemed to be controlling the dead army somehow!

"Aim for the beast!" King Julpen shouted as he pointed his sword towards the creature. "Take it down!"

Sir Hawkington heard the king's command and shouted the same tactic to nearby soldiers. The ones who weren't fighting the dead soldiers began to shoot more arrows at King Baffmit. But the arrows did not seem to be affecting the creature of darkness!

King Julpen realized that they were becoming out-numbered as more dead soldiers made their way over to the battle. Many of his men were being killed! The king noticed that as his men fell to the ground as lifeless corpses, the black mists that twirled upon the ground took the forms of strange creatures. The shadow creatures began to shroud their bodies and the soldiers began to become part of the army of darkness! The more his men fell the more out-numbered they were becoming!

King Julpen quickly glanced around. He was beginning to think that they were coming to an end as the cries of his men echoed in his ears. It was becoming too much. Darkness was winning again and would surely have him this time. His heart pounded and sweat poured down his brow.

All he could see was darkness and death all around him! There seemed to be no way out of the nightmare.

But as he looked, something quick and silent caught his eye. It was strange and stunning. It stuck out like light in a dark place. It was a massive white flying creature—a fowl of some sort. A large bird came, flying down from the dark sky like a quick blur of strange light. He noticed that it was white as snow and looked like some kind of owl. The massive bird flew towards King Baffmit like a charging wind as it stretched its sharp talons out. It fearlessly attacked King Baffmit, clutching its ugly head with its mighty talons while pounding its wings at the air. The bird's sturdy wings released a powerful blow that sent the creature crashing down to the ground.

King Baffmit smashed into a crowd of dead soldiers, making the ground rumble as it hit with full force. The earth began to tremble, making everyone falter.

Baffmit lost his concentration on the army and became enraged because of it. Strangely, the soldiers began to crumple to the ground as dead corpses again, as they were before. King Baffmit flew into the air with ear-piercing screams and roared out another cloud of fire, but this time towards the great owl. The owl used its powerful wings again and pounded the air with one quick motion, sending the fire back towards King Baffmit. The fire erupted in the dark air. Baffmit let out another scream as the fire came over his body. The creature looked like a fiery bird in the black sky. He thrashed around and pounded his large fiery wings against the foul air, then twisted them around his body. The fire went out and the black sky seemed to vanish. The thick dark mists that sat upon the clearing began to pulsate and swirl around King Baffmit in a mighty rush of air. The black opening in the sky began to diminish as King Baffmit seemed to dissipate into it.

Then it was all over.

King Julpen looked quickly all around the clearing. Everything was the way it was before. The sky was its usual dark-gray and it was quiet all around him. But as he looked, he noticed many of his men had been taken, lying lifelessly upon the clearing along with the other dead soldiers.

Sir Hawkington and the remaining men stood where they were, confused and carefully looking all around them. They began to run to their fallen comrades, checking their pulses to see if there was a lasting chance of life.

The great white owl glided down to the ground and perched on a nearby stone. King Julpen watched it with amazement as he thought of his childhood again. He remembered the owl and how it watched him from the trees when he was sad and alone in the castle gardens. The owl was his only friend during his flawed childhood, and amazingly it had come back again. When he had grown from childhood, he thought the owl was just a figment of his imagination. But now as the great owl perched before him many years later, he now believed. The owl was alive and was a beacon of hope.

"I remember you," he said as he just gazed upon the owl. "Thank you…"

The owl sat silently, speaking to King Julpen's heart. The owl seemed to send words and visions to Julpen with its deep stare. The words and images were quick and were laden with urgency. Julpen saw images of what was going to happen to them if they lingered around the clearing any longer.

"We must go! Quickly!" Julpen shouted as he rode his horse through the stunned crowd of soldiers. "Grab your weapons! Move quickly! We must leave with haste through the Black Forest! It will not be long until the creature called Baffmit sends another army of darkness upon us!"

Sir Hawkington shouted to the other men the same command then quickly rode to the king.

"What is happening, sire?! How do you know such things?!" the commander shouted to the king.

"The owl! It is no ordinary fowl of this world! He spoke to my heart and said that we must leave now if we want our lives spared! The one called Baffmit is plotting our demise! We must follow the owl with haste through the Black Forest! We must ride quickly—not stopping for anything!"

"But, Sire…," Sir Hawkington tried to call out.

"Now!" the king cut the commander off. "Move now if you want your life to be spared! Do not stop!"

Just then King Julpen rode quickly towards the Black Forest. The great owl took off from its perch and flew before the king. Sir Hawkington ordered the men to follow and rode quickly behind the king, feeling uncertain and nervous. The soldiers followed quickly with pounding hearts. They did not know what was going on but they rode quickly and vigilantly like they were commanded to do. The men followed the great owl into the Black Forest and did not look back.

The Black Forest welcomed them with threatening arms, shrouding them with shadows and images of an ill fate. King Julpen followed the great white owl quickly, with his men right behind him. As they went deeper into the forest, the king could hear cries and shouts from behind him, as if his men were falling victim to the Black Forest. He did not know if the cries were truly from his men or if they were from the shadows that grew thick all around the forest. He obeyed the warnings from the magnificent creature and did not stop. He kept his eyes on the keen owl and prayed that they would make it out of the treacherous forest alive…

✝✝✝

After what seemed like many hours of painstakingly dashing through the horrific forest, the owl led them out! The gray air that burst around them as they came out of the thick forest was invigorating.

King Julpen felt relieved as he followed right behind the owl and out into a field. He glanced behind him to see his army of men. They crashed out of the forest like a wave, quickly spreading over the field before them. They looked relieved as well but some had a look of fear over their countenance. As they all came into the field, King Julpen noticed how thin his army of men had become. It seemed as if the Black Forest had taken more of them. The king felt inundated with remorse as he looked before him.

A camp could be seen across the field and King Julpen's heart leapt with gratitude as they rode closer to it. But as they came nearer to the camp, a thick mist began to grow around them. The mist became black and moved quickly as if it were alive and thriving. King Julpen knew what the quick, swirling mists meant and he became nervous by it. He looked at the owl who flew ahead of them; it didn't seem discouraged as it dashed around the black mists, as if waiting for something. Then the owl disappeared behind the mists.

As the king and his men flew across the field with an anxious wind, the insidious black orb quickly came upon them. Shining eyes could be seen in it. It was King Baffmit! He had returned but this time with vengeance. The creature flew out of the black threshold of darkness like a quick shadow. It roared as its eyes gleamed with anger. It dashed down towards the ground and hit the earth right before the surprised men. The ground trembled and cracked as it quaked beneath them. They flew from their horses as the impact from the creature's landing pushed them away. Baffmit spread his massive wings as he slowly stood up before the incredulous men.

"You are foolish men! You thought you could defeat me!? Me, who is the most powerful being on earth, can not be stopped by mere mortals!" Baffmit roared out.

The king and his men just looked up at the relentless creature. King Julpen didn't quite know what to do as he began to search the black sky for the owl. The owl seemed to be nowhere in sight!

"I see you are looking for a savior," Baffmit said as he locked his flashing eyes on king Julpen. "You see—even the things you trust with your whole being, will disappear into the darkness... Now you will die…"

All around the king and his men, many dark forms began to grow from the mists. The black forms began to move about and make noises like beasts. It was as if a nightmare was coming alive before them. Gleaming eyes began to appear in the forms as their growls and shrieks became louder. The men began to crowd together as the beings of darkness surrounded them in the black mists.

"Your dead king has failed you, forgotten and betrayed you!" Baffmit roared out. "Yehoshua's name shall never be spoken again…"

The men began to cry out to King Julpen as all light seemed to be gone away from them. Their lives were coming to an end as the darkness grew thick around them. There seemed to be no way out this time.

But then, just as the black mists and wicked creatures seemed so close to them that their breath was beginning to falter, everything stopped... Everything became still. The black mists froze all around them. Everything was quiet as the men breathed heavily upon the cold air. Then the darkness began to disperse quickly! The glowing eyes of the monsters went out as they squealed as if afraid.

Then King Julpen could see why they were vanishing and squealing like terrified animals. Just as the black cloud of swirling mist dissipated, he could see hundreds of people quickly coming upon them! The people seemed to glow in the darkness and rode like the wind towards them on horses. The king could see other strange things in the dark sky: great white beasts that were being ridden by more of the glowing people.

Just then King Baffmit roared as it flew into the air. The remaining mists followed him as all of the creatures of darkness disappeared into the shadows.

"It is not over, King Julpen!" Baffmit roared as he hovered above them. "Your life has been spared from this squally morning! But your kingdom will pay for your folly by burning! You are weak and a pathetic man—you hold nothing in your feeble hands! A great king you think you are—but your people will be torn and eaten by char! After the moon glows red—your kingdom will be dead!"

Golden arrows began to fill the air as King Baffmit gave one last roar, followed by a wicked, thunderous laugh. He twisted in the dark air and then vanished into the black orb with a wicked laugh. Then shocking silence came over King Julpen and his men again.

King Julpen searched the gray sky again for his owl companion. The mysterious owl was nowhere in sight; it seemed to have disappeared into an oblivion... Wonder came over Julpen as his gaze left the sky and came over the people who now stood before him.

The people of light crowded silently all-around King Julpen and his men, surrounding them like a glowing wall. King Julpen looked at the people with an incredulous stare. He felt thankful that they had showed up at the right time to save their lives, but at the same time he was taken aback by them.

Just then one of the men came to King Julpen on his horse. He gazed at King Julpen with fearless, golden eyes.

"Follow me if you have hope to survive this, King Julpen," the being of light said with an inviting voice.

†

CHAPTER 5
Light in a Dark Place

Moral tightened her shawl beneath her chin as she made her way across the Great Field of Minslethrate. She carried a great bundle of stuff on her back that made her hunch over like an elderly person. The winds were much cooler that day, and stronger, so she made sure she was dressed properly. The sky was darker than it was the day before and looked like it was going to storm. But Moral didn't fear rain because it had been looking like it was going to rain for days—but rain never fell.

She decided that she was going to set up her shop. She had been in her little home in the forest all morning long creating bouquets from the wild flowers and herbs she had picked. Her hands throbbed because of her projects and she was going to stay home that day. But she decided that she wanted to decorate her shop. She was also excited to sell her bouquets of flowers for the Spring Festival that would be happening the following day.

The Spring Festival was her favorite event of the year. The marketplace would be decorated beautifully with thousands of flowers and there would be a grand celebration in the town square. Everyone in the kingdom would attend. From the commoners to the courtiers, everyone would be there. The festival would last all through the day and into the night, then the night would end in beautiful fireworks that would light up the sky.

Even though Moral knew that year's Spring Celebration would be drastically different, she still wanted to do her part. With the king gone and Marrisa missing, the celebration would not be the same. Even though their kingdom was heavy with burdens, she wanted to carry on as if nothing bad was happening.

Moral became relieved as she came upon the gates of the marketplace. Her back was beginning to ache because of the bundle she carried. As she made her way towards the gate, the winds seemed to pick up as something flew past her. Surprised, she nearly fell over. She quickly looked up to see what brought such a wind upon her. It was a large owl—the same large owl that she had seen outside of her window the other night!

Moral was stunned as she watched the wonderful creature soar through the dark air, then perch upon the tall wall of the marketplace entrance. The mighty bird became still upon the wall as it just watched her. Moral kept her eyes on the bird as she slowly walked over the drawbridge. She began to feel overpowered by peace. With the sounds of the water trickling below her in the moat and the winds upon the air and the owl, she felt overwhelmed with joy.

"What is it that you grace my presence again?" Moral asked in a low voice to herself as she began to smile.

Just then words of wisdom came upon her heart. She heard the words clearly as if they were spoken out loud. She knew that they were coming from the beautiful creature—and she knew that the owl was greater than anything living upon the earth. Then after a moment that seemed to last forever, the words that filled her heart became more urgent.

As quick as the wind, the owl spread its wings and flew off from its perch. It glided through the air as Moral watched. The mighty bird disappeared behind the forests that surrounded the field.

Moral stood for a moment and collected her thoughts. She came out of her daze then scurried into the marketplace. She didn't realize that she was already at her shop as the thoughts of the owl shrouded her mind. She rolled up the side walls of her tent-like shop and fastened them. She began to unpack her things as she thought of the words that came from the owl. Her spirit felt uneasy as she continued to work. She began to feel anxious as she hung the banners of flowers all around her small shop. She placed the bouquets all around the tables and rearranged everything she had.

She sat in her chair and fell into a daze again as she watched the other people around the marketplace. People were decorating their shops as well, and displaying bundles of flowers and other things like hats and headdresses that looked like crowns, which were made out of more flowers. Everyone seemed to have the same idea as she did: getting ready for the Spring Festival a day early. But she couldn't get excited as she thought of her second encounter with the mystic bird. She looked up into the dark-gray sky and thought of the owl once more.

"Go to the Kingdom of Hanon… Take up your husband's sword and go to the household of Timotheus…," Moral thought as she stared at the shadowed marketplace.

Those words kept repeating through her mind. The owl told her to go to the Kingdom of Hanon…and to take with her Timotheus' sword…but why? It didn't make any sense to her. Hanon was another small kingdom that sat to the east of Minslethrate. She hadn't been to Hanon in many years and wondered why she was urged to go there at that moment. She had no carriage to get there and wouldn't be able to just walk their safely; her body grew weary and would certainly fail her. But the one question that kept coming to her was about Timotheus' sword. What of her deceased husband's sword? It had been years since she saw the old sword.

Moral looked at the flower decorations that she had displayed all around her little shop. The flowers were beautiful and white and she had always loved them—because they were the same flowers that she planted upon her husband's grave. She didn't know before, but Moral realized just then that the flowers were a sign. To her the white blooms were a reminder of her husband and that's why she chose them to decorate her shop with. Then her thoughts switched to Timotheus' grave. The whereabouts of her husband's sword came into her mind like a sudden wind. She remembered that Tairren had driven her husband's sword into the head of his grave! She had forgotten about it long ago because the white blooms that she had planted upon the grave had grown and multiplied over the years, concealing the grave totally.

As Moral glanced all around the marketplace, the flowers kept catching her attention, reminding her of her late husband, his sword, and the words that came from the strange owl. Trying to ignore the idea of traveling to Hanon, Moral anxiously stood up and began to rearrange everything on her tables again.

"Moral," a voice said from behind her.

Moral jumped as she quickly turned around. "Oh dear, you gave me a fright!" she exclaimed as she placed her hand over her chest. "Hello Sora!"

Sora stood before her appearing tired and distressed. Her gown was dirty at the bottom where her feet were and her apron had smudges all over it.

"Hello," Sora said in a shaken voice, then gave Moral a small smile.

"Is everything well? Are you okay?" Moral asked as she noticed how distraught Sora looked.

Sora just began to cry as she brought her soiled apron to her face.

"Oh my, come and sit," Moral said as she rushed over to Sora.

Moral led her over to her chair, coaxing her to sit and rest.

"What has happened?" Moral asked with a worried tone.

"I—have nowhere—to go," she said between sobs.

"I don't understand. You do not serve for the Ducre' family any longer?!"

"Lady Christianne... She does not want me no longer," Sora said, as she wiped her dewy face again. "After I left your shop yesterday, the lady and I had gotten into an argument... She left me in the field! It took me all the rest of the day to get to the manor. When I got there, she told me that I was no longer welcomed there! She slammed the door on my face as if I were an animal! After many years of serving in the Ducre' household...I am no longer allowed in the manor!" Sora began to sob again as she buried her face into her hands.

"How terrible! Calm yourself, Sora," Moral said in a soft tone as she rubbed her back.

"I began to make my way back to the castle but it got dark out—so I slept in the field... I finally came here. And then I saw you, Moral... I'm so sorry for troubling you with my burdens—but I have no one to turn to!"

"You must be hungry and tired, my poor Sora," Moral said as she rushed over to her satchel. "Here, please take these."

Moral pulled out some fruit and biscuits that she brought for lunch and handed them to Sora.

"You are a saint, Moral...thank you," Sora said as tears rolled down her cheeks. "But I don't know what to do...it seems like my life is over...it might as well be!"

"You still have your life," Moral said in a more serious manner. "Don't ever speak those words of darkness upon yourself. You are a good woman! You must trust in the lord, Sora. Sometimes unexpected things happen—but they must be used to feed your spirit. That is how you grow. You will get through these hard times... You will. You must trust..." Moral's voice began to fade a little as she thought of her own words.

It occurred to her that her own words were also meant for her to hear. She realized that she must trust in God as well. She realized that she must trust in the words that came from the great white owl and the urges she had in her heart. She didn't understand it all, but somehow, she knew in her heart that the great owl and the God of Light were connected.

"Thank you, Moral," Sora said in a much calmer voice. "Your words are like water to the soul."

Moral nodded her head as her eyes went back towards the white flowers that adorned her shop. She then knew that she had to trust the great owl. Even though she didn't understand what was going on, and how it was all going to come together, she had to trust in what she had to do.

"I must go," Moral said to herself as she gazed at the blooms that moved about in the gray breezes.

"Where must you go?" Sora asked, but was startled by a coach that flew into the marketplace.

They both recognized the coach and watched as it stopped in the middle of the marketplace. It was one of the Ducre' coaches! They both watched as the coachman opened the door. They were expecting Lady Christianne to step out of the coach. But instead, it was a young, stout girl. She poked her round face out and shyly looked around.

"What is Alexa doing here?" Sora asked, surprised.

Alexa noticed Sora straight away and went to her quickly. "Oh my, Sora, I am so glad I've found you!" she squealed.

"What are you doing here alone?" Sora asked.

"Sora—something is terribly wrong at the manor—with Lady Christianne," she said with a shaken voice. "She has not slept all night and has been locked in her chamber all morning! Only cries and shouts could be heard through the door. She has not eaten since yesterday morning. I tried to get to the castle to ask for Lord Fernund, but servants are not allowed past the gates. So, I decided to come looking for you—you are the only servant in the household whom she speaks to! I've cried all morning—because I heard you were no longer welcome at the manor...and because Lady Christianne is acting strange again... I fear something terrible is going to happen to the lady again!"

Sora became alarmed. She knew what Alexa meant when she said that Lady Christianne was "acting strange again". No one in the kingdom knew about Lady Christianne's emotional state—and how she tried to take her own life once before when Lord Fernund was gone for months. Not even Natalia knew. Sora knew what her sister was capable of doing and became frightened at the thought of it. Even though Sora was always hurt by her younger sister, she would do anything for her.

"Oh Moral, I must go! But please, come with me," Sora said with wide eyes as she grabbed Moral's hands. "I am so sorry to invite you into my burden-filled world...but you are a very wise and strong woman. You seem to be like light in a dark place."

Moral watched Sora's frantic face. She thought of the owl again and how she was urged to go to Hanon. But then she thought of Sora and how she needed her help. She had compassion in her heart for Sora and wanted to help her in every way. She knew that supporting Sora in her time of need was more important at that moment. She knew in her heart that she would be blessed if she were to help someone in their time of need.

Moral pressed her lips together, then quickly nodded her head. "I will go with you, Sora," Moral said, then smiled.

Sora embraced Moral, then quickly helped her close up the shop.

Before Moral pulled the sides of her tent-like shop down to be closed and fastened, she noticed the white blooms again and picked one with a faint smile. She put the bloom in her hair, then continued to shut everything.

They quickly got into the coach. Then the coachman got his horses going hastily. The coach went through the gates and into the Great Fields of Minslethrate.

The three women sat in silence as the coach hurriedly went through the field.

Sora noticed that Alexa looked very uncomfortable and nervous. She kept glancing from the small window, back to Sora.

"I know that look like the back of my hand," Sora said, breaking the silence.

"What do you mean, Sora?" Alexa nervously asked as she kept rubbing her round hands together.

"This is not the time to hide secrets," Sora raised her voice a little as she gazed at Alexa. "You look more nervous than a convicted criminal. What's wrong?!"

"Well... I didn't want to say it in the marketplace because there were too many people about. But there is something else going on in the manor. There is something strange happening... I saw it the other night... Then I saw it last night in Lady Christianne's window...," Alexa stopped talking as she looked out of the window.

"Well?!" Sora said with wide eyes.

"I don't know exactly. At first, I thought it was my mind deceiving me...but when I saw it move, I knew it was real. But I saw—a moving shadow. It was black as night."

"Moving shadow?" Sora exclaimed with one eyebrow raised. "You've been secretly sipping the wine again, haven't you?!"

"No ma'am—I swear I haven't! On my own mother's grave, I swear!" Alexa squealed as her voice began to shake. "I saw the shadow creeping up the wall during the night! I swear I did! Then I saw it again in the marchioness' window!" Alexa nervously exclaimed as she kept glancing back and forth from Sora to Moral.

Both Sora and Moral sat quietly, not believing what they were hearing.

"Are you sure, dear? It could've been Lady Christianne looking out from her window." Moral spoke up, speaking in a soft tone.

"No ma'am," Alexa quickly shook her head. "It was not the marchioness…because it had glowing eyes."

Both Sora and Moral glanced at each other with a look of disbelief. An awkward silence came over the coach as it flew towards the Ducre' Provence.

✝

CHAPTER 6
Opened Doors

The chamber was dim. The windows were closed. The curtains were never opened that morning.   Only a few candles sat here and there in the dark chamber. The grand chamber was cold and the fireplace wasn't lit. The room held a disturbing presence and the silence around it was frightening.

The faint light from the candles danced on Lady Christianne's face and sparkled off of the tears that came down her cheeks. She sat at her vanity and stared at her reflection for what seemed like hours. She was dressed in her most beautiful gown and looked as if she were ready for a grand ball. Her hair was up beneath an exquisite headdress that was adorned with pearls and precious stones. She had been writing a letter, and when she was finished, she put her favorite pieces of jewelry on. She made up her elegant face and dabbed her favorite scented oils on her neck and chest.

Lady Christianne poured herself another goblet of wine. She had been drinking that whole morning to drown her emotions. She was frightened earlier that morning, but the heavy drinking relaxed her more. She thought she had seen someone in her chamber earlier that morning.   Then she thought it was only a shadow because the chamber was dark. But when she heard faint breathing, she knew it was much more than a shadow. So, all morning long she crept about her dim chamber with a candle. She didn't see anyone... No one was there... So, she decided that she was going mad because of her heavy emotions. So, she drank her wine for breakfast.

She sucked her new goblet down quickly and looked at her reflection once more. She always thought that she was beautiful, but that morning she didn't look her best. She appeared tired and spiritless. She knew it could've been because she hadn't slept that whole night before. So instead of rest, she thought that she could cover her tired appearance and feelings with her favorite materialistic things. She pretended that she was getting ready for another grand ball—where she could make other people feel envious of her.

But as she looked into her mirror, her eyes blurred a little...and she began to feel worthless again. Every now and then she felt that way. Depression usually came over her when she felt all alone. It got worse sometimes when her husband left her to go on his month-long business trips. She began to feel alone again ever since Lord Fernund took his temporary place at the castle and since Natalia had run away. And now that she had let Sora go, her own sister, and slammed the door on her face, she felt terrible.

But on any other normal day, she didn't understand why she felt so worthless sometimes. Being the Marchioness of Minslethrate, one would've thought that she had everything—which she did…but she had everything but true happiness. She did not have light in her heart, and was blinded by her possessions. She cared too much for her precious things to ever let them go.

She thought of what Sora had told her the day they got into an argument. Sora was right. She only seemed to care about wealth and power and social status. She thought of her past and the island she came from. She never wanted to live like that again: living in huts among the dirt and outdoors. She only wanted to be better than where she came from. But over time, she didn't realize how much she allowed wealth and social status to change her heart.

She was beginning to become ashamed of herself as she thought of everything…

She thought of her husband who was not there by her side. She thought of her daughter who was missing and how over time she had pushed her daughter away. She barely knew Natalia, and now that she was gone, she wished she could've spent more time with her only child. She thought of her sister, and how she always pushed her away too. She thought of all the terrible situations she had put her older sister through and how she never wanted anyone to know that they were truly related. She felt ashamed of herself as she thought of her sister—of everything. She took Sora for granted, and now that she was gone, she regretted it.

So instead of trying to make things better in her life, she piled on her jewelry and heavily scented oils, her face powders and her decadent gowns. She covered her body from head to toe to hide her true self. She was no longer Zorrina, but the Marchioness of Minslethrate.

Lady Christianne poured herself another goblet of wine and began to sip it this time. She was already drunken by the wine and continued to add to it. Her head whirled but she didn't care. Instead, she sloppily patted her face with more powder, then attempted to put another necklace on around her neck that already hung with diamonds and jewels.

Just then she heard something that made her skin crawl. The Marchioness turned her head quickly, dropping the necklace on the vanity.

She thought she had heard the sounds of breathing again. Her heart began to race as her head pounded.

"Hello… Who's there?" she said. Her words came together and sounded almost unrecognizable. "Sora?"

She sat for a moment, just staring into the dark shadows of her massive room. She brought her hand up to her whirling head. She realized that Sora was gone, so she turned back towards her mirror. She drank down the rest of her wine, then attempted to put the necklace on again. But as she looked back into her mirror, she noticed a black form standing right behind her! She gasped as she quickly turned with a pounding heart. The room began to spin as she tried to focus her eyes. No one was there…

"I do not wish to play these games," she said in a shaken voice.

Only silence answered...

She became afraid as she looked all around her room. No one was in her dark chamber. She sat for a while longer, allowing herself to calm down. The room was dreadfully silent and she could only hear her heart that seemed to boom with fear. She slowly turned her head as she cautiously looked back into her mirror. She only saw her reflection this time, staring blankly back at her. She began to chuckle a little at herself. She thought she was going mad.

"This madness shall kill me," Lady Christianne slurred as she attempted to pour herself another goblet of wine.

She didn't realize that her glass was already half full and began to overflow as she poured more wine into it. The wine spilled everywhere.

"Zorrina…," came a low voice from the darkness.

Startled, Lady Christianne dropped the decanter of wine on her vanity, spilling the rest of the wine out all over. She stood up quickly, nearly falling over as the room began to spin.

"Who's there?! Reveal—reveal yourself!" she shouted at some effort as she pushed her chair over. The sound of the chair hitting the floor seemed loud in the silent chamber.

There was no answer and the silence began to taunt her. The wet sound of the wine dripping and tapping upon the cold ground echoed in her ears. She moved away from her vanity towards her window, grabbing onto things as she went.

"You wish to steal from me?! You will be punished!" she shouted as she came to her window, nearly falling towards it. "Sora! Sora where are you?! Don't ignore me!"

She caught herself on the window ledge and quickly yanked open the curtains. "Show yourself!" she screamed out as she quickly turned around.

Her eyes widened as fear came over her like a heavy shroud. She began to scream with terror, breaking the heavy silence. Right before her was a dark form! It was black and loomed over her with its wicked presence. Its eyes flashed as it peered into her helpless soul. It let out a loud shriek that seemed to echo throughout the chamber.

Terrified, the marchioness flung herself back, swinging her arms at the dark form that threatened her. She crashed through the glass of the window and tumbled over the ledge! Her helpless body flung out among the empty air. Many shards of glass flew into the gray winds that swirled all around. She hopelessly flung down towards the stone ground as her jewelry twinkled like stars. Her mind went blank as she hit the ground with a disturbing crunch sound that erupted upon the hard stone.

Then there was a loud silence…

Her beautiful body lay lifelessly upon the cobble-stone ground as blood bloomed from beneath her head like a rose…

†

CHAPTER 7
Not Alone

Sora, Moral, and Alexa hurried out of the coach. They could see that something was wrong the moment they pulled up upon the Ducre' Manor. No one was outside working and there weren't any attendants outside of the door to greet them either. It was quiet and all around them seemed dead. All of the windows were dark and the entryway was even darker…

"Where is everyone?" asked Sora as they walked up the stairs to the large doors.

"I don't know," Alexa said as she hurried behind Sora.

The three women looked around as they made their way past shadowed columns and upon the massive threshold.

Sora pushed opened the door and went in first. The grand foyer was dark and the large candelabrum that hung in the center of the hall wasn't lit.

"So, this is how the manor is kept when I am gone from it?! This place looks like a nightmare! And where is everyone?!" Sora fussed as they looked around.

They peered into the nearby drawing-room and dining hall. Every hall they went into was dark and silent.

"Hellooo!" Sora yelled out, startling Moral and Alexa. Her loud voice echoed throughout the opened spaces of the manor.

"When I left early this morning the servants were up and about," Alexa said, nervously. "Maybe they are all out in the gardens."

"Child, go and check the kitchen and pantry," Sora said, eagerly. "There are always servants in those rooms. I will go up into the east wing— where Lady Christianne must be."

"Please let me come with you! I'm frightened!" Alexa whined as she came closer to Sora, who looked annoyed.

"I will go with you, Alexa," Moral said with a comforting smile.

"The manor is huge and old—you can get lost in the deeper halls," Sora said with wide eyes. "Stay close and I will meet you back here soon."

"Do be quick," Alexa said with a worried look on her face.

Sora quickly left them, going up the grand staircase towards the east wing. She glanced down at Moral and Alexa who quietly crept away towards the kitchen. Sora looked cautiously around as she went, remembering what Alexa had told her. She began to wish she had a lamp with her. She became nervous as the massive chambers and corridors created many shadows. There was no one anywhere around and only a couple of candles were lit here and there, which was very strange. On a normal day, especially a very dark and gloomy day, every candle and candelabrum would be lit and there would be a servant or two in every hall.

Something quick caught Sora's eyes as she turned the corner towards Lady Christianne's quarters. "H-hello...," she said nervously. She thought it might've been a servant, but no one was there...

She stopped with wide eyes as she placed her hand over her booming heart. "My Lord, protect me," she whispered to herself, feeling as if a panic attack was coming over her.

After a moment of staying still in the dim hallway, she decided that the quick movement she saw was just her eyes fooling her. She quickly went to Lady Christianne's door and knocked. There was no answer so she knocked again, louder.

"It's your sister, Sora!" she yelled, becoming nervous.

She realized that she still had all of the keys hanging beneath her apron, so she picked out the marchioness' chamber key and used it. She slowly opened the door and peered inside the chamber. The door creaked open, disturbing the silent air. The room was dark, having only a couple of candles lit. She looked all around as she came into the room. The bed wasn't made and the fireplace wasn't lit. There were different gowns thrown about the chamber as if Lady Christianne was trying them on one after another, then just carelessly threw them anywhere. Sora nearly tripped as she walked over a random shoe. She was blown away by the mess and carelessness.

"Zorrina...," Sora said in a low voice. "It's me—Sora."

The vanity stand caught her eye. She noticed that wine was spilt all over it and that the vanity chair was knocked over. She hurried over to it to inspect it. Oddly, it was unorganized and messy with jewelry and powders lying about it. Brushes and combs also lay about, sitting in spilt oils. There were tipped-over oil bottles, goblets, and a wine decanter. Spilled wine covered most of the vanity, which had splashed up and dried on the mirror in streaks. The heavy scents of tart wine and sweet oils filled her nostrils as she quickly glanced around.

"Dear God, what has come of my sister?" Sora said in a low tone.

She noticed a letter sitting off to the side of the vanity. It was signed to "Somebody" and it consisted of one disturbing line that was written very sloppily.

It read:

Dear Somebody,

I Am very alone.

Sora put her hand over her mouth as her eyes moistened with tears. She could tell that it was her sister's handwriting, but she could also tell by the penmanship that she had been heavily drinking when she wrote it. She knew that she had a drinking problem that got out of hand from time to time, but she didn't know that her sister truly had felt that way about herself—alone. Her heart broke for her younger sister, feeling horrible for the argument they had the day prior.

"Zorrina!" Sora shouted as she became frightened for her sister's sake. "Zorrina, where are you?!"

She looked around her sister's depressing chamber, feeling lost and panicky all of a sudden. The curtains that hung around her window rippled about as the gray wind from the day came in. She noticed that glass littered the floor near the window. She then realized that the opened window was not opened at all, but broken. Her heart skipped a beat as she ran over to the large window. She looked out as her heart seemed to leave her with the passing winds. She noticed that someone lay still upon a pool of blood. A scream left her mouth as she realized that the person upon the blood was her sister.

"My God! Zorrina!" Sora screamed out as she began to cry. My poor sister! Zorrina, what have you done?!"

She ran to the center of the room and fell upon her knees as her head whirled. She screamed and cried upon the rug, burying her face into it. Her heart pounded in her chest and she felt as if she were about to faint. She became sick and vomited. She wiped her face with her apron as more tears flowed.

"God! Why?! My little sister!" she bellowed out as she sat up on her knees. "I should've stayed! Oh, why didn't I refuse to leave?!"

After a moment, Sora looked up as she felt something strange in the air. She felt a presence she had not felt before, coming upon her like a cold breeze. She calmed down a little as she noticed something moving about the shadows of the room. Startled, she slowly stood up as she kept her eyes on the dark, moving entity. It looked like the shadows were moving and creeping all around. Her eyes widened as she thought of what Alexa had told her.

"What in God's name is happening here?" Sora said in a low tone as she slowly moved towards the doorway.

Just then the black form that looked like some kind of creature crawled out of the shadows! It crawled up the wall, towards the high ceiling! Two bright eyes flashed from the creature as it began to shriek!

Sora let out a scream as she ran towards the doorway. She flew through the door and down the hallway. She didn't even turn to look to see if the creature was chasing her. She began to hear cries coming from the main hall. It sounded like Moral and Alexa were screaming out her name! The cries echoed through the corridors and the dark shadows of the massive halls. Sora made her way out into the main hall where she found Moral holding onto Alexa who was distraught and trembling.

"Run! Get out of here!" Sora screamed as she ran down the main staircase.

Moral and Alexa ran across the hall and through the foyer with Sora right behind them. They flew through the massive doorway. Sora slammed the main door shut, then ran towards the coach where Moral and Alexa were waiting.

"Where's the coachman?!" Sora screamed out frantically as she noticed that he was gone. Where is he?!"

"I-don't-know!" Alexa screamed out between sobs. She took deep breaths as she panicked. "But—they all are—dead! Every one of them! All dead—with their chests torn open! Everyone that I've ever known is all dead! Something terrible is happening! We're all going to die!"

"Take hold of yourself!" Moral yelled as she grabbed Alexa's round face. "We will be safe! In God I stand and I'm declaring—we will be safe!" she said as she looked into her frightened eyes. "Get in the carriage!" She then directed her gaze on Sora who seemed to be in shock. "Sora can you manage the coach? We must get away from here! We must get to my cottage—then to Hanon—hurry!"

"I can… Get in, and quickly!" Sora said as she came to her senses. She then pulled herself onto the riding bench.

Moral got into the coach then quickly closed the door. She looked out towards the manor, shocked and bewildered. Her skin tingled as she thought of the many dead servants they came upon in the manor. Her eyes began to tear up as compassion came over her for them. She had never seen so many dead people before… She began to pet Alexa, who cried in her lap.

Sora anxiously got the horses going and left the mansion. She didn't look back until they were miles away from the manor. She turned her head to glance at the Ducre' Manor on its dark horizon. She began to cry as she thought of her sister. Tears flowed like water as she hurried out of the Ducre' Provence and towards the Great Field of Minslethrate.

†††

Every moment seemed to fly by like an urgent wind. It was like they were caught in a nightmare. They felt out of control, as if their very world was crashing and breaking and ending. They didn't know what was going on—but whatever was happening, they knew it was real.

They arrived at the edge of the Forest Provence. Sora stopped the coach as Moral hopped out.

"I will be back," she said as she looked up at Sora.

"You don't want us to come?" Sora asked, appearing nervous.

"I will be okay," Moral said, "just wait for me here, please, I must get to Hanon."

Sora quickly shook her head, "I will—please be careful, Moral."

Moral nodded at her, then quickly walked into the forest.

The forest was not the same as it usually was. It was dark just like the rest of Minslethrate, and carried an eerie presence. Moral moved with a fast pace, running halfway and then walking very quickly the next. She ignored the chilling look of the forest and kept her eyes on the uncertain quest before her. She had to get her husband's sword and she had to get to Hanon. She didn't know why she had to go, but her heart kept telling her that she must go.

She quickly passed her cottage. She knew that it wasn't long before she would come upon her husband's grave by the creek.

411

She thought of her son. She now knew why Tairren felt so strongly about going to the Forbidden Lands. She felt the same way, about going to Hanon, and she couldn't dare ignore it.

She could see the small mound that sat near the creek. It was covered in the white blooms and would've just looked like a large patch of flowers to anyone else. She quickly came upon her husband's grave. She looked down at the grave and thought of her husband. She slowly went to her knees, becoming surrounded by the white blooms.

"Hello, Timotheus," she said with a small smile.

She sat quietly as she thought of her husband. She wished that he was by her side, helping her through these dark days.

"I miss you so much…," she said as tears came upon her grey eyes. "I am so frightened… But I stay strong as I walk through these darkened days. I know that God is with me day after day. You have taught me that, Timotheus," she said as tears went down her cheeks. "And I have never told you—that I am so thankful that you have planted those seeds of light upon my life. I am strong because of you… Because of you…I know a God that strengthens me daily—even during the darkest of times. Thank you, Timotheus…and I know that I will see you one day… I love you…"

Moral picked the white bloom that was still tucked beneath her shawl, kissed it, then put it amongst the other flowers that surrounded her. She sat for a moment longer, then began to pray. Moments went by, and she finally felt at peace. She didn't feel overwhelmed or frightened any longer as she thought of what she must do.

"I must go, Timotheus," she said.

She quickly went to where the head of the grave would've been and began to dig through the flowers. She felt something hard sticking out from the ground. She knew it was the hilt of Timotheus' sword. It was still there, just where Tairren had left it many years ago. She grabbed the hilt and tugged at it a couple of times. It finally, slowly, started to come out. She gave it a couple more tugs, then it came out of the earth completely. She had forgotten how long the sword was as she held the muddy blade up. She became excited as she rushed to the creek to wash it off. After a moment of rubbing, it was clean and looked just as she had remembered it. She held it out and looked at it with a smile. It gleamed even in the pale light. She could feel her husband through the sword's hilt, and just then she never wanted to leave the sword alone again.

Moral ran through the shadowed forest to the little cottage. Inside, she packed a satchel of food to share and some other things she thought she would need. She looked upon her small abode one last time, and then she left.

Moral finally made it back to the edge of the forest where the coach was. She was relieved to see it. She quickly came upon the carriage, then put the sword and her satchel in it. She looked up at Sora who looked like she had been crying. Her eyelids were swollen and her eyes were red.

"Are you okay, Sora?" Moral asked as she walked to her.

"I'm fine, Moral…," she said as she looked off into the field. "Let's go quickly."

Alexa poked her round face out of the carriage. Her cheeks were red and glossy with tears. "Where should we go?" she said, anxiously.

"I must go to Hanon. The Kingdom of Hanon is a couple of hours east from here. If we leave now, we will make it before the sun goes down. We can take the Weeping Road along the Minslethratian River. It will take us past the town of Prat and into the moors. The road is small but it is the quickest way to Hanon. I know the way—my husband was from Hanon and I once lived in Prat in my younger days… Someone must go to see Lord Fernund…to tell him of the tragedy at Ducre' Manor," Moral said as she glanced at Sora.

Sora seemed to be in a daze. Silent tears came down her cheeks as she stared off into nowhere.

"Sora…," Moral said as she came close to her.

Sora glanced at Moral, then nodded her head. "Yes, we should go then… Alexa, you will go to Lord Fernund. He knows your face. Beg, plea, do whatever you need to—to speak to the Marquis! Moral is right—he must know…"

Alexa just nodded her head as she sat back into the carriage. Moral quickly got in, then they were off towards the castle.

Sora had the horses going as quickly as she could. She looked on with anxious eyes as her heart grew heavy with burdens.

†

CHAPTER 8
Wanderlust

Tairren and Rafiul had been riding through the Forbidden Lands for hours until they came upon the rocky terrain of Fiara Mountains. The mountains sat ruggedly upon dark skies, just before the Great Mountains of the south. It was around the middle of the day when they came upon the mountain range. The air around them was cool and strange. They grew tired and realized that they still had some time before them so they decided to take a small break by a creek.

"How long until the Fire Temple?" Tairren asked as he splashed some cold water on his face from the creek.

"We are close, Master Tairren," Rafiul said. "The temple should be somewhere to the east of here," he said, pointing.

Tairren looked off in the direction where Rafiul pointed. The Fire Temple was among jagged hills and cliffs and a black sky that swirled with haunting clouds. He placed his hand over Marrisa's heart-shaped necklace he found earlier that day. He wanted to get to Fiara quickly but at the same time he yearned to get to Marrisa.

He turned his eyes to where Marrisa was taken. It seemed as if he was almost there. He could see from where he was that the Dark Tower of Sacrifice sat at the bottom of treacherous mountains. The sky above the mountains was black, looking as if night loomed over it. A massive sloping field sat before the mountains; it looked like it went on for miles.

"We are so close," Tairren said has he gazed off towards the direction of the deep, deep South. "I could get to the Dark Tower of Sacrifice before dusk if I left now…"

"I'm sure of it, Master Tairren," Rafiul said as he glanced at Tairren, "but beyond that field, upon the dark fortress, there are things in which only light can break. You must be patient, Master Tairren. In time, everything will happen the way it should. Right now, your quest is at hand. The legendary sword of Yehoshua is waiting for you. You must rescue it from the wicked hands of Fiara. The golden blade was anointed and blessed long ago by the mighty words of King Yehoshua. Darkness must be pierced by this blade of truth—then will you truly see light break through the darkness."

Tairren grew silent as he thought of how far he came and how much he had changed. He thought of how far away he was from home. He felt as if he were on the other side of the world. He never would've thought that a peasant boy like himself was destined for something that was as great as this mission. It was hard for him to fathom it. He was surprised at his quest and that he was actually walking in his father's footsteps, by traveling the deep lands of Minslethrate. He would have never dreamt that he was meant for such an adventure. He knew that God's plan for him was great and couldn't be stopped. It seemed to him that just a couple of days ago he was lounging around in his small shop in peace, and now he was doing something that was greater than anything anyone could've dreamt of.

As he looked ahead to the Black Field of Old Blood and the Dark Tower of Sacrifice, he knew that something even greater would be happening soon. He began to think of Marrisa—his beloved Marrisa who's eyes shown like the sky during the clear days of winter. His mind kept drifting back to the times when his young life with Marrisa was innocent and carefree. He knew that he had changed—and he wondered if she had changed as well. He wondered if her eyes still sparkled with a loving blue light, and if her heart was still the same. He worried about her greatly and wanted her in his arms where he knew she would be safe.

"We must go," Rafiul said, waking Tairren from his daydream. "The night will catch us off guard in our travels if we linger too long."

Tairren pulled himself up onto Lilly as Rafiul hopped onto Cherbim's mighty back. They made their way over the rough terrain, towards the Fiara Mountains. The land became drier as they moved ahead and the greenery was scarce. The trees that stood around the mountain were all dead and gray and looked like stone. There was nothing about the Forbidden Lands that seemed blessed. Everything was cursed and nothing flourished. Even as they came upon the dead mountains of the Fire Temple, they could tell that no one had walked among it in many years. All of the south seemed untouched by life.

They came upon a terrain so rocky that it was even troubling for a horse to get through. The dry dirt rose beneath their feet in a powdery bloom. The air around them had no moisture in it at all. Their minds became uncomfortable as they looked up towards the uninviting mountain.

Tairren wondered how they were going to ascend it. There were deep cracks in the earth and the boulders and cliffs of the mountain were massive and high.

"So, this is the Fiara Mountains?" Tairren asked. He noticed an entrance in the stone which led to a broken path. "This mountain seems anything but sacred."

"Long ago, these parts flourished with green herbs and healthy animals. Today it is nothing but cursed—it is a desolate land of darkness and death." Rafiul said, as he hopped off of his tall beast. "When Minslethrate was young, after the fall of the first children of light, men came here to worship Fiara. She deceived men into thinking that she was the creator of fire. She blinded them with her sorcery and dark magic..."

"Magic and sorcery? How does a woman claim to create fire and then blind men with magic?" Tairren asked. "Men are not that easily deceived."

"The mind will believe what it sees. Magic is a power that should not be obtained by man—because it opens the doors to darkness. Long before Minslethrate came to be, there was a great war in the Kingdom of Nevaeh. Lucif, who turned against the Great King of Light, had many followers and brought them down with him. When Lucif and his followers were defeated and casted away unto the darkness, they loathed the king. So, they infiltrated this earth and Minslethrate, which was the first Settlement of Light. The eyes of the followers of Lucif fell upon the women of this world, and they came to know them.

"So, you see Tairren, Fiara is a descendent of darkness. When the followers of Lucif came upon the women of their liking, they taught them many things which were forbidden for humans to know. That is why magic is only obtained by some. Possessions like magic, and perceiving things that are beyond human senses, are powers that shouldn't be attained. Magic is a dark ability that comes from the mysterious realms unknown by man."

"Fiara is a descendent of the fallen legna?" Tairren asked, intrigued by Rafiul's knowledge.

"Yes Tairren, dark magic powers run heavily in her blood. She is not one to commune with. There are many forms of darkness in this world— and she is one of them."

Tairren began to become nervous as he thought of Fiara and her ways, which he wasn't familiar with. "How must I retrieve the legendary sword if it's guarded by an enchantress who is filled with dark powers? She could cast something dark upon me."

"Tairren—where does your help come from?" Rafiul questioned him.

"...From the God of Light," Tairren answered.

Rafiul smiled as he nodded his head. "You yourself have said that light is soaked heavily upon your heart. Darkness can not touch something that is guarded by light. It is up to you to allow such darkness to come over you… That is why Fiara does not use the sword for her ways—it is useless to her and she only keeps it as a remembrance of the fall of King Yehoshua. The sword is soaked with light and she can not touch it—it is the sword of truth… Little does she know that King Yehoshua is alive…"

Tairren grew quiet as his heart pounded with anxiousness. He was ready to face Fiara but he was incredibly nervous at the same time. He took in everything Rafiul had revealed to him as he looked up into the treacherous mountain before him.

"You must go now, Master Tairren," Rafiul said as he cast his golden stare upon him.

Tairren realized just then that he had to go alone. His eyebrows raised as his heart fluttered in his chest. "You are not coming?" he said. "What is the worth of having a guardian if I am not guarded?!"

Rafiul smiled a little at his mannerism. He placed his hand on Tairren's shoulder with a smirk. "Tairren you have something wondrous and far greater than I—right inside of you… Again—where does your help come from? Remember your answer, always. If Fiara saw me she would know right away that I am a follower of King Yehoshua. She would try to have us both killed straight away. Do not mention to her who you follow until the time is right. Any little slip up will reveal your true identity. I will stay here and wait for you. Lilly will not make it up the mountain side so I will keep her safe with Cherbim by my side."

Tairren just pressed his lips together while nodding his head. "I understand," he said.

He made sure that his sword was snug in its scabbard and his trusty dagger was by his side. He took his water pouch with him, strapping it to his belt. He left his bow and arrows and satchel so that he could move more easily up the mountain.

"The Fire Temple should be a little way through this path. Be careful and swift and remember that the moon shall rise quicker than you know. It will be as a red light tonight—just as it has been prophesied, Tairren… If you do not return by then, I will come up to get you with haste." Rafiul said reassuringly as he noticed the troubled look on Tairren's face.

Tairren left quickly towards the entrance of the path in the mountain. He looked back one more time towards Rafiul, then disappeared into the craggy entry way.

The path was rough and was surrounded by tall stone walls and jagged rocks. The pathway went up the side of the mountain, twisting around boulders, going around the steep sides of threatening cliffs, and over deep dark trenches. Everything was scorched and nothing new grew on the mountain. Tairren could tell that it was cursed. The dark clouds above him were invigorating; on a normal day Tairren could tell that the sun would've been brutal upon Fiara Mountain.

He stopped for a moment to take a breath. He went to take a drink from is water pouch, but it slipped out of his hand and fell down a deep trench. He became irritated at himself as he glanced around him. He looked down to see if he could see Rafiul. He couldn't see anything below because of the rugged view of the mountain side. He looked before him to see if there was any sign of the Fire Temple. He didn't see anything but boulders and cliffs.

He went a little further, then looked up. His heart jumped as he noticed something. Some ways up the mountain side, he could see that a cloud of smoke billowed out of it. The smoke spread out among the dark sky and mingled with it. He knew then that he was close.

Becoming anxious, Tairren went quickly up the rocky path. He made his way around a cliff then stopped before a wide opening. Tairren was intrigued by what he saw. The area before him opened out to a large staircase that was cut into the stone of the mountain. The steps seemed to go up for miles. He could see that the steep steps went up to a large dark opening in the mountain.

Tairren cautiously made his way up the stairs. He looked around at the architecture which must've been beautiful long ago. The steps were chipped and cracked and great columns lined them. Most of the columns were broken and cracked as well as the arches that went over them. Tairren climbed over the broken columns and under the fallen arches as he made his way up the steep path.

Something caught his eye. He was halfway up the steps when he noticed something moving quickly on a large boulder. It looked like someone dressed in dark garbs. He wasn't sure if it was a shadow or person, but he knew it was something alive. Someone or something had been watching him... He stopped climbing and stared, listening attentively. He heard small rocks falling and bouncing along the stone, indicating that someone was hurrying away. He moved quickly up the rest of the steps with a pounding heart.

Tairren stopped abruptly at the top of the rocky steps as his breath was taken away. He was amazed at the grand site. The open space before him was large and intimidating. The facade of the Fire Temple was carved into the side of the mountain and was adorned with mighty decorative columns. Right in the center of the open space, just before the large entrance of the temple, was a massive statue.

Tairren looked at it with amazement and wonder. The Statue was shocking and provocative. It seemed to be made out of marble and gold. It was a woman sitting on top of a mighty beast. The woman was naked and covered in jewels. She held out a great goblet, as if she were toasting to the opened sky. She wore a golden crown that looked like it would've gleamed brightly in the sunlight. Tairren knew that the idol was of Fiara.

The statue of Fiara sat in an inappropriate position on the beast with her legs out on each side. The ugly beast had many heads with snarling faces and was crouched down as if it were ready to attack. Great stone wings came out on either side of the beast, which were also covered in gold and jewels. A pit of fire roared beneath the beast as large flames came up in tattered peaks.

Tairren looked up as he slowly made his way across the open area of the temple. He noticed the large cloud of smoke that he had seen earlier. He could see that it came from further up the mountain and must've been from a massive fire. He nervously walked up the stone steps towards the entrance of the temple. The threshold of the temple consisted of more statues and beautiful columns. Over the threshold there was a large symbol that was carved into the stone. It was the symbol of Fiara.

Tairren was nervous but his spirit told him to be calm. All around him was quiet except for the sound of the great fire that burned beneath the statue behind him. He stopped before the grand temple entrance with a pounding heart. He peered in, looking all around the large space. It was dark in the inside except for randomly lit torches. He slowly walked into the temple, gripping his sword. The inside was cool and smelled sweet and smoky, as if incense were burning.

He walked a couple more steps into the dark temple. He didn't get too far when someone came quickly behind him like a dark shadow! Someone yanked Tairren's arm from behind him and put a cold blade to his neck!

"What do you want?" A muffled female voice said in his ear.

"I only come to see Fiara," Tairren said quickly.

He stayed still, not wanting to cause any strife. He thought of what Rafiul had said and didn't want to ruin his chances of getting the legendary sword.

"You grasp your sword as if you want to kill," the voice said quickly as pressure was put on his throat by the blade.

"I only come to see Fiara. The path before me is dark and I don't know what to expect." Tairren said quickly, trying to convince the threatening person behind him that he was of no harm.

After a quiet moment, the pressure of the blade against his neck was gone and the person swiftly stepped away from him. Tairren slowly turned to see who it was. It was a woman. She was tall and wore dark robes. Black linen was wrapped around her face and hands. All he could see were her eyes.

She silently gazed at Tairren, looking him up and down.

"I have not seen a man in many years…," she said as she came closer to him. "It seems as if it has been ages since anyone has come to see Fiara." She put her long blade back in its hilt. "Do you come to worship—or do you come for a potion or a hex? What is it that you want?"

"My business is my own," Tairren said.

She grew quiet as she just stared at him. "Follow me then," she finally said, then left swiftly into the temple.

Tairren followed her quickly down the massive entrance hall. He couldn't see much because of the minimal light that came from a few torches. Their footsteps echoed in the empty spaces around them as they went. They went through a corridor which was much brighter than the main hall. They walked in silence as they went through the long hallway, passing by many smaller chambers. The corridor was lined with many torches and the long walls were covered in ancient murals.

"Who are you?" Tairren asked, breaking the silence.

"…I am one of Fiara's loyal servants," she said.

"I saw you—you were watching me from the cliffs."

"I am the eyes of this mountain," she said quickly. "I have not seen anyone creep up this mountain in many years…"

They became quiet again as they made their way across the hallway. They came upon two large decorative doors. Each one had the image of a fair woman standing amongst a roaring fire.

"Behind these doors is Fiara's dwelling spot. The goddess Fiara is all powerful and will grant you things that you will never be able to accomplish on your own... Now give me your sword if you wish to proceed," she said. "Then you may go on with your business..."

Tairren looked at her for a moment. Her eyes strangely looked like translucent fire. He reluctantly obeyed her and pulled the golden sword form its sheath. He slowly handed her his sword, wondering if it was the wrong thing to do. As she took the golden blade, he swiftly covered his dagger with his cape.

"Now you may proceed," she said as she pushed open the large doors.

Tairren could feel a rush of warm air hit his face as soon as she opened them. He vigilantly walked into the large chamber, looking all around. The chamber was in the shape of a large circle and there was a mighty fire that roared in the center of the massive hall. The huge fire gave light and warmth to the hall. The ceiling was high and there was a large opening in the roof which allowed the smoke from the fire to escape. Tairren realized that this was the smoke he had seen on his way up the mountain. There were many tall columns around the hall, reaching up to the high ceiling. The columns casted dancing shadows everywhere as the fire burned brightly upon them. The floor was embellished by beautifully painted tiles that looked glossy in the firelight. On the walls that circled the hall were brightly painted frescos which had images of Fiara invoking dark powers, with people worshiping her.

The woman led Tairren past many columns to an area of the chamber which was closest to the great fire. It looked like some kind of resting area that consisted of beautiful pillows and furs. There was a large lounging chair that was draped with silk. A small golden table sat in the center of it all, holding different glass bottles and golden goblets.

"Come and sit," the woman said as she motioned her hand towards the beautiful lounge chair.

Tairren slowly sat down as he watched the dark, shrouded woman. She poured a goblet of water that sat on the small table. He thought of how he had lost his water vessel earlier along the cliffs. He watched as the clear liquid trickled into the sparkling goblet. He grew thirsty just by watching the clear liquid glisten in the fire light as she poured it.

She held the goblet out, offering it to him. "You must be parched after a long journey up the mountain," she said, then bowed her head to him.

Tairren took the goblet from her. His warm hand could feel the coolness from the liquid through the goblet. He quickly peered into it, noticing that it was indeed just water. He sniffed it as he brought it to his dry lips. It didn't smell like anything so he began to sip it. The water was cold and refreshing so he drank the rest down quickly.

The woman just watched him as she silently stood over him.

"Thank you," Tairren said as he gave the goblet back to her.

"Sit and rest, and then will you see Fiara," the woman said, then left quickly.

He watched her as she left with his sword. She went through the shadows of the chamber with quick foot-steps and disappeared behind the columns. Tairren heard the two doors close shut, indicating that he was alone.

Tairren began to relax as the aches in his muscles began to disperse. As he sat, a strange feeling began to come over him that he had never felt before. He began to feel like melted butter to a flame. His head slowly began to swirl and his vision became somewhat hazy. He sat back and rested his head on the pillows of the chair. The pillows felt soft beneath his head, inviting him to fall sleep. A strange feeling of euphoria came over him and his body began to like it. He felt good, as if ecstasy had come alive all over him. His skin began to feel like silk and his mind felt as if it became soft and warm.

Tairren realized then that something strange must've been in the water. Something in the cool water he drank made him feel like he was in a dream. But he didn't become alarmed. Instead his mind yielded to what he was feeling, slipping away into a thrilling oblivion.

Tairren tried to sit up, but his head felt too heavy and his neck was like air. Instead, he just gazed into the great fire that burned in the darkness before him. He watched it as he fell into a trance. The fire seemed to whisper to him and call out his name in rhythmic, soothing patterns. The colors of the fire began to come alive and pulsate. It danced and twirled in the dark air, sending colorful, sparkling light out into the warm chamber. The deep orange color of the flames began to pull Tairren's mind into it. The exhilarating flames danced and twirled as it slowly took the form of a woman. He could see her as clear as day in the fire, but strangely she was also part of the fire. The woman danced seductively like a slow image as the heat sparkled and whirled all around her.

Tairren's body was overwhelmed as he seemed to feel, see, hear, and smell everything in the chamber. He was drawn to the fire and just watched it as it pleased his senses. He could feel the heat radiate from the fire like passion. It came over him like a wave, making his skin erupt with pulsating tingles. He couldn't look away from the dancing orange heat. The dancing woman in the fire stood still, then began to slowly walk out of it! As her fiery body touched the air, flesh appeared. Feeling confused, Tairren closed his eyes, then opened them again. He realized that it was all real.

The woman slowly walked over to him with a stare that made his heart thrash around in his chest. Her eyes glowed like a faint light. Tairren thought she was one of the most beautiful women he had ever seen. She was tall and her skin looked like toasted honey, gleaming in the overwhelming air. She had long black hair which was adorned with fire-colored jewels. Long sheer fabric was wrapped around her waist, revealing the silhouette of her legs as the fire-light shown through it. Her top half was provocatively covered in precious stones that dangled and sparkled in the warm light, revealing skin beneath them.

She came to him slowly, leaning over his body as she gazed into his eyes.

"…Welcome," she said in a low, smooth voice.

Her accent was strange and dissolved in his ears. She caressed his face then smiled at him.

Tairren didn't say anything as he looked into her honey-colored eyes. Her eyes looked like living fire. She smelled of warm spices and sweet honey and her touch was hot.

"I am Fiara…," she said into his ear as she came over him like a warm cloak.

Her voice was sweet to his ears and made his skin become enveloped with goose-bumps. He was transfixed by her in every way and felt as if he was melting right before her. His senses were overwhelmed but tired at the same time. His heart pounded in his chest but sounded slow and rhythmic in his ears. He closed his eyes as he felt his thoughts go away from him.

His mind drifted away in an overpowering state of nirvana as a deep sleep came over him…

†

CHAPTER 9
Fair Haifen

Phillip splashed cold water on his warm face from a creek. He was feeling tired and anxious and sweated at the thought of his quest. He looked into the water at his reflection. He had not seen his reflection in so long it seemed, and it was strange for it to stare back at him. The ripples in the water caught his attention. He then thought of his life. The ripples in the cold water reminded him of how much he had grown spiritually. He felt that he used to be a small drop in a massive pond, and now he felt like one of the larger ripples that reached out to the edges.

Phillip's mind drifted away as his gaze sat still. He closed his eyes and breathed in and out. He thought of how he had learned to become patient and forgiving. He thought of how he learned to love. Then he thought of Natalia… She smiled in his mind, but her smile disappeared as he opened his eyes. He then caught Uriel's reflection bobbing in the water.

"Are you ready?" Uriel asked in a kind voice.

Phillip stood up as he wiped his face with his hands.

"As I will ever be," he said with a smile.

They were resting by a babbling creek for a while after a long ride. They were a short distance away from Haifen Falls. They were resting on the outer edges of the Black Forest. The terrain had changed the closer they got to the Water Temple. The ground sloped and dipped and had many creeks and large ponds scattered about. Where they sat, they could see Haifen Falls.

"Haifen Falls rests at the bottom of those small mountains," Uriel said. "Remember, the entrance is behind the waterfall."

Phillip quickly got his gear ready. He put his sword in its sheath then grabbed his shield.

"Thank you, Uriel—for your guidance," he said.

She smiled at him, "you are welcome, Prince Phillip. I'm glad that you are one of the three keys… Just remember that the king's shield must be obtained. The shield is a symbol of faith and will protect our hero from the wiles of physical darkness."

Phillip became inundated with his past regrets. All his life he had very little faith; his pride overpowered him.

424

"Uriel…I must confess something before I go… I—I do not have powerful faith as you think I do. Before I came this far…I had gotten into a fight with Tairren and mocked his faith. I was going to leave him in the forest days ago…because I didn't believe then. But I do now…and now I know why Tairren is the chosen hero in all of this. He is like a rock—and has faith that is just as strong," Phillip said.

A forlorn look came over his rugged face then as he looked away from Uriel's beauty.

"My dear, Prince Phillip," Uriel said with a soft smile as she came to him. She placed her hand on his shoulder and gazed into his eyes. "Do not ever doubt yourself—or your faith that you have come to know. Do not doubt something that many have died and live for… You being here now, standing before me—moments away from entering a legendary temple—reveals how much faith you truly possess. When you were awakened by light and then became baptized in the water, you silently exclaimed your faith. With your new belief in the God of Light whom you have not seen, shows that you have mighty faith. How do you believe in someone or something in which you have not seen? It is because you have strong faith—and it has blossomed in your heart and is beginning to take root in your spirit. You are a man of light now—you must not let your past hinder you. There is always a new day right before you," she said. She caressed his face as he looked back at her. "Phillip, answer me this… In your heart—deep down in your spirit, is there peace?"

He gazed off at the water of the creek and thought of the ripples that reminded him of how much he had changed. He realized that he did have peace in his heart. His spirit was calm, and his urge to find the king's shield was even stronger.

"Yes, Lady Uriel. I have peace deep down in my soul…and I've felt it before…" He smiled back at her.

"Then you will retrieve the shield of faith," Uriel said. "You must go now, Phillip. I will wait for you here," she smiled at him, then gestured for him to go.

He nodded his head with a subtle smile, then kissed Uriel's hand. He pulled himself onto Sable's back then left quickly.

They darted along a river towards Haifen Falls like a swift shadow. The trees were sparse and the shadows lay thin. Phillip felt thankful that the ride before him was easy and quick.

All he could think about then was obtaining the shield. He then realized that he didn't even ask Uriel about Haifen at all. He didn't know what lay before him or what he was going to experience; he just knew that he had peace about everything and that he was going to go through with his quest no matter what.

He slowed Sable as they came closer to the waterfall. He slid off of his horse and made his way to the pool in which the river led to.

He didn't notice it from afar, but there was a large statue jutting from the pool, right before the waterfall. The statue was of a beautiful woman sitting on a mound of large rocks. She was naked and held a large golden vessel that had water pouring from it. Phillip gazed at the statue with wonder as he noticed something strange about it. The statue of the woman didn't have any legs—but a long fish tail! Her long tail went down and around the rocks she sat on.

As Phillip went past the statue, he wondered what Haifen's true identity was. He wondered if she was just an old Minslethratian legend that was created long ago. He was beginning to wonder if she even existed at all.

He made his way around the pool to the rocky wall of the waterfall. Haifen Falls was massive and roared loudly. The rumble of the water bounced off of the large stones that sat all round him. The water fell from a shadowed cliff that was thick with dark trees, and crashed down into jagged rocks. A cold mist rose from the waterfall, chilling him to the bone. His heart raced with a sudden rush of excitement as he made his way around some large stones and behind Haifen Falls.

He followed a slippery path right behind the powerful wall of water. He could see that more water collected behind the falls and went deep into the entrance of the temple. He splashed through the entrance that was more of a rugged cave. Everything was dark. The stone walls of the cave were cold and slimy and the moist air had a strange smell to it. The sound of water dripping down from the dark ceiling could be heard. Heavy chills came over Phillip's skin as he waded his way through the cold, dark water.

He finally came to the end of the tunnel-like cave, which led to some stone steps. Phillip nearly slipped as he stepped onto the slimy stone. Dim light came down the steps, allowing him to see clearly. Phillip thought it was strange that he could hear noises from more waterfalls, emanating from the top of the stone staircase. He carefully made his way up, out of the cold water and into a large cavern. Strangely, light filled the cavern by a massive hole that was at the very top of the ceiling. The cavern walls went up and curved towards the hole. Water fell from the massive hole, creating a small waterfall. Phillip could see trees above him through the hole, and long vines and ivy that dangled from it. The cavern was majestic looking. There were many other small waterfalls that came from the sides of the cavern as well. All of the water collected in the center of the cavern and then got swept away in small cave-like openings all along the bottom of the stone walls.

He breathed in as he looked upon what appeared to be the main part of the Water Temple. The façade of the temple was carved into the farthest wall of the cavern and was lined with beautiful columns. There were also many other large columns that stood around the vicinity of the large cavern, sitting among jagged stones and reaching up to the rough ceiling.

Phillip swiftly made his way across the cold cavern. He waded through shallow water and climbed over slippery stones. He noticed that many bats hung about the top of the cavern, covering the ceiling like small dark shadows. He didn't want to disturb the bats so he went as quickly as he could. But the space all around him was too big and was easily disturbed. His footsteps echoed through the gray light and bounced off of the rough walls.

As Phillip climbed over a large rock, the rocks below it crumbled and fell. He jumped from the massive rock as it began to fall! The rock rolled down a rocky slope and crashed into the water, hitting one of the large pillars in the process. Phillip began to run as he noticed that the ancient pillar began to fall! It tumbled down in pieces and splashed into the water with a mighty crash! Stone began to fall from the ceiling where the column had touched, making another hole in the ceiling.

The bat-covered ceiling above him became startled and filled the air with loud shrills. The atmosphere of the cavern seemed to burst. Phillip ran beneath a large stone structure that looked like an arch. The massive plethora of bats grew angry and swirled around the cavern like a loud tornado. They thrashed about and made their way out through the massive holes in the ceiling.

Phillip noticed that the loud noises made more rocks crumble from the cavern ceiling. Alarmed, he held his shield up as he quickly ran towards the entrance of the Water Temple. He ran up the old crumbled steps as the bats finally began to disperse from behind him. It seemed that the loud noises disturbed the old temple, making it crumble. The cavern was ancient and delicate and Phillip knew that it probably wouldn't last for too much longer.

It seemed that if anything major happened on the earth above the cavern, the ceiling would fall and bury the entrance to the temple forever.

As soon as the last group of bats flocked away from the cavern, the atmosphere of the cavern became still again. Phillip's deep breaths seemed loud as all around him became silent. His heart pounded as he quickly came upon the entrance. For a moment he thought the cave would've collapse down on him.

He cautiously looked upon the ancient temple. The doorway of the temple looked like it was once majestic and beautiful. Phillip could tell that the decorative columns and statues once sat on either side of the threshold, and must've fallen over the years. He had to crawl beneath a smaller column and a fallen statue that partially blocked the ancient threshold. It seemed that over the many years, the temple began to crumble. It looked more like ancient ruins than a sacred temple.

As Phillip crept through the threshold and into a long hallway that stretched before him, he began to hear something that he didn't expect. He heard the voice of a woman. She seemed to be singing a strange melody he had never heard before. The beautiful voice came from deep within the temple. It was soft and low and bounced off of the smooth walls that stood on either side of him.

His heart quickened as he followed the voice. He suddenly became nervous as he realized that Haifen was real. He followed the hypnotizing voice until he came to another cavern. As he stepped into the open space of the temple, the singing voice suddenly stopped. Phillip looked all around the cavern. It was dark except for some light that came from high above the open space. There was another hole that allowed light from the outside to come in.

"Hello," Phillip called out in a low voice.

He was startled by the sound of a loud splash in the distance, as if someone quickly leapt into water.

Phillip quickly went deeper into the cavern. He was overwhelmed by what he saw. On the farthest side of the cavern, on a rock-like island that was surrounded by water, there was a mound of shiny things that consisted of gold and jewels. He saw different things like coins and crowns, and even stranger things like ancient pieces of armor and weaponry. The mound was tall and looked as if someone had just tossed the pieces of treasure on top of each other.

Phillip walked around the cavern, amazed by all of the treasure. Armor and swords lined the cavern walls and the stone ground was littered with coins and precious stones. He was then reminded of what he went there for and quickly began to search for the legendary shield. It all overwhelmed him. It then seemed to him that finding the shield would be like looking for a strand of hair in the dirt. He thought the shield was going to be impossible to find. There were shields everywhere! The hoard of shiny things was huge and must've been collected over decades.

As Phillip made his way around the water, he noticed that dead fish and bones also littered the stone ground. He realized that someone must've been eating the fish before he came into the cavern. His eyes fell upon a fish that had been bitten into, then he noticed one that was still alive. It wiggled around the ground as it gasped for air. Phillip kicked the fish back into the water and watched it as it quickly darted away. But as he looked, he saw something that startled him. At first, he thought it was another fish of some sort. Its movement caught his eyes as he peered closer into the silent water. As he looked, he noticed that it was a dark form staring right back at him!

Alarmed, Phillip inhaled a cold breath of air as he fell back. Just then something splashed out of the water and lunged at him with a strange shriek! Wide eyed, Phillip quickly crawled away on his back-side, slipping on random coins and jewels that encrusted the damp ground. The creature came at him quickly as it growled. It pulled itself quickly with its arms as the bottom half of its body dragged on the ground. It looked deviant and frightening the way it hurriedly shifted its weight from one arm to the other. It caught hold of Phillip's boots. It hissed as it pulled itself on top of him, pinning him down with its strong hands.

"Why are you touching my things?!" the creature screamed out.

Phillip's heart pounded in his chest as he realized that the creature was a woman! She hovered over him, coming closer to his face. She felt slimy and ice-cold against his body. Cold water dripped from her, covering Phillip with bone-drenching chills. Her face looked terrifying. It disturbed Phillip. The woman's face was white as snow and her eyes were large— glossy and brown, except for her massive black pupils. She had no nose and had some kind of gill-like slits on her thin cheeks that quivered as she breathed heavily. She had many small, sharp teeth beneath her thin, pale lips and her breath smelled of dead fish. Long black, wet hair fell upon Phillip's face as she stared down at him.

"Forgive me," Phillip said in a shaken voice as he just stared at her ugly face. "I mean no harm! I come, looking for the fair Haifen! I must see her!"

The strange woman just stared down at him as a small smile finally crept over her shiny face. After a moment, she came closer to him, nearly touching her face to his. "You are looking at her," she said, then chuckled.

After a moment, she slid off of him, leaving Phillip staring at the ceiling. He breathed heavily as his numb mind came back to him. He then heard the sound of water splashing so he got up quickly. He stood with a pounding heart as he saw the creature sitting at the edge of the water. Her spiny white back was towards him and she never turned to look at him. He slowly walked towards her, never taking his eyes off of the strange-looking woman.

"You—you are Haifen?" Phillip asked, startled, trying to catch his breath.

She slowly looked up at him and smiled. "I am she," she said, then turned her gaze away from him again.

He slowly crept towards her, then got down on his knees. But he kept his distance as he continued to stare at her. He looked at her long fish tail that dangled in the water. It was dark-green, almost black, and looked glossy but tough.

"You are…a sea creature. Was it you who I heard singing?" he said, amazed.

"Yes, it was I who was singing—I heard you coming, I heard you breathing… I have not heard footsteps in many years…and I am indeed from the deep waters of the sea," she said in a much softer voice.

She peered at Phillip through her long, wet hair that hung over her white face.

Phillip gazed at her with wonder and decided that she wasn't so terrifying after all. She just seemed like a lonely maiden. He noticed that she must've loved things that glistened. She wore many long golden chains and jeweled necklaces that dangled and sparkled with translucent pendants. She wore so many that they fell over her bare shoulders and down her back. He also noticed that she wore a head band that she must've made, consisting of shells, pearls and polished fish bones. She had a ring on every finger and silver bangles and diamond bracelets adorned both of her thin wrists.

"I am a maiden from the sea—man comes from afar to worship me… I am a long way from home," she said in a pitiful voice, "I have lived here almost all of my life… Long ago I left my kingdom from the deep waters that are on the other side of this mountain. I found an opening in the earth deep in the dark waters. So, I swam through the dark tunnels of the deep earth until I ended up here…" Her voice had a slight sadness to it and Phillip began to pity her. "The tunnels led to this cavern… I was stuck here long ago. But something happened when a man found me… He was intrigued by my tail and fin, just as you are—and worshiped me. He gave me shiny things so I told him to run and tell all of his people about me. They came by the hundreds—worshiping me and bringing me gifts," she said as she began to fiddle around with the jewels that covered the ground. "But it has been many years since I have seen a human…I am alone…"

She became quiet as she just stared into the water.

"I come from far away as well, Haifen," Phillip said, breaking the strange silence. "I am Prince Phillip from the Kingdom of Ishkar. I was sent here to marry a princess…"

Haifen looked intrigued then as she gazed at him. "A princess as striking as I should definitely catch his manly eye… A Prince?" she said, scooting closer to him. "I am the daughter of a king," she said with a smile. "Have you come for me?" she slowly reached out to Phillip's face with her webbed hand.

Phillip quickly moved his head back as she tried to place her cold, wet hand on his face. "I—actually come for something else," he said quickly.

"So, you come to worship me?" she asked quickly.

"No," Phillip said, looking around the cavern. "I come for a shield."

"A shield, a shield he comes for a shield—send him out and cut his heal! You do not come for ME!" Haifen yelled out, going from sweet to angry. "You do not come to *worship* ME!" she screamed even louder as she slapped her large tail fin against the water, splashing Phillip. "And you only come to touch and TAKE my precious treasure!!"

Her voice echoed throughout the cavern and bounced around in loud waves. Small bits of earth began to crumble from the cavern ceiling, falling into the water with small splashes.

"Please, forgive me," Phillip said quickly, trying to calm her down. He thought of how ancient the temple was and how the outer cavern ceiling had crumbled. "Please—allow me to speak to you…"

She became quiet again as she just glared at him, "What is it then, *Prince*?" she mocked. "What is it that you want from me?"

"Like I've said before, fair Haifen. I—I need," he said, nervously, "I need a shield…"

She sat quietly again, as if she were thinking about his request. She seemed to like to be called "fair" and even more, she seemed to like Phillip's company.

Many moments went by in the silent cavern as Phillip waited for her response.

"He has a handsome face and a sharp sword—my how he wants to touch my hoard," she said to herself as she looked at him. "Prince Phillip—I think I am very fond of you," she said with her strange smile. "I fancy you…"

Phillip was confused by her reaction, but disturbed at the same time. He was expecting for her to lash out at him again and felt uneasy by her attraction to him. She had different, strange personalities. One moment she was sweet, and the next she was explosive. She started her sentences with rhymes, which really got him thinking that she had gone mad from dwelling alone in the darkness for all those years. He decided then that he wasn't going to trust her or believe anything she had to say to him.

"I see his eyes wander, I smell his blood too—he wants to take a shield—that I'll let him do," she exclaimed out loud where he could hear her. "I will give you a shield… Pick one," she said as she just smiled at him, revealing her little sharp teeth. "I have too many anyway. There are plenty more by the walls if you like. Just simply pick one—if that is your desire."

He looked around with his eyes. He didn't see the golden shield he needed anywhere. All of the shields he saw around the wet cavern were either silver or dull and dented. The king's shield was nowhere in sight. He knew the legendary shield of faith had to be hidden somewhere in the cavern, somewhere his eyes were not allowed to look.

"That's very generous of you," Phillip said as he slowly stood up. "But the shield I need is no ordinary shield… I need a legendary shield… You know of what I speak, Haifen…"

"I do NOT!! I possess no such thing!" she shouted, cutting him off. Her face became angry as she glared up at him.

Phillip began to glance around quickly, becoming overwhelmed. "I know you have it, Haifen… I need King Yehoshua's shield…"

Haifen's pupils became large at the mention of King Yehoshua's name. Her strange eyes quickly appeared like two large black stones.

"Get OUT!!" she shrieked all of a sudden as she picked up a nearby helmet and threw it at him. "He speaks of a king that makes me sick—dead he is; his blood ran thick! Get out, get OUT!" she screamed even louder, then splashed into the water.

Phillip rushed over to the water's edge, searching quickly for her. She seemed to have disappeared somewhere deep below. His heart sunk; he couldn't fail his quest. He had to retrieve the shield, he had to! He thought he had lost his one and only chance of knowing where the shield was. He became irritated as he thought of all the time he was wasting. He kicked a pile of gold coins that sat near the stone edge. They flew into the air and fell into the water. He sat down on a nearby stone and watched the ripples that went out over the water where the coins hit. The cavern was silent and cold as he seemed to sit there for hours.

He waited to see if Haifen would come back out of the water, but she never did. He felt lost all of a sudden. He didn't know what to do and he couldn't fail his quest. He would never be able to forgive himself if he left without the legendary shield...

✝

CHAPTER 10
Tricks & Rhymes

Phillip began to get cold as he sat in the silent cavern. He knew he had to keep his mind on his quest or he would fail. He began to think of the legend of King Yehoshua. He knew his quest was for him and that if God sent him to it, He would certainly help him through it. He said a silent prayer in his head as he picked the golden wing-pendant out from beneath his tunic. He had forgotten about the golden necklace. He looked at it and noticed how it glistened in the pale light of the cavern. It was golden light in the dark place.

Just then a thought came into his head. He quickly stood up. The way the wing-pendant glistened reminded him of how much Haifen worshiped anything shiny.

He rushed over to the water's edge and pulled off his necklace. He thought he could temp Haifen with it. Thrilled that he had a plan, he held the necklace over the water, dangling it in the pale light that fell from the large hole in the roof of the cavern. The pendant twinkled in the dim air and casted flickers of golden light upon the water.

After a moment, Phillip could see Haifen beneath the water! She looked like a massive dark fish thrashing to and fro. She appeared anxious and disturbed. She burst up and out of the water, splashing cold drops everywhere. Phillip quickly moved as she tried to grab it from him.

"Give it to me! Foolish human, give it to me!" she roared, splashing water at Phillip. "I have not seen that before and it shall be mine! Give it to me, *prince*—or I'll…"

"Or you'll what?!" Phillip raised his voice, cutting her off. "I know you'll never allow me to leave without giving this to you first. I think it'll look beautiful among your things—or around your neck to match your rings," he mocked.

She sneered at him as she clenched her teeth together.

"I will have that even if I have to pry it from your dead hands! Give it to me!" she shouted again as she bobbed in the shaken water. "How dare you disrespect ME! I am a goddess! Now bow down and worship me and I will take that as a gift!"

"I will never worship you! I know only one God, and He is more powerful than an abomination like yourself!"

Haifen just glared at Phillip from the water. Her strange eyes were glued to his and her face quivered with anger. After a moment she disappeared beneath the surface of the dark water.

Phillip stood for a moment, looking for her. He could see her move quickly beneath the surface. She disappeared in what looked like a cave at the very bottom. After a few moments, he noticed that she came back out, but this time she had with her something large and golden. It was King Yehoshua's shield! Even below the water it glistened as if it were made from light.

Phillip's heart sped up as he gazed at it. She came back out of the water, holding the shield up. Water rolled off of the beautiful shield as the light from the ceiling reflected off of it. It was magnificent and had a mighty winged creature engraved on it with jewels embedded in the precious metal. It looked glorious and appeared more precious than any piece of weaponry he had ever seen.

"Is this what you have been looking for?" Haifen asked in a now sweet voice.

Phillip watched eagerly as she swam to the other side of the water with the shield. She threw it on the pile of gold and jewels that sat on the other side.

"My…my…you will never yield—until you get your beloved shield. I will make a fair deal with you, prince," she said, looking up at him from the water. "Give me that necklace and I will allow you to swim in my water— so you can fetch your precious shield." Her smile was deviant and carried a hint of deceit. "Come and swim so that the shield will be with you."

"I do not make deals with snakes! What is that shield to you?! It's nothing to you but another forgotten *object*, hidden in your hoard!" Phillip shouted as he became irritated.

"It's MINE! That is *my* shield!" she shrieked as she pounded the water with her fists. She became louder as she ranted on. "That was given to me long ago from King Baffmit—that is my gift from him, *my* PRIZE! What is this shield to *you*?! Answer me that, human! The king it came from is dead! Do you hear me, prince? Your god is DEAD! King Baffmit has killed him long ago! What is the worth of something from a DEAD king?!"

Phillip grew quiet as he glanced at the shield that gleamed on the pile of Haifen's treasures. The way the light shown from the shield was the way it gleamed in his spirit. He did not understand his faith totally, but he knew it was real. He knew that King Yehoshua was alive in his heart. He felt it like how he felt his heart pound in his chest. "You are wrong, Haifen… You know nothing and I pity you. You dwell in here in the darkness, worshiping your gold that cares nothing for you. Your gold sits in this cold, damp, disgusting cavern in silence. You have been deceived long ago, blinded by your hoard. You are not a goddess, Haifen. You are nothing but a deceiving serpent filled with tricks! You have been forgotten about long ago when King Yehoshua banished the Old Ways of Minslethrate. You will die here in the darkness, alone—and forgotten about…and I truly pity you… You will never be thought of again. No one will ever fall upon your tricks or deceiving words ever again!"

Haifen became angry by Phillip's words as he just calmly looked down at her. She shook her head violently and began to cry out, "No! No! NOOOO! You are a liar! You are nothing but a disgusting human! You lie you lie—I will never die! Do you hear me, human?! NEVER!!"

Phillip quickly put his necklace back on, then rushed to the edge of the water that dipped closest to Haifen's hoard of treasures. She hissed, revealing her sharp teeth as she quickly swam between Phillip and her precious belongings.

"You think you can outwit me, *prince*?" she said with a wet chuckle. "Try, try, and try again—I don't think he'll ever win! Just give me that necklace and I will allow you to swim in my water." She said in a calmer tone. "What is that necklace's worth to you? Is it not just a necklace?"

"It's a symbol of my faith—now get out of my way or your head shall swiftly be cut from you," he said calmly as he pulled his sword from its sheath.

Haifen began to laugh as she swam away from him. "Threats do not frighten me—I am like the dark waters of the sea! I'm not going anywhere, Prince. You will have to come in my water if you want my head! We can play this game for many years—your eyes will sting with bitter tears! I do not give in so quickly! Look down into my water and you will see how you will end up! Look down if you dare!"

Phillip walked closer to the water as he held on tightly to his sword. He peered down into the dark water. He could not see anything until his eyes met where the light hit it. He could see all kinds of things that gleamed under the water like armor, swords, golden goblets and coins. But then he noticed something else. He didn't notice them before, but he saw many bones and skulls sitting beneath the water! The mouths of the skulls hung open as if they were crying out from below Haifen's cold waters.

"You are nothing but a monster!" Phillip yelled, becoming angry.

Haifen just laughed at him then stuck out her long tongue to lick her lips. "You see what becomes of humans who try to steal from me—eat them up, back and thigh! Come and get your shield—I have not tasted human flesh in many years. I am tired of cold fish, and you look warm and tasty! Come and get your shield so I can eat from your flesh and suck your bones!"

As Haifen continued to patronize him, he thought of a quick plan of action. He quickly took his necklace back off and grasped it in his hand. As Haifen goaded him from the water, he closed his eyes and said a silent prayer. He opened his eyes and then allowed the pendant to fall from his hand as he held on tightly to the chain. When Haifen saw the golden pendant dangle from his tense hand, she began to lust for it again.

Her eyes became like two shiny, black stones.

"Do you really want this?!" Phillip yelled with wide eyes. "Go and fetch it you filthy serpent!"

Just then Phillip threw his necklace away from him, closer to the entrance of the cavern. It glistened in the air as it flew through the darkness. It landed on a rock that stuck out from the water. Haifen's eyes became wide as she let out a raspy hiss. She quickly followed it with her black eyes, reaching her webbed hands out to it as if it were her savior. She dashed towards it as she flicked her tail and slapped her large fin against the water.

Phillip acted quickly and dove into the water. The dark water was ice-cold and came over his body like a sheet of daggers. His skin became numb as chills soaked through. Adrenaline rushed through his veins as he kept his eyes on the shield. He swam as quickly as he could. He felt as if his heart was going to explode as he made it to the other side. Somewhat relieved, he grabbed the shield. The wet golden surface felt good beneath his trembling fingers. He began to swim as fast as he could but both his sword and the shield were slowing him down! He threw the shield to the other side as hard as he could. It landed on some large rocks that stuck out from the surface, a couple of feet from the edge of the water.

He quickly looked in the direction where Haifen swam off to. His heart nearly stopped as he noticed that she was gone! He saw nothing but shaken water! He quickly looked all around him as he began to panic. He nearly made it to the water's edge when something grabbed his ankle! He was pulled down into the water in a matter of seconds. Haifen came over him in the water like a dark shadow. She had her tail wrapped around his legs as she pulled him to the bottom of her dark waters.

Phillip's mind went numb for a moment as he began to panic. He had to get to the surface or he would drown and surely become another one of Haifen's victims! He realized that he still had his sword. He held on tightly to his sword with both hands and shoved it into Haifen's tail. It was like slow motion as the water pushed back against him. She let go quickly as black fluid rushed from her tail like a cloud. Phillip hurried to the surface, swimming with all of his might as he felt his breath creeping away from him. He exploded from the water. His first breath was intense as air filled his lungs again. He sucked in the cold air as he rushed to the stone edge.

Phillip went to pull himself up, but Haifen burst out of the water from behind him! She clung to his back, wrapping her slimy arms around his neck. She growled and shrieked loudly as she tried to pull him back down into the water. Phillip flung his elbow back as hard as he could, hitting her in the face. Her wet head flung back has her hold on him loosened. He quickly pulled himself out of the water and grabbed the shield that was pinned between a rock and the edge where he was standing.

Haifen began to scream and howl as he threw the shield away from her reach. She quickly pulled herself from the water and lunged at Phillip, pulling his legs from beneath him. He fell to the wet ground, hitting his head. His vision became blurry for a moment as Haifen's haunting voice echoed in his ears. She pulled herself on top of him as she continued to squeal and snarl. She bit his arm, sinking her many sharp teeth into it. Pain shot through his arm as he hit her in the head with the hilt of his sword. She let go of his arm and slid away from him. He knew he had to stop her before she grabbed the shield and went back into the water. Alarmed, he pounced on her back, pulling her arms back. He noticed that she still held on tightly to the wing-pendant. He pulled it from her slippery grasp as she thrashed her tail around.

"You have lost, Haifen!" Phillip yelled breathlessly in her ear.

He glanced at his sword that lay next to him on the stone. Normally he would've cut her head from her neck, then would've brought her head with him to show it off as if it were a trophy. But he couldn't bring himself to do it. He truly pitied Haifen. It seemed that her lust for gold punished her more than death itself.

"I will spare your life because I pity you, Haifen," Phillip said into her ear as her raspy breaths bounced off of the wet ground. "I bestow grace upon you just as my God has given me grace. Remember this, Haifen. As I leave you here in your lonely darkness, remember that there is only one God—and He covers darkness with his light."

Just then he put the wing pendant back on then grabbed his sword. He rushed to grab the shield, then swiftly went towards the entrance of Haifen's cavern.

Haifen rolled on her stomach to get a glimpse of Phillip. She began to cry, but then a look of anger came over her face as she watched Phillip leave with the golden shield. "Curses! CURSES!! Curses upon you and your bloodline! Curses upon your kingdom! Prince Phillip of Ishkar! I will never forget your name! CURSES!!"

Just then Haifen let out a loud shriek that could shatter glass. Her scream was relentless and seemed to release some kind of powerful wave in the air that hit the stone walls like a hammer. The powerful shriek shook the rough walls of the cavern as it bounced and vibrated in the wet air.

Phillip ran the rest of the way through the temple, holding his ears. Haifen's strange scream seemed as if it could crush his ears from the inside out. He rushed through the outer cavern as quickly as he could. Her screams disturbed the whole underground temple, making it quake and tremble. Stone began to fall from the ceiling of the large cavern! Large rocks crashed all around him, splashing in the water. The cavern was crumbling! Panicked, Phillip looked all around him as parts of the ceiling began to cave in. The mighty columns that sat around the cavern began to crumble and fall and the small waterfalls that came from the stone walls began to quiver and shake.

Phillip finally made it to the entrance of the great cavern. His breath shook from him as he realized that he was almost out. He glanced back at the Water Temple one last time before he hurried down the steps. The façade of the temple began to crumble, crashing down over the entrance to Haifen's pool. The remnants of the Old Ways were nearly gone as the ruins of the temple became nothing but a pile of stone.

He left quickly, splashing through the dark cave-tunnel that led to Haifen Falls. Phillip became nervous as he saw that the waters that fell from the waterfall began to shake! He realized that he would soon be buried beneath the earth if he didn't hurry! His heart pounded like a drum as he finally made it out from behind Haifen Falls. He quickly ran along the pool that sat at the bottom of the great waterfall. The water trembled and splashed as if an earthquake was happening.

He didn't see Sable where he left him! He made a loud whistle noise as he searched for his horse. Thankfully, Sable came running up to him along the river. Relieved, he quickly pulled himself onto Sable as he turned to look at Haifen Falls.

The powerful water of Haifen Falls continued to quake, splashing everywhere as if it were alive and enraged. The whole waterfall began to give way as the earth beneath it was falling! Water went flying from the earth as it came crashing down. The powerful water crashed against the glorious statue of Haifen, pushing it down into the water. The mighty sound of earth breaking filled the air. The ancient temple and idol of Haifen was no match for the creations of God. The earth and water destroyed Haifen's temple, making it become one with the stone and soil.

Phillip got Sable going as quickly as he could, racing along the river like a mad wind. The waters of the river quickly swelled up as Haifen Falls collapsed in a massive cloud of cold mist. A wave of water rushed down the river. Phillip's heart pumped with adrenaline as the sounds of the earth crumbling roared behind him.

A long way down the river, Phillip stopped to get a look at what had happened. He was shocked to see that in a matter of moments, it had completely changed. As the misty cloud dispersed, he could see that when the one mighty waterfall fell apart, it made many smaller waterfalls further back where the caverns had crumbled. All around the beginning of the river now looked like a lake as the waters flooded its surrounding area.

Phillip began to think of Haifen and how she would never be looked at again. Her treasure was now buried deep beneath the earth and water. She was lost below the ruble and darkness just as she had always been. The whole temple had vanished and everything in it had been buried. He began to feel bad for Haifen as he thought of her and her pathetic life. She had become buried alive with her treasure…

He then thought of the legendary shield that rested on his back. He had retrieved it and the struggle with Haifen was all over. He knew his life had changed greatly and he would never forget his experiences. He felt so proud. Even in his heart, he knew that the God of Light was very proud of him.

Phillip smiled as he petted Sable's neck. His heart pounded with joy. He then got Sable going back towards the little camp where he left Uriel. He grew excited as he hurried along. He had King Yehoshua's legendary shield safely upon his back, and he became overwhelmed with emotion because of it.

†

CHAPTER 11
Gone

"...Show forth the praises of him, who hath called you out of darkness into his marvelous light," Lord Fernund said as he looked out of the large window of the hall.

He sat in King Julpen's study and read from the ancient Book of Light. His spirit had become lightened and he wanted to know more about the God of Light. Ever since he had come to know the legends that Master Odwa had shared with him, he felt as if light was growing and becoming alive on the inside of him.

Master Odwa had been speaking to him about many things, and the legendary King of Light was one of them. Lord Fernund couldn't stop thinking of the legend, and wanted to know more of it. He felt as if he had changed overnight. He felt like a new person.

"My Lord," an old voice came from behind him.

It was Master Odwa. He had a serious look on his face and he was followed by one of the royal guards. The marquis stood up, noticing that there was another guard standing at the door.

"Yes, Master Odwa," Lord Fernund said as he watched the old man come before him.

"There is someone here who wishes to speak with you. She says it is urgent," the old man said as he looked up at him beneath his heavy eyebrows.

The marquis glanced at the guard who was standing near the door. "Let this person in," he said.

"He shall not be afraid of evil tidings: his heart is fixed, trusting in the lord," Master Odwa said quickly as he looked into the marquis' eyes.

Lord Fernund just gazed at the old man, wondering what he meant by his words. Just then his eyes caught a young maiden who walked solemnly into the hall. She looked like she had been crying, having a red face and swollen eyes.

The young servant girl stood before Lord Fernund. She nervously brought her eyes up to his as tears rolled down her cheeks.

"You work for my wife, Lady Christianne," he finally said, recognizing her round, freckled face.

"Yes, my lord…my name is Alexa and I am but a scullery maid in your house. But I come baring horrible news…," she said as she began to sob."

"Speak, young lady," Master Odwa said as he placed a friendly hand on her shoulder.

"I do not know what has happened, but you must come back to the manor, Lord Fernund… Everyone…everyone is dead," she said as she covered her face, beginning to cry again.

The Marquis stared at her. His heart dropped in his stomach. His eyes became wide as he slowly shook his head.

"What of my wife?!" he asked frantically, raising his voice.

"I—I don't know." Alexa exclaimed between sobs.

"I must go," Lord Fernund said to Master Odwa.

"Marquis," the old man said, looking into his shocked eyes. "Do not forget the light. Darkness walks to and fro, waiting to attack and will do so even harder… Do not forget the light inside of you..."

Lord Fernund just looked at Master Odwa, then slowly nodded his head. He left quickly as the guards followed behind him.

†††

The ride to the Ducre' Provence was agonizing as anxiety settled over Lord Fernund. The ride seemed longer. He kept thinking of what Alexa had said: "Everyone was dead…" Her shaken words repeated in his mind like a wicked chant. His heart pounded in his chest and sweat formed on his brow as they pulled up to the manor. A dozen soldiers had followed his carriage, armed and ready for whatever threatened his home.

He dashed out of his carriage as soon as they pulled up to the darkened manor. All around him was still and quiet and there was no lamp-post lit or soft light that would usually come from the windows. His home looked dead.

It seemed as if everyone could hear his heart pound as they came closer to the entrance. They made their way through the massive front doors of the manor, spreading out as they rushed into the foyer. Their feet upon the tile floor echoed in the hall as they quickly began to search everywhere.

It wasn't long till Lord Fernund heard shouts from the soldiers. Their voices sounded alarmed as they found many of the dead servants. Every one of the servants lie silently with their chests opened out to the air.

Lord Fernund shouted his wife's name as he made his way up the grand staircase and through the dark corridors.

He burst into Lady Christianne's chamber, frantically searching for her. He noticed the opened window and ran towards it. He looked out into the cold winds. The glass beneath his boots crunched. His heart raced in his chest as his eyes fell upon a puddle of blood down below. It looked like someone had fallen from the window...but there was no body among the dark blood...

"Christianne! Where are you?!" the marquis screamed out as he looked around her dark and quiet chamber.

His worried eyes fell upon the glass on the floor. He noticed dark-red fluid that looked like blood. It appeared as if someone had been bleeding upon the glass-stricken floor. His eyes followed the blood and noticed that it made a trail—right over the ledge and to the pool of blood down below! The trail of blood was also smeared down the stone wall, as if a bloodied person was pulled right up the side of the wall and into the room! The bloody trail led across the chamber and into the dark shadows that spread out thickly...

Lord Fernund stood frozen, trying to understand everything he had seen.

Oddly, the sound of strange breathing could be heard, as if it were right in his ears. Startled, the marquis quickly turned. His eyes widened as his skin felt as if it was about to crawl away from his bones. His heart nearly left him as he turned to find his wife standing in the shadows of her room.

"Christianne...you had me frightened," he said as his breaths became heavy.

He rushed over to his wife to embrace her but she quickly backed away from him. She stood in the dark shadows without a hint of emotion. Even though heavy shadows covered her face, she looked ravishing, as if she were ready for an engagement.

"Christianne...what's wrong? What has happened here?" he asked as he went to touch her face.

She flinched at his touch and moved away from him again. She then stood silently in the black shadows of the room; only her heavy breaths could be heard.

"One of your servants came to the palace to inform me that something terrible has happened here," he said, glancing around her untidy chamber.

She looked quickly towards the door. She began to look as if she were feeling threatened. Her eyes widened as a worried soldier came into the chamber.

A concerned look came over Fernund's face. "My love, speak to me," he said, noticing how strange she was acting.

She took her stare off of the soldier as she slowly came out of the heavy shadows. She moved closer to the marquis in the pale light. She slowly brought her hand to the back of her head. Her face was still emotionless, as if her spirit was gone from her body.

"The red life must be emptied… I must eat of the red," she said in a strange voice as she brought her hand away from the back of her head.

Lord Fernund noticed that her hand was covered in thick blood. He glanced behind her and realized that she had been standing in a puddle of it! Blood was leaking from the back of her opened head and ran down her back! He also noticed that her eyes were not the usual vibrant green, but black and cold looking.

"Christianne, are you hurt?!" the marquis asked, becoming alarmed as he came closer to her again.

Just then she let out a terrifying scream as she lunged at him! The marquis fell back as she hit him. Her sudden rage felt like iron. Her strength was surprising and her hands felt like cold stone. She pounced on him and began to strangle him as she growled like a vicious animal.

The soldier who stood by the door ran upon them, pulling his sword from its sheath. The sound of the sword sliding from its covering caught her attention. Her black eyes flashed as she showed her teeth. It was as if a creature was in her! The marchioness leapt from Lord Fernund, then darted towards the soldier like a quick wind. She rammed into the soldier, forcing him across the room! Shrieks left her mouth as she ran out into the dark corridor.

Lord Fernund hurried to his feet, shocked at what had happened. He chased after his strange wife, wondering what had come over her.

She was running towards the main hall and panted loudly as she went. The soldiers in the hall watched as Lady Christianne came running upon the balcony above them. Her screams echoed across the hall as she leapt from the balcony. She fell down towards the ground, landing like a crouching animal.

The soldiers pulled their swords out, surrounding the disturbed-looking woman. They were taken aback by the bizarre lady that growled before them.

A loud shriek erupted from her mouth as she clenched her fists. As the horrible sound came from deep within her, her mouth became unnaturally wide. Something began to come out of it! A strange mist crept out of her mouth like thick smoke, and then erupted into the air above her. Her body collapsed upon the hall floor as a black shadow swirled above her. The shadow rushed away from the main hall and flew out of the manor like a black wind.

Lord Fernund rushed down the stairs to his wife as the soldiers stared upon her with incredulous expressions. Her body lay silently. Her eyes were open, but they weren't black anymore; they were a pale-green. The marquis fell to his knees and checked her pulse. She was dead and cold as stone...

He just held her in his arms, as tears flooded his eyes. He let out a frustrated scream that seemed to come from his soul. He then wept upon her chest, crying like he had never done before. His heart broke for the first time as he screamed out her name...

✝✝✝

Many miles across the lands, far atop the Tower of Sacrifice, Lilith perked her head up as if she heard something. A wicked smile crept upon her face as she stood among the darkness of the chamber.

"It has begun," she said in a raspy voice. She began to chuckle. "It has BEGUN!!" she screamed out as she raised her bony hands into the air.

She tossed her thin hair back as a raspy laugh ripped from her throat. Her wild eyes darted back at Marrisa, who was chained to a wall.

Marrisa's long red hair hung over her face as she stood quietly.

"I hear the remorse—the CRIES! I hear pain and suffering! I smell the invigorating scent of carnage! I feel the dark energy growing ever so quickly as the people of this kingdom begin to fall!" She began to make her way towards Marrisa who just looked blankly at her. "Tonight—yes tonight, princess! Tonight, the moon will appear as blood, and the prophecy will begin to come alive! Tonight, will become the beginning of the end!"

Marrisa didn't say anything as she just stared at Lilith. She stood still as her arms reached out in opposite directions. Shackles squeezed tightly around her wrists and her ankles were tied together with rope. Her skin was clean and she wore a long black gown that appeared very old.

"You do not have to say anything, my sweet," Lilith said. "I can now hear your soul... You are prepared and anointed for the ceremony..."

Lilith became quiet as she just gazed at Marrisa. After a moment, she slowly shook her head.

"Your friends and family will die... Baffmit has showed himself to them, princess. It is good that you have given up," she said with a smile.

Marrisa just continued to blankly stare at her. Her eyes had no life in them and her mind was empty. She was in shock, stuck in an oblivion that seemed to never leave her.

Lilith silently walked back to the window that looked out over the dark lands of the south. She gazed upon the lands as a look of anger came over her ugly face.

"They think they are winning," she said in a low tone. "The dead king's people are infiltrating the lands...but father will stop them. Yes...darkness will rise like the mists and they will fall... Yes. They will fall..."

†

CHAPTER 12
Falling Leaves

The forest was dark and dead. Nothing was alive it seemed except for the shadows. There was no life at all; not even a single raven or creeping insect roamed about. The trees had no leaves and looked rotten. The dead bark reached up into the gray sky with its knotted and twisted branches, appearing as if they were crying out for life to touch them. The soil was black and bare. The atmosphere smelled of rotting earth and the air was cold and dry. This was the core of the Black Forest, the dwelling spot of the Forest Temple.

"Everything is dead," Natalia said in a low voice, almost whispering. "A forest should be filled with life."

"The Black Forest is cursed…and the Forest Temple is the heart of it," Gaibriul said as he peered through the darkness with his golden eyes. "I feel the sadness and death it holds—radiating from the earth as if it were a forbidden melody…"

They were slowly making their way through the forest, watching carefully as they silently rode their beasts. The ride to the center of the forest seemed to go by quickly. They rode steadfastly throughout their quest, but when they disturbed the darkness that slept around them, they decided to move with a much slower pace.

"I see something—through the trees," Natalia whispered, pointing her finger.

"That is the temple," Gaibriul said. "But we must move slowly, still. We shouldn't wake anything else that shouldn't be awakened," he said with keen eyes.

They quietly made their way to the temple. Everything was still and silent. The silence was so intense around them that it was hard to even breathe without being too loud. The closer they had gotten to the temple, the colder it got. They began to see their own misty breath.

They made it to the entrance of the temple, which looked more like ruins. They stared in silence at the depressing temple. It looked like the trees had taken over it, making the many columns and great walls fall. It looked like it was once beautiful, but death and many cursed years had taken hold of it.

"I do not like this—at all," Natalia said as her eyes fell upon a symbol above the entrance. "I feel depressed just by thinking of Dolsia."

"Do not forget the light, Natalia," Gaibriul said as he looked into her worried eyes. "Do not ever forget King Yehoshua or your quest. Darkness will try to have you...you must not yield to it. Remember the legendary armor of King Yehoshua, and wear it upon your heart. The armor of truth and righteousness is what will protect you from the wiles of darkness. The Dark Lord only wins when you succumb to the strongholds that he tries to blind you with... Remember, Natalia...evil will use your weaknesses against you..."

"...Is that how Dolsia fell?" she asked as she stared into the broken entrance.

"Yes...," Gaibriul said as a saddened look came over him. "She was blinded by the Dark Lord's deceiving words..."

Gaibriul became quiet for a moment as he too stared into the darkness of the temple. The cold air settled over them and made them tremble.

"This once used to be the most beautiful garden in all of the lands. The Garden of Nede was its name...but it was so long ago when life came from it... It's nothing but a desolate land of death and darkness... You must go Natalia; evening draws near and the forest will be crawling with nomed if we linger any longer than needed."

"I understand," Natalia said, reluctantly.

She became nervous all of a sudden as she slid off of Orchid's back. She looked back up at Gaibriul who nodded at her.

"Remember, Natalia... Wear the armor of truth and righteousness upon your heart. And do not leave without King Yehoshua's armor." Gaibriul became quiet for a moment. Something else seemed to be on his heart. "Natalia...Dolsia may still have hope deep in her spirit... But much time has passed since she has seen the light of our king. Have an opened heart for her...she is nearly gone... Please—remind Dolsia of the light she once had."

Natalia looked up at Gaibriul and nodded her head. She could tell that Dolsia seemed to be a very special companion to him, and that the thought of her being lost bothered him. She knew that companionship was important, and it touched her that Gaibriul wanted Dolsia to be helped.

But she began to think of the uncertain path before her. The thought of going into the temple made her overwhelmed with anxiousness. She swallowed down her fear as she pressed her lips together. Everything she had to do seemed easier said than done…

Natalia left him, and began to make her way into the Forest Temple. She glanced back at Gaibriul every now and then, who just watched her with a silent stare. She trusted Gaibriul, and deep down, she knew that with the light on the inside of her, she could do anything. As she pulled her cape tightly around her arms, she decided that nothing was going to stop her.

The air around her became colder as she walked into the silent temple. She looked around, thinking that she must've been in what was once a great hall. Twisting vines took over the crumbling walls, weaving in and out of the crevasses of the cracked stone. Natalia climbed over piles of stone and crawled under fallen columns as she made her way across. There was barely any ceiling left and random columns and statues stood here and there throughout the main hall, which seemed mostly filled with dead trees and naked bushes.

Natalia made it to a long corridor or passage-way of some sort. Large dead bushes lined the walls and the passage-way seemed to steadily go downwards. The dried branches of the bushes filled the passage-way, making it hard for her to swiftly follow the path. She realized that she was descending steps and nearly fell down them. She caught herself on a thick limb that stretched across the path. Most of the steps seemed cracked and broken, making it more difficult to get through.

She finally made her way down to the bottom of the horrid steps, feeling relieved that a great hall opened out before her. She looked around, amazed at the grand sight. She was standing in a massive hall that had tall ceilings and was filled with beautiful columns. The room seemed bigger than any hall she had ever seen. Most of the ceiling seemed to be intact, having only large holes in it. Pale light came in through the holes, allowing her to see the interior of the massive temple.

Natalia walked along the shadowed hall, searching with her eyes for Dolsia—or anyone for that matter. The hall seemed to be empty, and every one of her footsteps echoed in the dark air. She then noticed a large statue that stood in the center of the hall. The marble figure appeared to be of a woman: Her body was elegant and golden fabric that looked realistic hung from her frame. But strangely, the beautiful figure had no head. Natalia slowly passed the statue, looking up at its magnificence. A large hole let light in right above it, and as she passed it, she could see that its head laid right by its bare feet.

Chills went across Natalia's skin as she thought of the fall of Dolsia, and how the temple and the idol reflected her present state. She took her eyes away from the statue and focused on a grand threshold that led back outside. As she made her way to the threshold, she could tell that the other side was once a beautiful garden. The surrounding area of the garden was lined with tall walls; and arches, statues, and fountains could be seen among the dead garden.

As Natalia walked out among the gray atmosphere, she heard a singing voice… It resonated throughout the cold air. The voice was faint, as if someone was singing on the other side of the garden. Natalia thought that the voice was beautiful, but haunting. It sounded sad and filled the gray air with a strange ambience.

Natalia followed along a cold-looking stream, which seemed to lead to the singing voice. She knew the voice had to have been that of Dolsia. She thought of the haunting legend of the earth goddess that Tairren and Gaibriul had told her about.

"H-hello!" Natalia called out in a nervous voice.

The voice became quiet all of the sudden. Heavy silence fell upon the cold air again as Natalia stood still like a stone. She listened for a moment with keen eyes, but the voice never came again. She slowly made her way across a stone bridge that went over the creek. Mists seemed to come the further she went into the dead garden.

Natalia turned quickly as she heard the sounds of footsteps upon the dead earth. She looked with nervous eyes but there was no one there.

"Hello…," she said in a lower tone as her heart began to quicken.

She stood for a moment as she stared into the mists of the garden. Then she heard the noises again. She turned again—but this time someone was there. Someone stood in the distance, shrouded in a long black cloak! Natalia let out a scream that startled even the cloaked person. She hurried to cover her mouth. The dark silhouette just stood in the cold mists. Natalia trembled in the cold as the hooded person just gazed at her.

"Dolsia?" Natalia finally said with a shaken voice.

She didn't want to, but she started towards the person, slowly walking through the mists. Just then the hooded person began to move away as Natalia came closer.

"I will not hurt you," Natalia said as she stopped in her steps. "My name is the Lady…," she said, but paused. She was going to give her whole title and social rank in Minslethrate, but she thought just then that it didn't really matter anymore. "My name is Natalia… Are you Dolsia? I need your help…"

The shadowed person didn't say anything—didn't even move.

Natalia just stood quietly for a moment, then began to walk towards the person again. But she quickly stopped, noticing that the person began to move away from her again.

"Please…I need to talk with you," Natalia said as she brought her hands up. "I've been sent here to retrieve something of great importance."

The person was quiet for a moment, then moved a little. "Who has sent you and what do you want?" the cloaked stranger finally asked. The voice that came from the dark robes was that of a woman. Her voice sounded sweet, but carried a hint of melancholy.

"I've been sent here by the legna—to fetch King Yehoshua's armor," Natalia said. "I am a follower of the Legendary King Yehoshua and must complete my task."

"…Well, Nalalia, follower of King Yehoshua…tell your legna that they are not welcomed to have it," she said, then turned to walk away.

"Please, Dolsia… Do not leave—I beg of you!" Natalia said quickly as her heart began to race. "I must obtain it—for Tairren!"

Dolsia stopped, then turned to look at her again from her dark cloak. It seemed as if Tairren's name struck her.

"…Do you love Tairren?" she finally asked after a silent stare.

"I don't…Tairren is my friend," Natalia said as she rubbed her chilled arms.

"It's a pity—really… I saw you loving him in the forest," Dolsia said. "I saw you kissing the boy named Tairren among the forest of the legna's camp. Do not lie to me, human—if you wish to retrieve something of great value."

Natalia just gazed at her in disbelief. She wondered how she even knew about her and Tairren. She thought of that night when she had kissed Tairren… She remembered hearing footsteps in the forest and was beginning to wonder if it was her who was creeping around them that night.

"I don't understand… How do you know Tairren's name?" Natalia asked.

"I've seen him before…long ago," Dolsia said, looking away from Natalia's gaze. "He was a young boy then and was exploring the Black Forest with his father… The Black Forest was not as cold then," Dolsia said with a faint smile. Her smile faded away as she looked off into the garden.

"He doesn't know me, but I know him…his presence feels like that of the legna. So, I know it was him who you were loving in the forest…"

"It was you who was watching me from the legna's forest, then?" Natalia asked as she just gazed at Dolsia's darkened face.

"I am Dolsia…this is *my* forest," she said quickly. "I go wherever I please. I had to know what was threatening my lands. The legna think that they can do whatever they please! The legna infiltrated my lands…*my* lands! I am not welcome in their kingdom; and they think that they can walk upon my forest!"

"Your lands?" Natalia said, becoming irritated by Dolsia's ignorance. She gestured her hand out over the garden. "This desolate garden and broken temple are your lands? Is that why I only see death around me?! Why didn't you make yourself known when you saw the legna coming if you are so powerful? *You* say you are the earth goddess of Minslethrate— but you seem to know only broken darkness," Natalia said, raising her voice.

Dolsia just stood silently, then quickly turned away from Natalia to leave her.

"Wait!" Natalia said quickly as she made a couple of steps towards her. "Forgive me…sometimes my words are too bold… I—I just don't understand how a legna like yourself could fall victim to—this…when you possessed so much long ago…"

Dolsia just stood silently with her back facing Natalia. She slowly shook her head, then lowered it down towards the ground.

Natalia made her way to her, beginning to feel regretful of her outspoken opinions. She realized then that Dolsia was just a broken being that hid many dark wounds. She slowly walked around her, still keeping her distance. She placed her hand over her chest as she stood before the poor soul. Just then, Natalia realized that she wasn't a sacred being or a terrible, power-infested goddess—she was just a broken person.

Dolsia became startled by Natalia's presence and quickly pulled her hands away from her face. She just timidly gazed at Natalia from her dark hood. She appeared like a lost, scared child.

Natalia tried to look at her face, but the shadow from her hood was heavy and covered most of her countenance.

"Please—take your hood off…so that I may see who it is that I'm speaking to," she said as she stood before the tall woman.

Natalia noticed that Dolsia was covered from head to toe in old, dark garbs. Her arms and hands were wrapped with dirty strips of cloth and the only flesh Natalia could see was that of her face.

After a moment of cold silence, Dolsia slowly pulled her hood from her head. At first, she looked down at the ground, not wanting to even look at Natalia, but after a moment, she did.

Natalia's heart broke suddenly as she looked into Dolsia's saddened eyes. Her eyes were a pale-gold color—like a faint light. Her face was white as snow and looked like glass. Instead of having a golden circlet around her head like the other legna wore, she had a headband that was made with strips of bark and her own hair twisted together. Her long dull locks were almost white and fell down her back in long messy braids.

Natalia pressed her lips together. She felt like she was going to shed tears as she looked upon the faded legna. She knew Dolsia's story and broken past, which made her more sympathetic for her. She knew that she was once a beautiful legna, and sang in the court of Nevaeh. But she had no light in her anymore... Her countenance didn't even glow. Her soul seemed sick and her pale eyes revealed everything. She looked as if the many dark years washed her spirit away. She was tragic looking and her beauty was haunting.

"...Where has your light gone?" Natalia finally asked as she gazed into her pale eyes.

"It left me long ago... Light is but a passing thought that taunts me. I am not wanted by the legna—or loved by King Yehoshua anymore." She pulled her pale eyes away from Natalia's concerned face. "It seems as if you already know about me... So, I do not have to explain anything to you..."

"...My heart is breaking for you," Natalia said as she looked away from her. "I do know the legend of Dolsia... And—I know that everyone has a dark past... But you must not yield to it—there are always second chances..."

Dolsia didn't say anything. She looked numb, as if she really didn't have any passion within her. She seemed as if her heart had become a stone. Dolsia looked at Natalia for a moment, then turned quickly. "Follow me," she said.

Natalia obeyed her. She followed in silence as she kept her eyes on Dolsia's dark silhouette. She began to think of Dolsia's fallen life. She looked around as they went. The dead garden made her yearn for her homelands. Everything about the Garden of Nede seemed to cast a dark spell upon her. She thought of what Gaibriul had told her. She had to bring the light in the dark place. Even though she could feel the darkness all around her like a thick shroud, she was not going to let it change her how it had changed Dolsia. And somehow, she knew she had to remind Dolsia of the light she once held. She then thought of the armor of truth and righteousness, and knew she had to wear it upon her spirit.

Natalia came out of her thoughts and realized that they were walking upon a tree. Her eyes widened as she looked up at the beautiful thing. The tree sat in the center of the garden. The black soil sloped up to the tree and the creek that was in the garden circled around it. But strangely, it was the only tree that had leaves and fruit hanging from it.

"Beautiful," Natalia said as they crossed the shallow creek. A smile came over her face as her eyes glittered upon the dangling fruit.

"Even the most beautiful thing can cause tragedy," Dolsia said in a low tone, as if only to herself.

Dolsia walked to an ornate bench that sat at the foot of the tree and rested upon it. She just watched Natalia who seemed mesmerized by the wonderful piece of nature.

"What is this place?" Natalia asked with a smile.

Dolsia watched Natalia as she looked around at all of the fruit that hung from the low branches. A faint smile crept over her face, but then vanished as she noticed that Natalia went to pick up one of the attractive fruits that sat upon the black soil.

"…Do you like it?" Dolsia asked as Natalia stared at the fruit with intense eyes.

"It's lovely," Natalia exclaimed as she inspected the luscious fruit.

The strange fruit was vibrant and lovely and its cool skin was soft and smooth. It gleamed even in the pale light of the dead garden.

"You want to eat from it, do you not?" Dolsia said with a low tone.

"I am rather hungry and parched," Natalia said as she wiped the flesh of the fruit with the palm of her free hand.

"…Eat it," Dolsia said with a strange smile. "It is sweet and its juice is cool and fulfilling."

Natalia brought the fruit to her nose and sniffed it. It smelled so sweet. A smile came over her face as she closed her eyes. The fruit reminded her of the sweet berry pastries that Sora used to bake for her. It also reminded her of Marrisa… She thought of how much Marrisa loved to eat the glossy apples from the shaded castle orchard.

Dolsia intensely watched Natalia as she brought the fruit to her mouth. Another smile came over her face as Natalia bit into the fruit. The cool juice burst from the fruit and sprayed the side of her mouth.

"This is delicious," Natalia exclaimed, chewing the sweet fruit. She wiped her mouth with her sleeve as she swallowed it down.

"…I never thought that something so sweet could cause me to become so bitter," Dolsia said as her smile vanished quickly. "That is the forbidden fruit of the Garden of Nede," she said as she just glared at Natalia.

Natalia's eyes widened as fear came over her face. She looked like she was going to get sick. She spit the chewed fruit parts out of her mouth and grunted, throwing the apple into the creek.

"Don't worry, Natalia," Dolsia said, looking amused. "That fruit was only forbidden to eat upon long ago… It doesn't matter that you eat from it now—you being a human, you have been eating of it every day of your life... You already possess the knowledge of good and evil…just as I do. You have the propensity to sin and yield to darkness, because of the fall of the first children of light who once walked upon this garden—so long ago..." Dolsia looked off into the gray garden as a pensive look came over her face. "You know the legend in which I speak… Ages ago, when I ate from the fruit…I became something that I used to loath and fight against. Now, I am my worst enemy… And you wonder how a legna could even become something so pathetic like myself. I used to kiss my lord's feet before I sang for him—and look at me now—I kiss the dirt before I sing to the silent darkness around me…

"Humans are quick to judge, Natalia. But you know that I am a failure. It is no secret that I am a fallen legna. I am nothing but a wondering, restless human now. But death will never have me because I am cursed. The damned shall not even look upon me…because I deserve it not. My heart is bitter and I do not care for the light as I did before. Even the thought of King Yehoshua and the legna make me want to scream… The light and I are not companions…and never will be…"

Natalia walked to her as she shook her head, "…You are wrong, Dolsia," she said. "King Yehoshua loves you! He loves everything about you. You may not feel him—you may not ever feel him near you…but *he* loves you, Dolsia," she said with compassion. "I used to feel the same as you. I used to cry myself to sleep, thinking that I was all alone in this kingdom who felt the way I did. I had everything but felt that I had nothing! My companions used to be the only ones who made me feel—something... I used to get angry—for no reason at all. I used to despise my people in Minslethrate... I used to think that my existence on this earth was pointless—that my name and social stature was the only thing that was worth—anything at all!

"But I know that I am worth more—because I feel it now! When I decided to follow King Yehoshua...my life changed, I changed!" Natalia said with excitement as she placed her hands over her beating heart. "I used to crave the touch and love from anyone, from any man that looked upon me with twinkling eyes. And now I know that all I need is God's love and touch, his eyes only upon me! I have learned that no matter how dark the sky is, no matter how cold the shadows become around me—I will always have God's love-light in my heart... And knowing that—I feel as if I am a burning light in the darkness..."

Natalia became quiet as she noticed that Dolsia had been staring off into the distance. But she could tell that she had been listening carefully. She slowly sat next to her and watched her pale eyes.

"I...I don't know how to love...anymore," Dolsia said as she looked a Natalia. "I have not spoken to anyone but the darkness in many years. The silent darkness is all I've ever known—I am nothing without it. It is all I have..."

"Who has told you those things?" Natalia asked. "That is a lie...straight from the Lord of Darkness himself. That is a stronghold from the enemy that wishes your spirit dead!"

Dolsia became quiet as she stared back off into the distance of the dead garden. "Father, the only one that has loved me—told me that... The voices that come from the darkness tell me that," she said.

"Listen to me, Dolsia," Natalia said with a more urgent tone. "That is a lie... A father who loves his daughter would never say that. Love will never say that! Love is warm light—not cold darkness. The God of Light loves you!"

Dolsia's eyes flashed as she stared into Natalia's. "You say that with such assurance," she said as she raised her voice. "God loves me?! The God of *Light* loves me?!" she yelled. "He loves me enough to cast me away from Nevaeh?! He loves me enough to leave me here upon these dreadful lands?! Answer me this, *human*—does he love me enough to allow this?!" She began to frantically rip the bandages from her arms. Her breathing pattern began to shake as she revealed her white wrists and tender forearms. Purple scars and deep cuts could be seen all down her flesh, as if she had been cutting herself for many years. "And what of this?!" she shrieked. Her eyes widened as she pulled her dark robes from her neck. Her pale neck had scars and deep-red marks all around it.

Natalia put her hand over her mouth as tears swelled up in her green eyes. Her breath was taken away by all of the scars that plagued Dolsia's body. She couldn't stand to look at Dolsia's scars any longer so she turned her gaze away.

"If this is love, then I've been soaking in it every day!" Dolsia pulled her eyes away from Natalia. She took in a deep breath and began to speak calmly. "The first time that I ever cut myself...it felt like a kiss. You see, I became so numb that I had to feel something... The first time darkness touched my skin...it felt like an embrace... I began to connect pain with love. I began to indulge in father's words—and it resonated like a love song in my ears...

"But look at the path that has been set before me," Dolsia said as she looked back into Natalia's weeping eyes. "I've tried to take my life for many years—to rid myself from this world. I know I am only vermin upon the soil and must be rid of. I am not afraid to die, Natalia—because I've been dying with every breath that has filled me... I've tried everything...but death will not take me away from here. I'm cursed, Natalia," she said with a trembling voice as tears began to form in her pale eyes. "Do not blindly tell me that God loves me when I've never seen him or felt him for many years... Do not ever tell me anything about my pathetic life... Pain and suffering are all I've ever known..."

Natalia couldn't stop the tears that fell from her own eyes. She was taken aback and didn't know what to say. She went to touch one of Dolsia's scarred wrists, but Dolsia quickly pulled her arm away.

"Do not touch me!" she yelled, covering her arms with her long sleeves. "Do not ever touch me! Can't you see that everything I touch dies?!" She quickly stood up and walked away from Natalia. "Look all around you, human. Everything is DEAD!" Dolsia began to shake her head as she stared into the dark-gray sky. Tears flowed down her pale cheeks as her chin quivered. "The reason why this tree still stands is because I—I refuse to touch it... The thing that has brought such darkness upon me...is the only thing that brings me joy..."

Dolsia became quiet as she fell to her knees beneath the tree's low hanging branches. She sat for a moment and looked upon the fruit that rested upon the earth, then buried her face in her scarred hands. She began to cry, releasing her pain and suffering that she had carried upon her shoulders for many years. It seemed strange to her that warm tears came from her eyes.

Natalia slowly stood up and wiped the tears that flowed from her own eyes. Her heart broke for Dolsia, but she knew she had to stay strong. She knelt down by Dolsia's side and placed a caring hand upon her robe. She began to have the sudden urge to speak light over Dolsia. It was as if the light inside of her was beginning to swell up, and needed to come out.

"Dolsia…I am so very sorry… I will never understand what you have been through…what you go through every single day. I will never understand such torment. But I know that our God is a loving God. I know it! King Yehoshua was stripped from his armor and died long ago—for us all. He took all of the death, sickness, sadness, and darkness with him when he died… I do not know why darkness continues to walk upon this earth, or why we face hardships. I don't understand why we feel so alone or why we seem to be destined for darkness sometimes… But I do know that sometimes it is a test we must face upon this earth—and sometimes it's an attack from the enemy… The Dark Lord is everyone's enemy and uses our hardships to take hold of us…and our God uses those trials to make things better for us in the future. It is up to us how we face our trials, though…

"We must always remember that King Yehoshua is the last legend that we've come to know! He *is* the last legend! And I have to believe that, Dolsia—and so do you," Natalia said as more tears flooded her eyes. "We have to… In a world that has nothing to offer but darkness—we have to believe in something that saves our souls. Light is the only way! What is the worth of living upon the earth with a dark soul? What is the worth of living such a dark life? We have to believe in the light. We have to—now more than ever!

"You have said for yourself that we all contain the knowledge of *good* and evil because of the fall of the first children of light. That means there is still good. There is good upon the darkness of this world—and that *good* is the love-light of God! We are all blackened with sin, but that blackness was conquered long ago, you see. We must stay true and righteous to see the good in such a dark world. There are always second chances…and we must accept those chances before it is too late."

Dolsia pulled her hands from her face and rested them on her lap. Her eyes stayed still and gazed off into the gray light of the garden. But tears still continued to roll down her cheeks as she listened to Natalia's words.

"Call out to Him, Dolsia! He knows your pain and suffering. He is waiting for you! He will forgive you—he will! Ask him to be part of your life again. Ask him to lead you! He loves you—please believe me! Listen to me, because you will never hear it again after I leave you... I speak the truth...because darkness has nothing to offer but lies and pain and suffering... Learn to wear the armor of King Yehoshua on your heart again... Wear it just as I have. Darkness will always try to have you—but with strong faith and armor—it will never come upon you again!"

"But why would he want to forgive me?" Dolsia asked with a trembling voice. "I...I have been so angry with him for as long as I could remember... Why would he want to forgive someone who has boldly hated and cursed his name?" Dolsia's sad eyes fell away. She was ashamed of herself and couldn't even look back at Natalia's face.

"...How could a loving father not forgive his child?" Natalia asked. Dolsia quickly looked at Natalia. Her calling Dolsia, "His child", seemed to spark something in her heart. "A loving father will hold his arms out to his child in need. He will wait for his long-lost child...he will wait until the very last moment... Remember—you were forgiven long ago. And I believe he has been waiting for you... Go to him as you are, Dolsia..."

Dolsia continued to look at Natalia, into her passionate eyes. Her strong words and uplifting spirit began to awaken something on the inside of her. She sat for a moment longer, then finally stood up.

Natalia watched as Dolsia silently made her way to the tree. She stood for what seemed like forever, just staring at the tree that stood before her.

"You must complete what you came here for, Natalia," Dolsia finally said in a soft voice. "Go down the slope behind the tree and you will find what you came here for..."

Natalia looked up at her in silence. She nodded her head, then stood up. Her heart leapt with joy as she looked at Dolsia. "Thank you," she said as she came to her.

Dolsia nodded her head, then looked away from her. She seemed to be thinking of everything Natalia had told her.

Natalia could tell that the armor was special to her, even though she seemed to carry a strong grudge against the God of Light.

After a silent moment, Natalia went down the slope. She glanced up at Dolsia who was watching her. After a moment, she could no longer be seen as she crept behind the back side of the rocky hill. The bottom of the slope had a large hole in it. It looked like the entrance to a cave of some sort. Natalia slowly crept into the small cave. She noticed that a torch burned, giving faint light to its dark surroundings. She grabbed the torch that stuck out from the side of the dirt wall. As she went along the short dirt path, she noticed that roots of all sizes lined the walls and stuck out all over the cave like a massive spider web. She was right beneath the large tree. The rocky ceiling was just above her head. Her heart sped up with anxiousness as she breathed in the heavy air that smelled of dirt and fungus.

Natalia's heart skipped a beat as her eyes fell upon the legendary armor. The fire from the torch glistened off of the armor, sending warm light upon the dirt walls that looked like fireflies. The beautiful armor rested on the roots that came from the dirt ceiling, making it appear as if an apparition was wearing it. The armor was breathtaking and sparkled like the stars at night.

Natalia sat for hours it seemed, gazing up at the armor and thinking of King Yehoshua. Her eyes never wavered. Her love for Him became stronger at every waking moment.

When she finally came out of her thoughts, she placed her hands upon the smooth, cool armor. She lifted some parts of the armor, amazed at how light it was. Natalia looked at the armor one last time with a smile, then hauled it out from beneath the dark earth.

When Natalia came out of the small cave, falling leaves caught her attention. Dark leaves twirled among the cold sky and danced upon the shadows. She looked up at the tree that sat on the hill. Something was happening that took her breath away. The tree seemed to be dying! It was slowly turning dark-gray and the fruit was beginning to turn black. The vibrantly colored fruit was rotting right before her eyes, falling down to the black soil and bouncing down the side of the hill.

"Dolsia!" Natalia yelled out as she began to run up the slope, dragging the weightless armor as she went.

When she made it to the top, she found Dolsia sitting upon the base of the tree, just crying. The leaves from the tree fell like snow, getting caught in her white hair and the cold breezes of the garden.

"What's happening?" Natalia asked as she raised her hands up to the leaves that fell all around them.

"I did it, Natalia," Dolsia said as tears ran down her cheeks. Her voice held a strange tone of excitement. "I touched the tree… I killed it! But it is okay because—because I am free from its bondages! It shall no longer torment me! It shall no longer remind me of my sin and fall in this world! It's dead, just as my past is!"

A small smile crept over Natalia's face as she came to her. She was touched by Dolsia's growing faith. She looked as if she were changing right before her eyes. She stood over Dolsia, dropping the armor right before her.

Dolsia's watered eyes fell upon the armor. Her breath shook as she slowly placed her scarred, white hands upon the unworldly golden metal. The leaves from the tree fell on it like fallen petals. "This is it…the armor of righteousness and truth. It is the only thing that will not tarnish when I touch it." Silent tears rolled down her face and fell on the precious metal of the armor. "When my eyes fell upon this armor in the past, my heart became convicted and I thought of the God of Light… This armor was brought to me long ago by a very dark king—King Baffmit of the south. He told me his name, which I will never forget…because he was the one who stripped the armor from King Yehoshua, long ago… My heart only craved power then as revenge took over me. When the men of the south came to worship me—I wore this armor as if it were my crown… How ashamed I feel because of it! But that is my past—which I've let go—like the leaves that fall from this tree…

"But you are right, Natalia," Dolsia said with a smile as she looked up at Natalia. "I am loved by my God. And I am forgiven of my dark ways. And I felt his love when I gave up my burdens…," she said as she closed her eyes. She slowly breathed in and out, filling her lungs with new life. "I've always wondered why I kept the armor for this long…and now I know why. There were so many times when my thoughts told me to get rid of it…so I kept it down in the darkness of the earth instead. And I'm glad I've kept it all this time—because this armor has brought you here… You have awakened me—somehow."

Natalia softly smiled. She felt so blessed that she had planted a seed of light in Dolsia's life. She knew then that she had won in her quest and became overwhelmed with emotion because of it. She placed her hand over her chest and pulled her wing pendent from her white bodice. She looked at it with a smile, then took the necklace from her neck.

"Where is your light now?" Natalia asked with a gentle smile as she looked down at Dolsia.

Dolsia was quiet for a moment, then placed her hand over her heart. A smile crept back over her face. "It is within me," she said as her voice trembled with emotion. "…After I touched the tree, I—I spoke to Him, and he heard me… He did… He heard my voice and I am set free…and now know that I *am* loved. I am alive now. My flesh may be covered with scars but my spirit is new!"

Natalia wiped her eyes as she held back tears of joy. She slowly stuck out her hand to Dolsia. "Take my hand, Dolsia—and come with me, then."

Dolsia looked at her hand, beginning to feel nervous as her smile left her face. Thoughts of everything dying passed through her mind. But she began to think of the dying tree again and her being set free from her dark bondages, and those thoughts left her mind quickly. She was reluctant to touch Natalia's hand at first; but after a moment, she reached out her hand and grabbed Natalia's. That was the first time that she had ever felt another human's warm skin. Tears of joy came from her as Natalia helped her up.

"The curse has been lifted from me!" she said with excitement. "When I thought the Dark Lord permanently scarred me with the touch of death…my God has taken it from me! My touch did not take your life! I am forgiven! After all these years…I am finally set free!"

"That is your testimony…you must never forget that. Redeemed you are—by his grace. We cannot see him but we must know that he is near us now…and will always be with us. Now wear this always. Take it as a gift from me," Natalia said as she put her necklace around Dolsia's neck.

"I used to have one like this—but I lost it long ago," Dolsia said as she inspected it with shaken hands.

"It is yours now. Wear it with thanksgiving and never lose it again," Natalia said with a big smile as she gave Dolsia a friendly hug.

Dolsia was shocked at first, but then hugged her back as tears continued to flow. She felt speechless and blown away. She had not felt a loving touch in so long that it was strange to her to feel it then.

…Out of nowhere, a strange dark mist began to grow all around them. It was quick and frightening. It was as if the shadows were becoming alive before their very eyes. The atmosphere became colder and the sky was becoming black as if a dark shroud was being pulled over them.

"What's happening?" Natalia asked as she noticed how cold it had gotten.

"Father is coming…," Dolsia said with a nervous tone as she looked all around.

†

CHAPTER 13
Darkness Rising

"You must go, Natalia!" Dolsia said with wide eyes as she grabbed her arms.

The black mists of the Garden of Nede swirled and began to pulsate around them.

"I can't just leave you now," Natalia said as she grew worried. "If you will not run with me, I will stay with you!"

"Listen to me, Natalia," Dolsia said with flashing eyes. "I must face him alone—he is a stronghold that has haunted me my whole life upon this world. Just as you faced your quest by finding me—I must face mine!"

Natalia nodded her head as she pressed her lips together. She trusted Dolsia because she could now see the light coming from her golden eyes, but her spirit felt uneasy about it.

"Now take the armor and leave this place," Dolsia said with urgency.

Natalia did as she was told and quickly gathered the few pieces of armor together. She quickly ran towards the entrance of the temple, but stopped. She couldn't leave Dolsia now that she had changed. Instead of running, she decided to stay. Natalia quickly hid behind a large stone. She anxiously watched as the darkness all around the garden became thick…

Dolsia stood still as a dark form started to become visible before her. The form walked slowly out of the black mists that had come alive all around her. The tall form just stared at her from the darkness, appearing like an ancient shadow.

"Fa…," she paused, stopping herself from calling the dark form "father". "What do you want?!" she yelled, instead.

The dark form just stayed its distance from her. "I just wanted to speak with you… But I have no words for you now…because I see that you wear the symbol of the enemy upon your chest," it said in a whispered voice.

"No…*you* are the enemy," Dolsia said as her eyes became intense. "You are *my* enemy…"

The dark form became quiet as the black shadows that came from it began to pulsate. The shadows became bigger all around the figure as they began to shriek and growl. The feeling of anger radiated from it.

"You have changed... Come and worship me that I may know you again," the dark voice said.

Dolsia took a step backwards, slowly shaking her head. The shrieks that came from the darkness began to become so loud that it caused overwhelming pain in her ears. Dolsia put her hands over her ears, beginning to cringe. The angry screams and voices were trying to bring her back to the darkness! The shadows from the figure came over to her quickly like a shroud, making her fall to her knees. Dolsia screamed out as the dark figures began to take hold of her, forcing her to bow down to the darkness before her!

"Leave her alone!" Natalia screamed out as she made herself known.

The darkness relented around Dolsia and the creeping figures shrunk back down behind the menacing dark figure. The darkness did not like Natalia's voice.

The Dark Lord just watched Natalia closely as she walked before them.

"You can not have her!" Natalia said in a threatening voice as she now stood between Dolsia and the tall shadowy figure. "She has already devoted her life to the light of Yehoshua! In the name of King Yehoshua—I command you! You must leave this place!"

The figure backed away from Natalia quickly, appalled by her words. "Pathetic human," it whispered. "You speak his name as if he is alive!" it said in a more threatening tone. "Your God has left you long ago... Now listen to me...I am Lord and do not take orders from light-ridden vermin. Now bow down and worship me, human—serve me and I will spare your life just as I've spared Dolsia's all these years..."

Natalia's heart pounded in her chest. She felt her veins throb beneath her flesh as ill-feelings towards the darkness began to swell up inside of her. She began to feel something rise up inside of her like a burning fire. She gave the Dark Lord an intense stare that never faltered. She closed her eyes and said a silent prayer in her heart. When she opened her eyes again, she then noticed Dolsia who stood up proudly by her side. Natalia knew that the light was strong on her side. She noticed how bright Dolsia's eyes appeared in the dark air, as if the light was coming alive on the inside of her.

"We will never bow down to you! ...I will never give you my life again!" Dolsia said with a strong voice.

The Dark Lord that stood before them began to laugh. "Soon, the whole world will bow down to me! Tonight, the moon will glow like blood—and Marrisa's soul will meet its doom!" It began to laugh again, goading the women who stood strongly.

Natalia became angry by the Dark Lord's words. Tears flooded her eyes at the mention of her companion's fate. "Go back to the darkness where you hide! The legna are already on their way towards the Dark Temple of Sacrifice. You are no match for the light that is growing among us!" Natalia screamed out as she pulled her sword from its sheath.

The Dark Lord stood silently as the black mists that swirled around him started to quake.

"I did not come here to fight you, pathetic human," he said as he laughed at Natalia. "For if I did—you'd be dead where you stand." He then gazed at Dolsia, pointing his finger at her. "It is a shame, Dolsia…you have been such an advocate follower of the darkness from the very beginning… I will never forget the moment Natas brought you to me… I have given you eternal life upon this world—and you now decide to follow a pathetic lie. And for that—you will DIE!"

"I've been dead ever since you beguiled me long ago!" Dolsia yelled out with a trembling voice. "You've poisoned me with curses and lied to me ever since I saw you and Natas slither amongst this garden. You have tarnished something that was meant to be beautiful! I'd rather die a thousand times more, knowing that the God of Light loves me, than listen to your disgusting words!"

"So, you shall," the Dark Lord said as he began to levitate in the foul air. "Know this—I will forget you not! This is but a meeting. Because on the new day, you will drink from my WRATH! You will die when light and darkness clash on that new day! You…will…DIE!"

Just then a loud scream came from the Dark Lord as he raised his hands into the black air. A cold wind began to blow around him, taking the dark mists with it. A dark hole opened up behind the Dark Lord as the creeping forms that stood around the garden began to laugh and mock them. Just then the Dark Lord went into the black abyss before them, and vanished, taking the creeping nomed with him…

All around them became silent. It was as if the Dark Lord had never come to the garden. Their ears rang for a moment as they looked all around the dead Garden of Nede. Their breaths were heavy and their hearts thrashed about in their shaken chests. Their knees felt as if they were going to give out as their bodies released overwhelming stress.

"Thank you, Natalia," Dolsia said as she placed her hand on her shoulder. "You will never know how much you have saved my life. I barely know you and I feel as if we are sisters."

Natalia just looked back into her eyes, studying the light that now twinkled in them. "I feel very blessed knowing that I have done something that I would've never been able to do before I came here," she said with a reassuring smile. "But the Dark Lord's threats have made me nervous for you."

"He will have me dead…but I shall be proud to die for the God of Light who has lifted me from this cursed garden," Dolsia said as she placed her hand on Natalia's cheek. "I have been dead for a lifetime…and now that I feel alive, his threats do not frighten me. Do not fret… The flesh may die—time and time again, but the spirit shall live on… You have taught me that—and I will never forget it."

They both giggled as they embraced each other one last time before leaving the Garden of Nede. They obtained the armor and gladly began to make their way across the garden.

Just then something caught their attention as it flew down from the sky. The creature it rode on was quick and agile. It was Gaibriul! Both Natalia and Dolsia watched as Serafim glided smoothly down to the earth.

"I felt something dark stirring," Gaibriul said as he looked at the women from his mighty beast. "Is everything okay?"

Natalia looked at Dolsia with a proud smile. "Yes," she said.

Gaibriul stared at Dolsia who shyly stood before him. Their eyes met for the first time in ages. They locked their gaze on each other, becoming connected as if by a strong cord. A smile came over Gaibriul's face as he looked at her, giving her an understanding nod.

"It warms my heart to see an old friend," he said. "Your face is like a sunrise—just as I've remembered it… We've all been waiting for that sunrise…"

A bright smile came over her face. "…And It warms my heart knowing that I am still accepted by the light," she said, still looking into his eyes. "It is a new day and a new beginning…"

They left the Garden of Nede, never looking back. They understood that the garden was no longer a garden, but a portion of dead earth. They knew it was no longer cursed, and that one day the earth would begin to grow there, carrying on the nature that was meant to be.

Dolsia walked with them with a sense of peace in her heart. It was something that she hadn't felt since the beginning of time. She knew that she was no longer a victim of darkness, but a servant of the God of Light, just as she was meant to be. She was a legna…and was never going back to the darkness again…

†††

Miles away from the fallen Garden of Nede, an angry entity formed from the shadows. A darkened doorway opened up in the middle of a large chamber. The Dark Lord appeared from the misty orb like a shadow. His black silhouette hovered above the dirty stone floor like a quick apparition. His long black robe hung from his tall being and fluttered in the dark air as if it were alive.

The insidious form of the Dark Lord came upon a throne that sat at the back of the chamber. He settled over the throne like a shadow and sat quietly as his breaths cut the silence. His dark shadow became physical upon the throne beneath his black robe.

"My Lord," a voice came from the shadows. The voice was frightening and heavy. "I am not worthy to come before you…but I am your humble servant," the voice said as a large black form appeared. The form was tall and had mighty horns and wings that went out upon the cold chamber. "I must know what you have prepared for me."

The Dark Lord sat still on the large throne. Creeping shadows began to come from him as the darkness began to move all around the shadows of the chamber. nomed came from the shadows and scattered from the Dark Lord's presence, filling the chamber with hundreds of moving dark things.

"You failed me the first time when the boy was to be killed—he is still alive," the Dark Lord said in a low whisper. "You were supposed to smite his existence! You failed me again when the king and his army from the north infiltrated these lands… Now Dolsia has betrayed us and walks with a young girl who speaks his NAME! The foolish girl dared to stand in my presence…"

The black figures that crept about flinched and cowered as the Dark Lord's voice exploded with rage.

"Why do they speak his name when he is dead, Baffmit?!" A black sheet of air began to grow quickly as the Dark Lord became enraged. "I know why… The light keeps burning silently where I can not see it! It must be blown out! The dead king's name must never be spoken by human lips again! It is giving them power to rise against the darkness!"

"It won't be long before they begin to fall. The boy whom you spoke of has been at the Fire Temple," King Baffmit said.

"That means nothing to me!" the Dark Lord roared out. "My eye goes roaming about these lands as a misty shadow. I know his path—where he has been, where he is going! He must be stopped! ...I do not know this boy—my eye can not see his intensions... But he has been troubling me since the beginning." The evil lord began to laugh as he spoke of Tairren. "Does my ancient enemy use the boy to do his work?! A young boy is no match for the powers of darkness. What a fool the self-proclaimed *king* of *light* is! And what of this Ishkarian prince? He has left the Water Temple in ruins! And the girl—she has influenced Dolsia to leave the dark side! FOOLS! The Old Ways are vanishing from the south, falling victim to these filthy light-ridden humans! They are following the legna and must be stopped! If these humans break the barriers of darkness—you will join them upon my wrath, Baffmit!" Black vapors began to come from the Dark Lord as he spoke, appearing as dark flames.

"I will stop them, my lord," Baffmit said. "The wrath of my wings shall blow the light from them. I will redeem myself, my lord. I shall not move unless you command me to do so, great one. What shall you have me do to possess your trust once more?"

"Natas shall rid of them instead. My plans for you are far greater... You must lead the darkness against every living soul who walks upon these lands. I hear a war on the horizon... Hear me when I speak, my obedient nomed! When the moon glows like blood—there will be a new day... On that day, the human sacrifice shall be mine! I declare carnage upon the people of Minslethrate! Marrisa's body must begin to rule with her new power! The world will only breathe darkness. The God who thinks he has won—will be but a tiny flicker of light upon my eye. The legna and their followers will fall...and they will be mine. I command you Baffmit—when the new day comes, which is the last day of light—make your way to the Kingdom of Minslethrate—and kill them. Kill them all..."

"Yes, father," Baffmit said as he bowed his horned head upon the dark atmosphere. "I will do as you command, my lord. No one from the northern kingdom will be left alive!"

The dark chamber exploded with wicked laughter and strange noises. The nomed became excited by the Dark Lord's commands and King

Baffmit's response. The throne room of the Dark Temple of Sacrifice became filled with evil chants as the presence of the Dark Lord became stronger.

✝✝✝

The words of the Dark Lord and the wicked sounds that came from the nomed traveled through the dim halls of the temple. The evil words bounced off of the wet stone of the dark corridors and made its way up the tallest tower and into the chamber that sat at the very top.

Marrisa still hung upon the stone wall as the shackles hugged her raw wrists. Wisps of red hair fluttered across her frozen face as cold breezes masked the room. Her stare penetrated the air as the cold atmosphere licked her skin. Her pale-blue eyes gazed out of the taunting window that was opened right before her. The window was like a dream to her, opening to a world that she couldn't touch. The dark-gray clouds that slowly passed by was like a fresh vision to her. It seemed so close but terribly far away.

Her ears became disturbed as she heard the words that exploded from King Baffmit's mouth. The Dark Lord's declaration became embedded into her lost soul. Cold tears fell down her cheeks as the Dark Lord's threats became a chant in her ears. She thought that she had no more tears left to cry, but when she heard her companions being mentioned, her heart broke all over again. She knew that her loved ones were going to die…and she knew that she was already dead…

Lilith's eyes became like large black wells as she listened to her master's words that crept into the silent chamber. A wicked smile came over her ugly face as she stared at Marrisa's numb-looking countenance. Time was passing by quickly, and everything was going to change when the time was up. A laugh ripped from her rancid mouth and echoed in the dark chamber like a foul song.

"There is no more love left in this world, Marrisa," Lilith said with a cold voice. She stood nearby Marrisa, watching her from the shadows. "Life is full of darkness, is it not? You think your pathetic existence is miserable? The maid I live in now, Lilith, whom you were raised by—has lived a life tormented by the Dark Lord," the nomed inside of Lilith's flesh began to laugh, revealing its true voice. Its voice was heavy and frightening like an overwhelming nightmare. "Poor, sweet Lilith… Your beloved Moira used to love her so long ago. She loved her so much then, that she introduced her to the Dark Lord. I helped Moira teach Lilith how to open the doors to our world…

"Lilith was always meant to be one of us… She grew up in the south where all she knew was darkness! She did not have a chance as you did. It was so long ago… Your legendary God has tried so hard to bring her to the light over the years…failure is so sweet!" A wicked laugh exploded from Lilith's flesh as an ugly smile stretched upon her face. "You see, when you are wanted by the Dark Lord—you can not run! And when you are used by the Dark Lord, you will do great things. And when he is finished with you…your soul will never see the light of day!" A deep laugh rolled off of its tongue, bouncing off the chamber walls.

"Take me if you must," Marrisa's low voice came from her emotionless face. "But know that you will have me because you've stolen everything good away from me…"

Lilith sat quietly, dwelling on Marrisa's surprising voice. It was the first time that Marrisa had spoken that day.

"No…you have given up the night you ignored the owl," Lilith said, then let out a deep chuckle. "Just as Lilith ignored the being of light that tried to influence her, long ago—you have…"

Lilith grew quiet, continuing to stare at Marrisa.

She began to recite strange words, which sounded like dark lyrics.

Darkness is rising,
The light shall fall.
Hearts are sighing
In the dark hall.
The trees are breaking,
Their leaves drift away.
The cold water is trickling
Into another day.
Come with me, oh weary one,
Away from the light and from the sun.
Follow me child, into the Dark Lord's hands,
Away from the earth and from these lands.
You can not fight it; it must be done.
So ready your flesh, oh come.
Darkness is rising,
The light shall fall.

Your heart will awaken
Upon father's call.

Lilith stopped singing, becoming transfixed on Marrisa's beautiful face. "Breathe many breaths, princess… Nearly gone and dying, today will be the last day that you will ever feel life inside of you…"

†

CHAPTER 14
Unexpected Things

The sun was beginning to go down as Moral and Sora anxiously went across the wide-open heath of Prat. It seemed as if hours passed as they went across the sloping fields of the heath. The ground was covered in small bushes and white heather, which made the sky look bigger. The Weeping Road they went along was barely a road and looked like part of the fields. The wind was much powerful among the silent land and carried a cold chill with it. They had been riding in silence most of the way across the land, watching the pale sky on their journey as it slowly went from gray to dark-blue.

"The moors are breathtaking—much larger than I remembered," Moral said as they rode past the small town of Prat.

The town sat among the wide-open spaces of the heath and looked so close even though it was a way off.

A pensive look took hold of Moral's pink face as her gray eyes gazed at the small lights of Prat. "It was so long ago that I've seen Prat—or my parents. I don't even know if they are still living... All of my past is like a dream now, really," she said as her voice faded away.

Moral glanced at Sora who seemed to be lost in deep thought. She had been numb most of the way to Hanon, and Moral wanted to see her smile again.

"Where are you from, Sora?" Moral asked as she tightened her shawl beneath her chin. "Your accent tells me that you were not born in Minslethrate either.

Sora sat quietly for a moment. She looked sad as her eyes stayed focused on the road before them. She held on tightly to the reins and bounced a little as they went across the moors.

"I am from the small islands...many hours past the sea, across from Minslethrate," she finally said in a low voice. "We came here many years ago."

Moral glanced at Sora, having a curious look on her chapped face. "*We*? Who did you come to Minslethrate with?"

"Lady Christianne...she—she is my little sister," Sora said, stuttering. Her eyes looked frozen and her face was emotionless as she spoke. She didn't want to talk about her sister, but she knew she had to say something about her. "Her birth name is Zorrina—our father was the chief of our island... So long ago it was. The last time that I saw my family was before we were sold to Lord Fernund..."

Moral sat for a moment, shocked at what Sora had revealed. She understood her completely. She still remembered the day when her father sold her to Timotheus long ago—which was a blessing in disguise. She then thought of how different Sora and Lady Christianne were, then she thought of Natalia. She always thought that Natalia was both like her mother, and Sora: kind-hearted and stubborn at times.

"Then, Natalia is your niece?" Moral asked with wide eyes.

Sora sat quietly behind the trotting horse that pulled their carriage. She just stared off into the distance, answering her with a nodding head. Tears began to form in her dark eyes again and ran down her dark cheeks upon the cold wind.

Moral noticed the tears and became sad for her. "I'm so sorry, Sora," she said. "I didn't mean to upset you..."

"My sister is dead," Sora bluntly exclaimed, cutting her off. Her eyes watered but she didn't break down and sob as she did before.

"Dear," Moral said, putting her hand over her mouth. "I truly am sorry, Sora."

"Everything seems out of control... I feel as if my world is crashing down right before me! My niece is in the Forbidden Lands and my sister is dead! Everyone I've ever known at the manor...is dead! What am I going to do, Moral?" Sora cried out as tears flowed. She looked at Moral with eager eyes. "What am I going to do?"

Moral's heart broke for Sora as she looked into her frightened face. "You have to live on strong, Sora...that's what you have to do," Moral said as she placed a kind hand on her back. "When I lost my husband—I thought that my whole world was over... It was the darkest time of my life... During that time, I felt that my heart was finished. Timotheus was my everything... But when I looked into my son's sad eyes, I knew that my purpose was to be there for him...and his existence reminded me of God's love for me. My husband left behind a legacy of life that I will never forget...," Moral said as tears came to her eyes. "...But—I was so angry at God then—wondering why—why such a mighty God would allow my loving husband to die. How could a father allow his son to die?

Timotheus loved God with all of his heart—and he fell victim to the hands of darkness…

"But what keeps me smiling, Sora—is that I know I will see him one day in the afterlife," she said with a smile. "I believe it and I know I will see him one day, praising God with an open heart—just as he always did upon this earth… And over these many years, I've learned that our life on this earth is but a quick walk—filled with tests and struggles that make us stronger. Our real home is with God… I do not understand why we go through the things we do…why good people suffer… But I do know my God—and that makes every day worth it."

Sora's chin trembled as she looked at Moral. She wiped the tears from her eyes, trying to smile with some effort.

"But my sister…my sister never knew Him… Zorrina always told Natalia that the God of Light was nothing but a legend, a whimsical fairytale. *"It's foolishness,"* she would say…," Sora said, ashamed. "She never knew him…"

Moral grew quiet, then looked into her eyes. "…Do you *know* him?" she asked.

Sora sat silently, then shrugged her shoulders. Tears flooded her eyes again. "I…I don't know," she said. "All my life I've walked alone…taught to depend on myself and no one else… And I'm tired…," Sora said, looking at Moral. A tear glistened down her cheek as the cold wind blew upon her. "I want to always feel that I have something strong inside of me that will refresh me and keep me going. I want to know him, Moral… You have something special on the inside of you—and it keeps you strong. I want that…"

Moral softly smiled at her. "Then you shall know the secret to eternal life. All that call on Him, shall be saved… Say this sacred prayer after me and just believe," she said.

Moral said the prayer with a smile, which was the same prayer that Timotheus had blessed her and Tairren with many years ago.

Sora repeated after Moral, and after it was all said and over with, she strangely felt rejuvenated. She was beginning to feel refreshed, as if a yoke had been lifted from her shoulders. A soft smile came over her face as her heart fluttered with a sense of peace and joy. She knew that she had invited something powerful and special into her life; she could feel it with every beat of her heart.

"Thank you, Moral," Sora said as her tears dried on her cheeks. A large toothy smile came over her round face.

"Let this be a new beginning, Sora. Allow your old flesh to fade away…it shall be made new," Moral said.

Sora chuckled a little as she noticed how happy Moral looked. "Yes—it shall be made new," Sora repeated with a smile.

✝✝✝

They finally made it to the outer boundaries of Hanon just as the sun was going down. They saw in the distance, a manor estate that sat before the kingdom. Warm lights from the manor's windows could be seen among the dim sky of the evening. They began to grow anxious and weary as the cold night began to come upon them quickly.

Moral remembered that her husband had once told her that his family's home was the first to be seen after passing Prat. She could tell just by looking at the massive manor that the family of Timotheus was very wealthy. She became nervous just by looking at it. The manor looked like a small castle from afar.

They hurried to the Manor, passing its fields and crops, making it there just as the sky turned black.

They glanced at one another before hopping off the coach bench.

Moral grabbed the sword from the coach, and they quickly made their way to the entry-way doors. Moral glanced at Sora, then took a deep breath. She was incredibly nervous and felt unworthy to even stand before the doors. She thought she looked like a poor beggar woman standing upon the grand porch of the manor. She had never met her deceased husband's family before and didn't even know what she was supposed to say or do.

"…What am I doing here?" Moral said in a low tone as reality set in. She stared blankly at the doors. "These people have never seen me—nor do they know who I am… They may not even believe that Timotheus was my husband… I don't even know what I am to say to them. Will they even allow us to speak to them? How strange we must look…a peasant woman and a servant, knocking on doors as the sun goes down!" Moral said in a whispery voice.

"If you feel that God has sent you here, then you must knock," Sora said with wide eyes. She pressed her round lips together, then smiled. "Just this afternoon this meeting was urgent—now you question it? You said that the unworldly owl told you to come here with your husband's sword. You said it was written deeply within your heart to do so. You must do this, then. There must be a reason why you are here. Just as you've told me, I am telling you now…*trust* in Him," she said in a more serious tone.

Moral nodded her head as she tightened her grip on the hilt of the sword. The palms of her hands grew clammy and her heart began to pound with overwhelming nervousness. She quickly rested the tip of the sword upon the ground so that she didn't look threatening, then she cleared her throat. She took a deep breath, then boldly grabbed the door-knocker and hit it against the heavy door.

They stood in silence, waiting for someone to open it. They looked at each other with anxious eyes as silence became loud all around them. The wind swept through the porch, pushing at the leaves of all the potted plants that sat about. Then just as they were beginning to become worried, the door could be heard being unlatched from the inside. Their eyes shot open as their hearts sped up.

Moral quickly turned towards the door which slowly creaked open. "Hello," she said nervously, staring at the servant man who opened the door. "Forgive me for knocking at such a late hour. But—well…my name is Moral, and this is Sora… I'm so sorry for bothering the household, but, please—I must speak to the lord of the manor."

The man glared at Moral, then at Sora. "The lordship is entertaining his guests as we speak. He will not want to speak with peddler women at this hour," he said quickly, then began to pull the door shut.

Moral quickly stopped the man from closing the door. "Please, sir," she said in a shaken voice. "If only for a moment—I must speak with him!"

The servant continued to look at her, then noticed the sword she was holding. His eyes slightly widened as he glanced at Moral then at Sora, then back at the sword. He took in a deep breath as his eyes widened more, as if he had remembered something of great importance. He appeared as if he was looking at something that he had been longing to see.

"My, my… He's not gone mad after all…," the man said to himself as he put his hand over his mouth. "Please, do come in. Come in! You must be tired," he said quickly as he welcomed them into the manor.

They walked into the opened door, feeling surprised and confused by his strange reaction.

Moral glanced at Sora having an incredulous look on her face, then watched the frantic man as he quickly closed the door. Moral could tell by his attire that he must've been the head-servant of the household. She could also tell that he seemed to be really anxious and excited all of the sudden. He looked as if he were inviting royals into the manor. She watched as he beckoned a nearby servant girl, who came to him quickly. She couldn't hear what he was saying, but he said something quick and low into her ear; and then she bowed to them, and hurried into a nearby hall.

"Please, ladies," he said as he began to walk off quickly. "Follow me to the east wing and I will have you settled in with hot baths and fresh linens. The cook is settling the kitchen down, but I will have him prepare a meal for you. There is always something delicious to have prepared in the manor," he said quickly as he hurried through the great hall. Moral and Sora just followed him, looking all around the beautiful interior of the manor. "Come along ladies, don't be frightened," he said as he noticed the incredulous looks on their faces. "Yes, the manor is massive and quite a relic, but it is respectable and blessed with a face of elegance."

Moral followed close behind him, taking in the beauty of the manor. She had never set foot into a noble home before, and never thought that she ever would. Rushing through the elegant halls and up the magnificent staircases, she began to notice that many servants had stopped what they were doing just to take a look at them. She began to feel embarrassed, not fully understanding what was going on. It was strange to her that only moments before they were out in the dark cold, begging to speak with the head of the house; and now they were being welcomed into the grand home and treated like favorable guests.

"Here we are," the man said as he stopped in a quiet corridor, before a polished door. He opened the door, revealing an exquisite and rather large chamber. "These are your quarters for resting. Your handmaidens will be here quickly," he said as he gestured for them to enter.

Moral glanced at Sora, then walked into the room. Sora followed behind her, looking very nervous. Both of them glanced around the chamber, feeling strange that they weren't there to serve anyone.

"Shall I take your sword?" the man asked.

Moral kindly put it in his hands. "It was my husband's," she said with a smile as she brought her hand over her chest.

The man looked surprised at first, becoming quiet for a moment. But then he smiled at her and bowed his head to her. "Lady Valor," he said in a low tone. "I am pleased to finally meet you," he said.

Moral's smile faded as her mouth fell open. She was shocked and touched. She had not heard her last name spoken in many years. She herself hadn't uttered her married name ever since her husband had died. Her heart fluttered. She didn't know what was going on, and now she was confused as ever, realizing that a perfect stranger knew who she was.

"Forgive me, sir," Moral said as he turned to leave the room. "I only asked to speak with the lord of the manor. Your gesture is kind, but—we do not need to be waited upon," she said.

The man turned and just looked at her, surprised. "His lordship wishes it," he said.

Moral just stared at him, still having a confused look on her face. How could the lord wish it if she herself didn't even know that she was going to be there?

"Forgive me, Lady Valor," he said. "I thought you would've known." He cleared his voice and came closer to her. "We've been expecting you…both of you," he said as he watched both Moral and Sora look at each other with surprised looks on their faces. "I believe I've begun this all wrong; forgive me," he said, then cleared his throat again. "Welcome to the Valor Manor of Hanon," he said with a smile. "My name is Finagin, but you may call me Fin if you like, my lady. I am head-servant of the Valor Manor and have served in this household for many years… Lord Timotheus has made it known and very clear, that when you arrive, everything shall be in order… Now I must go, he will want to speak with you soon."

Then Finagin quickly left, closing the door behind them. The room became quiet as the women stood for a moment, taking in everything that had just happened within the short amount of time that had passed.

They walked around, looking at the high ceiling, beautiful marble columns, the grand fireplace that sat in the corner of the room, and the many lounging chairs that sat around, covered with lavish pillows. A beautiful golden candelabrum hung from the ceiling, and the walls were adorned with paintings and golden candlestick holders. Right in the center of the chamber was a massive arched threshold that led out to a balcony, and to complete the room, two welcoming beds sat on either end of the chamber. And on both sides of the beautiful room were doorways which led to bathing chambers.

"I feel as if I should be serving someone in this chamber," Sora said with a smile as she walked over to Moral. "I feel out of place," she said.

"I don't understand anything that is taking place," Moral said as she carefully sat down on one of the decorative couches. "How did they know we were coming?" Moral asked as she looked at Sora who sat next to her.

Sora shook her head. "This is stranger than any dream I get," she said. "And you were married into this noble family?" she asked with wide eyes.

"My husband was a nobleman—but left this life long ago. You see, I've always been a peasant. I was the daughter of a blacksmith from Prat. I met Timotheus as he passed through Prat…and we fell in love…" A smile came over Moral's face. "We traveled to Minslethrate and started a new life in the Forest Provence… We got married in Minslethrate and had Tairren in the forest. I've lived there in that quaint little cottage ever since…"

Moral became quiet as she thought of her deceased husband. She thought of how her husband had never really talked about his father's manor or his wealth. He never boasted of his family and accepted the peasant life with open arms. She thought they lived a rich life in the Forest Provence among Minslethrate. They didn't have wealth for the finest things in life, but she knew they were blessed, and she was thankful for the quaint life her husband had prepared for her. She wouldn't take that back for anything and thanked God daily for the simple life that she did live.

Just then there came a knock at their door. Sora quickly got up from her seat and rushed over to the door, opening it. Two young servant girls came into the room and smiled at them. They bowed their heads and introduced themselves as their personal hand-maidens for that evening. Then they led each one of them to their own bathing chamber where they prepared hot baths mixed with scented oils and herbs for them. After the women were finished bathing, the servant girls had them pick out their own gowns for that evening and fixed up their hair.

Both Moral and Sora accepted everything with thankful smiles, unable to contain the joy that rose in their hearts. As they thought that the showering of pleasantries was coming to an end, more servants came in and had a decadent meal prepared for them on a table in their room. The servants waited on them hand and foot, standing nearby their table like statues waiting to be called. Of course, they weren't needed that much as both of the women buttered their own bread and poured their own wine. Then after they thought that the meal was over, the servants brought them sweet pastries and decadent chocolate for dessert. After they joyfully chatted among each other while eating till they were full, they were led down to the drawing room to have wine with the lord of the house.

†

CHAPTER 15
A Divine Meeting

Moral and Sora sat in the drawing room, chatting quietly with one another as a quartet played a lovely piece of music in the background. They sat upon a decorative couch, in front of a large fireplace. The servants of the room offered and poured them a goblet of wine. They gladly accepted, feeling overwhelmed by the generous hospitality that was offered to them that evening.

Just then Finagin came into the room. He announced Lord Timotheus' and Lady Dilia's presence as they followed him. Moral and Sora stood up quickly and watched as Lord Timotheus hobbled into the room with a beautifully hand-crafted cane. He was followed by Lady Dilia who looked a little younger than him. They were both well stricken with age, but the kind smiles that they had on their faces made them look youthful. They were both dressed in fine garments and carried themselves with grace. They looked very happy to meet the women.

Both Moral and Sora respectfully bowed their heads as they came to them. Lord Timotheus gestured for them to sit as he slowly took his seat across from them. The women sat silently, waiting for Lord Timotheus to say something. They watched as Finagin poured them all a fresh goblet of dark-red wine.

Moral kept looking at the lord and lady, amazed at how much her deceased husband had looked like them, especially the lord. She realized that Timotheus looked exactly like his father. They had the same handsome facial structure and the same dark-blue eyes, which was passed down to Tairren, she thought. She thought the lord must've had black hair once, just as her husband did, but his was white as snow. She then glanced at the lady who sat upright and very proper. She noticed how she clasped and rested her hands on her lap and had a constant smile on her glowing face. Moral became slightly emotional at the thought of meeting Timotheus' parents for the first time.

"...Lord Timotheus," Moral finally said with a smile, "I feel so blessed that I am finally meeting you. My name is Moral and this is my lovely friend, Sora," she said as Sora smiled at both of them. "We thank you so much for welcoming us into your home and for sharing your kind hospitality with us. Anyone who sets foot in your house is truly blessed… We have traveled from Minslethrate to speak with you—and I'm thrilled that we finally get to."

Lord Timotheus smiled at her with twinkling eyes. He then gestured for Finagin to bring him something. Finagin scampered away quickly, then came back into the dim room moments later. He held the sword that Moral had brought with her. He gave it to the lord who accepted it with a great smile. Lord Timotheus looked over it for a moment with sparkling eyes. Tears began to form in his old eyes as he brought his hand across the old sword.

"This sword—is a very old sword," he finally said. His voice was low and sounded comforting. "This sword was passed down from generation to generation. It has been with the Valor men for many years. I gave it to my eldest when he turned of age." He looked at Moral who listened respectfully. "Time went by, and my bright-eyed son began a thirst for adventure, bringing that sword with him wherever he went. He loved traveling, and when he began his walk as a man, he left the manor." The old man looked back at the sword. "Timotheus was my eldest son, and I proudly named him after me…" He then looked back at Moral as a smile came over his face. "Moral Valor…I believe you are part of this family," he said. "I never thought I would get the chance to meet you."

Moral smiled as tears gathered in her gray eyes. It warmed her heart to be around family, especially her husband's, even if she never knew them before that night.

"Timotheus was a good son, who loved his parents very much," he said, looking at his wife who smiled at him lovingly. "He wrote us every month… He wrote of you, Moral, and how much he loved you," he said, noticing the tears that began to trickle down her cheeks. He pulled an unused handkerchief from his robe and handed it to her with a kind smile. "He wrote of your life in the forest. I was never surprised because I knew that he loved everything about the outdoors. I remember he seemed to be outside riding his horse or searching the lands more than he ate!" the lord said with a chuckle. "He always said that nature was the closest thing to God, besides his heart… He also wrote of his son, Tairren—my grandson… I never was able to write him back…I never knew where you were all living. A small cottage in the forest was all that he ever mentioned in his letters…"

Moral wiped her tears and nodded her head. She was touched that Timotheus had been writing to his parents that whole time. But she wished they could've visited when her husband was alive…so that Tairren could've met them. She never knew he continued to keep in contact with them, but she was very thankful that they knew of both her and Tairren.

"But the last letter that I received from my son…was the strangest of all. He wrote to me that he had a dream that two women with a sword came to my house—needing an army…"

Both Moral and Sora glanced at each other, speechless. They were confused as ever, thinking about everything that was going on. It was a strange coincidence that both her and Sora came to Lord Timotheus' door with his sword.

"That was long ago—about six years ago, I think," he said as he looked at his wife. She nodded her head, confirming that it was so. "And after that…I never received a letter from my son again…"

Moral began to cry as she brought the handkerchief to her eyes. Her heart broke as she sat before her deceased husband's parents. She didn't want to tell them that he had been dead for six years, and her heart cried out that they were speaking on about him.

Lord Timotheus placed his hand on Moral's shoulder. Small tears swelled in his old blue eyes; but he didn't cry. He seemed to already know of his son's passing and seemed to have peace about it.

"I already know… My son is with the great God of Light, living in a kingdom of eternal love," he said with a smile.

Moral stopped crying, surprised by the man. She peered at him from the moist handkerchief. She thought that he would've broken down by the thought of his son dying many years ago. She began to feel the sadness lift from her shoulders as she looked into his dark-blue eyes.

"I am so happy that you've finally come…because you sitting here with us in my home, confirms everything that was revealed to me long ago," he said, wiping a tear from Moral's cheek. "You will never understand the joy that leapt in my heart. When I was informed by one of my servants that you had arrived in your room I had prepared for you, I just laughed with joy. God is amazing and mysterious! You should've seen the looks on my guest's faces when I ended the night earlier than expected," Lord Timotheus said with an old chuckle. His laugh faded as he looked back at Moral.

"I'm going to tell you something that I've told my wife, and my entire staff of the Valor Manor," he then looked out of the massive window that took up much of the wall space. The night's sky was pitch black, having not even one star out. "It was not even a year after the last letter from my son, when it happened... I was sitting upon the gardens in the cool of the day, praying. I had been worried for my son's sake who had not written to me in many months... As I was praying, the sound of mighty feathers rustling in the breezes startled me. I looked up, and behold—a mighty bird that looked like it breathed light, sat upon a tree in the garden.

"At first, I thought I was daydreaming, then I thought it was my old eyes deceiving me like they sometimes do... I stared at it for what seemed like hours to me. I still remember to this day, how it spoke to me... It told me that my son had fallen victim to evil hands. I knew then that my son had died... But it also told me not to be sad or frightened, because he now lives in a land of eternal love and light... It also revealed to me that my son's wife, you Moral, and a companion would come to my household with his sword...and that I must prepare for them an army of strong men...

"You can only imagine the thoughts that went through my old head! The owl's words confirmed what my son had written to me about! The God of Light has been and is speaking to us! The owl revealed to me that darkness would have the Kingdom of Minslethrate—and that I would know when the time was near...for the two women would come to my door with his sword... All this time, over the years, most of my servants thought that I'd gone mad. And I was beginning to think that the owl was just a figment of my old imagination... But I told them all these years to keep their eyes out for two women and a sword... I didn't know the time or day that it would happen—but I had faith that it would. And now, here you are, both of you—sitting before me with my old sword!"

Moral placed her hand over her mouth, remembering everything that Tairren had told her days ago. She remembered how he mentioned the great owl, and how she had even seen the mysterious owl herself.

"I believe you, Lord Timotheus," Moral said in a low voice. "I have seen the owl two times... The first time the owl came to me—it spoke to my heart, telling me that my son was protected by the hand of God as he walked upon the Forbidden Lands of Minslethrate. Then the second time, the owl told me that I must come here to Hanon to Timotheus' house with his sword... It's all coming together... You see...there is something dark happening in our kingdom as we speak. The princess of Minslethrate has been kidnapped, and there are strange occurrences that have been happening in our kingdom. Tairren has gone to the south with Prince Phillip from Ishkar, and with Sora's niece, Lady Natalia. And King Julpen has also journeyed towards the south with his army..."

"Yes, there has been strange gossip among the courtiers of Hanon," Lady Dilia spoke up, having a concerned look on her elegant face. "We were there at Princess Marrisa's birthday celebration—but we were told that she had run away," she said, glancing at her husband, then back at the women. "...I fear that the gossip revolves around murders...and the sightings of strange beasts that are lurking upon Minslethrate."

Moral glanced at Sora who looked frightened by the news. She placed her hand on Sora's back, remembering that Sora had just lost her sister and companions by the dark hands of evil.

"That is the workings of evil that was revealed to me by the owl many years ago... Darkness such as that can not be spread to other kingdoms! Man will be threatened if it does... I've injured my leg long ago in a war," Lord Timotheus said, patting his right leg. "I can't feel much in it. But my point is that I've led my king in wars long ago in my youthful years. I was the commander of the Hannonites for many years. But after the injury of my leg, I retired to my father's house, this house, and carried on the cultivation of our crops that our great God has blessed us with...

"But to this day, I am still well respected by our king and the men of Hanon, you see. All these years that I've served the king of Hanon—he has blessed me back ten-fold. Old age has overcome him, but he is like my brother. You see, the king has rewarded me by allowing me to influence the army of Hanon if needed... What I'm trying to tell you is that—at my bidding, the Hannonites shall join Minslethrate in war if needed..."

"I see," Moral said, feeling speechless. She knew that strange things were happening in the lands, but she never expected that war would come upon them. "What are you saying that I should do?" Moral asked, becoming nervous.

"I propose this, and will see to it that the King of Hanon shall know it in the morning: I will send an army over to Minslethrate when the sky is much lighter, led by Sir Andor. Sir Andor followed under my wing like a son for many years when I led the Hannonite men... We shall negotiate with Minslethrate and join forces with them."

"Thank you, Lord Valor," Moral said with a smile. Even though she didn't know exactly what was happening, she was happy that Minslethrate would have a new stronghold of men. "Lord Fernund is sovereign over Minslethrate temporarily while King Julpen and his men journey across Minslethrate to find Marrisa. Sora knows Lord Fernund well—he is married to Lady Christianne, her sister...," Moral said, glancing at Sora with a kind face. "I believe that Lord Fernund will be more receptive to Sir Andor and the Hannonites coming if Sora meets with him as well."

A smile came over Lord Timotheus' face. "It warms my heart that you two are here. I feel blessed that I've kept my faith for all these years... You are a wise woman," he said. "You were destined to be part of our family. Courage runs in your veins... I know this is a divine meeting directed by God. We are all connected on some level, meant to be here... And knowing that my grandson, Tairren, is journeying across forbidden lands to save a princess—reveals how much character he has. My legacy is complete...and honors God to the fullest!"

Lord Timotheus then grabbed his cane, and pulled himself up. The women stood up as well, realizing how late it was getting.

"Now, let's depart and retire," he said with a smile. "Your quarters are ready for you and the morning shall come quickly," he said, looking at both Moral and Sora.

He embraced both of them with Lady Dilia doing the same thing. The lord and lady smiled at them, looking on them as if they were their daughters.

Both Moral and Sora respectfully bowed their heads to them with smiling faces, then watched as they hobbled out of the dim drawing room. Their young servant girls came into the room, then led them up the main staircase and back to their room. They walked silently to their chamber. The overwhelming thought of war settled over their minds as reality revealed itself to them. They thought of their loved ones and wondered if they were well...

Moral thought of Tairren; she wondered if he was warm and ate something that night. She thought of her husband and how proud she was of the legacy that he left behind him. She also thought of the Valor family— she was thankful that God had brought her to them. She didn't know what the morning was going to bring, but she had faith in God that everything was happening the way it was supposed to.

Sora thought of Natalia, wondering if she was safe and sound with Tairren and Prince Phillip. Her mind also drifted back and forth to her sister and to poor Lord Fernund. She wondered if Alexa was able to speak with the lord. She thought of Lord Fernund and wondered if he was heartbroken over the tragic news of her sister's death. She then hoped that Lord Fernund would stay strong while King Julpen was away. She thought of what the morning would bring and the look that would be on Lord Fernund's face when she would arrive at the castle. She didn't even know how she was going to tell Lord Fernund that she brought with her the Hannonite army when she did arrive.

The days just seemed to get darker and more uncertain. How was there going to be a war in the Kingdom of Minslethrate? Who would ever lead evil hands against the quiet and peaceful kingdom? Just then Sora hoped that everything was just a mistake. She hoped that Minslethrate would be spared from any war of any kind.

✝

CHAPTER 16
Penitence

Lord Fernund stared into the fireplace. His dark eyes were glazed over and his face was silent. He thought of his wife. He had been staring into the fire for what seemed like many hours. He still had dirt beneath his fingernails from digging a grave for his wife earlier that evening. He refused to let anyone else bury Lady Christianne, so his soiled hands and arms ached. He felt numb and drained as he sat. Even upon the warmth of the crackling flames, he felt cold. His eyes burned and his head throbbed. He sat still like a statue in the large chair of King Julpen's study. The hall was dark and the only light was from the roaring fireplace.

He thought of his wife's face. Her face was always something he adored about her. She was so beautiful and her eyes looked like the sea in the sunlight. But his image of her quickly changed when he thought of how black her eyes were before she collapsed... He thought of what she looked like when she screamed upon the Ducre' Manor earlier that evening. He didn't understand what had happened to his wife. He didn't understand why her eyes were so black or why her skin was cold as ice. The thought of blood then flashed through his aching mind. She seemed dead when he saw her. She had no life in her. She had not an ounce of life. And now her body lay dead beneath a pile of cold dirt... He thought of when she screamed like a Banshee; the black that came from her mouth was like thick, whirling smoke.

Goosebumps came over his flesh as his mind thought of the black shadow that came from her mouth. "What was it?" he thought.

It was something terrifying that lived inside of her. Why would it have picked her? Hadn't she been tortured enough in her own loneliness and madness?

The thing that forced itself inside of her was a cruel shadow of darkness. The shadow had eyes. It had eyes that flashed with anger.

He didn't understand it. He didn't understand anything that was going on. His world had been flipped upside down. He felt like he was stuck in a nightmare—a really long, horrible nightmare...

"I know what troubles you, Lord Fernund," an old voice said from behind him.

The marquis jumped in his skin, not realizing that Master Odwa had walked into the hall. He quickly sat up strait in the throne-like chair. He rubbed his unshaven face as the old man stood silently before him.

"What troubles me is that I cannot sleep anymore," the marquis mumbled.

Master Odwa was quiet for a moment, studying the anxious look on his face. He noticed that his eyes looked tired and his countenance was covered with sadness.

"We are breathing upon a world that knows only darkness," Master Odwa said as he placed his frail hand upon his shoulder. "You may wonder where the light must be in it all... I know that you buried your loved one this evening upon the gardens of your home," the old man said in a low tone. "I hear you made Lady Christianne a precious resting spot..."

"She used to love to walk in the gardens long ago when she first came to Minslethrate," the lord said with a solemn face, cutting him off. "That was so long ago...when life seemed much happier—when she was more alive..."

"...I did not know Lady Christianne personally, but she seemed like a wonderful woman," Master Odwa said.

"She changed over the years... There came a time when I barely knew her," the marquis said with some effort. His voice began to shake as emotion came over him. "I let her fall, Master Odwa," he said as he hunched over. He buried his face into his hands. "I let her change! Not only did I let her change but I taught her how to have a heart of greed! She began to love wealth more than her family...just as I did..." He looked up at the old man with frightened eyes. "And now she is gone... If I would've been at home instead of this retched castle, I could've done something for her!" He began to cry, not able to contain himself anymore. "I put my obligations before her as I've always done. What good is power when my family has fallen apart? I wanted wealth to feed my family—instead I have fed my family to wealth! I left my wife for months when I traveled! I left her all alone with her gowns and jewels, wine and money! It's my fault she had changed... It's my fault that she is dead...

"You would have gotten sick if you had seen her eyes, Master Odwa!" he yelled as he looked up at the old man. "Her eyes were black as night and had no life in them! Something had happened to her that I can't explain. Everyone, my staff, my cook, the gardeners, and even the young ones— were all dead! Dead! They all bled from their chests! I think Christianne killed them! She killed them all... What kind of man am I to leave my wife—only to drive her deep into a darkened state of madness?!"

The marquis brought his face to his shaken hands and began to sob. He had never cried like that and seemed to release emotions that he kept deep within himself. He felt like a mortified child again, sitting before his father.

Master Odwa placed his hand on the lord's head. "You have not done what you say, Lord Fernund... Your wife was a victim of the darkness that is covering Minslethrate. Your wife did not kill all those people... She was innocent upon the evil hands of darkness just as those poor servants were. It was the enemy who has taken your wife and servants. I've seen it before, Marquis... The black eyes, the blood, the shadows that move like creeping things... I've seen it before...and it is darkness becoming alive before us." His eyes widened below his feathery eyebrows. "We must stay strong, son. God help us—we must stay strong. We must have faith and stay strong with the almighty God's word upon our tongues!" Master Odwa's voice raised as passion whirled inside of his old heart.

"That is how I've gotten through the darkness that tried to have this kingdom long ago! Many years ago, many people were being killed as I sent praises to my God from deep down in the clutches of prison. God pulled me through because I knew he would. His plan for me was and is still happening... I thought that I would've been burned at the stake as a martyr! Evil hands could not take me. When I fell—I got back up in *His* name. When I fell again—I got back up stronger, in *His* name! It is a weapon, Marquis!" He raised his bony hands into the air.

"When you have the light inside of you—you must use that power to repel evil and its wicked attacks! You must! Now that you have the light inside of you, the enemy will attack again and again and again! Darkness is restless and will never stop until you yield to it. But you must never fall victim to darkness! Put it beneath your feet, Marquis. Tell your past to move! Shut up your flesh and push aside the strongholds that come over you. And when you do, marquis, you will become strong. Your spirit will grow and the light will burn within you like a great fire..."

Lord Fernund pressed his lips together and slowly nodded his head. Master Odwa's words were powerful and refreshing. A faint smile came over him as he took in everything the wise old man had said to him.

"Start now, Marquis. Tonight! Tonight, you become new—tonight you start as a fresh morning does in the springtime. These hard times of uncertainty are but tests...and you will become stronger because of them.

Thank the lord for your life! Use the rest of your life to change things, to set a legacy before you that God would be proud of... In time, God uses these broken things—and turns them into blessings. Tonight, your eyes are wide open... Now that you can see, spread the light that burns inside of you and spread it like a fire upon the darkness..."

Lord Fernund stood up and looked into the old man's sparkling eyes. Just then he thought he saw a light flash from them, looking like stars at night. He smiled and embraced the old man. He felt as if he were set on fire by the old man's words.

"Yes, Master Odwa," he said. "Tonight, I am new. Thank you... You inspire me like no other. I want to be that man whom you speak of so strongly."

Master Odwa smiled and chuckled a little. "So, you shall," he said. "Declaring it over yourself is the first step of many. Heavy burdens will come over you again—but you must push them aside!"

"Tomorrow is a new day, Master Odwa," the marquis said as he walked over to the great windows that looked out to the castle gardens. He looked out of the windows, noticing that the moon seemed to finally come out from the black clouds. "I feel as if I hadn't seen the moon in years... Tomorrow is the Spring Festival. Even during such a dark time—we will celebrate!" he said, feeling a little inspired. "We should carry on as if nothing has happened. We must encourage the people of Minslethrate just as you have encouraged me."

"Yes, Lord Fernund," the old man said as he stood next to the marquis. "But we should never allow danger to escape our minds... We should remember that anything could happen when we least expect it..."

They both stood quietly, looking out of the massive window as the fireplace roared behind them. They could see the garden that night as the moonlight glowed upon the earth. Everything looked peaceful and silent, which was something they hadn't seen or felt in a while. The moon poured its soft light down on them, filling the window with its charm. The surprising moon seemed larger that night, beginning to take on a warmer shade of light orange. The strange moon looked upon them with a full face... Its color was slowly changing as the night went by.

"The moon will be deviant this night," Master Odwa said as he gazed upon the glowing disc. "The spring equinox is at hand—the beginning of a new moon, a new day, and new year..."

†

CHAPTER 17
Bewitched

Tairren slowly opened his eyes. His eyelids felt heavy and his head pounded and ached. His vision was blurry at first, but after a moment the haziness went away. He realized that he was looking up at an orange moon in the night sky. The black sky was open above him and the moon was glowing upon him with its fullness. Tairren brought his hand to his forehead and sat up. He realized that his skin felt hot and wet. He looked all around, slowly awakening from what seemed like a deep, long sleep.

As he looked, he realized that he was sitting in a warm pool. The pool was in a rectangular shape and was filled with clear, warm water. The aroma of something spicy and sweet came from the water, reminding him of the scent of rosemary and other herbs. He searched with his eyes the room he was in, wondering where he was. He turned his head, surprised by a rush of wind that hit his back. His breath was taken away as he realized that he wasn't in a chamber at all, but a large area that looked like a veranda or terrace. There was no wall behind him and the space opened out to a vast, dark land of mountains. The mountains were steep and seemed to go on for miles and miles.

Marble Columns and arches stood tall all around him, holding up a ceiling that had a large opening in it so that the sky could be seen. Large pots of fire and torches crackled and glowed all around him, sending dancing shadows everywhere. The stone walls were painted with brightly colored, fascinating designs.

Tairren felt confused as he looked around. He didn't remember how he ended up in there. He didn't even remember what he was doing. His mind was cloudy, and he still felt tired. He realized that he had nothing on but an undergarment. He glanced around, trying to bring his thoughts together. His eyes wandered until they saw warm light that peeked through the black silhouettes of wide columns. He looked through the columns, becoming fascinated by the chamber on the other side. He noticed that the large cavern was filled with fire light. A glorious fire burned in the center of the cavern, filling it with waves of hot air.

As Tairren peered through the columns, he noticed a dark figure walking towards him. He couldn't see who it was until the fire from the terrace touched the figure's body.

The figure belonged to a woman—a very striking and exotic woman. She wore nothing but pearls and jewels that draped and dangled around the parts that shouldn't have been seen. Beneath the jewels, golden, sparkling paint could be seen. The gold paint had been blotched and smeared on her skin, making her appear like a lustrous idol. Her long black hair fell down her back and her head was adorned with a crown. She gazed at him with intense eyes as she walked into the terrace.

She slowly stepped into the warm water, silently moving towards him. Steam rose up from the water as she went, as if she were hot to the touch. The water went to her waist, and she caressed the surface with her fingertips as she moved.

"Hello, my god," she said in a voice that made Tairren's heart pound. "I've been waiting so long to gaze into your eyes of blue," she said.

She came so close to him, pressing her hot skin to his. Her face was inches from his and her honey-colored eyes pierced into his like hot daggers.

"…Who are you? I don't understand…what am I doing here?" Tairren asked, backing away from her intense presence.

Tairren's heart thrashed around as his skin seemed to melt at Fiara's delicate touch. He became nervous by her bold mannerism. He felt uneasy by her presence, but he liked it at the same time.

A lovely smile came over the woman's face. "I am Fiara," she said. "I am the fire of your heart… I am the heat that flows through your body and the passion that runs in your veins… You are here because you want to be…"

"No…there's someplace that I must be… There's something I need," Tairren said as he looked around the terrace with his worried eyes. "There's something I've been looking for… I lost something and I need it back— before it's too late…"

"No, my lord," Fiara said as she caressed her warm hand upon his cheek. "I have prayed for a dominion like you…to come before me. I need you here as my king—my god. I am a slave to you… You have everything here that you would ever need," she said as she turned his face to look into hers. Her eyes flashed like fire. "…Know me, love me, touch me—and I will give you more than what you could ever dream of… This is more than a connection…it's spiritual…no being of light could touch the love I have for you." She spoke softly, slowly bringing her face to his. "I am under your spell..."

She pressed her fiery mouth to his and kissed him passionately.

Tairren pulled away quickly, startled by her tongue that she slipped into his mouth.

"...My heart—belongs to another woman," Tairren said, breathlessly. "I'm flattered that you see me differently—but I can't..." He was beginning to realize that he had another life away from Fiara.

Fiara backed away from him, appearing offended for a moment. Her sensual eyes gleamed in the firelight as her face softened. She began to look as if an amusing thought came to her. She turned her gaze at him again as a faint smile came over her face. "Is her name—Marrisa?" she asked furtively.

Tairren sat up with a pounding heart. Marrisa burst into his mind like a rush of cold air. He had remembered what he was looking for...Marrisa! How could he have forgotten about the woman he loved? Her smile became embedded in his brain as his quest came over his heart.

"I've been poisoned—so that I would forget about Marrisa," Tairren said with an annoyed edge.

"You've been healed, my lord," Fiara said as she came over him again. She sat on his lap, bringing her golden legs around him. She pulled his arm from the warm water and caressed it with teasing fingers. "I healed you of your scars and wounds," she said, revealing the spots where Tairren had been injured from his journey. "That *is* love," she said.

Tairren looked at his arm and chest. To his surprise, his skin was clear and he had no scars at all.

"How—how did you do that?" Tairren asked, as he gazed at her.

"I can do many things no man on earth can do," she said as she caressed his chest. "I can bring fire to your loins and life to your mind," she said with a chuckle. "Do as God wishes and set me free."

Tairren pushed her hands away. "I must leave," he said.

She got off of his lap and sat next to him. She looked away from him for a moment, then brought her fiery eyes back to his face. "I can bring her to you...," she said.

Tairren looked at her with confused eyes. He wondered how she could bring Marrisa to him when he had been searching for her for days. He began to wonder if she could do such a thing. He wondered what kind of power she was really filled with.

"Do not be afraid," Fiara said in a whispery voice. "Close your eyes, Tairren…and you will see the one you love."

Tairren looked at her for a moment, searching her exotic eyes for any sign of deceit. Her face looked honest and she never took her golden gaze away from his. Tairren closed his eyes. The silence that sat all around him began to make him feel anxious. He didn't even hear the many fires crackle or the wind that blew behind him. It was as if everything had become frozen in the hot air. He began to become nervous as the silence became too intense.

"Fiara?" Tairren said, breathing harder.

"Open your eyes…," a sweet voice said.

Tairren shot open his eyes, recognizing the girl's voice. The soft voice was like a beautiful melody to his ears. Marrisa sat before him in the water! Her face was young and vibrant and her eyes sparkled like a bright-blue sky. Her long red locks dangled in the water and she wore a white gown that appeared as fine white light.

"Marrisa?!" Tairren gasped with a booming heart.

"Yes, Tairren," she said with a sweet smile. "I've been waiting for you…" She sat still, seeming to wait for Tairren to embrace her.

Tairren gazed at her. He felt overwhelmed as he moved closer to her. He felt as if he were in a sweet dream as he looked into her crystal-blue eyes. He wasn't sure if it was all real or not. It seemed to him as if he hadn't seen her beautiful face in years. He slowly brought his hand to her lovely countenance. He brought himself closer to her, never taking his eyes off of her.

"Kiss me, Tairren," she whispered. "Wrap your arms around me…"

Just as Tairren touched her cheek, he pulled his hand away quickly. Her cheek was hot to the touch and made his fingertips tingle. He studied her again, wondering if it was really her.

"Don't you love me?" she asked as her blue eyes became saddened.

"I love you, Marrisa…with all of my heart," he said.

Just then she giggled, and began to sing an old song that tugged at Tairren's heart. It was the old bard song that Marrisa used to always sing. When life was more pleasant, Tairren could listen to her singing it for hours.

As she sung, she came closer to him, reminding Tairren of all the special moments they shared together.

> Are you going to the spring time fair?
> Rosemary, love, and sunshine.
> Remember me when you go there,
> For he once was a hero of mine.
> Tell him to find me a castle of lace,
> Rosemary, love, and sunshine.
> By the saltwater—on a mountain's face,
> Then he'll be a true lover of mine…

Tairren's heart throbbed as his chest rose upon the warm water. He felt as if his heart was about to explode. He came to her slowly, bringing his lips to hers. He caressed her face as he leaned back against the side of the pool, pulling her against him. It was as if he were in a dream that had become real. It was overpowering and she felt warm and alive against him. She tasted just as he remembered her to—it was something that he would never forget. Her mouth was like honeysuckle. He felt just as he did the moment they fell in each other's embrace days ago in the forest.

The heat in the pool seemed as if it had intensified. Tairren winced in discomfort as his body became too hot. His mouth seemed as if it had been set ablaze. He quickly pulled himself away from Marrisa as her touch became like fire.

"What's wrong, Tairren?" Marrisa asked breathlessly.

Tairren brought his hand to his mouth, feeling the heat that came from it. He quickly got out of the water as his body tingled all over. His heart felt that it could explode because of his overheated body and intense feelings.

Marrisa stared at him from the water. "You will never be able to handle me," she said with a deviant smile. "Legendary—it really is…that a boy would travel across a country in the bowels of darkness…just for love…"

Tairren realized that her eyes were no longer sky-blue, but honey-colored. Her sweetness quickly faded away and she began to appear sensual and furtive. Her gown clung to her body like wet paper, revealing curves he didn't feel right gazing at. He knew he had been blinded again by Fiara's magic. He became angry, annoyed that she had played with his heart. "You are nothing but a wicked sorceress," he said between clenched teeth. "You've bewitched me."

Marrisa smiled as she slowly stepped out of the water. Her body transformed back into a tall, exotic-looking woman. Water ran down her body like silk and the jewels that adorned her skin sparkled in the firelight.

"You are pathetic," Fiara said as she walked towards him. "I've given you everything a man needs," she said. "I've healed your wounds, refreshed your body, quenched your thirst, and offered you carnality...and still you deny me..."

"You've poisoned me to forget my quest! You've stolen my things, and tricked me with charms and magic!" Tairren said with a strong voice. "It is already night. Failure is coming to me quickly because of your trickery!"

Fiara came to him again, hushing him. She softly moved a wet lock of hair that fell over his face. "Forgive me," she said as she looked into his eyes. "Forgiveness is what you were taught, is it not so? So, you must forgive me as God has forgiven you... There is nothing dark about me and my heart burns with fire..." She tenderly put her hand on his chest, wiping the water that dripped from it. "I only want to show you that I am good... The energy that flows between us is spiritual. Why would God deny that...us? I know the scripture, my love. Lay me down at your alter so that our spirits shall become one... I will reveal it all to you! You shall know the secrets of God if you just trust me!"

Tairren spotted his tunic and trousers and rushed to them. They were laying with his boots near the farthest end of the pool. He quickly got dressed, glancing up every now and then to only find Fiara watching him. "You know nothing of God...because if you did, you would know that He is the only one," Tairren said as he dressed quickly. "My spiritual body is with God—not you."

"If I know nothing of God...then you must not," Fiara said quickly. "Because I know what you know. We are all gods, Tairren. We are all filled with life and can do things with our inner powers... Why can't you see that?"

Tairren ignored her as he finished putting on his boots. As he stood up, his wing pendant necklace fell from his tunic. The sight of it refreshed his memory, and his full quest blossomed in his mind. He glanced all around for his sword and dagger, but didn't see them. Instead of searching for them, he left quickly. He made his way across the terrace and into the cavern where the great fire burned and danced.

"Where are you going, my god?" Fiara asked, following him.

"Do not call me that!" he exclaimed, stopping in his place. He glared at her. "I am but a humble servant to the God of Light. I do not seek power or magic as you do, Fiara."

"I seek the truth as you do," she argued back as she came to him. "And I see the truth as I look at you. Does that make me not know a god? Now you want to leave me when I am trying to help you? You came to me...remember that. You came to me for help, not God."

"You are lost, Fiara. You have lived blindly your whole life... I did come to you. But I came to you in search for the Legendary Sword," Tairren said with a strong voice.

"Aaaah...so you come for the Sword of Truth," she said, having a teasing tone. "So, you are lost as well...for you have no truth until you have the sword, I see. Why must you have something that you say you already have within you? Isn't that curious: Someone who has truth within them, still searches for it... You wish to *steal* the only thing that I have, to find truth? *Stealing* is a sin, my lord...but you already know that since you are so righteous," she teased.

Tairren looked at her curiously as she walked away from him. He was surprised that she seemed to know ideas from the Book of Light. But he wasn't too sure of her and knew that she still couldn't be trusted. She claimed she knew God and the light—but her actions said something totally different. She seemed like she knew the Book of Light, but she twisted its words, he thought. She seemed as if she were trying to confuse and influence him some kind of way.

"I know the word—just as I know the sword," she said with a smile as she made her way over to the great fire. The fire seemed to become excited as she came near it. "You see, if I know the word...then I must be a companion of yours...and a companion of God. We must be a spiritual family... I must have light inside of me that burns like fire—just as you do... Am I right—or wrong?"

Tairren began to wonder if what she said was truly in her heart. "How can I even trust what you are telling me if you have already tricked me before?" he asked.

Fiara stared into the fire as it reached its flames out to her. She closed her eyes, as if she were listening to something carefully. She seemed to be communicating with—something... She looked pleased as the fire seemed to whisper to her. Her eyes flashed open. She gazed at Tairren as if she were overcome by something she longed to tell him. It was as if the power she spoke to, suddenly revealed something to her. "Do you want to know who killed your father?" she bluntly asked.

Tairren looked at her as shock came over him. He wondered how she knew about his father and him being dead. He became inundated with curiosity. He truly wanted to know who killed his father, but at the same time he wasn't too sure if he wanted to know at all. He lived most of his life, thinking and dreaming of his father, and now Fiara wished to open a door that could change his life.

"A follower of darkness has killed my father," Tairren said with eager eyes. "I do not need to know from you…"

"Come to me, Tairren," she beckoned him. "You do want to know. You've been wondering ever since you were a young boy. You need to know… Why must you torture your inner being? God wants you to be happy, Tairren. Come and gaze into my fire…you will see things that only I can show you," she said.

Tairren slowly walked to the fire. He became nervous all of the sudden as he stared into its great orange flames. He stood still as thoughts of his father came over him. He began to wonder if the things he didn't know were supposed to be left unknown.

"Gaze into the flames…and you will see what has been revealed to me," she said.

Tairren began to get an uncomfortable feeling within him; but the flames of the fire pulled at his mind. He felt like an eager moth to an inviting flame. He was drawn to it, but he knew that nothing good would come out of it.

Fiara raised her hands out upon the great fire as she closed her eyes. She began to say a chant that was filled with an ancient tongue. Her chant grew louder as the flames began to become brighter and pulsate.

✝✝✝

Tairren seemed to become one with the fire as he looked into it. It was as if the fire had completely taken over his mind. All of a sudden, his mind was brought to another time! He was a young boy again, and walked through the forest. He recognized the beautiful forest, and realized that he was in the Forest Provence. He walked until he spotted his father…

"Father," Tairren whispered.

Timotheus was crouching down low with his bow and arrows. He was hunting a rabbit who nibbled at the grass. He was about to release an arrow when someone had swiftly stepped behind him. The rabbit became startled and ran away. He turned quickly to see who had crept behind him. It was a young woman. She stood before him, holding a sword. She breathed harshly and her face quivered with anger.

Tairren recognized her well as he watched from the distance. It was Lilith! She was much younger and appeared very disturbed.

"You are a threat to father," she said as she glared at Timotheus with black eyes. Her voice shook with intense emotion as tears rolled down her pale cheeks.

Timotheus looked at her strangely, trying to understand what she was talking about.

"You are a threat to me!" she shouted. "You are ruining father's plans. You must be stopped from altering the future. Father told me. Father told me! FATHER TOLD ME!!" she growled. "You must DIE!"

With one disturbingly quick motion, she forced the sword into his stomach until it came out of the other side. Blood erupted from his mouth as he stared at the disturbing face of Lilith.

Darkness came over his eyes as his spirit left him.

Tairren began to yell out as tears flooded his eyes. He closed his eyes shut, not wanting to see any more of it.

✝

CHAPTER 18
Into the Fire

Tairren shot open his eyes as tears flowed from them. He was out of breath and his heart raced as he quickly looked around. Everything was the same as it had been before his vision. He was standing before the great fire again. His thoughts raced all around his head like a wind. "All of these years," he thought, "a murderer and fiend has been living among us in Minslethrate, secretly living a dark life…" He thought of how Lilith had always watched them from the shadows. Little did they know then how truly evil she was.

Fiara was standing next to him and gazed at him with wide eyes. A faint smile came over her face as she watched his worried expression.

"Lilith," Tairren said in a low tone. "Lilith has killed my father! He yelled out in a shaken voice. "She has given me more of a reason to rid of her!"

"Yes, my love," Fiara said as she turned his face for him to look into her honey-colored eyes. "Lilith is the enemy. Lilith murdered your father and has kidnapped the princess—the one you love… I am not your enemy, Tairren…"

Tairren walked away from the fire. He wanted to get away from it. The thought of his father dying kept replaying in his mind. He brought his hands to his tense face and rubbed it. He didn't know what to think and felt stuck. He didn't quite know what to do. He stood for a moment, calming himself. His mind kept racing. He thought of the sword, his quest, his father, and even Marrisa. "How is this all going to come together?!" he thought.

He glanced at Fiara, noticing that she moved closer to the fire. The golden specks and smudges of paint that covered her dark skin sparkled in the light. She kept gazing at him as she went… He didn't want to watch her, but he couldn't help it. It was as if her presence and sensual body language pulled at his eyes. He thought she was indeed one of the most beautiful and exotic women whom he had ever seen. She made his senses thrash about and his mind wonder. He watched her body, forgetting about his stress…

Tairren gazed upon her as she brought her hands into the roaring fire. She moved them through the flames elegantly. She didn't even wince in pain as the fire consumed her hands. Instead, she closed her eyes as a look of ecstasy came over her face. She then looked at Tairren as she pulled her hands out of the fire and smiled at him. But even though she took them out, she still held the flames in her hands! She began to play with it, moving the bright orange flames around the air, somehow making it dance in her palms and around her arms.

"I *am* firelight," she said as she walked towards Tairren. "I have shown you the secret of your father's death—I have given light to your anxious mind… It is good that you follow me—to believe me with your pounding heart. You are like this flame upon my skin and must be mine to have… Isn't it strange that you are righteous, and your flesh still lusts for mine? I hear your heart as it pumps life now, as you wonder about me... Your blood is hot. I feel your eyes touching my flesh. I know the truth in which you seek and the words of God that you speak. We are all sinners, Tairren, and speak of God. But you hide your sin behind your flesh…you hide everything… We are the same. Forget your past and present…and follow me into your future… We shall breathe passing time together like a frozen dream."

Tairren watched her as she fondled the hot flames. She looked as if she were getting pleasure out of confusing him. But Tairren didn't allow her words to change his heart. He knew that she was trying everything to make him forget about his true identity and quest. He knew that she was trying to make him forget about who he was in Christ, Yehoshua.

"If you are a follower of truth…then fetch me the Sword of Truth…and I will believe you," Tairren said.

Fiara quit dancing with her flames, and looked at him for a moment. She searched his eyes with hers. The small flame she held vanished quickly just as her smile did.

"…You are testing me?" she asked with gleaming eyes. "My—how bold you are," she said. "I have shown you things that you have never seen before…and still you trust me not."

Tairren was silent as he peered at her. He wanted to show her that he was stronger than she thought. He knew that she could not touch the Legendary Sword of Truth with her bare hands. He knew that true evil could not stand up to King Yehoshua's mighty words, which were blessed upon the sword. The Sword of Truth would burn her, just as her fire could burn him.

Fiara glared at him. "Look closely into the fire again," she said, "and you will see the truth."

"I do not wish to see any more of your magic tricks," Tairren said, raising his voice.

"Look into the firelight, Tairren... You will see the truth," she exclaimed again, with a serious face.

Tairren looked again, peering into the hot, dancing flames. He watched as the flames roared and twirled in the air. This time his mind didn't become pulled into the flames. He looked harder and noticed something he did not before. He noticed the sword right in the center of the fire! The sword stuck out from an anvil, totally covered by the hot flames. Fiara had hid it in the fire so that no one could obtain it. Tairren hurried to the fire, searching all around it. There was no possible way that he could get to it. The fire was too large and powerful!

"Go in and get it...if you dare," Fiara said as she came to him. "Go and fetch it, righteous boy," she chuckled, "you can do anything—so it seems..."

Tairren searched all around the cavern with his anxious eyes. He thought that there must've been something that could kill the flames. His heart sunk as he realized that the only way he was going to get to the sword was if the fire went out with water. But the fire was too large and strong. It would be impossible to get water over it by himself even if there was water to do it. He looked up out of the massive hole that let the smoke from the fire out. The smoke billowed out of the hole like a thick cloud. He noticed that the sky was black but he could see the moon, which seemed as if it were a light shade of red!

Tairren became alarmed, realizing that the moon was on the verge of appearing as blood. It was the night of the spring equinox! The prophecy was at hand and nothing was going to stop it. He began to panic on the inside. The realization of precious time coming and going flooded his mind. He began to worry, remembering that darkness was going to have Marrisa in full after that night, during the twilight. He also thought of Gaibriul, who hadn't come for him yet. He remembered when Gaibriul had told him that he would come if he didn't return by the time the night had come.

"Where are you, Gaibriul?!" Tairren said to himself in a low tone, "I need your help." His voice was restrained but his mind bellowed out.

"Are you looking for someone?" Fiara asked in a low voice as she came to him. "I do believe that the light-being whom you seek is in trouble..." She began to circle around him like an animal upon its victim.

"Where is he!?" Tairren yelled as he followed her with his anxious eyes. "I don't have time for any more of your tricks!"

She could've been lying to him, like she had been doing. But he knew right then that she had done something. He knew by Gaibriul's absence that something was wrong. Gaibriul would've been there just as the sun went down, just as he said, and by the looks of the moon—the sun had been down for quite some time.

"Oh...you wish to know?" she said with a teasing tone. She stopped right in front of him, gazing her eyes into his. "But I thought I couldn't be trusted," she mocked. "...Both him and his beastly creature are somewhere locked away in my mountain." A smile then came over her face. "Their light is locked away..."

Tairren glanced up as something caught his attention. It was the white owl! It quietly flew through the massive hole and perched upon one of the tall statues. He looked at Fiara, who did not notice the bird at all.

Urgent words emanated from the bird, grabbing Tairren's heart and mind. "Go into the fire and fetch the sword...," it said. "Do not be afraid, Tairren...for I will be with you..." Its words were strong and pleasing.

Tairren became nervous as he glanced at the fire. He knew that the fire could devour him in moments. He took a deep breath and closed his eyes. "I trust you," he whispered.

He opened his eyes and quickly made his way to the fire. He walked boldly, feeling the owl's gaze upon his back. It all seemed impossible, but there was nothing else he could do. He had peace all of a sudden, knowing that he was protected. He felt a wave of courage and strength come over him like armor. He stood before the fire, staring into the hot flames. He could feel the intense heat on his face and arms, radiating over him like powerful sun-rays. Already he grew hot. Sweat began to accumulate on his brow. He watched the sword as the intense fire made it look like it was vibrating. The surrounding heat from the fire made everything look as if it had been liquefied upon the air. He closed his eyes again and took a deep breath. He then stepped towards the fire, keeping the eyes of his heart on the God of Light at all times.

Fiara laughed as she watched Tairren's foolishness. "You will burn to death, fool!" she yelled out. "Only I can withstand the powers of fire; only I can touch its flames!" she yelled.

Tairren ignored her, stepping into the flames with closed eyes. He took a couple more steps, wondering if he had even gone in. He slowly opened his eyes with a pounding heart. Fire was all around him but he did not feel a thing! He slowly raised his hands up, watching as the flames danced upon his skin. The flames whirled all around him, covering his body like an energized shroud. But it did not consume him! He didn't even feel the intense heat from it; he didn't feel heat at all! All he could feel was rapidly moving air and pulsating waves.

But he also felt something else… He became thrilled because he had felt it before. It was something that felt powerful and good. He realized that there was a hand on his shoulder. Tairren quickly looked up as a bright light caught his attention. The light was in the shape of a man! The man wore robes that were white as snow and his presence was overwhelming. It was the same man that he had seen in his dream! He knew that the being of light was the power of King Yehoshua. He could feel the intense peace and love from the figure as it touched him.

"As darkened hands try to take you…you are safe in my hands of light. Go, my son," the being of light said. "For I am with you always…"

Tairren breathed in the powerful presence and did as he was told. He began to make his way to the sword, understanding that the being of light was by his side. He stood before the sword, feeling overcome by joy. He slowly brought his hand to the sword and tightly grabbed the hilt. He could feel the power of the Lord within it! With one mighty pull, he pulled the sword from its anvil!

The sword was cool to the touch and was bright and golden, as if it were made from light. It was not even charred black from it being in the great fire for ages. The magnificent sword was beautifully crafted, consisting of intricate metal work that looked like clusters of fine feathers hanging from the guard. Luminous jewels adorned the hilt, and the pommel was iridescent and appeared like a large diamond that harbored light. A brilliant blue stone was embedded in the center of the guard, and all down the magnificent blade was an ancient writing of some sort that was inscribed on it.

He raised the sword into the bright orange fire that roared all around him. After a moment of joy, he looked back up at the figure.

"You have done well during your walk upon this world, obeying me and my commands...and for that—you will be blessed above all other kings," the being of light said. "Go now, Tairren."

Tairren gazed upon the being of light one last time, then bowed to him. He then left quickly, running through the hot flames. The flames rippled upon the air as he burst from them, coming out of the miraculous cool fire and upon the hot cavern.

"NO!!" Fiara screamed out as she saw that he was still alive and unharmed. She looked over him and shook her head as she realized that he had not been burned at all. "What impropriety is this?! You say that you are not a god, but you walk in fire as if you are one! You take what belongs to me as if you are a king! How dare you overstep me!"

"No, Fiara—God has protected me through the fire...I walked with God. He has blessed me with it," Tairren said as he held onto the sword tightly. "You see, if you truly knew my God, you would've known that there is only one God...and He reigns forever. You have only self-proclaimed magic and light within you and don't have the same light as I. You've lost Fiara," Tairren said in a steady voice. "Now tell me where Gaibriul is and I will spare your life."

Fiara glared at Tairren as she clenched her teeth. Her eyes became like fire and flashed with anger. "I am giving you one last chance, boy... Yield to me so that you may know the secrets from another world, unknown to man."

Tairren stared at her, slowly raising his glorious sword. "...No," he said with a tense face.

"...Then you have chosen the doors of death," she said with a blank face. "Now feel it open wide upon you."

Just then Fiara ran at him with full force, taking him by surprise. She was shockingly quick and brought a hot wind with her. Tairren went to swing his sword, but she was too quick and agile. She twisted her body and missed the golden blade. She swiftly twirled down to the ground, bringing her leg beneath Tairren, tripping him. Surprised, Tairren's feet flung up into the air as he crashed down onto his back.

Tairren quickly got up and watched as Fiara did impressive backflips towards the nearest wall of the cavern. He was amazed by her strength and agility. She looked weightless as she hurtled through the air. He ran after her, watching as she quickly stopped flipping and dashed up the wall. She grabbed two strange looking weapons that hung from it, and landed back down in a cat-like stance. She slowly stood up, glaring at Tairren behind fiery eyes.

"You've won the sword…but I will have your lovely head as my trophy," she said as she made her way to him.

Tairren stood still, grasping the sword tightly and positioning himself so that he could attack with full force. He watched with intense eyes and a bold face as Fiara came to him. His chest swelled as he sucked in the hot air.

Fiara twirled her strange looking blades around, trying to intimidate him. They hummed in the air, appearing blurry with great speed. Then she stopped twirling them abruptly and charged at him with a loud scream.

Their weapons clashed like quick heat, clinking in the warm air of the cavern. They moved together quickly, keeping their intense eyes on each other.

Tairren's swings were powerful, cutting through the air with the ancient sword of light. But as Tairren swung, Fiara would bend and turn, quickly dodging the powerful sword.

Fiara had more of an advantage, using her blades, quick moves, and agile body to counterattack. She flipped around Tairren like a quick flame, nearly catching him off guard and cutting him.

After what seemed like many moments of fighting, Tairren became accustomed to her flow and inhuman moves, and knew when to take her by surprise. The quick moment came, and he kicked her stomach, causing her to fling down to the ground with her blades flying into the air.

Tairren stopped her before she got up and crouched over her. "This will bring us nothing!" Tairren exclaimed with heavy breaths. "Follow me, Fiara, and the God of Light will spare you! He pities you!"

"I follow no one but my powers!" she grunted behind clenched teeth. Her eyes flashed with anger as the veins in her neck pulsated. "You will fail, boy." she spat.

Just then, somehow, she got her feet beneath Tairren and kicked into his stomach with a powerful force. Her hit sent him flying towards a statue! He crashed into it, groaning as he hit hard. The statue fell over, breaking and crumbling on the ground. His sword fell from his hand and landed a couple of feet away.

Fiara got up quickly and flipped towards one of the tall statues. She dashed up the side of the statue like an animal and stopped on the very top of it, perching upon it. The statue held a long spear with long blades that protruded from both ends. She glared at Tairren from the top of the tall statue and hurled the spear at him. The spear came down at him quickly, cutting through the air like a bolt of lightning.

Tairren moved quickly, nearly becoming impaired by the quick spear! It tore past him. Pieces of tile flew as it went straight into the ground. Tairren got up quickly and grabbed his sword. He watched as Fiara jumped from the statue and caught the arm of another tall standing statue. She hung onto the statue's arm, twirling around it, then flipped out into the air. She landed right before Tairren, grabbing the spear. She lunged towards Tairren with full force, pointing the spear at him. With one quick motion, she stabbed one of the daggers into the broken tile. She used the spear as leverage and shot her legs out towards Tairren before he could think. Her hit was like hot stone.

Surprised, Tairren's head flung back as the heels of her feet pounded into the side of his face. He hurled back and hit his head on a nearby column. His mind became darkened as he was knocked unconscious. Blood came from his head as he lie silently upon the ground...

Fiara slowly walked towards him, gazing at him with her fiery eyes. Her chest heaved as she stood over him. She silently stared down at Tairren, hovering over him like a menacing fiend. As Fiara looked upon his face, she closed her eyes, listening to a voice that spoke to her from another world. She opened her eyes, knowing what she had to do then...

"I have not lost... This is but a warning, foolish boy... Tonight, the moon shall glow as blood...and tomorrow we will meet again, my love. And you and your kind will taste my wrath," she said with an emotionless face. "You do not know the dark power that speaks deep within me," she said. "But soon you will..."

She looked down at him with her honey-colored eyes, then knelt over Tairren, bringing her hot lips to his. She softly kissed him, then quickly left his body alone on the stone...

†

CHAPTER 19
Restless Night

The cold night air blew across the Field of Old Blood like an anxious spirit. This night seemed colder than the nights before and the atmosphere contained a discouraging emotion that lay thick. The grass and shadows of the field seemed to scream out to the darkness as the winds scurried through them.

A strange presence, that held madness and turmoil, crept about the field. Its black body of pure darkness skulked about, then got caught up with the sour winds. Insidious emotions followed the black presence, and scurried up the side of the wild cliffs of the mountain. It came alive as it crawled up the side of the Dark Tower of Sacrifice. The window on the very top of the tower opened out to the cold night sky, allowing the creeping darkness to come in…

Lilith stood at the window, staring at the moon as it slowly turned into a shade that resembled blood. The moon looked haunting as it stared back from the strange, starless sky. She sniffed the air and closed her black eyes. The familiar presence of darkness came all around her, circling her like an exhilarating black mist. The mist left her rotting body, then slowly made its way over to Marrisa who hung from the wall like a silent ghost. The dark mist lingered around her for a moment, then disappeared into the heavy shadows on the other side of the chamber.

"Father, my lord of uncertainty," Lilith said as she bowed before the darkness upon the ground. "Lord of darkness who sees all… What is it that you have come before me?" she asked, bringing her black gaze towards the shadows.

A tall dark figure slowly came from the darkest area of the chamber. Its robe was black as night and fell upon the filthy ground. Small black shadows crept at the Dark Lord's feet in silence as it looked at Lilith.

"Natas…one of my most loyal nomed," it said in a whispery voice. "You have done well…but your task is not yet complete."

The dark lord slowly lifted his hands, bringing Lilith to her feet.

"What must I do? I've done everything you've asked of me, my lordship," Lilith said as she lowered her head. "Marrisa's body is ready and the moon is revealing that blood should be spilled soon…"

"Fool, your deeds do not matter to me!" it said in a much louder voice. The shadows around the Dark Lord's feet trembled as its voice echoed through the chamber.

"Forgive me, my lord," Lilith said, bowing her head. "I am vermin upon your feet."

"There is something that troubles me," the Dark Lord said. "I've seen lights from across the Black Field of Old Blood. These lights hold a presence that I loathe… These putrid feelings that come from the lights are from legna!" it roared out. "They must be stopped!"

"Stopped, indeed, your lordship," Lilith said as her black eyes shook. "The boy must be with them," Lilith said quickly. "The boy named Tairren is to blame for all of this! I've seen him, my lord. I've seen him speak of the light before! He has been in the way since the beginning!"

"I know whom you speak of," the Dark Lord said as he came closer to Lilith. "I sent you to kill his father long ago… His whole family should've died then!" the darkness screamed. The chamber became blacker, even covering the torches that burned on the cold walls. "The boy named Tairren must die…"

"Should I go to the lights that burn on the other side of the field?" Lilith asked. "He must be at the camp of the light folk…"

"You know nothing!" the Dark Lord screamed. The creeping shadows that scurried upon the floor repeated the Dark Lord's words. "Tairren is beaten and battered upon the Fire Temple… I have spoken to Fiara's mind and revealed to her what she must do."

"Forgive me, mighty lord," Lilith said.

"Hear me now, Natas!" the Dark Lord said in a frightening voice. "Go to the lights that have infiltrated these southern parts. Reveal to them their princess and that the prophecy is nigh… I shall be with you. Stop them from coming...for if you fail—you will be cast through the doors and into the fires of a thousand tormented souls!" the dark lord screamed out.

Then, with a loud growl, the Dark Lord pulled his stinking mists and creeping shadows away, and vanished into the dark shadows of the chamber.

Lilith stared into the darkness with silent black eyes. After a moment of madness, she turned her head towards Marrisa who dangled from the wall. Lilith slowly came to her with her wicked gaze. Marrisa stared silently at her. Her white face held no emotion and her blue eyes held no light. Lilith came to her, then caressed her cold cheek with her gray hand.

"You look at me but you cannot see," Lilith said. "Your ears are open but you cannot hear… Time draws near, princess. Yes—time draws near." Lilith began to chuckle as her eyes became large. "You will see the light one last time this very night. Then the moment we have all been waiting for will be upon us!"

Lilith took off the blood-red pendant that she had been wearing. She held it out in front of Marrisa who blankly stared at it. Her pale eyes didn't even flinch as the red jewel sparkled before them.

"You must wear it this night," Lilith said as she placed the golden chain over her head. The pendant gleamed on her chest and the black gown she was wearing. "The only piece that is missing is your crown. It will be added unto you soon, my pet," Lilith said with a wicked smile. "The crown of the dead king shall be yours as soon as the prophecy has been completed… Now we must go," Lilith brought her gray hand to Marrisa's face again and caressed her cheek softly. "Now sleep," she said in a frightening voice.

Just then Lilith grabbed Marrisa's forehead. She shoved her head back against the stone wall with a powerful force, knocking her unconscious.

Marrisa's eyes rolled behind her eyelids. Her mind fell back into the heavy darkness…

"You will wake no more, my precious," Lilith said as she gazed at her dangling head and long red tresses. "Your eyes belong to the Dark Lord now."

Lilith unlocked her shackles, allowing her body to fall upon the ground. She stared down at her with her black eyes. Marrisa's beauty glowed in the dim chamber like the moon. Lilith picked her up and threw her over her shoulder. Marrisa's long hair and jewel pendant moved in the winds that came in through the window.

Lilith walked into the shadows of the chamber, disappearing into the darkness with Marrisa hanging lifelessly over her shoulder.

†

CHAPTER 20
Be Still

Far across the Field of Old Blood, upon a steep precipice, a glowing camp sat. The camp was filled with soft fire light, music, laughter, and singing. The legna also made the camp glow, sending a soft flicker of light from their passionate bodies. The camp seemed to be filled with more joy than the last night it had come alive.

The legna had moved from the clearing in the Black Forest and set up their gleaming camp right before Skull Hill, which was directly across from the Dark Tower of Sacrifice. The precipice they dwelt upon overlooked the whole area of the south. The mighty Great Mountains of Minslethrate could be seen right before them, stretching as far as the eye could see. The majestic mountains loomed over the Black Field of Old Blood. The ancient battle ground appeared as rolling hills, having nothing in it but old bones and moving grasses.

All through the camp, legna rested and ate their delicious food and drank merrily with one another, just as they always had done. Another great fire sat in the middle of the camp, and all of the legna sat before it with one another, talking of the strange things that happened and the good things that were going to happen.

Lavish tents circled around the great fire. The largest tent, right in the front, held a solemn group of men who appeared anxious and worried. The men ate quietly with one another, speaking only randomly. King Julpen sat at the center of the table, and around him sat Sir Hawkington, Prince Phillip, and other men of importance.

Before they ate, they talked about the bizarre occurrences that they had all gone through. All of them were intrigued and seemed excited but worried at the same time. Everything they spoke of was unbelievable and outrageous. They weren't sure if they believed it or not, until a legna came into their view, then they believed all over again.

When the legna first came upon King Julpen, he and his men were frightened. But as soon as they saw and felt the kindness and love that came from them, they knew that they could be trusted. The legna held an entirely different presence than the black nomed that lurked about the lands. It was hard for King Julpen to take in everything he had seen and felt that day. But he felt thankful and relieved that the legna had come to them when they did.

"I did not think we were going to live another day," King Julpen said as he wiped his mouth. "I know that the God of Light is involved in all of this. These legna have shown me that light is even more powerful than the darkness that has been attacking Minslethrate."

"Yes, your majesty," Phillip said, as he finished up his food. "I too thought the end was near. But Tairren and Natalia helped me get through all of this. They have taught me that I can do anything through Christ, who strengthens me. Having faith, righteousness, and truth is all that we need to defend ourselves from the wiles of the enemy."

"My, how you have grown, Phillip," King Julpen said. "You seem like a different man from when I first met you days ago, prince… I did not know what to think when I first read the letter that you left for me… But now I am thankful—it has led me here," King Julpen said, then patted Phillip on the shoulder. "You will make a fine husband to my daughter."

Phillip glanced at the leftover food on his plate. He became quiet as he thought of Marrisa. It seemed like it was the first time that he had thought of her during his journey.

"I do hope my daughter is safe," King Julpen said, glancing at Phillip who looked lost in thought. "I will never forgive myself if anything shall happen to her," he said in a low tone. He glanced at the other men who ate their food and quietly talked among each other. "It sores me to think that Lilith is behind all of this…that she has succumbed to the darkness." He brought his ringed hand to his chin. "All of these years, she has been living in the palace, lying to me day and night—plotting on my family. All of these years… What a fool I have been. I have been blinded for so long!"

"We all have," Phillip said with a caring look.

"Yes, I suppose," King Julpen said. "And now there is word of war… I hope the legna are truthful in everything they say. But if they are…" He paused as a forlorn look came over his rugged face. "Our kingdom is in no state for any kind of war…"

"They are, sire," Phillip said. "At first I did not believe. Everything seemed like just ideas from false legends. But now I believe. We must be ready. Our hearts must be ready," Phillip said as he brought his hand over his chest. "The enemy will come quickly like a thief in the night, King Julpen. I have seen it and so have you… And that is only a taste of what is to come. There has always been war between light and darkness… We must stand strong… And we are nearly finished with our quests—Tairren, Natalia, and I."

"Yes—quests," King Julpen said as he sat back in his chair. He seemed interested. "The legna have mentioned something about that. But allow me to ask—who is this Tairren everyone has been speaking on about? I know every courtier and noble in Minslethrate—except him…"

"Tairren is a peasant, my king," Phillip said, glancing at him. "He is a wonderful young man who has risen above the darkness… He is the key to this whole puzzle…so the legna have said. He is from noble blood and it is said that his ancestors were followers of King Yehoshua."

King Julpen looked at Phillip with intrigued eyes. He leaned forward on the table, resting his elbows upon it. "I see," he said.

"Tairren is a good man—and a good friend," Phillip said with a smile. "He is like a brother to me… Your daughter and Natalia adore him."

"Aaaah, I see," King Julpen said with raised eyebrows. "The young lad who works in the marketplace, is he?"

Phillip nodded his head. "Yes, king… It's funny, how God works, really. Who would've ever known that a humble peasant would come from the ancestors of kings? Tairren has been chosen…"

"I must meet him," King Julpen said with a smile. "Where is this glorious man?"

Phillip's face turned serious for a moment as he looked across the table. "He has not returned from his quest yet… He went to the Fire Temple last night… I have not seen him since then."

Just then they were interrupted by a legna who quickly came into the tent. He looked excited with his wide eyes and bright smile.

"They have returned!" he exclaimed with a cheerful smile. "Lady Natalia and Gaibriul have returned! Your companion has completed her task! They have brought with them Dolsia!" He said, then quickly left the tent.

Phillip and King Julpen got up quickly and followed after the excited legna. As they came out of the tent, they could see that a large group of legna stood around Natalia and Gaibriul. They hadn't even gotten off of their beasts yet, and were already bombarded by many enthusiastic legna.

Phillip smiled as he watched Natalia. She sat upon her horse, having a lovely smile on her face. Phillip noticed that Gaibriul and a woman, who must've been Dolsia, hopped off of the mighty winged beast as it crouched down. He quickly hurried through the crowd of legna with King Julpen following right behind him.

"Natalia!" Phillip shouted with a smile as he rushed to her. He came to her and held his hands out to help her off of Orchid. "I'm relieved that you are okay!"

Natalia smiled at him and took his hand. She slid off of her horse and gave him a tender hug.

"Lady Natalia," King Julpen said, catching her attention. "My, how you are full of surprises." A smile came over his rugged face.

"King Julpen!" Natalia shrieked, bowing to him quickly. She rushed to him and embraced him as if she were hugging her own father. "You've come! I'm so happy that you've received Phillip's letter! I was wondering if you or anyone was going to come in search for Marrisa. Now you know what threatens this kingdom."

"Yes, my lady," he said with a smile. "The legna have awakened me. We've been through a nightmare, as you have, just to get here... We've lost some men on the way—but they will be redeemed. I've learned many things...and I am not stopping until Lilith and the darkness that is coming alive is stopped! Our Kingdom will not fall!"

Just then the crowd of legna that stood around them became quiet. The crowd opened up as Mikhal quickly came to them. The tall Archlegna stood before them, having a great smile on his face. He raised his hands up, joyfully welcoming them.

"Welcome back, Natalia! I am glad that Gaibriul has led you here safely! And have you retrieved the Armor of Righteousness?" he asked, gazing at her with his golden eyes.

"Yes, Mikhal," Natalia said excitedly as she pulled a bundle off of Orchid. The bundle was large and lumpy and was wrapped in her cape. A nearby legna received the armor and took it away for it to be cleaned. "Dolsia has given it to me and joined me in my quest."

Mikhal looked surprised as he glanced around the crowd. "Dolsia? Where is she?"

"I am here," Dolsia exclaimed from the quiet crowd. She slowly walked towards Mikhal, somewhat shy and looking out of place. She pulled her black robe from her head and looked away from him as if she were ashamed. Even though she was a legna, she still had human tendencies because of her fall. Her long pale hair fell over her shoulders and her eyes gleamed like an intense moon. "The God of Light has forgiven me..."

Everyone, including the legna and their beasts, looked on quietly. King Julpen and his men knew Dolsia's name by the legends she was centered around; and the legna knew her name by her notorious rebellion. Everyone waited for Mikhal's response.

The air was thick with silence as the cold winds of the night came over them.

Mikhal gazed at her for a moment. A smile came over his face as he looked into her golden eyes. He slowly came to her and placed his hand on her shoulder. Their eyes met as if by a cord. They could see each other's hearts right through their eyes. Mikhal bowed his head to her, understanding that even though she was human-like, she still contained the same light that he possessed.

"I have not seen your face...since I last saw you singing for His majesty in the court of light," he said in a low voice that was only to her. "Your face and voice were always compared to a sunrise," he said, noticing the tears that built up in her eyes.

He then noticed the scars on her neck and face. He gently touched her scars, peering back into her eyes.

Dolsia became insecure, realizing that he had noticed all of her scars, and even the ones on her heart. She began to feel unworthy all a sudden as she thought of them.

"A scar is a healed wound, Dolsia... Do not fret. Your sins have been forgiven and your light has been blessed. Now, child—it is as if you've haven't left us at all... Old things are passed away...all things are becoming new," he said with a smile.

Dolsia bowed her head to him, then smiled. She felt as if a ton of bricks had been lifted from her shoulders. She knew that she was forgiven, and always would be, but she was nervous that she wouldn't be accepted by her fellow legna. But now that she had faced Mikhal, she knew that there was nothing else to fear. She knew she was laden with scars, but she still had new light within her heart.

As a tear rolled down her cheek, Mikhal wiped it, then looked out over the crowd of curious legna. "Brothers and sisters of light—this night shall be a glorious one!" he shouted. "Natalia has retrieved the Armor of Righteousness, Dolsia has come back to us, Prince Phillip has obtained the Shield of Faith, and King Julpen and his men have decided to follow the light of God and join us!" he shouted out in a great voice, raising his hands into the night sky.

The surrounding legna rose up and cheered like a mighty wind. Their voices were loud. Joy that seemed multiplied fell over the camp like a fire.

After everyone had settled down, Mikhal began to speak out loud again. "As we all know, Tairren has not come back to us with the Sword of Truth. I feel that there is something strange that has happened with Tairren and Rafiul, but we must keep our hope and faith!"

The air became quiet all around the camp again. Natalia and Phillip glanced at each other, having concerned looks on their faces. The legna talked in a whispery tone all around the camp. Everyone knew that Tairren had to complete his quest in order to take on the trials that the following day would bring. Tairren and the sword were the main pieces in their precarious puzzle.

"It is uncertain and dreadful, I fear," he said as a concerned look came over his face. "I feel time slipping by as the moon changes right before us…but we must stand strong! I can not hear Tairren's spiritual voice—but I know that he is still alive! We must never forget the light that we are fighting for! Stand up and shout brothers and sisters! Stand up and shout!" Mikhal raised his hands into the air again as a bold look came over his face.

Everyone began to shout, raising their fists and hands into the air.

"Praise God for this day! Worship him for all that he has done! There may be uncertainty in the night, but joy will find us in the morning!" he shouted.

Everyone did. They shouted and praised the God of Light. They lifted their hands into the sky and sang out songs of love and joy to Him. They did not know what that night or the next day was going to bring, but they knew that God had everything under control. As they praised their God, the burdens of that day fell from their heads and shoulders, and everyone felt new.

Everyone began to dance as joyful music began to play. They held hands and danced around the tables and the great fire that burned brightly. The whole atmosphere became filled with joyful noise, making even the gloomy night look glorious.

But as they sang and shouted, a black hole began to form over the great fire. At first it was overlooked because of the smoke and the dark night sky. But as the mists began to pulsate and spread among the sky, everyone began to notice it, one by one…

✝

CHAPTER 21
Annunciation of Darkness

Something strange was beginning to happen as everyone became quiet. The black spot in the sky began to lower upon the fire, making the fire spread out around the black orb-like hole. An angry presence began to emit from the darkness, filling its surrounding area with ill-feelings. Everyone began to quickly back away from the fire as the flames began to spread out like tree limbs. The fire thrashed about as the strange orb threatened it. Just as the black orb came into the core of the great fire, the flames went out... The camp had quickly become dim as the fire became only swirling smoke. The camp suddenly became quiet and still. Everyone looked on anxiously as the black orb and mists came upon the burnt area of the ground, mingling with the thick smoke.

Mikhal and the other Archlegna slowly made their way closer to the black mists. Their golden gazes became locked onto the strange mists. Everyone stood still and looked on vigilantly. They knew where the mists were coming from…and they weren't going to dismiss it lightly.

Three black figures began to come from the black opening. At first, they could not be seen, but just as they stepped out of the mists and smoke, everyone knew who they were. A tall figure stood between two smaller figures. The tall figure was the Dark Lord and was shrouded from head to toe in a black hooded robe. Lilith stood at his left side, having a large wicked smile on her ugly face. Her eyes were black as the night sky. On the right was Marrisa! Her head dangled, as if she was unconscious. But she still stood upright. Black shadows came from the Dark Lord, holding Marrisa up as if she were their puppet.

"Marrisa!" King Julpen yelled out as he ran towards her.

Natalia and Phillip quickly followed suit, pulling their swords from their sheaths.

The Dark Lord raised his shadowy hand in their direction, then spread his fingers out upon the mists. Quick dark shadows came from the black mists and yanked them down! King Julpen, Phillip, and Natalia fell down to their knees as the dark shadows came over them like threatening shrouds!

"Let them go, Lucif!" Mikhal shouted out in a bold voice.

The Dark Lord just stared at him silently. "...I did not come to fight, Mikhal," he finally said. "Tell your followers to listen well..." His voice was whispery and frightening, but even though it was low, everyone could hear him clearly.

The Dark Lord lowered his hand and the black shadows relented. King Julpen, Phillip, and Natalia were freed. The legna who stood nearby quickly came to their aid. The legna pulled them back, so that they wouldn't interfere again.

"Fools," the Dark Lord said. "Light can not break the darkness so easily..."

Just then a couple of beasts that roared angrily at the growing darkness, flew up into the black air and went to attack the Dark Lord and his nomed. The Dark Lord raised his hands into the sky and the black mists became a solid mass in the air. The beasts crashed into the wall-like mists! Being taken by surprise, they fell to the ground with a crash. More legna became angry and began to attack. But the Dark Lord motioned towards them with his hands with his fingers spread out. Black mists that looked like giant thorns came out of the shadowed ground! The legna stopped abruptly, unable to get any closer.

"...I did not come to fight," the Dark Lord said again.

"Your day of reckoning draws near, Lucif," Mikhal said quickly with a threatening tone. "Have you come to receive it sooner?"

The Dark Lord began to laugh as the mists swirled and grew. The creatures that crept in the darkness of the mists began to laugh as well. The nomed's wicked chants and chuckles reverberated over the air like a foul wind.

"I come to warn you, Mikhal," the Dark Lord said with a sudden serious voice. "Leave my lands, or you will all die... The prophecy is at hand, and Marrisa and this world shall be mine! You have already lost...save yourself and leave!" he shouted. "That is my final warning..."

"You lost long ago, Lucif!" Mikhal shouted back. The light that glowed from him began to intensify. "I pity you! Our Lord loved you! You used to lead us! You let your lust for power take over you! Look at you now, Lucif! You fell from Nevaeh long ago, and after all this time, after all these ages—you are still lost! You have been planning the great God of Light's demise from the very beginning! Pity, it has been a waste of time—for you are already dead!"

The Dark Lord began to roar from the darkness like a beastly dragon. "The past is a shadow upon my eye... A lust for power, you say? I AM POWER! Do you not feel the world as it trembles below you, oh *mighty* Mikhal?! Do you see your precious princess, King Julpen?! Do you see her fragile face, Phillip?! Do you miss her, Natalia?!" he screamed out. "Know this, fools! This is the last moment that you will ever look upon her face again in this world! She is cursed! Just like this kingdom and this world...CURSED!" Just then Lucif began to laugh. "It was good that your God sent me away from your *precious* Kingdom of Light... It is far better to be feared than ridden with filthy light..."

The Dark Lord raised his hands, and Marrisa began to levitate into the sky. She appeared haunting as her head and appendages dangled lifelessly in the darkness. She hung over the Dark Lord like an insensible corpse. Just then the darkness and its mists began to quake! In a dashing moment, Marrisa and the Dark Lord disappeared into the black orb-like hole! Darkness and its creeping mists and nomed had vanished! Lilith was just left standing there in the smoke that came up from the ashes and soot where the fire once burned.

The night was still and cold and everyone watched Lilith quietly. She slowly moved her head, looking over the crowd like a hawk.

She looked up at the moon, which was now red as blood! "You are too late...it has begun," she said.

"You disgusting woman! You will die for this!" King Julpen screamed out as his emotions stirred.

"Julpen, you know nothing! You are nothing but a fatherless child!" Lilith shouted out in an accent that belonged to his deceased mother, Queen Karnidge. "Many will burn on your behalf!"

Julpen's eyes widened. He felt stunned all of a sudden. He began to breathe heavily as insecurities came over him. He felt like he was a child again standing before his abusive mother. He watched Lilith carefully as she slowly turned her gaze towards Natalia.

"Natalia...," Lilith said in a teasing tone. "I hear your selfish mother screaming out from the darkness. She is screaming for you... But her screams will never relent..."

"What do you know of my mother?!" Natalia asked, becoming concerned and panicked. "You know nothing!"

"She is DEAD!" Lilith screamed out, then began to laugh. "Darkness has taken her while you have been following your new *dead* king! You killed her! I hear her screaming right now!"

"Shut your disgusting mouth, Lilith!" Natalia screamed out as tears came over her eyes. She grabbed her sword tightly, wishing that Lilith's neck would hit against it quickly.

"Phillip, Phillip—Oh poor, Prince Phillip," Lilith teased again, now setting her black gaze on him. "Your father is dying, just as your kingdom will! You decided to stay in this weak kingdom while your sickly father waits for you—what a fool you are!"

Phillip clenched his teeth, holding his sword as if ready to strike.

"Your mouth has caused enough damage, Natas!" Mikhal yelled out. "Be gone with your wicked words, or your head shall fall just as your lord will!"

"Mikhal, you speak my name as if you know me," Lilith said as she slowly walked towards them. The atmosphere around her seemed to become black as she radiated with the Dark Lord's powers. She looked wicked as she crinkled her brow and scowled at them with her black eyes. "You must know how truly great I am if you know my name…"

Lilith suddenly stopped in her place. She silently glared at them then lifted her hands into the air. A large smile ripped across her sickening gray face, revealing a decaying mouth. "I shall release myself from this putrid body. I've been longing for this moment for ages! May the black air touch me once more! May my tail touch the feeble earth once again!" She pointed her face up to the black sky with the red moon right above her. "Release me now, my Dark Lord! Fill me with the powers of hell!!

Just then Lilith's mouth gaped open, stretching and breaking the rotten flesh around her mouth. A black smoke-like substance came from it, billowing out as if it were pushed with a strong force. Her putrid body shook and broke apart as it came from her. The smoke looked like black liquid in the air and swirled above her with wicked noises. It rose up and became a black form in the sky! After the blackness emptied out of Lilith, Lilith's body collapsed to the ground as a lifeless pile of dead flesh.

The black form crashed to the ground, becoming alive and physical! Its body became thick and black. It stretched its long arms and chest as it stood among the air. It was tall and looked like a massive serpent! Its torso was black and its long serpent-tale was covered in onyx-colored scales. It had a large head that had a long dog-like snout and large horns that spiraled from it. Its eyes were small and gleamed like the blood-red moon that hung in the black sky.

The legna and men held their ground as they grasped their weapons. Everyone looked at the nightmarish creature with wide eyes. Natas was massive and frightening. Besides King Baffmit, Natas was the largest nomed that they had seen so far on their journey! Their breath was taken away as they looked up at the mighty fiend.

"Hold on to the promises of God, children of light!" Mikhal shouted out to everyone with a mighty voice. He looked at Natas as he spoke. His eyes sparkled like the sun and his muscles tensed up beneath his glowing flesh. "This creature has no power over any of us!"

"POWER?!" it bellowed out in a raspy voice. "I shall show you what power I have!" As it spoke it grabbed Lilith's flesh with its black tail, hurling it at Mikhal with one quick motion.

Mikhal moved quickly as the corpse hit and tumbled upon the grass.

"You are pathetic, Mikhal! All of you shall become like Lilith: crying, screaming, dying, and breaking!" It yelled out as it loomed over the men with its black aura. "Lilith was foolish and weak! But her task has been completed!"

"You used to be kind!" Mikhal shouted out with a passionate voice. "You used to love the light that once shined inside of you! You have become like your master! Lucif has beguiled you just like he has done to every fallenlegna! What you have done to Lilith shall be done to you! I pity you, Natas! Lucif has blinded you just as you have blinded Lilith! You are cursed and sentenced to any eternity of relentless death!"

Natas growled as he slowly brought his mighty horned head to Mikhal. A long tongue came from Natas' snout and flickered about like that of a snake. "…Your words bounce off of me like water upon glass," he said. "Now you must die as my power consumes you!" he roared out.

Natas quickly swung its tail and hit Mikhal with a powerful blow, sending him across the field and into a group of legna.

Natas let out a mighty roar as he stretched out his arms. "Leave now and I will spare your lives!" he screamed out.

Mikhal got to his feet, standing tall and fierce. He glared at the creature with fiery eyes. "Go back to the darkness, Natas!"

"…Then I shall MAKE you leave, fools!" Natas roared out as he slithered with power towards them.

The legna began to attack quickly, shooting their arrows of light. The arrows darted through the black sky like streaks of firelight, pelting him like a fierce wave. The golden arrows pierced Natas' skin, making him scream out.

Natas quickly wiped the arrows from his skin and scaly tail as if it had not affected him. He then swung his tail quickly across the field of men, sending them flying into the air. He quickly slithered through the camp, knocking over the tents and tables that sat nearby. Things flew about the air, crashing onto the men. Natas laughed and mocked them as he terrorized the camp like a violent storm. He quickly grabbed men like small animals and plucked the limbs from their bodies, then threw them back into the crowds. He sent helpless legna flying and men screaming as he crushed them with his mighty tail.

The atmosphere became filled with pandemonium as Natas continued to slither upon the camp. King Julpen and his men, along with Mikhal and the legna, fought back with all of their might. It seemed as if grueling hours passed by them. There seemed to be no escape before them.

✝✝✝

Phillip, Natalia, and Dolsia ran together, looking around for a quick hiding spot to figure out what they had to do. They came to a large boulder that sat along the steep precipice of the camp. They quickly hid behind the boulder, pressing their backs against the cold stone to take satisfying breaths. A couple of feet away from the boulder, the cliff dropped down into a rock infested bottom, looking like a jagged wave of rocky glass.

"What are we to do?!" Natalia shrieked as she looked out over the cliff. "That serpent monster is tearing the camp apart! Men are dying!"

The roars of Natas could be heard behind them, followed by the cries of men and the loud crashing sounds of the camp falling.

"Lord help us!" Phillip cried out as he clenched his fists. "It's hard to believe that Lilith had been filled with that—snake!

"I know that serpent," Dolsia said quickly. Both Natalia and Phillip looked at her, wondering why she was talking about it then. "That is the serpent who tricked me long ago! I remember that voice and tail... Natas is the one who deceived me and led me to the Dark Lord!"

"You allowed that massive creature to deceive you?" Natalia asked, quickly. A look of disbelief covered her face.

523

"He was much smaller then—about my size…and he wore a robe," Dolsia exclaimed. "But his tail came from out the back of the robe! I saw it!"

"What is your point, Dolsia?!" Phillip asked quickly, becoming impatient as more screams could be heard in the distance.

"I think I should face him…I feel it in my heart!" she said, placing her hand over her chest. "I can trick him just as he has tricked me! I will speak to him, and with haste, both of you will cut his tail from him!" she exclaimed with wide glowing eyes. "His tail is what gives him power—we must take it from him!"

Both Natalia and Phillip glanced at each other, then back at Dolsia. They knew they had to do something, quickly, and anything worked for them. They quickly nodded their heads, agreeing with her.

"Where is King Yehoshua's weaponry?" Dolsia asked quickly.

✝✝✝

They quickly rushed through the outside of the camp. They could see Natas' horrifying head as he loomed above the broken camp. They rushed, dodging behind things and quickly running past tents that still stood upright.

Phillip remembered that the legna had placed the shield in Tairren's quarters, so he assumed that was where they put the armor. Tairren hadn't come back to the camp yet, so he knew that the armor should've been resting safely in his tent.

They quickly made their way towards the silent outer edges of the camp where their quarters were. Tents sat quietly, softy glowing as they ran past them. It was strange to see how much calmer the camp was away from Natas.

They made it to their quarters where no one walked about. They found Tairren's tent and burst through the doorway. They quickly looked around for the armor. The tent was dim and peaceful and glowed with soft candle light. They spotted the glorious armor hanging perfectly on a post near the back wall of the tent.

"It's all here!" Phillip exclaimed. "Its beauty is breathtaking—fit for a king of all kings!"

Natalia came to the armor, looking at it as they became quiet. The armor and shield were beautiful and had not one scratch or dent on them. She gently touched the breastplate of the armor, then brought her hand to

524

her chest. "All that is missing is the sword," she said in a low tone. "If only Tairren was here…"

Natalia looked back at Phillip and Dolsia who looked intrigued. Small pieces of light reflected from the armor and speckled their faces with luminous spots.

"The light and righteousness in it are strong," Dolsia said, gazing at it. "His shield of faith and armor of righteousness shall repel Natas…"

"Put them on, Dolsia—quickly!" Phillip urged with wide eyes.

Dolsia closed her eyes and placed her hands on her heart. "I am not worthy of your armor, my lord," she prayed softly. "But I am made new because of you, my king. May the sun rise for eternity upon my heart… Lead me and show me the way, Yehoshua…"

Dolsia opened her eyes, taking in a deep breath. She then looked at Phillip and Natalia who gazed at her silently, waiting for her to do something.

"So, it begins," Dolsia said.

†

CHAPTER 22
Unto Fire

Phillip and Natalia ran through the pandemonium-filled camp. Their hearts pumped furiously and adrenaline poured through their veins. They ran past tents that were ablaze with threatening fire and fallen bodies that were sprawled out on the sulking grass. Their hearts sunk with sadness because of the fallen men, but then became fiery as they came before the massive creature. They ran towards the creature with heavy breaths and swords held tightly in their clammy palms.

"NATAS!" Phillip screamed out with all of his might. "Pull your sickening gaze towards me, snake!" he yelled.

They came to him quickly, standing before his great size.

Natas turned his horned head quickly, gazing his beady red eyes at him. He held a screaming man in his hand, but dropped him as he fully turned towards Phillip and Natalia.

"I've been looking for you, my pets," he said in a deep voice. His eyes flashed and his mighty chest swelled as he sucked in the cold air of the night. "Come to me so that I may blow the light from you and crush your bones!"

Natas began to come to them quickly, prepared to destroy their bodies!

Just then a flying white beast dashed right in front of Natas' wicked countenance! It was quick and brought a gush of wind with its mighty wings. It was Serafim who was being ridden by Dolsia! The king's armor she wore gleamed brightly even in the dark sky and the shield seemed to cut the chilled air like glass.

"Natas!" Dolsia shouted, catching his full attention. Serafim hovered right in front of his face, flapping its feathered wings with deep pulses. "Let my people go and leave them be!" she shouted. "Your demise shall come quickly to you!"

"Who is this retched form of excrement?!" Natas asked with a booming voice. "I recognize a deep part of you which brings back forgotten thoughts… You wear the dead King's armor, but you are no king. You smell like a dirty legna!"

"I am Dolsia!" she shouted.

526

Natas looked at her with flashing eyes. A laugh came from him that erupted out over the crowd of weary onlookers.

"Dolsia? The pathetic whore of darkness? You can not fool me… You do stink of legna, but you are still part of this dark world—used up and ridden with filth! You are still human and bound to this world! I gave you to father long ago! Once broken…always broken…," he said.

"I am now set free by my lord and savior of light! You deceived me, Natas!" she yelled. "I was blinded and used to love you… I did fall—but I have been awakened again by the God of Light! I am no longer your concubine! I have found true love within my God! I will never become blackened in your doorway again! You have taken my past—but King Yehoshua sets my future before me! You may have left a path of destruction behind you, but you will not continue to walk upon this earth any longer…"

Just then Natalia and Phillip caught her attention, creeping quietly around Natas. She watched with a pounding heart as they quickly raised their swords. "Now you will feel the pain that you have bestowed upon the innocent!" she yelled. Just then she blew a horn that hung from her neck, then shouted, "A sword for the lord—and for Minslethrate!"

Just then Phillip and Natalia repeated after her and shouted the same thing. Astonishingly, the whole crowd of men screamed out, "A sword for the lord, and for Minslethrate!" They all raised their weapons into the air and screamed it out with mighty voices.

Then with all of the strength they possessed, Phillip and Natalia hit the creature's mighty tail with their swords. They quickly pounded at it as if they were cutting a tree. Natas let out a scream as his tail began to come away from him with spurts of stinking, black fluid.

"You shall never blind anyone again!" Dolsia screamed out, quickly shooting an arrow into each one of his eyes. "May your eyes come away from you, Natas!" The golden arrows stuck out from each of his red spectacles like golden rods.

Natas screamed as he brought his large hands to his face. He thrashed his head around and began to blindly swing among the air. He hit the armor and shield that Dolsia held on strongly to, but his hits slipped off of her like wind! His mighty hands didn't affect her, not even once!

Natas began to lash out angrily. Dolsia dodged his quick swings as he shrieked something terrifying.

"May you never deceive even one with your wicked words again!" Dolsia screamed out as she encouraged Serafim to fly at him.

They went with incredible speed. She held her sword out, quickly slicing his throat. Black fluid burst from his thick neck like a fountain.

Natalia and Phillip finally cut his tail from him completely, making him fall forward towards the ground. More black fluid came from his back side, releasing steam in the cold air. He landed on his chest with a mighty crash. He thrashed and writhed about like a wounded snake, trying to grab whatever he could. His long claws dug into the earth as he tried to pull himself upon the ground.

"May you never live again!" Dolsia cried out as she jumped from Serafim's back. She pointed her sword downwards as she fell towards him. She landed on Natas' back, pushing her sword deep into him with a powerful thrust.

Natas twitched about one last time as the sword sliced his insides. The light that came from the sword burned through him, releasing power within him that his body couldn't stand and tried to reject. He stopped moving as his black heart pumped no more. His breath left him with a gurgling sound as his back stopped moving. Black fluid oozed from his rancid flesh as silence came over him.

"May darkness die…in the name of Yehoshua," Dolsia said in a low tone as she stood upon his back.

Natas' body laid still and quiet, which was something it had never done on the earth before. His black eyes gazed out over the clearing, appearing empty and dead. The power of the Dark Lord had left him the moment that Dolsia's sword had pierced deep inside his heart—just how it had Left Lilith when she was no longer needed. Natas' death came over him because of the light… He lay not too far from Lilith's flesh—both unconscious on the path of destruction that darkness had set before them…

Sudden silence settled over the night as everyone gazed upon Dolsia. Looks of relief, happiness, and even shock appeared on their faces. It was hard for them to believe what they had seen. They didn't expect Dolsia to be the chosen one, and they would've never thought that she was able to defeat Natas. The prophecy had revealed itself two-fold. Evil did take on a new form—and it was Natas…and a chosen one did defeat a part of darkness—it was a fallenlegna who had been redeemed…

Phillip and Natalia went to her quickly with expressions of gratitude on their faces. They had thought that the armor and shield would've been for them to wear…but truly it was for Dolsia on that strange night.

Dolsia looked up, breathless and overwhelmed with emotion. She pulled the golden helmet from her fair head of hair, then looked at Natas one last time. She took her eyes from the fallen creature, then hopped off of his back. She pulled her sword out of Natas' strong back, noticing that Mikhal was making his way towards her.

"There are many who have fallen because of Natas," Dolsia said, looking around at the demolished camp. She wiped her blade on the grass, then slid it back into its sheath.

Random men and legna lay about the clearing, appearing dead. The camp was destroyed and burned in many spots. The atmosphere was filled with despair. The men looked weary, slowly walking or limping towards the fallen body of Natas.

"Natas is finished," Mikhal said. "Lucif shall be angry this night…but the God of Light smiles upon us," he said, placing his hand on Dolsia's shoulder. "He is pleased with you, Dolsia," he said with a smile. "You have amazed me by your bravery and wit."

Dolsia smiled as she nodded her head. Her eyes began to glisten with joyful tears. "My heart is filled with joy… Prince Phillip and Natalia have shown me the true meaning of companionship," she said, looking over at them who were listening carefully. "Without them…I might've failed."

Mikhal looked at her for a moment longer, then peered out over the fallen scene that lay all around him. "These men believed and fought hard for our God, just as you have… For that you and every fallen soul shall be blessed in His kingdom... Some have given up their ghost—but they will live for eternity… They were awakened by the light before Lucif and Natas arrived…for that—I am thankful…"

"Why have Lucif and Natas been so bold to come here?" Dolsia asked, concerned.

"The darkness is becoming stronger, Dolsia," Mikhal said. "But they are still no match for the light!"

"Mikhal," King Julpen said from behind him. He was standing with some of his men and looked saddened and worried. "What of my daughter?" he asked.

Mikhal gazed into his dark eyes. "King Julpen—Marrisa has fallen…," he said in a low tone. "But do not fret… Remember that blessed things will come from broken things," he said with a faint smile.

King Julpen lowered his head, glancing at the corpses of Natas and Lilith. It chilled his bones and boiled his blood to think that his precious daughter was destined for such a fate. He did not understand God's plans, but he trusted Him. He looked away from the corpses, wondering if he would ever see his daughter again…

Dolsia smiled as she placed her hand on King Julpen's shoulder. She thought about Mikhal's words and knew that they were true. "It is so," she said. "King Julpen—do not fret… You may wonder how we will ever awaken from this nightmare… Just know that there is always sunshine after a storm. We must stand strong against darkness during these times. We must keep this kingdom and world alive."

"Come away with me," Mikhal said as he motioned with his hand. His voice gave a sense of peace. "We must comfort the weary and make our men whole again!" he said in a loud voice, as if speaking out to the other legna. "We must stand up against darkness!" he shouted, catching everyone's attention. "We will fight for the ones who were lost! We will fight for the light that shines bright! Stand up with me men, and rise like the morning sun!" Just then the crowd of men and legna began to shout, becoming inspired once again.

As they shouted out glorious words to the God of Light, the legna began to walk about to look for wounded men.

Some men lay helplessly upon the ground with broken legs and others held on tightly to their bleeding flesh. Some cried out in pain, holding their joints where their arms and legs were torn away by Natas. They put their hands over their wounds while shouting out prayers to their God. Right before the men's eyes—they were being healed! It was something that was hard for them to understand, but it was happening none the less…

✝✝✝

Dolsia praised God as she touched each man that lay helplessly upon the ground. Natalia and Phillip watched as their skin became mended and their health became whole right before their shocked eyes.

They came to a man whose arm was totally missing from his body. He cried out in pain as Dolsia kneeled over him.

"Do you believe in miracles?" she asked, looking into his glossy eyes.

He quickly nodded his head with clenched teeth. He seemed to believe now more than ever because of the pain. "I do believe," he said with some effort.

Dolsia placed her hands over his bloody shoulder. "Pray with me Phillip, Natalia," she said as she closed her eyes.

They all kneeled over him, each one saying their own prayer. They began to feel something powerful and great swell up inside of them! They felt as if the light within them began to burn like fire! Right before their eyes, the man's arm began to grow! Phillip and Natalia stared as the man's arm became whole again right in front of them! His flesh was new and his pain went away from him as if it had never happened!

Tears swelled up in their eyes as their hearts pounded. They began to laugh with joy, then began to praise God again.

The healed men began to stand up one by one, excited and overwhelmed with emotion. They began to help one another as their hearts became restored. They began to pick up the pieces that Natas had torn apart. The whole camp was filled with light and a powerful presence that brought a strange mist. The mist was not gray or black—but it was golden and seemed to glow! The mist was lovely and invigorating, and they all knew that it was the miraculous presence of their Lord…

✝✝✝

As the night went by, another great fire burned brightly in the dark air. The night seemed strange as the fire danced below the red, full moon. Many gazed at the fire as Natas and Lilith lay inside the massive flames. From the fire they came, back to the fire they went. They had set Natas and Lilith's flesh ablaze, ridding the earth of their rotting and foul-smelling corpses. The silhouettes of their flesh seemed to vibrate in the heat of the orange flames, burning until their flesh became dust. The flames rose up high above their black bodies, reflecting the destruction of their spirits and the door that was set before them…

Everyone's eyes drifted from the great burning of Lilith and Natas, and up to the blood-red moon. They wondered what the following day would bring. What would they see? What would become of Marrisa and their precious kingdom? What darkness would Lucif pull over them? All of these questions whirled through their heads as they sat around the fire.

Everyone seemed to be in a trance as they meditated before the fire, below the ominous moon.

✝✝✝

After the great fire was ignited, Dolsia had been baptized in the water. Even though she carried legna-light inside of her, she still had human feelings and thoughts. Being human, she had to be born again unto the light, and she did so that moment in the Garden of Nede when Natalia left her to retrieve the armor... So, as a public testimony, she became baptized that night.

After her baptism, Dolsia walked in the clearing of the damaged camp. She became filled with joy and wanted to reach out to everyone. Her smile contained much beauty and compassion and she glowed with a light that had not been seen from her since the beginning of time.

She glanced around the camp, noticing how depressed a great number of people still looked. Even after the miraculous healings that happened earlier that night, some men still lingered about somberly. Many of their faces looked tired and weary. The damages of the camp and the worried looks that came from the men reminded her of her dark past. She thought of the darkness that killed her everyday back then... A deep feeling of sympathy came over her as her thoughts switched back over to the fallen men. She wanted to pull them from the darkness that was beginning to feel so real.

She began to sing a song that came from deep within her heart. Her voice started off low and sweet, then became loud and uplifting for everyone to hear. She grabbed everyone's attention as they moved about the camp. Men began to gaze upon her and legna began to gravitate towards her. She seemed like a glimpse of hope during that troubling time. She was fire in the night. Her voice was beautiful and was filled with light and joy, cutting the darkness that sat about the camp.

The legna smiled, remembering her voice when she used to sing for the God of Light. Her voice used to be the first thing they heard in the early morning and last sweet thing they heard before they rested. The great God of Light delighted in her voice and praises; and delighted in her just then as she sang that night.

Oh light, please fall,
Please fall upon us tonight.
You know I have cried and died, screamed
And lied—but you have forgotten it all.
I stumbled in the darkness, covered in
Shame and you have set me free again.
Hallelujah!
Praise the Lord on high.
Hallelujah!
Praise the King of Kings.
I will never cry again!
I am no longer covered with relentless sin!
I HAVE BEEN FORGIVEN!
I have been set free!
I praise you, my God!
You have filled me with light!
You have made me bright and filled me with
Your very being!
Thank you, my God, for you are good!
WE WILL PRAISE YOUR GREAT NAME!
The enemy of darkness shall tremble at your
Name, Yehoshua!
All the weak find their strength in you!
The fatherless find their rest in you!
The dead are raised and the broken are healed by You!
All the world will become awakened and will
Praise your mighty name!
YOU ARE OUR KING!
Hallelujah!
Praise the Lord on high!
Hallelujah!
Praise the King of Kings!

The whole camp became filled with an overwhelming presence of love and peace as they sang with Dolsia. Their voices rang out and filled the air with joy. The worship they were doing invited the God of Light's presence! They never saw their mysterious God, but they knew he was there right then as the golden mists appeared again. Light seemed to burst from everyone as the powerful presence filled the night. They knew that it was the God of Light's presence that covered them. Even though the moon glowed like blood above them, even though their camp was ruined, and even though they knew an uncertain day lay before them…they felt that nothing was wrong because of the peace and joy that covered them that night. Even as the moon became a vibrant-red color, revealing impending doom, they praised their God as if nothing threatened them. Even in the storms of life, they would praise Him!

†††

Gaibriul, King Julpen, Natalia, and Prince Phillip stood before the precipice of the camp, looking out to the deeper lands of the south. They had been talking about the healing and restoration that happened hours earlier. They were still filled with joy even though their minds had switched over to the present state that the kingdom was in.

The red moon glowed in the dark lands, giving off a strange light. They could see the dark, jagged mountains, the rolling hills of the Black Field of Old Blood, and even Skull Hill.

"This ominous night seems as if it is the last night," Natalia said as she rubbed her arms. "But it was filled with many blessings and miracles. I will never forget this night…"

"Around this time there is usually happiness in the air," King Julpen added. "Tomorrow is the Spring Celebration, the end of an old year and the beginning of a new one… I hope my people will carry on the tradition as if nothing has happened. Peace must be set in the kingdom…"

"Whatever the new day shall bring, we accept it as the beginning," Gaibriul said. "Every day is a new beginning… Do not forget the miracles that the lord bestowed upon us tonight… It is so easy to forget and become inundated with uncertainty."

"The moon glows like blood…war is on the horizon," Phillip said in a low tone. "I know it has to happen… But I also know that whatever happens—we will do it to honor our Lord…"

They gazed quietly at the moon. They thought of the prophecy and recited it in their heads: Following the night when the moon glows like blood, during the twilight when the morning star shines the brightest—evil will prevail and take on a new form… That was the prophecy that they had been worried about within the days that passed them. The moon glowing red was the beginning of it, and sent chills down their spines.

"Prophecy stirs, blood spills, light burns, and darkness screams...," Gaibriul said as he looked off into the lands. "Do you see that tree way down below, upon Skull Hill?" Gaibriul asked, breaking the silence. He pointed his finger and they followed with their eyes. "Long ago King Yehoshua was nailed to that tree... The ancestors of Minslethrate brought him there to die—and he did... But his death was not them winning. His death was him sacrificing himself for us all... After his burial he rose from death! You see, he won the battle long ago—and no monster in hell can stop that. He is the last legend... Every legend after Yehoshua does not matter... Lucif lost a long time ago...but he will carry on his darkness and will continue to cause death over this world until he is stopped..."

They gazed at the tree way down below them. Their minds wondered and their hearts fluttered because of the incredible legend.

"How can Lucif be stopped?" King Julpen asked.

"...Unto the end... Only the light of God can stop him... He must be casted down into the age-old pit of darkness..."

They grew quiet again as they thought of what Gaibriul had said. They understood everything now, as if their eyes were opened and their minds fully awakened.

King Yehoshua was, is, and still is the legend of time. He is the legend of all legends... He is the last legend...

†

CHAPTER 23
A New Dawn

The night was late in the land of Minslethrate. The winds picked up and became like ice-cold daggers. The earth was matted with darkness and the trees and animals yielded to it. The blood-moon became vibrant and glowed in the icy sky, casting a red overcast upon the lands. Morning was coming, breaking the night behind the thick clouds.

The clouds moved about the strange winds, whirling through them mightily. Something happened then… A strange star appeared in the sky… The star was bigger than any other star that gleamed brightly in the black sky. It was the first time in what seemed like ages that a sparkling star appeared during the night. It was the morning star, and appeared for what seemed like only moments. The glorious star meant that the sun would be rising soon over the lands…

It was now twilight in Minslethrate, and evil darkness celebrated during that ominous night…

Marrisa lay on a stone table, on top of the highest tower of the dark fortress. Her mind had left her like a traveling spirit. But her heart still pumped, sending physical life to her seemingly dead body. Her pale-blue eyes stared up at the red moon which appeared lighter and softer. The moon was beginning to fall away, presenting a new day that was coming quickly.

The morning star gleamed brightly above her like a dream that seemed so far away. It was so close it seemed, but she could not touch it. She never flinched or moved and her white skin seemed to glow in the twilight. Her long red locks moved about in the cold winds and the black gown she wore fell on the dirty stone.

Even when everything seemed gone away from her, an evil presence lingered near… The Dark Lord crept towards her like a shadow, looming over her frozen countenance. She stared up at him, not even aware that he had come to her.

He raised his hands into the cold air, over Marrisa. The cold winds just stopped and all around them now was nothing but thick, heavy silence. The air was freezing cold as the darkness around them became thicker.

"So, it begins… You are the last sacrifice, Marrisa. As a queen and goddess—the world will be your throne and the undoing of man shall come quickly to your feet," he whispered as he covered her with his darkness. "Everyone shall know your name… It shall be said in every prayer…and the light shall shine no more… He will shine—no—more…"

Just then the thick darkness twirled around Marrisa, silently thrashing all around her. The black wind seeped into her mouth, eyes, and pores, filling her with his presence.

Marrisa's body began to thrash around, becoming poisoned by the Dark Lord. Her eyes tightened shut and her chest swelled as she sucked in the cold air. Then after moments, she stopped... She lay silently on the stone table. Then after a moment, her chest slowly went up and down. The darkness was gone and the sky was beginning to become dark gray as the sun rose...

Everything was still and silent... The early morning atmosphere seemed peaceful and mysterious…

Marrisa sat up in the dim light, then silently stood up. Her cold white feet walked across the stone as her long black gown trailed behind her. She silently made her way down the freezing stair-well of the tower and into the throne-room. The chamber was dark except for a few lit torches.

The silence was loud and a terrifying presence filled the room as she walked through it.

The room was filled with dark creatures. They silently crept across the ground and up the walls and across the ceiling. As Marrisa walked across the chamber, the crowd of creatures split, giving way to her and bowing down to her... The dark nomed watched her carefully as she sat on the throne that stood tall and menacingly at the end of the dreary hall.

Marrisa sat still like a statue, grasping the arms of the throne with her ice-cold hands. Large dark creatures that breathed heavily brought to her a crown. The ancient crown used to shine brightly like a golden star. It was the legendary crown of King Yehoshua… But it now was covered in a thick black substance, appearing morbid and foul. The creatures placed the crown on her head as she gazed off into the dark chamber.

Her eyes stared across the dark hall and out over the large balcony that opened up across from her. Her haunting eyes stayed locked on the dreary morning that was coming over the lands.

Her eyes were no longer beautiful and blue… They were black as night and gleamed like onyx stone. She was filled with Lucif, the Dark Lord…

A wicked smile came over her pale face as she watched the dim sky transform into an early morning. Her red locks fell over her shoulders and her white skin seemed to glow in the darkness as pale light crept into the chamber.

Her haunting beauty radiated with rage and wickedness.

Her black eyes gazed out over the lands of Minslethrate as she caressed the red pendant that hung from her neck…

Blood was all she saw…

And when they shall have finished their testimony, the beast that ascendeth out of the bottomless pit shall make war against them, and shall overcome them, and kill them.
Revelation 11: 7 KJV

Book Three
FOREVER

Who is this? and what is here?
And in the lighted palace near
Died the sound of royal cheer;
And they cross'd themselves for fear,
All the knights at Camelot:
But Lancelot mused a little space;
He said, "She has a lovely face;
God in his mercy lend her grace,
The Lady of Shalott."
-Alfred, Lord Tennyson

For they got not the land in possession by their own sword, neither did their own arm save them: but thy right hand, and thine arm, and the light of thy countenance, because thou hadst a favour unto them.
Psalm 44:3

In the beginning was the word…and the word was with God, because the word was God… And in the beginning, the word became alive upon the Earth, flourishing in abundance. And over time, it became a legend…a legend that should never be forgotten.

After the Great War in the Kingdom of Nevaeh, when Lucif and his followers fell upon the Earth, the God of Light foresaw the fall of the world, because Lucif brought with him deceiving gifts of malice and seeds of destruction.

But the fruits of darkness had been overpowered when the God of Light became flesh upon the Earth. And when He brought light with Him, the legend began. After many years of torment by darkness, the God of Light came into the world by blessing an unlikely peasant girl with a child…

This child, born into poverty by innocence—was the son of God. He was the light of the world, the savior of man—the last legend. He was the king of the Children of Light. This child was Yehoshua: God with us…

Yehoshua was led by the God of Light, because Yehoshua was the God of Light. He fought against darkness and gave the people a glimpse of Nevaeh. He became a leader of the people and a beacon of hope. He was loved by many, even by the earthly king of Minslethrate, who was an ancestor of Tairren… Tairren's king ancestor gave his thrown to Yehoshua, and followed Yehoshua with his whole heart.

Yehoshua led the people during his walk upon the Earth as king and taught them many things about love and light. His love-light became strong, becoming the key to man's heart—and the door to the Kingdom of Nevaeh… He taught them that having the key of love-light in their hearts was the only way to love others, the only way to stand up against darkness—and the only way into the Kingdom of Nevaeh…

After much time and turmoil, King Yehoshua spread peace over the Kingdom of Minslethrate.

Lucif became aware of the light that was spreading upon the world, and he became like a dark lion, going about devouring every heart he could get to. And he did exceedingly. Over time, Lucif became the prince of the world, blinding people who did not know the light of God. You see, since Lucif was cast out of Nevaeh and onto the Earth, he was no longer welcomed back into the Kingdom of Light. Iniquity ran thick in his blood and he did not want the light near him. Light and darkness will never become one. Light can not comprehend darkness, and darkness loathes the light… Spiritual and physical warfare was inevitable… Out of spite and wrath, Lucif the Dark Lord, yearned that every man who walked upon the Earth should be cast away from Nevaeh as he was, and yanked into an eternity of endless torment upon the pits of Hell—just as he will be…

Just as Yehoshua led men into the light, Lucif led men into darkness…

Just as Lucif loathed light, he loathed every carrier of light, everything containing even the smallest glimpse of light. The Dark Lord influenced the followers of the world to fight against King Yehoshua and his men, his people—his whole kingdom.

Minslethrate soon became another blood-ridden war-ground.

An evil king of the south who was named Baffmit, who was filled with Lucif's followers of darkness, rose up against King Yehoshua and the Golden Lands, which was the northern Kingdom of Minslethrate. Fires roared by night and violence flourished by day. The Kingdom of Minslethrate was beginning to fall once again…

Out of love for humanity, King Yehoshua yielded to King Baffmit, and fought no longer against the south's attacks. The northern Kingdom of Minslethrate was saved by his grace… But the followers of darkness began to think that they had won as they brought King Yehoshua to the south, stripping him of his armor and hanging him to the tree upon Skull Hill. King Yehoshua was tortured and broken, submitting to a death that was conjured up by darkness.

Unknowingly, Lucif and his followers had truly lost their battle as soon as King Yehoshua's blood was shed. You see, King Yehoshua was killed, but he became the final sacrifice. He was part of the God of Light's own plan; a plan that saved mankind from darkness, forever… You see, God sent his only son, Yehoshua, to die a gruesome death—so that whoever believed in Him and his love-light that he shared, would live forever in the Kingdom of Light…

And so, after his death, King Yehoshua rose from his grave as love-soaked light and ascended into the Kingdom of Nevaeh and into the hearts of His followers…

Out of vengeance, Tairren's ancestor king rose up against King Baffmit, along with Yehoshua's followers, and overpowered them and defeated them… Tairren's ancestor died in war, but his ways of light lived on. The king's successor, who was another follower of Yehoshua and also Marrisa's ancestor, took over the Kingdom of Minslethrate and carried on the light that King Yehoshua left behind…

Over time, darkness fell once again, and the Old Ways of Minslethrate were forgotten, and crumbled. The old temples and goddesses of Minslethrate were then left in ruins…

Time passed and many more died.

There were many more attacks on Minslethrate from Lucif, the Dark Lord. Even though Lucif's followers had passed away with time, he still lingered in the dark places of Minslethrate, conjuring up many more deceived followers… Lucif did not understand that he had already been defeated long ago. As the world turns in circles, so does the warfare between light and darkness, which is a never-ending battle.

It will never stop until Yehoshua comes again upon the Earth, bringing forth a rain of light and power…

These tales will never be lost, for they rest deep down in the hearts of man, waiting to come out over and over again. The Last Legend was awakened long ago, unto the end…and forever…

And so, our story continues, beginning with the legends of old…

†

PROLOGUE
The Last Legend

The sky of the northern kingdom was filled with black smoke and the air held relentless chaos. Screams echoed across the kingdom as evil men continued to destroy the castle walls and its weakened contents. The marketplace was ablaze with roaring fires which were spreading to nearby buildings. Doom fell over the kingdom as the castle walls were being breached.

The Kingdom that used to hold beauty and tranquility—was now falling.

Inside the castle garden, the king of Minslethrate stood. The gardens were left untouched by evil hands, but would soon fall victim to fire. He had been praying as he walked upon the garden's beauty. Anguish sat heavily over him as sweat trickled like blood down his brow. His heart was heavy with sadness and his body grew anxious. He prayed that whole evening, that the God of Light would allow his quest to pass him by, but if not, to let His will be done.

His eyes were weary and his heart was subdued. He grasped a letter with his shaken hand that he had written earlier that afternoon. The cool winds of that evening felt sweet upon his tense skin, but did not relieve any of the overwhelming stress that lay thick upon him.

Then as if out of nowhere, a light appeared in the dark shadows of the garden, seeming to descend from another world. The light was like a breath of fresh air. The light came from an owl that flew into the garden, and perched right above the king on a tree branch. The site of the beautiful bird was like gazing upon the moon. The being of light strengthened him with mighty words and peace. The glowing light that came from the mighty bird seemed to become absorbed into his skin as he gazed at it. After what seemed like many hours, the bird spread its golden-tipped feathers and flew from its perch.

The light then faded in the dark garden.

The king watched as the bird seemed to disappear into the darkness of the morbid sky. His body felt relieved all of a sudden as he knew that his quest was nearly finished. His fate was coming quickly upon him.

"My Lord," a low voice said from behind him. It held nervousness. "What must we do?"

The king turned his passionate eyes on the man as he clenched the letter that was still in his hand. His blue-green eyes sparkled and held no sign of panic any longer. He possessed new strength that came from the owl.

"The spirit is willing but the flesh is weak, Peter...," he said, looking up at the other men who watched him. "But fear not this night..."

The men standing around him were his followers: his brethren and companions. They watched the king with solemn faces. They knew what lie before them, but it was hard for them to accept it. But they loved their king and trusted everything that he had taught and revealed to them—everything that was revolving around him and happening.

"Give this letter to the children and make sure they leave with haste to the Kingdom of Hanon," the king said as he handed the letter to Peter. "They are the children of time—they are your legacy, this kingdom's legacy..."

Peter nodded his head as he looked into the king's eyes, accepting the letter. Peter knew that it was important that the letter went with the children to Hanon. It was dire that the children left Minslethrate as soon as possible. He trusted the king with his children's destiny.

Peter had a servant's heart and wanted to serve his king more than anything. He used to lead Minslethrate, but gave up his throne to the mighty Yehoshua. He was a believer and knew that Yehoshua was the son of God, and that he would lead them into the light. He also knew that King Yehoshua loved his children—and that Yehoshua had a plan for his son and daughter...away from Minslethrate, in the Kingdom of Hanon.

"Give this to the boy," Yehoshua said as he took off the wing-shaped pendant that hung from his neck. The precious stones on the pendant sparkled just like his eyes did. "He must wear this pendant and keep it safe...for time knows what the future holds. Time is so precious in all of this... The future of this kingdom will depend on your son's fate..."

Just then the men were disturbed by a large group of people. The people were laden with shadows and their eyes glowed with madness. Their faces were frightening and covered with scars. The firelight from the torches they held gave them no justice. The men were rough-looking and were laden in tattered animal skins and matted fur. They held their weapons tightly in their hands. They carried no peace or love with them.

The leader of the men walked before them, grasping a long sword that had a hilt made of bones. He wore a black helmet that had long horns jutting from its sides. His helmet shadowed most of his frightening face. A long cape, covered in black feathers, fell down his broad back as sweat glistened off of his bulky arms.

From out of the crowd a man came. He slowly walked towards King Yehoshua, having a forlorn look on his face. He appeared nervous and ashamed as King Yehoshua's men looked at him with shock and confusion. King Yehoshua's followers became angry at the sight of him walking with the evil men. Because even though he walked with darkness, he was one of Yehoshua's followers. The man timidly stood before Yehoshua and slowly brought his lips to his cheek, kissing the king.

The mighty king looked into the man's nervous eyes. "You betray the son of man with a kiss, Iscariot?" King Yehoshua asked in a low voice as the man looked away from him.

Just then the leader of the wicked men tossed a small sack of coins to Iscariot. "For your information," the man said as his deep voice broke the silence. His tongue was like fire.

The foul men standing behind him began to laugh and mock King Yehoshua.

"You vile, traitor!" Peter yelled as he quickly came towards Iscariot. Emotion could be heard behind his voice.

Iscariot recoiled, moving back into the shadows.

The other men stood with Peter as their emotions flew. Looks of anger came from them as they glared at Iscariot. They were angry at their fellow companion for betraying their king.

Just then King Yehoshua raised his hand, silencing his flustered men. His face was calm. "Do what you must, Baffmit," the king said. His sparkling eyes never faltered as he looked at the evil man.

The ugly leader named Baffmit gestured with his head for his men to capture King Yehoshua. The dark men laughed and mocked Yehoshua's followers as they quickly came upon him, seizing him.

Yehoshua did not move as they grabbed his arms.

Peter's chin began to tremble as he watched his master become inundated by the foul men. Just then, Peter gave out a cry as anger swelled up inside of him. He quickly pulled out his sword and lunged at one of the men who grabbed Yehoshua. He swung his sword, grazing the side of his head. The man's ear flew off with a spray of blood, making him let go of Yehoshua.

The men began to fight as their emotions got the best of them. The garden suddenly became filled with angry shouts and the clanking of metal.

Iscariot looked on helplessly at his fellow brothers, becoming afraid. He then ran off into the darkness of the night to pursue his own fate, never to be seen by them or King Yehoshua again…

Yehoshua stood still, not moving from his spot. He didn't even try to fight back or escape the dark clutches of the men. "If violence is your first instinct, then violence will be your undoing!" King Yehoshua said in a stern voice to Peter as he looked at him and his men. "How must the prophecy be fulfilled if it does not happen this way?"

King Yehoshua's men became quiet as they obeyed their lord. Everyone became still. Their chests heaved with compassion and their eyes became sore as they looked upon Yehoshua's loving face.

Yehoshua looked at Baffmit who watched silently, then kneeled down to the man whose ear was cut from him. He placed a kind hand on the side of the man's bloody head, looking into his confused eyes. The man's breaths were hard as he cringed in pain. But as King Yehoshua pulled his hand away, the man's head was completely healed. A new ear could be seen!

Yehoshua quietly stood up, looking at the silent and shocked men that stood before him. His face appeared brave and unwavering.

Baffmit looked at him for a moment, then gestured for his men to arrest him. Even though he saw the kindness from King Yehoshua and the miracles he performed, his black heart still loathed him...

King Yehoshua's followers watched helplessly as the wicked band of men took him away. Their hearts stirred with a mixture of sadness and anger as King Yehoshua faded into the darkness of the garden with Baffmit and his men. Even though it was hard to watch their king be taken away from them and into an uncertain fate, they knew it had to be done. They knew their king was not only their king, but the king of man. He was their savior—mankind's savior...

Tears gathered in their eyes as he could be seen no more...

✝✝✝

The events that followed King Yehoshua's seize were too gruesome and unsettling to perceive. King Yehoshua had been forced into the Forbidden Lands by the heartless men. He had been stripped of His armor and crown by their wicked leader, King Baffmit, which were given to the ancient goddesses of Minslethrate. A crown of sharp barbs was forced onto his head and he was beaten. Blood lay thickly upon him. They mocked and laughed at him, spitting at his name. He was brutalized and humiliated by the evil men. The pain was unbearable and the site of it was agonizing. He was then nailed to a tree upon Skull Hill: A place where criminals were sent to die...

After many gruesome hours of torment, a dark soldier shoved his spear through King Yehoshua's side, just to make sure that his death was inevitable. Yehoshua's blood ran down like water as his body began to die on the tree. His blood saturated the soil around him, running deep down into the earth...

Darkness came over Minslethrate then as the land and sky began to quake. The Earth reflected the God of Light's emotions then as His only son died... The sky became filled with cold winds as the earth broke and cracked beneath the tree where his blood ran. It was all over then; his quest was finished. The son of man and God, died...

He gave up his life for his kingdom, and all mankind...

✝✝✝

Peter did as King Yehoshua wished. He gave the king's wing-pendant to his son, then quickly sent his children off towards the Kingdom of Hanon. He sent a servant with his son and daughter—praying that they would be protected on their journey. He didn't know his children's fate—but he knew his legacy would live on, forever…

From that moment on, Peter never saw his children again, but he knew in his heart that the God of Light would watch over them…

Peter thought of his children, the kingdom, and King Yehoshua as he hurried towards the south of Minslethrate with his men.

He and the followers of King Yehoshua grew weary at the thought of their king's death…

Peter, who was once the King of Minslethrate, before Yehoshua, led the followers of light against Baffmit and the dark men of the south.

His revenge held power.

A war grew among them as they fought in the treacherous valley before the tree King Yehoshua died on. Many hours had passed and much blood was shed as Peter avenged his King of Light. But as a blood-red moon rose upon the lands that night, Peter died before the enemy's sword… But even with the death of Peter, Baffmit and the men of the south were defeated that night. Their flesh and bones littered the earth.

The Black Field of Old Blood became its name, and the legend behind it became its roots.

King Baffmit, along with his wicked men, rotted upon the valley as time passed, but King Yehoshua rose from death and unto Neveah and the hearts of man.

King Yehoshua was risen…

But the time is now…and continues with Tairren: Peter's legacy and offspring—the hero, born from the children of time...

✝

CHAPTER 1
Trust

Tairren slowly opened his eyes. His vision was slightly blurred. Orange light that looked soft and warm slowly took shape before him. After a moment, his eyesight cleared and he could see why the light over him was orange. The light came from fire. The sounds of the crackling heat became audible as he slowly awakened. He brought his hand to his throbbing forehead, realizing that dried blood covered it in flakes. He slowly sat up, trying to collect his thoughts and memory. A puddle of coagulated blood could be seen where his head had been resting. A great fire burned before him, and suddenly his memory came back to him.

"Finally, you've awakened," a low voice came. It was a woman's voice.

Startled, Tairren turned his head towards where the voice came from. His tired eyes fell on a woman who sat before him on the ground. Her legs were folded and she rested her hands on her knees. He recognized the woman who stared at him, who was covered from head to toe in a black garb. She was the same woman who had led him to Fiara the day before.

"You... You are...," he stuttered, but stopped speaking.

He looked around, realizing that he was still in Fiara's cavern among the Fire Temple. The great fire roared before him, sending its heat out in waves. He was still in the same spot where Fiara had left him. Tairren began to look around quickly, expecting for Fiara to come out of the shadows of the cavern at any moment.

"She is no longer among us," the woman said as she gazed at Tairren.

Tairren looked into her eyes. Her eyes looked like golden honey, reminding him of Fiara's furtive eyes. Fiara ripped through his mind like an intense heat wave. "Where is she?" he asked.

The woman looked into his confused eyes for a moment longer, then turned her gaze to the golden sword that lay a couple of feet away from Tairren.

"Your sword...," she said.

Surprised, Tairren slowly stood up, gazing at the splendid sword. He went to the glorious blade, wondering why Fiara never bothered to hide it again from human eyes. He picked up the golden relic, amazed at how light and exquisite it was. When he had fought with it the night before, he couldn't pay much attention to it because of Fiara's attacks. But now his eyes looked over it as if it were a new treasure.

Tairren held the sword out, then swiftly swung it around, amazed at how it cut through the air so quickly.

"A relic as beautiful as that must mean the world to you," the strange woman said, slowly standing up.

Tairren noticed that she was tall, and had a long black braid that came from her hood and over her shoulder. She was clad in a loose black tunic and trouser and wore a long robe. All of her skin was covered, even her face. Only her eyes could be seen peering at him between two pieces of fabric that were wrapped around her head.

"You took my sword yesterday before I saw Fiara," Tairren said as he glanced at her strange-looking sword that hung by her side. "Why didn't you take this sword when you had the chance? Instead, you watched me sleep." He slid the legendary sword into his scabbard, which fit perfectly.

She was quiet and just stared at him, then turned to walk away from him.

"Who are you and where is Fiara?!" Tairren demanded.

The woman stopped, turning around again. "I've told you—I am the eyes of this mountain... And I've told you before, Fiara is no longer among us... Take your sword and go."

She turned to walk away again, moving towards the great entrance of the cavern.

Tairren went quickly to her, curious about her. He wondered why she let him take the ancient sword, and why she was letting him go so easily.

"You let me leave without a fight?" Tairren asked quickly. "You are Fiara's servant and you allow me to live?"

The woman began to laugh, not turning back to look at him. "You are queer, boy. Do you want me to kill you? Because, I will if that is your wish. Fiara is all powerful...if she wanted you locked up or dead—you wouldn't be talking to me now... Come with me, quickly."

Tairren followed her out of the cavern and through the great threshold. They went down a torch lit corridor and into another great hall, which was the main entrance hall. Natural light poured in from the entrance and they were walking straight towards it.

Tairren realized that they were walking to the outside of the Fire Temple. He wondered why the woman was leading him out and why Fiara did not kill him when she had the chance. The woman or Fiara could have easily ended his life when he lay unconscious throughout the night.

"Where are you taking me?" Tairren asked, confused.

"Have you forgotten about your strange companions already?" she asked.

"You are leading me to Rafiul? I don't believe you." Tairren said as they stopped right outside of the entryway.

"You do not trust me when I have already helped you?" she asked.

"I'm confused... You put your life in danger by helping me. Fiara will have you dead when she discovers your doing... You put your life in danger by trusting me. I could have killed you when you turned your back on me."

The woman laughed again. "You will not kill me. Like you just said—you had the chance, but didn't. I see it in your eyes—what kind of person you are..."

"Why are you helping me?" Tairren asked.

"Do you want to see your companions again, or not?" she asked quickly.

Tairren grew quiet, then nodded his head. He looked into her golden eyes, wondering what kind of person she truly was. How could someone who served darkness do good works? Tairren felt that he could trust her, but didn't know if she was truly trust-worthy or not.

Tairren followed her across the open space before the entrance of the temple, passing the massive golden idol of Fiara. They made their way to the other side, coming upon a large terrace that looked out over the lands. The view before them was breathtaking as they walked past the open space of the terrace. All of the south could be seen from where they were at.

Tairren looked towards the Great Mountains of Minslethrate where the Dark Tower of Sacrifice sat. Thick, black clouds loomed over the tower and the mountains, covering everything in dark shadows. Tairren's heart fluttered at the thought of him making his way closer to his destination. He could see that he was close, only having to descend Fiara Mountain and journey across the Black Field of Old Blood. It appeared easy, but he knew that looks were deceiving in the south.

"This way," the woman said, making a quick turn past a large boulder. She disappeared into an unseen passageway.

Tairren swallowed down his anxiousness and followed her through the narrow path along the mountainside. They went down many steps which led them into another open space in the mountain. They hurried past the open space towards what looked like an opening to another cavern.

"How did you get Rafiul and his beast all the way through here?" Tairren asked, wondering how one woman could capture a man and a large beast.

"I didn't...," she said.

"Fiara said that they were locked in the mountain," Tairren said quickly.

"They are not in the mountain," she said, sounding sly.

"But..."

"You are too inquisitive, boy!" she scolded, cutting Tairren off. "Follow me and you will see your companions."

Tairren looked at her curiously, wondering how much longer they had to go. She could've been leading him into a trap... They seemed to have trekked the mountainside for what seemed like hours. He glanced up Fiara Mountain and noticed that they had already descended half of it.

Tairren followed her into the cave. There was a torch sticking out of the wall, right inside the opening of the cavern. The cavern was dark and moist. Their footsteps could be heard bouncing off of the rocky walls of the cave. The strong scent of earth filled the air. The cave was massive and had many twists and turns. He would've gotten lost if the woman was not with him. They went down more steps, over cracked stone bridges, and under large archways.

Finally, after what seemed like hours more, Tairren could see gray light coming in through a narrow passage-way. They climbed over more large rocks and over deep cracks, coming upon a large pool of clear-blue water. The water looked cold and refreshing and tempted Tairren to drink from it.

Tairren went to the pool, looking into the deep-looking water. The water seemed to pull at his eyes.

"Do not drink from the pool," the woman said quickly. Her voice startled the quiet atmosphere, echoing throughout the massive cave. "The water is poisoned."

"Poisoned?" Tairren asked.

"The water has something in it that forces the mind to slip away for hours," she said, gazing into Tairren's eyes.

Tairren thought of the cool drink of water that she had given him before... He thought of how it had sent him into a state of oblivion.

"That is the water I drank yesterday," Tairren said quickly. "You offered it to me." He gave her a suspicious look.

"Fiara demanded that all of her guests drink from the water," the woman said, crouching over the edge of the pool. She stuck her fingertips into the clear liquid. "This water makes one see things that are not really there. This is what influences her guests to see her magic..."

"False magic," Tairren corrected quickly, becoming annoyed. "Great and powerful she is?!" Tairren's voice cut through the chilly cave. "She has no power."

"You know nothing, boy! Fiara is a dangerous sorceress! She does not need this water to call upon the powers from another world!" the woman yelled, becoming defensive. She hit the water, sending a splash out into the air. "Fiara *is* powerful!"

Tairren grew quiet, watching the woman's strange reaction. He kept his eyes on her, slowly backing away from her.

"Forgive me," she said, noticing how Tairren became suddenly cautious of her.

She became quiet for a moment, then began to make her way towards the narrow opening of the cave.

"Your companions were snooping about the base of the mountain. They found this cave and drank from the pool yesterday… They slept for hours and I tied them up. I didn't know if they could be trusted or not… Through here, you will find them," she said motioning with her free hand towards the outside light.

Tairren nodded his head, still aware of her movements. He looked at her for a moment longer, then quickly went through the passage-way.

Tairren rushed through the opening, noticing that he was at the bottom of the mountain. The passage-way opened out to the dry earth of the Forbidden Lands. A cold wind blew past him, sending his cape rippling out in the gray air. They had descended the whole mountain.

He quickly turned around, noticing that the woman slowly followed behind him, watching him.

Straight away as he turned towards the lands again, Tairren noticed Rafiul. He was tied to a dead tree while Cherbim lay near him, pinned down beneath a web of thick ropes. They had been bounded tightly and couldn't move, not even a little.

Tairren ran to Rafiul, anxious to cut him free. "Hold on, my friend," Tairren said, pulling his sword from his scabbard.

Rafiul's eyes widened with joy, noticing the glorious sword. "Tairren, this day the God of Light smiles upon you! You've retrieved the sword and are alive! And now you come to our rescue."

As Tairren cut the ropes from him, Rafiul noticed the shadowed woman standing nearby. His mannerism changed quickly by the sight of her. "You!" he yelled with flashing eyes. "You did this!"

The woman walked to them, not saying anything. Her long black cape moved through the air.

"No, Rafiul," Tairren said quickly. "She has helped me down the mountain. She led me to you… It was the water in the cave that made you sleep…"

Rafiul gazed at her with his intense eyes, then began to cut the web of ropes that covered Cherbim. "I know now, Tairren… I saw her watching us from afar. We drank from the pool in the cave—then I woke up tied to this tree… But she is forgiven… Her helping you shows something otherwise. But she still must not be fully trusted." He glared at the woman with intense eyes.

Just as Rafiul set Cherbim free, the mighty beast lunged at the woman, knocking her to the ground.

"Stop, Cherbim!" Rafiul yelled out in a strong voice.

The beast did not attack the woman, but just growled at her instead. His face was only inches from hers. He then slowly stepped backwards and sat down on his haunches. His large eyes were locked on her.

Rafiul quickly came to him, petting the beastly cat's wings which were folded back. "We need answers before she dies, Cherbim," he said while looking at her.

Tairren went quickly to the woman. She held her hand in front of her face with her eyes still glued to Cherbim. Tairren helped her up as she looked quickly at each one of them.

"Please, don't kill me," she pleaded. "I can help you. I know where you should go." She turned her fiery gaze on Tairren. "I can help you, Tairren. I know all of the hidden ways around the south. I can help you just as I helped you through the hidden path down the mountain."

Tairren looked at Rafiul who never took his gaze off of her. Rafiul watched her like how a hawk would watch its prey.

"Can you lead us to the Dark Tower of Sacrifice?" Tairren asked.

"She can not be trusted, Tairren," Rafiul said. "Anyone who serves darkness can not be trusted to do any good."

"I can be trusted, Tairren," she said quickly, never taking her golden stare off of Tairren. "You've trusted me this far... I know all ways upon these lands. I know secret paths that no man has walked upon before. You can ride your horse across the Black Field of Old Blood—but it is filled with deep trenches and creeping things. I know a way that is secret—much safer."

Tairren knew that Rafiul would always do what was good for him and his quest, but the woman seemed to be honest and knew things that even Rafiul did not. There was something about the woman that made Tairren want to believe her. He had compassion in his heart for everyone, even her, and did not want to see the woman who helped him, suffer.

"Lead us, then," Tairren said with a serious face, looking into the woman's eyes.

"We must go back to the camp, with haste," Rafiul said quickly. "You have done well thus far, but you are not ready, Tairren. We must go back to the legna with the sword. You must obtain the rest of the armor…"

"I *am* ready!" Tairren raised his voice, cutting Rafiul off. "I have obtained King Yehoshua's sword. The spirit of God has blessed me! This is *my* quest and *I* know that I am ready. This woman could lead us to the tower much quicker! We are wasting precious time! Marrisa needs me!"

"Tairren!" Rafiul said in a stern voice. His tone caught Tairren's attention. "Your labor should never be in vain. This is about God's timing—not our own!" He scolded as his yellow-gold eyes flashed. He glanced at the woman, then back at him. "Do not be unequally yoked with unbelievers…," he lowered his voice as he looked at Tairren caringly. "What good comes from fellowshipping with darkness?"

"I believe just as you do," the woman said convincingly, still looking at Tairren.

Tairren clenched his teeth, looking towards the Dark Tower again. They were so close. They were so close that Tairren's heart began to break at the thought of Marrisa again. "...I want to go further," Tairren said with a straight face, looking back at Rafiul.

Tairren felt strange for challenging his guardian, but he knew that nothing could stop him.

Rafiul silently looked at him for a moment, then nodded his head. "And I will be by your side," he said. "Today shall bring destruction quickly... We must go with haste, then."

Tairren began to feel ashamed of himself as he watched Rafiul walk away with Cherbim following.

"I have my own horse," the woman said, taking Tairren's attention away from Rafiul. She didn't seem to be bothered by Rafiul's warnings. "That is how I know my way around the south... I shall call him."

Tairren watched as she pulled the black fabric down off of the lower part of her face. She brought her fingers to her mouth and made a loud whistle sound. After a moment, a black horse came running from behind large boulders that were a way away from them. From afar the horse looked strong and agile.

Tairren smiled. "I know you are the eyes of Fiara Mountain, but— what's your name?" he asked. He didn't think that she would tell him because she ignored telling him many times before.

She stayed quiet as her horse galloped to her. The mighty black horse stopped abruptly before them, carrying a strange breeze with him. She patted the horse's neck then pulled herself onto him. "Jezebel," she finally said, looking down at Tairren.

"Alright...Jezebel," Tairren said, surprised that she shared her name with him.

He gave her one last look, speculating who she really was, then glanced over at Rafiul who kept watching them. He left Jezebel and walked past Rafiul, ignoring his stare. He spotted Lilly grazing on some grass not too far from where they stood. He started towards Lilly quickly, wanting to get going.

"Master Tairren," Rafiul said, catching his attention. He was sitting atop Cherbim's mighty back, petting the top of the beast's large head. "Stay vigilant, always... False believers will come to you in sheep's clothing...but inwardly, they are ravaging wolves."

Tairren just gazed at Rafiul, understanding what he was trying to tell him. He didn't respond, but just made his way to Lilly instead.

Then, after a short while, they were off, going further into the south towards the Dark Tower of Sacrifice.

The woman named Jezebel led them along the outer edges of the rugged mountains, around the Black Field of Old Blood and towards the Dark Tower—and to an uncertain fate.

†

CHAPTER 2
War on the Horizon

Moral looked out over the Kingdom of Hanon. The moors in which the kingdom sat were breathtaking, rolling and stretching as far as the eye could see. The flowers and bracken upon the lands gracefully swayed in the gusts of wind that bellowed by. She could tell that the sky would've looked like it was on fire in the mornings and evenings. But it seemed like impending doom was coming upon Hanon… The sky was cold and gray, appearing much like Minslethrate's skyward mantle.

Moral wrapped her shawl around her arms as she looked towards the south. She thought of her son as she noticed how much darker the south had appeared. The skies were thick and black, reminding her of the darkness that was coming upon her homelands.

"Good morning—even if it is a dreary one," a friendly voice said from behind her.

Moral turned to look at her dear friend, Sora. "Good morning to you, Sora," she said with a faint smile. "It's an ominous one at that… The clouds look as if they are about to cry... My heart seems to reflect the weather. I worry for our children and kingdom, Sora." Sora nodded her head, understanding completely what she was going through emotionally. "I've prayed all night that this day would be okay," Moral continued, "…and if not—that we would be safe…that the Lord our God would protect us against the workings of darkness." Moral looked back towards the south. "I wonder if Tairren is okay… Do you think they are safe, Sora?"

Sora walked to Moral, looking into her gray eyes. They sparkled as a layer of tears covered them. "I do…" She placed her round hand on Moral's shoulder. "Our eyes may be weary, but we are in good hands, Moral. It is all but a sunrise away—the goodness that is to come. We are but simple women—but we are strong women of God now…never forget that, Moral. I know you won't because you taught me that. Even if war draws near—we will know where our help comes from—the Lord…"

Moral nodded her head with a smile, amazed at how much Sora's faith had grown. She truly admired Sora's newfound strength and independence.

"Good morning, madam," Finagin said from behind the women as he quickly walked onto the balcony. "I hope breakfast was to your liking. I demanded that the best was prepared for you, my lady." He smiled as he spoke. "His Lordship wishes to speak with you now, before your departure."

Moral and Sora glanced at each other, then nodded reluctantly. They cringed on the inside at the word "departure". They were nervous to go back home and face the current situation their kingdom was in. The mention of war was embedded in their brains, which frightened them. Minslethrate had been in a period of grace for many years. No war of any kind had fallen over Minslethrate since they've been living. They heard of the legends of old about King Yehoshua leading is men into war, but war was something of the past. Their fate and the future of Minslethrate were unknown, and frightening to predict...

†††

Lord Timotheus stood quietly, staring out of the massive windows of his study. He looked out over the heath, becoming nervous by the black clouds that seemed to appear overnight. A pensive look settled over his old face and his dark-blue eyes glittered upon the pale light that came in through the window.

"My Lord," Finagin said in a low tone. He quietly walked into the study with the women following behind him. "Lady Moral and Mistress Sora are here now, just as you wished."

The old man nodded his head and motioned for them to come to him. Finagin left the room quickly. Lord Timotheus came away from his window and hobbled over to some chairs, which sat before a great fireplace. The fire was inviting and sent rays of warmth over them. The tap of his cane against the ground and the crackle of the fire added to the ominous atmosphere.

"Come and sit with me," the lord said as he slowly sat on his chair.

The women solemnly sat on the chairs across from his. They watched as Lord Timotheus gazed into the great fireplace. They waited for him to speak.

"The clouds are bringing something strange to Hanon," he finally said, looking over at them. "...Or, I should say, something strange is bringing the clouds."

The women looked out of the massive windows. Moral had felt the same way when she looked off of the balcony that morning. The dark clouds seemed to bring a morbid presence with it.

"Yes, I feel it too, my lord," Moral said in a low voice. "The feeling of impending doom came over my heart this morning when I awakened. I fear this day... I have to believe that God is going to remember us as the day becomes darker." She glanced at Sora, who looked very nervous.

Lord Timotheus brought his bony ringed hand to his white beard, then slowly nodded his head as if agreeing with her. "I have spoken to the king of Hanon early this morning. He has called upon Sir Andor and is gathering an army—as we speak."

558

Moral's eyes widened as her heart seemed to stop for a quick moment. Her bottom lip slowly dropped. Anxiousness came over her as she rubbed her arms. "Oh, my... It's hard for me to accept what is happening. War can not happen—but a strong hand is what Minslethrate needs..." She glanced at Sora again, then looked at the concerned lord. "I do not know such a word or what it brings... But I know we must accept what is happening...Lord Fernund must know for our king's sake. I must accept it... I know we must be strong during these times." Her voice began to shake with emotion. "It's strange, really. Just a couple of days ago I was content, having tea and tarts in my cottage among the forest— and today...I am about to embark upon unfamiliar circumstances." She slightly giggled out of nervousness as tears flooded her eyes. "...Why is this happening?" Moral asked in a shaken voice, unable to contain her emotion. She brought her hands to her face and began to cry. "Why is God allowing this to happen?!"

Sora placed her hand upon Moral's back, then looked at Lord Valor with uneasy eyes.

"My lady," he said, in a caring old voice. "Sometimes we must go through the valley—before reaching the mountain top... We do not know the grand scheme of things—what God's plans are... It is even hard sometimes to see the top of the mountain, because of mists or heavy clouds, but we must believe that it is there in order to reach it."

Moral stopped crying, wiping her eyes. She looked up at the lord, pleased by his words. She knew in her heart what he was talking about— she just had to hear it from someone else. "I'm sorry," she said, sniffling. "I'm blubbering like a child again."

"My lady, do not apologize for having emotions," he said with a faint smile. "We are only human. That's why we must never lean on our own understanding. We must trust that God has our fates already figured out. It is curious how one day brings the sun—and the next brings darkness. Each day brings trouble of its own... That is why we must trust in God every day." He smiled at her, then touched her wet cheek with a caring hand. "Now, don't let this day bring you despair, my lady."

Moral smiled with some effort as she glanced at both Sora and Lord Timotheus. "What should we do?" she asked.

"You amaze me, Moral," the lord said. "Sir Andor and his men will lead you back to Minslethrate. They will take care of you."

"You are not coming?" Moral asked, searching Lord Valor's blue eyes. It was nice having a father by her side.

He laughed, raising his heavy white eyebrows. "My dear, my old legs won't have that." He smiled as he patted his bad leg with his hand. "My body is in no shape for adventure. My days of quest seeking are over. If my cane ever gave out on me, your back would have to carry me," he said with a chuckle. His lightheartedness made the women giggle.

"That's the smile I'm sure my son fell in love with," the old man said with a twinkle in his old eyes. "Now, with that said, I do believe Sir Andor is waiting for us down in the foyer." Moral's smile faded a little. "Remember to always keep your heart up, my lady."

Then Lord Timotheus glanced up noticing someone in the doorway. He signaled for the person to come into the study.

It was Finagin, and he obeyed the lord's summon quickly. "A soldier is here to see you, my lord," he said.

"Let him in, Finagin," Lord Timotheus said quickly.

Finagin left quickly, then hurried back in with a soldier following right behind him.

The old man got up, noticing who the soldier was. "Aaah, Gideon, my boy," he said with a smile.

The soldier came quickly to them, bowing his head of blonde hair. Gideon was very young-looking and had a face that reminded Moral of Tairren. His blue eyes sparkled with tenacity and his face was smooth and untouched by stress.

"Sir Andor is waiting with the coach, My Lord," he said, looking at Lord Timotheus, then at the ladies.

"Yes, yes, thank you, lad," the lord said. "Ladies," he said, looking back at the women, "this is young Gideon. He is Sir Andor's newest squire and has been in training for weeks now to serve in the Legion of Hanon." The ladies smiled at him, nodding their heads. "This is Lady Moral Valor and Mistress Sora," he said.

"I'm pleased to meet you both," Gideon said, sounding nervous. "Shall I take you to the coach?" he asked, politely.

"That would be splendid," Lord Timotheus said. He guided them out into the corridor.

"Thank you, Lord Timotheus, for everything," Moral said with a kind smile. "I will always be proud to be part of the Valor family," she said, bowing her head.

Sora nodded and smiled, feeling thankful that she had been accepted by the Valor family as well.

The old man gave both of the women a warm hug, looking over them as if they were his daughters.

After a moment of embracing, Finagin led Gideon and the ladies down the corridor. Moral glanced back one last time before turning the corner, nodding at her husband's kind father.

The rest of the early afternoon went by quickly. Gideon led the nervous women to Sir Andor, who waited for them in the main hall. Sir Andor appeared to be about their age and had a serious, rugged face. His black beard fell onto his chest and his face had scars upon it from past wars.

Sir Andor nodded to them and led them to a coach that was waiting for them. "Gideon, my boy," he said. His voice was deep and intimidating. "Lead us out to the heath."

The young soldier did as he was told. He nodded his head, then pulled his helmet on. He got onto his horse then went before the carriage.

Moral turned back to look at Finagin who was watching them from the manor's great porch. He waved to them, making her smile. She then glanced up at the manor, feeling as if she were seeing it for the last time. Everything had felt like a dream then and happened so fast. She was thankful for everything that had happened, and relieved that she finally had the opportunity to speak to her husband's family.

She noticed that Lord Timotheus was watching from his window on the second floor. Moral looked at him for a moment before getting into the coach, then gave him one last nod.

Then they were off through the Valor Provence, following behind Gideon. They passed the many crops and workers of the manor, wondering if the servants had any clue of what was going on.

When they finally made it to the moors of Hanon, Moral was blown away by the sight of Sir Andor's army. Hundreds of men on horses waited for them upon the heath. They were lined up ever so perfectly, and their armor gleamed in the gray light of the early afternoon.

Moral and Sora gazed out of the window of their carriage, speechless and mesmerized by the army of men.

"The King of Hanon has sent his army with us," Sir Andor said, sitting across from the intimidated women. "Lord Timotheus has announced that a war is on the horizon of Minslethrate. Lord Timotheus feels that we should move with urgency. We have always looked upon Minslethrate as our brother-kingdom... We know that war is not the answer for Minslethrate, and if war shall ever come—we will be there... But, war against who? That, I do not know," he said, peering out of the window as they passed the mighty men of Hanon. "But we are ready..."

Moral listened well, but seemed to only hear bits and pieces as he spoke. She was surprised at all of the men. She knew what was going on, but didn't understand at the same time. She glanced down at her husband's sword that rested upon her lap. She squeezed the hilt and closed her eyes as Sir Andor continued to speak. She said a silent prayer in her heart and then thought of her husband... Everything was really happening, and there was no turning back. She wished that she was back at her cottage with Tairren by her side—but she knew that it wasn't going to happen. The days of her past seemed like a dream, and she felt as if those days were over. Her heart pounded as she looked back out of the window.

The carriage went off into the moors with half of the army leading them and the other half following. The young soldier named Gideon also rode close to them. She felt protected, but everything was uncertain at the same time…

✝

CHAPTER 3
Newfound Strength

The winds of the heath pushed at the carriage as they hurried towards Minslethrate. Noon was passing them by quickly and the sky was turning darker. They could feel the cold winds through the closed door of the carriage. It became dimmer inside as they rode in silence.

Moral continued to look out of her small window, watching the sloping heath of Hanon. Her eyes skipped around the patches of white heather that carpeted the earth. Her eyes then drifted up to the dark sky. Some parts of the sky were darker than others, but she could see that the sky above them was lighter than the southern sky.

"They just get darker—the clouds," Moral said in a low voice, breaking the silence.

"It's an omen," Sora said. "Something is happening…something that is greater than all of us."

"What do you mean?" Sir Andor asked, peering at them beneath his dark eyebrows. "Is it not just the weather turning?"

"I don't think this is normal weather," Moral said, tightening her hand around the hilt of her sword. "I believe it is darkness becoming stronger upon the lands. I fear it is spreading…"

Sir Andor looked at her strangely. The only thing he knew was strife between humans, not things like growing dark powers. "I don't understand, My Lady."

"It's hard to explain, Sir Andor," Moral said, becoming insecure. "There is evil in the world. But there is also light…" Moral took her eyes off of the man, then bit her bottom lip. He didn't look impressed. "Do you know of the Book of Light?" she asked, looking back at him.

"I know what you speak of. But I don't know much about Minslethratian lore," he said, looking out of the window. "I do not care for legends—only actual truth."

The carriage wobbled a little bit as a harsh wind blew against it.

Moral swallowed down her nervousness and continued to speak. "It isn't lore, Sir Andor… It *is* the truth. And we are living upon it now. Darkness comes as a thief in the night—and will catch you off guard when you least expect it. It devours the soul—darkness does. If we do not wear the armor of God upon our hearts, we will eventually succumb to darkness… It may all sound like nonsense to you, Sir Andor. But that's where faith comes in… We must have faith in the God of Light! Look out of the window, Sir Andor. That is physical darkness that is coming towards your kingdom now. Minslethrate has been wallowing in it for days!" Moral stopped talking for a moment because of her rising emotion.

563

She then looked at Sir Andor who was watching her curiously. "But...thank you, Sir Andor," Moral said, realizing that it was hard for other people to understand what was going on. "I appreciate you and your men..."

He nodded his head, then looked back out of the window. "I may not understand wholeheartedly, but I understand evil people... I've seen many men die because of the hands of evil ones..." He looked back at Moral, who sat silently. "And I understand that your kingdom may fall upon evil hands. I have always trusted in Lord Timotheus and his judgment. I gave him my word—that I would help your kingdom. If it wasn't for him, I would not be the man I am today... And that is why I am here now with you."

"Thank you, Sir Andor," Moral said, nodding her head. She placed her hand on his. "God will bless you for blessing others..."

Just then the carriage shuttered again as a strong wind hit against it. The powerful impact startled them. They held onto the walls, bracing themselves as they heard the squeals of the coach's horses.

All of a sudden, they could hear the men from outside the carriage. The men were yelling while their horses became frantic. The strange sound of horrific screams could be heard all around them. The screams sent chills over their skin as their eyes widened. Chaos seemed to erupt suddenly upon the heath. The carriage buckled again, then with a loud crash, something large and heavy smacked against the side of the carriage, sending it flying onto its side! They crashed and tumbled on their backs.

Shocked and confused, they quickly tried to get up. But they heard another scream as something hit the carriage again! The carriage tumbled again, falling down a rocky slope. They thrashed about, banging their heads against the interior of the carriage and bashing against each other. The carriage crashed upside down into a mound of bracken and blooming thistles.

"Get up, quickly!" Sir Andor yelled, pulling the women up and pushing them out of the carriage doorway.

The thistles clung to their dresses and scratched their arms. Blood trickled down their foreheads as their faces were well stricken with pain.

Moral fell on her stomach, screaming. She looked around quickly as panic came over her. Her eyes widened and her heart felt as if it was going to leave with her heavy breaths. The scene before her was like straight out of a nightmare. Large black creatures flew about, appearing like a swarm of hornets. The creatures squealed and screamed, pounding their massive bat-like wings against the cold winds. Moral watched helplessly as the creatures grabbed screaming men, pulling them into the air while ripping their limbs from them!

The heath of Hanon turned into a chaotic battle-ground as the men fought against the surprising black creatures. Swords swung and arrows flew into the air. Creatures flew about like angry bats and the air was filled with ear-piercing screams! It looked like hell was loosened upon them!

"Get up, Moral!" Sora screamed as she pulled at her arm. "We can not die here, not now!"

Moral finally snapped out of her shock as her husband's sword caught her attention. The shiny blade could be seen among the thick thistles. It must've flung out of the door when the carriage toppled over. Moral got up quickly, running towards the sword.

Sora noticed what she was doing and went to do the same thing. She spotted a sword nearby, upon the heather of the heath. She grabbed the sword and ran towards Moral. She was disturbed by the men who had fallen into death by the creature's power, already.

"You must get away from here!" Sir Andor screamed, shooting arrows at the flying creatures. "Take a horse and move with haste to Minslethrate! We will be right behind you!"

The breathless women nodded their heads and searched for a horse. The gusts of wind blew at their dresses, nearly pushing them over.

A squealing creature surprised them, angrily flying at them like a powerful wind. The creature began to attack Sora, trying to grab her! Sora screamed, blocking the creature's hands with her arms.

Moral began to scream as she swung her sword as hard as she could. She moved franticly, forcing her blade back and forth. Her sword caught the creature's wing, splitting its black flesh. The dark monster began to shriek, pounding its hurt wing in the air.

Sora began to swing her sword as well, realizing that she had to fight back if she wanted to survive. Moral's courageous act seemed to empower her. She became out of control, missing most of the time. But finally, her sword cut off one of the monster's large hands. A spray of black blood came from its wrist, covering Sora's gown.

"Go now, Moral!" Sir Andor screamed again, shooting his arrows at the screeching fiend.

After many arrows, the creature finally fell to the ground. Its body crumbled against the heath, releasing its black blood over a patch of nettles.

Moral quickly ran to the nearest horse, pulling herself onto it as fast as she could. She wasn't afraid to ride the horse and didn't even think about it. Her body was oblivious to everything but the dire situation she was in.

Sora did the same thing, then got her horse going towards Moral.

The men of Hanon seemed to be winning as most of the flying creatures fell to the ground. But many of the men had already fallen victim to darkness. Dead soldiers lie about the heath, along with their horses, broken and battered.

Suddenly, something massive and dark came crashing down to the ground. It surprised them, sending a loud crash through the air. The ground shook, making everyone falter. It was a large nomed, which was even bigger than the flying ones. The massive creature crouched down on its haunches, just staring at them. It then slowly stood up, revealing its whole body. It was tall like Baffmit, and had a massive head that looked like a cross between a human's and a bull's! It was ugly and carried a dark presence with it. It had a human torso and hairy legs that had large hooves. Its wide wings were covered in black fur and it had a long tail. Everything about the creature was horrifying.

The creature glared down at them with its beady red eyes as everyone stared up at it in shock.

"I am Baal...," it said in a low voice. "I am the Lord of the Abaddon..."

Sir Andor looked up at it, swallowing down his shock. "We've done nothing to deserve this," he said to the intimidating creature, still holding tightly to his bow and arrow.

"I do not care what you deserve... King Baffmit has sent us to destroy every kingdom upon this world... We are preparing a path for the Grand-High Mistress... You are the leader of these men, I see. I've come to warn you that your kingdom is my playground...and I play violently until death...," Baal became quiet as he stared at Sir Andor, then looked out over the men. "I saw you and your army from afar, leaving Hanon... Escaping your doom, I see?" It loomed over the men, bringing its ugly head closer to them. "Your frightened faces are becoming one with my mind—so that when Hanon is destroyed...you will be next..."

The monster named Baal quickly jumped into the dark sky like a twirling spear, then opened its massive wings out. "In the name of the Dark Lord, Lucif—ALL HAIL THE GRAND-HIGH MISTRESS!" it yelled in a mighty voice that tore through the sky. It looked at the bewildered men one last time, then flew into the windy sky. It let out a loud roar as it dashed away from the heath, going towards the Kingdom of Hanon.

They stood silently for a moment, collecting their thoughts and watching as Baal soared away.

"Look!" Moral yelled out in a shaken voice, pointing to the dark sky.

Sora and Sir Andor looked up to where Moral was pointing. It looked like the sky was moving! But when they looked closer, they realized that it was many black things moving among the low-hanging clouds! Hundreds of black creatures flew high in the dark sky, moving in different directions. They looked like they were moving towards other parts of the land—other parts of the world!

"Darkness is spreading like the winds," Moral said.

Sir Andor lowered his bow, understanding the dire predicament they were all in. His eyes widened as he realized that Baal and its army of creatures were migrating off to other unsuspecting lands, going not only to Hanon, but other distant kingdoms. "That is the darkness in which you speak of...," he said, shocked. "Not only is Hanon in grave danger, but everyone else is as well... God...help us all..."

"It has begun," Moral said, gazing off into the sky. "All of the world will taste of darkness' wrath..." Tears swelled up in her gray eyes as she became overwhelmed. So many innocent people were going to die. Many kingdoms were going to burn. She then thought of her own kingdom and people. "But we must do something. We have to get to Minslethrate! May God be with us!" she screamed.

Sir Andor realized that the heath was silent now as the last few flying creatures disappeared into the dark sky. His heart thrashed around in his chest as he thought of Baal's threats.

"Gideon! Come to me!" Sir Andor shouted, looking around. The young-looking soldier rode to him, quickly. "Lead half of the army back to Hanon!" he shouted to Gideon. "After you speak with the king, inform Lord Timotheus of this madness. Now is your chance to prove yourself to our legion, boy. Move with haste, now!"

Gideon quickly nodded his head, then gestured for the men to follow him.

Hanon had a great army with many leaders and Sir Andor knew that his kingdom was in strong hands. He would've left right then and went back to Hanon, but he wanted to keep his promise. He and the remainder of his men were going to help Minslethrate.

Gideon and the crowd of men left them, going back towards the east, while Sir Andor led Moral, Sora, and the remainder of his men, back towards Minslethrate.

Many thoughts rushed through Moral's head as she rode on her horse towards Minslethrate, alongside Sora and Sir Andor. She now understood fully what her son and loved ones were facing in the Forbidden Lands. But she felt empowered by her strength and courage and felt as if she could do anything right then and there. It didn't even occur to her that she and Sora were riding on horses with swords in their hands, being accompanied by an army. Adrenaline pumped through her veins and her body felt young again. It was something she had never experienced before. She knew that the God of Light was watching over her as a newfound strength came over her body. She knew that the newfound strength that came over her—was the presence of the God of Light. She felt like she was more than just a peasant woman, she felt like a warrior, a mighty woman of God who wasn't going to back down for anything. And she knew that Sora felt the same way.

They rode against the cold winds as quickly as they could, wanting to warn Minslethrate of their current situation. The dark creatures took their breaths away, making them wonder what else lay before them. They were taken over by the nightmare that had become their reality.

There were fewer Hanonnite men than before, but they still consisted of a great number. The cold afternoon was passing them by quickly and the clouds became blacker. Their hearts kept them warm as they rode on towards the small Kingdom of Minslethrate.

†

CHAPTER 4
The Darkness is Coming

"Fredrick! Oh, Fredrick, do hurry!" Lady Daleasa Vaughn shouted from inside their coach. "Hurry, fool!"

She waited impatiently for her twin brother, glaring out of the coach door. She watched as Lord Fredrick could finally be seen coming from their family's manor. He quickly got into the coach as the tired-looking coachman shut the door behind him.

"Forgive me, Sister," he said quickly, having an annoyed look on his face.

The coach gave a jolt as the horse got going.

"You are slower than anyone I know in Minslethrate!" she scolded, fanning herself irritably. "The son of a Baron—please... We must get to the marketplace, quickly! You know I need a new wardrobe for this evening," she said, rolling her blue eyes. "All the good trinkets have probably been sold already because of you!"

"Must you always shout?!" Fredrick scolded back.

"I shout as much as you wear that *stupid* hat!" she fussed, pulling his feathered hat from his blonde hair and throwing it out of the small window.

"Idiot!" Fredrick yelled back, snatching her feathered fan from her. He tossed it out of the window while glaring at her. "That is why everyone in the kingdom despises you."

Lady Daleasa quickly folded her arms and sat back in her seat. "And you are the loved one, dear brother? We were born at the same time—so you are just like me."

Lord Fredrick just glared at his twin sister, sitting back as well.

They rode in silence for a while, going towards the castle of Minslethrate. The clouds seemed to become blacker as they gazed out of their small windows. It became dim in the carriage as they noticed that the winds began to pick up.

"We might as well not go to the Spring Celebration this evening. The weather is horrid," Daleasa said in a low voice. "Besides, the peasants are welcome too...I hate them—disgusting, poor rats, they are."

"Everyone will be there, Daleasa," Fredrick said quickly. "We have to go if you care for your social stature. Everyone belonging to nobility must be there... Father would have our heads if we did not show up."

"Not everyone will be there," Daleasa said with a teasing tone. A small smile crept over her elegant face. "Lady Christianne and Natalia certainly won't..."

Her brother just stared at her, knowing what she was getting at. "You are cynical, dear sister."

"Well, she shouldn't have killed herself—that stupid woman." Daleasa said, defensively. "Lady Christianne was the richest woman in the kingdom. She was the Marchioness of Minslethrate for God's sake. I heard she jumped from the top window of the Ducre' Manor... And right before she took her own life...she killed everyone in the manor... Why would she give all that up? She probably killed herself because her trollop daughter ran away..."

"How do you know that?" Fredrick cut her off.

"I know everything about everyone in Minslethrate," she said with wide eyes. "And I know that Lady Natalia has run away with Marrisa. I hate Natalia—she shames nobility. I'm relieved that she has gone away. I hope she never comes back! The marquis is just going to have to deal with his wife being dead and his stupid daughter being missing. Can you believe the ruckus that family is causing?" Daleasa smiled, amused at what she was gossiping about. "I heard mother and father talking. King Julpen left to go look for Marrisa with an army and has trusted the marquis to rule the kingdom while he is gone. The idiot is going to ruin everything... Minslethrate doesn't have much of an army now. Do you understand what that means, brother dear?"

Fredrick sat quietly, shrugging his soldiers. "I don't care..."

"That means if something happens to our kingdom, foolish boys like you will have to serve in our legion," she laughed. "If that happens—this kingdom will burn."

"Nothing is going to happen, *stupid* girl," Fredrick said, annoyed. "Your mouth is bitter, Sister."

"Don't carry on like a child. You're just annoyed because you fancied Lady Natalia," Daleasa teased. "And now that she's gone for good, you can't take it!" Daleasa began to laugh, putting her hands on her stomach. "How could you fancy such a *dog*, anyway?"

Just then the coach shook as the winds picked up all around them. They smacked against the sides of the coach, hitting their heads on the windows. Then a loud shriek could be heard from outside the coach. The coach stopped abruptly, followed by a disturbing grunt sound. Then silence fell over them.

Daleasa became annoyed, hitting the seat with her hand. "Coachman!" she screamed out. She banged the wall behind her. "Coachman, you could've killed us, imbecile! Go now, we haven't any time to just sit about the field!"

Only the sound of the wind pushing against the carriage could be heard. The cold air whistled through the cracks of the doors as they stared at each other.

"Coachman!" Daleasa yelled again, but there was no answer. She looked at her nervous brother. "Fredrick, go see what has happened."

They sat for a moment longer, listening closely. The clouds seemed to get blacker, making the inside of the coach become filled with darkness.

"It's going to storm; we have to go!" Daleasa fussed at her brother. "Go and see…Fredrick!" She looked more worried as she spoke.

"Alright…," Fredrick said, reluctantly.

He slowly opened his door, peering out of the coach. He looked around cautiously. He stretched his neck as far as it could go, trying to take a peek at the front of the carriage. He couldn't see anything. "Coachman!" he yelled.

"Just go!" Daleasa fussed, pushing him out of the carriage with her feet.

Fredrick fell to the ground, getting a mouth full of grass. He got up quickly, spitting dirt. He cursed his sister under his breath, wiping the grit from his lips. He looked all around, realizing that they were in the middle of the Great Field of Minslethrate. He felt disturbed all of a sudden, feeling as if he were lost in the middle of nowhere. He could see the castle far off on the dark horizon. Civilization seemed many hours away. Another icy gust blew as he began to walk towards the front of the coach. His mouth began to quiver from the cold and uncomfortable situation.

He looked up at the coach's bench, nervously. The coachman was gone! He looked around quickly again. "Coachman!" he called. He rubbed his shoulders, getting a sudden feeling that something was— watching him.

He continued to slowly walk towards the front of the carriage. He was confused by how still the horse was. It looked like it was crumpled over, as if it were trying to sleep. But, why? His eyes widened as he realized why the horse was so still and falling over. Its head was missing! He panicked as his eyes flashed open. He looked around franticly, as fear came over him. His eyes stopped as he spotted something in the field. It was black as night and had large wings jutting from its sides! It was eating something. He could tell that the creature was pulling innards from a corpse with its jagged mouth. Fredrick realized that the horrifying creature was devouring—the coachman!

Fredrick stood in shock, scared to death. His heart pounded in his frozen ears. He felt as if he couldn't move! The tall thing slowly stood up, staring at Fredrick with large black eyes that looked like glass. It seemed to whisper his name…the creature knew his name! But he only heard the horrid voice in his head.

"Da…Daleasa!" Fredrick screamed out as he ran towards the coach door, nearly falling over.

Daleasa heard her brother's screams and poked her head out of the coach. "What is it?!" she fussed, annoyed. Her eyes became large as she noticed why her brother was screaming.

Just as soon as Fredrick made it to the coach, something pulled him into the air! He let out a scream as he disappeared from Daleasa's sight. His screams became gurgled cries, then it was quiet again...

"Fredrick!" Daleasa cried as she scooted away from the opened door. "Fredrick, come back! Fredrick!"

Her chest rose quickly as she sucked in the cold air. Her heart raced as tears filled her eyes. She pushed her back to the side of the coach, realizing that she couldn't go anywhere else. Intense fear settled over her body as a thick layer of goose-bumps exploded over her skin.

Just then Fredrick's body fell right before the doorway of the coach! The sound was disturbing as it hit against the ground. Daleasa began to scream frantically as she noticed that the bottom half of her brother was missing!

Strange whispers came into the coach, sounding like a terrifying chant.

Something landed on the coach, shaking it for a quick moment. Something was on the roof! Daleasa continued to scream as her eyes stayed glued to the opened coach doorway. Then, slowly, she could see the tips of black horns appearing from the top of the coach, pointing downward. The gruesome creature was on top of the coach and now peering down into the doorway! Its whole head could be seen now, as it slowly went into the coach. It just stared at her. Fear and ill feelings emitted from the creature as a wicked smile came over its gruesome black face.

Daleasa thrashed about, kicking her legs as her screams filled the small space of the coach.

"Daleasa...Father is waiting for you..." The creature's mouth did not move as it continued to smile, but whispers emitted from its sinister presence.

Daleasa pressed her hands against her ears as she continued to scream. The presence from the creature inundated her with ill-feelings.

Then, in a split second, it let out an ear-piercing shriek as it continued to crawl into the coach quickly. The coach began to shake violently.

The winds continued to howl as more shrieking creatures seemed to come from nowhere, circling around the carriage. They had found another victim...

No one heard Daleasa's screams as darkness came over her mind and soul...

✝✝✝

The Valor Manor became like a morose dream as black clouds covered the Kingdom of Hanon. The halls became filled with thick shadows as the dark air leaked in through the massive windows. Finagin hurried through the halls, along with other servants, lighting lanterns and candelabrums. The servants seemed disarrayed as the strange weather came quickly over the manor.

Finagin hurried to Lord Valor's study, stopping at the large doors. He poked his head in the dim chamber, searching for Lord Timotheus. He did not see the lord, so he hurried in, lighting candles as he went. The fireplace was the only source of light, sending dancing shadows across the hall. The shadows made Finagin nervous. He kept getting the urges to peer over his shoulder every now and then. The massive windows did not do much because of the dark sky that loomed over the kingdom.

"I fear it is upon us," a scruffy voice said from the darkened windows.

Finagin jumped, turning quickly. "My Lord, you gave me a fright," he said quickly, placing his hand on his chest. "I did not see you."

"I have been here. I've been looking out of my window all morning. It seems Moral has left a lasting impression on me," he said in a low voice as he continued to peer out of the massive window. Finagin silently came to him, carrying a candle. "I have worried for Moral all afternoon...but with the looks of the sky—I now worry for our kingdom..."

"It is very strange, indeed," Finagin said, standing next to Lord Timotheus. He gazed out of the window as well. "Should we worry, My Lord?" he asked.

"I do not know. But we should be on guard..."

Just then Lady Dilia quickly came into the dim hall. She breathed heavily, appearing frantic and overwhelmed with fear. He never saw his elegant wife so distraught before. "My Lord," she said with her hand over her bosom. "Some of our soldiers have come back—I fear they were attacked...many have died."

A soldier came quickly into the hall. His armor clanked loudly, breaking the heavy silence. "My Lord, we are under attack! Sir Andor and the women have hurried to Minslethrate. Many of our men have fallen! Wicked monsters with wings have spread out upon the lands. They are creatures that have been released from the deepest pits of hell!"

Lord Timotheus stood with wide eyes. He was bewildered by the news. "The darkness is coming," he said in a whispery voice. "The legends of old are coming alive..."

"Look!" Lady Dilia shouted, pointing towards the window. Horror came over her old face as she brought her hand over her mouth.

They all hurried, shocked at what they were looking at. Many black creatures flew through the dark sky, looking like large, monstrous birds.

They flew in massive groups, franticly spreading out in different directions.

"My God...," Lord Timotheus said, gazing out of the windows with wide eyes. "Help us..."

They stood speechlessly, watching as the dark forms searched the skies.

†

CHAPTER 5
Light Conquers All

Natalia sat atop of a rugged mound of boulders which looked out over the Black Field of Old Blood. The cliff below her jutted down, rolling out into a sea of grass and opening to a hill-filled valley. Her silent green eyes gazed at the black clouds that filled the sky. She could barely see the Black Tower which was in straight eye-sight.

The wind blew at her long brown hair as she hugged her knees. Sadness came over her as she thought of their present state. But she didn't think about Tairren, or even Marrisa, as she blankly stared. She thought of her mother… She couldn't help but think of what Lilith had revealed the night before. Was her mother really dead? Was she really lost in the screaming darkness? Tears filled her melancholy eyes, making them look like an ocean before a storm. She never looked away from the view of the mysterious mountains before her.

"You have been up here for many hours," a voice said from behind her. It was Gaibriul. He climbed up the rocks and sat next to her. His bright golden eyes watched the sadness that was coming from Natalia. "I hear your heart crying," he said as his white hair fluttered in the cold wind. He looked like a fleck of light among the dark atmosphere.

Natalia looked at him. Tears built up in her eyes, making them sparkle. "I'm scared… I'm frightened for my mother's sake… Last night, before the attack…Lilith said that my mother was dead…" She stopped talking for a moment as her emotions began to stir. "Is it true?" she asked, searching his eyes with hers. Her pretty face looked eager for information.

Gaibriul's face was serious but still held a hint of kindness. He had already known the truth about her mother. He just waited for the right time to inform her; and that moment was then. "The Lord spoke to my heart late in the night… Everyone is given the chance to find the love-light of God upon this world, Natalia. You have learned that. Some kind of way, whether it's a hint or an obvious sign, everyone is given a chance… Your mother did not accept that chance of knowing eternal life… The God of Light's eyes roam to and fro about the Earth, searching for hearts to cry out to Him. He never heard your mother's cry…" Gaibriul stopped for a moment, having compassion for Natalia as tears flowed down her cheeks.

Her breaths quickened as reality came over her. "She—is dead, then?" Natalia asked, choking up a little. Her chin quivered as her eyes became full of sadness.

"…It is far more devastating, knowing that one's spirit died—than knowing that their flesh has… I'm very sorry, Natalia—but your mother is gone…," Gaibriul finally said.

Natalia stared at him, trying to look for any sign of deceit. She searched his eyes with hers quickly. She shook her head, not wanting to believe him. It was hard for her to understand such a thing. But she knew that Gaibriul could not lie, and would never do so. Her eyes twinkled with despair as tears flowed from them. She looked away from Gaibriul, trying to find a glimpse of happiness—somewhere off in the distance. There was only darkness all around her. She took a couple of deep breaths as she ran her shaken hands through her hair.

She appeared as if shock hit her as she looked back at Gaibriul. She wiped her dewy face. "When?" Natalia asked in a shaken voice. "When was she ever given such a chance?!" she cried. "My mother lived bitterly in the lap of silent luxury! You're right—she did not go about searching for God! Material things don't speak of light. It was the wealth she idolized… And when she was alone, God never came to her. Why…didn't He have pity for her?!" Natalia shook her head as she looked out into the lands before her.

She had the urge to become angry with God, but she knew that everyone was given free will in the world. She then thought of Dolsia's past, understanding that it was easier telling someone to stay strong when they hadn't experienced what they've been through. She felt lost all of sudden. But she knew that there was no reason for her to, when God had poured his grace over her already.

Tears dripped off her shaken chin. "When my mother was alone, she drank her fill of wine. She never knew that I saw her many times in a drunken state. But I knew… She obsessed over her things…" She paused, thinking about how truly lost her mother had been all along. "Why didn't God try to reach her before she died, Gaibriul?! I could've seen her in her old age! I could've…" She became quiet again, suddenly appearing as if she were ashamed of herself. She looked back into Gaibriul's compassionate eyes. "I never told my mother that I loved her, Gaibriul… We never had a real relationship. Everything was a game…we only portrayed ourselves as happy for the people of Minslethrate. It didn't even matter because no one cared anyways! We had no peace between us, Gaibriul…and I never got to say goodbye…"

Natalia covered her face, crying harder than she had ever done before. She never appreciated her mother—and now that she was gone, she wanted her back. Her heart broke, realizing that she would never see her again. She knew that their eternal paths were destined for two totally opposite places. "I will never forgive myself… I could've done something to help my mother's fate—but I was too concerned about my own life! I shall never forgive myself, Gaibriul…"

Gaibriul placed his hand on her trembling back. She buried her face into her knees, hugging her shoulders tightly. She appeared like a lost child as she cried. Her cries came from deep within, spilling out like a heavy rain-fall.

"Natalia," Gaibriul said in a soft voice. "You have tried to reach out to your mother, before…"

Natalia stopped crying a little, wiping her nose. She slowly peered up at him, tears still flowing. She sniffled as she looked at him, anxiously, "How?"

A faint smile crept over Gaibriul's luminous face. He was the only glimpse of physical happiness before her. His cheeks seemed to sparkle with specks of light and his eyes gleamed like stars at night. "Remember, God's eyes go about, searching his children's hearts in this world. He yearns to hear His name mentioned, whispered—thought of, even… You tried to talk to your mother about God, about His light. When the God of Light's name is spoken, a spiritual door opens, you see. It is a way out of the darkness… Tairren taught you of the legends of old, and you repeated them back to your mother…"

"But she mocked them," Natalia said, finishing his sentence. "She told me that it was just a fairytale and that ladies did not talk of such things. She always said that it was far better to be beautiful than to live in a dream world. She said it was just ancient Minslethratian lore… But I knew that she said those things because she didn't care…" Natalia looked away from him. "How did you know that?" she asked, wiping her green eyes again.

"Have you seen the great white owl?" Gaibriul asked.

Natalia looked at him, curiously, wondering why the conversation switched so abruptly. She then thought of the owl. She had seen the owl, but the owl seemed dream-like, as if it were a figment of her imagination. She thought of its pure white feathers that had tips that looked like gold. She thought of its silent, mysterious eyes… "Yes," she said in a soft voice.

Her eyes drifted away from Gaibriul for a moment. She began thinking about all the times when the owl seemed to just watch them, protecting them from death. The owl seemed so close, but yet, so far away. She also thought of the time when Tairren had said that the owl was greater than any bird upon the Earth.

Gaibriul nodded his head, slowly smiling as he watched the sadness go away from her. He knew then that she was thinking of God. "He seems closer than your skin and further than your thoughts… Have you ever wondered how the owl always knew what was going on? He always showed up during the moments when you needed Him the most. Malakh is what he is called… He goes about on his own, painstakingly searching the lands, kingdoms—the world… He is the messenger—and eyes, of

God…" Gaibriul said with passion as Natalia seemed lost in thought. The light in his flesh seemed to glow as he smiled. His golden gaze sparkled. "He silently goes about the lands—watching and listening, revealing and loving…"

Natalia looked at him, speechlessly, wondering why she never realized that before. She sat silently, thinking of all the times God was watching over her and her companions. She realized that she had been blissfully unaware that she was on God's mind, always. She truly felt blessed all of a sudden. She wondered if the owl ever revealed himself to her mother—that, she would never know.

"Do not be dismayed, Natalia." Gaibriul continued, looking off towards the mountains. "You were a door for your mother to meet God…she just never walked through that door… Just like how you were a door for Dolsia to walk through—and she did… Do you realize that if it wasn't for you, Dolsia still would be living in darkness? You see, once you have the light inside of you—you possess the living God of Light! You contain power that should not be questioned. That is mighty! You are highly favored, Natalia, because you have accepted his love-light inside of you. You are his child… Always remember that you are a temple of light. And when your task is completed upon this world…you will live with Him in light, for eternity…"

Silent tears continued to flow down her cheeks. She was happy that her path before her was straight, but she was sad at the same time that her mother's was not. Knowing that her mother's spirit had died broke her heart, but remembering that she herself was saved by God's grace, mended it.

She then thought of Dolsia, and how she inspired her to call out to God. She understood that if one lived in the world without God's love-light, that soul was already dead. But if one lived upon the world with God's light embedded in them, that soul possessed everlasting life.

She gazed off into the mountains, thinking about her fate. She wondered what lay before her. She also kept thinking of her poor mother, and how she didn't want anyone else to suffer like her. She remembered what Gaibriul had said: It is far more devastating knowing that one's spirit died—than knowing that their flesh has…

She thought of how fragile life was, and how she was not afraid to die anymore. She knew that even though the darkness before her threatened her life—there was something greater waiting on the other side of time…

"I want to be alone," Natalia said in a low voice, not looking at Gaibriul.

Gaibriul got up silently, watching as silent tears continued to fall down her cheeks. He left her in her thoughts, understanding that she had to go through her human emotions.

Natalia didn't turn to watch Gaibriul leave. She just sat still with her twinkling eyes gazing at the dark horizon. After a while of sitting in the winds, she heard the sound of pebbles bouncing down the stone. She turned to see Phillip coming up towards her.

Phillip silently sat next to her as she ignored him.

"Natalia…I'm so very sorry…for your loss," he said in low a voice. "Some of the legna have informed me…"

She glanced over at him and wiped the tears from her green eyes. She then quickly looked away from him as he put his hand on her shoulder.

"Don't worry yourself about me," Natalia said, quickly, not sounding pleased. "Apparently, my mother's spirit died a long time ago… I don't need your comfort."

Phillip was quiet for a moment, sensing that she didn't want to talk to him or about her mother. He felt as if the "old" Natalia was coming back through her sadness. He took his hand away from her shoulder, still looking at her with worried eyes. "I…," he paused, taking in a breath, thinking about what he could say that wouldn't upset her any more than she was. "I'll—always worry about you, Natalia."

"Why?!" she asked, abruptly. She looked at him, looking more irritated than anything else. "You should be worrying about your princess bride who is chained up in the darkness, not me."

"Why do you say things like that? I only want to be there for you," Phillip said, becoming annoyed by her attitude.

"Why, Phillip?!" Natalia demanded. "You and I are not meant to be together! You do not need to worry about me, Phillip; I'm not a dainty child! You are constantly trying to protect me. You are not helping me!" Natalia shouted, standing up.

Phillip stood up quickly, standing right in front of her. "Natalia…I can not help that I love you!"

"Why do you love me, Phillip? I am a broken girl who just lost her mother, and about to lose her best friend and kingdom! How can you love me? I am the daughter of a marquis, but I have nothing to offer. I am just another broken girl in this world."

Phillip just looked down at her with his dark eyes. He took in a deep breath, slowly shaking his head. He then looked away from her. "…There seemed to be a breakthrough of light in you, once before. Now you seem as if you hadn't changed at all. It's as if the old Natalia is standing before me! What happened to you? Perhaps if I was Tairren you would accept me and listen!"

Natalia suddenly grew angry. Her eyes changed as she glared at him. "Do not bring Tairren into this. I just found out that my mother died, Phillip! She is DEAD! I will never see her again." Natalia's voice began to tremble. "How dare you judge me, Phillip!"

"You never wanted to see her before. Everything you ever said about your mother was negative; and now you want to see her?!" Phillip raised his voice. "My father is terribly sick, but I chose to come here to Minslethrate just as he wished. I respect my father and his wishes! Pity, you never know what you have until you lose it, Natalia!"

Natalia suddenly smacked him across the face, breathing hard as she glared at him. She was overwhelmed by her broken heart. She was surprised that she had even slapped him, but she couldn't help herself as anger rose up in her trembling body. She breathed quickly, looking into Phillip's surprised eyes. Shocked, she quickly brought her hand over her mouth.

Phillip just looked down at her, not saying anything else. He slowly looked away from her, then left her alone in the cold darkness.

Natalia watched silently as Phillip climbed down the boulder. More tears came up in her eyes. She sat back down on the stone, covering her face. She began to cry, not knowing what else to do.

After many moments, she heard a faint sound of conversation. She looked down from the boulders and noticed Phillip, Mikhal, and Dolsia, trek down the rugged path towards Skull Hill. Tears rolled down her cheeks as she watched them from afar. She felt ashamed of herself as she watched the legna place their hands on Phillip's back as they walked.

She realized then that she would never be perfect. She realized that she was more broken than she ever thought she was. When her guard was down, she became just like her mother. Her "old" ways tried to come back, just as Phillip had insinuated. She knew right away that she had to wear King Yehoshua's armor on her heart once again. "The Armor of Righteousness...," she thought to herself. When the days got darker, it was so easy to forget about the armor. During tough times, it was so easy to forget about the love-light of God within her. It was so easy to leave the God she had learned to trust and obey. Every moment of being alive seemed like a battle.

Natalia stared silently as the cold winds blew past her.

✝✝✝

The valley on which Skull Hill sat was rough-looking, filled with rocks, tall brown grass, and scraggly shrubbery. It looked much like the rest of the south—dead. Skull Hill slopped up upon the dark terrain, crowned with the legendary tree... Broken weapons and bones littered the earth all around the tree, for it was where criminals were executed, harshly.

But even though death seemed to surround the ancient tree, walking towards it was breathtaking. The tree stood tall, stretching its naked branches out upon the dark-gray sky. The tree looked like it had been

580

dead for a very long time. Its bark was almost black, appearing like stone. Giant nails stuck out of the tree's trunk and ropes and chains fell from the lower branches. Many other branches lay around the tree's roots, indicating its age and that it was rotting away with time.

Mikhal, Dolsia, and Phillip walked silently towards the tree, looking up at its magnificence. They were in awe as they slowly came upon the ancient, legendary tree.

"This is where it all happened," Mikhal said in a low tone. "This tree is just a tree. But it is a symbol of freedom. This tree signifies the death that King Yehoshua gave himself to. It is a reminder that he died for the human race long ago, so that humans can be covered by His grace. His blood was spilled upon this tree long ago, so that the darkness humans naturally carry with them, could be broken." Mikhal then looked at Phillip who stood silently. "He died for you, Natalia, Tairren, and everyone else living on this Earth. His legacy goes further than Minslethrate—all the way to the ends of the world. He is the true legend in all of this. He is the last legend…"

Phillip was quiet. He thought of Natalia and her brokenness. But he knew that he was broken just like she was. He felt overwhelmed as he looked upon the tree. He walked quietly to its black roots, feeling as if his heart was going to burst. Emotion came over him as he fell to his knees. He was inundated with something that he had never felt before. It was something that couldn't be compared to anything else. He touched the tree's black roots, closing his eyes. Tears rolled down his cheeks as he thought of all the brokenness in the world. Then he thought of the legendary King Yehoshua.

"This is it…," he said, quietly. "This is where He gave up his life. This represents the truth… Nothing else matters…," Phillip said, stricken with emotion. "What a fool I've been…"

Phillip felt ashamed, remembering when he had mocked the faith that he was now following. He realized that the Shield of Faith he had taken from Haifen, was more than a weapon…it was a symbol of his faith, much like the old tree…

It was only a story to him when he was back in his kingdom. He studied the legends of old and Minslethrate's history—but he didn't believe it. It was only a legend to him, then. And now, it was something powerful that had changed his life. It was more than a legend—it was the truth. He realized that he had been living a lie in the Kingdom of Ishkar. He was taught to follow false gods and idols. But now, he knew the one and only true God.

Phillip then thought of Natalia, wishing that she was by his side right then. He knew that they were all broken, and that was why King Yehoshua succumbed to the torture and death. He knew that King

Yehoshua's broken body was what lifted the curse of spiritual brokenness from man.

Phillip lifted his eyes as the tears flowed. "Thank you, my God," he said. "Thank you, Yehoshua, my king!" Mikhal and Dolsia kneeled down on each side of him, lowering their golden heads. "You are my savior, King Yehoshua," Phillip said with emotion as he raised his hands into the windy air. "I am nothing without you! Forgive me for not believing in the past... But I give you my heart now. Thank you for dying for me—for us!" Phillip fell to his face. His body couldn't take the emotion and mighty presence that came over him. It was like his spirit began to cry, releasing strange tears that he had never released before. "I love you, my God! Keep me, always!"

They sat upon the base of the tree for what seemed like hours. They thought of the last legend, King Yehoshua, as time slipped past them. The cold winds blew upon them as the dark clouds loomed above them. Even though the atmosphere was morbid, the peace that lay all around them was comforting. They could feel the love of God come down on them as they worshiped beneath the old tree.

Phillip finally sat up on his haunches, still looking at the tree. Everything felt like a dream to him then, but he knew it was all real. He looked at the tree's trunk and roots, noticing a deep crack in the earth that must've went deep below the tree. He touched the deep crack. He wondered if the King's blood was still below the tree, soaked deep down in the earth...

"When the earth shook, after King Yehoshua's death, the rock cracked beneath this tree, swallowing up His blood," Mikhal said. "His living blood, is what defeated darkness long ago. His blood gave order to the chaos that the world holds."

"For that, I give him my all—spirit, mind, and body," Phillip said in a low tone. He never took his dark eyes away from the tree.

"That is what we all must do," Dolsia said. "We must love Him with our whole beings. I've learned that there is no point in living, if we do not love Him," Dolsia's eyes fell away. She thought of Natalia, who had taught her that.

"It is good that we have come here," Mikhal said. His face was ardent and strong. "There is darkness on the horizon, but seeing this tree reminds us all that darkness was defeated by King Yehoshua. We must stay strong and do our Lord's work. We must take up the Sword of Truth, Shield of Faith, and Armor of Righteousness in our hearts. It is in our hearts that the light of Yehoshua resides." Mikhal stood up, placing his hand on the tree. "This is but a tree... When Yehoshua died long ago—he raised as light, days later. He reigns in our hearts, and in the Kingdom of Nevaeh. Light conquers all..."

Phillip and Dolsia stood up as well, standing with a new strength upon them. They began to leave the tree, understanding that they already had the armor of Yehoshua in their hearts and upon their spirits, because they possessed the God of Light's power.

They walked quietly together, looking up at the cliffs as they went. Natalia could be seen far atop the cliff. She seemed to be watching them.

Dolsia's heart broke as she looked up at Natalia. She knew that Natalia was grieving her mother's death. She understood greatly how sadness could take over one's heart. Dolsia quickly became angry as she thought of the pain that Natalia had been going through. She thought of the darkness that lingered around the kingdom. She wanted to rid the darkness that was causing so much pain. She was tired of seeing pain and suffering. Having human tendencies, she loathed the Dark Lord and his followers. She wanted to see them fall into an eternity of suffering. Just then, she made a promise to herself that she was going to die, if that's what it was going to take, to destroy everything dark.

✝

CHAPTER 6
Legion of Darkness

Everything was silent and still. The tower was quiet and cold, holding a presence that harbored anger and strife. The halls were chilled with a heavy breath of cold air, which covered the dewy walls and stone ground. Strange sounds echoed down the hallways sporadically, which were the whispers that came from the darkness. Shadows crept about the halls like low-crawling animals, anticipating the beckoning call from their Dark Lord. The winds moaned with a ghostly tone as the halls became suddenly loud by the growls and shrieks of the nomed. Their eyes searched the halls and their horns scraped the shadows as their whispers and heavy breaths shook in the air. The nomed knew when the Dark Lord stirred, and they became filled with anxiousness as Marrisa awakened with darkness upon her throne.

Marrisa sat up quickly, as if her body suddenly became filled with a shock of forced energy. She took a deep breath, filling her lungs with the sour air of the hall. She opened her eyes, searching the great, dark hall. Her eyes were black as night, glittering like a black lake. Dark-gray rings circled around her once beautiful eyes and her skin looked like fine porcelain. Her red hair fell over her face, fluttering in the wind that came in from the balcony before her. Her red pendant dangled upon her chest, glimmering like translucent blood.

It was exuberant for the Dark Lord to walk in human flesh once again…

Marrisa stood up from her throne, straightening her back and neck. Her black-crusted crown made her appear taller than what she was. She slowly made her way across the hall as the creeping nomed bowed at her feet. The tattered long train of her black gown trailed behind her, appearing like a moving shadow. She walked onto the balcony, looking out over the south of Minslethrate. The valley below her and the cliffs and hills before her was her playground. The wind blew at her hair and gown, making her dark beauty magnify.

"Look at your lands," she said to herself. "Your new eyes fall upon lands of old." Her voice spoke but they weren't her words. "Its destruction is at your fingertips… The world is rightfully yours… The King of Light is dead—dead as his people… Everyone who utters his name will die. Everyone who wears his sign will die. There will be no more light left! Only the ones who follow you will live…only the ones who bear your sign and darkness upon their hearts will live! Their spirits will die but their flesh will carry on… It is done! The world is your throne… The world is mine and all that inhabits it!"

A wicked smile came across her face as she stared at the sullen lands beneath her scowling face. "A mark shall fall upon the people—your mark. Your marking shall be three stars made from six dashes… You are the morning star—and the sixth sacrifice. You are of the sixth generation of the sixth day... It is the sign of the Grand-High Mistress." As she spoke, she pulled a dagger from her gown, then cut the marking of the three stars into her forearm.

The cuts dripped blood down her arm, forming a dark-red puddle on the stone.

After Marrisa was finished, she looked up into the sky, searching with her black eyes. "Baffmit, come to me, my pet," she said in a deep voice.

Her voice was low in the windy air, but all of darkness heard it.

Just then a black orb suddenly opened up in the sky before her. Stinking black mists came from the orb as Baffmit's dark shadow appeared, rising from the orb. King Baffmit's red eyes glowed as he stretched his massive body out. His mighty black feathered wings pounded against the cold air as he came before the balcony on which Marrisa stood.

The gusts from Baffmit's wings covered Marrisa's body, making her long red hair flutter away from her. She smiled again as she lifted her delicate hand into the air. Her white hand reached out to Baffmit, beckoning him to come closer. Her fingertips touched the cold air as Baffmit bowed to her.

"What is it that you have summoned me, oh great

Lord," Baffmit said in a low growl. His eyes glowed upon Marrisa's white face.

"The legna are drawing closer—I can feel their putrid presence already," she said, closing her eyes. "Something is happening that disturbs me." She paused for a moment as she sniffed the air. She shot open her black eyes. "I smell them from afar… The time has come, Baffmit," Marrisa said in a low voice. "Lilith has failed… The light-ridden vermin have sent Natas into oblivion!"

"I shall take the light folk down," Baffmit growled. "The legna will pay for their foolishness, greatly."

"No," Marrisa said. "What I have planned for you is greater. I shall not go to the north as planned…you will, instead… Go to the northern kingdom of these lands!" A dark voice erupted from Marrisa's mouth. It was low and filled with wrath. "Ignore the light folk—I will deal with them myself. Time is running out. I will not go to Ishkar as I have said before. Not now… The people of light shall be dealt with first…" Marrisa scowled, looking off towards the lands. "Show the people of the north this marking," she said, holding out her arm. "It shall be worn upon them all... If they refuse it—kill them. That will be a message to them! If they choose light—they choose death! You must not fail...for if you do...you will become like Natas," she threatened. "Break the Golden Lands, Baffmit! I command you!"

"I shall, My Lord," Baffmit said in a low growl. "They think they are winning...but darkness is growing. Your presence has magnified, soaring across the lands to many unsuspecting humans. I have sent Baal and the Abaddon out upon the skies. Their mouths have already tasted human blood! Baal will have the far-off kingdoms of this world conquered in your name!"

"Yes, Baffmit," she said in the evil voice again. "I will soon send Marrisa's flesh to Ishkar with the marking of the three stars, after Minslethrate has been conquered. She will rule as planned, and deceive them into thinking that darkness will be stopped. She will become their savior when Baal and the Abaddon stop suddenly... There will be peace then...it will be the calm before the storm. The pathetic humans will be blinded...and worship Marrisa. They will worship me... All of the world will be my throne!"

"You are great, oh mighty one," Baffmit said. "From the great war in Nevaeh, to the fall of the first humans in the beginning of time, to the destruction of the human king—and now... You are great, Dark Lord. Your dark power will never stop."

"Now, to my next conquest...the fall of Minslethrate...," she said, walking over to the stone balustrade of the balcony. She rested her hands on the cold stone. "Minslethrate WILL FALL!" she screamed out, as if yelling at the lands before her. The air around her became darker.

"Minslethrate almost fell long ago...when the filthy king ruled... Many times, Minslethrate has almost crumbled—but has not."

"FOOL!" she growled in the dark voice. A black shadow began to radiate all around her. "Minslethrate will fall! You will lead in its demise! And if the kingdom does not fall it is because YOU failed me! Darkness awaits your call! My nomed await your bidding, just as I commanded!"

"Show me, Dark Lord," Baffmit said, raising his hands into the dark air.

"I shall...," Marrisa said, closing her black eyes. "There will be hell on earth..."

Marrisa stretched her arms out, bringing her head back. She began to hover over the balcony, slowly rising into the air. Dark mists and shadows screamed as they pulsated around her. Her hair and gown fluttered out upon the air as her dark powers lifted her high in the sky. She levitated away from the balcony, floating in the dark sky.

Baffmit watched silently with his glowing red eyes. His ugly face followed her as he steadily flapped his massive wings.

"ARISE!" Marrisa screamed out in a loud, deep voice that sounded terrifying. Her black eyes shot open as a wicked smile came over her face.

She began to chant in a strange tongue as she froze in the air. The ground quaked as the earth split right below where she levitated. Black forms came from the opening in the earth, quickly spreading around the bottom of the temple. She freed the darkness from the bowels of the earth. Marrisa began to make a loud sound in the sky with a quivering face. Mists rose from the shadows of the ground and from the dark places of the temple. They moved quickly and took form, morphing into ugly creatures and snarling beasts!

Baffmit looked out over the massive army of darkness that now congregated around the bottom of the temple. Shrieks and growls could be heard from the sea of creatures as Baffmit bowed his horned goat head to Marrisa. All of the nomed did the same, bowing to Marrisa as she levitated above them.

"Baffmit, killer of men!" Marrisa roared as the clouds became blacker all around her, swirling in the cold wind. "This is your legion! Minslethrate will FALL! It will not stop until Hell is full and earth is Hell, all bowing to ME!! All of the God of Light's creations are mine! The world is MINE!"

Baffmit and all of the creatures began to scream and howl at Marrisa's proclamation.

"Now, go to the north…," Marrisa said in a low voice that was heard by all of the darkness in the south. "Bring with you the marking of the Grand-High Mistress. Wear it upon your flags and upon your flesh! Force it upon the people! Snatch their souls like you snatched the God of Light's son many ages ago, Baffmit. Repeat history…and force them into darkness—then kill them…kill them all…"

Baffmit roared as he spread out his black wings. He raised his hands into the sickly air as the army of darkness squealed and growled. Then, within seconds, Baffmit dashed into the sky. He roared as he flew like the wind towards the northern parts of Minslethrate. The army of darkness did the same, bringing with them hands of torment and destruction.

Marrisa watched from the sky with her shiny, black eyes. "Their blood will flow and their screams will shake the earth. The followers of light will crumble before darkness. All lights will go out… Every living soul will know my name… They will wear it upon their brows and their hands… The world is mine…," Marrisa said to herself as her eyes looked out over the lands. "You have failed, ruler of Nevaeh…you have failed…"

✝

CHAPTER 7
Come with Me

Tairren kneeled over a clear rivulet, splashing cold water onto his face. The brisk liquid gave him a jolt of energy. He drank from it quickly, trying to get his fill before they continued on their journey. He looked to the sky, noticing how dark it had gotten. It looked as if the sun was going down.

They sat in a cluster of trees near the edge of the mountain range, resting for a quick moment. After a ride that had lasted for many hours, Rafiul decided that it was late-noon and time for them to sit a while.

"Where are we?" Tairren asked, looking at Jezebel, who silently stood near her horse.

Jezebel had been looking into the sky, as if sensing something, but Tairren disturbed her. "We are upon the Great Mountains of Minslethrate, also known as Fiara Mountains," she said. Her honey-colored eyes turned as she pointed in the southwestern area of the mountain range. "Over there, across the Black Field of Old Blood, is the Dark Tower. It sits on the lowest cliff of the mountains."

They glanced at where she was pointing to. They could see the temple. It looked like a small castle, sitting among ruins. There was a tall tower that stuck out the center of it, appearing haunting and ancient. The temple was so dark that it blended in with the mountains.

"The Black Field of Old Blood has many trenches and death spots about it. Things that can devour you live among the dark trenches. Their bite is worse than their presence... We must continue our journey along the mountains, around the valley. I know a secret path that leads to the temple."

Rafiul glanced at her, suspiciously. He still did not trust her or the strange feeling he got from her. She always seemed as if she were hiding something... But suddenly, Rafiul's attention was grabbed by a strange phenomenon. He felt a disturbing presence fill the air. He quickly looked up into the sky. His golden eyes pierced the cold air and his ears perked up. He quickly grabbed his sword, appearing vigilant and serious.

"What is it, Rafiul?" Tairren asked quickly as he grabbed his sword as well.

Rafiul quickly raised his hand, silencing him. "Hide," he said.

They grabbed their horse's reins and hurried to some nearby boulders. The shadows behind the boulders were dark. They hid behind the massive rocks, being heavily concealed by a tree that loomed over them. They stood quietly for a moment, just staring and listening. Only the gusts of wind could be heard, blowing dirt across the rugged earth. Everything was ominously silent.

Then, in the blink of an eye, a dark mist began to grow quickly, covering the terrain around them. The mists were cold and thick. Their eyes fell upon a large black cloud that seemed to move with the quick winds over the land. They realized that it wasn't a cloud at all. The sky became filled with hundreds of creatures! Large, horrifying creatures flew quickly together in the sky, being led by a massive nomed. Hundreds of other black creatures ran among the ground, moving quickly like powerful beasts. The sounds of growls and shrieks filled the air.

"That is King Baffmit," Mikhal said, quietly. "He is leading the nomed towards the north."

"That is the Nomed that attacked me the other morning!" Tairren said, alarmed. "They are moving towards the north? Why?!" Tairren became frightened for his mother and kingdom as he watched the hundreds of nomed move like wild shadows across the Black Field of Old Blood!

They looked on with wide eyes, watching as the wicked stampede seemed to never end.

"The northern kingdom is in grave danger," Rafiul said, quickly.

"What must we do?!" Tairren asked, overwhelmed.

"Nothing," Rafiul said, never taking his eyes off of the monsters. "We must continue towards the tower and pray that the legna and the others are prepared for what's to come. We have gone too far and it is too late to turn back now. We must attempt to stop the core of darkness, which is the one who dwells in the Dark Tower of Sacrifice."

"God, help our kingdom," Tairren said under his breath, watching with sore eyes. "…Watch over my mother, my Lord."

After a while, the sky seemed to clear up as the nomed's shrieks relented. They seemed to be the only ones in the south again. They slowly walked out of there hiding place, cautiously looking around them. The cold winds continued to blow and the dark sky continued to churn.

"They're gone…," Tairren said, still looking into the sky. "We must get going."

They seemed to be safe as they crept out from behind the boulders, walking further away from the mountain's side. They began their travels again in silence, but something sinister made them come to a halt once again.

They stopped abruptly, looking around. At first, they caught the scent of something putrid, and then they noticed something that they didn't before. They weren't sure if they had passed it earlier or if they stumbled upon it just then. There was a small cave sitting before them; the smell of foul things emitted from it and was surrounded by jagged rocks. They could see bones spilling out of the cave's opening, as if the whole cave was filled with them. The entrance to the cave was black and howled as the wind blew into it.

Jezebel raised her hand, signaling them to be still and quiet. "We must not go this way," she said in a whispery voice. "Where there are bones—there are things that are hungry…"

"We must leave, quickly," Rafiul said, looking around cautiously. "The smell of death fills the air."

The cave caught their attention again as the winds howled through it. As they stared, an uncomfortable silence settled all around them. Their hearts quickened as the feeling of impending doom came over them. They looked around with their hearts beating quickly. A disturbing sound suddenly came from the cave, sounding like a growl or grunt. They jumped. It could've been the wind, but when glowing red eyes appeared, they knew it wasn't. Then, in seconds, many red eyes appeared, being followed by frightening, loud growls and howls.

"Move!" Rafiul yelled, going to pull himself onto Cherbim.

Black things darted from the black cave! The bones around the stone flew as the shadowy creatures rushed upon them. At first, they didn't know what the things were, but after a moment, they realized that they were gazing at animals of some kind. But they weren't normal animals. The creatures looked like ghastly dogs. Their eyes glowed brilliantly like red firelight and their razor-sharp teeth gnashed and chomped behind their wet bark. Their black flesh was missing in some areas, revealing rotting bones and tissue. They were smaller than the other nomed, but they came in large threatening groups!

One of the hellhounds dashed at Jezebel. Its jaws chomped wildly as it ran at her in full speed. She swiftly pulled her sword from her sheath and swung upwards as it lunged towards her head. She was quick and agile. Its body broke in the air as her sword ripped through it.

Growling louder, the creatures began to attack! Tairren swung his mighty sword through the cold air. The creatures seemed fragile against the powerful golden blade. The blade flashed in the air. The sword seemed to burn the dogs simultaneously as it went through them. They howled as light wisps of steam rose from the parts where the sword hit. Tairren was amazed by the sizzling sounds that came when his powerful sword sliced into the nomed.

Rafiul used his bow and arrows as he sat upon Cherbim's back. The golden arrows looked like beams of light as they hit the creatures, one after another. Cherbim chomped at the dogs with his mighty jaws, catching and throwing them across the stones. "Sweep them, Cherbim!" Rafiul shouted as he continued to shoot the attacking creatures. Cherbim did as he was commanded and opened his glorious wings. He sent out a gust of wind as he pounded his powerful wings against the air. The creatures squealed as they went hurling yards away.

They fought hard, protecting themselves and the horses as the creatures continued to attack.

After a while, Tairren looked up quickly, noticing that more creatures continued to skulk out from the cave! "There are too many!" he shouted.

Rafiul looked up, continuing to shoot his swift arrows at the ferocious fiends. He saw the crowds of black hellhounds erupt from the cave like a colony of angry ants that had been disturbed. They were becoming too much to handle! Their growls and shrieks rumbled across the foul air.

"We must get away from here!" Rafiul shouted.

Jezebel and Tairren swiftly pulled themselves onto their horses, continuing to swing their swords as the dogs gathered closely around them.

Then, strangely, the creatures stopped attacking as they just congregated around them. They were so close that heat could be felt from their rancid breaths. They growled as their eyes glowed brightly. The nomed circled around them like a mighty ring of darkness.

Tairren's spirit began to become troubled as the creatures stared at them. He felt like something dark was trying to force itself upon his spirit.

"...Tairren..." They began to speak to him! Their frightening whispers came together and reverberated across the air. The voices seemed to come from their glowing eyes. Tairren could feel the whispers crawl all over his body.

"I hear them trying to get to you, Tairren!" Rafiul yelled, trying to make them back away. "Do not listen to them!"

The heavy scent of death covered them, along with the presence of evil, as the hellhounds continued to circle around them. Their horses' jumped, kicking their legs and Cherbim let out its mighty roar. The frightening dogs backed away quickly, but they still continued to surround them.

"Do not look into their eyes!" Rafiul shouted in a strong voice. "If you stare into their eyes too long, they will take you down! They are trying to pull you closer to death!"

"I will not yield!" Tairren shouted. "Leave us, in the name of Yehoshua!" Tairren commanded in a strong voice that broke the dark air. His voice spread over them like a wave.

The hellhounds began to cower at the bold mention of Yehoshua's name. Many of them quickly crouched down, hiding their ugly faces. Howls and whimpers began to fill the cold air.

"Run like the wind!" Rafiul shouted. "Follow me, now!" He got Cherbim going quickly, bursting through the crowd of dogs.

They quickly followed behind Rafiul as Cherbim took the lead, sending the dogs flying. They finally got out of the crowd of hellhounds, but they weren't safe yet. They quickly turned their heads only to see that the massive pack of dogs were chasing after them!

They dashed across the field, jumping over small trenches and cold rivulets. Cherbim flew into the gray air, flying low enough while Rafiul continued to shoot the creatures with his bow and arrows. They were outnumbered! They looked small compared to the massive black wave of nomed. The hounds were just yards behind them, howling and screaming behind them like wild Banshees.

Rafiul quickly flew higher into the air, searching for anything that could help them. After a moment, his intense eyes fell upon a bridge. It was a wooden bridge that crossed a deep trench. He didn't know how strong it was, but he knew it was better to attempt the bridge than to give in to the creatures. The trench was wide and black, appearing very deep. Rafiul quickly directed Cherbim back down to Tairren, flying near him so that he could communicate to him.

"Follow me, Tairren!" he yelled, "I know a way out of this!"

Tairren nodded his head, then motioned for Jezebel to follow him. They took a sharp right, being led by Cherbim and Rafiul. They were headed straight to a wide cliff! Tairren's heart thrashed in his chest as he became worried, but his anxiousness quickly went away from him as he kept his eyes on Rafiul. He knew he could trust him. He realized that they were going straight towards a bridge!

Tairren turned his head, feeling overwhelmed as the massive group of hellhounds came closer. Their eyes burned in the dark atmosphere and the noises they made seemed to come from everywhere. The snap of their teeth echoed in his throbbing ears. He felt like he was stuck in a never-ending nightmare.

After an intense moment, they burst onto the bridge. The wooden bridge shook as their weight came upon it. Tairren looked down below the creaking bridge, realizing that they were miles above a black abyss! The bridge began to rock a little as the wave of hellhounds followed them onto it! Tairren looked quickly, noticing that many of the dogs flung off of the bridge, disappearing down into the darkness.

Just then Tairren saw a man at the very end of the bridge! He was waving at them to hurry. Surprised, Tairren got Lilly going even faster. As they came closer to the end of the bridge, he noticed Rafiul waiting for them, along with the strange man. Tairren realized that the man began chopping at the thick rope of the bridge with an ax! Alarmed, Tairren motioned for Jezebel to hurry behind him, noticing that she was a little way away from him. They were moments from falling to their death!

Tairren finally made it to the other end of the bridge with Jezebel right behind him! Relieved, Tairren burst onto the earth, turning his eager head to watch Rafiul and Cherbim. He then glanced at the man who continued to vigorously chop at the rope. He noticed that Rafiul commanded Cherbim to sweep his wings again just as the man finished chopping the rope.

Tairren realized what they were doing. They were trying to tip the bridge over! One side of the bridge began to fall a little as some of the advancing hellhounds slid off. They thrashed around in the air, franticly. Cherbim pounded his wings against the wind many times, making the bridge sway. The forceful gusts knocked against the bridge like a storm. The bridge soon began to sway so hard that the nomed were forced off of it! Cherbim gave one last powerful strike with his massive wings, then the bridge flipped over. The massive pack of dogs looked like black water pouring from the bridge as they fell into the deep trench. Their howls echoed down into the darkness as their red eyes disappeared.

Tairren raised his sword into the air and shouted as he watched the last of the hellhounds disappear into the black abyss.

Cherbim glided down to the ground, perching near the man who helped them. Rafiul hopped off of the beast's back and walked to the man. He was cautious but he wasn't frightened by the man. All of the men of the south were said to be vile, but Rafiul could see that the strange man carried with him God's light. "Thank you," he said. "May God forever remember you."

The man looked at Rafiul, curiously. He appeared excited as his eyes widened. He looked happy but had an incredulous look on his rugged face at the same time. "You are a legna?!" the man shouted. "The owl was right! The eyes of God have fallen upon me!" The man's loud voice erupted in the air as he lifted his eyes up to the sky.

Tairren came to them, having a strange look on his face. "You know the light, then?" Tairren asked.

The man nodded his frazzled head as he excitedly shook their hands. "I do, I do, son! He draws near! The end draws near and He will come again soon!" he said in a loud voice.

Tairren smiled at his excitement. Tairren noticed that the man must've lived among the wild for many years. His beard was long, as well as his hair, and his clothing consisted of fur, dried animal flesh, and leaves. His skin was laden with scars and his face was dark. Even though his appearance was rough and his voice was loud, Tairren could tell that he was a kind man. "Thank you for helping us," Tairren said, looking at his gloating face. "My name is Tairren, and this is Rafiul and the woman over there is Jezebel."

"My name is John," he said, looking at each one of them. His dark eyes were wild. He nodded at Jezebel who kept her distance from him. "Those Jakals would've chased you until death. Do you know what a Jakal is?" he asked, staring his dark eyes into Tairren's. Tairren just shook his head. "Jakals are the gatekeepers of the dark realm… They will pull you into a state of oblivion, waiting to maul you and take you into the darkness… Darkness is rising because the end draws near! But they could not get to you, my lad!" he said with a chuckle as he slapped Tairren's arm. "I know you are strong," John said with a smile. "I saw the owl. The owl told me to keep watch of the bridge. But I did not know why, until now. Always listen to God's words, son. Always listen whole heartedly for his voice... Come with me," he said quickly.

Tairren wasn't too sure if he should trust John at first. John seemed as if he hadn't spoken to anyone in a long time. He seemed frenzied and rambled on about things Tairren hadn't heard of before. Tairren glanced at Rafiul, who nodded his head. He knew then that he could fully trust the eccentric man.

They quickly followed the man across the rugged terrain, looking around for any oncoming nomed. They were going towards a cave that glowed with a soft light. The cave was surrounded by large rocks from the mountain's side.

John gestured for them to follow him into the cave. Rafiul went in first, leaving Tairren and Jezebel on the outside.

"Tairren," Jezebel said, catching his attention. She stood away from the cave.

Tairren stopped quickly, turning towards her. He gazed at her, wondering why she had been acting so aloof. "What is it?"

"I must check our surroundings," she said, quickly, looking around the windy mountainside. "I know the path is near—we shouldn't linger too long with this strange man."

Tairren nodded his head. "Should I go with you?" he asked.

"No," she responded quickly. "I'll be back..." Then she left furtively, disappearing behind a rock.

Tairren stood for a moment, standing among the cold winds that blew upon him. He looked out over the lands, glancing towards the north. Then he went inside quickly.

Tairren stopped for a moment, looking around the cozy-looking cave. He instantly felt comforted, going from the cold outside air, into the inviting cave. The small cavern was filled with warm firelight. Furs and dried herbs hung about the cave, and the stone ground was covered with leaves and dried grass. The small home had a large flat stone that sat in the center that John used as a table; and against the far wall was a pile of leaves and sticks that must've been his bed.

"Come in, come in," he said, gesturing at Tairren. "Come and rest for a moment as I speak to you."

Tairren did as he was told, sitting next to Rafiul who had already made himself at home.

John poured them some hot tea that was brewing over the fire. The small cups they used were made from sundried mud mixed with stone and bones. He stuck some herbs and dried flower petals into the tea and then put in front of them plates of wild honey and dead locusts. He then smiled at them, urging them to eat them.

Tairren smiled a little, looking at the fat locusts that lay in a pool of dark honey. "Thank you," Tairren said, then cleared his throat. "John, how did you get these things? I have not seen anything alive since we've been in the south," Tairren said.

John sat next to them, looking at their plates. "I am a nomadic man, my boy," he said, nodding his hairy head. "This is my permanent home, but I travel about the south and other wild lands, proclaiming the word of God to other travelers! I do my Lord's work. The end draws near, so I must continue His work unto the end! So, you see, I pick up things as I go, and eat from the lands. I don't eat much, but I save the best foods like this for special occasions," he said with a large toothy smile.

Tairren smiled, then went to stick his finger into the sticky honey.

"Wait, son!" John said, making Tairren jump in his seat. "We must thank the Lord for this feast we are about to partake in. Remember to always thank Him."

John said a quick prayer in a loud voice. Just as soon as he was finished, he scooped up a handful of dead bugs and tossed them into his mouth. He smiled and nodded as he crunched on the bitter locusts.

"So, what did you want to speak to us about?" Tairren asked, glancing at a couple of bug legs that hung from John's whiskers.

John took a gulp of his tea, washing the crumbles down with the hot liquid. "The owl, who is the eyes of God, has told me to wait by the bridge, and I did," he said as he wiped his beard. "You know the owl too. The owl speaks to me during rare moments... So, everything that comes from the great owl is precious and must be taken seriously. So—I did wait by the bridge only to help you and your companions... But, why? Why are you so special, boy? So, as I led you all to my home, I thought—your quest must be something precious, indeed... So, you must tell me why the lands are changing, now," he said as his dark eyes became serious. "I know that darkness is growing... I can tell as the winds get colder and the sky gets darker. I feel something in the air that is not of God. My heart has been yearning to speak of the light even stronger! You must know something. Tell me what you know, boy."

Tairren nodded his head, taking a sip of his tea. "This kingdom is in danger." John's heavy eyebrows rose at Tairren's straight forward response. "Marrisa, the princess of this kingdom, was captured days ago. The evil work of Lucif threatens the lands. As we speak, an army of darkness is making its way towards the north."

"So, you are making your way to the Dark Tower, then?" John asked.

"Yes. The core of darkness resides in the tower," Rafiul added. We must try everything to stop it. A great war is coming upon these lands, John. You must know that you are in danger as long as you live here."

"I do not know of any wars, but I know that I must continue to do the God of Light's work!" John said loudly. "I will die as a martyr, if that is what it takes, for the lost to know Him! Light the world, we must! We must feed His sheep!"

Rafiul nodded with a smile, he put his hand on the passionate man's shoulder. "It warms my heart to see a man do the King of Light's work. You continue to do His work, and you will be blessed in the Kingdom of Nevaeh."

"Thank you, friend," John said, nodding his head. "I am not afraid of anything and I will help you!"

"Thank you, Tairren said. "I feel so blessed to meet companions as I continue on the quest that God has set before me. He has brought us all together. Even Jezebel has agreed to help..."

"Ah, yes, the woman in dark garbs," John said, looking around. "She did not want to rest with us? Anybody is invited into my home and should not be ashamed."

"She is checking our surroundings... She knows a path nearby," Tairren said, glancing at Rafiul.

Rafiul just gazed at Tairren, as if he was in deep thought.

"She is a brave woman! When you all go, go with caution," John said. "The Jakals are a glimpse of things to come..."

They sat for a moment, finishing up their tea. It was warming to sit in a cozy abode with good company. They spoke of their adventures, laughing and sharing their experiences. They jokingly compared whose adventure was the most intense. John shared his strange stories of his missionary work as Tairren and Rafiul smirked at his overdramatic hand motions. After a while, they finished up, thinking about the next part of their quest. They could've talked for hours, but knew time was limited.

"I'm sure you must leave, but first I must ask you something, Tairren," John said, running his hand over his beard. "I know you have God's light inside of your heart—and I know you believe in King Yehoshua...but have you been baptized upon the water?"

Tairren sat for a moment, peering at John. He was amazed at John's faith. He thought for a moment, realizing that he had never been baptized. He knew what it was all about, but he had never been offered the opportunity. He realized then that he would've been baptized if it wasn't for him sneaking away from the legna's camp.

"No," Tairren said softly. "I would've been, but I missed my chance."

"Your chance is now, my boy," John said, smiling. He stood up, quickly walking towards a blanket of furs that hung on the wall. "God brought you here for a reason. Follow me."

Tairren stood up, glancing at Rafiul. Rafiul smiled at Tairren, then gestured with his head to follow John.

"Come along," John said. He pulled the furs open, revealing a narrow tunnel in the stone wall.

They carefully followed John through the tunnel, stepping over large stones and ducking under low spots in the rocky ceiling. They made it to an exit, which opened up to another small cave.

Tairren went into the cave, realizing that it wasn't a cave at all. It was an opening in the side of the mountain. There was no ceiling, and the rocky walls went high up, surrounding a crystal-clear pool. The gray light from the early evening came down into the water, showing off the water's splendor. The water looked like glass. Tairren gazed at the water, noticing the large stones that sat beneath it.

"What is this place?" Tairren asked in amazement.

"This is where I baptize travelers who want to be washed of their darkness… I have not baptized anyone in a long time. The world is becoming fewer of believers… But the time is now!"

Just then John stepped into the water, disturbing its peaceful surface. The glass-like surface broke, spreading ripples towards the stone walls. "Come into the water, Tairren." John smiled at him, beckoning him with his hands.

Tairren quietly stepped into the water, not caring that he still had his boots and clothes on. He walked into the cold water as it came to his waist. His blue eyes stared into the water, then up into the sky as he thought of his destination.

"This is a reflection of King Yehoshua's death and risen life… This signifies the death of your darkness and rising of your light!" John said. His voice echoed up the rocky walls. "Close your eyes and succumb to the water…"

Tairren looked into John's passionate eyes while nodding his head. He glanced at Rafiul who was watching attentively. He felt his heart pound as something stirred on the inside of him. He felt that the God of Light was literally looking down on him. He felt he was doing something mighty and sacred, something that was drawing him nearer to God. He closed his eyes, then stood for a moment. He felt John tug his arms. Tairren could feel himself being lowered down into the water. The water rushed over him like an invigorating mantle.

He felt new as he opened his eyes below the clear water. Then, in that quick moment, he saw something that took his breath away. It happened for only a second but it seemed to him like many minuets. He saw a bright light descending from the sky, coming over him. He could see John's silhouette above him, above the surface of the water. But even though it was John above him, he could see the King of Light looking down at him through the cold water. He could feel His mighty presence radiate over him like warm sunrays. Then, in a quick motion, John pulled him back up above the surface.

Tairren splashed out, quickly looking around. His excited heart pounded beneath his cold chest. His skin seemed to glow. He wiped his eyes and face and looked into the sky. He stroked his hands over his wet hair as he continued to look into the gray opening above him.

Rafiul and John looked into the sky as well, catching a glimpse at what Tairren was intrigued by. A being of light came down upon Tairren, looking like a mighty bird of some sort. The beautiful light gracefully came upon Tairren as he raised his hands into the air. The light glowed over Tairren, touching his fingertips and coming upon him like a cloak. The beautiful light seemed to become absorbed into Tairren's skin and blood, making its way into his pounding heart.

"You are my child of light, whom I am proud of," a mighty voice said from the sky and from the light that came into the small opening of the mountain.

Rafiul and John glanced at each other, then at Tairren. Each one of them heard the voice, and they knew where the voice came from. Smiles covered their faces as they stood for what seemed like hours.

At that moment, Tairren became filled with a power he had never felt before. He knew of the power of God, but he had never experienced it before. He felt like he was on fire. He felt like every cell in his body and every inch of his skin radiated with God's light.

He felt new. And just then, he knew that he would never be the same again. He knew then that there was no stopping the plan that God had prepared for him.

✝

CHAPTER 8
Tribulations

Lord Fernund looked out over the town square. He felt a sense of hope as he watched the people of Minslethrate mingle about. The town square and marketplace were decorated heavily with all sorts of flowers and colorful banners. People of all different social rankings walked around in brightly colored costumes and masks. Even though the sky grew black, the colors of the flowers and costumes made the Spring Celebration carry on with excitement. Torches were lit all around the town square and marketplace, along with many softly glowing paper lanterns and colorful candles. The people of the kingdom danced to the cheerful music of the bards while many others clapped and sung with smiling faces. Everything looked splendid and grand, and Lord Fernund felt proud to be leading such a celebration. He knew that the celebration would get even better, when the night would end with more music and glorious fireworks.

The marquis had been going about the kingdom on his horse, making sure that everything was going as planned. The thought of his deceased wife and missing daughter never crossed his mind as he kept busy. He smiled as he watched the people from his horse. He hadn't seen such happiness in the kingdom since Marrisa's birthday, and even that ended horribly. He promised himself that nothing was going to stop the happiness that was coming alive over Minslethrate.

The marquis sat peacefully, until he noticed a group of flustered soldiers hurrying to him. His peace instantly vanished as he noticed the looks on the men's faces.

"Lord Fernund, I'm afraid something terrible has happened," one of the soldiers said, breathlessly.

Lord Fernund looked around quickly, making sure that they were unheard by the nearby people. He looked at the frightened soldier. "What is it, soldier?" he asked, becoming irritated.

"We found something in the field," he said, taking a gulp of cold air. "A lady and lord, were…" He stopped quickly, swallowing down his rising fear.

"What is it?!" Lord Fernund demanded.

"I recognized them—the young lord and lady of the Vaughn household… My Lord—they were mutilated…"

Lord Fernund gazed at the soldier, then glanced at the other ones who looked at him silently. He shook his head, trying to understand him. "Mutilated, soldier? Are you certain?" He couldn't believe what he was hearing. "Perhaps the field is littered with drunkards and trash…"

He shook his head, "no, My Lordship. It is true! They have been killed—along with a servant and horse... Parts of their bodies were thrown about the field..."

Lord Fernund looked up at the crowd of people who danced and laughed among the festival. He felt sick all of a sudden. He brought his fist up to his mouth and took in a deep breath as realization came over him. "This can't be happening...," he said as his voice trailed off. "This can't be happening!" he yelled.

He closed his eyes as Lady Christianne burst into his thoughts. Blood and shadows clouded his mind. He felt inundated with remorse and anxiousness as the feeling of doom began to come over him again. He blankly looked at the soldiers who waited for a response. "I can't do this...," he said to himself in a low voice. His mind seemed to go blank right before the anxious soldiers.

"What should we do, My Lord?!" the soldier asked with wide eyes. "There is a killer on the prowl! It must be the same lunatic who has killed your..." The soldier silenced himself, realizing that he was about to bring up the marquis' deceased wife and household. He looked away quickly, feeling mortified.

Lord Fernund just stared at him silently. He felt numb and didn't realize what the soldier was saying. But then he was disturbed by one of the gatekeepers who rode quickly on horseback towards him. The gate keeper came tearing through the crowds of surprised people. "Why have you left your post?!" he shouted, unable to contain his composer any longer.

"Marquis, you must come out to the field!" he said in a shaken voice. "Hannonite soldiers are outside the main gate!"

Lord Fernund glared at him in disbelief. He nodded his head, then gestured for the gatekeeper to leave. He casually got his horse going behind him with the other soldiers following suit. Lord Fernund looked around, noticing that some people had been watching them, curiously. He noticed how some of them whispered in each other's ears as they gawked at him. But most of the people were too caught up in that evening's festivities to notice anything at all.

The men quickly rode through the small town and out of the main gates that led to the fields. They were amazed. They gazed at the hundreds of Hannonite men that sat on horseback before them.

Lord Fernund looked around at the hundreds of men. They had torches and weapons in their hands, while the front soldiers held flags and banners. The Hannonite colors and symbols flashed on their flags as the cold winds pushed at them.

A soldier came to the marquis quickly, bowing his head. "Lord Fernund, I presume?" The marquis nodded his confused head, still looking out over the army of men. "I am Sir Andor, from the Kingdom of Hanon. We come in peace—we come to help."

"Sir Andor, I don't understand," Lord Fernund said, looking down at him from his horse. "His Majesty, King Julpen of Minslethrate, has gone off on a mission to the southern lands of this kingdom... I am only the ruler until he returns..."

"If you are their ruler now—then you should know that your kingdom is in grave danger," Sir Andor said. His tone was serious as he looked into Lord Fernund's confused eyes. "The Kingdom of Hanon is being threatened as we speak. Minslethrate is next..."

Lord Fernund shook his head. He wasn't ready to hear anything that was happening all of a sudden. He was only a merchant who knew only wealth. He didn't know anything of war or how to truly rule a kingdom. "I am only the Marquis of Minslethrate... I don't understand what's happening!" Lord Fernund began to panic as the heavy burdens of his falling kingdom and broken family began to jump heavily upon his shoulders.

Lord Fernund began to breathe heavily as a sudden panic attack began to come over him. His heart pounded in his chest and sweat formed on his brow. His stomach churned and the ringing in his ears became louder. He quickly glanced around, only seeing a sea of shadowed faces. Just then he wished that he would just disappear within those shadows.

"My Lord...," a low voice came from his other side. The woman's voice caught his attention and calmed him a bit. It was a familiar voice that made him think of his wife. Her accent brought nostalgia over him. His eyes widened as he saw Sora standing by him. "They have come to help you understand," she said, placing a caring hand on his boot.

He stared down at her, amazed and bewildered. His eyes grew wide as he realized who the woman was. At first, he thought he was daydreaming, but after looking at Sora's face his mind became whole again. "Sora...," he said as he thought of Lady Christianne and his dead household. Emotion came over Lord Fernund as he hopped off of his horse. He came to Sora, looking into her eyes. He thought that she was dead, just like everyone else. "My dear, Sora!" Lord Fernund said in a shaken voice as he hugged her. "The Lord has spared your life!" He fought back his tears as he held her. He felt like he was hugging his wife again.

Moral silently watched from her horse. She placed her hand over her mouth. She was touched by the marquis. She had never seen Lord Fernund act the way he did just then. She pitied him as he appeared like a lost child. She could tell that his experiences had truly humbled him.

"My Lord," Sora said in a soft voice, pulling away from the marquis. "Something is happening this very day. Darkness is covering the lands. Flying monsters from the deepest pits of Hell are already attacking far off kingdoms. A monster named Baal is leading them… We are all in grave danger." Lord Fernund searched her dark eyes as a tear fell from his weary face. "The King of Hanon has graciously sent half of his army to help us…" Lord Fernund just blankly stared at her with his bloodshot eyes. "We are breathing upon a time that knows only darkness, My Lord. You may wonder where the light is in it all…" Sora's voice began to tremble as emotion stirred inside of her. "…I know you've buried my sister, Marquis… I know it is the darkness that has taken her. And my heart is broken because of it…"

Lord Fernund began to sob, unable to contain himself any longer. The stress of his darkened life was rising up from his aching heart.

"But we must fight on…for Zorrina," Sora said, placing her shaken hands on his face. Sora's words and the mention of his wife's birth name seemed to ignite something in him. He had not heard Zorrina's true name be spoken in many years. He looked into her dark eyes, amazed by her strength. "We must avenge my sister! We must avenge, Natalia, your daughter—my niece! We must avenge the princess and this kingdom!" Sora said as passion rose inside of her. "We must avenge all who have fallen victim to the darkness! We must fight this, Marquis! We must bring the light back to the kingdom! It has been far too long that we've slept. We must awaken our spirits and fight for our Lord God!"

Lord Fernund began to breathe heavily as he fed off of Sora's uplifting words. Her words reminded him of Master Odwa and his inspiration. Her passion reminded him of the God of Light. Her face reminded him of his own strength. He realized if it wasn't for him seeing her, he might've gotten lost in his ill feelings… Just then he pressed his dry lips together and nodded his head. He inhaled a deep breath, then exhaled. He placed his hand on Sora's cheek and faintly smiled at her, then looked out over the Hannonite men.

He then glanced at the group of Minslethratian soldiers who were watching him. Silence sat heavily. "Go tell the other soldiers that Hanon will be joining us this evening."

They obeyed him and quickly rode back through the main gate.

The marquis then pulled himself onto his horse, looking down at Sora and Sir Andor. "We must fight for the light, then…"

✝✝✝

Lord Fernund quickly rode into the main gate, followed by Sora, Moral, Sir Andor, and the massive army of Hanon. The clatter of the horse's hooves against the cobblestone filled the air. Some of the people of Minslethrate, who noticed, watched as the Hannonite soldiers poured in through the gates and gathered around the walls and courtyard of the castle.

Lord Fernund, followed by Sir Andor and the women, hurried into the castle. They met in the study chamber of the castle wanting to speak in privacy, away from the people of Minslethrate. Master Odwa met them in the chamber as well, not appearing panicked or frightened at all. They casually greeted one another as Sora told Lord Fernund about their visit to the Kingdom of Hanon. They then began to talk of more serious matters like the kingdom's present state and the journey the Hanonnites made from their kingdom to Minslethrate. There was no laughter or smiles in the room; only grim attitudes and pensive looks filled the hall. The fire place roared behind them, sending their shadows dancing upon the dim stone.

"I don't want there to be any chaos in the kingdom," Lord Fernund said, gazing out of the massive window that looked out over the castle gardens. The whole celebration could be seen as well. Torches and colorful lanterns and banners could be seen dancing in the evening air. "I'm sure there is gossip going on because of the many soldiers you've brought here. This is the first time since the princess' celebration, that the people of Minslethrate appear happy. We must allow the Spring Celebration to continue without any kind of notion of war... But if anything happens, which I pray it does not, the soldiers will be ready."

"Marquis, you don't want to send the people back to their homes to safety?" Master Odwa asked. "If anything does happen—there will be chaos and death upon the people."

"No," Lord Fernund said, quickly. "What if nothing happens at all? I do not see any sign of danger..." He stopped talking as he watched the distant firelight of the festival.

He thought about what the soldiers had told him earlier. Images of the Lord and Lady Vaughn mangled upon the fields flashed into his mind. He closed his eyes tightly, bringing his hand to his forehead. He didn't know what was truly out there in the darkness. If it was one man or a group of men doing the killings, the soldiers could easily stop them. But what if it wasn't men who were killing? The thought of his wife's blood and startling black eyes came into his mind. Could darkness possibly come alive and walk around like man? He didn't know what to believe anymore.

"I've seen the darkness, My Lord," Sora spoke up. Lord Fernund glanced at her. "I've seen the creatures that look like they were made from fire and pure evil... I've seen them yank soldiers into the air and rip them apart as if they were paper..."

Moral turned away towards the window. She didn't want to engage in the conversation any longer. Everything was beginning to feel real, but dream-like at the same time. The thought of the creatures destroying the soldiers made her feel sick.

"My soldiers will line the walls of the castle," Sir Andor said, catching Lord Fernund's attention. "They will be the castle's eyes. They will be ready—if something does happen…"

Lord Fernund walked over to the fireplace and gazed into the fire. He became lost in the flames as they danced and crackled. The orange flames soothed his mind. "Have a soldier around every corner. Line them inside and outside of the walls," he said, turning towards them. "Send more soldiers out upon the fields as well…," he said, thinking of Lady Daleasa and Lord Fredrick. "Our kingdom shall be heavily guarded this night. Our kingdom shall be safe! I promised our king—Minslethrate shall be safe."

"Yes, My Lord," Sir Andor said quickly, then rushed out of the study hall.

Lord Fernund walked over to the window, looking out over the lands. After a moment, he watched as Sir Andor could be seen rushing towards the gates with some of his men following him.

"My Lord," Moral said in a low tone. "…I am so sorry, for everything… I give you my condolences," she stammered. He looked at her, not saying anything. Silence grew between them. "Forgive me, we have not properly met," Moral said, breaking the uncomfortable silence again. "My name is Moral… My son, Tairren, ventured off towards the south with Lady Natalia and Prince Phillip."

Lord Fernund was silent for a moment. "I see," he finally said, continuing to peer through the glass. "I've heard my daughter mention your son's name before… Natalia is stubborn—much like her mother," he said with a faint smile. "I've never really known who she associated with—or what she did on a daily basis…" He became quiet for a moment longer as his smile faded away. He realized then that he didn't really know his maturing daughter anymore. He was too busy—for everything and everyone. "If it wasn't for my daughter leaving…she might've been dead by now." He looked at Moral, having a straight face. "I'm happy she's gone with your son…"

"If you don't mind me saying this, My Lord… Your daughter is very precious, Marquis. She is bold, but sweet," Moral said with a smile. "Her boldness is what makes her a special young lady. She has helped my son come out of his shyness… She always made me laugh with her dramatic ways," Moral said with a chuckle.

"You know my daughter more than I do," Lord Fernund said, appearing ashamed. "But I'm glad she knows someone like you. You seem like a wonderful woman…"

Moral felt sad as she looked out of the window. She thought of all the times in the past when Natalia mentioned how she barely saw her parents. "There are always second chances," she said, looking up at him. Her voice was low where he could only hear her. "Yes, life is too precious and short…but during life, there are always second chances… When this is all finished…you hold your daughter in your arms and never let her go. In a world of second chances, we only have but one life, marquis. Just remember that…"

Lord Fernund looked at her quickly. He stared at the wise woman. She softly smiled at him as her gray eyes twinkled. He nodded at her, appreciating her comfort and kind words.

"When this is all finished…," Lord Fernund repeated in a low voice. Those words gave him hope. He smiled back at her. "It amazes me how we are all connected. It's as if God chose us just for this moment—this day. It makes me think that we are all pieces in a grand puzzle."

"The Lord works in mysterious ways, Marquis. We are all but a glimmer of dust upon his hand," Moral said. "We must have faith in our God…because without faith, we have no reason to be here…" She smiled up at Lord Fernund, patted his arm, then turned to leave him in his thoughts.

Lord Fernund grew quiet as he continued to look out of the window. He wondered how it all was going to come together…if it even was going to come together at all. He wondered why, if they were all part of a larger scheme, were they forced into trials and tribulations? How much darkness were they to go through before seeing the light at the end? Lord Fernund had faith, but it was hard for him to totally believe when he did not see any good from his current situation.

His eyes fell upon the festival again. He hoped that everything was going to be good. It was hard for him to see the goodness as he looked further towards the south. The clouds were as black as night and they brought with them cold winds and foul smells. The ominous sky made him feel a sense of doom come over his spirit.

There had to be light somewhere behind those clouds…but he could not see it…

†

CHAPTER 9
Darkness in the Moors

Across the windy heaths, among the old village of Prat, an old woman sat silently. She slouched beneath a tree on a rickety wooden chair, smoking her dirty old pipe. She inhaled the sweet herbs, filling her lungs with its heavy smoke. A white plume of slow-moving smoke poured out from her cracked lips. A strange gust of wind blew into the village suddenly, making her white hair flutter in front of her wrinkly face. Her glorious plume of scented smoke flew away with the winds. She moved her hair out of her eyes, looking into the sky as the winds began to blow harder. The sky became blacker and moved closer to the village, as if the thick, dark clouds began to blanket the earth. The threatening sky seemed to come alive suddenly.

"A strange storm is coming, madam," a young man said, walking past the old woman.

The boy stopped, noticing that the old woman began beckoning him. He walked to her, looking at her curiously.

"You better hide your handsome face from those clouds..." She stared her cataract-filled eyes at him. "That's no regular storm, son," she said, taking a big puff on her pipe. She exhaled, releasing coughs and smoke into the cold air.

"What do you mean, ma'am?" the boy asked, rubbing his arms with his dirty hands. He felt the temperature drop all around him.

"The darkness is coming...," she said, looking up at the boy with her gray eyes. She smiled an old smile, which turned into a toothless grin. She began to laugh, spitting as she did. "It's gonna get ya!" she shouted, pointing her knobby finger at him. "The darkness is coming!"

The boy looked at her strangely, slowly backing away from her as she continued to laugh. He looked at her with disgust, quickly turning away from the strange old woman. He looked around nervously, startled by what the woman had said to him.

He realized that he was all alone. Warm lights glowed from the windows of the small storefronts and the streets were clear of people. Everyone must've rushed indoors because of the ominous weather.

The wind blew trash and leaves across the cobblestone as he hurried towards an alleyway. He became nervous, having a strange feeling come over him as if something was watching him... A loud shriek erupted in the air, followed by a raspy scream. Panicked, the boy quickly turned around to see what the commotion was all about. He looked for the old woman—but to his surprise, she was gone! Her old chair was left beneath the tree, tipped over.

The boy began to panic as his breaths quickened. He looked around quickly then ran down the alleyway, towards his home. He thought of the village legends and ghost stories, about the creatures that would come when there was no light at all in the world... The stories were just common-folk lore, but he had believed in them his whole young life. He looked up into the sky as goose-bumps filled his flesh. The sky looked black, making the torches shine brightly in the dark alleyway.

Suddenly something fell from the sky, plopping down right in front of him. The boy stopped quickly, looking down at the object. It was round, and had two eyes and a gaping mouth. His heart seemed to go out when he realized that the round thing was—the old woman's head! Her gray eyes stared at him as the hairs on the back of his neck stood up. He let out a loud scream, running to the nearest door in the alley. He banged on the door, screaming for help. Random people looked out of their windows for a moment, but then slammed their shutters closed and pulled their curtains together tightly.

The boy continued to run down the alley as darkness filled the atmosphere. It was as if a black mist began to form all around him. A loud shriek rang out above his head. Startled by the high-pitch scream, the boy looked up. Something large and black flew over the alley! It had large wings and eyes that glowed intensely! The boy screamed, becoming petrified. He breathed harshly, looking down the alleyway. He was nearly home! He began to run as fast as he could through the darkness. His panting breath seemed louder than the echo of his feet hitting against the cobblestone.

The boy stopped abruptly as a large black shadow fell from the sky. The dark figure landed quickly, making a strange sound when it hit the ground. The shadow crouched down in the middle of the alleyway, appearing like a large mound of black stone. The young man stood still, frozen. He breathed hard as his eyes stared wide open. His face was white as a ghost as he shook with fear. The shadow before him slowly stood up. It was tall and haunting as its eyes glowed silently. Suddenly, like a quick wind, it rushed towards the boy with a loud scream!

The boy screamed for help, but his screams were muffled. Then silence came over the alleyway as darkness covered his body...

The black sky loomed over Prat, filling the old village with icy air. Many flying shadows infested the dark air, covering the small village with fear and terror...

✝✝✝

Miles away from Prat, across the quiet moors of the eastern kingdom, Hanon sat in a state of panic. The flying Abaddon, led by Baal, terrorized the kingdom. The flying army was killing many innocent people. Much blood was spilled as the Hannonite Army fought against the nomed's evil clutches. The kingdom was filled with chaos, falling against the powers of darkness. Most of the kingdom fell victim to the ferocious Abaddon, filling the dark air with chilling screams.

Further away from the castle of Hanon, on the outer edges of the kingdom nearer to Prat, the Valor Manor sat in silence. The feeling of despair filled the manor. No one knew when the enemy was going to attack. The black clouds loomed above the manor and the mists sat heavily upon the earth.

Lord Timotheus talked with the young soldier named Gideon, upon the balcony of his study. His heart grew heavy at the realization of his kingdom being taken over by the flying creatures. The mention of death came from the soldier's shaken lips. Lord Timotheus listened on, shaking his head at the terrible news.

"Our army is great but the monsters are too powerful. Their strength is unnatural," Gideon said quickly. "The dark army of flying creatures is being led by a monster named Baal. They fly to torment, my Lord. It's as if it will never stop!"

"We will carry on unto the end!" Lord Timotheus said with a scruffy voice. "We shall not fall, in the name of King Yehoshua! We shall not fall! If my leg did not hold me back, I would have the monsters screaming upon my sword!"

"We will carry on," Gideon tried to say in a strong voice. "But the king thinks that we should go into hiding soon, below the moors. The creatures are relentless and the deep caverns are our only safe haven."

"Aye, his majesty is very old, much like myself," the lord said, looking into the dark sky. "If that is what he commands, that is what the kingdom must do. Go below the moors when the time is right. Give my king inspiration and let him know that I am praying for him and our kingdom."

Gideon nodded his head, looking into the old man's concerned eyes. He became silent for a moment. He looked away, appearing insecure all of a sudden.

"What is it, son?" Lord Timotheus asked, noticing the pensive look on his face.

"I'm...," he stopped for a moment, shaking his head a little. "I'm only a baker's son," he said finally, looking into the old man's eyes. "I am not mighty like you or Sir Andor. I don't feel that I am capable for any of this. The king wants me to lead the people down below the moors when the time is needed... The monsters are much bigger than I, and much faster... What if I lead the people astray?"

Lord Timotheus looked into the young soldier's eyes. Timotheus knew that Gideon was only about seventeen and only recently became summoned to join the army of Hanon. He knew that he worked at the mill most of his life. Going from a miller to a warrior was extreme, but Lord Timotheus knew that being a warrior was his calling. He had faith in the young man.

"Why do you doubt yourself now? Son, you once told me that the Lord spoke to you. You said that the God of Light told you to join the legion, is that not so?" Lord Timotheus said, looking into his eyes.

Gideon looked at him, then finally nodded his head. "Yes, my lord."

"Then it is so! The Lord of Light will be with you, Gideon! You may be the son of a baker, but you have the heart of a warrior! Do not be afraid and always remember where your strength comes from." Lord Timotheus smiled at him. "I will pray for you, my boy. I will pray for us all!"

Gideon nodded his head as his face lightened.

"Thank you, Lord Timotheus—you are right. I will remember those words. And I shall pray as well..."

The lord put his old hand on his soldier. His dark-blue eyes twinkled. "We all must... Let us never forget what we are called to do. Let us never forget the power of God! Now go quickly, and may God watch over you, my boy," he said in a passionate voice. "King Yehoshua is with you, mighty warrior!"

The young soldier pressed his lips together, nodding his head. He held his chin up, appearing bolder than before. Then he was off quickly, disappearing in the shadows of the study.

Lord Timotheus stared into the shadows for a while, thinking of that young soldier and all of the soldiers who were fighting and dying for their kingdom. He slowly turned to the dark sky, looking at the way the winds blew the strange mists all around. The mists twirled upon the sky, then settled down as a soft sheet of gray air again.

"My God," he said out to the sky. "Watch over us... Watch over my kingdom. Burn fierce among the darkness that is covering the lands! Lead Gideon and the other soldiers! Lead my people as war settles over us! Give the king of Hanon strength in his old heart. Please do not turn your eyes away from us. Remember us, as we remember you! Please, my God, protect us..."

After his prayer, Lord Timotheus stood quietly upon the balcony. His old eyes never left the sky. His eyes drifted away, looking towards the blackness that covered the direction where Minslethrate was. He thought of Moral and Sora, hoping that they were okay. It seemed as if darkness was covering the whole Earth then. He said a silent prayer for the women, Sir Andor, and the rest of his army.

His eyes fell away from the dark skies, falling upon the lands his manor sat upon. Just then he was reminded how truly blessed he was. He was thankful that the creatures had not attacked his manor as they were doing his kingdom. He looked around, realizing that there were no creatures in the sky or lurking in his lands. He had seen them before in the skies—but they had vanished. It seemed as if the Lord had put a blanket of protection over his home. He was suddenly reminded in his spirit that God had not forgotten about him, and protected him from the growing darkness.

The old man closed his eyes, thanking the Lord in his heart. A sudden feeling of peace came over him as tears filled his blue eyes.

He continued to pray for his kingdom, Minslethrate, and the whole world. He fell to his knees, praying with all the passion he had.

He never stopped praying as the cold air covered him.

†

CHAPTER 10
Dark Fire

Above the Black Field of Old Blood, upon the cliffs, the legna and Minslethratians were preparing for battle. They readied themselves by putting on their armor, and praying. They sharpened their blades and filled their quivers with arrows. Their belts were fastened and their shields were buffed. But even though their armor was ready—they needed to prepare their spirits and minds even more.

The whole army had been quiet as anxiousness settled over them. Mentally, they weren't prepared for a battle of any kind. They didn't know what to expect or what hour it would happen—but they knew it was going to happen soon. They knew a war was on the horizon. They could feel their spirits shake as the feeling of impending doom rose in their hearts. The sky became as black as night and dark mists covered the earth. The air was cold and a strange wind blew among the sky. Something was going to happen—but they didn't know what.

King Julpen, Sir Hawkington, and their men stood silently upon the cliffs, looking over the Black Field of Old Blood. It was hard to see because of the black sky and mists. They held their torches tightly in their clammy palms. Small plumes of mist escaped their mouths as they breathed with nervousness upon the cold air. The wait was unbearable and the silence was intense. Even though it was cold that evening, sweat still collected on their brows, dripping from their helmets.

The legna were mixed in with the crowd of Minslethratians, appearing as specks of luminous lights in the crowd of solemn faces. Their golden armor gleamed in the dark light. Their golden eyes gave an intense stare as their faces held no fear. They stood tall and unwavering.

"Are you certain that something will happen soon, Mikhal?" King Julpen asked in a low tone. He sat on his horse, peering into the silent mists before him.

Mikhal stood next to him, appearing much taller. "I am certain, Your Majesty," he said, still staring. "I feel it growing, even now as we speak… We must go down into the valley."

"Nothing can be seen," Phillip said quickly. He stood next to Dolsia. "We'll be going in blind."

"We will get taken by surprise. We might as well move with our eyes closed," Dolsia added.

Natalia stood away from them, just watching them with curiosity. She stood along with Uriel and other legna who had befriended her over their journey.

"We must go down into the valley," Mikhal said again. "How must we reach the top of a mountain if we do not move from the bottom first? Our God is the light—and will lead us through the darkness," Mikhal said.

"I see," King Julpen said. He took in a deep breath. "Let's move, then. Waiting in the dark silence is what torments the mind."

They all glanced at each other, coming to a silent agreement. They got their armor ready and made sure that their weaponry was secured. The men hopped onto their horses as some of the legna pulled themselves onto their beasts. The army began to move about as their hearts fluttered with anxiousness.

Mikhal shouted out a command in the ancient tongue to his fellow legna, then looked out over the crowd of men. "This evening, we ride to our victory!" he shouted. "The darkness is thick, but we must not fear it! Remember, whatever happens—it happens for our Lord!" He raised his sword into the dark air as the men began to shout. Their voices were loud but their faces still had worried looks on them.

They began to descend the cliffs, going around the steep edges and down the slopes where it was manageable. Their torches burned brightly, dancing in the air as the dark mists gave way. The strange mists split, moving around the men as if it didn't want to touch them.

Phillip and Dolsia, with Natalia walking nearby with Uriel, went together on foot like many of the other men and legna. They wore the legna's golden armor, which made them appear strong and mighty. They moved swiftly together. Their eyes searched the darkness around them; they were prepared for anything it seemed. But they were not prepared for what was to come next.

Suddenly, the winds picked up. Faint noises could be heard, as if something was coming upon them quickly. A powerful, cold burst of wind came over them like a strong wave. The whole crowd of men nearly fell over. Some surprised men tumbled down the dales of the valley as some crashed into the boulders. The noises became louder as ghastly shrieks and grunts began to fill the air. Red, glowing eyes appeared in the distance, starting as faint specks. More red eyes appeared as they came closer. All of a sudden, everything became chaotic all around them. A stampede of nomed were coming straight towards them!

"Stand guard!" Mikhal shouted. The other captains and Archlegnas commanded the same thing.

King Baffmit flew over them in an angry wind, sending a massive cloud of fire over them. The men blocked his wrathful flames with their shields. King Baffmit was leading hundreds of ferocious Nomed! The black creatures roared loudly, flying past them in a quick blur of loud shrieks.

It was as if they were caught in a wild storm. The legna began shooting their arrows and swinging their swords as the black wave of nomed tore through the crowd. The passing nomed squealed as their arrows and swords caught them. The nomed didn't even fight back. They seemed to just ignore their attacks!

"What's happening?!" King Julpen shouted to Mikhal over the loud sounds of the nomed.

"I fear they are going towards the northern kingdom!" Mikhal shouted, swinging his sword as the Nomed burst past him.

After a moment of intensity, the field became silent again and the winds died down. The nomed vanished up the cliffs as their loud sounds slowly dissipated. Everything became quiet again. The men's breaths and the clanking of armor filled the air. It was like nothing had come at all. They stood still, confused by what had just happened.

Phillip breathed hard, looking around with wide eyes. "Where are they going?!" he asked, lowering his sword.

"The north is in grave danger!" Mikhal shouted over the crowd of bewildered men. "The nomed did not want to fight us—so they are attacking the weak and innocent, instead!"

The men became angry as they all looked at each other. Fear followed as they thought of their loved ones.

"No!" Natalia shouted. "Our kingdom can not take a war! Many will perish! Cowards, the nomed are!"

"Lucif is making things worse by attacking the innocent," Uriel said. Her golden eyes gleamed intensely. "He will stop at nothing to destroy everything."

"Darkness must be stopped!" King Julpen shouted, becoming enraged. He thought of his kingdom and everyone within it. His heart broke as innocent faces came into his mind. "There are so many women and children! They will not have a chance!"

The men of Minslethrate became frantic as worry and fear came over them. Their voices rose in the air as remorse grew upon them.

Mikhal looked towards the sky, hoping to see a sign. He knew something was out there. He felt a strong presence come quickly before him. The presence was completely opposite of what the nomed brought, and carried with it, power. His golden eyes searched the black skies, eagerly looking for the beacon of hope that was coming near them.

The symbol of light and hope came quickly, just as Mikhal thought. The white owl showed up in the sky. He looked like a soft apparition in the black, misty sky. He flew over the crowd of men, looking down with its dark, starry eyes. He glided down towards the earth, soaring peacefully with its wings spread out. The golden tips of its feathers sparkled upon the firelight of the men. The beautiful white owl perched on the ancient tree on top of Skull Hill. He rustled his large white wings, then settled down in the windy air. He glowed in the dark sky like a lamp.

The whole crowd became quiet, taking notice of the mysterious bird. They gazed at it with wonder, not saying anything as their minds began to rest. The bird's powerful presence pushed every dark feeling away from them.

"I Am, that I Am...," a voice said from the owl. Intense light seemed to come from the owl's aura, brightening with its words. The mighty voice resonated in their hearts and spread out among the field in pulsating motions.

The owl reminded them of all God's promises as he sat upon the tree's branches. They were reminded of King Yehoshua, and the war that took place long ago on that same field. They were reminded that King Yehoshua had won the war long ago, and that no matter what happened— they had already won. They were reminded of their inner strength and the power they harbored. Each and every person upon the field had become enlightened just then.

After many quiet moments, the owl spread its white wings out, then flew into the air. Its mighty wings pounded against the sky, sending out a rhythmic pulse sound until the great white owl had vanished.

The men looked at each other, trying to see if they had all experienced the same thing. Time seemed to have stopped as they realized that the God of Light was just speaking to them through the glorious bird.

"Do you believe?" Mikhal asked, looking at the bewildered faces of the men. "Answer me this—Do-you-believe?!" he asked in a louder voice. "Don't you see, men? That's what this is all about! When you believe with all your heart, not even the strongest powers in Hell can stop you! BELIEVE, I say to you! Believe God's promises! Believe in King Yehoshua's words! The God of Light has spoken to us all!" Mikhal said, raising his hands into the air. "We must carry on through the valley! Each and every one of you carries a power that should not be put away! Nothing shall smite it! Even when your flesh dies, it will not subside! Rise up, men, and believe! This field holds countless bones from your ancestors! The ground is saturated with blood that was spilled so long ago, not only by your ancestors, but by the King of Kings—King Yehoshua! We shall redeem the princess and all who have fallen in the hands of darkness! We shall redeem them all as we fight for this kingdom...and the whole world!"

Just then everyone gave out a shout as their hearts lifted.

"Now go together as men and light! You are one!" Mikhal shouted as he raised his sword. "Time has run out. God have mercy on the people of Minslethrate. We must go to the Dark Tower and take it down! Lucif will be punished!"

The men and legna shouted again as they came together in unison. Their hearts were stronger and their minds were clear of fear, just then. They began to march into the Black Field of Old Blood.

"I must go," Mikhal said, only to King Julpen. "The God of Light spoke to me and told me to go to the tower with haste. I can move quickly upon my beast. Something is happening as we speak. Tairren is alive... I felt a jolt inside of me and saw Tairren becoming inundated with light, in my spirit's mind."

King Julpen nodded his head, amazed by Mikhal.

"You must lead them, King Julpen," Mikhal said, placing his hand on his shoulder. "You must lead them into battle. Lucif will send another army; it is definite. Avenge your kingdom and your people...God will be with you!" Mikhal patted his chest, then pulled himself onto his mighty beast.

King Julpen watched as Mikhal quickly flew off into the dark air.

"A sword for my God...and for Minslethrate," he said, then rode off on his horse.

†††

Across the valley, upon the Great Mountains of Minslethrate, Tairren and Rafiul made their way up the mountain's rugged path. They were alone and had to make the rest of their journey on foot. The mountains were impossible to travel upon with a horse, so Rafiul sent Lilly and Cherbim away into the Black Field of Old Blood. He spoke to their minds and commanded them to look for the legna, where they would be safe. Cherbim would protect Lilly, they thought. They missed them at first, but knew it would be impossible to travel with them.

They had just left John's cave after the visit from God's light, and began their way towards the Dark Tower. John gave them torches because of the black sky and more locusts to eat on their journey. They graciously accepted the dead bugs, even though they didn't have the appetite for them. John also prayed for them and their beasts, that they all would be safe. As soon as they left John's abode, they searched for Jezebel, who was nowhere in sight. They could not wait for her so they began their own way, using Tairren's old map and compass.

"Where has she gone? I knew I should've gone with her. It's too dangerous out here," Tairren said, looking at his compass. "Without Lilly and Cherbim, I fear it will take us longer."

"According to your father's map, the Dark Tower of Sacrifice should be southwest from here. I sense something past the trees," Rafiul said, looking up the rugged mountainside. "We shouldn't have to ascend the mountain for too much longer. The temple is towards the bottom of the mountains, so the journey should not be as strenuous."

After a few more glances, Tairren folded up his tattered map and put it away. He followed his old compass, grateful that he had it in his possession.

615

They trekked up the mountain, climbing up large boulders and steep stone-walls. Dead trees stood tall, twisting around each other in clusters. As they went through the trees, the earth steadily rose up. Their legs began to ache as they pressed on.

Tairren glanced down where they were at. They seemed to have made a lot of ground. It was hard to see because of the dark clouds, but they could tell that they were high. If they had slipped or fell, they would've surely tumbled down towards the deep valleys and trenches that surrounded the mountains. Tairren noticed something strange as he continued to peer off from the mountainside. Many small lights could be seen, far off towards the north from where they hiked.

"Look, over there, towards the north. Do you see the lights?" Tairren said, pointing.

Rafiul stared, noticing the small specks of light as well. "Firelight," he said, "thousands of torches and fires. The legna are coming."

"Do you think the legna allowed the nomed to pass them?" Tairren asked, thinking about his kingdom and the storm of nomed that were going towards the north.

"That, I do not know...," Rafiul said, turning his gaze back up the mountain. "We still have a journey ahead of us so we mustn't linger."

Rafiul left Tairren staring at the tiny specks of firelight. They looked like small fireflies on the morbid horizon. Tairren thought of his mother and loved ones, hoping that they were safe. He thought of the Forest Provence of the north and the rolling fields that always stayed green and vibrant. He thought of the apple orchards and the many colors nature possessed in the north. Even the air was much pleasant there. It all felt like a dream to him. It felt like the pleasantries of Minslethrate were far gone. It had been many days since he saw the sun and green plants, the skittering animals and the birds. He wondered if he would see them again. He longed to smell the fresh scents of the earth and feel the fresh air against his face again. He was in love with his kingdom. His heart broke to see how ill-looking the sky had gotten over the days that passed him by.

"We must go," Rafiul said, breaking his thoughts.

Tairren quickly glanced at him, then followed him up the mountain.

After many quiet moments of lurking up the rough terrain of the mountainside, Rafiul stopped abruptly. His keen eyes stared.

"What is it?" Tairren asked, noticing Rafiul's cautious mannerism.

"There's a fire burning," he said in a low tone. "Someone is talking nearby."

Tairren looked around the dark mountainside. He moved his torch around to see clearly. He didn't see any fire of any kind; he only seen dark trees and shadowed rocks. The mountain was quiet.

"Follow me," he whispered.

They lurked through the trees, coming upon a cliff that looked over a small dip in the mountain. They could see more dead trees, and in the midst of the trees was a small fire. The fire sent dancing shadows upon the rocks and trees. A dark form crouched in front of the fire, staying still like a statue.

They slowly made it down into the small wooded valley, keeping their eyes on the still figure. They crept towards the trees a couple of yards away from the fire.

"Jezebel…," Tairren whispered, staring at the woman in black robes. "What's she doing?"

They peered closer at her. She seemed to be talking to the fire… Her lips would move a little, and then the fire seemed to respond by flickering.

"She's communicating with another entity," Rafiul said, grabbing the hilt of his sword. "Deceitful, wolf," Rafiul grumbled with flashing eyes.

He got up quickly from the shadows of the trees, pulling his sword form its jeweled scabbard.

"Wait, Rafiul!" Tairren rushed behind him, worried that he would cut Jezebel's head clean off.

Jezebel stood up quickly. Her golden eyes became wide. She swiftly pulled her sword from its sheath, ready to swing it. She held it up towards them while the fire burned behind her.

"Who are you speaking with?!" Rafiul demanded, rushing upon her. His face was intense with anger.

Jezebel raised her sword, prepared to block his strike. Her honey-colored eyes flashed, looking like fire. She didn't say anything as she glared at Rafiul from her black hood.

"Stop!" Tairren shouted, dashing between them. He raised his arms out to block Rafiul's sword.

"Tairren, get out of my way! She can't be trusted—just as I warned you!" Rafiul said, looming over them. Being much taller than both of them, he could've easily thrown Tairren aside to get to Jezebel, but didn't.

"There are worse things to worry about this night," Tairren said quickly, not moving. The firelight bounced off of his serious face.

Rafiul looked at Tairren, then lowered his golden sword. "I'm surprised at you, Tairren," he said. His face softened a bit. "I didn't think that you were one to think foolishly…"

"I've done nothing!" Jezebel shouted, stopping Rafiul from speaking. "I searched the mountain for danger—for you, Tairren. I lost my way so I built this fire—the sky has gotten darker. I couldn't see my way!"

"You said you knew these lands," Rafiul said quickly, still holding his sword tightly. "You've lied, and have been lying to us all along!"

"No! No, I didn't!" she said, grabbing Tairren's attention. He turned to look at her. He noticed how fiery her eyes looked. "Tairren, I've helped you this far. You trust me no longer?"

Tairren felt torn between his two companions. He had compassion for Jezebel, but he wanted to trust everything Rafiul was saying about her.

"I am no threat," she said, putting her sword back into its sheath.

Rafiul gazed at her for a moment, then slowly put his sword back as well. "Who were you talking to?" he asked again.

Jezebel glared at him, then quickly turned away from them. She sat on a fallen tree near the fire. "I was talking to no one," she said, not looking at them.

Tairren looked at Rafiul who didn't appear satisfied. Tairren watched as he sat close to Jezebel. He followed Rafiul and sat near him.

"Why are you fully covered?" Rafiul asked, trying to reveal who she truly was.

Jezebel looked into the fire, silently. She seemed to be in deep thought, ignoring Rafiul. "...I apologize," she finally said, looking at Rafiul. "I did not mean to frighten or alarm you..."

Rafiul looked into the fire. His golden eyes shined and his face glistened. "If I catch you in a lie again—you will not live to look upon the fire any longer."

Jezebel glanced over at him quickly, glaring at him.

"Whose side are you on, Jezebel?" Rafiul finally asked, antagonizing her.

Jezebel just looked at him, then at Tairren. She quickly got up from her seat, silently going towards the trees to leave them.

Tairren irritably glanced at Rafiul, who didn't move from his spot, then got up to follow her.

"Tairren, let her go," Rafiul commanded.

Tairren stopped for a moment, staring into his eyes, then left him quickly. He ignored Rafiul's command and intense gaze.

Tairren followed Jezebel, who stopped abruptly. "Where are you going?" he asked.

She turned to him slowly, looking him up and down with her furtive eyes. Her strange eyes glowed among her black shrouds. "I am not wanted. And besides, you don't need me any longer," she said. "You know the way to the Dark Tower... It's just an hour from here. Go now—to fulfill your quest," she said.

"Thank you," Tairren said, "for everything... I would give you a payment, but I have nothing to offer you but my gratitude."

"Jezebel looked into his eyes, then giggled beneath her dark garbs. "I don't need anything from you... But *I* will give you something," she said, swiftly pulling something from her robes.

Tairren backed away quickly, looking down at her hands. He watched as she pulled a beautiful golden vessel out, quickly holding it up to him. His eyes fell upon the jeweled flask. The colorful stones sparkled from the light of the fire that flickered between the trees.

"I can't take that from you," Tairren said, watching how the firelight bounced off of the gold and jewels. "It's too precious of a keepsake."

"When you traveled up Fiara Mountain yesterday, I saw when you dropped your water vessel." Tairren looked at her strangely. "Remember, I see all upon that mountain, Tairren. I watched as you boldly climbed it… Drink from it when you become tired and weary," she said, nudging it against his chest. "You are thirsty now—I can tell by your lips… I filled it at a stream when I searched the mountainside. It's still cold. It'll be refreshing upon your mouth…"

Tairren watched her honey-colored eyes. Her eyes were like deep pools of fire and light. Tairren slowly took it from her as she watched him intently.

Then, like a quick shadow, she disappeared into the shadows behind the trees. She barely made a sound as she left quickly.

Tairren stood for a moment, listening to her faint footsteps as she left him. He looked at the vessel again, rubbing his hand across the precious metal. It was cold to the touch and he could feel the liquid move within it. Tairren looked into the darkness again, then hung his gleaming flask beneath his cape. He then quickly made his way back to Rafiul.

Rafiul was still sitting by the fire. He rested his elbows on his knees as he watched Tairren walk into the firelight.

"She's gone," Tairren said. He sat next to Rafiul as an awkward silence fell between them. "Forgive me, Rafiul," Tairren finally said, "for dishonoring you."

"I only see the truth—I only follow the truth," Rafiul said, nudging at Tairren's sword with his boot. "That sword you have by your side once belonged to a mighty king… Honor your king and follow truth, always… I forgive you…" A faint smile came over his face as his golden eyes gleamed. "This journey has changed us—but we must never forget our purpose." Rafiul stood up. "We must go. We lingered too long here and still have much mountain to cover before the Dark Tower. But first, let us fill our flasks before we continue our journey. A cool drink is what we need."

"Here, drink from mine," Tairren said, pulling the dazzling vessel out that Jezebel had given him. "The stream is a way off and will set us back. I saw it on our way here."

Rafiul took the water vessel from Tairren, bringing it to his lips. The water was cold and refreshing. Rafiul smiled at Tairren, passing it back to him. "Thank you, Master Tairren."

Tairren took the vessel from him, then gulped some of the water down. The cold drink immediately quenched his thirsty. "This water is like honey," he said, putting the gold top back on, then strapped it back to his belt.

They were off quickly, walking through the trees. But something happened then that brought back memories to Tairren. As they walked, a feeling came over them. The feeling was heavy but made them feel as if they were about to float away…

"Tairren," Rafiul said, stopping in his place. He brought his hand up to his forehead as he began to falter. He caught himself by grabbing a tree. "This is strange… Where did you get that water from?"

"Jezebel…," Tairren said with some effort, but suddenly stopped talking. The way he felt made him think of when Jezebel had given him the water at the Fire Temple.

"It's—poisoned…," Rafiul tried to say. He stammered more, then fell to the ground. He fell down the slope, back to the fire. He lay on his back as heavy sleep came over him.

The feeling of euphoria came over Tairren like a powerful wave. He could barely make out what Rafiul had said. He didn't even notice that Rafiul had blacked out. Tairren breathed hard, trying to open his eyes as wide as they could go. A fiery feeling of nirvana came over him as his muscles felt like they were melting away. He fell back, tumbling to the ground near Rafiul. He looked up into the sky as sleep was trying to take over him. His eyelids became heavy as he tried to keep them open.

The firelight slowly faded away in their eyes as oblivion came quickly over them. Their heartbeats became loud in their ears as their breaths slowed.

Jezebel skulked through the trees, slowly making her way to the fallen men. She crouched over them, staring her honey colored eyes at their silent faces. She pulled off her hood as her long black braid fell from her head. She yanked the cloth off from her face, revealing her exotic, beautiful countenance. Her eyes flashed like fire.

Tairren looked up at the woman's face as his eyesight slowly left him. It all became blurry. "Fiara…," he tried to say, but his words left him as darkness covered his eyes.

"You should never trust the Jakals," Fiara said with flashing eyes. She caressed Tairren's face, bringing hers closer to his. Her lips touched his ear as she whispered, "Like I've told you before, my love… You will lose…"

†

CHAPTER 11
Entrapment

Hours went by as the sun began to go down behind the black clouds. Dusk fell upon the lands of Minslethrate as the sour winds picked up. Everything seemed ominously peaceful, like the calm before a storm. As every human-being walked upon the kingdom—an impending, malicious storm was churning, coming closer, ready to release its darkness and wrath…

†††

High atop the Black Field of Old Blood, inside the Dark Tower of Sacrifice, Tairren hung from chains in the darkness…

Low whispery voices echoed down the silent hall, bouncing into the chamber and into Tairren's burning ears. Tairren roused as the voices reverberated in his mind. He slowly opened his eyes. His heavy eyelids opened and closed a couple times, then opened fully. His eyesight was blurry at first, but after a moment of focusing on a burning torch, his vision came clearly to him. He looked around. His head whirled slightly, but then the dizziness subsided. He realized that his hands were chained, reaching out in opposite directions. He began to look around quickly. He was confused at first, but the firelight from the torch reminded him of the fire that he and Rafiul sat among in the mountains. He thought of Jezebel… Then Fiara tore through his mind as his breaths quickened.

He realized that Jezebel was really Fiara all along. Tairren felt like a fool, suddenly. He thought of all Rafiul's warnings, and how he ignored them all. Tairren began to look around for his guardian legna, but he was nowhere in sight. His heart sunk as he realized that his foolishness put them in danger.

Tairren yanked at his chains, but they were too tight. He felt lost all of a sudden. He looked around for his dagger and sword. They were gone!

"Fiara!" he shouted out, becoming angry. "You deceiving, witch! Where are you?!"

After a moment, the voices that had been echoing down the hall stopped, as if his yells disturbed a secret conversation. It became quiet all of a sudden as Tairren's breaths swept through the air. He listened intently. At first, the only thing that could be heard was the howling winds that came in through the window across from him. Then the sound of footsteps began. Tairren listened carefully as the footsteps echoed across the cold stone, becoming louder. Tairren looked closely, noticing the flicker of firelight slowly cutting the darkness. The light became brighter as someone holding a torch appeared in the doorway.

"Well, well, well," an exotic-sounding voice rippled into the chamber. It was Fiara. "The hero has finally awakened," she chuckled as she came into the chamber.

She furtively walked before Tairren, staring her golden eyes at him. She was no longer covered in black garbs. She wore jeweled, golden pieces of armor that covered her breasts and arms and her bottom half was cloaked with sheer, red fabric. Her dark skin was covered in gold paint that glittered in the firelight and her black hair fell over her shoulders in long intricate braids.

"You've tricked me again," Tairren grunted, glaring at her from beneath his black eyebrows. "This time I will not pity you as I have before. Where's my sword and companions?!"

Fiara laughed, shaking her head. "Foolish boy—who always lets feminine wiles control you... You are truly pathetic. Are you thirsty?" she mocked, then laughed at him. She grabbed the jeweled vessel that hung from his waist, yanking it from his belt. She held the vessel up in front of his face. "You drank from the water of Fiara Mountain, twice. Why not have one more drink of ecstasy?" She chuckled, then threw the vessel across the chamber. "At first I didn't think you would fall for it— but the powers in the fire told me that you would..." She smiled, standing right in front of him. Her eyes flashed like the torch's light. "Your sword and companions can not help you now..."

Tairren clenched his teeth while shaking his head. "So, the woman that guards your mountain is..."

"Is really me," Fiara mocked, cutting him off. "I have no servants! *I am* a servant of fire! *I am* the mountain! *I am* the eyes of the mountain!" she yelled. She searched his eyes. "...Jezebel was a name I was called long ago," she said in a calmer voice. "You see, my love. I am very ancient, and hold a power that was taught to me by the fallen legna, long ago. When Minslethrate was younger, my name was Jezebel... I was a queen! I was taught magic by the fallen legna...and I became all powerful! The fire speaks to me and feeds me with its burning powers and desires... The powers in the fire tell me what to do—and I obey them."

"You are truly the foolish one, Fiara," Tairren spat. "The entity you speak to comes from the powers of Lucif! He cares nothing for you and only needs you to do his evil deeds! You follow darkness like a blinded FOOL!"

Fiara slapped Tairren across the face quickly, sending his head to the side. The sound of the slap echoed in the cold chamber. "Shut your mouth, boy!" she yelled. "You do not know what you are dealing with!"

After a quick second, Fiara caressed his face where she had smacked him and began shushing him, coming closer. "My sweet, Tairren," she said in a now low voice. "You don't understand. We could've been royalty over the south... You could've been my king. But your heart will not accept the power that is being offered to you. I've tried to grant you this power many times before..." She came so close to him that their mouths barely touched. "Instead you accept a foolish power that comes from a dead king... Tairren—remember...we are all the same. We shall shine in the darkness without the light! Because when everything is finished, there will still be darkness. Can't you see that light can not exist without darkness? Light is darkness—and darkness is light..." She stared into his eyes, then pressed her mouth to his.

After a moment of kissing him, she pulled her fiery mouth away from his.

Tairren just silently looked at her, not fazed by her bold kiss. "God is light, and in him there is no darkness at all... I'd rather follow the powers from that king than follow yours," he said quickly.

Fiara just gazed at him, slowly stepping away from him. Her intense eyes never left his. "I am of the new way...where light and darkness mesh together as one." She chuckled, noticing that he was becoming irritated.

"Why play these games?!" Tairren shouted. "Why didn't you just kill me when you had the chance?" Tairren asked, watching her as she walked to the shadows near the chamber wall. "You are truly foolish, Fiara. You could've led me astray, but have led me closer to the place I have been fighting to get to! You only lead me closer to my destination!"

Fiara silently stuck her torch onto the wall, then picked up something that was on the ground. The smaller object sparkled in the torch light. Tairren noticed that it was his dagger, along with something else that was wrapped in black cloth.

"I did not kill you because the powers in the fire told me not to. I led you here because the fire told me to. Can't you see that I only listen to the fire?" She slowly went to him, holding his dagger in one hand and the wrapped item in the other.

He watched as she slipped his dagger snugly between her waist and garment. She then held up the wrapped object in front of him. "Do you know where your sword is?" she asked, smiling.

Tairren then knew what was wrapped in the black fabric, and Fiara seemed to be amused by it. Tairren glared at her as she held the wrapped sword up to him. He looked at the cloth, noticing that it was loosely wrapped. He remembered how Rafiul had once told him that she couldn't touch the Sword of Truth with her bare hands.

"Do you want this back?" she asked, still smiling. "Here...," she said, raising one eyebrow. "Take it back now if you want it... If not, I will get rid of it for good."

Tairren yanked at his hands, but couldn't move. The chains clanked in the cold air as Fiara began to laugh. He clenched his teeth, glaring at her as his heart raced. "You are vile, woman!" Tairren shouted.

"I guess you don't want it since your hands aren't upon it," she mocked. "It's a shame, really... You must want me to throw this beautiful, *powerful*, relic away..."

She turned around, holding the wrapped sword out in front of her as she walked to the wall across from him. The window upon the wall opened out to the black sky. She quickly walked to the window, then carelessly threw the sword out upon the cold winds.

"No!" Tairren screamed, watching helplessly as the sword twirled upon the dark air.

The black fabric came from the sword, revealing the sword's splendor upon the black sky. The golden blade flung down to the earth, twirling in the winds until it crashed into the rocks below the temple. The majestic sword stuck into the stone, making it stand up straight like a beam of pure light.

Fiara laughed as she turned to Tairren. "The sword is gone just like its king! We shall make way for our new king of the world..."

"It does not matter what you do, Fiara. I know TRUTH! You may not see it, but I still have *His* power within me!" Tairren shouted.

"The nasty, wild man named John has helped ignite such a thing!" Fiara yelled, rushing towards him. "It doesn't matter what I do, you say?!

She pulled his dagger from her cloak then came upon him like a wild, screaming Banshee. She pressed her body against his as she got a handful of Tairren's hair, forcefully yanking his head back. She breathed loudly as she pushed the cold dagger to his throat. "You speak of this putrid light as if it is alive!" she screamed. "Do you want to know how your king died long ago!? You want to know how his blood flowed?!"

"His blood is what conquered you and Lucif long ago." Tairren grunted, closing his eyes as he could feel the cold blade press harder into his neck.

Fiara pushed the dagger into his skin, but not deep enough where it would kill him. A small stream of blood came from his neck, trickling down his white throat. Fiara got off of him, then screamed as she swung the blade across the palm of one of his hands. Tairren winced in pain as blood quickly flowed from his trembling hand. She angrily went to his other hand, shoving the dagger into it with angry strength. The blade came out the other side, along with a spurt of blood. She twisted the blade, spitting with clenched teeth as she did. She then yanked the bloody dagger from his palm, stepping backwards as she breathed heavily. Her eyes were large and wild; they were no longer golden—but black and shiny.

Tairren let out a scream as the pain became unbearable. His chest heaved as he sucked in the cold air. Sweat accumulated on his brow as he closed his eyes tightly. Blood ran down his arms and dripped onto the stone ground.

Fiara lowered the bloody dagger, lifting her face as his blood formed a puddle on the ground below him. She slowly closed her black eyes, taking in deep breaths. She then looked back at him; her eyes were no longer black but golden, once again. She glared at him, then threw the blade at his feet.

"Fiara…," a voice came from the doorway of the chamber. The voice was low and haunting.

Fiara turned quickly.

Marrisa stood in the doorway. Heavy shadows covered her body as only pieces of her could be seen. Her face was covered in the thick shadows and she stood still.

"Pay John a visit with the marking of the Grand-High Mistress upon your brow… Send the legna a message…," Marrisa said in a whispery voice.

The shadowed figure of Marrisa raised her hand into the air as a black hole opened up. The black hole filled the whole space of the chamber.

Fiara looked at Marrisa, silently bowing her head. Marrisa' voice was like the fire to her. She understood her… She knew what she had to do just then. She looked at the black orb and quickly went into the hole, becoming one with the darkness. She vanished as the black misty orb faded away.

Tairren slowly opened his eyes as the pain from his hands traveled down his arms. He breathed heavily, searching for Fiara. He didn't even notice that she had left quickly.

Tairren's eyes searched the chamber, not realizing that Marrisa was watching him from the darkened threshold. After a moment, his weary eyes caught her standing still like a statue. Tairren stared at her for a moment, wondering who she was at first. He could only see the black silhouette of a woman.

"Marrisa?" Tairren said, breathing quickly as the pain in his hands intensified.

His heart pounded as he tried to study the black silhouette. His energy was leaving him with his blood as his face turned white. His eyesight was slowly slipping away from him as the blood from his hands oozed out. He began to feel nauseated and light-headed.

Marrisa moved to him slowly, gliding across the stone floor. She gazed at him silently as the torch light slowly reached her white face.

Tairren's blood continued to trickle to the ground, tapping loudly onto the stone, and in his ears. The sounds of his blood echoed in his head as he could now see Marrisa's large, black eyes… His mind suddenly slipped away as his eyes rolled back. Darkness came over him as he fell into a deep sleep.

†††

John collected his things in his warm cave. He packed a satchel, filling it with things to eat and other items he thought he needed. He walked about his humble abode, looking around. His dark eyes searched his home one last time. He then decided that he was going to miss his home because after praying, he had the urge to leave. And when those strong urges came to him, he obeyed them. His spirit told him that something was going to happen. He thought of what his visitors told him earlier that afternoon. He thought of what Tairren and Rafiul had said about darkness becoming stronger, and that a war was on the horizon. He didn't know exactly what to do, but he knew he had to do something.

He grabbed his ax and wooden staff that sat near his doorway. He looked one last time at his abode, combed his beard with his hand, then left quickly.

John walked out into the cold air, amazed at how dark it had gotten outside. He knew the sun was just now setting, but it looked like it was night out already. He grabbed his torch that stuck out near his doorway, then began to move away from his cave. The winds blew, making the fire from the torch falter, becoming thin as it quickly fluttered. He blocked some of the winds with his hands, trying to save his only source of light.

He looked out over his cliff, noticing the many torch lights that could be seen from far away. He gazed at them with wonder, realizing that it was a massive army of some kind. The army seemed to be coming closer towards the mountains. Just then he realized that something serious was about to take place in the south…

"Hello, John," a voice came from behind him. The sultry voice startled him.

John turned quickly. At first, he couldn't see, but after a moment, his eyes caught a tall woman wearing a long black cloak. Her cape rippled through the cold air like a black phantom, revealing her golden undergarments.

"Who are you and what do you want?" John asked, peering at her through his torch's light.

She walked towards him, pulling her hood from her head. Her long braids danced down her shoulders and her beautiful face gleamed in the dim torch light.

"I am Fiara, the goddess of firelight," she said, gazing at him. "I come for you…"

"Follower of darkness!" John yelled. "Your kind is not welcomed here! Go back to the stinking pits of the black abyss!"

Fiara laughed as her golden eyes flickered. "You are mistaken, John. I do follow light, just as your flesh contains seeds of darkness… We are all one, dancing around upon the fires of life and the shadows of uncertainty… Perhaps if you follow me, I shall show you the truth…"

John just glared at her, slowly shaking his head.

Fiara gazed at him with a smile, then lifted one of her finely shaped eyebrows. "I didn't expect a blinded buffoon as yourself to understand… I have a message for the legna," she said, coming closer to him. "I need you to help me deliver that message…"

"You, harlot of darkness! I stand with the legna, with all that is good! I do not commune with monsters such as yourself! Back away! Get back I say, in the name of light!" He began to franticly swing his torch at her. "Back with you—you, Jakal!" John shouted, then threw his torch at her. He pulled his ax out, ready to fight.

Fiara dodged his flying torch, then quickly swung her cape open, revealing her golden body and bright armor. She pulled her sword from her side, beginning to circle around him like a furtive dog circling its prey. "Then I will take you myself!"

She flew towards John, swinging her sword quickly. She was fast and went with the winds that blew upon them.

John dodged her, swinging his heavy ax upon the air. The heavy cleaver nearly caught her leg, flying into the stone. He tugged, pulling the ax up and swung at her again. This time his ax caught her robe, making her fall.

Fiara crawled from her robe quickly as John's ax came down at her again. She rolled quickly, missing the massive blade. Light sparked from the ax as it pounded into the stone, sending shards flying.

"Get away from here!" John yelled, franticly swinging his ax with his large arms.

Fiara did a swift back flip away from him. She stood a couple of feet from him, watching him as he stood hunched over with his heavy weapon.

"If I can not take you myself—perhaps my pets can," she said from the dark shadows.

Suddenly, many red eyes began to appear from the darkness. Creeping things skulked out of the shadows, growling and barking loudly. Fiara had brought with her, Jakals!

John's eyes became large as the hellhounds began to surround him on the cliff. The winds circled around him as he looked quickly all around the darkness. A putrid scent filled the air as they came closer to him, bringing with them the strange mists. He swung his ax, trying his best to keep them away, but they only dodged his swings.

"We must deliver a message," Fiara said in a low voice as the dogs barked louder. "Bring him to me…," she said, standing menacingly in the shadows.

✝

CHAPTER 12
The Martyr

Phillip, along with the legna, trekked across the Black Field of Old Blood. By legend, it was called a "field," but it was more like a dangerous valley, consisting of massive stones and deep holes. The great valley was ridden with steep cliffs and large trenches. The terrain was intense and jagged and nothing grew upon it.

As they traveled across the valley together, Phillip wondered what the ancestors of Minslethrate went through when they fought in the great-war, long ago. The battle must've been brutal, they thought.

The army of legna and Minslethratians had found a large piece of flat land. They were near the middle of the great valley and decided to rest up a bit before continuing. The journey across the Black Field of Old Blood was treacherous and took their breaths from them; so, an ample rest was crucial.

Phillip found a resting spot upon a small cliff. The cliff looked out over the area where the remainder of the men rested. The wind blew all around him, howling as it slipped between the stone and through the deep trenches. He could see all of the dips and valleys where he sat. It seemed as if he was nearly there; the mountains appeared so close. But he knew it was just a trick of the eye. They all still had many miles of traveling before them.

Phillip watched the legna and men below. He also looked for Natalia, but didn't see her. He hadn't spoken to her since their argument. He inhaled a troubled breath, thinking of her as he always did.

Suddenly a noise startled him. He turned his head quickly, only to find Natalia slowly walking towards him. She looked nervous. He turned his head away from her as she came closer to him.

"Phillip...," Natalia said in a low voice as she stood by him. She looked down at him as he ignored her. "Uriel told me that you'd be here... Can I sit with you?" she asked.

Phillip looked up at her again, then nodded his head.

She sat next to him, looking off of the small cliff. She inhaled, then glanced at him. "Phillip...can we put all of this hostility behind us?" she asked.

He looked at her, gazing into her green eyes. His heart thrashed in his chest. "Everything is so convenient for you, isn't it," he said, looking away from her. "I've poured my heart out to you time and time again and you continue to crush me. And now you wish to put it all behind us?! Perhaps you take me for a fool, walking all over my heart like some kind of siren."

628

Natalia sat silently, looking over at him. She bit her bottom lip. She felt remorseful for everything she had put him through over their journey. "My emotions always get the best of me... I know that's something I need to change... I try to be so perfect... Please forgive me, Phillip," she said in a soft voice.

He just stared at her for a moment, then finally nodded his head. "You know I will always forgive you, Natalia," Phillip said.

Natalia looked into his dark eyes, then glanced off towards the south. "We are so close...," she said, wrapping her cape around her arms tightly. She gazed out over the valley, looking towards the black mountains that stood before them.

Phillip watched her, noticing how much she had changed over their journey. He knew that when they had gotten into a fight, it was only because they were stuck in a moment of weakness. He knew that it was the light within them that continued to pull them out of the brokenness and darkness. He smiled, gazing at her as her hair fluttered in the cold winds. Not only was her mannerism different, but she just looked different. She didn't look like the spoiled daughter of a marquis anymore. She seemed as if she had turned into a strong woman overnight.

"I'm sorry, Natalia...for judging you...," Phillip said, looking away from her. It wasn't long before he brought his eager gaze back over to her. "Earlier today, when I brought up Tairren...forgive me... I just wanted to know why you can not accept me the way you do him..."

Natalia peered at him, feeling surprised that it had bothered him greatly that whole time. "Phillip, Tairren has a heart unlike any man I've ever known...that's what attracted me to him so."

Phillip nodded his head, looking away from her. His heart sunk like a rock in a lake.

"But your heart seems to have grown... I can truly see how extraordinary you truly are, Prince." She looked at him, having a serious look on her face. "I'm still learning to love... But I do believe you have stolen my heart, Phillip..."

He looked back at her quickly. His heart thrashed in his chest, rising back up like the sun. "Thank you, My Lady... But you should know that I never stole it. I accepted it the moment I gave mine to you..."

A soft smile came over her face as she studied his for a moment. She nodded her head, looking away from his intense gaze. "It's so strange," she said, in a low voice, "how everything could change within days... I feel as if it was only yesterday that I was putting on my lavish gowns and having tea with Marrisa...and now I'm deep in the south, with you...about to come upon a war." She looked up at Phillip again who continued to gaze at her. Her heart quickened as she felt herself being pulled into his presence for the first time. "I just met you days ago—and I feel as if I've known you forever... We've fought, laughed, and cried together... It's as if everything we've been through has brought us closer together..." She smiled at him, looking away. "You are the only man who's made me feel every human emotion in just one day," she said with a giggle.

"I'm a different person than who I was when I first came here...when I first met you," Phillip said as he looked off towards the mountains. "Whatever happens...I know it is because of something much grander than what we perceive, is orchestrating it. I wouldn't take back anything from this journey...and I wouldn't take back the first moment I met you, Natalia."

Natalia smiled at him again. She realized that Phillip was no longer a presumptuous prince as he was before. He was no longer a large child as she thought he was. He seemed more like a kind-hearted man to her just then. She could truly see that his heart had grown with passion for life.

"Do you remember when you frightened me at the castle stable?" Natalia asked, then giggled. A large smile came over Phillip's face as he nodded. "I shall never forget how you fell to the ground. Your eyes were as if they've seen a ghost. I nearly injured you that night."

They both laughed.

"It was only because you startled me. But you mustn't tell anyone," he said, nudging her shoulder with his. "You'd scar my pride forever."

They both looked into each other's eyes as their laughs faded away. They felt closer than ever as their eyes stayed locked onto each other's. With everything that they had been through, they felt inseparable. They felt as if they knew each other more than anyone else.

Natalia smiled at him, then leaned against him, putting her head on his shoulder. He responded back by putting his arm around her. They sat for a while, becoming cozy as their bodies touched.

"Phillip...," Natalia said in a low voice as she stared off into the valley. "When I found out that my mother had died...I felt as if I had been shattered into a million pieces... It's hard for me to think that I can come back together again... I couldn't breathe then... I felt so ashamed of myself, to the point that I wanted to hate myself... I..." She stopped talking for a moment, stopping the emotion that tried to creep over her. "When I sat atop the cliff by myself, when I didn't think of my mother...I thought of you..."

Phillip looked down at her as she continued to lay her head on his shoulder. He was surprised by her words and didn't really know how to respond.

"I thought of how you had mentioned that your father was very sick," she continued. "Losing a parent is something I would never wish on anybody..."

Phillip stayed quiet for a moment. He rubbed her arm as the winds continued to sweep across them. "I'm so very sorry, Natalia," he said. "My heart breaks for you with every breath I take, knowing that I can do nothing to help you… Just knowing that tragedy has stricken both you and your family is unsettling to me."

Natalia looked up at him, thinking about how great of a man he had become. He was humbler and more honest and put a spark in her heart. "You are sweet to me, Phillip," she said with a faint smile. "I feel as if I am the only one whom you care for…"

"You are, Natalia," he said with a serious face. "I would do anything for you… Taking on this quest and going on this adventure with you is more than I could ever ask for." He held her tighter, bringing her closer to him. "I think…well, I know that…I love you," he said, still looking into her green eyes.

Natalia just looked back at him. She was amazed by his perseverance. She thought of their conversations within the last couple of days, and every conversation seemed to bring her closer to him. She studied his face and his dark eyes. She thought of everything she had been through and just finding out about her mother's death. She thought of all the times she denied Phillip, and yet, he still loved her.

"Why do you love me?" she asked in a low voice. "I've done nothing but disappoint you… I'm more shattered than you truly know… I'm not the dainty noble woman whom you've met many days ago. Don't be fooled by my smile. I'm not that girl any longer. And I…I find that the closer I get to God…the more broken I discover myself to truly be."

He looked at her silently. His eyes never left hers. "No one in this world is perfect, Natalia. Don't ever believe that you are the only one who feels that way… We will always be filled with scars…but at least we understand why… When I stood before the tree, I understood completely why we were put on this earth. I've learned that we were not put on this earth to flaunt ourselves as perfect and mighty, because we're not; no one is. We were put on earth to worship the Lord, to love him back as he loved us, and to love others… But we should always know that having the light inside of us does not mean that we are perfect…it means that we know who to look towards when we fall—and that is the almighty God! I too saw how broken we all are, and that only God could make us whole again. King Yehoshua's body was broken for us, Natalia. A mighty king as perfect as he…was broken for us all; that's true love… Do you not see that? So why can't we be shattered together, and live for him, Natalia?" he asked. His question was honest and passionate.

Natalia was quiet for a moment. His words struck her. It was as if his words had awakened her mind. A smile came over her face as she continued to stare into his. "You are a mighty man of God now, Phillip… All this time I have been the lost one… We shall be shattered together…but you must fix me first…," she said, laying her head back on his shoulder.

"You are already fixed, Natalia…by the grace of God…," Phillip said as he rested his head on hers, holding her tighter. He kissed the top of her head, then looked out over the valley.

A sweet moment of silence came over them. It was a moment they had never shared with one another before. They accepted each other as they were, feeling something between them they had not felt before. It wasn't about sharing a passionate kiss or a fire-kindled conversation with one another. Their honest moment was about sharing the newfound love they had for each other, that came from their righteous hearts.

It was as if they had sat that way for many moments. But time slipped past them quickly. As they sat together, they noticed that the area of land below them became darker. It seemed as if a thick mist was coming from nowhere. They could see that the men began to notice the whirling mists, standing up quickly. Their minds quickly slipped back into reality.

"Do you see that?" Phillip asked, taking his arm from around her. "The mists are growing!"

"We have to get down there, quickly!" Natalia said, alarmed.

They knew what the sudden black mists meant… Darkness was coming.

They rushed down the cliff, nearly falling down as the dry earth beneath their feet crumbled. They got to the small clearing quickly, joining the alarmed men.

"Stand together, men," Phillip shouted. "Something approaches us!"

Dolsia joined their side, looking around quickly. "The powers of Lucif are getting stronger," she said in a low tone." Her pale eyes glowed in the dark atmosphere.

They quickly found King Julpen who was standing with Sir Hawkington and the Archlegna. They grabbed their weapons, prepared for their unseen enemies.

"Get ready, Men!" King Julpen shouted. "The black mists always bring trouble!"

Everyone became alert, standing together with their weapons held tightly in their sweaty palms.

Right in the center of the crowd of men, a black orb began to grow. The men noticed it, moving away quickly. The black orb pulsated, bringing with it more mists and winds.

"Get back!" Gaibriul shouted as he and the other Archlegna quickly gestured for everyone to move. "Do not touch the orb! It is a doorway which only leads to darkness—anything can grab you into it if you are not prepared!"

The men spread out, circling around the black orb. They stood armed and ready, leaving a couple of yards between them and the malicious black hole. They stood silently, waiting for the nomed to come out of it.

They could see a black form slowly step out of the darkness—but it was not a nomed. The dark form was too elegant to be that of a nomed's. A tall woman walked out of it. She was clad in golden, sparkling armor that fit snugly around random body parts, and the rest of her bare skin was slathered in gold paint. Her eyes flashed like golden honey and her long black hair fell down in jeweled braids. A golden crown sat on her head as she stared at all of the men. She was beautiful, but the darkness that came with her said otherwise. She turned around slowly to look at everyone as her golden skin sparkled in the torch-light. She elegantly brought her golden hand upon her forehead, revealing a cluster of three black stars that were painted on her brow.

"Who are you?!" King Julpen demanded, coming before her. "That doorway only brings evil—so you must be our enemy!"

She turned her head quickly towards him, staring her beautiful face intensely at him. Her eyes glittered as a smirk came over her golden face.

"I am the very legend that your ancestors obsessed over, ages ago. My name is written in many books and poems... I am Fiara, the one who will light your way...," she said, looking around. The men whispered among each other, surprised by her presence. "You know very well who I am..."

King Julpen was quiet for a moment, shocked that the legendary woman was standing before him. All his years living upon the lands of Minslethrate, he had never seen the mysterious woman. He was shocked that she even still existed. "I am King Julpen," he finally said.

"I know who you are," she said, quickly. "I finally get to meet the king of this retched kingdom," she said, looking at him with disgust. "When I ruled the lands, during the ancient times, this kingdom was all powerful... It was a shining beacon, then! Pity—it has fallen just like its present king." She laughed as her eyes flashed.

"You're being deceived, Fiara!" Dolsia shouted, feeling compelled to speak out. Fiara's eyes flashed as she quickly turned towards her. "I am Dolsia. Man knows me as the Earth Goddess of Minslethrate. But I've always known that there is only one God! I was blinded by darkness and walked the path you do now... But I am now changed—I realized that I was fooled, all these ages! Lucif only comes to destroy! He has been plotting this since the beginning, Fiara—before you've even ceased to exist. Why can't you see that you follow Lucif? How can a goddess follow, Fiara? Doesn't a godly one lead?"

Fiara glared at her. Her face looked like she had tasted something bitter. "You disgust me, Dolsia... You were never a goddess, you pathetic being! You were nothing but a dead symbol! I *am* the only goddess of the south! You and Haifen mean nothing to me. I've always resented the fact that these Minslethratian idiots believe that we are sisters... YOU and that bottom-feeder, *Haifen,* were only good for stories... How dare you compare yourself to Fiara! It would be a waste of time to even think about you. Nothing you were—and nothing you still are! But I...I am more than that... I am the truth and the burning desires of every heart. I am the fire of the mind and the door to eternal bliss. I come from a bloodline of powerful beings... Now stand back, *Dolsia*! Take your place beneath my feet!" she spat.

"What do you want?!" King Julpen demanded, interrupting her terrible words.

"I come to deliver a message!" Fiara said as her face became serious. She looked at everyone, feeding off of their worried looks.

A smile appeared slowly on her face as she looked back into King Julpen's eyes. She gracefully gestured with her arm towards the massive black hole that was opened behind her. Suddenly, red eyes appeared in the black orb, then growls and howls began to emit from it.

The men stared into the massive hole before them. They watched with wide eyes as many rotting dogs came from the hole. Some of the ferocious dogs had cords in their mouths, which were attached to something that was still in the black orb. The hellhounds growled and barked at the men as they watched nervously. The dogs that held the cords yanked hard at them, then a bounded man fell out of the orb! The dogs shrieked loudly as if they became excited.

Fiara laughed as the man wiggled about. He thrashed his head around as his muffled screams filled the silent air. The man's whole body was swathed in rope and his mouth was bounded with a black piece of cloth.

"What is this?!" King Julpen demanded, noticing that the man was trying to shout out something.

"You'll see...," she said with a smile.

She walked towards the man, then kneeled over him. She gazed at him as she touched his long beard. She kissed his forehead, then pulled the piece of cloth from his mouth.

"This is a warning to you all, to your children, and to your children's children!" she shouted, looking out over the men.

She turned her fiery gaze back down at the man who continued to shake his frazzled head. She looked over his face, softly smiling at him. "Can I put the marking of power upon your brow?" she asked in a sweet voice. "It is a marking that symbolizes unity of light and darkness; it is a marking of power that will show others who you follow." The man shook his head, scowling at her. "Whom do you follow, my wild man?" she asked in a soft voice.

"Go back to the stinking abyss, harlot of darkness!" the man shouted angrily at her. "She lies to us all! She is a deceiving, false prophet who speaks of false beliefs! She sets the way for the one who hates King Yehoshua! That mark is the sign of the great dragon! Listen to me, all of you! I am John, the follower of light! The end is near, my brothers!" he shouted towards the onlookers. "Never give in to the dragon! Keep the light within your hearts and never cease to believe! Become clean like the light! No matter what happens, know that King Yehoshua is king of all! Darkness will fall because He is coming back soon! LONG LIVE, KING YEHOSHUA!" he shouted out.

"SILENCE!" Fiara screamed angrily, hitting him in the face. She began rewrapping the cloth forcefully around his head, pulling it tight over his mouth.

She growled, standing up quickly as she glared at the crowd. Her beautiful face changed into a vicious one. She began to chant something which sounded like an ancient, evil tongue. She closed her eyes as she got louder. She lifted her golden arms into the cold air as the mists began to swirl all around her. Her eyes flashed open, appearing like fire. The heavy mists around her lifted the squirming man, making him stand straight up like a stiff board. The frightening mists circled around him, making him unable to move at all. His body became frozen!

"Listen well, infidels!" Fiara shouted as the darkness circled around her. "This man speaks of a dead king whose name should never be spoken of! This man has defiled the lands with his mouth which speaks nothing but lies! His punishment is a message to you ALL! Your king is DEAD! The Grand-High Mistress of Darkness is now your king! Her voice is in the fire and in the dark light of my powers! She demands that every follower of the dead king and every light-bearing soul—be cut away from this world! Only the light of fire and darkness shall breathe upon the human heart! Light and darkness must become one after the Earth is cleansed! Unity is the world's future! This day, and every day to come, shall be a reign of darkness if you do not yield to the Grand-High Mistress! That darkness shall cleanse the whole world, setting before us a future containing POWER! You and your offspring, or anyone else upon this world, will never speak, or even whisper, the dead king's name again! No one in this world will eat, drink, or even breathe if they do not wear the marking of the Grand-High Mistress upon them! The Old Ways have come back, King Julpen... But the new ways of unity and peace are set before us, legna. This is your message—and do not forget it..."

She became silent, then walked towards John. She stood before him as he just helplessly looked at her. She pulled her sword from her jeweled sheath, then slowly brought it into the air.

John didn't appear frightened or overcome with darkness or despair. He continued to stare at the evil woman, never looking away. He then said a prayer as he slowly closed his eyes. He kept his mind and spiritual eyes on the God of Light. He didn't hear anything as the hellhounds all around him became louder. He mentally and spiritually pulled himself away from the world around him. He thought of his King of Light. The only thing he heard in his head was the powerful words of King Yehoshua. His words lifted his heart. He knew then that his flesh was going to die…and dying for his king made his heart flutter. But he was not frightened of the death before him, and didn't even feel it come upon him as he kept his eyes on the Lord. He knew his spirit would live on forever…

Just then the dogs' barks and shrieks filled the dark air as King Julpen and some of the men tried to help the man named John. The air became chaotic all around the black orb. The dogs kept the men back as their excited shrieks filled the air. They gnashed their wet teeth and threatened them with their jagged mouths. The Jakals wouldn't allow the men to pass them, or even come close to John.

The legna shot their arrows and the beasts tried to attack from overhead, but the strange mists pushed them all back, making them fly to the ground.

Fiara screamed in the black atmosphere as her eyes became large and black. Her face quivered and the veins in her neck pulsated as she frantically shook her head in the dark air. She swung her sword in the cold winds. It appeared as a quick blur and made a humming sound. The metal flashed like her glossy eyes as it cut through the air, quickly slicing John's tender neck. The blade was so fast that his body did not comprehend the slash at first. In a quick moment, John's head fell from his neck, tumbling and rolling upon the ground. Then his body crumbled to the ground.

Everyone in the crowd became stunned. Some quickly looked away while others shouted angrily.

Fiara laughed, then in a quick moment, she and her Jakals vanished into the black hole. "Your demise is coming quickly to you all! ALL HAIL THE GRAND-HIGH MISTRESS!" her voice echoed in the darkness as it dispersed.

All around them became quiet again.

Everyone stood silently as they looked upon John's body. A vibrant-red puddle of blood slowly formed around his opened neck and head.

Nearby legna rushed to John's body, covering it with their capes. They gathered around John's stiff corpse, looking at it as sadness covered them.

Natalia closed her eyes as she covered her mouth. She buried her face in Phillip's chest as he wrapped his arms around her.

Dolsia went to King Julpen's side as he continued to stare at the man he didn't know. His heart cried out for the man, and all the other men who had died. She placed her hand on his back as she could tell that internally, he wasn't doing so well just then. "Stay strong, King Julpen," she said with care.

Everyone stood quietly, shocked, realizing that they had just witnessed not only a frightening threat, but a public execution.

"We will not stand down," Gaibriul said, looking as if slight emotion was coming over him. "We will NOT stand down!" he shouted. "Fiara is a tyrant that must be stopped! She is an ancient nuisance and a liar! She is so blinded by Lucif that she doesn't even realize that she is being used! But she will pay for this; all evil will pay! The wrath of our God will not come diluted! Darkness will drink from it... John was a good man—a follower of King Yehoshua! He had peace on his face because he knew that even though death was upon him—he was dying for the light! He, as well as everyone else who dies as martyrs, will be blessed in the Kingdom of Nevaeh!" The solemn men watched Gaibriul as he glowed with passion. "We must continue on, men! We must not let darkness control us! They will use fear and death to take hold of us—but we will not stand down! We will rise like the light of day upon the twilight!"

The men cheered as they came together. Their hearts fluttered because of Gaibriul's words. Their emotions soared. They were scared of what lay before them, but they knew that in the end, God would be there...

That evening, they wrapped John's body up, then burned it among the fire. The sweet flames rose high in the cold air of the south. They knew that John was celebrating in the kingdom of light, away from the darkened world. They had John on their minds as they continued through the Black Field of Old Blood. Darkness was not going to stop them...

King Julpen sat alone on his steed, watching as his army moved with their weapons and torches. His eyes then fell on the lingering fire that engulfed John's body. He felt like his past was coming upon him, when his mother burned and killed many innocent people. He realized that it wasn't going to stop. Darkness would continue to attack all of God's creations as long as the world spun. It was a constant battle that always had been, and always will be. He knew that he had to be strong as he continued to walk the miles of his life. He knew that no matter what happened to him and his kingdom, he was going to fight for the light. He was giving it all up to the creator of the Earth...

Gaibriul came to him with Uriel and Dolsia by his side. They stood tall as King Julpen looked into their faces.

"Gaibriul, who is this Grand-High Mistress?" King Julpen asked.

Gaibriul glanced at the others, then back into his weary eyes. "Darkness never looked so beautiful...," he said.

King Julpen peered at him, having a confused look on his face.

"I fear this Grand-High Mistress is...your daughter...," he said in a low voice.

King Julpen grew quiet as he looked off towards the Dark Tower with his saddened face.

Gaibriul placed a kind hand on his shoulder, understanding that devastation would not leave him alone.

They stood quietly for a moment as the winds continued to blow past them.

†

CHAPTER 13
Legion of Baal

The Kingdom of Hanon was consumed in complete chaos. Abaddon flew through the black sky like a storm of monstrous wasps, shrieking as they destroyed everything they came upon. Their black wings broke the cold air, sending the surrounding mists twirling and forcing fires to consume other parts of the kingdom. Dead bodies and blood covered the streets, fires rose from the homes and trees, and sounds of devastation, joined with screams, filled the air. Even though Hanon's legion consisted of hundreds, the flying army of destruction was becoming too much for the Hannonite army to handle. The Kingdom of Hanon was breaking in the hands of darkness.

A soldier blew his horn, catching as many people's attention as possible. "Everyone must move to the gateway!" the soldier shouted, forcing people to run faster. "Move below the moors, by orders of His Majesty!"

Many soldiers began to act quickly, blowing their horns and calling out the same commands while trying to round up the people of Hanon. They all ran together, running through the chaotic streets towards the center of the marketplace. They appeared like a mighty stampede as everyone began to make their way towards the marketplace.

In the center of the marketplace was a large building that sat tall. It rose up to the sky, scraping the low-hanging clouds with its steeples and decorative gables. The beautiful building was the gateway which led to the bowels of the moors. It had mighty columns and tall doorways and stained-glass windows.

The gateway was actually a sanctuary where the Hannonites worshiped the God of Light together. The massive threshold of the gateway opened up to a large sanctuary. Behind the sanctuary was another massive gateway which led to an old, dark stairwell. The stairwell went down below the earth, leading to the moist caves beneath the moors. The gateway was ancient and hadn't been used in many ages, so nobody truly knew how trustworthy it was—but it was their only option...

Gideon moved quickly, remembering what Lord Timotheus had told him earlier that afternoon. He trusted in the God of Light and tried everything in his power to keep the people safe. He was not an experienced soldier, but he had a bold heart. He directed the frantic people into the church, trying to keep them calm. He looked around. Everything seemed out of control. People were falling and trampling on one another while the sanctuary became filled with loud echoes.

The loud shriek of children crying caught Gideon's attention. He looked quickly, noticing a little boy and girl cowering to the side, nearby him. They were looking around quickly, screaming out for their mother. Gideon rushed to them, picking them up quickly. "I will bring you to safety, children," he said, trying to calm them down as they continued to cry.

Gideon rushed along with the crowd, making his way towards the massive stairwell. Screams filled the air as peopled rushed past him, nearly knocking him over. He looked around, noticing a woman who ran with her older child. She was coming right past him.

"You, ma'am!" Gideon shouted, catching her attention. "Take these children to safety with you, please!"

The woman nodded her head as tears fell down her red cheeks. She noticed that he was a soldier so she did as she was told. She took the children, then hurried down the dark stairwell.

Gideon felt proud as he glanced around. He ran back to the entryway of the church, helping more people as he went. Many people were frazzled and scared. After what seemed like hours of people flooding into the church, the last few people came in, screaming as they went. Something was chasing them from outside the church.

"That looks as if that's all of the people!" a nearby soldier shouted to Gideon from his horse. "God help the ones who have not made it!" he shouted as he quickly looked around.

"Shut the gates!" another soldier screamed from the entryway. "The creatures are coming! Shut the gates, now!"

Gideon ran quickly towards the main gate. He didn't want to get shut in. "Close the main doors!" Gideon shouted as he ran through the threshold. He hurried towards a crowd of soldiers who guarded the entryway. "Shut the doors! Lower the gates!" he screamed out again.

"Are you mad, Gideon?!" a nearby commander yelled at him. "You need to get below the moors with the people; you aren't trained for this!"

The doors behind them slammed shut as the gate lowered.

"Our all mighty God has commanded me to do so!" Gideon shouted, surprising the older man. "I will fight with all I have within me! I am a warrior of Hanon, and a warrior of God!" His passion grew as he appeared like a young man, filled with wisdom. He didn't look like an adolescent any longer.

The commander looked at him for a moment, then at the gate as it closed to the ground with a clank. He nodded his head. "Ready yourself, men!" the commander yelled, looking towards the sky. "The storm is coming!" He pointed his sword into the air as the darkness above them became heavy.

They looked up, noticing that the Abaddon were swarming all around them. They circled around the building in the sky, filling the dark sky with loud, disturbing screams and howls. They looked like a twisting, solid cloud. The wind became stronger as the black mists filled the atmosphere.

The men began to back away, noticing that the largest of the creatures was coming closer to them.

Gideon recognized the repulsive creature from the moors; it was Baal, Lord of the Abaddon.

Baal came upon them, flapping his large hairy wings right above them. He stretched his arms out as he glared at them with his gleaming eyes. His horns and long fingernails scraped against the winds.

"Foolish people," he said in a growling voice. "You can try to run and hide…but you will not get away… Hiding beneath the stone will not save you."

"You will pay for this!" Gideon shouted, looking up at Baal.

The commander glanced at him, shaking his head for him to stop speaking. "Gideon!" he grunted in a low tone.

Baal began to laugh. The flying Abaddon roared above him, seeming to become excited. Baal pointed at Gideon with his long fingernail, becoming dangerously serious.

"You, boy…," Baal said, "come here."

Gideon looked around at all of the soldiers who appeared frightened for him. He wasn't afraid, though. Gideon didn't even appear intimidated as he lifted his chin. He slowly walked towards Baal who silently loomed over him. Gideon's clean armor gleamed as the nearby fires reflected off it.

"Whatever you do to me will not stop the God of Light's wrath towards you," Gideon said, looking fearlessly at him. "The time will come when darkness will be locked away…"

Baal continued to look down at him as his eyes became brighter. "Your light has no power!" Baal roared out in a loud voice that startled the men. "Light is dead, just as your people will be! Foolish boy, you have cursed your own people!"

Suddenly Baal flew up into the dark sky towards the storm of Abaddon. "Kill the ones beneath the stone, dominion!" Baal roared as the flying creatures franticly flocked through the air. "KILL THEM ALL!"

The men grabbed their weapons and began to shoot their arrows at the flying fiends. The army of Hannonites had become smaller, but there were still hundreds of men left.

Gideon grabbed his sword, watching as the Abaddon began to fly down towards the church and ground. They soared quickly without stopping, crashing into the earth and stone, appearing like black bolts of lightning. Gideon ran towards the creatures as they attacked upon the ground. He swung his sword with all of his might as the other soldiers did the same thing.

The Abaddon continued to ram themselves into the ground, not caring that the impact was killing some of them.

"They are trying to cave in the underground haven!" the commander shouted.

The church began to crumble as the Abaddon continued to attack. The stone walls and columns began to fall, crashing down over some of the soldiers. The heavy sounds of stone falling filled the air.

Gideon watched helplessly as the glass and stone of the church tumbled to the ground. He ran to help up some fallen soldiers, dodging the Abaddon as they continued to crash down upon the ground.

"Shoot them down!" the commander ordered.

Arrows continued to fly, killing some of the Abaddon. The flying creatures came hurtling down as if the sky was falling apart.

The ground shook as the Abaddon attempted to cave in the underground haven.

Hope began to run thin as their chances of survival began to shrink.

†††

Down below the earth, the people of Hanon continued to flock. The air was dark and damp in the massive cave. They splashed through the puddles of dark water, becoming chilled to the bone. Torch light filled the moist air and cries and shouts echoed throughout the darkness. Women and children huddled together as the men tried to lead and comfort everyone. The people could do nothing but stand in the darkness, waiting to meet their fate.

They could hear the crashes above them. The noises frightened the people, making them think that their world was coming to an end. Rock fell from the earth above as the noises continued on. The cave seemed to tremble and shake, bringing terror over them.

"We're going to die!" a woman screamed between sobs, hugging against her husband.

Children cried and screamed as the darkness and loud noises frightened them. "Those monsters are gonna eat us!" a little girl kept screaming out, clinging to her mother.

Then suddenly, towards the entrance of the cavern, more people began to scream. Loud noises rumbled throughout the cold air.

"The church is crumbling!" a man screamed out over the noises. "The creatures are getting in!"

Everyone began to panic, filling the dark air with loud pandemonium.

Another loud crash came above them as the cave shook again. Small rocks and dirt fell from the ceiling, falling on the disturbed people. Parts of the ceiling began to cave in! Areas of the heavy earth above them fell onto some people, burying them beneath the stone.

Panic ravaged the air as fear and doom moved throughout the cave. Their demise was coming upon them quickly.

††††

Gideon panicked, looking all around at the chaos. The Abaddon were beginning to break the earth-barrier between them and the people of Hanon. Sink-holes in many areas began to grow as the earth rumbled and broke. The earth began to fall in, crashing down on the helpless people of Hanon.

"My God!" Gideon cried out to the sky so hard that his heart shook. "Help us! Show me what to do!"

He began to run, ducking the creature's attacks. They flew past him, wildly crashing into the ground. He quickly spotted a horse and pulled himself upon it. The horse franticly began to run around. He looked around as the horse flew, noticing the faces of all the fighting soldiers. They appeared frightened and disturbed. The light and hope they had before seemed to falter as it seemed to them that the end was near. Then he spotted a horn hanging from the waist of one of the soldiers. The horn stood out, gleaming in the dark air. He looked around himself, noticing that the horse he sat on still had a horn in one of its saddle-bags. He pulled the horn out quickly, having the urge to blow it. The horn signified attention and warning.

He blew the horn, making the familiar sound into the air. The sound was low but loud at the same time. He looked around, noticing that some of the soldiers had looked at him. He blew the horn again, then raised his sword towards the sky. He got the horse going past the fighting soldiers.

"A SWORD FOR HANON, AND FOR THE LORD!" he screamed out as loud as he could. He blew his horn again, now grabbing the attention of all the men.

He continued to go as fast as he could, blowing his horn and screaming out, "A sword for Hanon, and for the Lord!"

All of the soldiers started to catch on, beginning to blow their horns and yell out the same thing. Soon the whole atmosphere was filled with the sounds of the horns and their shouts. The hundreds of soldiers filled the air with the noises that began to come together in one mighty sound. The atmosphere became chaotic and overpowering.

The Abaddon began to look disoriented and lost. The loud noises seemed to confuse them! They began to fly around, going every which way. They bashed into each other, spinning around and crashing into the earth and buildings.

Gideon looked up, surprised. "It's helping us!" he yelled. He continued to blow his horn, running all around the chaos.

The soldiers began to slaughter the creatures that fell to the ground. They continued to blow their horns and shout as they noticed that many of the Abaddon were failing!

"NO!" Baal shouted as it flew to and fro, quickly looking around at his fallen legion.

Baal flew down at Gideon, becoming enraged. "YOU WILL PAY!!" he screamed, flying down towards the soldiers with an angry roar.

Gideon noticed Baal as it came dashing down towards him in an angry wind. He got the horse going, dashing through the fighting army. He jumped over the crumpled Abaddon and soared through the burning streets.

Gideon turned his head, noticing that Baal was dashing right behind him! He blew his horn as he rode, flying around the marketplace and back into the crowd of soldiers.

The soldiers gave way to Gideon as he tore through the crowd. They realized that Baal was chasing him so they began shooting it with their arrows.

Gideon dashed towards the crumbled church, stopping abruptly. His eyes widened as Baal came roaring towards him, filling his ears with its thunderous scream. He moved quickly, jumping off of the horse as Baal flew past him.

Baal went crashing into the crumbled building, making more stone fall down. The stone tumbled down with a loud rumble, covering Baal as his wings thrashed about.

Gideon stared at the pile of stone as dust rose. His heart pounded as reality set in. He looked around, noticing that the sky only had a few Abaddon flying among its winds. He turned around, pulling his helmet from his head.

The soldiers stood still, watching him, silently. They were amazed by the young soldier's courage. The fires burned behind them as the atmosphere became quiet. Shock settled over their faces as they looked surprised, just staring at Gideon. They could not comprehend how a young, inexperienced squire could face such a threatening foe.

Gideon inhaled, looking back at the pile of heavy stone. Sweat dripped from his brow and blonde hair that clung to his face. He breathed heavily, wondering if it was all over…

†

CHAPTER 14
The Other Doorway

Mikhal soared through the black sky on his mighty steed. His beast pounded its glorious wings as the cold winds knocked against them. He held on tightly, peering intensely through thick air of the south. He could tell that they were coming before the Dark Temple quickly. He noticed the tall black fortress, sitting atop jagged cliffs that looked out over the south.

Mikhal looked on intently as they sailed through the winds. He noticed how ancient the tower appeared, even from afar. The towers of the temple looked as if they were crumbling and the staircases and bridges that led from one tower to the next, were broken. The ancient tower looked more like ruins than anything else. He noticed a tower that still looked intact, standing the tallest right in the center. The tower had a large balcony and many windows that went down the sides of the structure.

Mikhal slowed his beast down some. They were coming quickly upon the Dark Tower and he didn't want to be seen. He looked for a quick spot to land, but his eyes fell down towards the bottom of the cliff. Something was speaking to his spirit. He felt a strong urge to go down towards the stone that sat below the tower. Something was pulling at him as he led his beast towards the rocky cliff bottom. As they came closer, Mikhal noticed something gleaming in the dark air. From afar, it looked like a small light or twinkling star. He came closer, eagerly looking through the mists that sat around the earth.

Mikhal's golden eyes became intense as he realized what the twinkling light was coming from. It was the Sword of Truth! His spirit leapt as he looked upon the ancient sword.

Mikhal led his beast safely down to the earth, landing on top of a large boulder. The cold wind blew past him, bringing a strange scent to his nose. Ignoring the smell, he slid off of his mighty beast, then quickly climbed down the stone. As he came closer to the golden sword, he realized that it was sticking out of the stone. He looked up towards the Dark Tower that loomed high above him. The tallest tower with the balcony was straight above him. He realized that Tairren must've been in the Dark Tower, and somehow, he must've lost his sword.

Mikhal's golden eyes fell upon the sword as his spirit seemed to ignite with fire. He became overwhelmed with joy as he slowly reached towards the hilt of the sword. "My master's sword," he said to himself. His eyes sparkled like the mighty blade.

He touched the pommel of the sword, watching how light stirred within it. He grasped the jeweled hilt, then closed his eyes. "Lead me in these times of trouble, my God. Let your truth rain down quickly upon the lands. Let your sword be a shining beacon, upon the lands and within the hearts of man!"

Mikhal grabbed the sword, then pulled it from the stone. The blade gleamed like a star as he lifted it into the dark air. Mikhal watched its power pulsate as the black mists dispersed away from the blade and back into the shadows.

Mikhal turned quickly as a low moan seemed to come from the earth. It sounded like the stone itself was crying out. The strange scent came to his nose again. His eyes flashed as he turned his head towards the sounds and smell. He followed his senses as he held the sword tightly. He climbed over the stone, making his way to a small cliff. The sound of rapidly moving water began to fill the foul-smelling air. A black river crashed over the stones below him, quickly going off towards the ends of the south. He looked over the cliff, peering down at the wild river. He then heard the strange noises again, which sounded louder. He quickly looked across the rapid river.

He peered through the darkness that sat before him. As his eyes gleamed, he noticed something he had not before. "No...," he said to himself, with wide eyes. Across from the black river, a deep abyss could be seen. As the mists faltered, he could see that the dark abyss was massive. Low moans and strange sounds came up from the abyss, sounding unlike anything he had ever heard before. "The cries of the damned...," he said. Black mists slowly billowed out of the abyss, collecting in the sky above it like smoke.

Mikhal realized that the black abyss was another doorway that led to the Dark Realm. It was the doorway that Marrisa had opened up... Darkness was spilling from it like smoke from a great fire. The darkness upon the south was stronger because of the opened door! Mikhal clenched his teeth as the thought of Lucif's powers growing shrouded his mind. He gazed at the mists as they twirled together, rising from the abyss like a shadow. The mists brought with it screams and growls.

He then looked at the sword. The sword glowed brightly, pulsing in the dark air. He waved the glorious blade through the air, watching as it repelled the black mists. The light from the sword broke the darkness, driving it away. He could literally hear the black mists sizzle as he waved the Sword of Truth through the heavy air.

Mikhal knew that the God of Light's truth and power would send the stinking dark powers back down into the bowels of torment. He knew that the sword could've stopped the abyss and could close it forever. In the twinkling of an eye, it could happen...

Suddenly, an urgent vision came into his mind and spirit. He closed his eyes as his heart thrashed about. He saw Fiara... She was in disguise as a woman named Jezebel, but had revealed herself to Tairren her true self. He saw her prophesying lies and making way for the beast of darkness. He saw her again in a quick horrifying flash, cutting the head from an innocent man of light... His name was John... Mikhal squeezed his eyes as his heart broke. He opened his eyes quickly, becoming overwhelmed with irritation and remorse. "Innocent blood continues to spill," he said to himself.

Overwhelmed, Mikhal looked back down into the treacherous abyss, watching as dark shadows continued to slowly rise up from it, becoming one with the atmosphere. His eyes flashed as he began to become angry at the current situation Minslethrate was in. He wanted to rid the earth of darkness suddenly as passion rose up in his spirit. He clenched his teeth, taking in a deep breath. Still holding the blade, he brought his hand back, then swung the sword out into the sky. He watched the sword twirl among the sky, cutting through the black mists with ease.

The sword flashed as it flew towards the black abyss, creating a clear path behind it as the mists shrunk back. But strangely, the sword stopped falling, seeming to get caught in the air. It froze in the sky as if unseen hands were holding it! A bright light began to grow all around it, burning the darkness that came too close! The sounds of darkness screaming and rushing away filled Mikhal's ears as the air around the sword became clear.

"It is not time yet, Mikhal," a mighty voice said, catching Mikhal off guard.

He looked around quickly, then realized that the voice seemed to come from the light that burned around the sword! The sword gleamed brightly, appearing like a burning star.

Mikhal brought his hands to his eyes, protecting his eyes from the intense light. He fell to his knees, then bowed down towards the ground. "Forgive me, my Lord!" he cried, covering his face.

"The time of my coming draws near, Mikhal," the mighty voice said. "Wait patiently, and do what I commanded of you. It is not over until all ears fall before my name..."

The bright light and sword suddenly grew quiet. The burning light around it slowly vanished as the blade became golden like it was before. The intense light went away, leaving Mikhal in the dark atmosphere. The powerful blade then flew among the air towards Mikhal like a bolt of lightning, crashing right before him. The sound of the sword, ripping through the darkness, vibrated in his ears. The mighty blade penetrated the stone, sending shards and stone flying at him.

Mikhal looked up slowly. His eyes fell upon the sword that stuck straight out from the cold stone right before him. He slowly got up, then pulled the Sword of Truth from the cracked earth. "You are mighty, my Lord," Mikhal said, looking into the sky. "And I will always be your humble servant, oh mighty one... You are magnanimous. All will know your name..."

He looked up at his beast who had been watching him the whole time. His fur and feathers moved about in the cold winds. The beast gave Mikhal one big nod of his massive head, revealing that he knew what to do as well, then looked up towards the tower. Mikhal hurried to him with the Sword of Truth in his hand. He quickly pulled himself onto the beast's back as it spread its golden wings out. The mighty cat crouched down, ready to leap into the air.

"Wait," Mikhal said, as if something had caught his attention. He quickly looked up towards the east of the Dark Tower. He stared for a moment, as if he was listening for something. His eyes didn't move. "Something stirs within my spirit again... I see Rafiul lying upon the earth...he is near...," Mikhal said.

He got the sudden feeling that Rafiul was somewhere upon the mountain! As quick as the wind, the beast leapt into the windy, dark sky. They flew towards the east of the temple, taking action to a call that came within their spirits.

†††

Rafiul lay near the embers of the fire that had died sometime in the evening. The orange embers glowed in the dark air, slowly going out. The dead forest on the mountain was quiet as the wind blew through the bare trees. Rafiul slowly opened his eyes. His vision slowly came to him as his head whirled for a moment. He slowly sat up, bringing his hand to his head.

Rafiul realized where he was at, looking all around the dark woods that surrounded him. "Tairren!" he shouted, remembering what had happened to him.

He stood up, nearly falling over. He caught himself on a tree. "Wicked snake...," he grunted, becoming irritated. "Jezebel will pay for this," he said in a low tone as he searched the ground for his weapons.

He picked up his spilled arrows and made sure his sword had been secured. He looked up the rugged mountain before him, then began to make his way towards the Dark Tower. He knew that he was close, but he didn't know exactly how far away he was from the temple.

Rafiul made his way up the mountain's side, thinking of Tairren and his fellow legna. He quickly stopped as his spirit began to stir. He felt something coming closer to him. It was like a golden cord was becoming one in his spirit as the feeling of peace was coming over him.

Then out of nowhere, it seemed, the trees began to quake as a blast of wind came down into the forest. Rafiul looked up quickly, catching a glimpse of the glowing legna as his spirit leapt.

"Rafiul!" Mikhal shouted to him as he and his beast soared down to the earth.

647

The beast landed quickly, sending a gust of air over Rafiul. He flapped his great wings a couple of times, then folded them back.

"My brothers!" Rafiul shouted, becoming joyful. "It has been many days, it seems, that I've felt my fellow legna's presence!"

"Come, Rafiul," Mikhal said, nodding his head. "It is urgent that we leave, now."

Rafiul quickly pulled himself onto the mighty beast, behind Mikhal. "Tairren has been captured, by a woman named Jezebel," Rafiul said quickly.

Mikhal shouted to the beast, then they flew into the air, bursting from the dead forest.

"This Jezebel you speak of is Fiara," Mikhal said. "She has beheaded the missionary, John... She prophesied the world's fate and the coming of the dark dragon, the Grand-High Mistress... I saw her in a vision..."

Rafiul sat quietly, looking out over the mountain as they flew. He could see the Dark Temple already from where they were at. He thought of John, who was a mighty man of God. He became angry at the thought of his death. His eyes flashed as he thought of Jezebel, who was really Fiara, and how he should've gotten rid of her when he had the chance.

"Something is wrong with Tairren, Rafiul," Mikhal added, turning his head towards him. "I retrieved the Sword of Truth from the bottom of the cliffs... I fear Tairren is in danger... There is something else...Lucif has opened the doorway to the Dark Realm... It is only a matter of time now, Rafiul..."

Rafiul understood everything. He didn't say anything as he looked out over the mountain. He thought of Tairren. He had compassion for his young companion. He had an uneasy feeling in his spirit as he thought of him, though. He knew that he was alive, but he didn't know what kind of shape he was in.

They soared through the black sky, coming closer to the Dark Tower. The Dark Tower had no lights within it and sat on a jagged cliff, looming over the Black Field of Old Blood.

†

CHAPTER 15
The Marking

Night fell over Minslethrate, making the sky appear like a dark abyss. The sun had been sickly all day long, and now that night had fallen, the sky looked like blackened death. The air was strangely cold, feeling more like winter than spring, and the winds carried a foul scent with them from the south. But even though the weather was unnatural and ominous, the people of Minslethrate continued to celebrate. They were blissfully unaware of what was to come…

The Spring Celebration held no sign of turmoil or sadness as the night went on. Everyone, rich and poor, were there. The people were dressed in brightly colored garbs and wild-looking masks and headdresses. Vibrant colored streamers and festoons of flowers adorned every building and shop around the marketplace and town square. Even the castle was decorated. Flower petals littered the cobblestone while banners and colorful paper lanterns filled the air right above their heads. Children ran about the streets, wearing flowers in their hair and having streamers in their hands. Laugher filled the atmosphere, along with music and loud conversation.

The soldiers looked on at the people vigilantly. Both Hannonite and Minslethratian soldiers lined both the interior and exterior of the castle walls. Soldiers walked about the marketplace and town square, while others stood silently. The whole castle and its surrounding areas were heavily guarded by the alert soldiers.

Lord Fernund, Moral, Sora, and Sir Andor sat upon a grand platform before the cheerful celebration. They ate and watched the people in silence, appearing to be the only ones who were not excited about the Spring Festival. Castle servants served them wine and decadent food, but both their plates and goblets still sat full. The table was covered with untouched meet and fruit. The worry and intensity of that night lay thick upon them, making their stomachs turn sour.

"The sky lights will begin soon, My Lord," a nearby servant said, offering them more wine.

Lord Fernund held his hand up, signaling that he didn't want any more wine. He nodded his head, then the servant left quickly.

"The fireworks have always been my favorite part of the celebration…," Moral said with a faint smile. Her mind drifted away. "I remember when Tairren, Marrisa and Natalia used to laugh cheerily among my shop, just waiting for the sky lights to burn brightly upon the night…," Moral said with a smile. Her smile faded as she continued to watch the excited people. "It seemed so long ago…"

"I've never seen them," Sora said, taking a sip of her wine. "My sister went every year, though…," she added, but stopped herself from speaking any longer. She glanced at Lord Fernund who didn't seem to pay any attention.

Sir Andor sat quietly, looking around the scene of people. He looked nervous and uptight and hadn't said anything since he first sat down with them.

Suddenly a loud sound filled the air as the first set of fireworks erupted in the black sky. The vibrant colors burst out, sparkling like massive flower blooms.

"Oohs" and "aahs" filled the air as the sky became filled with colorful, fiery lights. The loud booms spread across the sky.

Everyone in the kingdom looked up at the magnificent sight. Their eyes sparkled like the fireworks.

"I do hope the sky lights end the celebration quickly," Sir Andor said, catching their attention.

"The night will not end so soon," Moral said. "Everyone will celebrate into the late hours of the night."

"Perhaps, we will be spared," Lord Fernund said, looking into the sky.

"I don't understand," Sir Andor said, looking around with his anxious eyes. "Other kingdoms are being attacked as we speak while Minslethrate sits in peace."

"I assure you, Sir Andor," Moral said with a serious tone. "This is the calm before the storm. My son was awakened by a being of light days ago, warning him of what was to come. We shouldn't be fooled by this ominous peace."

"I hope you are wrong," Lord Fernund said. "I will do whatever I need to, to keep the peace upon this kingdom. It is the least I could do for King Julpen."

"But we must not be blinded," Moral said quickly, speaking boldly. It was something she had never done before in the past. "We must be prepared for anything…"

"You are right, Moral," Sir Andor said, nodding his head. "But whatever is to come from afar, the soldiers standing guard in the fields will notify us by sounding their horns," he said, then sipped his goblet of wine.

The fireworks carried on, filling the black sky with loud colors. The music continued to play and the people continued to dance and sing, adding to the noises.

Everything seemed to be going as planned…until a strange feeling settled in the air.

"Do you feel that?" Moral asked, looking around.

"What is it, Moral?" Sora asked quickly, putting her goblet down. Her dark eyes became large.

"I don't know…but I feel uneasy in my spirit," she said. Tingles went across her skin as she rubbed her arms.

Sir Andor looked at her, then looked up into the sky. He felt it too, but he didn't say anything…

†††

Right outside of the castle walls, upon the Great Field of Minslethrate, many soldiers stood quietly. They watched the bright colors of the sky lights, seeming to forget about what they were waiting for. The loud sounds filled the air and music could be heard from where they stood. The noises from the celebration sounded spectacular, making them wish to be there.

But far off in the distance, a strange sound that wasn't part of the celebration could be heard. At first it was not known because of the ruckus of the Spring Celebration, but after a few more moments, some of the soldiers began to hear it.

Some of the soldiers shuttered as a feeling of doom came over them. They rubbed their arms as the temperature seemed to drop. "Something is happening…," one of the soldiers said to another, searching the sky.

"Listen!" another soldier shouted out across the field. "Do you hear it?!"

They all stood in silence, listening for something strange. Their eyes became big and their ears perked up.

"I hear nothing but the sky lights," a nearby soldier called back.

The men sat still on their horses, becoming aware of the dreadful feeling that was coming over them. After a moment, some of the soldiers began to become disturbed and paranoid, looking around frantically as their breaths sped up.

Then, even louder, the sounds of distant shrieks could be heard!

"There it is again!" the soldier shouted. "They're coming!" Overwhelmed with nervousness, he began to blow his horn, catching the other soldier's attention who stood from afar.

But in an instant, something pulled him off of his horse! He screamed as a strong force threw him across the field! His alarmed voice disappeared in the air as something else caught him. The disturbing sounds of his body being broken could be heard. Then another soldier was snatched from his horse, then another! The soldiers became frightened, looking frantically all around them as a black mist began to creep above the ground. The night was so thick and dark that their torches could barely be seen. The sounds of the fireworks could still be heard, covering their screams, but the thick mists began to obscure their view of the bright colors.

The other soldiers noticed quickly, becoming alarmed as dark creatures flew down at them from the black sky! The terrible screams of the flying nomed suddenly filled the air as something rumbled in the distance. Roaring creatures that looked like wild animals began to crash against their horses, taking them by surprise.

They began to blow their horns, signaling that danger was upon them. The sounds of the many horns joined with the loud ruckus of the celebration.

✝✝✝

Inside the walls of the kingdom, Sir Andor heard the familiar sounds of the Hannonite horns. He stood up quickly, grabbing his sword from his sheath. "Something is happening! Listen!"

Lord Fernund and the women stood up as well, looking all around the sky with their wide eyes. They all faintly heard the sounds of the horns.

Moral raised her hands to her mouth, looking at Sora who glanced everywhere with her panicked face. "They're here," she said, alarmed.

"We must get the people out of here!" Lord Fernund shouted.

"We can not send them home; it'll be too late. Does your kingdom have a safe haven?!" Sir Andor asked with wide eyes. He searched Lord Fernund's confused eyes as he looked as if he had not the slightest idea what to do. "Is there not a place of refuge?!"

"We are but a small kingdom, we have nowhere to hide...," Lord Fernund said, looking around as the horns got louder.

Some of the people of the kingdom began to notice the sounds of the horns too. They began to look around with confused faces.

"The church and the castle are our only chance, then!" Sir Andor said quickly.

"Have the other soldiers ready!" Sir Andor shouted to a group of nearby soldiers. "Lead the people to their safety—to the church and castle, now!" Sir Andor shouted.

The soldiers did as they were commanded, going quickly.

"People of Minslethrate!" Sir Andor shouted as loud as he could with Lord Fernund standing by his side. "We are under attack! Move with haste to the sanctuary and castle if you wish to keep your life!"

The people looked at Sir Andor curiously, beginning to talk amongst each other. The music stopped and everyone began to become quiet. They didn't move at first as the fireworks continued to burst in the air. Some people laughed and others ignored him. Some looked at Lord Fernund, wondering if they should believe Sir Andor or not.

"My fellow people, Sir Andor is correct—we are under attack. Move with haste if you wish to live!" Lord Fernund shouted. "Be aware of women, children, and the elderly!" Lord Fernund began to fear for his people after he spoke.

Some people began to move quickly as the many soldiers forced them to move. Then in a matter of moments, everyone began to become frightened as the crowds rushed towards the castle and church. Cheer dispersed quickly away from the celebration as pandemonium began to come alive.

Screams filled the air suddenly as a massive creature came from nowhere! It flew over the crowd of people, spreading its feathery wings out upon the fireworks. Everyone looked up, including Lord Fernund and his companions. Shock seemed to cover the people as they couldn't take their eyes off of the massive creature and his horns.

The ugly nomed flew towards the wall, landing upon it like a mighty bird. It folded its mighty wings back, hunching over. Its massive horns and body could be seen clearly in front of the bright fireworks. Its eyes glowed as it silently peered down at them. Black mists followed it, filling the marketplace and town square with swirling darkness.

"People of Minslethrate—I am the great King Baffmit... I've come before you all, to deliver a message from the Dark Lord!" He announced in a loud voice. As he spoke, more dark creatures began to surround them, creeping in through the entrances and flying above them in the sky.

"I've brought with me, witnesses," he said, gesturing out towards the many nomed.

Squeals and growls began to surround the people, making them cringe and cry.

"A kingdom without a king...," he goaded with a strange smile. "A vulnerable kingdom you are. I greeted your king in the south... Poor King Julpen...I wanted to help him find your princess, but he did not want my help..." Baffmit looked out over the people as his red eyes gleamed. His appearance was horrifying but his voice seemed to hold a sense of assurance. "I've come to help you now... Who is the one that leads this kingdom?" he asked in a not so threatening voice.

The fireworks had stopped and the air became dreadfully quiet as even the nomed stopped making noise. The air was disturbingly quiet. Only the crackle of torches could be heard.

"I am," Lord Fernund spoke up, looking up at the dark creature. His face was fearless but his nervous voice said otherwise.

Lord Baffmit quickly flew from the wall, landing right in front of Lord Fernund and his companions. A gust of wind came with him, pushing at them lightly. They flinched as his mighty feathered wings flapped. His feathers rustled in the silence as he folded his wings back. The people screamed and gasped, moving away from the tall creature, quickly.

Sir Andor and Lord Fernund grabbed their swords, looking up at him with intense eyes.

Moral grabbed her sword as well, trying her best to stay strong as Sora stood by her side.

"Aaah," Baffmit said in a low tone that rippled out over the people. "The strong leaders of Minslethrate, you must be… Brave and silent, you are. I only want to speak with you, then…"

Everyone just looked on with wide eyes, becoming quiet and nervous. The heavy presence of the creature lay thickly over them.

"…If my king did not want your help, Baffmit—nor do I," Lord Fernund said, holding his sword tightly. He tried to stay calm.

Baffmit looked down at them as a wicked smile came over his ugly face. He leaned over, bringing his horned head closer to them. His red eyes intensified, glowing in the black air. "I only want to offer your kingdom something that it has not been offered before…"

Lord Fernund glanced at Sir Andor who looked unsure of the creature. He looked back at the tall creature, not saying anything.

"My lord does not trust me?" Baffmit asked with a chuckle. "…I offer you power, stability, and GREATNESS!" he said, raising his voice. His deep voice made their hearts falter. "The Grand-High Mistress has great powers… She will be your new king…"

Lord Fernund just peered up at him, shaking his head. "Like I've said before…," he said, nervously. "I—I don't want your help…"

Silence fell over Baffmit as he glared down at them. The silence was so heavy that only the breaths from the great creature could be heard. He moved his wings as his feathers ruffled up. The sound of his black feathers made their skin crawl. Many uncomfortable moments seemed to go by as he looked down at them. "Foolish…like your king…," he finally said. "The Grand-High Mistress wishes to leave you all a message…"

King Baffmit took his intense glare off of Lord Fernund and looked out over the crowd of people. The people looked back at him, crying and cowering as his intense eyes searched them. In a quick second, Baffmit opened his massive wings and flew into the air. He was like a quick shadow. He swooped down into the frantic crowd. The people erupted with screams as Baffmit snatched up an unsuspecting soldier. He wrapped his great arms tightly around the soldier, then brought him into the air! He hovered over the crowd as the soldier screamed and thrashed about, trying to get free.

"Let him go!" Lord Fernund shouted, becoming alarmed.

"Listen well, humans!" Baffmit roared out, squeezing the soldier tighter as his helmet fell off. "This will be your fate if you ignore the wishes of the Dark Lord! Death will have you!"

Baffmit growled loudly, then grabbed the soldier's head in his great hand. He pulled the frightened soldier's head quickly, yanking it from his body! A spray of blood came out over the crowd as they began to scream and panic. Baffmit threw the soldier's body into the crowd, still holding onto his head.

"Shoot him down!" Lord Fernund shouted in a shaken voice.

The soldiers began to shoot at Baffmit. A wave of arrows filled the air. The crowd continued to scream as some of the arrows came down at them. The creature stretched out his long arms, blowing out a cloud of fire over the soldiers. Screams and cries filled the atmosphere as the fire enveloped the soldiers.

"Your stupidity will cost you, Lord Fernund!" Baffmit shouted as he flew back into the air. "I suggest you listen well, or torment and death shall come quickly upon you."

The soldiers stopped shooting as Lord Fernund gestured for them to halt. The arrows were not affecting Baffmit and seemed to make the situation worse. He looked out over the crowd of screaming and crying people. He then looked at the group of burnt soldiers who lay upon the ground. Their faces of anguish and terror took hold of his heart. He then looked at the terrified women and children, beginning to become inundated with heartache. His heart pounded in his chest as fear began to come over him.

Lord Baffmit soared into the air, still holding the soldier's head. He flew to the largest flag that rippled through the air. He dipped his long fingers into the opened neck of the head, then threw the head down at the screaming people. He then grabbed the white flag and marked it with his bloody fingers. The marking was of three stars, each star consisting of six dashes.

Baffmit then grabbed the pole the flag was attached to and broke it off. He quickly flew above the crowd where everyone could see it clearly. "Your message: Everyone must wear this sign upon your flesh—or your head shall come away from you in a mighty splash of blood!" Baffmit roared out. He then flew to the top of the castle and shoved the pole into the tallest tower, where everyone could see it. "I declare Minslethrate: The first settlement of the Dark Lord! ALL HAIL, THE GRAND-HIGH MISTRESS!"

The people of Minslethrate began to cry out, not knowing what to do. Screams filled the air as fear and chaos settled over them. Doom came over them as hope and light continued to vanish.

Lord Fernund looked out over the people, becoming alarmed and sickened. He panicked, not knowing what to do. He thought of his people and his king. He just wanted everything to stop. He closed his eyes, wishing that everything would just disappear. He quickly opened them again, looking at the faces of the frightened people. They were all looking at him, pleading for him to end the nightmare.

"If we wear the sign as you wish—will you leave us be?!" Lord Fernund shouted, not thinking before he spoke. He just wanted the anguish to stop just as the people did.

Moral's eyes flashed as she looked at him. A look of disbelief came over her flustered face. She shook her head, feeling an overwhelming sensation boil up in her heart. She knew she had to say something just then. Her breaths sped up as her head pounded.

King Baffmit flew back down to him, coming upon him in a rush of cold air. A smile came over his face as his eyes flashed. "…Yes…," he said in a low voice. "Submit, and wear the sign, Lord Fernund…and you and your people will be set free…"

Lord Fernund looked up at him as his ears rung. He just peered into his bright, red eyes. His heart pounded in his chest as sweat formed on his brow. He looked out over the frantic people again, taking in a deep breath. He had to agree with Baffmit's offer, he thought. He forgot about the God of Light as the thought of him saving his people came over him. But he didn't know that he couldn't save them. Lord Fernund looked back up at him. He slowly nodded his head, concurring with Baffmit's wish. He was about to agree with Baffmit…

"Do not listen to him, Lord Fernund!" Moral spoke up. Her voice was bold and unwavering. "He is lying! Remember, Lord Fernund, he is one of them who has killed your wife! He is one of them who is trying to force our kingdom into the bowels of Hell! That marking is the symbol of destruction, death and darkness! That is the marking of a beast! We must wear the light upon us, Lord Fernund, not the marking of the beast!"

Baffmit quickly turned his horned head towards her, glaring at her with his burning eyes. "Who are you, woman?!" he demanded. "Silence yourself or you will be the second fool to die before this castle this very night!"

"Your threats don't frighten me!" she shouted, holding her sword tightly. "I know that I have something more powerful than you, *lord* Baffmit! I have the power of light within me, and it will never falter! In the name of King Yehoshua, I-STAND!"

King Baffmit flew back, away from her and the sound of the great king's name. He held his great hand up, spreading his long nails in the cold air. His eyes became brighter as he growled like a vicious animal. "You have already broken one of the Grand-High Mistress' commandments! DO-NOT-SPEAK-HIS-NAME!"

The nomed all around them began to growl and shriek as the mists became thicker. Moral seemed to enrage them all. The atmosphere exploded with loud chaos as the darkness grew.

"I follow King Yehoshua, who is LORD OF ALL!" Moral shouted out in a mighty voice, coming closer to Baffmit. Her strength and boldness made him falter in the air. "And I am abiding by His commandments: There is no other God before HIM!" Power began to swell up inside of Moral as she shouted at Baffmit. She thrust her sword into the air as everyone stared at her with shock and amazement. The intensity of the light within her was so strong that her eyes literally flashed with a bright light! "Stand down, Baffmit, in the name of KING YEHOSHUA!!"

Suddenly a powerful force seemed to erupt from Moral's spirit, pushing Baffmit away from her. Everyone saw it with their own eyes, the way the unseen power forced Baffmit away. Moral had the power of God within her!

Baffmit screamed as the force threw him away from Moral and into the air. His mighty wings fluttered about, trying to catch the air. The powerful force propelled him quickly into the wall, making it crack and crumble as he hit it.

Everyone, including Lord Fernund, gazed at Moral as she stood boldly with her sword in hand. He became empowered by her and felt a surge of strength within him.

Sora and Sir Andor rushed to Moral's side, standing tall alongside her. Their chests heaved as they sucked in the cold air.

A loud roar burst from King Baffmit as he jumped from the heavy stones that fell around him. His anger exploded from him. He opened up his feathered wings and sucked in the cold air. His wings stretched out, revealing its true width. His chest swelled as he opened his arms. He let out another loud roar as a mighty plume of fire erupted from his mouth. The fire went out over the people, burning some of them in the hot cloud.

Screams filled the air.

"Make your way to a safe place!" Lord Fernund shouted.

The atmosphere became filled with chaos as the people began to run. The crowds rushed through the gates to the castle and church.

"ATTACK!" Sir Andor yelled. "We shall fight to the death!" He raised his sword into the air as he gave a shout.

A war suddenly became alive before the castle. The soldiers shot their arrows and swung their swords as the nomed began to attack them. The sounds of swords and armor filled the air as the nomed sent their shrieks and growls out. The atmosphere was loud with screams as the people continued to rush into the courtyards of the castle and church.

Baffmit continued to spill his fire out over the houses and buildings of the kingdom, sending flames high into the black sky. The flowers and decorations of the festival became engulfed in massive flames, filling the air with bright-orange light. He flew into the black sky, looking down at his progress as the kingdom began to fall. "There shall be no one left alive!" he roared out.

Black smoke billowed out from the flames, covering the streets in thick darkness. People's bodies lay upon the cold stone and glass and fallen shops fell into the alleyways and streets. The wind blew, sending the fiery destruction to other parts of the castle.

Baffmit flew to the highest tower of the castle, hovering over the chaos next to the bloody flag. The flag rippled through the air, revealing the markings of the Grand-High Mistress...

✝

CHAPTER 16
Dreams & Visions

Tairren slowly opened his tired eyes. His mind became filled with confusion as he slowly sat up. The fresh scent of green grass and cherry blossom filled his nostrils. The sun was bright, trickling through the leaves and pink blooms that rustled above his head. Small shadows from the dancing leaves moved about his skin as the fresh spring breezes blew all around him. The air was cool and the grass below him was even cooler. He sat in a shady grove of flowering trees, looking around as wonder came over him. Everything was so sweet, everything so still. The presence of the outdoors was magical, and it seemed like it had been ages since he felt its calming atmosphere.

"Tairren," a sweet voice said from behind him. He turned quickly to the maiden's call. "You've been sleeping all afternoon," the maiden said, giggling.

Tairren smiled, running his hand through his black hair. The strands of his bangs danced over his dark-blue eyes. "I guess I have," he said, looking around the beautiful grove. He looked back at the maiden, realizing just then that the sweet girl was Marrisa.

She smiled down at him as the pink blooms of the trees rustled in the breezes above her. The blooms filled the air, gliding through the blue sky and over the tall green grass.

"Are you going to the spring-time fair?" she asked, sitting next to him. She smiled a sweet smile as her clear-blue eyes sparkled.

"I... I don't know...," he said, becoming mesmerized by her beautiful face.

A brisk wind blew, making her red curls flutter in front of her fair face. Her red hair, along with her vibrant blue eyes, was something Tairren had always loved about her. Flower petals got caught in her long tresses as the tree continued to sprinkle its velvety blooms upon them. She moved her hair, pulling it to one side as she stared into his dark-blue eyes. "Rosemary, love, and sunshine...," she finally said after a sweet moment.

Tairren just looked at her, confused. "What?" he asked.

She caressed his cheek lightly, smiling at him.

"...Remember me when you go there—for he once was a hero of mine...," Marrisa added, just looking into his eyes. Her sweet smile slowly faded as she looked away from him.

Tairren realized just then that her words were from the old bard song that she loved. Suddenly a charming memory came back to him as he thought of when she sang the song in the Forest Provence of Minslethrate.

So long ago it seemed to him, and it was a memory he never wanted to forget.

"Tell him to make me a golden crown...rosemary, love, and sunshine." Her voice slowed as her mind seemed to drift away. Her eyes looked saddened all of a sudden, as if a terrible thought came into her mind. She continued to just stare away from Tairren. She was slowly slipping away from him. "...Without metal...made with feather-down... Then...he'll be a...true love of mine..." She stopped singing as the soft colors of her aura left her.

She suddenly appeared as if her spirit had died... "Save me, Tairren...," she said in a faltering voice. "Wake me up and save me..." Her eyes drifted away.

"Marrisa?" Tairren said, trying to catch her attention. He waved his hand in front of her face.

Marrisa just stared silently as her bright-blue eyes twinkled no longer.

"Marrisa?!" Tairren became alarmed, shaking her shoulders. "Stay here with me, Marrisa!" He touched her white cheek, noticing how cold it was.

The temperature began to drop suddenly as the sun went away. The flowering tree stopped releasing its petals and the grass below them became as rough stone. Darkness began to cover them as a strange mist filled the air.

Marrisa slowly looked at him, appearing as if confusion was coming over her. She looked as if she didn't know Tairren at all. "...It's so cold...," she said, staring off blankly.

"Mar...!" Tairren yelled, but couldn't finish her name before his mind awakened to reality...

†††

"...risa!" Tairren screamed out, shooting open his eyes.

His breaths were quick as a cold sweat trickled down his white face. He swallowed down his panic, looking all around him. Sour, damp air filled his lungs. He was no longer in the sweet, sunny grove, but in a dark and dingy chamber. He moved his arms as the familiar sound of heavy chains rattled. He realized that he was still chained up like a criminal. He glanced at his hands which were still pulled to the right and left of him. They throbbed with pain and discomfort while dark, dried blood was still caked on them. He apprehended that he was still in the Dark Tower—still held captive.

He looked around the small chamber. It was colder than he remembered as a strange wind blew in from the window. The memory of Fiara slashing his palm and shoving his dagger into the other came into his mind as he looked down. The dagger was sitting at his feet, in a puddle of his own dried blood. He glanced at his dirty arms, noticing all the blood that had dried down them. He brought his weary eyes to the window. The sky was totally black, filled with icy winds.

He thought of his dream as the firelight from the torch still flickered about. The sound of the soft flame soothed him as his mind drifted away. The precious memory of Marrisa made his heart ache. The thought of her falling into darkness made him sick. He thought of what she was saying in his dream… He remembered clearly that she was stating the lyrics of the old song to him. At first, he didn't know the significance of the song, but after a moment of thinking about it, he realized that the lyrics of the song had come to him on many occasions. The song was more significant than he thought. His heart fluttered as he realized that the dream must've been a sign, the lyrics must've been a sign!

He thought of the words and recited them in his head. The melody played sweetly in his aching mind as he thought of it…

> Are you going to the spring-time fair?
> Rosemary, love, and sunshine.
> Remember me when you go there,
> For he once was a hero of mine.
> Tell him to make me a golden crown,
> Rosemary, love, and sunshine.
> Without metal—and made with feather-down,
> Then he'll be a true love of mine…

He remembered that when Marrisa used to sing it, he'd think it was just a tease, a silly poem of impossible quests for a man to take on for his bride. But it wasn't… It was a test of love…but a different kind of love…

Tairren's heart raced as he figured out what Marrisa was trying to tell him in his vision-like dream. The song that had never made sense to him became clear to him all of a sudden. He became overwhelmed as he realized that the song was a riddle! To anyone else the song would've been just an old folksong of forbidden love, but to Tairren it was a mysterious poem. The song that Marrisa had sung for many years was actually a riddle that could only be solved if one understood the light of God!

The question, "Are you going to the spring-time fair?" was pertaining to the Spring Celebration. The Spring Celebration was to honor the gifts of God…and the life of King Yehoshua… He realized that the Spring Celebration would've been going on at that very moment during that ominous night.

The statement, "Rosemary, love, and sunshine," were the things that represented "good omens". They were things that made Marrisa happy. Rosemary was also used in weddings, Tairren realized. The memory of

Marrisa singing the old folksong in the Forest Provence came back into his mind. He smiled as he remembered when he had picked the herbs for his mother, and dropped them on the ground. He thought of when Marrisa picked the aromatic herb up and caressed his cheek with it, saying that it bound them together, as if they were promised to each other. Tairren remembered her saying that rosemary represented—love… Love and sunshine was something that made Marrisa flourish…which had gone away from Minslethrate many days ago.

Tairren thought of the next line, "Remember me when you go there." She was letting him know not to forget about her. And the following line, "For he once was a true hero of mine," was the belief in God she once had, before she turned away from light and succumbed to darkness… God is the only hero, he thought. Tairren thought more of the rest of the lines in his dream. "Tell him to make me a golden crown…without metal—and made with feather-down… Then he'll be a true love of mine…" He realized that she was asking for a crown, but not the physical royal crown made of golden metal…she wanted the crown of light! Light is weightless, just like feather-down. If she had the crown of life, then she could love and be with the God of Light, forever!

Tairren thought of how all along the song was part of their fates! He thought that God must've put the vision and lyrics in his head, reminding him that it was not too late for Marrisa. Marrisa was not forever cursed like everyone had been saying… Marrisa's heart, even though it seemed lost in the darkness, still had a small flame that burned deep within it. Her heart's flame was weak and sickly, but it was still there...

"Marrisa…," Tairren whispered to himself. "There is still time—and a second chance…"

A noise caught Tairren's attention, making him look up quickly. His eyes widened as he realized that someone had been watching him the whole time! He saw a black form standing in the shadowy doorway of the chamber.

"Marrisa?!" he shouted. His heart raced as he peered into the darkness. The form stood quietly, then slowly faded back into the blackened doorway. "Marrisa, come back!" he shouted. He thought of the end of his dream when Marrisa seemed to slowly slip into the cold darkness, fading away from him. "MARRISA!!" he screamed out as tears came to his eyes.

His voice echoed in the torch-lit chamber, becoming lost in the shadows.

Tairren closed his burning eyes, trying to take his mind off of the darkness. He thought of the memories he had shared with Marrisa back in the northern kingdom. He thought of her beautiful face and voice. He thought of the love he had for her. He thought of the innocent and pleasant times, the moments in their lives when everything seemed simple and perfect.

"She is here no longer, Tairren," a familiar voice came from the shadows of the doorway. It was the exotic voice of Fiara, a voice he began to loathe.

Startled, Tairren opened his eyes as Fiara began to walk upon him. He quickly felt anger come over him. He peered at her, noticing how much her appearance had changed. She was clad in golden armor, which looked much like the legna's, and her beautiful face was glittery, having gold paint splotched on it. Long red and purple fabric hung from her arms and waist, fluttering elegantly in the winds that came into the chamber. The fabric was sheer and sparkled with small jewels. Her long black hair fell over her shoulders in braids and was covered in more jewels. She looked like a gleaming idol.

"Where is she?!" Tairren screamed out, breathing hard.

"Far away from here," she said with a smile. As she walked towards him, her armor gleamed and the sheer fabric seemed to come alive upon the cold air.

Tairren clenched his teeth as she stood before him. He noticed that her forehead had three stars painted on it. He then looked into her honey-colored eyes which glowed in the firelight.

"You noticed her marking…," she said.

"You said she is not here!" Tairren spat.

"Her spirit is not here—but her flesh is… The mark on my forehead that your eyes fell upon is the symbol of the Grand-High Mistress… Marrisa is the Grand-High Mistress," she said, gazing into his eyes. "And tonight, we shall celebrate her coming with the shedding of blood in a great cleansing… She is the new sovereign of Minslethrate…and will be the priestess of the world and the GOD OF MEN!" she shouted.

"Leave her alone!" Tairren yelled, pulling at the chains. "She has done nothing to you! If she has given in to the darkness it is because of you!"

Fiara laughed, bringing her long fingernail across his lips. "You had the chance to follow the powers, but did not." She grabbed his face, bringing hers closer to his. "Remember, Tairren, you have power inside of you—you just don't know how to awaken it."

Tairren yanked his head away from her grasp. "I have the power of God inside of me!" he shouted, glaring at her beneath his brow. "It's something you know nothing about."

Fiara just quietly glared at him as the firelight gleamed off of her golden armor. The silence between them was thick.

"…Do you remember when my power revealed your father's death to you, Tairren?" she asked, breaking the tension between them.

Tairren just glared at her, breathing hard as his heart pounded. He clenched his teeth, not saying anything.

"I can show you Marrisa with my powers...," she whispered, tempting him.

Tairren looked away from her. "I want nothing to do with you and your magic tricks."

Fiara turned away from him, going towards the torch. The sound of the fabric hanging from her armor rustled in the air as another wind blew in.

Tairren peered at her. He watched as she brought her hands up to the firelight of the torch. She stuck her hands into the fire and closed her eyes. Tairren stared silently as the fire danced around her hands.

"Look into the fire," she said, bringing her hands away from the torch. As she stuck her hands out towards Tairren, the fire followed them. The fire began to grow in the palms of her hands! "I will show you Marrisa," she said with a smile.

Tairren stared at the fire, then looked into her eyes. Her eyes glowed as the fire rippled in the dark air, beginning to pulsate. "No," Tairren said, having no emotion.

Fiara walked into the middle of the chamber. She began to chant something. Her voice became louder as the fire grew right before Tairren. She took her hands out of the fire, stepping back as she continued to chant. The fire floated in midair! The sounds it made was not like any other fire, and the flames that came from the center stretched out in all directions. It looked like a massive burning mirror.

Tairren brought his gaze away from the magical fire. He could feel the heat from it, tingling on his face and arms. He closed his eyes tightly, not able to do anything else.

"Look into the fire, Tairren!" Fiara screamed out as her eyes turned terrifyingly black.

"NO!" Tairren shouted again, keeping his eyes tightly closed. He didn't want to see what she offered him.

Silence came over them as the only sound was that of the strange fiery mirror. The small chamber became bright and hot as the fiery mirror pulsated. The atmosphere became stifling.

"Tairren...," a voice said that wasn't Fiara's. It was Marrisa's voice. "Look at me...," she whispered. The voice was soft and peaceful.

Tairren couldn't help himself as Marrisa's voice made his heart quicken. He slowly opened his eyes, obeying Marrisa's sweet whispers. Bright fiery light filled his eyes, mesmerizing him instantly like a moth to a flame.

Tairren stared into the fire, noticing someone standing on the other side of it. It was Marrisa. He could see her silhouette move on the other side. He could see her face and her long red hair. He could smell her sweet scent and feel her cool breath. She was like a cool drink of water to his spirit. His senses began to quake as his mind began to slip away from his body. "Marrisa...," Tairren whispered, never taking his eyes off of her.

His mind began to become pulled into the fire. He did not notice as the magical fire took over him. His mind slipped away, quickly bursting into the fiery mirror like a rush of air. He was suddenly forced into another realm as he followed Marrisa through the fire, leaving his body in the morbid chamber...

†††

Tairren looked around, realizing that he was no longer in the chamber. His chains were gone and he looked the way he did before his world had changed. His body had not one single bruise or cut on it and his clothes were clean.

He was standing in the middle of a rundown kingdom. His eyes searched his surroundings, becoming taken aback by what he saw. The buildings were dark as smoke billowed from them and everything appeared to be destroyed. The kingdom looked as if a mighty war had taken life away from it. The trees were dead and the ground was littered with thick dust and trash. The silence that lay thick even felt sickly.

"Look for the one you love...," Fiara's voice said. Strangely, her voice seemed to come from all around Tairren, reverberating throughout the broken kingdom.

Tairren looked around, searching for Fiara. But he was all alone. He looked into the sky which was dark with heavy clouds and smoke. Soft white flurries slowly glided down to the gray ground. Tairren thought it was snowing. A flurry fell upon his cheek, feeling not cold at all to the touch. He brought his fingers to the soft speck. As he looked at his fingers, he realized that the white flurries were not snow at all, but ash and soot. The sky was filled with the quiet and graceful soot.

"The sun has gone out...," Tairren whispered as he looked at the gray filth that smeared across his fingers.

The sun was dead... The air was ice cold and no light came from anywhere. Death was all around him.

Tairren began to walk through the destroyed town. The streets were covered with black stones and thick ash. He passed by rundown shops and dirty fountains. He walked over skeletons and broken things. "Where am I?" he said to himself.

Suddenly the sound of whimpers caught Tairren's attention. Someone, somewhere, was crying. He followed the pitiful voice into the great castle. "Hello," Tairren said. His voice echoed in the darkness of the silent castle.

He cautiously walked through the great doors, looking all around him. Everything was dark and dingy. The air smelled foul and the floor and staircases were matted with more ash and dust.

The crying voice came to him again. He looked quickly, following the voice through a massive doorway.

He realized he was now standing in the middle of a huge throne room. The hall was darker than the outside hall, and even colder. His eyes fell upon the mighty throne which sat across from him. It was empty. The whimpers came again, sounding louder. Tairren realized that the cries were coming from behind the throne!

"I'm coming," Tairren said, making his way quickly towards the throne. His voice echoed throughout the great hall.

Tairren came before the throne, noticing that the top was adorned with a cluster of three stars. All three stars were shaped with six dashes, forming some kind of pyramid. Tairren's eyes widened as he remembered the same marking on Fiara's forehead. "The Grand-High Mistress...," Tairren whispered.

The whimpers came again, startling Tairren. He quickly went behind the throne, looking for the crying person. To his surprise, it was Marrisa! She was chained up behind the throne! Her mouth and eyes her bound with black cloth and she looked as if she was dying.

Tairren panicked as his heart quickened. He ran to her, quickly pulling the bounds from her face. "I'm here now, Marrisa," he said in a shaken voice. "Don't be frightened, I'm here."

As he took her bounds off, she seemed to become weakened. Her blue eyes looked dull and her dried lips were white like her cheeks. Her white skin was like ice. "She's coming...," Marrisa whispered in a feeble voice, closing her weary eyes. She suddenly became unconscious. Her long red hair fell back as she hung from the chains like a corpse.

Tairren frantically tried to wake her up, but nothing was working! "Marrisa, please stay with me," he said, breathlessly. "You can not die!"

Suddenly a loud sound rumbled in the dark air. A heavy presence began to fill the chamber. Tairren stood for a moment, then turned slowly, recognizing the morbid feeling of darkness approaching him. No one was there... He slowly crept out from behind the throne and upon the dark hall, looking all around the black shadows. The shadows were heavy and the air was uncomfortable.

Tairren turned quickly as he felt someone standing behind him, looming over him. He could feel breaths on the back of his head, making the hairs on his cold neck stand up.

"WHY ARE YOU HERE?!!" a deep voice roared out, making Tairren's heart quake.

Tairren's eyes widened with fear as he fell back. He got away quickly from the woman standing before him.

The evil woman was Marrisa! But she didn't look like his sweet Marrisa he had always thought of. It couldn't be her. She stood tall in a shining black gown. Her long gown looked as if small gleaming stars were sown onto it and the collar of it rose up high behind her head. Her long cape fell down upon the stone as she looked angrily at him. Her white face gleamed like glass and her eyes were heavy with black shadows.

A cloud of smoky ash surrounded Tairren, covering his eyes. He quickly closed his burning eyes, breathing quickly.

The sounds all around him changed suddenly. He opened his eyes, looking around quickly as his heart raced. The smoky ash was gone and the air was clear. He was no longer in the dark throne room! He looked around for the darkened Marrisa, but she was nowhere to be found.

He stood up quickly, confused at what he was seeing and experiencing. He was now standing in the middle of another kingdom. The kingdom was darker than the last. It was uglier than the last. Everyone in the kingdom walked about solemnly. Their faces were dirty and their clothes were like rags. They looked like they were dead but still living simultaneously. Everyone was chained, aimlessly walking around like spiritless corpses. Tairren peered at the disturbing people, wondering where he was at.

"Tairren," another whisper came. But this time the whisper came from a man. "Tairren, over here," the whisper said, urgently.

Tairren followed the man's voice to a dead tree that sat in the middle of the rundown kingdom.

Tairren's confused face flashed with relief as he noticed who the man was. "John!" Tairren shouted, rushing to him.

John hushed him, bringing his hand over his mouth quickly. "You must be quiet," he whispered loudly. "We mustn't be seen."

"What is this place?" Tairren asked quickly in a low tone.

John looked around quickly, crouching down low behind the tree. "This is what is to come… These are the days ahead of you. I am not supposed to be here so I must speak quickly. I was sent here to let you know that Marrisa must be destroyed…"

Tairren looked at him with disbelief. He felt as if his heart dropped into his stomach. His eyes widened as he slowly shook his head. He fell to his knees near John as he inhaled a shaken breath. His eyes fell away from John as he looked at the world around him.

"Tairren, if Marrisa is not destroyed—this will be your new world," he said, gesturing out over the dark land.

Tairren looked around. Everything was dead and dark. Rotten smells lingered in the air, dancing with the feeling of turmoil. The sun was gone and the wind was icy. There was no light at all. It was like everything good had been pulled away from the world. "What happened to the light? I thought the light has already won."

"It has, Tairren... But this is the future of your kingdom, and every other kingdom. This is what will become of the world when light is taken away from it. One day, King Yehoshua will come back, and take his people of light with him! This is the world with the God of Light gone from it!"

"I don't understand," Tairren said.

"I was sent here to tell you that it is not time yet. So, you must do whatever you can to stop Marrisa from ruling the world. When everyone upon the world hears King Yehoshua's name, then will he come back and take his people and the light from it. There will be a new Earth…but there will be a time of absolute darkness before that happens…"

"What must I do?" Tairren asked, nervously looking into John's eyes.

"…Stop the Grand-High Mistress," he said. "The only way to stop her is by using God's truth…the Sword of Truth…."

Tairren just stared at him. "Are—are you asking me to kill her?" he asked. He shook his head. "I…I can't kill her… I can't… Can't you see that I've come all this way to save her? Now you are telling me that I should kill her?!"

John pressed his lips together, understanding his pain. "Look over there, Tairren," John said, becoming more serious. He pointed towards a dark mountain that loomed over them.

Tairren looked, becoming overwhelmed. He saw Marrisa sitting atop the mountain upon a great throne. She was covered in black garbs and a tall crown sat upon her head. Her white forehead was marked with three bloody stars and her face was emotionless. She held a great sword in one hand, and a scepter in the other. She was looking out over the sullen lands. Her black eyes roamed about, intensely.

"I've seen this in a dream," Tairren said, quietly. "She was sitting upon a dark mountain…made of dead bodies…" His skin crawled as he thought of the frightening dream he had once before.

"Yes, Tairren…this will happen," John concurred, holding his hand out. "Everyone you know and love will be locked up, tormented, and beheaded if they refuse the marking of the Grand-High Mistress. Anyone who even mentions the great king's name…will be brutally killed… Everyone who loves the light will be casted away like soiled rags. A world with darkness does not want the light. Do you want that?!"

Tairren shook his head quickly, becoming nervous. His eyes became filled with tears as he looked back up at Marrisa. He barely recognized her. "I will do what my God wants me to do… Even if that means ridding of the only person I have ever loved in this world…" Tears began to accumulate in his eyes as he looked away from Marrisa's dark form.

It was hard for him to understand why it had to happen that way. Why couldn't God just stop the darkness from rising? Why didn't he just reveal his power like the morning sun? Tairren was confused, but knew that there was a reason for everything happening the way it was. He just didn't understand. But he knew it was not for him to understand right then.

John nodded his head as a faint smile came over his face. "You will be blessed, son. God smiles down on you now. God will mend every tear and reveal everything to you in the end... You will get through this, Tairren... He will be with you, even down in the darkest valley."

Tairren solemnly nodded his head.

John looked up quickly. Someone was coming! "I must go!" he said, beginning to get up.

"Wait, John!" Tairren said, grabbing his tunic. "I wanted to ask you... How did you get here?"

John smiled a little, looking at young Tairren. "Just know that I live among God's light now... Nevaeh is my home now..."

Tairren let go of his collar, realizing what he meant. He looked at the mighty man and nodded his head.

"Remember your calling, Tairren," John said, placing his hand on Tairren's shoulder. "I will see you again one day," he said with a smile, then left quickly.

Tairren looked, but John had already vanished. He looked around the silent darkness quickly, realizing that the person who spotted them was now standing over him! Tairren stood up quickly as the person grabbed him!

"You can not speak to him!" Fiara's voice boomed in his ears.

Tairren realized that it was Fiara who had grabbed him, sending him back to reality with a mighty push...

†††

Tairren quickly opened his eyes, taking in a deep breath. His body shook. He looked around quickly, disturbed by the fact that he was chained back up in the dim chamber! The fiery mirror was gone and Fiara stood right before him.

"What did he tell you?!" Fiara demanded, picking up the dagger that had been lying on the stone. "Tell me or pain shall come over you quickly!" She shoved the blade against his side as she stood before him.

Tairren winced in pain, feeling the blade digging into his flesh. "You sent me there and you didn't know he would be there?!" he spat, angrily. "It doesn't matter what he said, because I've seen what will happen to this world! I've seen what will become of Marrisa!"

Fiara breathed heavily as she looked into his angry eyes. She then slowly backed away from him, pulling the dagger away from his side. She smirked, raising one of her eyebrows. She took in a deep breath, then looked away from him. "You're right, Tairren... It doesn't really matter what he told you—because he is dead just like this world." She smirked, looking back into his eyes. "I cut his head from him many hours ago."

"You, filthy monster!" Tairren shouted, thrashing his arms around. "He didn't deserve to die!"

"YOU, just like all the others, killed him, Tairren!" she screamed. "You did—because you continue to walk a path that comes from a dead king."

Tairren just glared at her, shaking his head.

Fiara began to chuckle, tapping the dagger against the palm of her hand. "I cut his head from him because he denied the Grand-High Mistress. It was a message to all of the men who continued to travel this way... I warned you, Tairren." She chuckled again as she turned her head towards the window. "Time is passing quickly, Tairren. It would've been you to be executed first—but there are other plans for you." She turned her head towards Tairren and smiled. "The Grand-High Mistress wishes to use you for something greater, before taking your head... You will be a message to the whole world. The message will be: Worship the Grand-High Mistress...or die..."

Suddenly she stopped talking, quickly turning her head back towards the window as if sensing something. Something caught her attention. She stood silently, listening intently. She looked uneasy all of a sudden, as if she felt something threatening. "They're here, somewhere," she whispered.

She slowly walked towards the window, stopping right before it. She looked out as the winds blew upon her. She looked around at the broken temple, seeming to search for someone. After a moment, she turned away from the cold window, glaring at Tairren. She then left the chamber quickly, disappearing into the black doorway.

✝

CHAPTER 17
Willing Spirit

Mikhal and Rafiul had been vigilantly searching the surrounding area of the Dark Tower, circling around the tops of its towers and cliffs. They were searching for a safe spot to land their beastly companion upon. There seemed to be no place large enough or sturdy enough to land. They looked to see if they could find some kind of firelight, revealing that someone was near, but found nothing. The longer they searched overhead, the more they became irritated. Every window and threshold were black and almost all of the large balconies that they could've landed on crumbled when they came too close. Most of the temple was falling apart, and there seemed no easy way of getting into it.

"Tairren is near!" Rafiul shouted through the winds as they searched from the sky. "I feel his troubled spirit! Fly low, Mikhal, he has to be close!"

Mikhal nodded then got the beast to fly nearer to the bottom of the temple. They swiftly went under arches and between the tall towers. They swooped around collapsing drawbridges and through opened chambers. "I see no sign of life anywhere," Mikhal said, trying to peer through the thick black mist.

"Over there!" Rafiul shouted, pointing. "There is a faint light from a fire of some sort!"

Mikhal saw it too. The faint firelight came from a window that was nearly hidden by the large stones and crumbling towers. It seemed as if they had passed by that area plenty of times, but did not notice it before. They had to swoop below a balcony and fly between two towers to get closer to the window.

Mikhal landed his beast on a rocky cliff that sat below the dimly-lit window. The beast perched atop a boulder as they looked around.

"We have to climb," Mikhal said in a low tone. "It will be hard to fly close to the window without being seen."

Rafiul quickly got off of the beast, then began to climb down the boulder. Mikhal commanded his beast to watch for anything odd, then swiftly followed behind Rafiul.

After jumping from boulder to boulder, they began to climb up the jagged stones. The path was filled with danger and took their breath away. They had to leap across deep trenches and scale along steep cliffs. Every now and then they glanced down, peering at the black river that roared miles below them. The sounds of the violent river bounced up the trenches and stone, sounding closer than it really was. After a while, they finally made it closer to the window. The warm light from inside the window looked haunting. They looked back down, realizing how high they were. They could see the beast's fur and wings down below, glowing in the darkness. The winds picked up, nearly knocking them from the cliff. They held on tightly, then when the cold winds subsided, they hurried up one last rocky ledge, right beneath the window.

Rafiul crouched below the window, pressing against the stone wall. He slowly peeked into the chamber. He saw Tairren right away, chained up, appearing tired and beaten.

"Tairren's in here," Rafiul said in a low voice, looking down at Mikhal.

Rafiul looked into the window again, then slowly climbed into it.

Tairren saw him right away. His eyes widened as he glanced towards the dark doorway where Fiara had left not too long ago. "Rafiul!" Tairren whispered loudly. He smiled with some effort, appearing relieved. "Move quickly, Fiara will be back!" he whispered.

Rafiul crept into the chamber, bringing his finger over his lips, shushing him. His eyes looked cunning as he quickly glanced around at his surroundings. Even in the dim light, his eyes gleamed. He quickly crept to the doorway, looking through it. The corridor it led to was dark and empty. No one was nearby so he hurried to Tairren.

Mikhal climbed through the window, quickly looking around as well.

Surprised, Tairren looked over at Mikhal as hope came over him. "God has heard my cries," Tairren said quickly. "Thank you," he said, then looked at Rafiul who was inspecting his wounds and the chains that held him captive. "...I'm sorry, Rafiul," Tairren said, catching his attention. "My foolishness has done this. I should have taken your advice."

Rafiul looked at him for a moment, then nodded his head. "You are forgiven, Tairren. You are learning—every step you make is a test in your walk... You just have to grow from it."

Mikhal came to Tairren quickly, pulling the Sword of Truth out before him. "Look what I've retrieved, Tairren," he said.

"Thank you, Mikhal," Tairren said, amazed. "Fiara stole it and threw it out of the window... Fiara beheaded John," Tairren said, looking back at Rafiul. "But I saw John in a vision." He looked at both of them, wide-eyed. "He has prophesied something that disturbs my very being..."

Rafiul glanced at Mikhal, as if they'd already known.

"Yes, I know. I felt it in my spirit when John left this world. I have seen and felt it time and time again. I have seen people of light, like yourself, become locked away in the darkness just for following King Yehoshua... John died as a martyr—but now lives forever in the kingdom of light. Darkness will not stop until it is stopped first... Fiara will be punished. Her intensions of trying to stop God's work will not be forgotten and will not be dismissed lightly," he said with a serious face.

"She is the Grand-High Mistress' pawn and the mother of harlots and abominations of this world. She is against light and spreads false prophecy, speaking of power that is not of God. She will not move without a vicious fight. So, we must move with haste."

Rafiul stepped aside quickly as Mikhal raised the mighty sword into the dark air. "Your bondages shall be broken. Not even chains of iron can withstand the mighty Sword of Truth," Mikhal said. He swung the golden sword quickly, swiftly cutting the chains from Tairren's arms and ankles. The iron chains unraveled and fell to the ground with a heavy clunk.

Tairren rubbed his red wrists, quickly looking towards the darkened doorway. He looked at his hands, becoming aware that they looked infected. He winced in pain as he tried to move his fingers and the muscles of his palms.

Rafiul took his hands, inspecting them. "These wounds are deep," he said, looking at Tairren. "They will rot and die if they aren't healed quickly." His strong hands looked clean against Tairren's. "Remember when God healed your wounds once before, days ago, Tairren?" Rafiul asked, looking down at him. "King Yehoshua died for your wounds and set you free long ago. You just have to believe..."

"I do," Tairren said in a low tone. "You know I do."

Rafiul smiled at him while his golden eyes twinkled. He took a small vessel from his belt, then poured oil from it onto his wounds. He closed his eyes and both him and Mikhal laid their hands on his. They began to say a prayer of healing as Tairren closed his eyes. After a moment they stopped praying.

Tairren opened his eyes, bringing his hands up. He looked at them with amazement. He felt overwhelmed as he noticed that the wounds were gone. His skin was made new! He wiped the dried blood from his palms and smiled. Solid skin was revealed.

"Take the Sword of Truth in your healed palms, and know that God is mighty," Mikhal said, handing him the beautiful blade. "Use King Yehoshua's ancient sword and smite the darkness with it. Never forget the truth of God, brother."

Tairren gazed at the glorious sword, then looked up at Mikhal. "Should we go back to the camp? I don't have the armor or shield," he said.

Mikhal smiled at him, placing his hand on his shoulder. "No, Brother Tairren. You have the Armor of Righteousness upon you. You wear the armor upon your heart, and always have," he said, placing his hand on Tairren's chest, above his beating heart. "You've shown that when you completed your quest for the sword. You've denied Fiara and retrieved the Sword of Truth...only a righteous man could do that!" Mikhal said with a smile. "Your faith is strong—you have the Shield of Faith, already. You've shown that as well, many times. You are the only one who has believed from the very beginning… You have always had faith…that is why you are the chosen one. Your faith is childlike, but strong…and only the ones who have childlike faith will see the God of Light… You need only the Sword of Truth—because darkness has neither righteousness nor faith. Drive the Sword of Truth deep into the belly of darkness—and then, will darkness be defeated…"

Tairren gazed at him. He looked at the sword again, then back up to Mikhal's gleaming eyes. "I understand," he said in a low tone that held sadness.

Even though it was hard, he accepted what he had to do. He accepted everything that was going on, and everything that was going to happen… His heart seemed to pump with every emotion rattling in it. He squeezed the jeweled hilt of the sword as he thought of Marrisa.

"…She is not the same woman whom you fell in love with long ago," Mikhal finally said. His tone was low and caring.

Tairren's eyes became glossy at Mikhal's comment. He bit his bottom lip then looked away from Mikhal as he took in a deep breath. He thought of Marrisa again as he had always done time and time again over his journey. He thought of how much he still loved her, how he promised to do anything to save her. He knew that he still loved her because that was why he endeared so much pain and suffering. He then thought of his strange dream he had of her… There had to be another chance for her. There had to be another chance…

Her beautiful eyes kept flashing in his mind. Her smile and giggle ripped through his heart. He closed his eyes tightly. He then thought of King Yehoshua. He understood King Yehoshua's legend and quest. He understood why Yehoshua died for them long ago…because He loved them… He realized that King Yehoshua was the root of everything—love was the root everything. Love was the reason why God gave His only son, Yehoshua; and love was why Tairren risked his life for Marrisa.

A tear fell down Tairren's cheek as he walked away from Mikhal. His heart ached, but he knew that King Yehoshua's heart had ached even greater, long ago.

Tairren opened his eyes. "It shall be done," Tairren said quickly, looking out of the window. "…But, please, let your will be done quickly, my God." Tairren continued in a low voice, looking out into the black sky. "My flesh is weak—but my spirit is willing…"

Mikhal silently nodded his head. He glanced at Rafiul, then back at Tairren again. "You must go, Tairren… This is your quest... Rafiul and I will guide you to the Grand-High Mistress. We will be ready for what is to come… And we will take care of the false prophet, Fiara."

Tairren looked back at Mikhal, then nodded his head. He took in a deep breath, then turned towards the darkened doorway. His heart quickened as they went to look for Fiara, and Marrisa: The Grand High Mistress of Darkness…

†

CHAPTER 18

It Is Not Over

Silence lay thickly around the Kingdom of Hanon. The air was filled with dust as the crumbled and burning kingdom began to settle. The distant shrieks of Baal's flying army could be heard as the Hannonite soldiers killed the rest of them. A grey veil hung over the kingdom as the sky burned with an incredible orange hue. After many moments, the shocked people of Hanon began to emerge from the underground caverns. Random coughs and whimpers could be heard throughout the haunting, smoky air. Tears filled their eyes and stained their dirty faces. Many people had fallen because of the attack, and the number of deaths was high.

Gideon peered through the heavy grey atmosphere, trying to get a glimpse at all of the people who had survived.   He wiped the dripping sweat from his face and rubbed his burning eyes. His heart thrashed in his chest as his weary eyes fell upon the destruction of his kingdom. He looked around, wondering when the nightmare would end. As he looked, he noticed the many soldiers were helping each other and the injured people of Hanon.

He watched as the people looked upon the fallen army of Baal. The massive dead creatures lay throughout the kingdom, appearing as dark mounds upon the stone. His eyes went back to the pile of stone before him. He still had an uneasy feeling about the creature that seemed dead beneath the crumbled church. He didn't want to leave his spot, still looking intently at the mound of stone.

"You have done well, Gideon," a deep voice said from behind him. It was one of the tall captains of the Hannonite Legion.

Gideon just nodded his head.

"I believe you are the hero," the large man said, patting his shoulder.

"It is not over until I know that the monster is dead," Gideon said with a serious tone.

He looked down at Gideon, then nodded his head. He patted his shoulder again with his large hand, then turned to leave him.

Gideon watched as many people rose from the stone. Anguish filled the air. Some people limped around while others stayed in their spots, unable to move. His heart broke as he watched many people cry over their fallen loved ones. Death was all around him.

It appeared that they had won, but the destruction said otherwise.

Gideon turned his head quickly towards the rubble. He heard a noise below the stone. He stared vigilantly at the fallen rock, listening sharply.

"It is not over," Gideon said to himself.

Suddenly the stone began to rumble as a low moaning sound came from deep below the mound of rock!

Gideon slowly stepped back, coming away from the large stones. His eyes were wide as he grabbed his sword. His heart sped up as his thoughts ran wild.

The other people and soldiers heard the noise as well. One by one, the people began to pay attention to Gideon and the rumble of the stone as the noise became louder.

"Everyone run for safety!" Gideon yelled out.

Suddenly the stones on the top of the mound began to topple over and tumble down to the earth. The rocks began to move and fall. A loud roar could be heard below the stone as more fallen rock crashed down.

Lord Baal could suddenly be seen, crawling from the pile of stone. He pushed the rubble away with his horns and his great arms. His screams were loud and his great wings moved about, flapping in the cloudy air.

Gideon's heart sunk as he saw that the monster was still alive.

The soldiers began to act quickly as the many people began to scream and hide.

Gideon looked up with wide eyes as Baal stood tall among the pile of rubble. He stretched his wings and arms out upon the smoky air. His eyes glowed behind the wisps of smoke and his growls rippled out over the fallen kingdom. Everything and everyone seemed to freeze in the frightening atmosphere.

"My demise will not come quickly," Lord Baal said as he slowly walked down the stone mound.

Gideon held his sword tightly, watching as the massive creature came closer.

"You may have destroyed our kingdom, but you have not destroyed our hearts!" Gideon shouted out.

"YOU!" Baal shouted, coming closer to Gideon. "You will pay for my fallen legion!"

"You will pay for my fallen kingdom!" Gideon yelled back.

Baal became angry, beginning to scream. He ran full force at Gideon, bringing with him a violent wind. He flapped his hairy wings, beginning to soar through the smoky air. His bulky body flew low, charging Gideon like a mad bull.

Gideon swung his sword as Baal came over him like a mighty shadow. It was hard for him to see through the smoke and dust, so he began to blindly swing his blade like a mad man. Lord Baal was too quick. Gideon groaned as Baal grabbed him, picking him up into the rancid air. Gideon shouted, trying to swing his sword again, but Baal was too powerful and his grip was too strong.

Lord Baal brought him high into the air, over the large flames and towards the castle of Hanon. The smoke and fire billowed below them like a tormenting, scorching sea. His once peaceful kingdom was engulfed in fire.

The castle stood on a high precipice, looking out over the large village of Hanon. As they came towards the castle, Baal began to fly faster. Soaring through the air, the monster threw Gideon towards a large balcony that adorned the front of the majestic castle.

Gideon crashed into the balcony, groaning as he hit the hard stone. He rolled, dropping his sword. He lay for a moment, struggling to get up. His heart shook as he heard Baal's heavy body hit the balcony behind him.

"Get up, human," Baal said in a wicked voice, looking down at the weary boy with his ugly face.

Gideon slowly looked up, breathing hard as the monster stood over him. Blood dripped from his nose and bottom lip. Gideon looked around for his sword, then faltered a bit as he reached for it. He finally got up, wincing in pain as he struggled to stand.

"Your death shall come...but your strife shall come first as I show you the path of the Grand-High Mistress...," Baal said, gesturing his hairy arm out over the lands.

As Baal stepped aside, Gideon could see the full destruction of the lands around him. The skies were black, and orange light could be seen below him as the fires grew. He looked beyond his kingdom at the far-off kingdoms of the land. He could see faint firelight from the far-off civilizations, indicating that they were also ablaze and destroyed.

"No...," Gideon said as tears filled his weary eyes.

"Yes, boy... You may have beaten this fraction of my flying tormentors, but other parts of my great Abaddon legion have already made their way to other kingdoms and villages. Behold! This is the new world-order: Worship the powers of the Grand-High Mistress, who is sovereign of all, or SUFFER!"

Gideon shook his head as his heart thrashed about in his chest. His eyes burned as he looked out over the sullen lands. Darkness was winning, it seemed. He closed his eyes as he thought of his kingdom before that day. He was overwhelmed with emotion as he thought of his loved ones and people. He suddenly thought of Lord Timotheus and his mighty words. "If God is for you...who can be against you?" Gideon's thoughts grew with determination as Lord Timotheus' words resonated in his aching mind.

He opened his eyes, looking up at the ferocious fiend. "It is not over yet," he said.

Lord Baal looked down at him, coming closer. His horns were black and his body was massive. His eyes gleamed and his breaths were loud.

"It is not over until King Yehoshua returns," Gideon said with a straight face.

Baal let out a loud roar that rung in Gideon's ears, then swung his great arm quickly. He hit Gideon hard, sending him flying into a pillar.

Gideon fell to the ground again. His sword fell, clanking against the stone. He slowly stood up, looking up into Baal's threatening eyes.

"The king in which you speak of is dead!" Baal roared out as his eyes flashed. He snorted and shook his mighty head. "The Grand-High Mistress is your king…" Lord Baal stood over the feeble boy. "I want to hear you say your new savior's name… Who is your king, boy?" Baal asked in a threatening voice.

Gideon just helplessly looked up at him.

"SAY IT!!" Lord Baal roared out. His fiery breath came over Gideon as he brought his horned head closer to him.

Gideon flinched as his great voice rung in his ears. He looked up at the massive creature as he leaned against the pillar. He held his arm as his body screamed out in pain. "…King Yehoshua…," he finally said in a feeble voice.

Baal roared again as he slammed his mighty fist into Gideon's body.

Gideon groaned as his body felt broken in the inside. He leaned over as sharp pain exploded over his body, taking his breath away. The pillar behind him cracked when his back was forced into it. He fell to his knees, panting for air. He spit blood as Baal loomed over him.

"I'll ask you one last time, pathetic human. Who-is-your-king?"

Gideon breathed sharply as he sucked in the stale air. He held onto his stomach as the anguish in his body grew. He closed his eyes tightly, knowing that Baal would kill him if he didn't say what the nomed wanted to hear. He quickly opened his eyes. He noticed his sword. He winced in pain as he went to grab his sword that lay below him.

"WHO IS YOUR KING?!!" Baal roared out above him. His eyes flashed like red fire as wisps of steam came from his wet nostrils.

Gideon closed his eyes again, breathing harder. He could feel the heat from Baal's breath all over him. The nomed's raspy breaths and loud snorts echoed in his throbbing ears. His heart pounded, sending drumming pulses throughout his aching body.

But strangely, as he opened his burning eyes, he felt a strange sensation in him, as if a power was coming alive on inside of him. He grabbed the hilt of his sword, squeezing it tightly as he clenched his teeth. Drops of sweat fell from his brow and spit shot from his mouth as passion and anger swelled up inside of him.

"KING YEHOSHUA!" he screamed out, turning quickly with his sword.

Strange power rushed through his arms as he forced his sword into Baal's gut. He screamed, pushing as hard as he could until only the hilt of his sword could be seen upon Baal's stomach. Black fluid gushed from the wound as his sword stayed deep inside of him.

Baal screamed out, quickly grabbing the hilt of Gideon's sword. He pulled the sword from his hairy stomach, allowing more black fluid to spurt from it.

Gideon crawled away from Baal as quickly as he could, hiding behind another large pillar.

Lord Baal let out another loud roar as he swung his bulky arms, hitting them into the pillars. The stone fell, tumbling down upon the edge of the balcony. Baal threw Gideon's sword from the balcony, then crashed his arms into another pillar.

"I will not die so easily! Lucif's power is soaked heavily upon me. But YOU will die!" Baal screamed as more stone fell onto the balcony. "Your body will be crushed!"

Gideon quickly crawled away, hiding behind another pillar that was further away from Baal.

Baal continued to destroy the balcony, pulling more pillars down. He roared as the weight of the fallen stone began to make the large balcony crack. Pieces of the room began to crumble, falling down on their heads.

Gideon grew frantic as he felt the balcony tremble beneath his bruised hands. He pushed himself up, dodging the threatening stones. He looked around quickly, realizing that the balcony was massive, and the only way he was going to survive was if he got off of it and into the castle.

Baal roared again as the balcony began to quake. He continued to walk through the pillars, breaking and smashing them as he went.

Gideon got up quickly, wincing in pain as he pulled himself up. He hobbled over to the next pillar, clenching his teeth as the pain became intense.

Baal noticed him and became angry. He screamed as he began to run towards Gideon. As he ran, the balcony began to crumble and fall down!

Gideon rushed to the threshold as fast as he could go as the stone crashed down behind him. He could hear the loud sounds of the balcony falling and Baal's threatening screams as if they were right behind him. Gideon finally made it to the threshold, falling down as he came into the hall of the castle. He turned quickly as his heart pounded in his chest.

He could see the stone roof and balcony fall right before him. He breathed sharply as he watched Lord Baal roar out. Baal thrashed his arms around as he pounded his large wings against the cold air. The massive nomed fell down with the heavy stone, crashing down to the cliff below them. Gideon closed his eyes as the crashing sounds became fainter.

Gideon fell back, resting on the cold stone of the castle as he tried to catch his breath. He brought his shaken hands to his dirty face, wiping the sweat from his brow and the blood from his nose.

He took in a couple deep breaths, then looked back towards where the balcony was. There was nothing there but dark sky and the glowing orange hue of fire light. He slowly sat up, clenching his teeth as he did.

He stared off into the destroyed lands, breathing deeply as shock began to settle over him.

†

CHAPTER 19
Happenings

Cold winds rippled through the Black Field of Old Blood, howling through the dark trenches and over the rough terrain. The Minslethratian soldiers shuttered as the night became colder. The men's flags rippled and the flames of their torches danced and stretched in the strange winds. The stars and moon seemed to have been dead, absent from that night. The night seemed so black that it was hard to see even yards ahead of them.

It seemed as if the sun set behind the dark clouds a long time ago. The legna and men had been trekking across the Black Field of Old Blood for hours, finding themselves in bizarre areas of the valley. Ancient bones and armor littered the stone, revealing the war that had happened so long ago.

"It seems as if this valley lasts for days," Natalia said, peering through the cold darkness. "There is not one star out... It seems as if morning shall never come."

"Darkness dwells thickly upon these lands," Gaibriul said, holding a torch up. The firelight covered his face. "We must continue to press on."

"How long will it be until we get to the Dark Tower of Sacrifice?" Phillip asked.

"We are closer than you think," Gaibriul said. "I feel a presence as we get closer... I feel it even in the earth below us. It seems as if even the ground and bones are sopped with darkness. These old bones we walk over are the bones of Minslethrate's fallen warriors...and the ancient bones of the enemy..."

A grimaced look came over their faces as they looked down at the old bones. Some of the bones were massive, as if they belonged to huge beings. Other bones looked like they belonged to unearthly beings, having horns jutting from their skulls and long claws protruding from their bony hands. They belonged to nomed most likely, they thought.

"Long ago, during the ancient wars of these lands, many fought, including legna and nomed. You see, there has always been a war between light and darkness, and always will be until the end of time."

"When will it ever stop?" King Julpen asked. He rode on his horse beside them, moving along with the solemn soldiers.

"It never will as long as this world survives," Gaibriul said. "Only when King Yehoshua returns, will it end."

"When will this happen, Gaibriul?" Natalia asked, peering up at him.

"That is the only question I can not answer, for I do not know," Gaibriul responded. "Only He knows."

They grew quiet, continuing to travel the lands. The winds seemed to grow colder, and the air seemed to get thicker the closer they went. The winds blew at their armor, making them shutter every now and then. Most of the men seemed to have grown tired, and their faces held anxiousness. The thought of war lay heavily on their minds. No one knew what that night would bring, and that was the most terrifying thought of all.

As they continued to move, something came flying down from the sky. It caught Dolsia's attention first, making her become more alert.

"There is something in the sky!" Dolsia said, pointing.

The swift creature caught everyone's attention then. It swooped through the black sky then glided down towards the ground. They all recognized the glorious creature. It was Cherbim! His glorious wings and feathers spread beautifully as his white fur moved in the winds.

Shortly after Cherbim landed upon a large boulder, Lilly galloped out from the darkness as well. Her white body and long main stood out in the shadows.

"Lilly!" Natalia exclaimed, excitedly. Her heart fluttered at the sight of Marrisa's horse. "But where is Tairren?"

Gaibriul quickly went to Lilly, calming her by touching her course hair and placing his hands upon her neck. Gaibriul closed his eyes, sensing and listening to Lilly's emotions. "Tairren and Rafiul have set them free… They went up the mountain towards the temple." After a moment, Gaibriul opened his eyes, glancing up at Cherbim who sat quietly. "They are safe then," he said, looking over at Phillip and Natalia.

"They are safe," Natalia repeated, as if to herself.

"How shall we get the armor to Tairren?" Dolsia asked.

Gaibriul looked over at Natalia and Phillip, faintly smiling at them. "The armor and shield are for the ones who sought them," he said out loud as he pulled himself back onto his beast.

Natalia and Phillip glanced at each other, then back at Gaibriul. They were surprised and never expected the armor to be for them. They thought it was for the one true hero.

"Uriel, bless them with their armor," Gaibriul said, catching her attention. He looked back at them again. "When one searches for true faith and righteousness, it shall be addend unto them."

"But, forgive me if I'm wrong," Phillip spoke up. "I thought the armor was for Tairren, who is the key and hero in this whole—quandary."

"Phillip, you are all a key and a hero in this whole *quandary*, as you have put it," Gaibriul said, looking at each one of them. "Everyone who is involved in this is a piece in the grand scheme of this world."

"Every one of you is a hero," Uriel added, standing next to her angelic beast, Eralim.

Natalia and Phillip watched as Uriel pulled the armor and shield from Eralim's large back. She gave Phillip the Shield of Faith first, then gave

Natalia the Armor of Righteousness. "Wear this upon your being in war, and upon your heart, always," she said with a loving smile.

Uriel looked at Phillip, then smiled a lovely smile. "Phillip, remember when you first came to our congregation, and received your wing pendant?" she asked. Phillip nodded his head as he pulled his pendant from his tunic. "Mikhal prophesied over you then. Remember his words?" Phillip's eyes contained confusion as he peered at her. "He said that you are like the mighty beast upon the earth—and that you would do great things because of your dedication and bravery. Now I shall reveal something to you... Your shield shall block darkness and death... In time, your kingdom shall rise up on mighty wings just as your faith has." She smiled again at Phillip, making him smile back.

"And you, Lady Natalia," she said, directing her attention on her. Natalia's eyes lit up. "Mikhal prophesied something for our witty and compassionate lady," Uriel said with a smile. "He said that you would help a lost soul because of your love and wit. That lost soul was the one who wears your wing pendant now..." Uriel motioned towards Dolsia. Natalia and Dolsia glanced at each other, softly smiling. "And, because of you, she is no longer lost... And now I must prophesy something over you. Your spirit shall never die...and your legacy of strength and courage will carry on in the hearts of others..." Uriel watched as Natalia looked away, as if she were thinking hard about what Uriel had said. "Do not fret, Natalia. Armor may not protect your body wholly, but your righteousness and faith shall protect your spirit for eternity."

Uriel glanced at both Phillip and Natalia, smiling at them with her luminous eyes. She softly took their hands and brought them to one another, gently cupping them together. "Married hearts never die," Uriel said in a soft tone, only so they could hear.

Natalia and Phillip looked at each other, still holding each other's hands. Their faces were serious at first, because of their nervousness. After a moment, they smiled at one another.

King Julpen watched from his horse, having a faint smile upon his face. He felt blessed because of them being young and filled with bravery and strength.

"Tairren has the Sword of Truth," Gaibriul added, looking at King Julpen.

King Julpen was quiet for a moment as he thought of the young commoner boy. "Tairren must be a mighty man to possess such greatness," King Julpen said.

"Tairren has extraordinary blood running through his veins. His ancestors once ruled these lands." King Julpen raised his eyebrows, becoming taken aback by Gaibriul's words. "Tairren is the rightful Prince of Minslethrate," Gaibriul exclaimed.

Everyone standing near him heard him, and looked very surprised. Even King Julpen looked surprised, not knowing what to say.

"Tairren is a mighty young man who contains a servant's heart... He is the ancestor of King Peter, who was one of the followers of King Yehoshua. These kings are in written legends, and are part of history. Tairren is the Prince of Minslethrate..."

Gaibriul's face was serious but truthful at the same time. His eyes seemed to glow even in the darkness.

King Julpen looked into his eyes, not saying anything. He nodded his head, then glanced at Sir Hawkington. "All these years...I've wondered who the heir to my throne was. All these years I wondered why my legacy seemed dead..."

"You are part of a grand scheme," Gaibriul said, having a softer look on his face. "Your path has been set before you by the great God of Light."

"All these years I thought I've been cursed," King Julpen said, looking away from Gaibriul. "I've often wondered why such tragedy was brought over my life."

"Your past is ridden with tragedy, but your future holds a path that will bring an end to this madness, and Tairren is part of it." Gaibriul looked around at everyone who was listening, then brought his gaze back over to King Julpen. "This kingdom was blessed by God a long time ago. It may seem like the end, but when the morning comes...the sun will rise again." He looked back out over the crowd of men who watched. "Remember, the sun will rise again!"

King Julpen nodded his head as everyone began to perk up.

"If Tairren is the future king of Minslethrate...then he should be kept safe," King Julpen said.

"He is upon the temple as we speak," Gaibriul said quickly. "Whatever happens...it happens because it is meant to." Gaibriul looked out over the men. "Lead your men, King Julpen. We are near the bowels of darkness and they must be led."

King Julpen looked at Gaibriul, nodding his head. He knew that everything the Archlegna said was from truth. He respected everything he said, wanting to honor him and the God of Light.

"Ride on, men!" King Julpen shouted. "Keep your wits and hearts near the light as we come near the Dark Tower!"

The crowd of men and legna began to move. They held their torches and weapons tightly as they moved together.

✞✞✞

Tairren crept through the dark halls of the tower, following closely behind Rafiul and Mikhal. The light from their torches sent shadows dancing on the walls all around them as they went. The halls were cold and dreadfully silent. The firelight sat over them as they went. But as they crept through the quiet halls, strange shadows seemed to follow them. Wherever the light touched, the shadowy creatures that stalked them would shrink back quickly.

"We are surrounded," Mikhal said in a low, calm voice. "But don't worry, they will not touch us."

Tairren looked around him, noticing that if he looked hard enough, he could see movement in the darkness. The black nomed mingled with the shadows and flittered about. He could see them move even by the corners of his eyes. He looked back into the firelight, keeping his thoughts away from the thick darkness.

"Why haven't they tried to attack us yet?" Tairren asked.

"They are frightened of us," Rafiul answered, holding his torch out. His eyes glared below his white brows.

They continued to move through the old corridor, realizing that they were advancing into a large chamber. The chamber was black and soft sounds of raspy whispers could be heard all throughout the place. They slowly made it to the center of the cold chamber, moving with wide eyes. They stood with their backs touching, holding their torches out in the air. They could only see the perspiration from their breaths among the moving torch light. They peered intently into the darkness, noticing that relentless nomed moved all around them. The nomed came close, breathing in their ears and crowding all around them. There squeals and raspy throats became loud. They could see that they were surrounded by many nomed, but the darkness of the chamber covered most of them.

"We need more light," Tairren said.

After a moment, he heard someone walking towards them. It sounded like metal clanking as the person came closer. They could hear the creeping nomed move quickly, giving way to the approaching person.

"Who's there?!" Mikhal demanded.

It was quiet for a moment, then they could see someone slowly stepping into the soft firelight of their torches. It was a tall woman, clad in golden armor which revealed parts of her lean body. The soft firelight touched her protected feet first, then went up her body as she approached them. Her armor sparkled like precious jewels. Long, sheer fabric fell from her waist and arms. She nearly looked like some kind of being of light... But the thing that made the woman appear startling, was the skull that covered her face. She wore a large ram's skull on her head, as if it were her crown. The skull was massive and covered her whole head like a helmet. It had large horns that spiraled out and the whole skull was painted gold. The eye sockets of the skull were black and haunting. She looked like a mixture of both nomed and legna.

"It is Fiara," Tairren said through clenched teeth.

Fiara suddenly lifted her hands. Then, as if by magic, the hall became filled with light as the torches on the walls and the large candelabrum above them became filled with firelight. They quickly looked around. As the light filled the chamber, the dark creatures that lurked around them began to disappear into the room's dancing shadows.

"Welcome," she said.

They held their swords, glaring at the mysterious, golden woman.

"Jezebel," Rafiul grunted between clenched teeth.

Fiara just chuckled.

"Where is Marrisa?!" Tairren demanded.

Fiara slowly walked towards them, placing her hands behind her back. Her armor gleamed as she moved. "The Grand-High Mistress is in the throne room, Tairren. She is waiting for blood to be spilled as the legna and men of Minslethrate draw closer."

Tairren looked around, noticing another doorway on the other side of the chamber. It was the only way out besides the door they came through. He had a chance to find Marrisa. He held the Sword of Truth tightly as he slowly crept towards the door, never taking his eyes off of Fiara.

"I see the legna have helped you, once again, Tairren… You may have been cut from your bounds and gifted with your sword…but they shall not save you in the end." Fiara said calmly, looking back at Rafiul and Mikhal as she spoke.

Tairren glanced at Mikhal quickly as he backed up towards the doorway. Mikhal nodded his head at him, signaling for him to go quickly. Tairren obeyed and hurried into the darkened doorway, knowing that Fiara would never turn her back on the legna.

"Fools, you all are," Fiara smirked, pulling two swords from behind her back. Her long golden swords were incredibly sharp looking and curved elegantly. "So, the boy runs to his death. He may run, but it is the Grand-High Mistress who has pulled him here…" She stared at them from the ugly skull head that masked her face. She chuckled again, studying their glowing faces. "I have been longing to see a legna… And now that I look upon your light-ridden faces; I've decided that, I…despise you. I despise every one of you light-ridden beasts."

"You will be punished, Fiara," Mikhal said, glaring at her. "You are the symbol of false beliefs. You speak of unity and peace…but your fruit says otherwise. Your workings of darkness will not be dismissed lightly. Your destruction will cause you much pain in your future…"

"Are your words designed to frighten me? Spare me the weak threats, *legna*," Fiara chuckled as she held both of her swords up, one in front of her and the other above her head. She quickly went into a fighting stance, arching her back and bending her knees. "I can take both of you rotten legna. You are no match for me. I've taken John's head from his body already. Oh, how I would love to take yours."

"I pity you, Fiara," Mikhal said. "Being born from fallen legna, deceiving followers of Lucif, you can't even help it that you are destined for an eternity of fiery death."

Fiara glared at them. "I *AM* fire!" she shouted.

The legna stood tall, not moving as Fiara remained still like a statue. The tension was heavy as they never looked away from each other. After many intense moments, they began to fight! Their swords clashed loudly, bouncing off of the stone walls.

Fiara was quick, spinning and slashing her swords upon the air. Her blades were fast and made humming sounds in the cold air. She dodged the legna's strikes as if she knew their every move. Every move they made, she retaliated back at them, even faster than what they had delivered.

The legna jumped over her sweeping kicks and quickly dashed beneath her powerful swings. Sparks flew from their swords as their blades smashed against each other.

Rafiul swung hard at Fiara, making her drop one of her swords. But she retaliated quickly by spinning and sweeping her leg beneath him, making him fall to the ground. Mikhal swung his sword down at her, nearly taking her head off. She dodged his blade by moving quickly, doing a back flip away from them.

She grabbed her sword quickly from the ground, then ran away from them down the dark corridor.

"Loathsome, cowardice!" Rafiul shouted, chasing after her.

Mikhal dashed behind Rafiul, following right behind them down the dark hallway.

They ran quickly, realizing that they came into a much smaller chamber. The chamber was dark and had no light in it, except for the faint light that came in through the window, which was not much at all. They searched the small chamber, quickly. They stood for a moment, catching their breaths. But before they could move again, someone caught them by surprise; angry swords swung in the dark air. Both the legna sensed the attack and swung their swords back, catching the hit in midair. A large spark lit up the small chamber for a brief moment, revealing that it was Fiara. Her Golden ram's skull flashed in the black room.

Fiara growled, then ran towards the window, quickly jumping onto the ledge like an animal. She disappeared through the window as Rafiul and Mikhal dashed towards her.

"Go after her!" Mikhal commanded quickly, peering out of the window. He could see her armor as she swiftly moved down the side of the mountain. "She is making her way towards the Black Field of Old Blood. She is prepared for battle and it will begin soon... I will go find Tairren."

Rafiul nodded his head, then quickly climbed through the window, disappearing behind the stone wall.

Mikhal left quickly, running back through the corridors and towards the throne room of the tower.

✝✝✝

Fiara jumped from rock to rock, crouching down and appearing like that of a swift cat. She climbed down the mountain with ease, making her way towards the valley.

She stopped abruptly, sensing a familiar power she had always lusted for. She stood up straight, looking up towards the tall tower that loomed over her. She pulled off her skull headdress, searching for the entity that was pulling at her darkened spirit. Her golden eyes flashed as she caught the Grand-High Mistress watching her from a large balcony that stuck out from the front of the gloomy tower.

Even in the murky night, she could see the devious silhouette of her new master. The tall shadowy queen silently stared at her, standing still like a statue. The thick mists flittered around her body, moving through the air as if electricity controlled it.

"Receive your gift at the door," a dark voice said in Fiara's head. The voice was deep and wicked, but alluring to Fiara's ears. "The beast shall rise at your command…"

Fiara stared at the Grand-High Mistress, never looking away. After a moment of deranged bliss, she quickly looked towards the deep trench. Her eyes became large, yearning to see what dwelled in the bowels of darkness for her. She put the large skull back over her head, then started to creep towards the black doorway in the earth. Her heart thrashed with madness. As she came closer, she could hear the low moans and growls that came from the deep recesses of the earth. Fiara stood at the edge, looking down into the black abyss. Black mists billowed out, covering her body with its treacherous hands. Her heart pounded and her flesh tingled.

"Powers of the dark fire!" Fiara shouted out. Her voice echoed into the deep trench. She stretched her arms out as the mists swirled around them. "I accept the gift you offer to me! In the name of the Grand-High Mistress, RISE!"

Suddenly the mists became blacker as they erupted from the trench, appearing like ash. The deep growls and moans became louder, reverberating out of the darkness like an overwhelming alarm. The earth began to quake as something massive came nearer to the opening of the abyss. Many fiery eyes could be seen through the murky mists, coming closer.

Fiara began to laugh, raising her hands into the air as a great monstrous creature crawled out from the darkness! It had many heads that roared and screamed. Anyone could hear its screams from miles away, it seemed.

"Yessss! Come to me, dragon of darkness!" Fiara screamed out as the massive creature pulled itself from the abyss. It crouched right before her, gazing down at her with its many fiery eyes.

The creature was bigger than any earthly animal. It walked on all fours and had a massive tail that was as big as a tree trunk. It had great fanged paws and its body was covered in black scales and course hair. It had seven heads with each one having a long, pointed horn; except for the main head, which had four horns that resembled a jagged crown. The ugly heads looked like a cross between that of a ferocious dog and a serpent, having roaring, toothy snouts and beady eyes. All of its eyes glowed red through the black mists. Fire seemed to burn within the evil creature.

The beast beckoned Fiara to ride among its massive back by pulling at her with the dark mists that surrounded them. She obeyed its wishes, quietly walking before the insidious fiend. The heavy darkness around her elevated her into the air, bringing her upon its back. Its touch vitalized her, filling her with loathsome anger and sinister powers. She threw her head back as she became one with the beast.

Fiara opened her eyes, gazing into the valley before her. "We shall rule the south. We shall be worshiped by the world!" she shouted. "Bring forth your powers of darkness, and smite them! Bring the fire of destruction upon them all!" she commanded. "The Earth shall be cleansed and the new commandments shall rise!" She screamed out excitedly as she raised her arms into the black mists. "The infidels shall be CRUCIFIED!"

The mighty beast roared out from its many heads, sending a loud noise upon the south that made the earth quake. Fire burned behind its many eyes and in its many mouths as it looked around the lands. Suddenly, it leapt over the trench, landing on the other side with a crash.

The commands from Fiara and the screams from the beast awakened their new army. Right behind the monster, many nomed, by the hundreds, began to rise out from the opened doorway, pouring and spreading out upon the earth like dark waters. The dark army screamed and growled, beginning to make its way into the Black Field of Old Blood.

The Grand-High Mistress watched from the balcony with her shiny black eyes. The powers within her became so strong that her aura could literally be seen all around her, moving about in the air as black smoke. A wicked smile came over her white face as the beginnings of a great war began to come alive upon the south.

✝✝✝

Rafiul crouched behind a large boulder. He squeezed the hilt of his sword as he watched Fiara sit atop the great beast. The golden ram skull on her head glowed among the great beast's eyes.

He became inundated with anger towards Lucif and his darkness as his eyes gazed upon the blasphemy that rose with power in the south. He watched with a heavy heart as the thousands of eager nomed rushed upon the valley. He grew irritated at the thought of Fiara. There were so many times he could've killed her, but missed his chance every time. She became the bane of even his quest upon the earth.

He closed his eyes as he heard and felt the destruction of the world all around him. He could feel far off kingdoms screaming out. He could feel their pain even on his fingertips. "Help us, Father of Lights," he prayed.

He opened his golden eyes, noticing that Fiara was beginning to lead Lucif's army into the Black Field of Old Blood. He looked further into the valley. He could see light from many torches off in the distance. His fellow people and Minslethratian brothers were coming closer. His eyes intensified as he could literally see the war between light and darkness beginning to unfold right before him.

"Fly to me my brother, Cherbim," Rafiul said in a low voice. He called to the beast, communicating with Cherbim with his mind.

He searched the sky with his eager eyes. Cherbim was the only way he could get to his comrades quickly. He could sense his friend nearby, so he called again to Cherbim with his mind, even stronger. He knew he had to get to his fellow people, quickly. He thought of Tairren, but he knew that Mikhal would be with him.

As he waited for Cherbim, he crept among the shadows of the jagged rocks, following alongside the army of darkness.

He never took his eyes off of Fiara as he squeezed the hilt of his sword. His hand began to tingle. No matter the danger, no matter what was going to happen, he knew that destroying her was his yearning.

†

CHAPTER 20
Fire and Ash

Fire fell from the black sky, sending ash and heat all over the northern Kingdom of Minslethrate. The Golden Land was matted with the destruction of darkness. Bright orange firelight consumed many parts of the kingdom, sending billows of black smoke around the tall castle. It seemed as if all of Hell was loosened upon the small kingdom.

Pandemonium filled the atmosphere. Screams and cries rose loudly as the people fought their way inside the strong walls of the castle and church of the town-square. The streets were filled with fallen buildings and the marketplace was ablaze with roaring flames. The once peaceful and beautiful kingdom was falling apart, reflecting its damaged past.

The beasts of darkness would not relent. The flying nomed continued to snatch running people from the streets and the running nomed mauled the people who tried to fight back. Their lust for blood was strong. They continued to spread the fires among the buildings and trees. Their main goal was to destroy, punishing everyone who denied the Grand-High Mistress.

The soldiers fought their hardest, trying to keep the nomed away from the castle and church. But their energy and hope began to fade as the nomed continued to grow in numbers.

King Baffmit flew through the air, watching as his legion terrorized the kingdom. His large, feathered wings kept pounding the air, keeping his body still as his horned head gazed down at the running people and burning buildings. His evil eyes roamed about the chaos below him, searching for anyone who was not yielding to the darkness.

But Baffmit mainly had his mind on the ones who tried to stop him earlier that night. He wanted the ones, who had spoken of the legendary king's name, dead. He wanted them to suffer, especially the woman, and the man who was Minslethrate's temporary leader. The woman named Moral and the man called Lord Fernund were on his mind, and they were the main ones he wanted dead.

†††

Moral and Sora ran together, trying not to get lost in the chaos. One moment they were fighting the nomed near Sir Andor and Lord Fernund, and the next, they were lost in the frantic crowds. They were moving towards the castle, trying to get through the throngs of people as they went.

They held onto their swords tightly, trying to protect themselves and other unarmed people from the treacherous nomed. They used their swords more than they could count, swinging at the nomed that charged them among the ground and the flying ones that dove down at them. They saw many people get plucked from the ground, being taken somewhere into the sky. Their hearts were heavy. They witnessed many people dying, feeling terrible for not being able to help them all.

They were almost to the castle gates! Moral's eyes lit up as she saw that the castle still stood. The fires hadn't even come near the castle. She grabbed Sora's hand, pulling her quickly towards the tall iron gates.

"We are nearly there!" Moral shouted, turning her head to look at Sora.

Sora's eyes were wide as she franticly looked all around at the madness. People were pushing each other, fighting their way into the safe places. Many soldiers acted as the peacekeepers, shouting commands to calm them down and steady the flow of the frantic people. Other soldiers continued to fight off the nomed that relentlessly attacked.

"Look into the sky, Moral!" Sora shouted, grabbing Moral's arm.

Moral turned quickly, looking into the chaotic sky. At first, she just saw the relentless smoke and random flying nomed, but then she saw two bright red lights that glowed like fire. Her gray eyes widened as she noticed what Sora was yelling about.

A large winged shadow with terrifying eyes was flying straight for them. It was King Baffmit! He stretched his long arms and fingers towards them as he roared. He sounded like thunder. His feathery wings flapped powerfully, beating against the smoky veil.

"Run!" Moral screamed. "Everyone, take cover!"

People looked into the sky, beginning to scream louder. The crowds dispersed as much as they could as the mighty nomed came at them with vengeance.

As Baffmit came closer, they could see that fire was building up in his retched jaws, ready to come pouring out over them!

Moral and Sora ran through the chaos and into the courtyard of the castle, franticly looking for a place to hide.

"It's too late!" Sora shouted. "We're trapped!"

Baffmit came down in a heavy wind, sending out his roars as the hot fire began to spark out from his mouth.

They ran along the wall, looking up as Baffmit spread his wings above them. He stopped abruptly, bringing his ugly horned head back. He screamed again, forcing flames out of his snout. Moral and Sora ran between the trees as fast as they could, dodging the heat. The massive flames spilled out over the trees, filling it with Baffmit's orange wrath.

"There's a side door," Moral shrieked, spotting the small door that was the same shade of gray as the stone of the castle.

They ran towards the side door with nervousness upon them. Their hearts thrashed in their bosoms as they came closer to their safety. They looked up, noticing that Baffmit was roaring in the sky right above them in the black smoke. His eyes glowed behind the smoke. They could tell that he was angry and building up fire in his throat again.

They screamed as they got to the door, yanking at it. It was locked! Moral hit the heavy door until her hands throbbed. "Open the door, please!" she screamed out as tears built up in her frantic eyes.

Sora began to bang on the door as well with her heavy fists. "Open up, hurry!" she screamed out over Moral's cries.

They noticed that Baffmit was flying down at them, quickly. His wings opened up in the smoky air as he inhaled a deep breath. The frantic women began to scream as they pushed themselves into the door. Their eyes widened as orange light began to swirl around in Baffmit's jaws, spreading out around his ugly muzzle.

"God, help us!" Moral cried out.

Baffmit roared out another powerful stream of fire. The flames were bigger and went out over the women in a bright plume of consuming light.

Just when they thought they were going meet their death in the fire, the door opened. They flew into the doorway, falling down onto the hard ground. The frantic woman who opened the door quickly slammed it shut. They scurried away from the door as Baffmit's fiery wrath could be heard hitting the other side. Their hearts thrashed about as they saw the flames dancing in the crack below the door.

"Thank you! Thank you!" Moral cried out.

Both of them stood up, looking all around them. They were standing in the servant's quarters. The room was filled with crying, frantic people. The woman who let them in was a castle servant. She was older and looked at them nervously as sweat dripped down her wrinkled brow.

"I heard your cries," the woman said. She quickly locked the iron door, flinching at first because of the heat that radiated from it.

Just as she finished locking it, loud sounds could be heard on the other side. The women backed away from the door, bringing their hands to their mouths. The sounds were loud and intimidating, as if the massive creature was pounding on the other side. His loud roars and growls shook them as the door shuttered with every heavy hit. The people inside the room began to cry and scream. Then, after a moment, it became quiet. Everyone in the room became quiet as they stared at the door. Moments passed, revealing that Baffmit had gone away.

"It will find a way in!" the woman said, franticly. She shook her head as she brought her hands over her face. She began to cry.

"We must stay calm," Moral said, placing her hands on the woman's arms. "We must stay strong!" she yelled out to the room of weary people. "My Lord, watch over these people and give them strength, as you have given me," Moral prayed with closed eyes.

The people looked at one another, watching Moral curiously.

"Yes, we are frightened! And we are tired and confused," she said as she looked at everyone. "We wonder where God is in all of this. We wonder why things are the way they are... But we must be strong, unto the end. When the world falls, He shall be there to pick us back up in the end! Let's hold onto King Yehoshua in our hearts. Let's hold onto His promises! Let's hold onto each other... I know you are frightened," Moral said in a softer voice, "for I am frightened too. But we must not let fear consume us... Light shall come when it is all over," Moral faintly smiled, comforting them. "We must believe that...light shall come..."

Moral looked over at Sora, who smiled and nodded her head. They understood each other, and they understood that they had to help others. The women quickly walked to the other people, comforting them. They were the light in that chamber. Among the fear and sadness, they were the light.

Loud bangs and roars started again outside the door as Baffmit continued to try and burst through the stone wall...

†††

Lord Fernund ran towards the castle as anger pumped in his heart. Earlier he saw King Baffmit blowing fire towards the castle, terrorizing the people. He saw his people crying and falling down upon the ashes and soot. He saw his once beautiful kingdom shake beneath the powers of darkness. There were so many frightened people. There were so many people dying.

Screams echoed in his ears as his heart beat loudly. Sweat dripped down his face as adrenaline rushed through his throbbing veins. He squeezed the hilt of his sword until his clammy hand became numb.

"Baffmit!" Lord Fernund screamed out, noticing that the monster was releasing fire into the courtyard of the castle.

The fires consumed the blooming trees that lined the walls.

He ran faster. His gaze was locked on Baffmit. Right then he wanted the king of the nomed dead. He wanted his horned head off, rolling upon the ground.

"Lord Fernund!" Sir Andor yelled, trying to catch his attention. He noticed that Lord Fernund was running straight for King Baffmit. "My Lord!"

Lord Fernund stopped right before the courtyard, bringing his sword up. Smoke filled the empty spaces of the once charming courtyard.

"My Lord, don't act irrationally!" Sir Andor shouted, pulling his shoulder. "He can not be stopped by merely one man!"

"Irrationally?!" Lord Fernund spat. "This thing has brought madness upon us all! My family is torn apart because of the likes of him!" Lord

Fernund shouted, grabbing Sir Andor's tunic. "I shall die trying to kill him!"

Sir Andor looked into his shaken face. His intense, dark eyes glittered with emotion and madness. He understood his troubles and the pain he was going through. He pressed his lips together, taking in a deep breath. He responded to Lord Fernund by nodding his head.

Lord Fernund released his tunic, then turned his gaze back on the roaring fiend.

"Baffmit!" Lord Fernund shouted out in a strong voice. "Look at me, you disgusting creature!"

Baffmit was pounding at a small door, trying to force his way into it.

Lord Fernund walked into the middle of the courtyard. The trees were on fire, sending smoke all around him. Cold winds blew at the smoke, making it whirl in the dark sky. The firelight from the trees glowed off of his rugged face. He glared at the creature, never taking his burning eyes from him.

Baffmit suddenly stopped punching at the door, turning his head towards Lord Fernund. He stood up straight, spreading his black wings out among the dreadful air. His eyes burned like the fire.

Lord Fernund stayed quiet, taking deep breaths as his heart pounded in his aching chest. He pressed his dried lips together. He could feel his blood throbbing through his skin as he looked up at the massive nomed.

"You... I've been looking for you... Foolish man, you are," Baffmit said, coming closer to him. "You wish to fight the most powerful nomed alive?!"

Baffmit let out a loud raspy chuckle, bringing his taunting gaze closer to him.

Lord Fernund glared up at him as his muscles quivered. He looked small compared to the beastly creature, but he wasn't backing down. He breathed quickly. Anger covered his face as he brought his sword up. "You will die, Baffmit," he said in a shaken voice. "Every breath that I have will be used to kill you."

Baffmit laughed again. His eyes flashed behind the smoke that wisped past him. "So be it..."

Baffmit looked down at him, waiting for him to move. He studied his nervous mannerism and his intense, human eyes. Baffmit's wicked eyes began to burn brightly as growls rumbled deep down in his throat. His gaze was frightening. The man's bravery and boldness angered him. He roared loudly, showing his jagged teeth. He brought his hands out and thrashed his feathered wings. His wings glistened like black fluid in the firelight. He let out a loud sound that broke the tension, then quickly lunged at Lord Fernund.

Lord Fernund moved quickly, swinging his sword at the massive creature. He hadn't fought with a sword in many years, but he still had his agility. His silver blade reflected the fiery light, slicing through the smoke that danced between him and the massive nomed. He cut King Baffmit's large hand off. He felt Baffmit's strength as his blade went through. Fernund inhaled quickly, falling down to the ground because of Baffmit's resilient, swinging arm.

Baffmit screamed out, crinkling his ugly face as he held his wrist. His massive hand tumbled across the grass as black fluid squirted from his opened wrist.

Lord Fernund got up quickly. His heart fluttered with empowerment as he looked at Baffmit's wounded wrist. He held his sword tightly and stood strong. He breathed quickly as he watched King Baffmit move.

The mighty nomed's eyes darted at Lord Fernund. He swung his arms, trying to hit Fernund with his other fist. His wings sprung open and his snout release a cloud of perspiration.

The lord retaliated, fighting back with his sword. Being half Baffmit's size, he dodged most of his powerful blows.

Sir Andor watched from afar, feeling empowered by Lord Fernund's bravery. He knew that Lord Fernund was not a warlord, but only a nobleman and merchant. Lord Fernund's boldness revealed how courageous he truly was. Right then he knew he had to do something. He couldn't just watch Lord Fernund fight the beast alone. He looked around quickly, signaling to a group of soldiers. They obeyed, coming to Sir Andor quickly.

"Shoot him!" Sir Andor shouted. He motioned his sword through the air.

The sounds of their bows popping in the air filled Sir Andor's ears with excitement. Swift arrows pelted Baffmit's side, making him scream out. He looked quickly over at the men, shaking his horned head as he let out an angry cry.

Lord Fernund ceased that perfect timing, shoving his sword deep into Baffmit's stomach. He yelled out with frustration, pushing his blade as hard as he could into Baffmit's massive body. Black blood speckled his face as the nomed's stomach gave in to his sword.

King Baffmit let out a terrifying scream as he hit Lord Fernund away from him, sending him flying to the ground.

Then, something happened suddenly that took Lord Fernund off guard. It all occurred so fast, shocking even Sir Andor and his soldiers. King Baffmit came at him with an angry cry, pulling the sword from his stomach. The blade slid out in a flash, dripping with black fluid. He held Lord Fernund's sword up in his one massive hand. Lord Fernund went to move, but it was too late. Baffmit heaved the sword down, pushing it into Lord Fernund's tender stomach.

Lord Fernund's eyes shot open as he felt the sharp blade continue to go down through his muscles and intestines. Pain surged throughout his shaken body. Baffmit had driven the sword deep into the earth below him, nailing him to the ground. Bright red blood shot from his lips, trickling down his quivering chin and cheek. Only the hilt could be seen.

Lord Fernund quickly brought his shaken hands to his stomach, feeling the solid hilt that seemed like part of his body. He took quick breaths. Blood shot from his mouth as he looked up at the dark creature standing menacingly above him.

He didn't hear any more of the chaos around him as he stared. Even King Baffmit began to slowly fade away from his sight. At first there was a ringing, but then silence came over him as he could feel the life inside of him slowly leaving his shaken body. Quick images flashed before his eyes. He saw the many seasons of his life all at once. He saw his precious daughter, Natalia. He saw Sora and her graciousness. And he saw his wife... Then, after thousands of thoughts ran before his eyes which only lasted a second, he saw a strange light...

Peaceful light came over his mind's eyes as heavy silence settled over his dead flesh. His cold body lay silent and still as the chaos of the kingdom burst all around it.

Sir Andor saw it. He saw Lord Fernund die below the evil presence of King Baffmit. He grew angry as he watched King Baffmit let out a loud, roaring laugh into the sky.

Sir Andor began to shout, saliva flying. He angrily thrust his sword into the smoky air. His voice cried out with emotion as he began to run towards Baffmit. He lost all control. Many soldiers began to follow suit, charging the massive creature with their weapons raised. More arrows blanketed the air, falling down at King Baffmit.

They screamed out with intensity, avenging Lord Fernund, the fallen kingdom, and the many people who had died upon the hands of darkness.

†

CHAPTER 21
Into the Bowels of Darkness

Tairren hurried through a dark corridor. His heart raced as he continued to look for Marrisa. She had to be near. He remembered that Fiara had said that she was in the throne room. But where was the throne room? As he ran through the Dark Tower, he realized how great it was. There were many old chambers and corridors, and a number of dirty halls and staircases. Some of the chambers and corridors had fallen in long ago, allowing cold winds to rush through.

He quickly came to an old wooden door. The light from his torch danced on the heavy door, making shadows move all around him. He pushed at the door, making it creek open. He stood in the threshold as the sound and feeling of wind rushed over him. His flame moved about quickly, indicating that it was being played with by the winds. Tairren slowly crept in at first like he did every corridor and hall. He became irritated. He had entered into another long hallway. But there were tall windows on the right wall. The door on the other side seemed far away.

He moved cautiously into the narrow corridor, realizing that he was the only one in it. He began to move quicker, glancing out of the windows that lined the wall as he went. The sound of low roars echoed up the side of the tower, coming through the window and into the hallway.

He stopped abruptly at one of the windows. The cold wind rushed past his face. He peered out of it, wondering what the loud, ferocious sound was. The low, rumbling sound was coming from the valley below him. His attention was quickly grabbed by the sea of lights that covered the valley below the Dark Tower of Sacrifice. It seemed so close but so far away. A gust of wind came over him again, along with another distant roar, sending tingles across his skin. His mind raced as he became overwhelmed by the many torches that glowed way down below.

"No…," he whispered to himself as he saw hundreds of glowing eyes moving towards the sea of lights.

Then he saw where the roars were coming from… The thunderous screams were coming from a behemoth that led the dark army towards the lights. He was taken aback by the sight. His heart raced as war was coming alive before him. He wanted to help his people, but couldn't, and his heart shook because of it. But they seemed to not be fighting yet, because it seemed that miles of valley sat between the nomed and the many lights. But he knew it would begin soon because of the great speed that the nomed possessed.

He realized that he had to find Marrisa, quickly. He continued to look out of the window, trying to get an idea of where he was at. He brought his burning eyes away from the valley and up the cliffs, towards another faint light. He saw the firelight glowing a little way away from where he stood, across the black abyss below him. He could see that the light came from another tower. He peered through the darkness, understanding that the tower was the tallest tower in the temple. He could make out a large balcony, jutting from the side of the great tower. Just then he knew the tower that he was gazing at was where the throne room resided.

Tairren's heart sped up as he began to run down the windy hallway. Knowing that he was close empowered him.

As he made it to the other side of the corridor, the sound of running footsteps startled him.

"Tairren!" a familiar voice echoed down the hallway.

Tairren turned quickly, watching the torchlight that followed the voice bounce in the darkness towards him. As the figure came into the windy corridor, he realized that it was Mikhal.

"Mikhal!" Tairren shouted back.

"Yes, Tairren, it is I," Mikhal said, rushing towards him. He seemed slightly out of breath, as if he ran the whole way.

"The throne room is close, Mikhal," Tairren exclaimed, pointing out of the window closest to them. "The main tower is just across the trench, away from this corridor."

"Well done, Tairren," Mikhal said, looking out of the window. "We must get to the Grand-High Mistress."

Tairren just looked at Mikhal. He didn't like that he kept calling her that. "Marrisa is near," he said in a lower voice, looking away.

Mikhal raised his eyebrows, watching Tairren as he seemed to become pensive all of a sudden. "Tairren," Mikhal said in a lower voice. "Marrisa is no longer here."

Tairren looked up at him quickly. His face was serious. He didn't say anything as he turned to open the door.

Tairren pushed open the heavy door. His breath was taken away by the surprising chamber before him. The right wall and roof were gone, opening out to a black sky. Tairren went in, looking around. The chamber had nothing in it but rubble and stone which must've been the remnants of the roof. He cautiously went to the edge of the chamber, looking out over the lands. The feeling of standing on the brink of death made him feel odd. They were high atop a cliff which loomed over a steep, jagged mountain side and a black, roaring waterway that gurgled loudly below them.

"Careful, Tairren," Mikhal said, coming up behind him. "This temple is ancient, and has been crumbling for years."

The winds pushed at them as they looked off into the dark lands before them. Faint orange could be seen far off on the horizon. It looked like small patches of glowing light.

"What are those faint lights coming from?" Tairren asked.

"I'm afraid those are other kingdoms and villages…burning," Mikhal said in a somber voice.

Tairren shook his head. He knew destruction was coming, but it was hard for him to look at it. It was becoming so real. He looked far off towards the northern part of Minslethrate. He couldn't see it at first, but after a moment, he realized that the northern kingdom was ablaze as well.

"Mother…," Tairren said in a faint voice. Tears swelled up in his eyes, dripping down his dirty cheeks.

Just then he knew he had to look past the thought of Marrisa. His own kingdom and people were dying right before his eyes. It only took days for his once peaceful world to flip upside down.

"John revealed this to me, Mikhal," Tairren said, trying to cover his emotion. "I know John is dead now… But he came to me when Fiara had me under a spell. He showed me the future of the world. He showed me Minslethrate's fate…" Tairren stopped talking, becoming scared for their future.

"What else did you see?" Mikhal asked.

"I saw…Marrisa…," Tairren said with little effort. "I saw Marrisa sitting upon a darkened throne… Darkness ruled the lands and there was no light at all. Everything, including the sun, was dead…"

Mikhal placed his hand on Tairren's shoulder. "But it can be stopped…," he said.

Tairren turned to look up at him. He was quiet, looking into his golden eyes. He was amazed at how the light glowed from Mikhal, even though darkness grew so thickly around them. It gave him hope. "The light still shines inside of you…," Tairren said in a quiet voice.

"These times may seem bleak, but God has not forgotten about us. The light is what continues to burn inside of you. That light is what we fight for in this dark world," Mikhal responded back.

Tairren looked away from him. He grabbed the beautiful hilt of his sword, remembering the God of Light's truthful words. He dwelled on the words of God that he learned to trust with his whole being. He thought of his quest. He thought of everything that had happened up until then. He brought his hand up to his chest, pulling the wing pendant from the collar of his soiled tunic. He gazed at the jeweled necklace, thinking of his father, his ancestor king, and King Yehoshua.

Just then he closed his eyes and inhaled the cold air that danced all around him. Just then the thought of Marrisa's beautiful eyes ripped through his mind. He opened his eyes quickly, putting the necklace back into his tunic. As he put the pendant back, he felt the rough heart-shaped stone below his tunic. He pulled the necklace out. He had forgotten about it. The blue stone was rough, and symbolized the love he had for Marrisa. He looked up, thinking of Marrisa again. The love was still there, and always would be.

He quickly put his necklace back. "We must go," Tairren finally said, looking back up at Mikhal.

Tairren quickly made his way to the door on the other side. Mikhal didn't hesitate to follow. They climbed over a mound of stone. From where they climbed, they could see into the next chamber. The door hung from one of its hinges, blocking the doorway. They climbed over the broken door, looking in, vigilantly.

The chamber was dark and quiet, and unsuspectingly massive. Only small torches were lit here and there, indicating that someone was there. The ceiling went high up with unlit candelabrums hanging from it. Tall windows lined the walls, along with old paintings which portrayed ancient kings from Minslethrate's past. Large, decorative marble pillars sat about the hall, sending haunting shadows everywhere. The floor was decorated with black and white tiles that made a checker pattern. It was a design that Tairren thought was strange. Old skeletons lay upon the floor, along with broken furniture and dusty candelabrums that must've fallen from the ceiling long ago.

As they walked into the hall, they could see that it went further in. Tairren looked around, amazed. He could tell that the old chamber used to once be a grand hall. It was probably used for congregations, he thought. He could tell that it used to be fit for royalty and nobility.

"This hall looks as if it was meant for royals at one time," Tairren said, moving his torch out in the dark air.

"Long ago, before King Yehoshua was born into this world, Minslethrate used to worship the pagan goddesses of this land, unknowingly worshiping Lucif. The elite of Minslethrate used to come here to celebrate the gifts of nature: water, earth, and fire. But it is untold, that even the elite from far off kingdoms would attend... There would be a grand feast and celebration once a year, when the moon was full and red... They would bring a virgin maiden here to this tower and sacrifice her on the top of this very tower. But Marrisa was the final sacrifice... Dark times, they were...and that is why it is called the Dark Tower of Sacrifice..."

"I know the legend," Tairren said, never taking his eyes off of his surroundings. "The people of Minslethrate used to tell old lore about Minslethrate's past... I never thought that I would ever live to see this place..."

"And you are the only one who has...," Mikhal said, quickly. "Ever since these parts of Minslethrate were declared as the Forbidden Lands, no one has ever gotten this far into the Dark Tower, and lived to tell the tale...

But now this tower sits in ruins. It reflects the fall of darkness; King Yehoshua conquered darkness long ago when he died on the tree and rose from death, unto eternity. The last legend was awakened, unto the end, and forever… Light shall live forever…"

They continued to walk through the great, morbid hall. Every now and then, they could feel the cold winds come in through the broken windows. The air was icy and smelled very old, as if it had been untouched by humans for generations. Their feet left footprints in the thick dust, upon the black and white checker tile. They walked past a long banquet table. Old, dusty goblets, dishware, and candlesticks sat on the table, covered in spider webs. Everything was made of gold, but they couldn't tell because of the thick dust and spider webs.

The shadows of the giant pillars danced across the checker floor as they continued to follow through the hall. Firelight was coming from the furthest side of the hall. The hall slightly curved as they went; and as they came around the bend of the hall, a massive fireplace roared out a great fire. Tairren realized that firelight must've been what he saw from the other corridor.

They crept into the open space before the fireplace. The warmth from the roaring fire felt good on their skin. But the warmth trickled away as they felt a cold wind burst into the chamber. They looked quickly, noticing that there was a massive threshold to the right of them where the cold wind came. The threshold opened out to a balcony. They crept further into the warmly lit open space, and noticed that on their left was a large throne.

"This is it," Mikhal said in a low tone.

They looked all around them, noticing how the pillars circled around the open space. The black and white tile below their feet made a strange circular pattern. And right above them was an unlit, decadent light fixture.

"The three stars…," Tairren said in a low voice, "and the three ancient goddesses of Minslethrate…"

He pointed towards the throne. Right above the throne was an indention in the stone that contained three women, sculpted from marble. The strange sculptures looked down at them with blank, cold eyes. They were tall and beautifully crafted. The statue on the left was a woman with a serpent's tail, sitting upon a stone in the water. He guessed it was Haifen. The statue on the right was standing among a tree, which he assumed was Dolsia. Tairren recognized the woman in the center very well; she stood upon fire. "Fiara…," Tairren whispered to himself.

Right above the three idols was a grand panel that contained three decorous stars that twinkled in the firelight. They were made of gold and jewels. Each mysterious star was made from six dashes.

"That is the sign of the beast…," Mikhal said. "And the pagan goddesses from Minslethrate's past are part of it… That marking is what's to be forced upon the people of the world if we do not stop it from happening!"

Suddenly, a strange, cold feeling began to come over them. Not even the warmth from the fire could stand up to the surprising cold air. Their breaths could suddenly be seen as the temperature drastically dropped. A dark mist began to come into the hall, swirling around their feet. Strange whispers began to fill the hall, echoing off of the dark walls.

"Voices from the darkness," Mikhal confirmed, quickly.

Their eyes widened as the warm firelight around them became dim. They glanced at each other, understanding what was happening. They grabbed their swords, swiftly bringing them out upon the firelight. The whispers began to disperse as their golden swords glowed. The light from the swords repelled the darkness that was surrounding them. They stood, quiet and still, holding their swords in their palms.

Just then a loud noise came from behind them. It sounded like a scream and growl mixed together. It came from the threshold that led to the balcony. They stared at the doorway, noticing that a massive, dark spot grew between them and the balcony. The dark spot appeared like a hole, pulsating upon the mists that circled it. More blackness came from the hole as a shadow slowly came out of it. The shadow was tall and menacing. Black substances began to move all around the shadowed person, shifting about like electricity.

Tairren gazed at the form. His heart throbbed in his chest, sending loud booms in his ears. His chest heaved as his insides began to become anxious. He licked his lips, watching closely as the figure came closer to them. He nervously held his sword up, squeezing it until his sweaty palm tingled. Finally, he could see who it was as the darkness stood before them and the firelight. And his heart nearly left him as he realized who the ugly, frightening person was.

"Marrisa…," Tairren said, choking up.

"Remember, Tairren! That is no longer Marrisa!" Mikhal said in a loud voice.

She levitated before them, appearing like a dark goddess. Tairren couldn't believe that it was Marrisa he was looking at. He couldn't believe that the black eyes that stared at him belonged to Marrisa. It was hard for him to understand that the tall, lifeless, wicked, queen that hovered above the ground before them, was…Marrisa. His heart ached as he realized that his nemesis was the one he loved with his whole heart. He came to rescue Marrisa…only to battle her…

Marrisa, who was now the Grand-High Mistress, glared at him from the shadows that consumed her. Her face was white as marble and on her forehead were three black stars. Her long red hair was pulled up below a black crown that was encrusted with a thick, black substance. She wore a long black gown that had a decorative collar which went high up behind her head in jagged points. Her long black gown spread out among the cold air, dancing in the black mists that surrounded her. And she wore the red pendant that King Julpen had given Marrisa on the night of her celebration. The red stone glistened as the silent firelight touched it.

Tairren backed away from her. He never took his eyes from her shiny, black ones. He couldn't help but gaze at her.

"Your God has led you here to die," a deep voice said from Marrisa's lips. "…But it is I who has led you here to offer you life…"

The wicked voice stirred up disgust inside of Tairren and Mikhal, because it was the voice of Lucif, the Dark Lord.

"My God has sent me here to stop you," Tairren said.

The Grand-High Mistress just stared at him, pouring her gaze over Tairren like a black storm.

"You hide behind an innocent woman, Lucif?" Mikhal said in a strong voice. "It's just as you've always done! Wicked, tyrant!"

"Silence!" she screamed out in Lucif's dreadful voice.

She quickly raised her hand into the air, sending a rush of black mist towards him. The darkness pushed Mikhal with a strong force, sending him crashing into the wall.

"Why give in to the darkness, Marrisa?!" Tairren yelled out.

Her dark eyes gazed at Tairren again.

Tairren breathed quickly, becoming nervous.

"She was weak, Tairren," she finally said. "But she is the greatest sacrifice… Now, she is all powerful, because of my greatness. She will become the goddess of the world."

Mikhal got up, standing off to the side. He watched vigilantly, knowing that it was Tairren's battle. But he would guard him every step of the way.

"Why continue to fight this, Lucif?" Tairren asked in a low voice. He felt brave enough to ask. "The light has already won, long ago… You've already lost."

The Grand-High Mistress just stared at him. Her face was silent and haunting.

"I wish to only spread unity upon the world," she finally said in a softer voice. Surprisingly, the voice was Marrisa's.

Tairren's heart quickened as he breathed in the intense air. "Marrisa?" he said, gazing at her.

"Light and darkness shall become one… There shall be one belief, one faith, one mighty congregation upon the world," she said, then smiled at him. "The meaning of life is unity, Tairren. Why refuse such a glorious gift? I will lead this world, in peace…"

"Light and darkness can not comprehend each other… God is light, and in him, there is no darkness at all. It has been that way since the beginning of time."

"Perhaps you are correct, Tairren," Marrisa's voice said from the darkness. "But that is why there will be a new world, a new kingdom, and one new ruler! UNITY!"

"You lie!" Tairren yelled. "Death is not peace. Turmoil and malice do not come from peace!"

"The world is being cleansed, Tairren... We must rid of the old... Enlightenment shall come upon the world. Every person upon the world shall worship their inner being, coming together in one unstoppable kingdom of Unity! Life shall not be about light vs. darkness, Tairren. It shall be about the gray areas."

"That is a false belief that is not of light. That is Luciferian beliefs! It's seeds of darkness straight from the bowels of Lucif!" Tairren grunted. "You have been plotting the world's demise since the very beginning, Lucif! You loathe the God of Light and his creations because you can not have any part of it. You are pure darkness! You will never mix light with darkness, because you do not understand light! I pity your wicked soul. You can only force people to love you! You can only trick and blind people to worship you! Your false word of uniting light and darkness is part of your plan to get the world to worship you over God! Your ancient goddesses have failed you...so you use a new age belief to continue to thrive... But you are already dead, Lucif."

"You don't understand, Tairren. I do. Rule with me, Tairren," Marrisa pleaded. "Be my king and you shall see the power. If you love me, you would rule the world with me."

Tairren continued to look into Marrisa's black eyes as she loomed over him. "You are not Marrisa," he said as his teary eyes glistened in the firelight. "Marrisa is beautiful like God's creations, because she is one of God's creations. Marrisa is warm, and full of love for humanity. The woman I love is not filled with wicked philosophy! I do not follow darkness... I will never follow you... I follow the light, which has already won..."

"And the light continues to win as your kingdom, other kingdoms, and the world, burns and DIES!" she shouted. Her white face crinkled up as the deep voice of Lucif came back, echoing throughout the hall.

Tairren backed away from her a little. His eyes continued to swell with tears as he looked upon Marrisa's evil face. He remembered how her face used to shine like the stars. He glanced at Mikhal who watched intently. He then looked back at her frozen countenance, shaking his head.

"You only come to lie, steal, kill and destroy...," he said between clenched teeth. "But in the end...you will burn upon the wrath of GOD!" Tairren shouted.

"I AM GOD!" Lucif screamed out, making the dark air around them shake.

The darkness from her began to thrash around Tairren, moving around as if it were filled with energy.

"You will never be great like my God!" Tairren screamed out. The cold darkness began to move around the hall as Lucif became enraged.

Mikhal came quickly to Tairren's side, still holding on to his sword.

"You will always be doomed, Lucif!" Tairren continued to shout as the dark winds began to scream all around him. The wind became so loud that he could barely hear his voice over it. "KING YEHOSHUA IS GOD!" he shouted with a mighty sound.

Suddenly Marrisa began to scream, releasing dark mists from her pale mouth. The mists quickly formed into ugly creatures! Their misty forms became flesh and their eyes flashed like fiery light. They circled around Mikhal and Tairren, surrounding them. They growled and screamed, moving quickly as if they were filled with power and energy.

The dark entities began to fight them. Their arms were like weapons as they swung at them. Their claws were like blades as they clashed with the swords of light. But they were no match for Tairren and Mikhal's light-soaked swords! The dark creatures shrieked as the swords went through their black flesh. One by one, the nomed fell to the ground. Tairren and Mikhal watched breathlessly as the nomed's dead corpses melted into the mists, becoming one with the darkness again.

"You are no match for the power of Yehoshua!" Mikhal shouted.

The Grand-High Mistress screamed out again, beginning to levitate above them! She hovered in the air as her black eyes became large. She scowled at them, bringing her arms out. She yelled out in a strange voice as the darkness grew upon her hands and arms. As the strange mists grew around her arms, Mikhal and Tairren seemed to become surrounded by black shadows, simultaneously.

She swung her arms as the dark mists came over them like a wave. She was controlling the shadows and mists! The darkness around them screamed and roared out as they quickly dodged it.

They swung their swords, keeping the veil of darkness away from them.

The Grand-High Mistress became angry, screaming again. "You can not stop me!" she roared out.

Tairren and Mikhal ran, finding a way through the thick shadows. They made their way through with their gleaming swords. The mists sizzled and shrieked as the golden light touched them.

They quickly came out onto the massive balcony. They franticly looked around as the winds circled around them. The sky was black like everything else. The only thing they could see was the sea of torchlight way down below them.

"We are trapped, Mikhal!" Tairren said, franticly.

"This is it, Tairren! This is where it all ends!" Mikhal shouted back. The winds howled loudly all around them. "Darkness will continue to grow from her if you do not stop her!"

Tairren turned quickly as the Grand-High Mistress exploded out onto the balcony. Her face looked like a skeleton as her dark eyes and mouth blended in with the shadows. She slowly levitated towards them, bringing her power with her. Her black gown moved in the air as she stretched her arms out.

"Since you do not yield to me…you choose DEATH!"

"You will die, in the name of King Yehoshua!" Mikhal shouted back, bringing his sword up.

Marrisa shrieked out a horrifying noise as she quickly brought her darkness around Mikhal. Mikhal swung his sword, but the powers of Lucif came from all around him. The powerful darkness surrounded him, beginning to choke him! Mikhal dropped his sword as Marrisa lifted him into the black sky. His sword got caught by a gust of wind, flying off the side of the balcony and down into the darkness below.

"Your light will be gone from you!" she screamed out with her ugly face. "DIE, son of filth!"

Mikhal thrashed around in the air, helplessly, pulling at the darkness that choked him. It seemed as if Lucif was winning. "Tairren!" he yelled out with some effort. "Do it now, before it is too late!"

Tairren swallowed down his nervousness as his heart thrashed around in his burning chest. Sweat came down his brow as he looked up at Marrisa with sore eyes. He clenched his teeth. He quickly closed his eyes as Mikhal continued to yell to him. He felt panicked and out of control. Marrisa's beautiful blue eyes flashed in his mind. He heard her giggle as he thought of her. He thought of how much he loved her, how he would do anything for her.

His heart ached as the Grand-High Mistress' screams grabbed him from his pensive state. He opened his eyes quickly, tears sparkling. He looked at the evil being as she continued to strangle Mikhal.

It had to stop!

Tairren began to scream as he pulled his sword back with tense muscles. Spit shot from his mouth as his emotions flew. His head pounded. Tears fell down his quivering cheeks. Blood rushed through his veins like a mighty river as his heart raced. The blade glowed intensely in the darkness as Tairren squeezed the hilt with his shaken hands. He squeezed the hilt even harder, feeling the sweat move between his hands and the precious metal. Then he thrust as if his elbows released built up tension. He jabbed the golden blade forward, straight into Marrisa's stomach. He did it with all of the strength he had. He released his anger, sadness, and burdens all at once as he pushed the Sword of Truth straight through her.

He began to sob as he realized that he was killing Marrisa, still pushing the sword until it went no further.

Sweet images of Marrisa flew through Tairren's mind and across his teary eyes as he continued to scream from his deep emotions. His mind began to deceive him. He saw Marrisa's face. He saw her smiling at him and her wrapping her frail arms around him. He saw them kissing in the beautiful Forest Provence and laughing in the cool breezes of the castle gardens. He saw how much he loved Princess Marrisa... He saw her teary blue eyes, sparkling like crystals as they let go of each other's hands. Then he saw Marrisa leaving him, breaking his heart in the darkness that grew all around them.

The images seemed so real upon Tairren, but reality settled over him as his teary eyes caught Marrisa screaming out into the black sky. He realized the powerful sword was still in her.

Tairren suddenly fell back as a burst of light surged through Marrisa's body. It looked like bright light behind paper. The light glowed beneath her skin, revealing her veins and organs right through her flesh. Then after a moment, the light left her quickly as her skin's color faded. She arched her back and threw her head back as a mighty roar ripped out of her mouth.

Tairren got up quickly, running to Mikhal who had fallen onto the ground. They both looked up at Marrisa as her body thrashed around. Dark mists continued to bellow out of her mouth like a mighty stream of black smoke. Lucif was being forced from her body!

Then, Marrisa's broken body fell to the ground as the darkness stopped pouring from her. Lucif had left her completely. The crown she wore fell to the ground, clanking as it tumbled across the cold stone. The black substance that caked the old crown, crumbled off, revealing its original golden metal.

Tairren ran to Marrisa's lifeless body. He looked over her franticly. All he could see was the sword going straight through her body. He yanked the blade from her belly. He couldn't think straight as his shaken hands touched her face and neck. Blood rushed from her stomach, oozing out. "Marrisa!" he cried, trying to contain his emotions. He pushed his hands over her stomach, trying to stop the blood that rushed out. "Marrisa, I'm here!" he uttered as tears dripped down his eyes.

Her pale face looked peaceful as she lay lifelessly. Tairren pulled her onto his lap, holding onto her tightly. He knew right then that she was dead... He closed his eyes, hugging her as his silent tears continued to flow.

"It is not over, yet!" Mikhal screamed out as he grabbed Tairren's sword. "Marrisa was just a domicile to Lucif! When the Sword of Truth went through her, the light sent Lucif's spirit away from her! The sword was the only way to get him out for good!"

Tairren looked up at Mikhal, watching as he ran towards the massive black mists that whirled and screamed upon the balcony.

Mikhal stood before the roaring darkness. "You have failed, Lucif!" he shouted. "Now fall upon the ground and worship your new king!"

The power of Lucif grew angry, roaring and whirling among the balcony like a storm. "No…you all have failed. Look around and you shall see the fruit of my work, my legacy! Now I shall show you greatness!" he roared. "Look upon my true form and worship me, you infidel!"

The black swirling mists began to shake violently, transforming into a wicked monster. He stretched his arms and body, revealing his true form. Lucif was bigger than all of the nomed.

His disturbing appearance was different than any other nomed. He had no horns or jagged teeth. He had no tail or monstrous claws. And his flesh didn't seem like flesh at all, but more of a moving black, misty substance. His face was strange, looking like a cross between a human skull and an unearthly beast. But strangest of all was that his eyes were not totally black or fiery red. They glowed with a strange light, as if they were once made of light long ago, but faded into black light. They were like smoky, black fire.

His body mingled with the black mists that moved around him. The strange mists that moved energetically seemed to be drawn to him, slowly moving towards him. He had large wings that were made out of the dark mists, and his strange body never touched the ground.

Mikhal looked up at the fiend as he brought the Sword of Truth up into the air. Time seemed to stop as the winds all around them ceased. All he could hear was Lucif's loud breaths.

It was suddenly quiet upon the balcony as both Tairren and Mikhal watched the wicked entity loom over them.

†

CHAPTER 22
Brave Hearts

King Julpen led his fellow people and legna towards the Dark Tower. They marched quietly; their hearts pumped with anxiousness. They held their weapons and torches high, feeling as if they were blindly walking to their deaths. Their eyes stared at the uncertainty before them. They could hear shouts and screams from hundreds, thousands even, of vile nomed. The sounds of the dark army ahead of them shook the horizon, making the ground below them softly rumble. The howls that blew through the trenches and past the large boulders even sounded louder. Because of it, their bodies grew nervous and uneasy. The roars of the nomed became more intense with every step they took.

"Hold on to your faith, men!" King Julpen shouted out. "Nothing shall stop us as we fight for the days ahead!"

The men responded by shouting, but they still carried fear in their hearts.

Another loud roar came from the eerie distance, sounding like a mighty crash of lightning. They all knew that the army was advancing nearer. They could see the small red lights of their eyes coming closer.

Suddenly a low glowing light came down from the black, misty sky. It was Rafiul, riding atop Cherbim! The flying beast glided down, landing beside King Julpen and the other Archlegna.

"Hello, my brethren," he said with sparkling eyes. I am glad to see your faces again. But I am stricken with bad news. The beast as risen from the black pit."

Everyone glanced at each other. They looked worried.

"We are happy you are with us," Gaibriul said, nodding his head. "But this news makes us uneasy. I feel the earth tremor with every cry the beast makes on the horizon. I foresaw the beast coming, but the men of Minslethrate are not in the right state of mind to look upon such an entity."

"Their minds must regain strength. Now. Fiara is riding upon the beast of darkness, and leading an army of thousands," Rafiul continued.

King Julpen grew frantic, looking around. Their army seemed greater than his. He pressed is lips together, looking towards the Archlegna for guidance. "What must we do?" he asked.

"We shall do what we were brought here to do—fight," Rafiul said, boldly. "We shall fight until there is nothing left to fight."

"We shall trust in the Lord of Light," Uriel added, nodding her head.

"Just as Mikhal and Tairren are standing up to darkness, now as we speak...so shall we," Gaibriul said, quickly.

Dolsia stood with Natalia and Phillip, but watched their serious conversation intently. She couldn't help but listen. She was no longer an Archlegna, but she still felt that she could help. She knew that it was all much easier said than done; the legna did not understand that a human could be controlled by their emotions and thoughts. Being half human and legna, she knew how it felt to be terrified, not knowing what was to come next. She knew how heart-aching it was to feel all alone with human emotions. She knew how it was to not see... But she also knew that she had to lean on something greater if she was going to get through the darkness, and that "something greater" was the God of Light.

"King Julpen...," Dolsia said timidly from where she stood.

King Julpen glanced up at her as the Archlegna turned their golden gazes over to her.

Dolsia suddenly felt insecure as she walked upon the other legna. They were much brighter than her, and braver.

"Speak up, Dolsia," Gaibriul said kindly, nodding at her.

She stood tall, looking at all of them, then only at King Julpen. "Your Majesty, I know how you feel... But we must remain strong. Even the littlest glimpse of fear can set us astray. Trust in God, that no matter what, your quest shall be completed as He wishes..." She stopped talking, looking into his dark eyes.

"Your sweet tone and strong words inspire me, Dolsia," King Julpen said. "Thank you..."

Dolsia knew that he truly still felt lost. She could see it in his weary eyes. "...May I sing to you?" she finally asked, catching his attention again.

King Julpen looked at the other weary people surrounding them, then he looked at his army as a whole. He knew they all needed comforting.

He gazed back into her pale eyes. "Sing to us all, Lady Dolsia," he said. He faintly smiled at her.

Dolsia nodded her head, then looked around. She felt the fear and sadness from the onlookers. She felt the pain and suffering from the lands. And she felt the uncertainty that lay before them. She closed her eyes and thought of her inspiration. She thought of the God of Light and his grace, and she thought of her life. It was her "testimony" that inspired her, which was what Natalia had called it. Her life was broken for so long after she fell away from God, but now that she had returned to the light of God again, she had a reason to sing.

She opened her pale-yellow eyes, then began to sing as she looked off into the frightening horizon. Her beautiful voice resonated over the cold night, catching everyone's attention.

The night shall fall.
The winds are cold.
They say
Do not ignore God's call,
Be bold.
Though we are far from home,
And death welcomes us,
We shall do what was shown,
And trust.
But the eye is blinded and can not see.
The eye yearns for light from He.
Rescue us,
Oh, rescue us!
Break these chains
Oh God,
And lead us through the valley of darkness.
Wipe our tears away.
We're restless!
But still we trust.
Still we fight!
We must
For the light!
The sun can not hear us.
The day is lost.
The lands are broken
And still we trust!
Come down like rain
And set us free!
Take this pain,
Oh, God, please!
But the Lord is my light
And my salvation.
Whom shall I fear?
The Lord is the strength of my life,
Whom shall I be afraid?
The waters are deep,
And the fires overtake.
The valleys are steep
And the shadows quake.
But You fight my every battle
Oh, God!
The winds get colder,
The waters turn to rust.
The fires take over,

And still we trust?
Blood is spilled from heavy hearts,
Being forced to leak by poisonous darts.
But we still trust in God,
Because he is our Lord and King!
We put our trust in him with everything!
Our hearts grow heavy
And our minds grow numb.
But our God makes our spirits steady,
That's why we sing this song!
We shall not fear.
We will not cry.
We will not believe in the Dark Lord's lie.
We are free!
We must fight!
You are our shield and sword of light!
We must press on for all mankind!
We will rise up on wings of eagles!
We shall smite this movement of evil!
The Lord is my light
And my salvation!
Whom shall I fear?
The Lord is the strength of my life,
Whom shall I be afraid?

Everyone began to sing together, bringing a great sound across the dark valley. It seemed to raise their spirits as they marched together in song.

Dolsia rode on horseback, smiling as she listened to all of the men and legna sing her song in unison. She glanced over at King Julpen. He didn't seem as if anxiety held onto him any longer; he looked in higher spirits. She looked over at the other Archlegna, who appeared very pleased. She felt as if she had done what she was meant to do, and that was sooth people's souls through song. She believed she was meant to sing and worship her God of Light. She looked up into the black sky and smiled. She wasn't afraid of that night, and knew that whatever happened, it was because it was meant to…

But suddenly, the whole atmosphere changed as a thunderous roar came out over them. Their army stopped, looking towards the treacherous sounds. And what they saw was not pleasing or uplifting.

The dark army of Lucif was coming upon them. They could see Fiara leading the army, sitting upon a great beast that looked like a mountain. All of their eyes, including Fiara's, looked as if fire burned behind them.

†††

King Julpen sat on his horse upon a small precipice. He held his sword tightly as he gazed out over the massive army before him. He saw how they restlessly moved about; their eyes twinkling like dark stars. He saw how some of them were small and some of them were massive; some looked like wild animals and while others looked like ferocious creatures he had never seen before. Some even looked human, but distorted and ugly. He saw many horns move around and many ugly wings move about. But the worst thing to him was the noises he heard. The sounds the nomed made were even more terrifying than any nightmare.

King Julpen looked out over his army. They now stood fearlessly. The light of the legna glowed and the mannerism of the men showed confidence and bravery. He brought his eyes back over to the dark army, noticing Fiara clad in golden armor. She sat upon the beast of darkness, which had many heads and eyes. The noise that came from the beast was louder than any other nomed.

"I trust you, God," King Julpen said. "Lead me as I fight against the enemy."

He then thought of the great white owl, wondering where the creature was through all of this. The strange bird seemed to leave them… But he knew that even though he did not see or feel God's presence, the almighty God was still there…

He then thought of his kingdom and his daughter. He thought of Tairren, who he had never met, and how he was the rightful prince of Minslethrate. Then he thought of his own life, and how it all led up to that moment.

He brought his eyes to Prince Phillip and Lady Natalia. He smiled as he watched how they seemed to have fallen in love with each other, reminding him of his sweet memories of his deceased wife… His eyes gazed back to the dark horizon as he thought of his wife. He knew that she was in the Kingdom of Nevaeh, the wonderful kingdom that the legna spoke about.

He watched as the Archlegna took their commanding places near different parts of their army. He took a deep breath, then mentally prepared himself for war.

†††

Phillip and Natalia stood close to each other, having their horses by their sides. They stood near Dolsia, who watched Rafiul intently. Rafiul commanded their part of the army. They all stood strong on the frontlines. Rafiul led them, shouting out commands and words of wisdom, riding on his beast. Because of where they stood, they couldn't quiet see the dark army approaching them. But they heard the loud sounds they made.

Their horses were nervous, so they tried to calm them down the best they could. Just by being close to them calmed them down a bit.

"Are you ready?" Phillip asked.

He held the Shield of Faith on his arm, which sparkled in the firelight of the torches. He patted Sable's neck, looking over at Natalia every now and then.

"I have to say that I am…," she said, faintly smiling back at him. She caressed Orchid's brown face, looking into her kind eye. She then brought her gaze back to Phillip.

"It's strange how that armor fits you so well," Phillip said, trying to make the intense situation a little more light-hearted, which seemed impossible.

Natalia wore the Armor of Righteousness, and it did fit her like a glove. The golden armor was mysterious and reflected that it was meant for everyone.

"It's no ordinary armor, Prince. It fits the person who wears it," she said, grasping her helmet in her arm. "Even a big lummox like yourself could wear it if given the chance." She smiled, nudging his arm with hers.

They chuckled a little to themselves. But the sounds of the threatening army ahead of them disturbed them. They became quiet, studying each other's face. They gazed into each other's eyes, becoming pensive.

"Promise me, Phillip, that no matter what happens…you will overcome this and lead Ishkar into the light of God." Natalia pressed her lips together. "Do not forget this, ever."

Phillip gently nodded his head. "I promise," he said. "I will lead my kingdom to the power of King Yehoshua, just as you have led me, Natalia. Darkness will not take Ishkar away from me…"

Natalia smiled, caressing his cheek.

"I worry for you, Natalia," Phillip continued. "You are not meant for war… I don't want to lose you," he said. He touched her hand, pulling it away from his cheek, grasping it tightly. He touched her face, still looking into her vibrant-green eyes.

They grew quiet, never looking away from one another.

"I have always been a fighter… I shall fight just as my heart always has," she finally said.

"I love you," he said, quickly.

He slowly brought his face to hers.

He wanted to kiss her. But he paused a little, giving her the chance to stop him. But since she drew closer to him, he knew that she wanted to kiss him back.

Natalia closed her eyes as their lips went to touch. "I love you too," she finally said in a soft voice.

It was the first time that Natalia had said that she loved him. And it was the first time that Phillip felt true love as he kissed her. Their hearts beat together as they turned towards each other. They held each other's hands and kissed one another, never wanting to leave each other.

They kissed as if it was their first and last kiss, never minding the threatening army that came closer to them.

✝

CHAPTER 23
Fight Until Death

The loud army of darkness stopped moving abruptly. Their blood-soaked flags that held the sign of the Grand-High Mistress waved through the cold air. Their eyes gleamed and the mists of their heavy breaths bloomed out in the air. There was still some land between them and the light folk.

Fiara sat tall upon the beast, her golden ram's skull glistened like a crown. The nomed howled and roared all around her.

But then the loud sounds stopped as Fiara raised her hand into the air.

Heavy silence fell upon the south as the two armies gazed at each other.

Fiara's fiery eyes met the legna's golden stare. Even their emotions began to clash as they stood before one another.

"People of Minslethrate, hear me now!" Fiara shouted. "Your world is falling upon the Dark Lord's hand! Kingdoms burn, succumbing to the new order of this world! We must all make way for the path of enlightenment! Follow the Dark Lord and wear the sign of the Grand-High Mistress upon you so that your life shall be spared!" Her powerful voice echoed throughout the valley.

The legna and men of Minslethrate just stood strong, watching their enemy's every move. The Archlegna held their arms out, commanding the men to stay put and vigilant. They stood quietly, holding their torches and weapons, ready for battle.

Fiara gazed out over the silent crowd of men. She chuckled to herself as her eyes flashed. "Your silence reveals it all," she exclaimed. She was quiet for a moment, then raised her hand back into the black air. "So, they choose death!" she shouted out.

The nomed began to make loud noises again by shrieking and howling and stomping their feet against the ground.

Fiara let out a loud scream as she swiftly grabbed one of her golden swords, thrusting it out towards the legna. "KILL THEM ALL!" she roared.

Her army sounded like a mad storm as they obeyed her commands. They began to charge the legna, beginning the war, and a new path of destruction.

✝✝✝

King Julpen saw Fiara's movement, then let out a loud shout. He thrust his sword into the black sky. He commanded the army, beginning to

718

run towards them with full force. There was no turning back. Adrenaline raced through his tense body as he commanded his army.

The Archlegna followed suit, commanding their parts of the legion to go. They raised their golden swords into the air as they sat upon their mighty beasts. Even their beasts roared into the cold air, sending a loud sound towards the advancing nomed.

Chaos exploded upon the Black Field of Old Blood immediately as they began to fight. Arrows pelted the air, flying towards the frontline of the nomed's army. The great white beasts roared in the sky as they attacked the flying Nomed and the men hollered as they fought among the ground.

Everyone upon the grounds, sky, and the whole world, was battling in a war. It was a war between light and darkness that began long ago.

The air was filled with the loud sounds of clashing metal and shouting voices.

✝✝✝

Phillip and Natalia rode on their horses, flying through the nomed with their swords waving. Their armor gleamed like the legna's. Their swords slashed and dismembered as they went.

The nomed had no physical weapons, but they had their gnashing jaws and their sharp claws, and their strength. They howled and screamed as they swung at them, trying to pull them down.

Natalia swung her sword as hard as she could, fighting off the ugly nomed. She fought hard, as she always had done, not afraid of the threatening creatures. She had a brave heart, which had become more courageous over her journey.

Phillip swung his sword swiftly, looking up at Natalia every now and then. It was hard for him to concentrate when the woman he loved was fighting right before him. But when his mind went back to the nomed, he pushed on to destroy them. He used his strength to behead the nomed that were tall enough for his sword's reach. The nomed seemed to fall easily. They screamed at the touch of his mighty shield and sharp sword.

Natalia noticed Fiara sitting upon her great beast. She grunted as she noticed that the wicked sorceress had the upper hand, commanding her beast to devour and destroy everyone who came near her. Many soldiers were being crushed beneath the beast. She also noticed Dolsia, who was running among the earth, towards Fiara. Natalia thought that she must've lost her horse. Natalia instantly became worried for her new companion. Her heart quickened as she realized that Dolsia was going to take on Fiara alone.

Natalia quickly got Orchid to dash through the nomed, towards Dolsia.

Phillip noticed Natalia moving quickly, going towards Fiara and the beast. His heart sped up as he swung his sword, killing an attacking nomed. He then quickly got Sable going towards Natalia. He knew Natalia was bold, but he didn't think she would attempt to take on such a beast.

"Natalia!" he shouted, grabbing her attention as he rode next to her. "What are you doing?!"

"Dolsia is going take on the beast!" she hollered back. "She needs help!"

Phillip looked up, bringing his eyes to Fiara and the beast. He saw Dolsia running quickly towards Fiara, dashing past nomed and ignoring them in the process.

They quickly rode, swinging their swords and killing nomed as they went. They got to Dolsia, following her with speed.

They were nearly to the beast when Natalia's horse stumbled down an unseen drop! Surprised, Natalia screamed as she went flying over Orchid's head. She hit the ground, tumbling down a small slope.

"Natalia!" Phillip screamed out.

He grew frantic. He saw her flip over her horse, disappearing into the fighting crowd. His heart thudded in his chest as he jumped off of his horse, running towards her. He could see that she quickly got up, swinging her sword as the nomed attacked. He was relieved, but now they were in a bad position among the ground.

Phillip was taken off guard as a tall creature attacked him from behind! The creature looked like an ugly shadowy human, but had large black eyes and horns that twisted from its head. Phillip swung his sword quickly, but the creature retaliated by moving with great speed. Phillip looked towards Natalia, noticing that she was making her way towards the beast. The nomed made a shrieking sound as he took him off guard again, hitting him into the ground with a powerful force.

✝✝✝

"Dolsia!" Natalia shouted, making her way towards her.

She kept her eyes on Dolsia's white hair that fell from her helmet, which stood out among the darkness. She fought her way to Dolsia, who was now standing before the great beast. Natalia finished a nomed off she was fighting, then ran to them. She stopped quickly, shocked at the beast's size.

They both looked up at Fiara who sat upon the beast. The beast roared at them from its many heads as Fiara looked down at them. They became intimidated as many fiery eyes glared down at them all at once. It felt scary being in Fiara and the beast's presence, but they were not backing down. "Whom shall I fear?" they kept repeating in their pounding heads.

"Aah, Dolsia," Fiara said, surprised. "So, you come to fight, have you?!"

"I come to kill you!" Dolsia screamed.

Fiara laughed as her fiery eyes flashed beneath her golden skull. She stared at them from the intimidating beast, then patted its back. "I shall be glad to take up such a challenge." She quickly stood up on the beast's mighty back. "My pet," she said, speaking to the behemoth. "Go and destroy as I rid of these vermin!"

Fiara flipped off of the beast, landing right in front of Dolsia and Natalia. The beast roared out with its many heads, then began to trample across the crowds of men, doing as she commanded.

Fiara pulled the skull from her head, throwing it to the ground. Her exotic face smiled as her eyes flashed like fire. Three jeweled stars twinkled on her forehead, revealing who she followed. She slowly walked towards them, pulling her swords from her back.

Dolsia and Natalia stood tall, holding their swords tightly.

"Dolsia and a little girl," Fiara teased with a wicked smile. "Oh, how I will love killing you."

"You will die, Fiara!" Dolsia screamed out in a shaken voice.

"YOU, shall die, *Dolsia!*" Fiara screamed. "You, disgusting woman who follows a dead king, shall feel the wrath of the dark fire! When I kill you, only the dirt upon your body will mourn you."

Fiara quickly glanced at Natalia, looking her up and down. Her stare was intimidating, making Natalia nervous. "And you, little girl... You wear the dead king's armor... I can smell the filth from it..."

She turned her intense gaze back over to Dolsia. "Pathetic... You give a human your prize? You weak, foolish, human-lover..." Fiara's eyes grew ugly as she sneered at Dolsia. "You once had power... You've become like them! INFEDILS! He is dead, his humans are dead, and this world is dying. And yet, you still follow him?" Fiara spit at Dolsia, then smirked. "Worthless...just like your king."

Dolsia swallowed down her emotions as Fiara continued to goad her. Her heart thrashed in her chest as tears built up in her pale eyes. She clenched her teeth as she began to breathe harder. She closed her eyes. "You are my strength, King Yehoshua," she said to herself in a low voice. She opened her eyes, looking back at the evil woman.

Fiara's eyes flashed with anger. She heard Dolsia speak His name, the name above all names that was forbidden to say. Instantly she became provoked. She screamed as the dark powers inside of her influenced her to destroy.

She lunged at Dolsia like a wild animal, swinging her two swords quickly. Dolsia retaliated by blocking her hit.

Natalia swung her sword with all the strength she had, hitting one of Fiara's swords with hers. Her heart quivered as she watched Fiara falter because of her hit.

The three women began to fight, catching the nomed's attention. A crowd of nomed began to circle around them, watching and growling.

Fiara took on both of them at the same time, swiftly moving and swinging her swords at them. She had unimaginable strength, making them shutter at every swing. They moved about the earth, like a dance. They moved with each other's hits, blocking and swiftly dodging each other.

Natalia grunted as she fought. She yearned for Fiara to fall, to get hit, or trip even; but she was too swift and strong. It seemed to her that they had been fighting forever. She was the smallest out of all of the women, and she wasn't as strong. But she fought until her muscles began to ache. Sweat trickled down her brow as she became overwhelmed. But Fiara was not relenting, moving with power and speed.

Fiara's attention seemed to be more on Dolsia. She forced all of her power on her, giving her the brunt of her wrath.

Natalia raised her sword from behind Fiara. She had the perfect chance to stop Fiara! But just as she swung downwards with her sword, Fiara turned like a fast wind, elbowing Natalia in the face, hard. Natalia fell back, hitting against a pile of rock as her sword fell. Her helmet came off, tumbling across the rock. Natalia got up quickly. Her nose trickled blood and her face throbbed. She saw Dolsia struggling. She could see the pain in her fare face and the intensity in her pale eyes.

Dolsia continued to fight, but Fiara's attacks were too strong! Dolsia lost control as Fiara did a powerful kick into her stomach, making her fall to the ground. Dolsia moaned out in pain as she crashed into a large stone.

Fiara raised her swords into the air, screaming. Her eyes flashed as she looked out into the crowds of nomed who carefully watched. The nomed all around them began to shriek with praises. Their praises filled her with energy. She quickly looked back down at Dolsia. She threw one of her swords down, chuckling as Dolsia slowly tried to get up. Her eyes began to glow with a strange black light. She growled, then spun quickly, kicking Dolsia in the head. Her hit was powerful, making Dolsia's helmet fly off.

Dolsia slammed on her side as the rest of her white air fell over her face. Her head pounded as her ears rung. She grunted as tears swelled in her pale eyes. Blood came down her nose and the side of her head. She felt overwhelming human pain and emotions come over her body like a vicious wave.

"Dolsia!" Natalia cried out, beginning to run to help her.

"Hold her down!" Fiara commanded, shouting to a large nomed standing nearby.

The ugly nomed rushed upon Natalia, snarling as it grabbed her arms from behind her. It forced her down to her knees, making it hard for her to get back up.

Fiara looked down at Dolsia, watching her struggle to get up. "Dolsia, follow my powers and I will spare you," she said in a serious tone.

Dolsia looked up at her. Blood came down her bruised face and one of her eyes was beginning to swell. Dolsia slowly shook her head, helplessly looking up at her. "No...," she said in a shaken voice.

Fiara's face crinkled into a scowl as she let out a growl. She quickly raised her leg, bringing it down hard into her back. Her powerful hit pounded her body back down into the ground.

"Leave her alone!" Natalia screamed out as her emotions rose. She struggled, trying to get loose from the growling nomed.

Dolsia lay for a moment, breathing hard. Her body felt broken. Blood and spit fell from her opened mouth as she slowly pushed herself up from her stomach. She could barely move as tears went down her dirty, bloody face.

"WHO DO YOU FOLLOW?!" Fiara roared. Her face shook as veins pulsated in her neck. Her voice became frightening as the dark fire glowed from her evil eyes.

Dolsia looked up, shaken and battered. "King Yehoshua...," she uttered in a broken voice.

Fiara sucked in the cold air, then turned her head towards the large nomed who held Natalia. "Make her watch!" she screamed at it.

The nomed all around them began to stomp their feet and scream into the sky as they yearned for their deaths.

Natalia struggled, trying to move as the monster grabbed her head. She cried as she watched Dolsia look up at Fiara, helplessly. Dolsia needed her help...and she couldn't help her.

"Die for your king, since that is your wish," Fiara scowled. She slowly circled around Dolsia, looking down at her with disgust.

"My body—shall break...but my spirit...shall live forever," Dolsia murmured. "If my flesh—is to die...I am...proud...to die as a human...," she struggled to say, breathing harder, "...for my king."

"And so, you shall!" Fiara screamed out. Without warning, she swiftly swung her sword from behind Dolsia's helpless body.

Fiara moved quickly like the wind. Her brutal strength was magnified. Her golden sword hummed in the cold air, cutting through Dolsia's neck. The hit was so powerful that it flung Dolsia's wing-shaped pendant from her neck.

The nomed roared out, pleased at what they saw. All around them chaos flourished.

"NOO!" Natalia cried out, watching as Dolsia's head fell from her body.

Natalia closed her burning eyes as tears drenched her face. Her heart felt like it was about to go out. She felt sick. She screamed out as the image of Dolsia's head being cut away scarred her mind. She cried out as her tears ran, but no one could hear her.

Fiara slowly kneeled over Dolsia's head. She looked at the bright-red blood that puddled all around her, then smiled. She caressed Dolsia's white face then grabbed a handful of her hair. The nomed all around them filled the air with loud roars and noises as she raised Dolsia's head out into the cold wind. A wicked smile came across her face as she held the head for all to see it.

Fiara's vicious eyes fell on the wing-shaped pendant that had flung off of Dolsia's neck. She glanced at Natalia then threw Dolsia's head next to her. Blood splatted across Natalia's cheek. Fiara quickly picked up the wing pendant, then looked at Natalia's distraught face. She squeezed the golden pendant in her palm.

"Let her go," Fiara commanded, slowly walking towards Natalia.

The nomed snarled, pushing her down into the ground.

"Get up!" Fiara screamed, glaring down at her.

Natalia slowly got to her knees, looking up at Fiara. Her body trembled as tears continued to fall from her weary eyes. She sucked in the air, trying to calm down. She tried to swallow down her fear. But she felt like she couldn't catch her breath as her emotions sat strongly over her.

Fiara stood over her. She had no compassion and her eyes burned with an evil glare. Her armor was the only thing that sparkled in the air. She held the pendant in front of Natalia's sore face, letting it dangle from her hand. Blood trickled down the necklace, landing in drops before her.

The golden wing-pendant swung back and forth in the wind, taunting Natalia.

All Natalia could do was look at it. The image of her giving it to Dolsia ripped through her mind. She screamed out, then started to sob.

"Where is *He* now?" Fiara asked, taunting her. "Where is the *son* of *God* now? Tell me, girl, where is the *light*? Where did it go?" Fiara chuckled, then threw the necklace in her face. Then Fiara brought her bloody sword up to Natalia's neck, threatening her. "Long live the king, they say… Death—shall be the only way to cleanse this world of such foolishness!"

Natalia grew angry, watching Dolsia's blood drip from Fiara's sword. Her chest ached as the thought of Dolsia dying crashed through her mind again. Her spirit cried out at the thought of her lands falling. She thought of Marrisa, and her mother. She thought of everyone who was dying because of the darkness. She grew mad as the noises of the excited nomed rung in her ears. The noise was so loud that she cringed.

Natalia screamed out as her emotions flew. The passion and sorrow in her inner being cried out. Her muscles tensed up. She grabbed her sword quickly, hitting Fiara with surprising strength.

Taken off guard, Fiara faltered a little, then growled as she raised her sword into the air.

They battled, their swords clashing with anger. Their armor gleamed in the faint firelight as the nomed continued to scream and snarl all around them.

"Natalia!" a voice cried from behind her.

It was Phillip, who was trying to fight through the crowd of nomed. The nomed were strong, attacking him and pulling him back as he fought them.

Natalia did not hear him as she continued to fight.

Fiara saw Phillip fighting to help Natalia, so she struck Natalia as hard as she could, sending her tumbling across the rough terrain.

Natalia winced in pain as she landed on her stomach. She released a big breath, pushing the dirt across the ground. She struggled to push herself up, slowly getting to her knees. She brought her busted hand to her pounding head. Blood dripped from her forehead and her face was bruised and gashed.

But as she went to rise up, she felt an intense, painful force explode in her back. She screamed out in agony as the pain overwhelmed her, saliva flying from her bloody mouth. She felt the intense pain soar through her chest. With sore tears in her eyes she quickly brought her hands to her chest, feeling a wet blade stick out of it. Blood came from her mouth, dripping onto her cold armor. Her ears rung as she gasped for air.

"NOO!" Phillip cried out. "NATALIA!" Anger built up in his chest as he fought through the relentless nomed.

He saw Fiara swiftly run behind Natalia, thrusting her blade into Natalia's back. He grew frantic as he saw the blade come out from her chest.

Fiara smiled wickedly, yanking her bloody sword from Natalia's back with one quick movement.

Natalia fell back onto the cold stone. Her body lay lifelessly as she stared up into the black sky. Blood blossomed below her golden armor as the warm life she held on to, slowly left her. Her vibrant-green eyes stared into the starless sky, her vision fading with every faint breath she had left. Silent tears fell from her eyes, drying on the sides of her face. No more tears fell as her body settled... Her mind drifted away... Then, her heart stopped pumping as it ran out of blood and strength.

Her last breath left her, blooming out into the cold air. Her eyelids slowly closed, forever...

"NATALIA!" Phillip cried out. His heart burst with emotion as he angrily swung his sword.

He let out his grief as he destroyed the Nomed around him. The nomed's heads and arms flew as Phillip fought with vengeance.

"FIARA!! You will die for this!" Phillip threatened with an emotional roar. "You will die!! You hear me, witch?! YOU WILL DIE!" Phillip cried out. He couldn't contain his emotion any longer.

Fiara's eyes flashed as she quickly looked towards Phillip. She let out a toothy roar, then ran up a rocky precipice as Phillip swung his sword after her. She disappeared into the chaos of the war, escaping him.

Phillip ran to Natalia, falling by her side. Blood was everywhere. His distraught eyes searched her. He franticly checked to see if she had a pulse in her neck. There was nothing but cold flesh. Phillip looked at her silent face, caressing her cheek and hair with his shaken hand. He began to sob, gently bringing her head to his chest. He held her tightly as he released anguish from deep within him. His heart broke as tears dripped down his contorted face.

He screamed out in grief, not letting her go as the constant chaos of war exploded all around him.

✝✝✝

Rafiul soared through the air above the fighting men. He felt the screams from his comrades in his heart. He anxiously looked around through the vicious fight. Then he saw Phillip holding onto Natalia. He knew she was dead by the silence that came from her spirit. His heart shook as he noticed Dolsia's dead body lying near them. Her head was gone as blood covered the stone among them. He saw red puddles everywhere.

Rafiul grew angry, clenching his jaw and fists. Then he noticed Fiara darting among the cliffs, away from where Natalia's and Dolsia's dead bodies lay. The light in him moved about quickly as he kept his eyes on Fiara. Now was his chance to stop the evil woman for good.

†

CHAPTER 24
Beasts and Black Fire

King Julpen and Gaibriul fought the great beast as it roared down at them. Bits of fire and brimstone shot from the beast's many mouths as they roared. Nearby soldiers shot arrows at it while others tried to attack from the ground with their swords. But the beast was too great, thrashing its massive tail as the crowds of men went flying. Gaibriul managed to cut one of the beast's ugly heads from its neck. He soared through the air on Serafim's back, weaving in and out of the beast's necks. He shot his golden arrows into its eyes and its other fiery throats. The beast roared, lifting its front paws into the air. It came back down in a mighty crash. The ground shook, knocking everyone to the ground.

A great sound continued to fill the atmosphere as the relentless war carried on. The ground became littered with dead bodies and weapons. It seemed as if the darkness was winning…

Gaibriul stopped shooting his arrows. He felt something that took him by surprise. He suddenly became inundated with a strange, intense feeling as he continued to soar through the cold air. Natalia and Dolsia were dead… He felt their spirits leave. He saw the golden cords of their spirits break from the world. He became filled with passion, shooting more arrows at the great beast. He shouted loudly as the light within him glowed.

King Julpen rode his horse quickly around the beast, looking around. He saw that they were becoming overwhelmed with nomed! More of his soldiers were falling. The nomed seemed to grow in number! They crawled from the dark shadows of the trenches and from the black mists that lingered above the ground. They were becoming inundated. It was never going to end!

King Julpen got his horse going below Gaibriul. He got his attention. "Gaibriul! We must draw back!" he shouted.

Gaibriul flew near him with intense eyes. "There is nowhere to draw to!" he yelled out. "Fight or run; that is it! But know that you *must* fight because we are near the end! We have to press on! As long as Lucif lives, darkness shall continue to grow, all across the world!" Gaibriul shot more arrows up at the tormenting beast. "It is all up to Tairren and Mikhal!" Gaibriul looked at King Julpen one last time, then got Serafim to fly higher towards the great beast's heads.

King Julpen shouted, swinging his sword as the nomed continued to try and pull him off of his horse.

†††

Rafiul soared through the air, eagerly looking for Fiara. She had disappeared into the chaos of the fight. He looked intently for her golden armor, but his eyes were being distracted by the armor of the many legna. He got Cherbim to fly lower. After a moment, he saw Fiara running among the jagged cliffs above the ruckus. Rafiul became filled with eagerness as he directed Cherbim to dash towards her. They came down at her quickly like lightning.

Rafiul jumped from Cherbim's back, tackling Fiara down to the ground. Their armor smacked together with a hard hit. Fiara grunted, being taken by surprise as her sword fell from her hand. They rolled upon the stone, yelling as anger rose up between them.

Fiara's eyes glowed with the black light. They were no longer golden as before, but black and shiny. The darkness was becoming stronger in her, and she was consumed. She realized who had attacked her, and she cursed him. She instantly became like a wild animal.

Rafiul pounded her body into the ground, forcefully bringing his sword to her neck.

Fiara spat as she brought her legs beneath him, pushing him off of her. She quickly grabbed her sword as Rafiul came at her again.

They began to fight. Their swords were quick and powerful. Intensity rose in their eyes, never leaving each other. Power grew inside of them. Light glowed throughout Rafiul's body as darkness pulsated through Fiara's. They wanted each other dead, more than anything, and they weren't going to stop until it happened.

Rafiul swung his sword down hard upon Fiara, making her flinch. His hits became stronger as the light glowed in his eyes.

Fiara had finally met her match. She clenched her teeth as she scowled at Rafiul with her ugly, black eyes. "Die like your king!" she screamed out in an ugly voice.

"My king is alive!" Rafiul grunted, blocking her swings. "And when He comes back, your regrets will overtake you!" he shouted back, louder.

He swiftly swung his sword with passion, catching her off guard. His hit was so strong that it went through her armor, slicing her shoulder and arm off.

Fiara screamed out as she fell to the ground. Her arm lay next to her in a puddle of black blood. Fiara growled like a ferocious nomed, then swung her leg beneath him.

Rafiul fell down but got up quickly just as Fiara did. He looked at her with intense eyes as she panted crazily. Her eyes were large and black and she licked her lips. Her having one arm didn't even stop her.

Fiara roared like a beast as she lunged at Rafiul, swinging with her one arm. She growled and made strange noises as they continued to fight.

She jabbed with her arm, forcing her blade into Rafiul's side. Her blade went through, piercing his insides.

Rafiul grunted, not aware that he was standing on the edge of the small cliff. He grabbed his side, becoming distracted. Fiara lunged at him, pushing him off the edge. He landed on his back, groaning as he hit the stone.

Fiara leapt off, coming down over him like a wild animal. She screamed as she pointed her sword down towards him. Rafiul moved quickly, just in time so that Fiara's blade hit the stone with a spark. Rafiul got up, holding his side. He watched Fiara get to her knees. She looked weakened and tired as she pulled herself up by the boulder that sat next to her. She panted, leaning over, still holding her sword. Black fluid continued to leak from her body, going down the side of her armor.

"It will never end," she growled, breathing hard. "The world…shall fall upon the Dark Lord's hand…"

Rafiul stood up straight, staring at her with his intense eyes. "It will end when the creator of it all, the almighty Lord of Light, says it is done."

Fiara didn't say anything as she glared up at Rafiul with her strange, black eyes. She breathed loudly, beginning to twitch a little. The darkness in her seemed to magnify with her anger. Steam seemed to literally come from her as her body began to glow like fire. She started towards Rafiul, growling as she did.

Rafiul swung his sword again, dismembering her other arm. More black fluid came from her other shoulder, oozing out onto the ground. She stopped moving, glaring at Rafiul as her eyes became large and frightening. She ran at Rafiul with a mighty roar. Puddles of black fluid trailed behind her.

Rafiul thrust his sword into her stomach where there was not much protection. Her body jerked, tensing up. She silently looked into his eyes as more black blood gurgled from her mouth and punctured flesh. But her eyes still glowed like a dark fire. She opened her mouth, panting as the fluid poured out.

Then, something happened that took Rafiul off guard. Fiara thrashed her head around as a terrifying noise came from her throat. As she roared louder, her eyes burned brightly and her face quivered. Steam came out of her flesh and hair. Her skin opened in some places as dark flames came from it. Her flesh began to melt right before Rafiul's eyes!

Rafiul flinched, backing away quickly as Fiara's body became ablaze in the strange fire. She became so fiery hot that her armor and jewels melted from her body! The black fluid that sat in great puddles around her also became ablaze. Fire circled around Fiara as she began to grow in size. Her flesh totally burned away, revealing her true form.

The spirit that came from inside of her looked like a fiery skeleton. But the fire was black! The black fire danced around its skull and upon a crown of horns that jutted from its head. Strange things moved about its bones, looking like moving scorched flesh and serpents, and strange black electricity. The grotesque substances slithered around its rib cage and black eye sockets. The spirit had many arms, moving around. Its mighty arms looked like fiery serpents, releasing black smoke all above its terrifying body.

The spirit of Fiara gazed down at Rafiul. "Watch them burn…," it said in a low voice that was deep and crackly.

The fiery monster turned towards the valley, then sent out a massive wave of black fire from its many arms and mouth. Black smoke billowed up as parts of the valley became scorched while other parts turned into lakes of fire.

Rafiul grabbed his sword from the black ground, holding tight. He did not falter or weaken, or show any sign of fear. "The earth shall scorch upon your fiery arms, but our light shall burn greater!" he shouted out angrily.

The spirit of Fiara quickly turned back towards Rafiul, glowing like a black star. A deep chuckled rumbled from the fire. Then the spirit of Fiara quickly spit fire out towards Rafiul, making it rain down upon him.

Rafiul moved quickly, rolling away from the deathly substance. He hit some with his sword, making it fall away from him. Just then, Rafiul didn't know how he was going to get past the entity's wrath, but he knew that the God of Light was strong.

They continued to fight before the fiery, dark valley. It seemed as if the end of the world was upon them all…

✝✝✝

Far across the screaming lands of Minslethrate, through the cold heaths and past the burning village of Prat, the Kingdom of Hanon sat silently among the relentless fires. It seemed as if the hand of destruction had come and gone away from the silent kingdom. A heavy black cloud lingered over the kingdom, filling it with ash and soot. An orange glow lit up the destroyed kingdom, lingering off of the weary people's dirty faces. People walked through the falling ash, calling for loved ones and looking upon the wreckage. It seemed as if hell had opened its arms to them.

Gideon looked out over his kingdom with his weary eyes. He limped before the opening that once held the grand balcony. He leaned against the stone, gazing out over the destruction of his homeland. His eyes looked further, trying to search for other kingdoms, but the smoke had become too thick. He couldn't see anything but the destruction of Hanon.

He thought about his family. He wondered if Sir Andor and the kind women who he went with were alright. He thought of Lord Timotheus, and his strong words. Everything seemed like a dream. He thought he would awaken from it at any moment. But he never did.

His eyes sparkled with tears, wondering if the torment would ever end. He wondered what good would come out of this, if any at all…

But his thoughts left him as a strange sound grabbed his attention. It sounded like thudding noises. He looked over the edge, peering down into the smoke that passed through the cold air. He couldn't see anything. But then he saw something that made his heart become full of sorrow. Two bright-red eyes came glowing up through the heavy smoke!

Gideon shook his head, slowly backing away from the edge. He swallowed down his fear that tried to come back up.

A mighty roar broke the heavy silence as Baal came up, out of the smoke!

Gideon fell down. He franticly looked up at Baal, pushing himself away from the opening as best as he could. He thought it had ended…but he was wrong. And now he was sure he was going to die.

Baal crashed onto the edge, flapping its mighty wings. He growled as his eyes glowed in the darkness. "It is not over until you die," he said with a growl. "As the world falls, it shall be cleansed of humans like you…"

Gideon slowly shook his head. He tried to get away from the beast, but his battered body wouldn't allow it. He lay on the ground, closing his eyes. He said a prayer as tears came down the sides of his smudged face. He knew death was upon him as he looked up at the high ceiling of the castle. The cold wind from the outside blew over his body as faint a song came to his aching heart.

He began to softly sing to the Lord of Light, sending a sweet melody into the air as Baal's flickering shadow came into the chamber…

I wait in the dark.
I need your light.
I'm trying to hold on to you.
I need you to rescue us.
Come and save us.

The soft melody of his song rose up into the air, trickling away in the cold wind that came in.

†

CHAPTER 25
Remember the Light

Moral ran through the castle halls. Her sword, much like her heart and mind, was becoming heavy. Her heart pounded as tears swelled up in her gray eyes. She had just heard the news of Lord Fernund's death and was running to inform Sora. She tried to hide her emotion as she rushed through the threshold of the library hall.

She stopped running, only walking quickly. She nervously looked around. They went into the hall for providence earlier that night, being led by Master Odwa. The grand hall was filled with many people. They huddled all around the dim chamber, hiding between book shelves and below tables. The cold air was filled with cries and whimpers as the loud sounds of the war outside seeped through the stone walls.

Every now and then the walls shook, as if creatures were pounding into them. Dust and crumbles of stone fell from the high ceiling as the candelabrums swayed back and forth. The grand stain-glass window glowed with warm colors of amber and gold as the great fires burned on the other side of it. The great leafless tree that was formed by the stain-glass could be seen beautifully as the glass glistened. The massive window was the only thing in the room that gave hope to the eye.

Moral hurried solemnly into the hall. She walked over injured people and past groups of crying women and children. Her heart broke as everything seemed out of control and dreadful. She thought of Lord Fernund and the news of his death.

She wished she hadn't even gone to fetch cold water and rags. Because when she did, a soldier saw her and told her of the horrible news. But he also had informed her that Sir Andor was leading many soldiers against Baffmit, pushing him and the nomed away from the castle and church. But judging by the noises and tremors of the walls, it seemed as if the nomed were ceasing the castle.

Moral saw Sora and Alexa standing with Master Odwa and a crowd of people. They all congregated in front of the tree off the stain-glass window. The old man was comforting them and the other people who stood listening. She walked quietly, gently making her way through the crowd of weary people.

Master Odwa looked at her, noticing how distraught she looked. He stopped talking as everyone glanced at her.

"I have more terrible news…," Moral said, looking at Master Odwa, then at Sora.

"Speak, child," the old man said, quickly.

"Lord Fernund...," Moral said, trying to cover her emotion. She spoke to the whole crowd but only looked at Sora. "He is dead..."

The crowd of people gasped, beginning to fret and cry. They became frightened as doom fell over them. They had no leader and their kingdom was falling as their fellow people were dying.

Sora slowly shook her head, bringing her hands over her mouth. She closed her eyes, turning around. Tears seeped beneath her eyelids as she began to cry.

Moral and Alexa rushed to her, trying to comfort her.

Master Odwa glanced at Sora, then looked down, slowly shaking his head. Compassion grew in him. "God help us all," he said in a low voice.

Master Odwa walked over to the small stand where the Book of Light sat. The people watched him with teary eyes as he opened the large book. "This old book...holds the ancient words of our God... This word was of the past, of our present, and of our future. It shall never die..." The book creaked as he opened it flat. He gently flipped through the old pages, slowly running his old finger down.

He caught everyone's attention, one by one. The people seemed to yearn for hope, something that would give them light. The old man looked up at the weary people beneath his white eyebrows. His old eyes sparkled.

"History is the past that unravels the present...opening the doors to an unstoppable future. And time is the present which passes by like a faint breeze." The people peered at him anxiously as he spoke. "This book, the Book of Light, has been through many ages...and yet, here you see it, right before you. His word...is powerful! In the beginning was the word...and the word was with God, because the word was God... And in the beginning, the living word became alive upon the Earth, flourishing in abundance. And over time, it became a legend...a legend that should never be forgotten...

"People of Minslethrate," he said in a louder voice. Everyone became quiet as the outside noises from the war could only be heard. "We are breathing upon darkness. We are living upon a time that is ruled by dominions and powers of the Dark Lord!" Everyone glanced at each other as tears fell from their smudged cheeks. "But I say to you now, people of Minslethrate, do not fear! The darkness that is killing and destroying, shall not take the light from us! King Yehoshua died for us, this kingdom, other kingdoms—this whole world! Whom shall we fear?" His eyes lit up as passion rose in his old heart.

The people listened carefully, being drawn to his words.

"We shall fear no one!" the old man shouted. "We shall fear no evil being that is conjured up by darkness!" His eyes glistened as he became quiet for a moment. His face became serious as deep thoughts seemed to come to him. "...Long ago, when the tyrant queen, Queen Karnidge, ruled Minslethrate...I was thrown down into the bowels of prison. I know her cursed name must never be uttered…but I must tell you this… I cried out to God every night! I was beaten, I was starved, I was forced away from the light for five years! FIVE YEARS!! But I refused to let my light be broken, I refused to let go of God! Because I knew that God was with me… He heard my cries! And when the torment stopped because of Queen Karnidge's death, I rose from my cell…and I praised GOD! Because I was brought away from the darkness, my chains were broken, and I was lifted from the mire!" He lifted his hands into the air as his voice shook.

"I know you are frightened and weary. I know the darkness grows before you, but we must not forget about the light! And now we have no leader, but that is why we must trust in God's word, stronger than ever now! King Yehoshua is our leader, our confidence, our savior! But, people of Minslethrate, you must believe first in your heart—in your whole being! If you do not know what I am speaking on about now, then you must open the eyes of your heart upon the Light of God! Open your heart to King Yehoshua! Some say he is only a legend; some say he was only a king… NO, I tell you! He is the King of Kings and Lord of Lords and He shall be praised!"

The people became influenced by the old man, beginning to perk up. They nodded their heads as their hearts fluttered. The loud sounds of the war outside the castle didn't even discourage them.

"Ask King Yehoshua into your hearts, now. NOW, I tell you! BELIEVE!" he shouted, raising his frail arms into the cold air. He seemed more youthful all of a sudden as he spoke. "Do not delay, because as darkness bangs the walls of our castle, the end draws near!"

The people slowly stood up, one by one. Tears dried on their cheeks as they placed their hands on their hearts.

"For the God of Light loved this world, loved US so much, that he gave his only son, King Yehoshua." Master Odwa became quiet for a moment as his old voice trembled with emotion. "Yes, my fellow people…God loved us so much, that he gave his only son up… Did you hear me? And He still loves us. That's why we are saved by his grace, now!"

He looked all around at the people as they watched and listened intently. Even the children and injured ones listened.

"God LOVES you! He gave up his only son so that whoever BELIEVES…shall not parish, but live everlasting life… That's something we should never forget! When the world comes crashing down on us, when darkness brings death and all lights go out, when there seems to be no way out, we shall rise up and proclaim that Yehoshua lives FOREVER!"

One by one the people in the room began to cheer, making noises as hope grew in them.

"Believe now, people of Minslethrate! And hold on to that faith with all of strength you have. Put on the Armor of Righteousness; hold the Sword of Truth and the Shield of Faith! The time is now, people of Minslethrate...," the old man's voice grew quiet as he gazed at them. "Darkness never looked so beautiful, knowing that your darkness was broken by King Yehoshua long ago, on the tree... Be the light in a dark place... Remember the light... Hold on until the end...because *He* is coming back... He is coming back..."

The whole chamber sat in silence as the wise old man stopped speaking. They were filled with inspiration and wonder. The noises continued to grow outside of the castle, but their hearts grew with light. Tears dried on their faces and their minds throbbed with the words they heard.

Sora and Moral smiled at Master Odwa, touched by his testimony and words. They wiped tears from their eyes as they looked around the calmed chamber. Master Odwa nodded his head at them, then smiled with twinkling eyes.

But the silence ended quickly when a blast of fire hit the other side of the window. The roar was loud and the heat could be felt radiating from the glass. They all noticed, and backed away quickly. The black tree on the stain-glass window stood out sharply among the bright-orange pieces of the surrounding glass.

"Stand strong, my people!" Master Odwa shouted.

Loud cracking sounds came from the window as the glass turned black. Suddenly, the glass burst. Fire erupted into the great library. The fire dispersed quickly, leaving a large plume of black smoke. The loud sounds of the war came in, followed by a gust of cold air and deep thud sounds.

Everyone backed away quickly, peering through the smoke. Gasps and loud breaths came across the people as red eyes could be seen glowing in the smoke.

King Baffmit slowly walked into the hall, crunching the glass beneath his large hooves. Steam rose up from the glass, circling around his massive body. His horns stood out as great fires roared behind him, around the castle. His handless arm dripped black fluid which sizzled in steamy puddles. He flapped his mighty feathery wings, then folded them back behind his broad shoulders. He balled his one fist, gazing over the massive crowd of people.

"I've been looking for you all..." he said in a voice that growled across the silent people. "You all will pay for the severance of my hand."

"Leave! You have no power here!" Master Odwa shouted. He stood boldly before the powerful creature, appearing small and frail.

King Baffmit chuckled, peering down at the old man with his glowing eyes.

"I am power, old man," he said.

King Baffmit sneered, rustling his feather. Then he thrashed out both of his mighty wings. The crackle of his wings ripped through the intense atmosphere. The power of his wings hit Master Odwa, sending the old man into a pillar.

The people screamed, shocked at what they saw. Some people began to cry a little, bringing their hands over their faces. Others covered the eyes of their children, trying to comfort them.

Moral and Sora rushed over to Master Odwa, franticly looking over him. His head had bashed into the marble, hard. Blood came from the side of his head, heavily pouring out.

"Master Odwa!" Moral shrieked, pulling her bloody hand from his head. Her hands shook as her heart raced. She rested his head on her lap, looking down at his old face caringly. Blood soaked her dress and ran onto the cold tile.

"Do not cry," the old man said in a fading voice. "Remember...the light..." He suddenly stopped speaking, closing his sparkling eyes. His last breath left him as his body became limp.

Sora brought her hands over her mouth, "Oh, God help us all."

Some people who surrounded them began to cry, looking at the wise old man as their hearts broke.

"Master Odwa?" Moral said in a shaken voice. "Master Odwa?!" She shook him gently, beginning to cry. Tears came down her pink cheeks.

The outside firelight played on his face. He looked as if he was in a deep sleep. His old face looked peaceful.

Moral began to breathe hard as she slowly looked up at Baffmit. "You, beast!" she screamed out with a shaken voice. She glared at the evil being from where she sat.

Baffmit chuckled again, taking his gaze off of her. "I wanted you dead, woman. But it seems as if you have led me to a whole crowd of weak humans..."

The fires burned brightly behind Baffmit, sending black smoke everywhere. The people looked up at him. Their eyes silently stared. They did not know what to do as the war went on. But they remembered Master Odwa's words...and they remembered the light.

✝✝✝

The lands grew darker. The fires flourished higher. The winds blew colder. The world they knew was falling apart, beneath the power of Lucif. All the way from Minslethrate, to the consumed Village of Prat, and past the scorched Kingdom of Hanon, the whole world became blanketed in smoke and insidious mists. The sky loomed low to the earth like a black mantle, devouring any kind of light. All of the world's hope seemed to be lost…

But among the fallen world, there was still a great multitude of people who followed and remembered the light. It seemed as if darkness was winning. But through all of the pain and suffering, the light still burned inside the yearning hearts of believers.

That light within them all cried out in one voice, going up to the Kingdom of Nevaeh like a mighty prayer. The God of Light who seemed to have left them, did not, but was closer to them than they knew. He heard their cries, never forgetting them. He opened up the windows of heaven, releasing a quenching rain down upon the earth.

Then, something happened that would change the world, forever…

✝✝✝

†

CHAPTER 26
Return of the King

Mikhal had been battling Lucif upon the balcony of the Dark Tower of Sacrifice. The Dark Lord grew, becoming an overwhelmingly massive entity. He loomed over the Dark Tower, bringing his dark mists upon Mikhal. The mists were like shadows and battled Mikhal relentlessly. But Mikhal continued to fight, bringing a mighty shout into the air as passion grew within him.

A mile away from the tower, the mighty war between the legna and nomed ravaged on. Fires roared all around the south, sending its rancid smoke all over. The cries and sounds of despair filled the air as the great beast and the spirit of Fiara seemed to rule the battle.

All over the kingdom, there was an anguish-filled encounter. It seemed as if it would never end. It seemed as if the end was upon them, until, a mighty sound came from behind the heavy, black sky...

The rumbles started low, then became louder. The ground began to quake in the south, bringing a loud cracking sound into the air. The sound came from the earth ripping apart! The great trench that released darkness, opened wider, stretching across the battlefield. Many faltered, falling to the ground as the ground shook violently!

Rain fell from the dark sky as mighty lightning suddenly crashed. The strange weather stunned everyone. Many began to glance up, surprised by the sudden rain and lightning. The lightning began to light up the sky with its power, sending loud crashes across the land. The heavy rain fell upon the lands, drowning the many fires. The rain quickly washed some nomed away! The waters threw them into the dark trench that was caused by the earthquake.

Some continued to fight in the rain, not giving up as the nomed fought even harder. But among the war of the world, the rain continued to fall, drowning the great fires from all of the kingdoms. Smoke and steam rose into the sky as the embers of the once flourishing fires, stopped. Then, after the fires died, the rain mysteriously became a light drizzle.

All across the lands, people recognized the strange weather, becoming alarmed and somewhat relieved.

The skies made another loud sound! All across the lands, people began to look to the skies. Even the nomed took note. The sound was strange, sounding like a mixture between a loud trumpet sound and thunder!

The noises became louder until it grabbed the attention of every living soul upon the earth.

†††

Mikhal and the Dark Lord continued to fight. The Dark Lord ignored the sounds that the sky made, yearning to smite Mikhal and his army.

The sounds grew louder, catching Mikhal's attention.

Mikhal knew something was going to happen. He felt it in his spirit, and it burned greatly. As he fought, he called out to the flying beasts within his spirit. He knew he had to get them off of the balcony before it was too late. He felt the beasts answer his call right away.

"Tairren, we must go, now!" he screamed out. "Be ready!"

Tairren looked quickly, holding onto Marrisa's body with all of his strength. The winds blew hard upon them as the strange lightning crashed in the black sky. The sky was terrifying and chaotic! He picked Marrisa's lifeless body up, looking up at Lucif's mighty entity.

"Lucif, it is your turn to suffer!" Mikhal shouted out, swinging his sword at the dark powers that came from Lucif.

Lucif sent a mighty roar into the sky, sounding like a mighty dragon. "Darkness shall continue to take your precious humans! Darkness will not die!" Lucif screamed out. "LONG LIVE DARKNESS, THE KING OF THE WORLD!!" Lucif brought his dark mists into the air, screaming out into the chaotic sky.

Suddenly, something happened that took everyone's breath away. Everyone saw it, every living person, young and old, male and female, and every living animal upon the Earth, saw it. The legna looked up with zeal in their hearts while the nomed trembled. Lucif roared like an angry beast. His screams ripped through the sky, along with the shrieks from the great beast and the spirit of Fiara. They all knew what was taking place! The legna rejoiced while the powers of darkness looked suddenly confused and afraid. It was the first time that the nomed and the great dominions of darkness looked terrified!

The skies opened up upon the lands! The black clouds and mists quickly shrunk back, giving way to a bright, blinding light! The light contained many colors, shining gloriously. The light ripped through the darkness, shining down like a beam of light.

Then, as every eye watched, an entity that looked like fire came from the glorious hole in the black sky! The beautiful form sat on a grand, white horse that glowed like the moon. The form was of a mighty king! A crown of light sat upon his head and his clothes looked pure-white, pulsing like fire. King Yehoshua rode on His glowing white horse, being followed by a massive army of legna! The people of light blew their loud trumpets, alerting the whole world of King Yehoshua's return. They poured down upon the earth like a massive wave of light.

The world was seeing King Yehoshua's return for the first time; and He brought with him love, peace, justice, and wrath...

739

The nomed screamed out in pain as the trickle of rain that fell from the sky turned into fiery light. The fiery raindrops sparkled, pelting the nomed like arrows. The nomed fell to the ground, screaming out as they melted into the mists that trembled on the grounds. King Yehoshua's presence made the mists scream out as well. The ancient king's power forced the darkness into the trench that stretched across the valley. The army of King Yehoshua spread out upon the lands, avenging every living soul!

The spirit of Fiara and the great beast fell to their knees. The power of light was too much for them. They yielded to the power of King Yehoshua, falling upon the light, face down. They screamed and growled, but the light drowned their horrible screams. Their bodies thrashed about as the ground began to tremble again. The earth took them, forcing them deep down into the bowels of the earth. Their cries and screams vanished as they disappeared in the darkness.

"NOOO!" Lucif cried out as his voice faltered in the air.

The light from Yehoshua and from the opening in the sky spread out over the lands like water, forcing the darkness back into the deep abyss!

Mikhal and Tairren watched with eager eyes as they fell on their knees. They were anxious and relieved. The sight of King Yehoshua and his army was breathtaking, filling the whole south with beautiful light. The colors of the power of King Yehoshua made their hearts melt.

Some flying beasts that Mikhal had called earlier swooped down towards them, quickly landing on the balcony. They roared, alarming them. Mikhal and Tairren were suddenly taken out of their trance. They had to get off of the balcony, quickly!

The Dark Tower rumbled and shook as they quickly dashed towards the beasts. The tower was beginning to crumble down as the ground continued to shake! As Mikhal ran to the beast, he spotted the king's ancient crown that fell from Marrisa's head, sitting upon the ground. He quickly grabbed the crown, then got onto the beast, looking at Tairren. Tairren pulled Marrisa's body onto the beast with him just as the top of the tower came falling down, saving her flesh from its fate of burning in the eternal lake of fire… They held on tightly as the beasts leapt into the air, spreading their wings to take flight. The balcony began to fall as the rest of the tower crumbled, crashing down towards the bottom of the great mountains.

The abyss below the temple roared as the stone and rubble fell into it. All of the darkness was being sent down into the black abyss and the trenches, forced into the fiery lake for eternity.

King Yehoshua, followed by His massive army, brought light back to the world, destroying the darkness that lingered! He and his legna filled the sky, making the black clouds shake and dissolve in the air! The forgotten colors of the sky began to come through as the mists faded, bringing sunlight back!

Lucif screamed out in a deep voice as King Yehoshua flew over him like the sun above the earth. Light came from King Yehoshua, falling upon Lucif like a mighty ray of powerful sunlight. Lucif screamed out, falling to the ground with a mighty crash. He bowed before the mighty king, shaking as he did. Then after bowing before the almighty lord, he then fell into the black abyss with a loud roar. He disappeared, along with the rest of his lingering mists, falling deep into the abyss.

Then, the ground began to quake as the fiery rain drops continued to fall. The great abyss and trench closed back up, making a loud sound in the air. The earth was locking the darkness in the lake of fire!

Everyone across the lands walked out into the cool air, bringing their hands into the air as the soft fiery rain drops fell upon their bodies. The rain drops sparkled like beautiful light, not burning them, but filling them with the love-light of God, instead. Cheers and happiness erupted into the air as the sky gave way to an early morning sun. The sky was a brilliant blue with vibrant pink, orange, and gold hues splashed about it. As the sun peeked above the mountains, the sky revealed the glorious colors of King Yehoshua. It was a sight they had forgotten, and it filled their hearts with joy.

But something else strange happened as the sparkling rain drops continued to fall. The return of King Yehoshua brought life upon the earth! The people who had died with light in their hearts had awakened from death! They opened their new eyes. King Yehoshua was filled with so much light and life, that his presence upon the world brought the dead back to life! Even the colors in the kingdom and in the nature seemed to brighten, becoming vibrant among the King of Light's presence.

The one's who died with light in their hearts stood up. Their bodies were new and unbroken. They knew that their time on Earth was short; they were going home to the kingdom of light. Their hearts glowed with joy, anticipating the moment when King Yehoshua would take them back to the Kingdom of Nevaeh with Him…

✝✝✝

All across the world, it happened this way. From Minslethrate all the way to Hanon and beyond, the world was becoming new under the power of Yehoshua. Just when they had thought that it was all over, the coming of Yehoshua suddenly forced them under the influence of power.

All the people of the world saw it with their own eyes.

The Northern Kingdom of Minslethrate saw Baffmit fall under the power of God as the mighty legna came over them all. Just as soon as Sir Andor led his men towards Baffmit, they witnessed him fall to his knees and bow just before the great legna dragged him off into an oblivion. Sir Andor and his men lowered their swords then, submitting to the light that fell upon them. They were amazed and joyful as they saw the sky open up with the light pouring out of it. Sir Andor, Moral, Sora, and the people, rejoiced as the radiant light filled the castle and the kingdom. The nomed sizzled and screamed out in the sky upon the majestic light as the destructive fires went out. They too rejoiced as the drizzle of light fell from the sky, falling onto the faces of the ones who died for King Yehoshua. Tears of joy fell from the people's eyes as they saw the fallen believers of light rise from their deaths...

Even so, far off in the Kingdom of Hanon, the weary people saw the rain of light fall upon their kingdom, sending the smoke and fires away. They too saw life and light and love come suddenly as the skies opened up. Gideon, as well as many others, saw Baal fall to his knees like a shadow submitting to the early morning sun. Gideon got up, looking into the light as his wounds healed, just as he saw Baal being taken away right before him. He fell before the Lord, crying out with praises... They all witnessed Baal roar out as the legna and the light of King Yehoshua come and force him away from Gideon, away from them all. They saw how the dead bodies of the nomed melted away with the heavy shadows and smoke!

It was this way, everywhere. Everyone saw the coming of King Yehoshua simultaneously, having the same experiences and feelings. The whole world exploded with mighty colors and light as it rejoiced the coming of their Lord of Light. The followers of the light rejoiced as the non-believers began to believe.

†

CHAPTER 27
Rapturous Light

The men of Minslethrate and the legna jumped and shouted praises as the darkness vanished from the valley. Sunlight poured over the lands, revealing a crisp sky that they had almost forgotten. The cold winds went away, along with the smoke and heavy shadows. The land was filled with a joyful noise as everyone shouted and cried out praises.

Phillip couldn't stop smiling as he saw the love-light of God fall over the lands. He stood up, looking at the glorious light that fell from the sky.

"We've won," a voice said from behind him.

He heard it above the noise, because it was a voice that he loved.

Phillip turned quickly. It seemed as if time stood still all around him. Tears glistened in his eyes as he caught a glimpse of Natalia standing before him. His heart leapt for joy as he grabbed her in his arms, swinging her around. They laughed with joy as Phillip stopped swinging her, standing her before him. They grew quiet, gazing into each other's eyes.

"I thought you were dead," Phillip said, placing his hand on her cheek.

He smiled at her, noticing how bright and beautiful she looked. She was filled with a light he had not seen in her before. Her green eyes looked like the ocean and her skin glowed like luscious honey. Even her hair glistened, every strand reflecting the sunlight.

"Remember when Uriel prophesied over me, Phillip?" she asked, touching his cheek. Phillip nodded his head, looking intently into her vibrant eyes. "It has been done. She prophesied my death, Phillip... I did what I was supposed to do; my quest on this earth has been fulfilled," she said, smiling. "And...I believe it was to help you... When Mikhal prophesied that I would save a soul, I thought it was Dolsia... But it was you...," she said, never taking her eyes from his. "It was you, all along, Phillip. Remember when you told me that you had a vision, that the hand of God pulled you from the darkness and said that your kingdom was great, that you would do great things?"

Phillip nodded his head as a tear went down his cheek, "Yes," he responded.

"I believe that is why you are here, why you were influenced by me and the light... You will do great things in Ishkar, Phillip," Natalia said, smiling bigger. "You promised me that no matter what, that you would rise from this and lead your kingdom under the influence of God! And so, you must and you will! You are the heir to the throne of Ishkar, and you will lead your people like the great man of God you are!"

743

Phillip nodded his head as tears continued to go down his cheeks. He knew that this was her farewell to him…

"I will…," he said.

Natalia smiled at him, searching his eyes, then embraced him again.

"The light of King Yehoshua has brought me back…," she said. Her voice was low but happy. "But this world is not my home… I must go with King Yehoshua and the other believers to the Kingdom of Nevaeh." Her face glowed as a beautiful smile lit up her face.

They embraced each other again as the cheers of the people continued to erupt all around them.

Phillip understood her. Even though he loved her with all of his heart, he knew that they had to do what was planned by the God of Light. He knew that God did have great plans for him back at his Kingdom of Ishkar, without Natalia. But he also knew that Natalia's new home in Nevaeh was far greater, and that he would see her one day…

"I must go," Natalia finally said, looking up into Phillip's passionate eyes.

Phillip nodded his head as tears sparkled in his dark eyes. He then gently kissed her lips. After a moment, he looked back into her glowing face.

Natalia smiled a soft smile, caressing his cheek. She wiped the tears from his face. "Don't ever forget about me," she said.

Phillip just looked into her eyes. He tried to hold onto the emotion that was trying to spill out of him. "I will see you one day…" He held her hands, squeezing them.

Natalia slowly walked away from him. She let go of his hand, then turned one last time to look at him. She smiled softly, then turned to leave him.

Phillip just watched as she walked towards a great light. He closed his eyes as tears ran down his face. He thought of Natalia, and how she did change his life, influencing him to follow King Yehoshua. He knew that he was saved by King Yehoshua's grace and set free from his past. He opened his eyes; Natalia was gone. But he knew where she was going, and that made his heart become filled with joy.

Phillip looked into the beautiful sky as he continued to think of Natalia. The images of Lady Natalia made him want to do great things. And he wanted to lead his kingdom to greatness, just as he promised her, so that he would see her one day in the Kingdom of Nevaeh…

Phillip's attention went back to the present situation as he noticed a crowd of men and legna forming, further towards where the Dark Tower used to be.

✝✝✝

Mikhal stood before King Julpen. He handed him the ancient crown he had retrieved, looking into his dazed eyes. "This is Tairren's crown," Mikhal said.

King Julpen looked up at him, taking the crown from him. He understood completely. He nodded his head, not saying anything. He felt speechless.

Mikhal looked at him with his yellow-gold eyes, then patted him on the shoulder. "Till next time, King Julpen," he said, smiling. Then he turned to walk away with the other legna.

King Julpen watched as the mighty legna left.

The light around the south seemed to come together in one spot in the center of the valley. The light looked like a massive, colorful, living fire. All of the legna and great white beasts stood around the mighty fire. The light of the legna and the fire came together, making much of the valley glow. Right in the center, stood King Yehoshua. Everyone who had rose from the dead all around the world made their way to the light, being welcomed into the light with love and peace.

The mighty beasts glided down to the ground and all of the legna turned towards the mighty king who stood among the light. Everyone began to bow before King Yehoshua. Even the risen ones and the men of Minslethrate bowed before the Lord. The atmosphere was filled with something no one could explain.

Then, something spectacular happened. As the light spilled over the earth with King Yehoshua's presence, green grass and flowers of many colors began to grow upon the ground. The Black Field of Old Blood became a beautiful valley, full of the richness of nature and new life. The southern parts of Minslethrate resembled the northern parts. The kingdom became one, no longer divided and ridden with forbidden lands.

King Julpen and his men stood and watched; they were amazed. They watched the beautiful light among the luscious grass and herbs. They saw the Archlegna standing together in the glorious light. They saw Mikhal, Gaibriul, Rafiul, Uriel, and even Dolsia. Dolsia stood in the center of them, appearing happy and at peace. They nodded their glorious heads and smiled at them all. It was a farewell gesture. But they knew that they would see them again…

King Julpen also noticed Natalia and Master Odwa standing near each other. He took a deep breath and pressed his lips together as both sorrow and happiness came over him. But then he noticed people that he had not noticed before. He saw his beloved wife, Queen O'nessa… His eyes became teary as he noticed her standing and smiling at him. He gently waved to her. And when she nodded back at him, his heart quickened. He brought his hand over his heart as tears came down his cheeks. He knew right then that he wanted to see her again, one day.

"Live for me unto the ends of the world, and you will too see me in the Kingdom of Nevaeh," King Julpen heard. It was the voice of King Yehoshua. "Lift Minslethrate up like the sun, Julpen. I will be with you…"

King Julpen bowed before the voice of Yehoshua as his heart throbbed.

Everyone who stood before the mighty light heard the voice of King Yehoshua in their hearts. But they heard their own blessing from Yehoshua. And they heard what they must do to finish their quests upon the Earth.

Then, the mighty light exploded out into the atmosphere as the light spread out. The flash of great wings came from the intense light, appearing like the great wings of the mighty owl… After a quick moment, the light was gone.

Everyone looked around with passion in their hearts. It was strange how silent it had gotten. Only the sounds of the breezes pushing past the earth could be heard. The new flowers and tall grasses waved in the air as the sound of peace came over the lands. The colors of the earth were not as vibrant as they were when the light of King Yehoshua touched them, but they were still breathtaking.

"We shall go home, men of Minslethrate!" King Julpen shouted. "Our kingdom shall rise up, in the name of King Yehoshua!"

Everyone began to shout, filling the south with joyful noise once again.

†††

Tairren kneeled quietly, pensive because of what he had seen. He saw his dear companion, Natalia, standing in the light with the other people and legna. He also saw a man who he had seen in his dreams before. The man was his father, Timotheus… He knew it was his father because of what he felt. His father had watched him from the light, and he watched his father, who appeared proud of him.

Tairren also saw the herbs and grass spring up, out of the earth. He too witnessed the glorious light vanish in an oblivion. He heard the great sound of joyful noise erupt all around him.

But it was hard for him to celebrate like everyone else. He was still stricken with remorse. He wanted to cry out, but he refused to show his emotions anymore.

"Tairren, take your rightful place upon Minslethrate. For I give you this kingdom, and all in it…," the great voice said to Tairren. The mighty voice sounded out right before the light of Yehoshua vanished.

Tairren looked into the sky, still on his knees. The sky was a beautiful blue. The blue of the sky reminded him of Marrisa's crystal-clear eyes. He closed his eyes, listening to the breezes moving across the tall grasses and the joyful shouts of the soldiers.

He had been kneeling upon the grass, over Marrisa's body. He opened his eyes, looking back down at her. Her skin was white as snow and her face looked peaceful. Her red hair fluttered upon her face and neck. Flower petals danced over her, then fluttered away with the breezes.

Tairren's attention was taken away from Marrisa as King Julpen kneeled on the other side of him. He watched the king as he lovingly looked down at his daughter. He watched with an aching heart as the king placed his dirty hands upon her clasped, cold hands. He watched as a tear came down the king's rugged face.

King Julpen looked up at Tairren with silent tears in his eyes. "You've loved my daughter very much…," he said.

Tairren was quiet for a moment, then nodded his head. His dark-blue eyes sparkled, but he refused to let them release anymore tears. "I still do," he finally said, bringing his gaze back down to Marrisa. "My name is Tairren, Your Majesty," he said. "And I love your daughter more than my own life…"

King Julpen just looked at him, touched by his passion. Right then, he realized that a young man with so much love in his heart, was going to lead his kingdom in the future…

"I know who you are…," King Julpen finally said, resting his hand on Tairren's shoulder. "And I know that you would've been the best suitor for my daughter…"

Tairren looked up at the king quickly. He was surprised by the king's words, by someone he had never met.

King Julpen patted his shoulder, then stood up, leaving Tairren with Marrisa's body.

Tairren just gazed down at Marrisa. He didn't want to pull his eyes from her. He thought of all the moments they shared together. He thought of her smile and her giggle. He thought of their care-free days, which seemed like ages ago. He thought of how much she loved humanity… And he also thought of what could've happened before she was kidnapped. He thought of what could've happened while Lilith had her, while she was locked away in the retched Dark Tower. "What happened to you?" he thought. "Why did you give up on your spirit?" he wondered. He touched her cold cheek, wondering where her spirit was just then…

She was the only one out of the people he loved, who did not rise because of King Yehoshua's return. She was the only one who was still dead…

†

CHAPTER 28
Ashes to Gold

Among the Kingdom of Hanon, a grand celebration was held. After days of cleaning and rebuilding, the once great kingdom was beginning to become whole again. They held a great celebration, lifting up the everlasting light of God. They also commemorated Gideon's bravery as Lord Timotheus proudly dubbed him a knight. Sir Andor was also honored for his bravery and compassion as the old king of Hanon announced that he was their future king. He also announced that they were going to be helping the small village of Prat and other nearby civilizations.

Their hearts beat with compassion and happiness. They were humbled by the war that tried to destroy them. It seemed as if the darkness that tried to stop them, helped them to grow. But it wasn't that darkness had helped them, but it was that God turned their broken pieces into blessings...

†††

Hanon grew from the darkness that tried to stop them, but miles across the lands, the Minslethratians still moved with the feelings of uncertainty and sadness.

Days seemed to pass by slowly. And the remaining survivors of the Minslethratian army traveled back to the northern part of Minslethrate. As they went, their emotions went back and forth. They were happy to be going back home, but they were anxious because of the uncertainty of their kingdom. They were also saddened because of the loss of their princess... They traveled for days, trekking across the beautiful lands. It was strange not having the legna by their side any longer. But they were at ease by knowing that Minslethrate was saved by the God of Light's grace.

They carried Marrisa in a wooden vessel that Tairren had produced for her. The casket was nicely built and was filled with many types of flowers. Only Marrisa's face would be seen peeking through the flowers if one were to open it.

King Julpen wished to have a ceremony for his daughter, so that everyone in the kingdom could see her one last time before burning her flesh into the air...

†††

Arriving to the kingdom was bitter sweet. It was early in the day, and the people were beginning to clean and pick up the destruction of their kingdom. The soldiers, who were left alive, went back to their families. There was a grand celebration in the kingdom. The people of Minslethrate were relieved to see that their king was still alive and well. And King Julpen was taken aback to see that much of his kingdom and castle had been spared. And even though the marketplace and town square had been destroyed and charred, he knew that their horizon was new and that great things were to come. He knew that the rebuild of his kingdom would be far greater than anything he could dream of.

Everyone embraced each other as joyful tears fell from their eyes.

†††

Moral looked up at everyone embracing. Her heart raced as she franticly searched for her son. She hurried through the crowd of men, but didn't see him. She grew frantic, bringing her hands over her face. She searched the weary faces of the returning men, yearning to see her son.

"Mother!" a voice called to her.

She turned quickly. Her eyes widened with tears; she saw her son walking towards her. Her chin quivered as her face contorted with emotion. She cried tears of joy at the sight of him. "Oh, Tairren, my son!" she shrieked with emotion.

Moral ran through the crowd, finally making it to Tairren. She joyfully wrapped her arms around him, releasing all the emotion she had bottled up within her. "My brave son!" she cried, holding him tightly.

Tairren quietly wrapped his arms around her, closing his tired eyes. "It seems we all are heroes in this... I'm glad you're safe, mother," he said, closing his eyes. He was relieved that she was well, and happy to be home and alive. But his heart held a sadness that only he understood.

She pulled away from him, glancing into his sad eyes. She smiled, caringly looking at her son.

"I saw father," Tairren said. "I know that he lives forever in the Kingdom of Nevaeh."

"I saw him too," she responded. Her voice was soft. "I saw him in the great light that came from the sky..."

Tears fell down her cheeks as she caressed Tairren's solemn face. "He would be so proud of you...just as I am," she said.

Tairren became quiet, looking away from her. He was thankful for his mother's words and comfort, because he didn't feel proud of himself at all. He kept thinking about Marrisa... She was the reason why he left, and he felt that he had failed her. Even though they had won—he felt as if he had lost...

"What's wrong, my son?" Moral asked.

She looked into her son's face. His face didn't look as young and fresh as she remembered it. He looked as if he had matured overnight. He had bags under his once bright eyes and his face looked thinner. He looked more rugged, having dirt smudged all over his skin. She saw that he had a sadness about him and that his eyes were glassy and red.

"Marrisa...," he finally said, but paused for a moment. "She's gone..."

Moral just looked up at him. She was quiet for a moment, then pressed her lips together. She touched his cheek, trying not to show any remorse. She just gently nodded her head. "I'm sorry, son," she finally said, quietly hugging him.

After a moment, Tairren kissed his mother's forehead, then silently pulled away from her. "I'm tired," he said.

"Yes, Tairren, go and get cleaned up and rest." Her voice shook. She touched his cheek again, understanding his pain. She understood the hurt of losing a loved one...

Tairren nodded his head, then turned to leave.

"Tairren," she called, catching his attention. "I'm so proud of you. Thank you...for all you have done..."

Tairren just looked at her for a moment, responding with a faint nod of his head. He then left, fading into the crowds of people.

Moral stood silently, just watching. Tears built up in her gray eyes as she brought her hands to her mouth. She thought that their happy ending was slipping away from them. She looked around, then noticed Sora.

Sora seemed to be frantically looking around for someone. She rushed about, speaking to anyone who crossed her path. Sora spotted Moral, then quickly rushed over to her.

"Oh, Moral," she said, breathlessly. "Have you seen Natalia?" she asked. "I've looked all over!" Her eyes were wide and anxious.

Moral just silently looked at her, responding by shaking her head. With the thought of Marrisa being dead, she had a bad feeling about Natalia too. But she didn't want to say anything.

Sora quickly noticed King Julpen walking with a young man. She rushed over to him, abruptly leaving Moral's side.

Moral watched as Sora pushed through towards King Julpen and the young man. She watched Sora franticly speak with the king, who looked sad all of a sudden. Moral noticed how the king put his hand on Sora's shoulder, slowly shaking his head. Sora took a couple of steps backwards, bringing her shaken hands to her mouth. Moral's heart broke as she watched Sora begin to sob. She knew right then that Natalia was gone...

She hurried to Sora with tears in her eyes. They embraced each other, sobbing.

"I thought she was safe, Moral!" Sora cried out. "I thought God had his hands over her!"

Moral just silently held onto Sora as she buried her face into her shoulder. She didn't know what to say to Sora. Her heart broke as she looked into the sky with tears in her eyes.

After a moment of sorrow, Sora felt a hand on her back, followed by a man's voice. "I'm so sorry for your loss," he said softly.

Both Sora and Moral looked up with dewy faces. He was the young man who they had seen walking with King Julpen. Sora didn't know who he was, but Moral recognized his face.

"Natalia was a wonderful woman," he said with a faint smile. "She helped me in a way that I can't explain… It hurts…but just know that she is in a far better place, right now…" The young man looked at them, then smiled softly again. "…I saw her with King Yehoshua…" He looked at them one last time, then turned away.

They watched as he left, walking towards King Julpen.

"Prince Phillip…," Moral faintly said to herself. She remembered him before Minslethrate had changed. She watched the prince as he and King Julpen walked through the crowds of people.

Sora inhaled, wiping her face. She stared off, thoughtfully thinking of her niece. "She's in the light…," she finally said.

The women held each other as they thought of their loved ones. Their world had been flipped upside down. But the words from the prince helped them, which, he would never know…

All around them was a mixture of sadness and happiness. But they knew in their hearts that everything was going to be okay…

✝✝✝

As the day slowly progressed, King Julpen ordered the kingdom to rest. Then, in the following morning, the king had many people go out to the Ducre' Provence to clean and prepare the deceased Lord Fernund's home. He declared that Sora was the new Lady of the house, which instantly ranked her as a noble.

Also, that day, the kingdom commemorated everyone who had died, lifting their families up in prayer. King Julpen also spoke of Master Odwa during that time, honoring him and his life. The whole kingdom stood among the Great Field of Minslethrate, holding flower petals and letting them go into the wind.

Then, as the solemn day went by, they began to prepare for Marrisa's ceremony and cremation. It was put together nicely, but the people of Minslethrate were apprehensive about it. As the day went by, they anxiously waited for it to begin. The ceremony was to be that evening in the courtyard of the castle. And, because of the kingdom's current tragic state, everyone was welcome to attend.

✝✝✝

The new day went by like a faint breeze. The sky looked like fire as the sun began to set. Early evening was upon the kingdom. The air became cool and crisp, welcoming the night with glorious arms.

Across the Field of Minslethrate, among the Ducre' Provence, Sora sat alone in the manor gardens. She quietly rested in a veranda that was covered in vines. Magenta colored flowers hung from the vines, beginning to close up as the sun went down. Her eyes were still as she thought of her experiences. Echoes of familiar voices she once knew resonated in her mind. Her experiences were strange to her, and she would never forget them.

She had been crying that whole day and the night before. She felt she couldn't cry anymore. She sipped on a cup of hot tea, continuing to stare out into the gardens with her swollen eyes. The flowers reminded her of Natalia... She began to think of the loss of her family and beloved niece. She felt like her emotions were a mess, wanting to cry again.

She began to think of the blessings that followed the Ducre' family's death. She was instantly blessed with the label of "Lady of Ducre" because of her bravery and loyalty. She took over the selling of Lord Fernund's crops, which she planned on hiring someone to do. She also hired Alexa as her head servant, who had plans to build the manor back up. Sora took over the Ducre' fortune, which she was content to do, but her mind kept drifting back to her sweet niece.

She thought of Natalia every moment of the day. Everything about the manor reminded her of the moments she shared with her niece. She always looked at Natalia as if she was her own daughter.

Sora brought the hot tea to her lips, remembering how she and Natalia used to have tea in her room. Just then she knew that it was going to be very different. Sora looked out into the garden as she sniffed the sweet aroma of her herbal tea. The sun was beginning to go down, painting the sky with many warm colors. The cool breezes went by Sora, pushing the steam away from her hot tea.

Sora decided that she wasn't going to attend Marrisa's ceremony. She wanted to stay home when the sun went down. She knew she wouldn't be able to withstand it. After her experiences with darkness that had risen against them, staying home was all she looked forward to. But she wasn't going to let loneliness consume her life; for she knew that having God in it was the only way to get through the days.

Something suddenly caught Sora's attention. She heard a faint laugh. She looked through the vines that surrounded the quaint veranda. She thought she saw movement, as if someone was approaching her from across the garden. She put her tea cup back down, peering through the leaves and flowers.

752

"Alexa, is that you?" she asked. There was no answer, so she got up from her seat to see who it was. "I'm coming, child," she said, thinking that it was Alexa. She knew that supper would be served soon. "You need to ready the fire for…," she said, stopping in mid-sentence.

Sora stopped abruptly, standing still like a statue. She was overwhelmed by what she saw. She quickly raised her hands to her mouth. Her eyes became wide as she gazed at who it was. At first, she thought it was a couple of strangers, but when she realized who the people were; her heart nearly stopped.

She saw them, plain as day. But she couldn't believe it. She saw them standing with one another. They must've been ghosts, but were they? They were speaking to a tall person who glowed like light!

"Natalia?!" Sora exclaimed, beginning to walk out of the veranda.

She saw Natalia and her father, Lord Fernund, being accompanied by a legna!

Sora's emotions flew as she began to run through the garden. She cried as she noticed Natalia running towards her with open arms.

It really was Natalia, Sora realized. They ran to each other, filled with overwhelming joy. Sora saw that Lord Fernund was walking towards them as well, while the legna stayed where he was at.

"Oh, Natalia!" Sora cried out. Tears ran down her cheeks as she embraced her niece.

She knew that Natalia was gone, but she didn't look dead. She was beaming with vivacity. She felt warm and alive and looked more vibrant than when she was alive. They hugged for what seemed like hours.

Lord Fernund walked up to them, having a smile on his bright face. He put his arm around Sora's back.

"I've come to tell you that it is not over, Sora," Natalia said, smiling up at her. "There is another life away from here, and you have a home there waiting for you." She wiped the tears from Sora's face. "Don't cry, my sweet Sora. I'm safe, living among the kingdom of light."

Sora's eyes looked her over, checking her out to see if she was unharmed and healthy, just how she always had done. She smiled, placing her hands on Natalia's warm cheeks.

Sora glanced at both Natalia and Lord Fernund. They seemed to glow. They looked radiant in their white and gold clothing. They looked unworldly, as if they were made of light.

"We have only little time, Sora," Natalia said, looking back at the legna who was watching them. "Gaibriul says that we must be quick… But I had to see you one last time… I love you, Sora. You will always be in my memory as a mother. Your face has always given me strength since I was a child. Stay strong, and remember that I will see you again…"

"I want to go with you," Sora said in a shaken voice.

Natalia placed her warm hand on her cheek. "You will, in time. Your quest in this world is not finished yet, Sora…"

"What must I do?" Sora quickly asked.

Natalia smiled. "…Seek the King of Light first…then you shall know…"

Tears went down Sora's cheeks as she quickly nodded her head. She smiled a toothy smile at her niece, then looked up at Lord Fernund.

Natalia smiled back, then gave her one last hug. "Never forget the light, Sora…," she said in a voice that seemed to fade away…

"Sora!" Alexa called from behind her. "Supper is ready, ma'am!"

Sora turned quickly, wiping the tears from her eyes. But she had a peaceful smile on her face. She saw Alexa approaching her. She looked back towards Natalia, only to find that all of them were gone. She gazed off at the sunset that burned upon the gardens, having peace in her heart.

"Sora," Alexa said, grabbing her attention.

Sora looked at her quickly, still smiling. "Did you see them?" she asked, looking back into the sunset.

Alexa had a strange look on her round face. "See who, Sora?" she asked, confused.

Sora just grinned, slowly shaking her head.

"Forgive me," Alexa said, quickly. "I meant, *Lady* Sora," she giggled.

"I will never get used to that label," Sora said, chuckling.

They began to walk together, wrapping friendly arms around each other's backs. They laughed together as they walked towards the great Manor of Ducre'. The sun was nearly down, and a sprinkle of twinkling stars was beginning to come out.

It was going to be a clear, beautiful night.

Sora wasn't too sure if the vision of Natalia and Lord Fernund was real or not, but she would never forget it. She felt that Natalia and the light were closer to her than she knew, and it inspired her. Seeing Natalia and knowing that she would see her again one day, made her sadness leave her.

It was a new night. It was a new year. And it was going to be a new life for Sora. And as she looked into the evening sky, she promised herself, that no matter what, she was going to keep the words of her niece, and live for the God of Light, forever…

✝✝✝

The winds had strength, but were refreshing among the coast. The sun was setting nicely, reflecting its beautiful colors off of the bouncing waters. The salty sea released its fragrance into the air with every wave it produced. Seagulls called out in the cool air, flying above the ship.

Phillip quietly walked up a wooden ramp, onto a ship that King Julpen had prepared for him. He was happy to see the ocean again and was excited to go back home. He looked around, watching the sailors as they readied the ship for their long journey to Ishkar.

King Julpen requested that he stayed for Marrisa's ceremony, but he declined, anxious to go home. But he informed the king that Ishkar would continue to be a friend of Minslethrate. King Julpen respected him for that, and he greatly respected the king and Minslethrate.

Phillip took his experiences as a life-changing event. He would never forget any of it. He received nothing physical out of going to Minslethrate, but he knew that he obtained the most important thing of all, and that was having the light of God in his spirit. He was forever changed, and was going to lead his kingdom in such a way that would change their lives for the good.

Phillip stood upon the ship, thankful for everything. He pulled his wing-pendant from his tunic, looking at its splendor. He rubbed his thumb on the golden pendant, looking out into the sunset. He could see the stars coming out, which reminded him of Natalia. He picked a star in the sky that shined the brightest and mentally attached Natalia's name to it. He would always think of Natalia when he looked into the stars...

Prince Phillip inhaled the cool, salty air as he closed his eyes. He smiled to himself, looking off towards the direction where he would be going. The wind blew past him, invigorating his heart. He was suddenly ready for another adventure; he was ready to change lives; and he was ready to be part of the greatness of his kingdom that God had promised him.

He knew that he was about to embark on a path that was set before him by God, and he was eager to face every moment of it.

†

CHAPTER 29
Heart's Desire

As the sun set behind the horizon, the warm colors in the sky became intense for a moment. The pinks and oranges faded, then changed into a quiet shade of dark blue. The sky became a dappled veil, shadowing Minslethrate beneath its starry face.

Sorrow filled the courtyard of the castle as King Julpen commemorated his daughter. He spoke out to his people, talking about Marrisa's loving heart and her amazing mind. He spoke in a calm voice that would break every now and then. He also spoke of Tairren and Marrisa's relationship, and how blessed he was to know that Tairren loved his daughter and risked his own life for her and his kingdom.

After the heartfelt utterance, King Julpen left the people's attention. Heavy silence came over the people as they took a moment to dwell on their thoughts of her... The sound of whimpers and crackling torches lingered in the miserable air. Soon, the courtyard was filled with faint conversation as the night progressed.

Tairren silently stood over Marrisa, gazing at her silent beauty. He grasped the heart-shaped pendant that hung from his neck, squeezing it. He remembered telling her to hold the pendant and think of him when she became sad or felt lost... And now it was him who was doing it. It was him who felt lost... He took the blue pendant off from around his neck. The cerulean-colored stone glistened like a tear as the torchlight touched it. It reminded him of Marrisa's eyes, which he hadn't seen in so long. He gently placed the pendant in her cold hands, closing her fingers around it. It was a gift from him, from his heart, and even in death he wanted her to have it.

The heavy scent of oil which saturated the platform didn't bother him. It was as if all of his senses were in tuned with Marrisa. He had been close to her that whole afternoon and evening. He couldn't pull his weary eyes away from her. Even in death, she was the loveliest woman he had ever known. No one could ever replace the love he had for her. He would lock that love up in his heart forever. He felt that he couldn't even leave her side, because it would be the last time he would ever see her...

Her face was so still and silent and glowed in the light from the torches that circled her body. She looked like a being of light, but there was no light within her.

King Julpen had some handmaidens prepare Marrisa's body for the ceremony earlier that morning. The women had cleaned her and anointed her with scented oils and herbs. They fixed her hair beneath a jeweled crown and dressed her in a lacey white gown. She looked hauntingly beautiful, lying upon a bed of white flowers and rose petals, atop a platform of oil-soaked wood. She was ready to be burned into the air.

Tairren's face was quiet and serious. He never showed any emotion, holding it all in. He had held his brokenness in since he left the south. His eyes were blood-shot and looked glassy. He looked up, realizing that the cremation would begin soon, which made him edgy.

He glanced around, noticing that almost everyone in the kingdom was there. The people filled the courtyard of the castle, talking softly amongst each other. Some people were crying while others stared silently; but everyone was impacted some kind of way by Marrisa's death. He saw his mother speaking solemnly with King Julpen and some other people. Most of the people he didn't know, but he was overwhelmed by the emotion they showed for Marrisa.

He clenched his teeth and closed his eyes tightly. The moments when she was alive kept running through his mind. They were special to him, and he would never let them go. Then, he kept thinking of her face when she was filled with darkness... Her screams haunted his mind as the terrible image of him thrusting the sword into her belly overcame him. He didn't understand why it had to be this way. He couldn't get the taunting images out of his throbbing head. He couldn't get over the fact that he killed the one he dearly loved. He trusted God and had done what he was commanded. But then why was he enveloped in such sadness? He didn't feel like he could become himself again. He knew he did it to save the land and to stop the dark powers of Lucif, but remorse kept coming over him.

He quickly opened his burning eyes, looking into her face again. Her red hair had flower petals in it and her lovely countenance appeared like fine porcelain glass. He wanted the image of her peaceful, elegant face to stay embedded in his mind forever.

He caressed her cold cheek one last time, slowly leaning over to gently kiss her cold lips. The thought of her eyes opening at the touch of his kiss trickled over him. If only fairytales were true... If only there was no death among true love.

"I love you, Marrisa," he whispered.

Her dead silence and lifeless face broke his heart all over again.

Tairren was startled by the gentle touch of a hand on his back. He turned to find King Julpen looking over him.

"It's time, Tairren," he said in a low voice that held underlying sadness.

Tairren just looked up at him, not saying anything. His heart throbbed at the thought of her body being burned. He became so overwhelmed that he was beginning to feel sick. He couldn't say anything to the king as he just blankly stared at him. His mind seemed to leave him for a second. After a feverish moment, he reluctantly backed away from the platform. He watched as King Julpen quietly walked over to one of the torches, hesitating to grab it at first.

King Julpen went to the platform as tears collected in his weary eyes. His hand shook slightly as he slowly brought the torch to the platform. He was about to set his only child's body ablaze, which was something he never thought he would ever do.

Tairren's heart began to thrash in his chest as a knot seemed to grow in his throat. His mouth became dry and sweat formed on his cold brow. He breathed hard as tears collected in his eyes. He was beginning to panic. He glanced at her elegant hands that loosely held the blue pendant. There was still love there; that overwhelming sensation of never seeing her again inundated him with sudden fear. The love he had for her, which hung on for dear life, was forbidden. He would never see his cursed love again, and knowing that, was putting him on the brink of insanity.

He then looked around at the crying people, and at his mother who had her hands over her gloomy face. His heart felt like it was about to explode, pumping loudly in his ears. Why was this happening? His eyes flashed back at the flames. They were taunting him. He fearfully watched as the torch came inches away from the platform.

"STOP!" Tairren bellowed out, startling the king. His voice echoed all throughout the intense atmosphere of the courtyard.

Everyone, including King Julpen, curiously looked at him.

"WHY?!" Tairren screamed out, shaking his head. "Why God?!" he cried out as tears fell from his eyes.

His heavy emotions spilled out of him like a waterfall. He couldn't contain himself as the realization of Marrisa being cursed and dead forever hit him like a satchel of bricks.

He sobbed as he bellowed out to the starry sky. "I've done everything you've commanded me to do; and still you deny me the only thing my heart aches for?! Please, God! PLEASE! Have pity on her! I love her! She never deserved to die! She never deserved to be punished!" Tairren buried his face into her stomach, releasing his tears.

Everyone looked on, becoming overwhelmed by Tairren's sudden emotion. Even his mother began to cry, watching her son become broken. King Julpen didn't know what to say or do as he just watched Tairren cry over his daughter.

"If you would've been there, she would not have DIED!" he screamed out to the atmosphere. "Hasn't she suffered enough?! She wasn't in the light; and now she is to burn for eternity?! Where is the love in that?!" He buried his face into his shaken hands. "I did everything you asked of me! Why wasn't she saved, GOD?! I need her...," he sobbed in a shaken voice to himself. "I would have the world become inundated in darkness again...JUST TO SAVE HER!! I would...travel to the bowels of hell…just to save her… I would give up my life for hers… I would take her place…"

Everyone was touched by Tairren's passion and tenacity. To put himself in danger and in harm's way, and to want to give up his whole life, just for love, showed how true Tairren was. Tairren had a heart that reminded them of King Yehoshua. He had a heart of gold that was unlike any other man. And his heart was what brought power.

Tairren's spirit cried as he buried his face into his hands again. His inner being ached so badly that even his body began to feel torn. He revealed his brokenness in front of the whole kingdom. And because of that, he was given respect by everyone there.

But, as Tairren wallowed in the lowest state of his existence, something unexpected and unusual happened then. It was like a dream. It was something that had never happened before. And it happened facing the whole kingdom, taking everyone's breath away. And that glorious sight made everyone in the courtyard fall to their knees. One by one, everyone went to their knees.

A bright light appeared near Tairren. It seemed to come from nowhere, from another world. He noticed the light through the cracks of his fingers. He slowly pulled his hands away, looking into an illumination he would never forget. The light was in the shape of a man, and Tairren knew right away who it was. He inhaled, falling before King Yehoshua. Every feeling that could make one feel overwhelmed with adoration came from the king. It was a feeling that inundated his heart and spirit. It was like a surge of life. He cried, yielding before the king's feet. He felt that he wasn't even worthy to kneel before the king's presence.

King Yehoshua's light fell over Tairren, blanketing him in His power. He covered Tairren with His love-light, which he yearned to feel.

"Tairren, do you believe that I Am the resurrection and the life?" a mighty voice asked from the magnificent light that radiated over him.

Tairren slowly looked up. He was inundated with emotion. Tears fell from his cheeks as the light of God sparkled upon him. "I do…," he finally said in a shaken voice. "I have always believed, my God."

"Then you should know that whoever believes in me, shall not parish, but live everlasting life…" The King of Light radiated as He spoke.

Tairren's breath shook as he gazed up at King Yehoshua. He understood clearly what the almighty God meant. He knew that Marrisa had given up on the light sometime during her capture. He knew that she was cursed… But it was too hard for him to merely accept it. He knew that the ones, who believed, would escape spiritual death and darkness. And Marrisa's spirit had been dead for some time…

Tairren closed his eyes tightly, bringing his face back down to the ground. He was speechless.

King Yehoshua's gaze was intense as He looked down at his child. His heart ached for both Tairren and Marrisa. Just as He loved the whole world, He loved his children, even if they fell away from Him. Even though He was a jealous God, He had a deep love for them that they would never understand. And even though He was a God of his word, He would always be a God of miracles. He would always be a magnanimous God of life.

Suddenly, King Yehoshua's light became brighter, looking like fire. His glorious presence filled the whole kingdom, taking everyone's breath away. It was as if the sun had fallen over them.

"MARRISA, AWAKEN!!" King Yehoshua commanded in a mighty voice that shook everyone's spirit. Even the stars and moon in the night sky pulsated with intense light as He spoke. His light became forceful as the power of his voice disturbed Marrisa's dead spirit.

Miraculously, just as Yehoshua commanded, Marrisa awakened from death, opening her eyes. She inhaled the first breath of life!

Tairren slowly stood up. He was in a daze. He was overwhelmed with everything that had happened. He stared at Marrisa's body. Was she really alive? He never took his sparkling eyes off of her. He slowly came closer to Marrisa with a booming heart as King Yehoshua's light burned behind him like the sun. His heart pounded in his ears as he stood over her. He noticed her eyes first. He had nearly forgotten how bright-blue they were.

"Tairren?" she said in a faint voice.

Tairren's eyes watered as he responded by nodding his head. A smile came over his face as every emotion settled over him. "Yes, it's me...," he said in a shaken voice.

He caressed her face as she looked up at him, softly smiling. He was filled with passion and joy that he had never felt before when he was with her. He kissed her, then pulled her up off of the platform. He held her in his arms as she responded by tightly holding him back.

He didn't want to ever let her go.

The courtyard of the castle was instantly filled with a joyful noise. They were all overwhelmed. The people were taken aback and filled with excitement at the same time. Their hearts seemed to jump as they all truly believed in the God of Light that night. It was a miracle. Witnessing Marrisa rise from the dead made them yearn for more of God. It made them all want to know King Yehoshua even more. Everyone in the courtyard sent out praises to King Yehoshua, lifting his name up on high. The whole courtyard was filled with light as King Yehoshua's presence grew. Power filled the place, sending any form of sadness or madness away. It appeared as if it was daylight as everything intensified with lively colors.

King Yehoshua suddenly dispersed into the air, spreading out upon the people. And even though He was no longer physically there, they could feel Him upon their bodies as if He was closer than their own skin. The lights softly dimmed as the night sky ruled over the kingdom once again, but they still cheered and shouted.

"I was so frightened...I was alone," Marrisa said, looking into Tairren's glittery eyes. "I was locked away and screamed out for help. But, as soon as I saw the hand made of light...I grabbed it... I wanted so badly to be rescued, Tairren. And I was... I wanted life so badly...and it pulled me from the darkness. I heard a voice and it woke me up! Then I saw the bright light...and you, Tairren."

Tairren smiled at her, looking into her beautiful face. "You were saved by the grace of God," he said.

They kissed again before the audience of people. It seemed as if the joyful noise would never end. The feeling was so wonderful that nobody wanted to leave that night...

✝✝✝

But that night did end. It ended unlike any other night, and it would never be forgotten. For that night became celebrated, and every year during that night, the kingdom would celebrate the God of Light, and life. The miracles that King Yehoshua had displayed thrust the kingdom into a powerful position, full of faith.

Minslethrate would become a powerful kingdom, ruled by a king that was filled with love and anointed by God. Tairren would soon become that new king of Minslethrate, continuing to lead the people towards the Light of God. And for that, Minslethrate would continue to be blessed and highly favored.

Days after the miracle, there was a series of exciting events. First, there was a coronation. The whole kingdom watched as Tairren was ordained to the throne. King Julpen happily placed the old crown on Tairren's head that was rescued from the south, which was given to him by Mikhal. Tairren felt proud to wear the crown, which was worn by his ancestors...and by King Yehoshua.

Soon after, Minslethrate held a grand celebration and a wedding ceremony. Prince Tairren and Princess Marrisa were married. They shared a love for each other that no one could break. And as King Julpen placed a crown of rosemary on each of their heads, they were bound together until death.

And Moral, who became the first lady of the castle, lived with them, supporting them like no other. She became a mother to Marrisa, and King Julpen a father to Tairren. And just like all of the other nobility in

Minslethrate, Moral and Sora became close companions, having tea with one another and going to every event the kingdom held.

Every event that happened in Minslethrate was blessed by God. There was never a time of sadness or strife, for the curse was lifted from the kingdom.

God blessed Tairren and Marrisa's marriage, also blessing them with a child. The child was a boy, and a new heir to the throne...

†

CHAPTER 30
Unending Story

Tairren and Marrisa strolled through the Forest Provence. They held hands, casually talking to each other. Their giggles and loving mannerisms sprinkled the air. Their crowns sparkled on their heads as sunlight trickled through the green canopy above them. Sweet smelling breezes played past them, gently moving the branches and the long grasses and flowers.

"We're nearly there," Tairren said, peering past the blooming trees.

"It's been so long," Marrisa said, smiling at him. "This forest holds so many memories..."

The sound of a child's laughter broke the quietness of the forest. "I found one; I found one!" the young boy shouted excitedly. He held up a large frog.

"Oh, Joshua," Marrisa said, giggling. "You're all wet."

"I found him in the creek!" the young boy shrieked.

"We're almost to nanna's cottage, Joshua," Tairren said, pointing through the forest.

The little boy smiled up at his father, handing him the frog. His bright-blue eyes sparkled and his red curls bounced in the breezes.

Tairren smiled at his son, patting his head.

Marrisa laughed as Tairren held the fat frog, just staring at it.

They made it to the cottage, standing before the small abode. It was overtaken by blooming vines and shrubbery. It was barely recognizable. But even though the quaint little cottage was aging, it still stood strong. It was a symbol of love and strength that would always be part of their hearts and memories.

Tairren would always bring his little family to the cottage every now and then, never wanting them to forget where he came from. He wanted his son to appreciate nature, and the gifts of God. And when he was there, he thought of his father, and all of his childhood memories. The cottage was nostalgic, and would always be part of the forest and part of Tairren.

"Let's make the picnic," Joshua said, jumping up and down. His face glowed with innocence.

They spread out the blanket, arranging everything to their liking. They settled down, talking about the forest and the old cottage. Tairren told Joshua about his adventures in the forest and how he and his father used to search the woods for treasures...

"Tell me a story, father," Joshua said, eating a sweet pastry his nanna had made for him.

Tairren smiled, appreciating his son's company.

"Oh, let's see...I know lots of stories," he said, diving into his thoughts. "I can tell you a story about a beautiful princess," he said, smiling at Marrisa. He then noticed his son's sudden uninterested face. "Or, I can tell you a tale about warriors who are made from light." His son then became wide-eyed with fascination. "I can also tell you a story about a noble lady and a prince who searched far off lands for the lost armor of a great king... I can even tell you a tale about an evil witch that used magic to control fire!" He smirked, becoming entertained by his bright-eyed son and his young expressions. "But I know a legend of all legends, son. And I'll tell it to you because it should never be forgotten." The young prince stared up at his father, crumbs falling from his mouth. He gave him his full attention. "It's about a mighty king... And this king is from the legend of all legends! He is the last legend..."

Joshua bounced up and down, squeezing his pastry till it broke everywhere. His sweet face warmed Tairren's heart.

"Do you want to know that one, son?" Tairren asked, teasing him.

"Yes, father! Tell me; tell me!" he shouted, excitedly. He made his parents laugh.

"Okay, son, listen well, because it shall be a story you can tell anyone, even your friends... Once, upon a time, long ago, there was a King of Light. And this king loved his people and the world very much..."

Tairren began the legend, lovingly looking at his family as he spoke...

✝✝✝

In the wind-blown canopy, above Tairren and his family, a mighty owl perched on the highest branch. It sat mysteriously among the dappled shade of the tree, quietly gazing down at them with its starry eyes. Its golden-tipped feathers glowed as the sunlight flickered upon it. Then, after a thoughtful moment, the magnificent owl took wing into the sky, soaring with its glorious feathers.

The watchful owl traveled through the air above the lands, looking for the next believer, the next life-changer, and the next hero...

These tales will never be lost, for they rest deep down in the hearts of man, waiting to come out over and over again…

Some say that it's just a story, others say that it's just a dream, but I say that it's the world's memoir: life's chronicles that is as old as time. And when you look deep down into your heart, you will find The Last Legend; because He is waiting for you…

And when you finally meet Him, He will be back as quick as a flash of lightning, waiting to take you home with Him.

So, hold onto the Light and never forget it. Remember it always. Darkness will knock at the doors of your heart and mind, but that is when you fasten the strings of your spiritual armor and take up your sword…and fight.

As you walk through your life, remember that your quest in this world is your story, your poem, and your testimony.

God will always be there, watching from the glowing branches of your heart's eyes. And when you finally learn what He has instore for you, you will take flight and soar above it all, with Him by your side.

Never forget the light of Jesus, my friend.   Because He is The Last Legend, and was awakened long ago, unto the end…and forever.

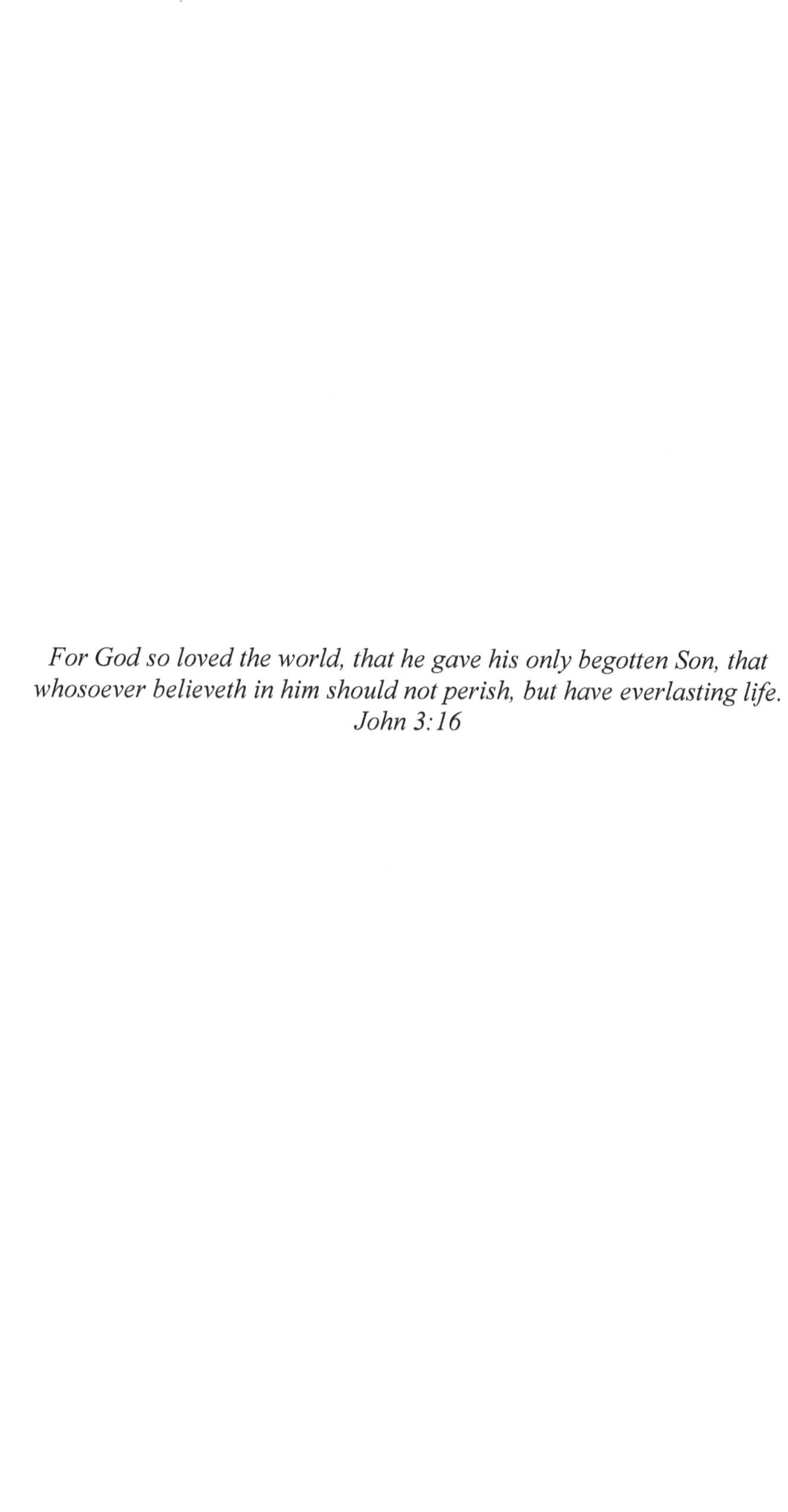

For God so loved the world, that he gave his only begotten Son, that whosoever believeth in him should not perish, but have everlasting life.
John 3:16

Reflect

The spiritual world is real and upon us every day.
The Bible tells us that it's not flesh and blood we wrestle against, but the principalities of darkness…
Ephesians 6:12
The characters in this story were inspired by my own walk on this earth: physical, emotional, and spiritual. God has changed my life so much. Darkness will never cover my heart again—it may knock but it will never get in. During my literary journey with *The Last Legend*, I prayed daily that this book would touch the readers—and that a seed of light will become planted and take root.
Let it bloom.
The Bible reveals to us that God loved the world so much, that he sent his only son, Jesus Christ, to die a gruesome death for us—so that all of our sins may be forgiven. If you confess with your mouth and believe with your heart that Jesus is your lord and savior—your sins will be forgiven and you will be saved…
John 3:16 & Romans 10:9-13
✝
That's true love.
You can live with The King of Light forever.
Talk to Him:
Dear God, thank you for loving me unconditionally and coming to earth to die on the cross for my sins. I believe that you died and rose from the grave for me. You are my lord and savior. Please come into my heart and lead me.

I love you, Jesus. Amen.

About the Author

I am an artist with a passion for literary creativity, visual story-telling, and a loving God of light.

My yearning is to use the gifts that God has blessed me with to help plant seeds of light—and change lives one day at a time. I believe that's my quest on this earth. I am also a children's book illustrator and have worked on many charming children's picture books.

Personal Anecdotes: Everyone has stories within them to tell—and there are so many ways to tell them...

When I was a preteen, I was fascinated with Greek mythology and Medieval art and literature. During that time, I had just gotten accepted into the Talented Arts Program at my junior high—and that's when my story ideas unfolded. I would draw characters and create stories about them. That's when I began to write. *The Last Legend* began as art work and a faint storyline—then grew into one incredible story. For thirteen years, my story became stronger and grew in my heart. It wasn't until 2010 that I started writing *The Last Legend.* During those years I rededicated my life to Christ, and that's when my story turned into something more than just another fantasy—it became a testimony, my own poem and a beacon of hope. You see, the situations that my beloved characters go through in *The Last Legend* are inspired by broken experiences that we all go through every day—but just with an epic twist. Just as I experienced the dark-side of our world, so do my characters in the story. It's ironic how over many years ago, my story inspired by poems dealing with many gods, is now inspired by our *one* and *only* true God. Over the years, my story had many names and main themes—but now its name and themes are complete.

The Last Legend: Awakened, is book one in the Epic-Fantasy Thriller, followed by book two, ***Unto The End,*** and book three, ***Forever.***

Chronicles of The Last Legend: Awakened Unto The End Forever is the trilogy as a whole.

Check out www.TheLastLegendAwakened.com for more of Joshua's art and work.

Joshua B. Wichterich

What is **The Last Legend** about?

The first time poor-boy Tairren saw Princess Marrisa's stunning red hair and
gazed into her angelic blue eyes, he was stricken with a deep love for her no
one would understand, not even himself. They say that young love is blind.
It's no wonder he didn't see that loving her was deadly…and the catalyst to
the collapse of not only the Kingdom of Minslethrate, but the world.

It was on Marrisa's sixteenth birthday, her engagement to Prince Phillip and
the day before her enthronement to the powerful Kingdom of Ishkar, when it
happened. Chaos was unleashed by a silent follower of darkness that had
been creeping in the royal bloodline of Minslethrate for ages. When Marrisa
is betrayed and kidnapped by her guardian she had been entrusted to since
birth, Tairren realizes that the childhood myths of light and darkness that
were told to him by his deceased father were very real and upon them. As
Marrisa is forced to face her fate that had cursed her bloodline since the
beginning of time, something moves in the spiritual realm that unlocks the
doorways of Hell.

When Tairren quickly responds to Marrisa's fate, he is awakened by a living
creature of light, and learns that he and Marrisa are the main keys to a
prophecy that would disturb evil, awaken forgotten legends, and light the
fire of a threatening world war that would end life on earth. His ancestors
and true bloodline that had been kept a secret by his deceased father and
loving mother are revealed to him, confirming that he is part of a dire quest.
With the company of his very different comrades, the unconventional and
bold Lady Natalia, Marrisa's unbelieving fiancé Prince Phillip of Ishkar, and
a peculiar guild of glowing beings called legna, Tairren travels across the
uncertain lands of Minslethrate while being inundated with the yearning to
save the only girl he loved more than himself.

They begin to realize that their precarious situation is dealing with more
than just themselves and their kidnapped princess, that's just the beginning.
Not only are the three young adventurers who are connected to Marrisa
involved in the world's fate, but everyone bridged to them are as well.
Destiny and fate reveal themselves in trials and tribulation as followers of
darkness, called nomed, rise against them all. They not only have to face
their inner demons, but are caught in the middle of an ancient warfare
between the enigmatic worlds of darkness, light, and the legends that
brought the origin of Minslethrate, and the world, into existence.